SEVERED HEART

Also by Kate Stewart

The Ravenhood

Flock
Exodus
The Finish Line

The Ravenhood Legacy

One Last Rainy Day
Severed Heart
Birds of a Feather

LEGACY
SEVERED HEART

KATE STEWART

kensingtonbooks.com

Content notice: *Severed Heart* contains depictions of domestic abuse; child abuse/severe neglect; sexual abuse; self-harm; explicit language; explicit sex; acts of violence, including but not limited to mentions of murder and gun violence; references to human atrocities, including the human slave trade; terminal and mental illness; PTSD resulting from military service; and PTSD resulting from abuse/neglect.

KENSINGTON BOOKS are published by:

Kensington Publishing Corp.
900 Third Avenue
New York, NY 10022

kensingtonbooks.com

Copyright © 2025 by Kate Stewart

All rights reserved. This book or any portion thereof may not be reproduced or used in any manner whatsoever without the express written permission of the publisher except for the use of brief quotations in a book review.

All Kensington titles, imprints, and distributed lines are available at special quantity discounts for bulk purchases for sales promotions, premiums, fundraising, educational, or institutional use.

Special book excerpts or customized printings can also be created to fit specific needs. For details, write or phone the office of the Kensington sales manager: Kensington Publishing Corp., 900 Third Avenue, New York, NY 10022, attn: Sales Department; phone 1-800-221-2647.

The K with book logo Reg US Pat. & TM Off.

This is a work of fiction. All of the characters, organizations, and events portrayed in this novel are either products of the author's imagination or are used fictitiously.

ISBN 978-1-4967-5701-2 (trade paperback)

eISBN 978-1-4967-5702-9 (ebook)

First Kensington Trade Paperback Printing: July 2025

10 9 8 7 6 5 4 3 2 1

Printed in the United States of America

The authorized representative in the EU for product safety and compliance is eucomply OU, Parnu mnt 139b-14, Apt 123
Tallinn, Berlin 11317, hello@eucompliancepartner.com

For our true modern-day heroes, the men and women of the armed forces, "thank you for your service" will never be enough.
EVER.

Prologue

Tyler

U.S. PRESIDENT: PRESTON J MONROE | 2021–2029
Present Day

Sweat slicked, a few drops glide down my temples before I lift my ballcap to clear it with the side of my glove. Laser-focused on the door, I idle in the bucket seat as a welcome breeze sweeps over me. The slight chill at the edge of it indicating the end of summer as it caresses my heated skin.

Closing my eyes, I can picture her so vividly, peering back at me from the porch. Feet bare, hand raised over her brow in a salute to shield her silver-gray eyes from the sun, as the windswept tips of her long, onyx hair dance along the small of her back. A serene smile lifting her lips as I drew near—her expression, combined with the look in her eyes, rendering me speechless.

Love emanates from her being, from her every pore, where she stands in summons to me only feet away.

A love so pure, so tangible, and unconditional bouncing between us. The only safe space I have ever truly known beating inside her chest as I draw closer to it, pounding over the wood planks to answer her summons and feast on a love that blankets me. A love that protects me and brings me peace while keeping me whole. A love so mine, so ours.

A love and place we made together, against all odds. Our darkness mingling and molding, pouring our foundation, and erecting the frame while we decorated the walls with the memories we made. Filling every shelf and lining every cabinet, creating our forever home within one another.

The engine purrs beneath me as if telling me to get on with it while my recollection keeps me idle as I awaken memories. All of which I'm choosing to draw upon, bringing them from the recess of my mind where I've kept them safe and untarnished—not a second forgotten.

"Please don't mourn me."

As if I ever had a choice. As if either of us ever had control over anything in that respect—her ask impossible.

I know better now because I've lived long enough to know better. Which has me thinking that maybe she never discovered this secret before she left. Or maybe she did and just wanted to push her will and hope for me into her plea.

But on this, I consider myself the wiser of the two of us. I couldn't make or keep that promise any more than she could change her fate against the cancer that ravaged her before it stole her last breath.

Just like I haven't had a choice to breathe deeply since I watched her take it. I'm convinced at this point that my shallow breaths since her departure are part of the price for having such perfection. For having found true peace for a moment in time.

She once told me life could happen in a blink, but it's a series of blinks that brought us together. It was life *happening to us* which ended with the same close of the eyes, leaving me on the other side of it without her. I understand that now more than ever. Because I know the difference between living your life and life happening to you, and they are distinctly different.

Severed Heart

Living life is making choices—what to wear, when to eat, whether or not to cut your hair. These are the easy decisions we get to make—to have some say or a hand in.

Life happening to you is vastly different. It comes by way of a powerful reckoning force that cements your path for better or worse. It's only in the wake of it that you realize the easy decisions are the only choices you have any real say in.

The hard stuff—the really hard stuff—that's life *happening to you.*

And since I'm a contingency man, I've figured my way around allowing life to happen to me.

I've found the trick, the loophole, a way to take away the power it can wield over me, and now, *I happen to my life and the lives of others.* Not the other way around. At this point, it's up to me to remember the blinks of the days before and after I mastered it.

Blinks I'm choosing to remember now. Some of them slow and meant to be savored. Many of them so fast it doesn't feel like they're real, but delivered by a force so powerful, it's undeniable it exists. A force she prayed to and called God.

Something I never fought her on and still don't exactly disagree with. While her faith was unshakable, mine remains in her—in us.

Either way, as I ready myself to happen to life in the years ahead, I close my eyes, summoning every close and clear of them that brought me here—that brought us together—before I'm forced to blink it all away.

PART 1

"A BOY BECOMES A man when a man is needed."
—John Steinbeck

Chapter One

Delphine

US PRESIDENT: RONALD REAGAN | 1981–1989

I TURN THE DIAL on the radio to find our favorite new Johnny Hallyday song when a woman's voice sounds *very loud* through the speakers, making me jump. "... *le président Américain Reagan a été abattu devant un hôtel Hilton à Washington—*" US President Reagan was shot in front of a Hilton in Washington—

I turn it down so it doesn't wake Papa from his nap and jump when someone pounds on the front door. "Matiiiis!"

He says Papa's name again like we do when we play hide and seek. "*Matiiisss!*"

I move toward the door when the latch catches and stop when I see the man with the burnt face staring at me through the gap on the other side. "Delphine, where is Matis?"

When I don't answer him, he smiles at me with crooked teeth. I hate the burnt man. He always tries to touch me when Papa doesn't look, and Papa *never looks* when he plays cards.

"Open the door, Delphine," he orders before he smacks the wood *hard* to scare me. I push at the door to show him he doesn't frighten me and to try to close it in his ugly face. "Go away, my papa is sleeping, and you're going to wake him up!"

He laughs in a way that's not funny and yells at me to open it. When I don't, he disappears from the door, and I push it closed. Turning to get Papa, the burnt man kicks the door open, and it hits me in the back. Screaming, I fall to the floor. When the man reaches for me, I jump to my feet as Papa runs into the room and starts to wrestle him while shouting at me. "Delphine, to the barn! *Go!*"

I know I should follow his orders like his good soldier, but I see the shiny side of a knife in the burnt man's hand and warn Papa instead.

"The . . . barn, go!" Papa yells again, wrestling the burnt man for the knife as I look around for something to help him fight. Papa always tells me, 'a man who doesn't choose a side is a man in the way,' and I'll be in his way if I don't choose his side and try to help him. When the burnt man smiles at Papa, pushing the knife closer to his throat, my tummy flips. "Don't worry, Matis. By nightfall, she'll be a woman."

"Delphine, go!" Papa yells again the way he does when he's *really mad* at me while he pushes the sharp side of the knife away from his neck. Turning to follow orders, I crash into another man and hear him curse. Looking up and up, my head starts to burn as water drips down the back of it to my neck. The man tilts his head as he stares down at me, and Papa screams at him not to touch me. When I look back at Papa, I watch him push the knife toward the burnt man's throat before the man in front of me knocks me to the floor. My eyes go fuzzy, and I stop and wipe the water away with my hand so I can see. When Papa calls for me, I crawl toward his voice, but when I put my hand back on the floor, I see it's not water in my eyes—it's *blood*.

Feeling dizzy, I lay on the floor and try not to fall asleep as Papa and the second man shout at each other. Rolling on the carpet toward Papa's voice, I stop when I see the burnt man's open eyes staring back at me.

He's dead.

Papa killed him.

I'm glad. He is not a good man. Papa said so. He said he plays cards with bad men to find out their secrets.

Looking back up at Papa as he stands from the floor, I see he's very, very angry as the man he's yelling at kicks me in the stomach. "It's much too late, Matis. Your payment is due, and it's time to collect."

"The only thing you're collecting today, you fucking pig, is your death, one I'm all too happy to give you," Papa says through his teeth, his voice still very angry but very quiet. When Papa moves toward the man to deliver his death, I wonder if he's going to punish me for not following his order to go to the barn. Maybe he is proud of me for fighting. Before I can ask him, I fall asleep.

***

"Wake up, little flower. Please don't break my heart. *Please*," he whispers, his hand on my cheek.

"Papa," I call for him. "I can't open my eyes."

His breath tickles my nose as he does his tired sigh, like when I break a dish or dirty the carpet after playing in the creek.

"You can see, little flower. Open your eyes."

I try hard and open them to see that Papa's eyes are red and puffy. He's been crying. I know because he cried for a long, *long* time after Maman told us to 'rot in our filthy life.' I wasn't sad when Maman left like Papa was. She was mean to me and slept *all the time*.

Papa was the only one who would play with me. Brush my hair. Bring me toys. It was always Papa who read me stories and tucked me into bed.

"Papa." I wipe at the little spot of blood on his cheek. "Did you hit your head, too?"

"No, little flower." Papa closes his eyes and begins to cry. "Forgive me, Delphine."

"Matis, if you want to save her from your fate, we have to leave *now*." The voice comes from a man standing at my bedroom door. I try to look at him, but Papa uses his finger to turn my face to his. The light from the chandelier hanging above him hurts my eyes. Papa gave it to me as a birthday present and told me all princesses have rooms with chandeliers. I told him that I wanted to be the *prince* because they got to fight. He laughed and laughed before promising not to bring me anything else for a princess and brought me a sword the next time he came back from playing cards—my sword! I should have gotten my sword when the burnt man came.

"Delphine, do you remember when I told you one day you would have to be a soldier?"

"Yes, I am ready!" I tell him, trying to sit up, but he keeps me in bed.

"Good. I need you to follow orders now and do exactly as I tell you, understand?"

"Yes, Papa."

"We have to go now!" the man shouts from my door. "I'm not dying for your kid, Matis!"

"I need you to go with this man and do what he tells you," Papa says, lifting me from my bed. He walks over and puts me into the man's arms, handing him my suitcase with the wildflowers that look like the flowers we dance in. The man stares down at me, and I decide I don't want to follow orders tonight, but Papa shushes me.

"I'm begging you . . . bring her to my nephew. Francis will raise her as his own. Please get her there safely," he tells the man. "I'll pay you any price you ask."

"As if you'll survive," the man tells Papa. "Making promises you can't keep is what got you in this mess, Matis."

"Forget how you feel about me, just this once, *please*."

"I'm here, aren't I?" He talks funny when he doesn't speak French. Papa told me these people are called the British.

"Papa, I don't want to follow orders tonight. My head hurts," I tell him, and he jerks his chin to quiet me.

"Here." Papa puts a roll of money in the man's hands.

"This is all I have. I was trying to save enough to get her out of here, but I don't understand . . . why aren't they here?" Papa starts to cry again.

"Even now, you're still maintaining the lie?" the British man says.

"I don't have time to argue with you," Papa sighs, wiping his face.

"You could try to run," he tells Papa before looking at me like I'm filthy, "and save me the headache."

Papa shakes his head. "It's too late. They'll never stop now. Above all else, just make sure you aren't followed."

"For old times' sake, Matis." He looks at Papa like he's filthy too. "Honestly, those bastards are doing us all a favor by ridding the world of you, and you have my word that if it's within my power, no harm will come to her tonight. Though for that to be a possibility, we have to leave right fucking *now*."

"P-papa?" I whisper, looking at the man and back to Papa. I do *not* like this man or the way he talks to my papa, but he nods to the British man before he looks down at me, his eyes getting redder.

"I love you, little flower," he whispers before bending and kissing my head next to where it hurts so much. "I'm so sorry. I'm so sorry. Forgive me." Papa does the sign of the cross on my forehead with his finger, closes his eyes, and speaks English to the British man. "Take her. Go."

"N-no, no, Papa!" I scream as the man starts to walk away, and Papa cries into his hands. "Papa, no, no orders tonight. Please!" I shout, feeling sleepy again as the man holds me tighter to him, walking faster.

"P-please, Papa!" I wiggle in the man's arms. "I'm ready to be *your soldier*, not *his*!" I shout over the British man's shoulder as Papa comes out of my room and grabs my hand, following the man holding me down the hall.

"Close your eyes, Delphine," Papa orders me so I won't see the men he delivered death to in the living room. Closing my eyes, I hold Papa's hand really tight so he can't let go. When we are outside, snow hits my nose and cheeks, and the wind makes my head hurt more. "I'm sorry I didn't go to the barn. I'm sorry," I tell Papa. "I'll be good. I promise. I'll follow orders, *your* orders!"

"Wait, *please* . . . one more minute," Papa cries to the man.

"Enough with the melodrama, Matis! It's probably already too late!"

Papa cries harder and follows us down the creaky porch steps before kissing my hand. "Remember what I taught you?"

"Yes, Papa."

"Remember, little flower. Remember everything I told you. Never forget!"

"I'll remember, I promise!"

Closing his eyes, Papa kisses my hand one more time before he lets it go, and I scream for him as the British man starts to run with me in his arms. Papa calls after me through the snow and tells me that it's okay. That it's all going to be okay and to go with the man—that he will keep me safe. That he loves me. That I'm his good soldier. That he's sorry, but he cries the whole time! If everything is okay, he wouldn't cry so hard!

"No! Papa!" I slap the British man's face, and he curses and drops my suitcase. It falls open on the ground as the man puts me into his car. I kick at him over and over as he gathers my clothes, cursing as he pushes my legs and suitcase inside. "Papa, please don't let him take me! I'm sorry I didn't go to the barn! I'm sorry!"

"Delphine, be my soldier and do as you're told!" Papa yells through the wind, but I can't see him anymore through so much snow! The man slams the door on me as lights flash through the window of his car.

"They're here!" the man calls back to Papa before he gets into the car.

"Get her out of here!" Papa yells, and the man starts to drive away before I throw up on the floor.

"Oh, bloody fucking hell," the British man says, his eyes on the lights coming through the glass before a loud bang comes from the house behind us. I know that sound. Papa is shooting from his big, *big* gun. The cars with lights have more bad men coming, and Papa is shooting at them to stay away. He's fighting again.

"I have to go back!" I scream at the British man. "I have to fight!"

I pull at the car door handle, but the man pulls my arm to keep me inside and goes faster.

"Come on, Matis." The man says Papa's name like he's praying as another loud bang comes from the house and shakes our car.

Papa shoots at the lights coming again and again, and one car lights fire before it goes into the river. More lights come as the man goes faster and faster, turning this way and that way.

"Take me back!" I order like Papa does.

"Shut up," the British man tells me as he turns the wheel. "Keep going, Matis, just a little longer," he whispers, looking into the mirror on the glass.

"Are you stupid?" I tell the British man. "He can't hear you whisper!"

He laughs like I told him a joke before I count three cars turning onto our road. The man drives faster and faster, and I close my eyes to ask God to give Papa enough bullets for the big guns to shoot all the bad men.

"Don't look back," the man tells me as he starts to drive *really, really, really fast*. Snow makes it hard to see through the window, and my tummy hurts when I can't see our house anymore.

"We go far way now!" I shout in English. "I am Matis soldier! Not for yours! Take Delphine back house, help fight!"

The man continues to drive, and I know I said the words right.

"You understand my English!" I yell at him. "I tell you

to back!" When he doesn't listen, *again*, I curse at him. "*Imbecile!*"

"Definitely Matis's daughter," the man laughs, and I know he's making fun of me and Papa. I decide I do not like British men.

"I am *Matis soldier!*"

"Sure you are, kid." He says this as if he doesn't believe me. But *I am* a soldier. Papa taught me how to march and salute. How to make fires. How to fish. How to shoot—not the big gun yet. How to skin a rabbit and take out its entrails. To cook. Which mushrooms are poisonous, and which flavor food. He taught me tactics and intelligence he learned when he was a special soldier. He taught me that keeping clean keeps you close to God. He reads to me the stories of other soldiers. Of wars. Of the news. I decide the man driving does not know Papa. I stare at the side of his head as I speak more English. "You make Delphine *very* angry."

He smiles. "Get used to it."

He is not a nice man, but I know he doesn't want to hurt me like the burnt man did. Papa says he will keep me safe, and I believe him.

"You soldier, like Matis?" I ask in English.

"Yes. Long ago, when he was a *respectable* man." The British man goes faster, screaming when his car spins round and round before it finally stops. He curses when I throw up on his floor again and on my clothes and my suitcase. I wipe my mouth and look around to see lights shining through the back window of the car.

"The bad men are chasing us!"

"I'm aware, Delphine, *Christ*, be quiet! And I'm taking you away from the *bad man*," he yells back, rolling down his window. He shoots a gun at the car chasing us over and over again until we can't see the lights anymore, and lets out a long breath.

We drive for a long, long time before the British man stops the car and tells me to get down in my seat while he watches the road for more lights. After a long time, I try hard not to fall asleep when he finally speaks.

"Your father might have borne the worst luck, but as it seems, you won't be suffering the same tonight. Looks like you live to see another day." He presses his hand to his face. "Christ, that was close."

"Take Delphine back house. Matis need . . ." I try to think of the English word. "His medisis-medicines spoon. *I* know where. Only *I* help him."

"Life is cruel, and it would do you a bit of good to learn it early." He turns in his seat toward me. "As intelligent as you might be for one so young, you're utterly ignorant in judgment of allegiance because your papa *is* the *bad* man, *little flower*. A weak, pathetic drug addict." The man curses and shakes his head as he turns the key. "So weak that he made another bad bet because he didn't have anything to fill his precious spoon."

"Papa *not* bad man," I whisper, staring at the side of his head. I hope he can see he's making me angry and that I think he is an imbecile. "You tell lies."

"You don't seem to be a soldier that follows orders"— he looks down at me in my seat—"so maybe that's why he *bet you.*"

Chapter Two

Tyler

US PRESIDENT: WILLIAM J. CLINTON | 1993–2001

"BARRETT, OVER HERE!" I holler before climbing up a few steps of the ladder Mom told me *pacifically not* to climb. She won't see me now because she's too busy going goo-goo, ga-ga over my twin cousins Jasper and Jessie.

All I know is that babies make adults act *stupid*. That's all I know. Barrett and I have been able to get away easy today from our parents' eagle eyes because they can't stop gushing over how cute they are. I don't see the big deal. All they do is cry, poop, and throw up all over everything. Jasper pooped and throwed up on *me* when I held him.

"Barrett," I holler louder, and he drops the stick he was poking the dead squirrel with and runs over to me as I try to figure which apple to pick. We came to the farm today because Mom, Dad, and my aunts and uncles spent all day helping clean and fix up the boarding houses to get them ready for the laborers.

During harvest, all our 'stended family comes from Georgia and Florida. Daddy doesn't let Barrett and me come to the farm when they're here because he says a lot of them 'don't have the sense God gave them,' and they drink and curse too much.

Severed Heart

Barrett squints up at me from where he stands at the bottom of the ladder as I reach as high as I can from the middle of it.

"Tyeeelerrr," he whines, "Uncle Carter said *not* to pick apples." He looks over to where our parents are grilling chicken and drinking beer next to a big bonfire. Right now, the smoke is risin' to the sky and giving us some needed cover.

"They aren't payin' us no attention. Uncle Grayson's talkin' about that Kurt Cobana guy again, who shot his own head, but Daddy's going off about the Major League strike. 'Sides it's just *one* apple, and Pawpaw said this land is as good as ours, and if we want to be real farmers, we need to start getting our hands dirty *early on* and work our land."

"Well, you can be a farmer, but *I'm* not gonna be no *alfalfa desperado*."

"You don't even know what that means." I roll my eyes.

"Yeah, I do. I'm not gonna be just a farmer who grows apples and vegetables. I'm gonna raise *livestock* too, so I can be a *real cowboy*."

"Well, I won't have time to be a cowboy 'cause I'm going to be a *Marine* like Uncle Gray, Daddy, and Pawpaw."

"Then you're gonna be just a farmer. *Alfalfa desperado!*" he teases, pointing at me.

"Shut up!" Tired from reaching, I wiggle my shoulders. "I guess I could be a cowboy, too. Maybe I can put a horse and cows on your land, and you can watch after 'em while I'm a Marine?"

"Maybe."

"Until then, we have to be grunts," I tell him.

"What's that?"

"I don't know. I think a laborer. Grunts have to start with apples."

"Fine." He looks back towards the bonfire. "But if your daddy catches us, he's going to smoke our butts."

"So what?" I swat a fly from my nose. "I can take an ass-whoopin'. I don't cry like you do."

"I don't cry," he calls up to me.

"Yeah, you do. You cry louder than Jasper and Jessie when you get a whoopin'. Bet they could pick apples better than you anyway."

"Shut up." Barrett wipes his nose with his shirt. "They're just babies. They don't know they own land yet or even have apples to pick because they have baby brains. *Duh.*"

"Which means I'm the oldest cousin *and the boss*. Now hold my legs, crybaby, and hurry up."

"*I* don't *cry*," he lies as he reaches up and holds my legs. Twisting the apple on the branch, it finally comes free, and I hold it down for Barrett. "See, no big deal. They'll never know one is missing."

"Let me pick one," he says as I start to climb down.

"You have to work your *own land*."

He scrunches his nose as I take the last step down. "Where's my land going to be again?"

"Gah, you never listen." I nod toward the other side of the highway. "Over there. From the road, up the hill, and then some behind Pawpaw's house."

"We can't go over there! It's 'cross the highway. If we go 'cross the highway, we'll both get whoopin's."

"It's not a highway," I tell him. "It's just a road, and you're *always* scared."

"Am not, and Mom says I'll be as big as my daddy someday."

"We're not big like them yet 'cause we haven't hit our growth spurt."

"What's that?" Barrett asks.

"When you get hair in your armpits," I tell him, "and," I whisper low, "I heard Uncle Grayson say our balls will drop."

"Drop where?"

"I dunno." I scrunch my nose, wondering where my balls will drop to.

"Till my balls drop, Tyler, let me pick one of your apples on *your* land."

"Nope," I say, wiping my apple on my shirt before taking a bite. "You have to work *your own land*. Those are the rules."

"Fine," he puffs. "But you got to help me carry the ladder 'cross the highway."

"Why? I can carry it by myself."

"Liar, I saw Uncle Carter carry it over here!"

"Boys!" Mom calls. "Dinner!"

"Shit," I mumble. "You're gonna have to wait."

"Come on, cousin," Barrett whines, "let me pick one of your apples. I'll be quick."

I toss my apple and cross my arms. "What are you going to give me for it?"

"I don't have any more money in my piggy bank. You already tooked it all," he huffs out.

"Fine." I tug down my ballcap. "You owe me two dollars next time you have money. Spit shake on it."

"I'll never have any money if *you* keep *taking it*."

"That's tough shit," I say like Daddy does. "That's the price of pickin' on *my* land."

Barrett moves around me to get to the ladder, and I block him and shake my head. "Nuh uh, spit and shake on it. Two dollars."

"Fine. Two dollars."

We both spit in our hands and shake to make it a real deal between men.

"All right. Get on up, and I'll hold your legs."

"I should make *you* pick it for two whole dollars."

"Barrett, you want to be a real farmer who works his land or not?"

"Yes!" he shouts as I shush him when Mom calls us again for dinner.

"Coming, Mama," I holler back, ducking so she can't see where we are in the orchard. "Tell her you're coming and hurry up," I order Barrett. He hollers at them and climbs the ladder. When he gets as far as he can with me holding him, I point out one he can reach.

"Almost . . . got . . . it," he says, stretching to grab the apple. When he finally picks it, I lose my grip on his legs, and he screams as he starts to fall. Daddy appears and catches him before he hits the ground. I straighten my spine as Daddy turns toward me with Barrett wiggling in his arms, Barrett's eyes as wide as mine.

"Daddy, that was *so, so* fast," I tell him. "How'd you get here so fast?"

"Nice lecture, Son," Dad says in his 'thortive tone. "This boy was a foot away from his first break," he says in a way that tells me I've earned a whoopin', and it's going to hurt. I lift my hand to the sun to see how mad he is and can only see him shake his head. That means he's disappointed. "For a boy who likes to give orders, you sure have a horrible salute."

"Sorry, Daddy," I say, putting my hand down. "I wasn't salutin'. The sun was in my eyes. I was just . . . well, Barrett—"

"Best think a little longer before lying to me, Tyler," Daddy warns.

"I was just—"

"Oh, I heard what you were telling him," he says in the same way he does when he's playing with me. I squint at him as he tosses Barrett around, making him giggle.

"Every single word, Son, including your curses." He sounds like he's playing with me again, and I swear I see him smile, but the sun blocks it. He spins Barrett 'round one more time, and Barrett squeals before he lets him down.

"Thanks for catchin' me, Uncle Carter. I'm sorry we didn't listen. I tried to tell Tyler we would get in trouble. Are you gonna whoop me too?"

"We'll see. You can spend dinner thinking about what you've done." Daddy puts a hand on Barrett's shoulder. "Now, go get washed up and take your seat at the table for grace."

"K," Barrett says, making big eyes at me behind Daddy's back.

"Sorry, what was that?" Dad calls after him.

"I mean, *yessir*," Barrett shouts behind him as he runs toward the porch.

Daddy kneels next to me and picks up the apple I bit into and tossed on the ground. "Son, if you're going to take responsibility for being the oldest and in charge, you best know what you're doing before you start doling out orders and lectures."

"But I've been watching you, Pawpaw, and Uncle Grayson, so I know what to do."

He smiles and shakes his head. "Is that right?"

"Yes, sir."

"All right then. Tell me, son, how much is an apple?"

"Pardon?"

"Buying time and being polite won't give you the answer. So, I'm going to ask you again. Do you know the cost of an apple?"

I swallow and swat a fly away from my nose. "No sir, I don't."

"And why is that?"

"Because we don't have to buy them." I smile and stretch my arms out. "We own a farm!"

"True, but we *do* have to *sell* the apples to make money, and you just cost your Pawpaw the money for that apple, which you will pay for." He picks up Barrett's apple. "Think we can sell a bruised apple?"

"No, sir, I'm sorry—"

"Your apology doesn't count, Tyler. You're not apologizing because you're sorry—only because you got caught. If you want to be a real man, apologize when you mean it, or it never will count for anyone. And don't think you can fool them. People know when you mean it and when you don't."

"Yes, sir."

He lifts my ballcap and ruffles my hair. "You'll be a man soon enough, but until you are, you have no business lecturing another boy on how to be something you aren't. Understood?"

"Yes, sir," I tell him as he pulls my cap back down.

"Now come on, your mother's called you *twice* for dinner, so if you want to keep some hide on that butt, I suggest you get washed up and to the table."

I nod as we start to walk toward the patio where the family sits on picnic benches. "Hey, Daddy?"

"Yes?"

"How much will be mine? You know... when I become a man?"

Stopping, he lifts me above his head and onto his shoulders. I laugh because I know I'm getting too big, but he's so strong he can still carry me. Everyone says I'm the spitting image of him, and I know I'll be as strong as him one day. He points toward one of the hills ahead of us. "Straight ahead up that valley—"

"Twelve o'clock," I tell him, knowing it'll make him proud.

"Exactly. See that tree line out there?"

"Yes, sir."

"From twelve o'clock to four o'clock and then all the way to the back of Uncle Grayson's house, to the road, and back where we're standing right here."

"That much is all mine?"

"Yes, son, it will all be yours."

"Why don't you want to work on our land? Pawpaw said you didn't take your share to work it."

"I guess I wanted to be a Marine more."

"Do I have to choose?"

"Nah, you can be both if you want."

"Pawpaw was both," I tell him.

"Yeah, well, Pawpaw is a better man than me."

"No way he's not," I say, ruffling his hair like he does mine, and he laughs.

"That's what I'm going to do. I'm going to be a Marine and cowboy, not no friggin' alfalfa desperado neither."

"Out of the mouths of babes," he laughs as he lifts me from his shoulders to stand in front of him. "It's something I couldn't manage, but I believe if anyone can do it, it'll be you. But do me a favor for a bit?"

"What?"

"Stay a boy just a little while longer, for your mom and me? Think you can manage that?"

"If I stay a boy for a bit, can we play catch after dinner?"

"Always the barterer," he laughs and tugs my ballcap down over my eyes.

"What's that?"

"Your nature," he chuckles as I put my hat back right. "And it's a deal, but try not to break any more of your cousin's bones this weekend and apologize for cursing in your prayers tonight."

"K . . . so . . . are you going to whoop me? Cause Mom told me 'pacifically to stay off the ladder."

"That's *specifically*, and no whoopin' today, but now you know better." He grabs my hand as we walk toward the porch, and I hold it tight. He stares down at me as we walk, and I can tell by his eyes that he's proud. "Love you, son."

"Love you too, Daddy."

We walk a few more steps. "Daddy?"

"Yes?"

"Thanks for saving it for me . . . the land. I can't wait to be a Marine and cowboy."

"Welcome."

"Hey, Daddy?"

"Good Lord, son, what now?"

"How much *is* an apple?"

Chapter Three

Delphine

US PRESIDENT: RONALD REAGAN | 1981–1989

"Salope" rings out in taunt before I slam Celine's car door, glaring back at the girl through my window before she trots off triumphantly. It's the third time today, and I know she planned it. They always plan it.

"Ignore them," Celine says with a sigh, tenderly running her manicured nails through my hair before pulling away from the curb. "They're only mad because you are prettier than they are, and you have boobs."

"I've had boobs since I was *nine*."

"How could I forget? You showed them to me along with the rest of the family at the dinner table," she laughs, and I roll my eyes.

"They're mad because they think I kissed their boyfriends... and *I did*. I kissed her boyfriend"—I nod back toward the school—"Lyam, during lunch. He uses too much tongue."

Celine gasps as I face her, wearing my own triumphant smile while clicking my seatbelt.

"You aren't going to make any friends that way," she warns.

"I don't want to be friends with them," I tell her. And I don't. I don't want to talk about boys all the time—or dresses, makeup, shopping, or going to concerts. I want to fish the river, and shoot, and make campfires. I want to be back in Levallois-Perret and living as *Matis's* daughter. Not pretending to be Celine's little sister—though no one believes it inside the family but Celine.

"You shouldn't be kissing so many boys. Nine was not that long ago," Celine scorns, taking a turn toward home. A home where the drapes have ruffles, the floors don't creak, and the windows don't have a thick layer of the filth that Maman told us to rot in. Every day, I wish for my life back in our house just outside Levallois-Perret, and every day, I live like a princess instead of a soldier. A home where we have house staff to do our washing and who keep eyes on my every move and then report them to Papa's nephew, Francis, and his wife, Marine.

"Where is Ezekiel?" I ask, glancing toward the empty back seat as she turns up the radio to "Lucky Star." Madonna, *again*. *Always Madonna*. I like Prince.

"He's with Maman for the night, so you'll see him when I drop you home."

"Why is he with her?"

"*Why?*" She bulges her eyes, and I laugh, knowing very well what a tyrant my three-year-old 'nephew' is. "So I can get some needed rest," she sighs and glances at me. "And I kiss *one* man," she reprimands, refusing to let my confession go. "*One man* I'm hoping to be able to kiss tonight without a demanding audience."

"This is why you're boring. Already tied to one man *forever, imbecile*." I poke like I always do, and she smiles—like she always does—never taking my insults seriously, even when I mean them.

Celine had embraced me the minute I was dropped at her front door. Handling my temperament easily because she never seems to get angry. I did all I could to get her to the point of hitting me back during my first few months in her house. Though there are many bedrooms, we shared a room before she moved out and eloped with Abijah. My suspicion is that we only shared a room because Celine decided before I got there that I was the sibling she had always longed for. During that time, I did my best to make her think otherwise. I stole her clothes and even claimed her favorite necklace as my own. When I did, she shrugged and said she would have given it to me if I had asked. Possessions mean nothing to Celine—probably because she grew up with so many of them.

At first, I hated that she never got mad, but instead of fighting back, she hugged me. She said I needed hugs. Though I don't like her hugs, I let her hug me because I think *she* is the one who needs them.

Though Celine and I have become close, it remains different with her parents. Francis, a much older cousin I had never met before the night I came to live with him, now plays as a parent to me. Though I make Francis laugh, his wife, Marine, only tolerates me. I overheard Marine speak her opinion of me not long after I was dropped like garbage at their door.

"She came to us from the slums, and she acts like it. He did not raise a girl—he raised a future criminal who is rude with no manners."

Marine's view of me has not changed much in our years together. She still looks at me the way she did and declares all her efforts have been wasted because I am 'still rude with no manners.'

Francis had come to my defense that night, as he often does now, by reminding her they were the only family I had left. Which I knew to be true because my uncle Aloïs—Matis's only brother and Francis's father—had also been a soldier but died in Vietnam. From what Celine told me through late-night whispers in our bedroom, Francis and Marine had been activists up until Celine became a teenager. I can only assume by her behavior that Marine was the one who put a stop to it, though I have my suspicions that Francis remains involved without her knowledge.

At the dinner table, Celine's mother always silences Francis from telling stories about their time as activists.

She also quiets Francis when he mentions Papa or his *own dead father,* Aloïs. But I refuse to forget my father or my promise to him to remember what he taught me. Most nights, to keep my memories safe, I stare up at my ceiling and relive the time with him after Maman left us—my happiest days. Most of the time, I pretend he didn't die that night in the snow. That the British man lied and that my father didn't sell me for a spoon of drugs. I pretend a lot because I still want to be with him—there. Always. Forever dancing in the wildflowers.

For me, this life is no life at all. There are no outdoor adventures, no fields of flowers to dance in or nearby rivers to fish from, and no animals to target and shoot. All of this city is concrete, and there are way too many eyes. Too many people. I don't blame Celine in the least for leaving the house, though she foolishly didn't move out of the city.

"The man I kiss is changing the world," Celine chimes happily as I change the station, Reagan's words, "Mr. Gorbachev, tear down this wall!" being played, again, as they have for the *millionth time* since the US President spoke them months ago.

"Yeah, yeah, and you're going to help him," I mumble.

Though they have now been together for years, Celine is *always* talking about Abijah. When we still shared a room, I would eavesdrop on their conversations when she would sneak him in at night. Sometimes, they would passionately kiss when they thought I was asleep.

When they weren't kissing, he would tell her stories of our government and the corrupt people inside of it. Of a group he was in—Pardi Radical—and of the changes being made in leadership. He would often tell stories of his friend, Alain, whose papa was killed in a bombing, as well as their plans to change things together.

I would listen because it reminded me of Papa's stories as Abijah reminded me of the soldier my papa was.

Celine hung onto his every word and got arrested with him weekly for protesting after she left home. Up until she got pregnant with Ezekiel, Celine was living more of a soldier's life than I was. To my aunt and uncle, *I* had suddenly become the *good daughter*.

Even though I think most boys are imbeciles, I can understand why Celine fell so madly in love with Abijah. He's not only a true street soldier but very, very handsome. With dark black hair, eyes that glow like fire, and a smooth, silky voice. He always speaks so excitedly about his plans that I sometimes believe him like Celine does.

"I told you I'm done helping him for now, for a much better purpose," she says fondly, speaking of the other love of her life, her son, as she takes a turn I don't recognize.

"Celine, this is not the way home," I point out, glancing her way.

"It is for me." She looks back at me, a twinkle of mischief in her eyes. "You always ask me to take you to my apartment to meet our friends."

I turn fully toward her in my seat, finally excited about something. "Today? We're going right now?"

"Yes, but you have to promise to behave. Don't backtalk Abijah this time with your politics. Just listen."

"I promise," I agree easily, anticipation thrumming through me at the idea of talking about more than shades of lipstick.

"Don't make me regret this." She rolls her eyes as Prince starts to sing "When Doves Cry."

"I promise," I tell her before I turn it up.

***

Standing just inside the tiny kitchen, I study the map Abijah marked as Celine's laughter reaches me from their bedroom. Rolling my eyes, I walk along a table full of guns—most of them dropped on the tabletop as their friends came in. Celine's giggles quiet when someone turns the record player up, as even more smoke fills the small apartment. Most of the nicotine cloud rapidly filling the room exhaled from the half dozen of their friends crowding their second-story balcony. Shivering due to the crisp fall breeze sweeping through the room, I scour the mostly unimpressive inventory of firearms before pausing on a gun that looks similar to one of Papa's. Just next to it sits a large box of tools and tubs that have powder inside them. When I reach out to open one of them, someone whispers a "BOOM!" in my ear.

Jumping, I turn and see a man, or . . . boy. He's somewhere in between, his eyes light brown, his hair as dark as Abijah's. Studying him closer, I decide he is almost as handsome as Abijah—though his teeth are a little crooked when he smiles at me. "I wouldn't play with that. It's not a toy."

"I wasn't *playing*. I'm not a little girl."

"You are Celine's sister? Non?" he says in English.

"Oui, but—" I pause to think of the word. "I . . . curious."

"Curiosity kills the cat," he laughs, taking a sip of his beer. He is dressed in jeans and a T-shirt, but his shoes look new and expensive.

"Do I look like cat? You look like imbecile," I utter, humiliated by my English again as I am most days. I've spent every year since Marine enrolled me trying to catch up with my fluent classmates because Matis never once put me in school when I came of age after Maman left.

The boy flashes me a full smile as if he knows something I don't. "No . . . you, you're a spirit-filled little girl."

"I'm no more *girl* than you are *boy*," I counter in French.

"Hmm. I see. Please, take no offense, little sister." He might not be laughing at me now, but his eyes are, and I scowl at him before picking up a rifle I'm familiar with.

"This is old," I say, "MAS 49/56, ten-round magazine. Standard-issue French army in the *sixties*. This is a relic that requires *gas* to shoot and needs to be *buried*."

His brows shoot up in confusion. "How do you know this?"

"That's my business. Who are you?"

"I guess you'll have to stay curious, but I've got my eyes on you, little sister."

"You can keep those eyes to yourself," I snap, unsure why my heart is pounding so fast as he glances over my shoulder. I follow his stare to see a girl waving him over to her.

He lifts his chin toward her before he slowly brings his eyes back to me. My chest aches a little as he watches me for a few long seconds. "It was nice to meet you, Delphine."

"I will not say it's nice to meet you," I tell him. "You better go to her, that is, if you like being told what to do."

He laughs, sips his beer again, and keeps his eyes on me even as he walks toward the girl. Celine comes out of the bedroom, cutting off my view just after he disappears into the smoke on the balcony. The second he's out of sight, I hate that I can't see him anymore.

"Ready to go?" Celine asks me.

I nod and follow her toward the door, looking back one last time to see if the dark-headed boy is watching me. Abijah emerges from their bedroom just after and stops at the door, watching us go—watching *Celine* go. He's just as obsessed with her, and in seeing it, I find myself wanting someone to look at me the way Abijah looks at his wife.

"Celine?" I ask, looking back at the balcony again for any sign of him.

"Yes," she replies absently, seeming to be locked in the flames dancing in her husband's eyes. As she does this, she smiles at him with confidence, and I know it's because of the way he watches her—never taking his eyes away once, even for those who call his name. Anyone in the room can tell they love each other. They only have to look to see it. In watching them, I decide that I want to feel the same confidence when a boy looks at me.

"Celine, who was the boy who just went out onto the balcony? The one wearing the blue shirt."

"The blue shirt? *Oh*, that was Alain."

"*That* was Alain?" I gawk, shocked he's so young because of the way Abijah speaks so highly of him—as if he's someone of authority to respect.

"Hmm," she confirms as we exit the apartment before taking the stairs down to her car, my attention lingering on the boy I just met. Alain must be at least sixteen—seventeen at the most. This means I would be forbidden from kissing him, and only makes me want to kiss him more.

As Celine pulls away from the apartment, I search for and find him on the balcony, only to see he's laughing with the girl who summoned him. As we drive away, I decide I'm done kissing boys like Lyam.

Chapter Four

Tyler

US PRESIDENT: WILLIAM J. CLINTON | 1993–2001

My arms burn as I cut the corner with the mower the way Daddy taught me before stopping to wipe some of the sweat from under my ball cap. When I look up, I see the same two boys riding their bikes past my house. I know one of them from school. Sean. And I see him sometimes at the Pitt Stop. His daddy owns it, and my daddy knows his daddy and loves their burgers. We go there for grub after church sometimes. The other boy moved into the neighborhood a while back. Daddy calls their yard a 'shit show' 'cause they never cut their grass. Daddy says, 'A man who takes no pride in his yard has no pride at all.'

Sean waves at me the next time they pass, and I wave back. They ride by my house two more times before Sean pulls up into our driveway, shouting something at me. I shake my head to tell him I can't hear him and cut the mower.

"What?" I yell over from where I stand in the yard.

"Why doesn't your daddy cut your grass?!" Sean hollers back.

I walk over as the other boy pulls up and stops next to Sean. He doesn't say anything but just stares at me.

"He's deployed," I tell Sean, still staring back at the

dark-haired boy. His eyes look like the metal on one of Daddy's guns.

"Oh," Sean says before tilting his head. "What's that mean?"

"It means he's a Marine, and he's protecting you and me from all enemies, foreign and domestic. I'm the man of the house while he's away, so I cut the grass."

The dark boy laughs, and I cut my eyes at him. "*Your yard* is a *shit show*. Why doesn't *your daddy* mow it?"

The dark boy only stares at me.

"His daddy is dead. His momma too," Sean tells me.

"Oh," I say, wiping my forehead with my shirt.

"Aren't you going to ask how they died?" Sean asks.

"It's not polite to ask things like that," I tell him. "He can tell me if he wants to." The boy doesn't say anything and just keeps looking at me. "If you want to, you can tell me."

He nods, but he doesn't tell me. Now I wish I did ask.

"Is your daddy deployed all the time?" Sean asks.

"Sometimes for a long time. He was deployed when the Desert Storm came years back. You hear about that?"

"Nope," Sean says and looks to the boy. "You hear about that?" The boy shakes his head.

"Well, it was *a bad* storm," I tell them. "When my daddy has no choice, he has to kill the bad guys."

Sean's eyes get big. "How did he do that in a storm?"

"He won't tell me sometimes. It's secret Marine stuff."

"Huh . . . well, I'm Sean." Hands on his handlebars, he tilts his head toward the dark-headed boy. "This is Dom. He moved here with his brother and his Tatie. That means aunt in French 'cause they're French. You're Tyler Jennings. I seen you at school. You're a grade up from me."

"Yeah, I seen you too."

"Well . . . want to be in our club?" Sean asks.

"What club?"

"We sneak out at night, get on our bikes, and ride into the woods. We bring flashlights."

"And do what?" I ask him.

"All kinds of things, right, Dom?"

Dom nods, and I wonder if he can talk at all.

"He doesn't talk all the time," Sean tells me. "But he's nice. You don't have to look at him like he's weird. He's not weird. I made sure."

"Okay." I tug my ballcap.

"Well," Sean says, "if you want to be in our club, you have to bring a snack." Dom looks at Sean as if he's telling a lie but stays quiet.

"What kind of snack?" I ask.

"Any snack, and as much as you can bring. I like Fruit Roll-Ups."

"I have a box of berry," I tell him.

Sean nods. "That will work. But we stay up *really* late, sometimes past midnight. One time, we stayed up until *one o'clock*. Think you can stay up that late?"

"I've stayed up later than that," I tell him.

"Oh, well then, meet us on Dom's street at the second light post after dark if you can come tonight."

"Yeah. All right."

"Don't forget the Roll-Ups if you want to be in our club."

"I'll bring them."

"K. See ya." Sean pedals away, and Dom still stares at me. I wonder if Sean feels sorry for him, and *he is* weird because he still doesn't talk.

"It's rude to stare at people," I tell Dom. Then I feel bad because I know not having my daddy would be hard. I probably wouldn't talk a lot. Before I can think of anything else to say, Dom pedals away and looks back at me one more time. He smiles a little at me, and it's a nice one.

***

Hoping I still have enough gas, I push the mower up the driveway, look around the yard and then back to the street. This is going to take a lot longer than I thought it would. Deciding to try, I push it onto the grass to start the first row. Dandelions shoot out, and I know that's not good because it will only spread the seeds and grow more weeds. I'm almost done with the second row when I look up to see an older, dark-headed boy on the porch, watching me. When he sees me watching him back, he walks down the steps and over to me, and I stop mowing.

"Why are you mowing my yard?" he yells over the mower. "Did my aunt hire you?"

"Uh, no." I take off my ball cap. "You Dom's brother?"

"Yes. I'm Tobias."

He sounds very French.

"Oh, well, I'm Tyler, and I just met Sean and Dom, and Sean told me you didn't have . . . uh, that your daddy isn't here anymore to mow your yard, and my daddy said your yard was a, uh, needs to be mowed. So, I thought I would mow it for you. My daddy is overseas. He's a Marine, and he's deployed. Do you know what that means?"

He nods.

"Well, he says if you ever find someone that has a need you can fill, then you should fill it."

Tobias smiles at me like he's about to laugh. "Thank you, Tyler, but I can mow my own yard."

"Oh. Okay. I didn't know you were the man of the house."

He nods. "I am."

"Okay then. Well, I can go." Feeling stupid, I start to push the mower back to my house.

"Tyler," Tobias calls after me, and I look back at him. "I don't have a mower *right now*. Would it be okay if I borrowed yours?"

"Oh, yeah," I say, letting off the gas and stepping away from it. "It's a real good one. A John Deere. You ever heard of him?"

He glances at the mower. "No."

"Well, it's one of the best there is. It's self-propld or somethin'. That means it pushes itself. You can try if you want. But don't cut it off 'cause it's really hard to start. K?"

He nods and smiles at me like *I'm the one* that talks French. "Thank you."

"Welcome."

Standing at the edge of the driveway, I watch Tobias mow his yard. A little while later, the front door opens, and Dom comes out with a cup of water. He walks over and holds it out to me.

"Thanks," I tell him, drinking the whole glass. He still doesn't talk, but he looks over and stares at me as he drops to sit on the driveway. After a bit, he scoots over to give me a spot to sit next to him. I take a seat, and we both watch Tobias mow for a while.

"Is it fun to have a brother?" I finally ask him. "Sometimes, I wish I had one. I got my cousin, Barrett, but he's younger and a crybaby."

Dom laughs and finally talks. "It's okay. He tells me what to do—*a lot*."

Dom doesn't speak French like his brother, but I don't ask him why. Maybe he'll tell me that tonight, too.

Chapter Five

Delphine

US PRESIDENT: RONALD REAGAN | 1981–1989

I TAKE A PUFF of my cigarette as the woman watching me from the aisle seat across from mine finally speaks her mind. "You look too young to smoke."

"You look *old*," I tell her, and her mouth drops open.

"How very rude," she gasps.

"Yes"—I roll my eyes—"*rude* for *stranger* to make observations and speak them." I blow my exhale her way, wishing I had gotten the window seat. An older man snores next to me, his head tilted away from the wasted view.

"Who are you traveling with? I wonder if they would approve of your behavior." She eyes the wheezing man next to me. "Is that your father?"

I bark out a laugh as I smooth my hand down Celine's dress and ash my cigarette, staring back at the woman. "My papa rots in the ground."

"Oh," she says, taken aback by the way I tell her this. I never understand why people are so polite about revealing the truth when it's not pleasant. It's as if people are hiding from real life, but some truths can never be pleasant, no matter how they're worded or spoken. "And your mother?"

I inhale again, considering if I want to reveal so much to her, and decide to have a little fun. This woman considers me a mystery to solve, much like my aunt and uncle did. Not only that, but it will also give me a chance to practice my English.

"Left me when I five. *Poof.*" I snap loud, and the woman jumps back in her seat. She is intimidated by me—*me*—a girl at least twenty years younger in age. Alain says intimidation is one of my gifts.

"My papa dies the night partner comes to collect me from a card game. I was"—I lean toward her—"*I was bet, last bet he* makes."

The woman gasps in shock as I lean in further, blowing more smoke in her face, which she now ignores for my story.

"Sold me for a spoon of . . . the *needle* drugs." I take another cigarette out of my pack sitting on the tray table.

"Heroin?" She asks, eyes bulging.

"Yes, heroin. So if you want to talk parents how rude I behave, you will have *hard times* to reach them."

"My God." Her eyes soften with pity. "I'm so sorry to hear that."

"What is your name?" I ask.

"Janet," she tells me, her eyes scouring my face and dress—nothing I am not used to. Women and men alike are *always* watching me. Alain says they cannot help themselves because I am *painfully* beautiful.

"Do not pity me, Janet . . . I very, I'm fortunate."

"Oh? How so?"

"When I land in America, I marry a *soldier.*"

She gapes at me. "But you can't be more than what, sixteen?"

Her guess discourages me even as I fill out one of Celine's more sophisticated dresses after applying thick makeup. I'm failing to conceal my age as much as I hoped. I decide it is better to start rehearsing the lie I'll be living very soon.

"I am *eighteen.*"

"Oh?" Perspiration dots her upper lip as I shake out my match. "Well . . . congratulations. You'll make a beautiful bride. You're just gorgeous, honey."

"Merci, Janet. You have nice..." I look her up and down to try and find a way to be kind with my reply, "Eyes."

"Oh, thank you." She smiles, and I smile back for an entirely different reason. Within the length of a plane ride, I will be legally eighteen in the eyes of United States law and be able to work and marry. Alain told me that in America, if the paperwork says so, it must be.

And I will marry him because after kissing too many Lyams, I found the only soldier for me the night Celine brought me to her apartment—a soldier who had been fighting alongside Abijah in the *new Pardi Radical* until he evaded arrest just weeks ago. Declaring his time in France over after, he promised he would send for me once he found us a place to live and work—as well as a good place to re-establish his movement. He fled France with a few of his most trusted men and writes that he has been *very* successful. Yesterday morning I received a letter with a ticket as promised.

I left school early, faking an illness to start packing. I decided to bring very little of my clothes and leave all those meant for a modest little girl. I packed just enough to fit in my wildflower suitcase—all I have left of life with my papa. But the life I had with him, I've been promised to have again with Alain.

Excitement fills me as I think of Alain's description of North Carolina. My dream written in his handwriting, in black and white, of the town of Triple Falls. He wrote that there are many rivers and lakes for me to fish—along with abundant wildlife—and not nearly as many people as the city I so despise. After getting to know Alain, I found out his dream was mine, too.

It's still a mystery to me how we kept our relationship from both Abijah *and* Celine these past months. We almost got caught once or twice but managed to escape all suspicion that we were a couple—which we weren't—not at first. It was only yesterday that I finally told Celine of our relationship and future plans.

"You can't be serious," Celine gasps as Ezekiel keeps a firm grip on my hands, leading me around their kitchen table. As she gawks at my admission, I notice a fresh bruise on her cheek.

"Did Abijah do that?"

She jerks her chin. "No, he did," she laughs, nodding toward Ezekiel, her eyes soft as they always are with him, which I recognize as a mother's love. "He hit me with one of his bath toys."

"Don't lie to me, Celine," I warn.

"I told you, Abijah doesn't hit me. Not like that, and don't change the subject," she snaps. "You can't just tell me you've been with Alain all this time and nothing more. Did you start seeing him right after you met?"

"No." I shake my head. "No, no, not at first. He said I was too young. It took him a very long time to consider me for himself—years—but I finally convinced him." I smile at her, but she does not smile back.

"God, it was happening right under my nose!"

"You were busy," I say, picking up the reason for her distraction and holding him up for my inspection. Ezekiel stares back at me with his father's firelight eyes and pats my cheek with his open hand. "So much of Abijah in you," I tell him, and he giggles.

"Don't remind me," Celine sighs.

"No, that bruise will remind you," I say, turning to her.

"For the last time, Abijah is not violent with me," she insists. "Just the once, and it was an accident."

"If it happened once, Celine, it will happen again. I have seen how he behaves—his paranoia—and he is not well."

"Since when did you become an expert on men? You've dated only one."

"So have you," I point out, and she sighs again.

"But Alain, he is good to you?"

"He's perfect to me," I tell her, my attention still on Ezekiel as he jabbers on about one of his toys. "He treats me like I matter more to him than anything else, even his cause."

"Abijah was like that too," she relays in warning, "and he hasn't been the same since . . ." She trails off, but I know exactly what she's referring to.

"All they did was make their stance known. It was just."

"Not the right way," Celine says in a whisper. "Not the right way, Delphine, and you know it."

"Alain lost his father in a bombing," I argue. "If he didn't think it was necessary, he wouldn't have done it. You have to trust them."

"Trust them?" She gawks. "Alain fled because—"

"I know what he did. He's honest with me and wouldn't have left if Abijah hadn't overreacted and exiled him."

"As he should have. Say all you want about Abijah, but Alain is far more dangerous."

"I believe his reasons and . . . I've been helping him. Since we met."

"What?" Celine pales. "Jesus, Delphine. What have you done?"

"I was not there that night, but I go to the meetings and hear of their plans, their ambitions. I run errands for them, messages, trade guns, things of that nature. All they want is audience and—"

"Don't," she shouts, scaring Ezekiel, who jumps in my arms. "Don't tell me anything else! I will not lose my son for any cause! Not for Abijah or you and Alain! Do you hear me? I'm done with it all!"

"Fine," I say, tired of the same argument we've been having since Alain left—which is also why I don't visit when Abijah is here.

Though we both want to drop it, she shakes her head. "Jesus, Delphine."

"It's what soldiers do."

"Soldiers sign up to be soldiers and serve in the French Army. Why can't you do that?"

"It's going to be a different world when the Berlin Wall falls, and minds will change with it! They've already seen many politicians forever stuck in the old ways, leaving soldiers to obey exhausted orders of oppression and control. The new soldier has become the common man who turns street warrior to fight for a new world without selfish motive. That is the soldier my Alain is and the soldier I want to be."

She shakes her head gently. "Maybe, but I don't agree with you, Abijah, or Alain with the tactics you choose. The Pardi has already denied any of those inciting violence like Alain. I am for peace."

"Peace," I scoff. "Since when has peace brought change? The cost of peace is being compliant to whatever our government decides without our say. That's not peace, that's enslavement. Alain says the same corruption stands just beneath the veil of American capitalism and is ready to join the fight to liberate them."

"Fight how? Violence only leads to more violence. So, I don't agree with you. Or Abijah. In fact, I don't agree anymore on anything with Abijah." She wrings the towel in her hands. "I am afraid, Delphine."

She takes Ezekiel from me and presses a kiss to his head, and I fear the conversation will only get worse with my next admission, but she speaks first. "As long as we're confessing, I've met someone. I don't know how . . . but it just happened."

Shock instantly fills me. "My God, Celine—"

"He's a good man," she defends, "a wonderful man, Delphine, and he wants to take me away from Abijah. He wants me to leave him."

I freeze, my fear for her and Ezekiel overtaking any need to confess about my departure as she grips him tightly to her. "Abijah will kill him if he finds out."

"I know," she whispers. "But he doesn't care. He would take me away now if I allowed it. And I think, no, I know I'm in love with him." Her eyes fill. "I know it's wrong, and I feel so guilty, Delphine." She shakes her head, her tears falling steadily. "How did this happen?"

I hesitate but only briefly with the truth. "I envied

you," I admit, "your connection and bond, and if I thought for one second it could be salvaged, I would urge you to try. To stay, but he is only becoming more dangerous."

"He leaves us for weeks at a time now without a word and comes back different each time. The man I married is just . . . gone. I can't raise my son with what he's becoming, and I don't know what to do."

"Come with me," I offer instantly. "I'm leaving for America tomorrow to be with Alain. He sent for me as he promised. We're to be married once I get there."

She pales again, this time pulling out a chair and sitting with Ezekiel in her lap. "You can't be serious. You're far too young—"

"You know that's not true. My age does not match my intelligence. Even my body agrees and does not match my years. I'm nothing like the other girls at school. I'm far more evolved."

"Yes, yes"—she waves—"you are a soldier."

"I am," I declare with confidence. "Come with me, Abijah won't ever find you where I'm going. Please, Celine, think of Ezekiel," I utter, terrified for them both. I know she shares my fear as we stare off for long seconds.

"Mamannnn," Ezekiel draws out, wanting her attention as she stares at me—through me—lost in thought. She's so beautiful, my cousin who insists she's my sister. And I allow her to believe it because I feel the bond now as truth. Aside from Alain, Celine is all that remains.

"Wait here," she finally says before disappearing into her bedroom. Not long after, she emerges with a bag that holds a few dresses, shoes, and makeup, as well as a smaller purse full of money.

"It's all I have, but it should help you until you find work. How will you work, Delphine?"

"Abijah has found a factory where the boss helps to get visas for all who come to work for him. You could work there too. We could both start a new life together."

She bites her lip.

"Please, consider it." I glance at Ezekiel, my throat burning. "Please, Celine. If this new man truly loves you—"

"Beau, his name is Beau."

"If Beau loves you, he will follow you there. Leave Abijah. As you said, he is gone, and I am convinced of it too."

She swallows, her expression solemn, before she breaks it with a smile. "He has red hair."

"Who?"

"Beau," she whispers before shaking her head. "What am I doing, Delphine?"

"You already know what you're doing. You're simply stalling from seeing it through because you're scared, but it's the right thing."

"And you're so sure you want this?"

I nod. "He's good to me. He's beyond his age, like me. He's my match, and I'm most myself when I'm with him. I'm sure."

She nods and sets Ezekiel on his feet, his little shoes slapping the floor as he runs toward me and crashes into my legs. Laughing, I lift him up and speak to him. "Take care of your maman for me, okay?"

Ezekiel nods very slowly as if he's making a promise to me. "La poursuite, Tatie," he squeaks in demand to play our game.

"Not today," I tell him regretfully as my throat burns that I can't promise to play tomorrow.

"Soon, you'll have your own son or daughter," Celine whispers fondly. "You're so good with him."

"Only because he is yours," I say, setting him on his feet. "I will have no children. They will only get in the way."

She lifts a brow. "Does Alain know that? You might want to tell him that before you marry him."

"I will. I'm not afraid to tell him what I want."

She smiles. "Always so sure of everything. I admire you for that. Are you not scared at all?"

"What is there to fear?"

"So much," she says, *"but maybe I won't worry too much for you. I believe you scare even Abijah sometimes."*

We both laugh and spend the rest of the day together until I know I must leave to prepare to sneak away tomorrow.

After promising her no less than a dozen times to write—with the decision that I address my letters to Celine's best friend to keep them from Abijah's reach—she finally frees me. Kneeling next to Ezekiel at the top of her apartment stairs, they both wave me off. Celine's tears fall freely as Ezekiel calls after me. "Au revoir, Tatie!"

"Au revoir, Ézéchiel." Goodbye, Ezekiel.

The image of the two of them on the top of those stairs imprints in my mind and heart as I roll the lit part of my cigarette along the curve of the ashtray. In that moment, I vow to keep Celine in my life. Aside from Papa and now Alain, Celine is the only other person who has ever accepted me exactly as I am. As I catch a glimpse of the ocean out of the window past the snoring man, I feel little remorse for my decision to leave. My gut telling me they won't be far behind.

In hours, I'll have a home and husband. I'll have a purpose, and we won't have to hide our love, nor will I from who I truly am. I can finally rid my life of the ruffles and the lie of being a little girl with a woman's mind and start my true life as a soldier and wife.

My heart beats faster at that knowledge as the flight attendant stops her cart next to me, eyeing my cigarette and dress.

"How long to airport?" I ask.

"We have about three hours left. Can I get you something to drink?"

"Vodka. No ice. Merci."

She pauses. "Vodka?"

"I am"—I briefly struggle to find the English word—"celebrates. I marry tomorrow."

"Oh? Congratulations, I'll get that drink for you."

When I have my vodka in hand and the attendant moves to the next passenger, Janet lifts a brow at me.

"You know, I'm not worried about you at all. You're going to be just fine, but I am a little worried for your fiancé."

I laugh at her joke, but Alain knows how to handle me when I get too cross.

My love.

For years, I had to make him see me as the woman I am. Not Celine's little sister or a little girl, but as an equal and soldier. For years, he denied me, but all the waiting has proven worth it. Soon, we will be together the way real couples are together. Physically, intimately, and completely. Hours until I become his—entirely his.

My heart pounds as the minutes pass, and I drink down the vodka in celebration of the new life that awaits me.

Chapter Six

Tyler

US PRESIDENT: GEORGE W. BUSH | 2001–2009

"For christ's sake, Regina, *stop!*" Dad snaps at Mom for her tears as he packs his duffle while I pace in my room, making noise here and there so they assume I'm busy. I've already cleaned it to the point that I could eat chow from the floor and ensure my bed sheets passed the quarter bounce test. A lecture I'd been given when Dad returned from his last deployment.

"If you can't figure out how to properly make your own bed, Son, how in the fuck do you expect to defend your country?"

For days on end, I spent my free time trying to get the sheets tight enough for the quarter to bounce—which was nowhere near as easy as I thought it would be. When I'd pulled Dad into my room to show him, instead of giving me the proud grin I've come to expect, he'd whispered a sarcastic "congratulations," rolled his eyes, and walked out of the room.

As he stalked out, for the first time ever, I felt something bordering hate for him, or at least that side of him. Last year and in the years prior, he'd taken me hunting every chance he got and spent hours on end prepping me for my own time in the service. He didn't stop there, teaching me mechanical basics, including fixing the plumbing, air conditioner, and other things to help 'spruce up the house' and maintain it.

This year, it had been the opposite. He just expected me to know things—to have figured them out for myself. Not only that, but he also seemed to be weighing my intelligence and worth on whether I could figure them out on my own. I was thankful when, more often than not, I could.

"Excuses are for the lazy and weak," he'd said when I failed, all patience gone—for me, for Mom, for my uncles, and his oldest friends. They stopped coming around when he got home this time, and I can't blame them. He argued with them every chance he got, and when they weren't arguing, he'd start one.

For years, I always thought I had it better than Tobias and Dom—until this one. When Dom was still of single-digit age, their aunt Delphine was a horrible bitch, and at times, still can be. Especially when she's drunk—which is most nights. For years, she used to torture Dom with mind games, but even when we were younger, he usually came out on top. I used to feel sorry for him because she picked on him the most. Back then, she was exceedingly miserable and tried to make everyone around her feel the same.

That's my dad *now.*

He was angrier after he got back from this last deployment and harder to get a laugh or smile from, and at times, to get him to simply function. It's been nearly impossible to keep his attention, even in short spurts. Worse than that, my parents started to fight all the time, and Mom spent most of their arguments defending herself. I stepped in a time or two, but I might as well have been a fly on the wall and was treated as such, swatted away with Dad's backhand one of those times. He didn't strike me hard, but the blow itself ruined me for weeks. He never apologized, and that hurt worse than anything.

After a few minutes, Mom's cries settle, and the landline rings. I don't have to see them where they are in their bedroom to know they're both staring at the phone. Standing with one foot in the hallway where I can quickly retreat into my room if their door opens, I strain to hear them answer.

"Hello? Hi Sean. No, I'm sorry, sweetheart, Tyler can't come to the phone right now. He's seeing his daddy off. Uh-huh. Okay, I'll have him call you tomorrow."

That's not happening. As soon as Dad leaves, I'm taking the nails out of the window he hammered shut when he caught me sneaking out. By midnight, I'll be around the fire with Sean and Dom. It's what we always do when one of us has shit going on, and these days, one of us *always* has shit going on. Not only that, but Tobias is also due for a visit from France any day, and I don't miss a minute of his visits if I can help it.

When she hangs up, Mom's cries start up again, and I know it's due to disappointment that Dad's orders to report haven't changed. It's like, somehow, she still believes Dad's deployments are optional. Something he can get out of. Like calling in sick, and he says as much as her low cries somehow start to fill the entirety of our house.

"You married a Marine, Regina," Dad reminds her. "I don't see how this is still surprising to you."

"I just got you back," she says, her voice clogged. Though technically, he's been home for a while, her remark is due to his behavior. "And I know who I married," she snaps, "and he just barely came back to me. Did you have to re-enlist?"

"Stop it, God dammit, stop it. You're seriously going to guilt me right now? I'm a career fucking Marine, and we're at war. Weren't you there? Did you not see the fucking planes?"

I shiver at his comment the way I always do when he refers to that day—that morning. No matter how hard I try to blur the vision, I can see the footage so vividly. A sunny day, a clear morning, the first plane enveloped by the tower, its course steady, eerily steady, as if it was natural for the plane to fly straight into the New York skyscraper.

Our whole family had gathered at the farm that day. Without so much as a phone call to meet up, it was a given. Car by car, every relative in and around Triple Falls filed in, embracing one another with fear-riddled and devastated expressions. A majority of them were active or ex-military, including my Uncle Grayson, who chose not to re-enlist in lieu of taking over the farm full-time.

Barrett and I kept the fire stoked as our mothers cried for hours and hours, and our fathers talked and drank. Dad had called a few in his old company and only got amped and angrier with each beer. Even with the lingering high of the annual Apple Festival—in which Jennings & Sons had sponsored one of the larger tents—none of us talked about it or dared change the subject.

Later that night, Dad and Uncle Grayson had wandered out into the orchard for hours, not coming back until sunrise. It was a long night, and no one could be comforted. I was the last one waiting by the fire when they got back. The look in Dad's eyes was one I'll never forget as he passed right by me and went into the house. Uncle Grayson had stopped and gripped my shoulder, only telling me to get some shut-eye.

The last few weeks, things have only gotten worse, what with Dad receiving his report date—which came faster than expected—to the fights they've been having. I've done everything I can to stay out as late as possible to avoid home—something I never used to do. And I got away with it until Mom's paranoia got me busted sneaking in.

Even as a trained psychologist equipped to handle situations such as these, she's been acting irrationally and gets up in arms about everything. Curiously watching me and Dad as we eat breakfast and do other everyday shit. One night, I caught her watching me sleep from the door of my bedroom before the phone rang, and once again, she had to pick Dad up from the bar because he was too drunk to drive.

Last night was Dad's last supper. He'd asked for steak and a sweet potato. We ate in silence, and when Dad finished his plate, Mom swiped it from the table not a second later, turning quickly so he couldn't see the tears in her eyes.

"Carter, I just want—" Mom starts to say, and I flinch when the sound of shattering glass reaches me. Hauling ass toward their bedroom across the hall, I pause just outside of it when Mom sounds up.

"Break anything you want. It'll be a mess I can clean, but what mess will you be in when you get home? Do you think they care about that? About your family, about you? Your father—"

"Don't you fucking dare," Dad snaps. "That man has gone through hell and back to defend his country, and you should respect that."

"I do," she defends, "you know I do, but *they* don't."

They meaning the United States Marine Corps. Though I'm with Dad most of the time when it comes to patriotic duty, I'm starting to think Mom's way when it comes to limiting the *amount* of service.

Though it seems they are never late with a paycheck or to offer up a benefit, I've been researching more on the long-term effects because of the way Dad is acting. What I've learned is that a lot of soldiers don't bounce back after too much exposure to war. The more I dug in, the more the statistics and bodies piled up because of soldiers who take their own lives after not being able to acclimate once they get home.

I've also been sneaking Mom's psychology books into my bedroom. The more I learn, the more I'm starting to realize that Dad has oversimplified his job. My thinking had always been simple as well—you enlist, train, go to war if called to fight, follow orders to the letter, and come home. Once home, you get out your tools and spruce up the house, barbecue, catch up with friends, work on your truck, and wait for the call to go back.

It's a kid's perception, and Dad has made sure recently that I have very little of those kinds of thoughts left in me.

He's always made it seem so uncomplicated, but thanks to my research—and as my parents scream at each other—I'm not so sure any of it is simple.

"You don't respect shit," Dad snaps. "You say you do, but you don't because you didn't grow up with a militant father and in a house filled with respect for the uniform. You grew up getting what you wanted on a whim."

"So now I'm spoiled because I want my husband home and safe?"

"I'm done with this. If you can't get behind me, don't bother seeing me off."

"Carter, don't—"

"God damn you, Regina!"

"I love you," she cries. "But every time you come back, it becomes harder and harder to recognize the *family man* I married. If you want a reason why we didn't have another baby, there's your damned reason."

The air in the house grows thick, and it becomes harder to breathe due to the loaded silence.

"You took birth control." He doesn't ask it. He knows. A cry of outrage leaves my father as I take another step toward their door. "How long?" Dad roars. "How low have you been sabotaging this family?"

"C-Carter, please don't see it that way. You're a wonderful father—"

"How long?!"

"I never stopped," she admits before another crash sounds in the bedroom.

I'm not supposed to hear this, but they do little to hide the fact that they fight anymore. They used to go out to the garage, but that stopped this year. I used to turn up my stereo to avoid it, but Dad walked in, lifted it, and drop-kicked it the last time I did. I can still hear the echo as it smacked against my drywall and dented it, one of the shattered pieces narrowly missing me.

"How could you?" Dad asks, heartbreak soaking his voice.

"I've already got one son who's had to sacrifice seeing his father in the stands at his ball games. I'm not doing that to another child."

"Well, you bid your time and made sure it was too late, denying me the one thing I truly wanted."

"And we aren't enough? Tyler and I aren't enough?"

"Stop twisting this. You betrayed me! I'll never forgive you, Regina!"

Though my father is ripped up about Mom using birth control, I can't help but be glad about it. I don't want a little brother or sister to know this version of Carter Jennings, and I get why she's scared. I am, too. Is Dad one deployment away from never coming back?

Back in my room after hearing Dad and Mom speaking more softly to one another, I lay on my bed and stare blankly up at the ceiling while vowing never to mistreat my wife or my kids no matter what I face on my missions.

A knock on my bedroom window jars me, and I pull back my curtains to see Sean straining to lift it. When the pane doesn't give, his eyes drop to the nails before he slowly brings them back to me.

Embarrassed, I point toward our fence, ordering him to leave.

Expression full of concern and refusing to go, his voice sounds on the other side of the window, and I know if I can hear it, my dad might, too. Cutting my hand through the air desperately to shut him the hell up, I urgently point behind him with the other to try and get him to leave. In the next second, his bare ass is pressed against the glass before he turns his head, producing a joint in his fingers and nodding toward the fence, or rather, the woods behind them, while mouthing a "later."

"Idiot," I mouth back, nodding as he tucks his ass back in his pants, and I grip my curtains. It's when he pauses and stiffens that I know he hears the yelling resuming, and his eyes snap to mine. Dropping my gaze, I draw the curtains on him.

Not long after, my bedroom door opens, and Dad looks over to me. "What are you doing?"

"I was just about to come to you. Uncle Grayson here yet?" Dad stopped letting us see him off after his last deployment and only allows Uncle Grayson to take him now. I know it's 'cause of the state it leaves Mom in. I guess he thinks it's easier on her if he walks out of the front door as if he's running an errand.

One hell of a fucking errand.

"Yeah, he just pulled up," he says, running a hand through his hair. It's just now grown to the length Mom likes, and when he comes back, it'll be time to start all over again. But he does it because he still loves her, and even I can tell she's only fighting because she'll miss him. At least there's that.

"You know the drill, Son. Do your chores, your school-work, and as your mom tells you."

"Yes, sir."

"Please don't give her any reason to bitch to me. I want good reports only, understood?"

"Yes, sir."

He smiles, but it's forced. "You too old to give your dad a hug?"

"Not yet." I grin as he pulls me to him.

His words come out stunted and sincere as he keeps me in his tight grip. "I love you, Son."

"You too, Dad."

"Fuck," he croaks, "I hope you know I still hate this... leaving you. I hope I never make it look easy."

"You don't, and I'm proud of you. You're a good Marine and father." Though the words come harder this time, I still mean them.

His eyes shimmer, and he looks away briefly before turning back to me. "I'm proud of you too, Tyler. Really proud. I couldn't have asked for a better son. Never forget that, okay?"

"I won't," I swear, trying to tamp down the fear that, one way or another, this might be the very last time I lay eyes on Carter Jennings.

Chapter Seven

Delphine

US PRESIDENT: GEORGE BUSH | 1989–1993

Feeling the heavy weight of a stare on my profile, I crush my cigarette into our large, overflowing marble ashtray and stand suddenly from the table. Without looking up, Alain stops me as I move past his chair with a palm on my hip. "Where are you going?"

"Make coffee," I whisper low as Ormand glances over to me for the second time in mere minutes, his eyes lowering to Alain's palm before floating back up to mine.

Alain sharply nods and releases me as I walk through the ever-present cloud of smoke while the arguments ensue over our kitchen table. Dreading the long hours ahead, I'm spooning coffee from the tin when I feel him approach.

"Your neck," he whispers hoarsely. "Is he hurting you?" He asks in French, and I reply in our tongue, thankful that Ormand always makes it easy for me—whereas Alain often uses my limited English to humiliate me.

"It's my marriage you're asking about and none of your concern."

"Not private when he marks you for us all to see," he scolds.

The sound of Alain's laughter allows me enough time to glance at Ormand, who I can't deny is attractive. He's taller than Alain and has lighter brown hair and kind eyes, but behind that kindness lies the capability of doing very unkind things for very good reasons. He's been with Alain since they were young boys, which is where the last of his allegiance remains. It's inside his eyes that I see that allegiance fading when I glimpse a look I've seen one too many times before. One I can't seem to escape. "Don't forget yourself, Ormand. I am Alain's wife."

"He keeps you a recluse when it's not your nature," he states, seemingly outraged for me. "He silences you when you have so much to offer."

"He's been a good friend to you, has he not? Friends since you were young children."

"Things have changed, and he's not the same." He glances back toward the table to see Alain occupied before I feel his eyes tracing my face again. "Not since we got here. We've been talking."

"Don't speak of this to me," I whisper harshly, more a plea as I fill the pot with water from the sink. "Don't."

"He's becoming a directionless drunk. This is not what we came for. We believe you should start to run the meetings."

"He is my husband," I state in warning.

"You are unhappy. Any fool can see that."

"He is not a fool," I warn, "and he sees much," I emphasize, pulling more cups from the cabinet to busy my hands. "Even things that aren't real."

"We could turn him into the American authorities to be sent back to France to face judgment for his crimes. No one has to know."

"I will know," I snap, looking over at him. "I will know. It's still very early. He is adjusting to life here. Give him time."

"He hurts you, quiets you, diminishes you, and you still love him?"

"He's my husband," I repeat as I have to myself so many times since I landed in America. "I am his only family. His papa—"

"That's not an excuse. Delphine," he whispers, and I brace myself for what's coming. "You must sense by now I have—"

"Stop," I whisper roughly. "He's my family, we're a family. You are part of that family."

His eyes glaze over as I continue.

"Whatever you entertain in your mind about me is imagination."

"I could never hurt you," he murmurs. "I'm in love with you and have been since France, and I'm tired of pretending I'm not. Sometimes I feel you look at me too—"

"I am not worth losing your station or friendship with him," I tell him. "The work you're doing is important—"

"We won't be with him much longer. Come with me."

"What?"

"Let me take you away from here, from him. I plan to return to France. I have inherited my father's land."

"Delphine!" Alain snaps, and we both turn to face him. His eyes roam from me to Ormand before he lifts his glass in silent demand for more vodka.

"Coming," I say, turning back, pouring a cup as the coffee still brewing drips, sizzling on the burner.

"You're shaking," Ormand says.

"You say you would never hurt me"—I swallow—"but who do you think pays for your long stares?" I glance over to see his eyes drop before he speaks.

"I only want to give you a better life." When he turns his back, I stop him with my whisper.

"You give me a better life by staying." I know he hears me when his shoulders draw tight. "Please don't take this from him and don't yet go back to France. He's not well . . . but if we give him more time, maybe he can be the Alain we both love again."

He turns back to me quickly. "You're fooling yourself."

"Please don't go," I ask him, knowing how selfish my request is. "Please understand, I can't leave. Not now."

His eyes implore mine. "But you will consider it?"

"Ormand," Alain snaps, this time not looking up at

either of us. Grabbing the vodka bottle from the fridge, I hear Ormand's whisper as he passes. "I will stay as long as it takes."

***

Celine,

It is time to admit I have been stubborn in writing this confession. As you predicted before I left France, I have made a horrible mistake. I'm sorry I was not honest until now. I wanted so much to believe in the dream I came for, but after enduring these last few months, I'm certain that that dream has died.

When I first arrived not long ago, my letters were truthful, and my happiness with Alain was real, but I can no longer deny that my life now feels more like a nightmare.

I used to think I was smart. So smart. That I was steps ahead of other women, but now I am making the very same mistakes of lovesick fools and living a life I refused to believe I would have for myself. All I feel is the need to get things right, to try to reason with and see the Alain I once knew, but I feel it may no longer be possible.

I'm quickly becoming convinced he brought me here to support and care for him. That I am nothing but a paycheck. Somehow, I know that he assumed that at my age, I would never put it together, that a child bride would never realize his manipulation, but you know that I cannot be deceived so easily. And yet I was because now I live the deception.

Since I've lost the baby, it is as if I'm living outside of myself, my mind and body. Am I paying because I never wanted it?

As I examine my bruises in the mirror, I find no trace of that fearless girl you spoke of before I left, and I no longer recognize myself.

I don't know where the soldier in me went, but I feel like the longer I stay this way, the further from her I become.

I don't know why I'm letting him convince me of his lies, and each day, start to believe them as truth. As it stands, I cannot stop loving him, no matter how hard I try. And if I can love such a monster, what does that make me?

Why am I not worth loving, Celine? Why do the men I trust and care for with all my heart holds treat me so terribly? It is not just the men in my life. It is the women, too. What is it about me that tells people it is okay to insult and hurt me?

I know I am not a kind, gentle woman. I know this much of myself, and still, I'm treated as though I'm no one to be wary of and earn no respect.

My father threw me away, and my own husband hates me and considers me a possession.

Is love so much of a weakness, and that is why we make such fools of ourselves? I am drinking now—more than I ever have. I'm ashamed to admit that I drink before my shift some days.

Please write to me soon with word from France.

What of Marine and Francis?

What of my nephew, Ezekiel? Is he growing strong?

Please, Celine, teach him to be protective of you and of women so that he will never resemble the men we have so horribly chosen. Tell him there is so much strength and honor in treating women with respect and care. I'm ashamed and scared, and I've never felt so alone. Alain's mind has taken a turn for the worse, and I fear his plans. His friends and allies are slowly losing faith, as am I.

Alain continues to take all my checks so I cannot escape him or travel home. What of your plans to come here? Am I holding onto false hope?

Could you visit? Maybe to remind me of who I was such a short time ago, and maybe I will do the same for you?

If you cannot come, please, for yourself and Ezekiel, do what I cannot and leave Abijah. Maybe if you do, I'll find the strength to do the same. Please write back.

Chapter Eight

Tyler

US PRESIDENT: GEORGE W. BUSH | 2001–2009

WALKING INTO THE house, I release the strap of my bookbag and am about to toss it when I'm stopped dead in my tracks.

Frozen at the entryway, my eyes fix on the family portrait hanging in the gap across the hall between my and my parents' bedrooms. The sound reaches me again, disbelief turning into rage as my blood begins to boil because there are two things I'm certain of. One—my mom's car isn't in the driveway, and two—she's at work.

This is confirmed a second later when a woman's shrieks engulf me, a woman who is unmistakably *not* Regina Jennings, as her enthusiasm rings out.

"Fuck, oh, God, Carter. God, yes!"

He must be too drunk to realize the time, knowing good and fucking well I would be getting home from school. He has to be.

The woman's enthusiastic groans and pleas sicken me, and shortly after, I'm granted the added bonus of slapping skin.

My instinct to act on my fury threatens to overtake me, and it's the fear of what that might look like that has me pulling my bag back on and slamming my way out of the house, away from what's happening inside it.

And what's happening . . . is that my father is cheating on my mother in their marital fucking bed.

In the home she built for him, for us. Years of her love's labor make up every room. It's our haven and refuge against the outside world, and Dad might as well have lit a match to it. I feel that truth now as flames engulf me from head to foot.

Just like I feared, Carter Jennings disappeared somewhere overseas, and Master Sergeant Jennings took his place, invading the home Carter left.

Every hope I had that it could be rectified—and that he could be redeemed—leaves me as waves of memories surface, all involving my parents. The two of them stealing bordering-inappropriate, lengthy kisses next to the bonfire. The hysterical laugh that only my mom seemed to be able to draw out of him just before Dad pulled her to him and nuzzled her with adoration.

My mother is the best of women—a dutiful and doting mother and wife, a respected career woman, and a staple in the community. In recent years, she's put up with more shit from Dad than any woman ever should for her husband—Marine or not—and he repays her *this way*?

Devastation fights with the rage for dominance as I realize I just lost every ounce of respect I have left for my father. Blinded by the ingrained image of our family photo and the accompanying noise I now and will forever associate with the sight of it, rage overtakes me, and I go black.

***

". . . one, inhale, two, exhale, out, three," the firm voice speaks. I know the source, the accent, familiar with the curl used around certain letters and words, but I gravitate toward the command inside them, leaning into it. "Count with me."

"One," she says.
"One," I repeat.
"Two," she says.
"Two," I repeat.
"Three."
"Three."
"Again."

We repeat the count as I ease back into a sense of familiarity from the space I'm in—some foreign, endless abyss. A darkness I drift further and further away from toward the voice summoning me back: "... your breaths and body are all that matters. This you control. One. Two."

Breathing on count, I fixate on the solid, dark twin pinpricks behind my lids, ignoring all muted light surrounding it—no outside images or noise, only my body and each breath. Counting again and again as I slowly come to.

"... again. One. Two. Three."

"One," inhale, exhale. "Two," inhale, exhale. "Three," inhale, exhale. Within the next breath, I exist only inside the black and remain there until the next command is spoken.

"Open your eyes, Tyler."

When I do, all surrounding light temporarily blinds me, and I look down to see Delphine standing directly in front of me, staring up at me keenly from where I hover above her short stature. For the first few seconds, we simply stare at one another, me speechless, shaken, and feeling transported. Especially since I have no fucking idea how I came to stand in the middle of Dom's living room. Utterly stupefied, as I come further into myself, I note my state—heart rate steady, breaths even, the sweat on my neck and back has long since dried.

"How did I get here?" I ask Delphine, who stares back at me attentively. "I found you here," she replies in a tone a little above a whisper.

"How long were we doing that?"

"Not sure, ten minutes, maybe longer," she says in the same sleepy tone she used throughout the exercise, though her return stare remains intent.

"How did you know how to do that?" I ask, not exactly sure what *that* is.

"It is common for some and can be mastered with many, many hours of practice," she relays calmly while seeming to search me for any sign of the opposite. Of any of the remaining rage I know that brought me here.

It's then I realize how numb I am to what set me off other than what I'm currently experiencing—fear and . . . shock. Whatever the hell she just led me through worked miracles. The anger is still there . . . but distant—as if it's in a faraway place that I can reach if I need it. It dawns on me then what *it* might be. "You mean suppressing emotion?"

She shakes her head. "Non, not exactly."

I've read up about this. While something similar is a part of military training, it's been a hard concept for me to grasp. From the minute the door closes between recruits and the outside world, they teach them to ignore their own free will, opinions, and comfort. They eventually put them and keep them in the mindset of survival mode, only thinking of the mission—the mission being the most important. So, while their tactic is not to suppress emotions because they don't want a heartless military, the goal is to get them to compartmentalize the emotions for a later time for the sake of completing the mission.

I'm still a few years away from that training, but I can't understand how this tiny woman in front of me is so familiar with it, to the point that she seems to have mastered it and guided me through it so flawlessly.

"The fuck?" I say aloud, still shaken. To my surprise, Delphine laughs. Memory kicks in of what waits at home for me, and my residual anger suppresses any return smile I could possibly give her.

"Is this how you escape?" I ask, knowing such a

personal question to her will probably go unanswered, but she surprises me again with a reply.

"There is no escape. Your problem is still there, is it not?"

I nod.

"But maybe who you're mad at has more of a chance to get away, at least temporarily."

I don't bother to defend that this wasn't some teen angst drama I brought to her doorstep and that my home-life just imploded—though her joke indicates that's her belief. Right now, I don't have the energy to correct her. "That was some Jedi mind trick," I tell her.

"Ah"—her eyes light—"you speak of Star Wars. I *love* Star Wars."

This time, I can't help but grin. "Do you?"

"Yes, I watch every time there is a marathon."

Tilting my head, I take note of the playfulness in her eyes. One I've never seen before, though I've never been this close to Delphine. Not in all my years of knowing her.

Of course, I've noticed her beauty once or twice. It's fucking impossible not to, but her behavior, along with her aggressive, cruel posturing over the years, has made it easy to ignore. As I stare down at her now, the adult lens associated with her presence in my life starts to dissipate as she comes into clear view, far more dimensional.

"Dom is at Sean's . . . if you want to see him."

"Thank you," I say on autopilot as I drink in more of her details. Silver-gray eyes peer back at me, slight confusion marring her expression as I consider her for the first time, and not as a background presence or authoritative prop. Or the woman I habitually help Dom gather from whatever foundation we find her passed out on—last time, it was the backyard, and she was barely conscious.

Within seconds of my first real look at her, I take another greedy pass while a dozen questions start to accumulate, my curiosity running rampant. It's when I'm tempted to sweep her again that I know I need to see myself out. And so I do, but not without pausing at the storm door and looking back as she walks into her kitchen. It's only when her head starts to turn in my direction that I rip my eyes away and slip out of her front door.

Chapter Nine

Delphine

US PRESIDENT: GEORGE W. BUSH | 2001–2009

"That man cannot hides his desire for you," I tell her in a hushed tone, knowing every woman's eyes are on Roman. He's a rare type of handsome that is not common in Triple Falls—the face and build of a movie star, not a man who owns a factory.

However, as he walks through the floor each day, his eyes drift to only one woman, and it's always the woman to my right. He has been enchanted by Diane since she started at the factory.

"He's beautiful," she agrees just as quietly, keeping her eyes down and continuing her work, "though everyone here hates him."

"He is a thief," I tell her, and she looks over to me.

"He shorts checks because we have no choices but to work here. If we report, we lose work visa. This is corruption I fight for. Corrupt mens like your Roman Horner."

"I'm so sorry, and I promise you, he's not *my* Roman Horner."

"Can you not speak about what he does to our checks?"

"I can barely talk to him, period. Our relationship isn't in that place right now. And don't change the subject again. Tell me about your Alain."

"Nothing to report," I say.

"Don't clam up on me." She pushes her arm to mine in a nudge, adding a tight smile.

"Clam?" I ask.

"Close up like a clam. Don't shut me out."

"Oh," I say as her eyes search mine. Aside from Celine and Beau, Diane is my only ally working at the factory, and for good reason—one of them approaching us now.

"By lunch," Donna snaps, dumping a plastic bin to purposefully ruin our progress, making it impossible to know which products we've already sorted.

"Bitch," I snap, and Diane grabs my arm to stop me from gripping Donna's hair and slapping her *again*. The woman laughs and waves her fingers behind her to taunt me.

"Your husband looks to me because you are *ugly*," I taunt back, and Donna turns around and rushes toward me. Diane steps in front of her, and I laugh at her feeble attempt to charge me, waving my fingers like she did.

"Let her go, Diane," I laugh, "I would love to show her who to respect."

"For the love of God, Delphine," Diane huffs, struggling to keep her back. "You're going to get us both fired."

"Worth it to teach this hag how to regard me!"

"Stay away from my husband, you whore!" Donna yells.

"Maybe if you know how to *fuck*, he would not swells his cock for *me*."

"Your insults could use some work," Diane chortles, still struggling.

"She understands my point," I say, bored by the woman's snapping jaws.

"Stop egging her on," Diane grunts before shoving her back. "Enough!"

Diane finally pushes Donna away from our part of the line. Half of the factory takes notice as Donna stumbles, and Diane speaks up for those whispering and watching the spectacle. "If your husbands have wandering eyes when they pick you up, it's not her fault. Check your *men*, ladies. They're the ones with frothing mouths. Grow the hell up!"

I stick my tongue out at Donna before she stalks off. Diane gives me wary eyes as I tighten my gloves and turn back to sort out the mess the woman made.

"It will take *all day* for us to fix this," I hiss.

"You can't lose this job," she scolds.

"I wish I did get fired. Then *something* changes things. Then maybe Alain will do his parts and work."

"He's a deadbeat, and I meant what I said. You're so beautiful, Delphine. Half the men in this town are in love with you. You can do so much better."

"And you propose another man is the solution? *Non*, and what you believe is blessing is not for me."

"What do you mean?" she asks.

"Looking this way causes me to suffer." I grab another bin as Diane starts to sort.

"How?"

I bite my lip and look over to her. I have trusted Diane with many secrets. Secrets I have told no one. Not even Celine, because of our constant arguments about Alain and my inability to leave him. That I'm ashamed I've endured so much in the hope the boy I met and married will return to me, only to bury that hope in the bottle as the years pass. A bottle I ache to sip from now, knowing where it waits in the bathroom stall. The endless cycle strangling me.

Staring over at Diane now, I see her eagerness to hear me, to understand my reasoning. Both of us well aware we are not good for the other in sharing our reasonings for being with men we have no business being with. When Celine and Beau first came to America mere months after I arrived here, I had a brief reprieve from Alain's abuse. My suspicions are that Beau put a temporary stop to it. These past years, he's been more volatile than ever, growing more paranoid about Ormand's affections. The last time he suspected an affair, I wasn't able to work for two days. Aching for a drink and disgusted by the memory,

I let out a long exhale as Diane waits for my response, and I decide to give her some truth.

"When I was very young, too young, my papa friends gave me much attention, which led to much conflicts." To his death, but I do not admit that much. "In school when I was young, girls treats me much same as they do here. Now, if Alain's friend compliments me, I . . ." I shake my head. "One friend, Ormand, tells me I look beautiful in my dress on my birthday and have not been allowed to have dinner with any friends again." Just after, Alain stopped allowing me to participate in many of the meetings, making it impossible for me to be the soldier I desire. Which only led me to drink more.

"Not that I'm defending him," Diane says, "but you are the kind of beautiful that drives men crazy."

"I know," I say, chewing on my lip.

"Modest, too," she laughs.

"I *know*," I tell her, "this is not too much confidence. Is too much attention. I hate it. But what do I do? *Ugly* myself?"

"Not much you can do."

"I can get fat," I say. "But I do not want to."

"That's ridiculous. You don't throw looks like yours away because of other people's insecurities."

"Alain is so . . ." I pause, searching for the word. "Jealousyness."

"Jealous?"

"Yes, so many days I feel a prisoner of our house." I blow out a long breath. "I look like that hag"—I point to Donna—"I become free of many conflicts."

Diane grips my wrist. "I'm sorry things are so hard for you here, Delphine. I know this isn't the life you pictured, but things will get better. They will."

"I do not see this," I say, aching to sip the bottle in the stall.

"Yeah, honestly, I'm not feeling too optimistic myself these days." She turns to me, her eyes shining with fear. "I have something to tell you, and I haven't told anyone yet." Just as she opens her mouth to speak her confession, we both jump at the sound of her summons.

"Johnston," our crew leader snaps from feet away, and I know it is on Roman's behalf.

Diane turns to me, a gleam in her eyes but an apology on her lips.

"I'm sorry. I told him to stop doing this."

"Go, be the happy one for us both." I wave her away, knowing I will be the one spending the next half hour of my shift to work alone.

"I promise that's not the case," she relays mournfully before she stalks away.

Not long after I've taken long sips of the bottle I hide in the bathroom stall, I study my reflection in the breakroom mirror—the yellow bruise on my chin noticeably lighter today. Alain has been too preoccupied lately to do more than the minimum to keep me obedient and rutting into me before he passes out. Even with that attention, he can barely finish. Back aching and dreading the long hours ahead, I turn and exit the bathroom and am stopped short when I see Donna and a few of the whispering women in wait for me.

"Your bodyguard isn't here now, bitch." Rolling my eyes down her frame, I pause them on the pair of purple boots Donna often wears. I think Diane called them Doc Martens.

"I like your boots," I compliment as she smiles back at me menacingly.

"You're about to hate them," she relays in threat.

"Oh?" Manufactured by drink or not, a boldness I almost forgotten I'd possessed fills me as I step up and punch her in the mouth before another insult can leave her hag lips. That familiar feeling is almost worth the beating from the women that renders me unconscious before Diane finds me. And the added beating Alain gives me just a few hours later for risking getting fired.

Chapter Ten

Tyler

US PRESIDENT: GEORGE W. BUSH | 2001–2009
FALL 2004

"So, what's this I hear about you and Amy Miller? Because apparently, she can't stop talking about *our boy*," Sean chirps, poking his head between Dom and me, where I sit in the driver's seat of my mom's van.

A van that's on its last leg and which Mom refuses to part with. A van we're also in desperate need to keep running, thanks to Mom's constant consent to let me chauffer the three of us around since I aged out, being the first of us to get my license.

The situation being temporary until we can finish restoring the classics Sean's uncle gave us by way of a massive heart attack. The process to get them street-ready has been and will be slow and agonizing due to the expense, but one we deem will eventually be worth the wait.

Sean's uncle's widow opted to hand them over with no strings as long as we got them hauled off within her allotted time frame.

We jumped on it, and the minute she opened the yard, I spotted and stalked straight to the '66 C20. Sean and Dom had done the same with their own cars. It was a fated feeling that day, as if all three vehicles were waiting, predestined for each of us. All three vehicles are now stripped and waiting at King's—a garage Dom bought with his parents' death settlement money, paid for, and titled the day after he turned sixteen.

To help with restoration, I called upon Russell, who's worked on tractor equipment at Jennings & Sons during the last three harvests. All three of us took up with Russell fast before letting him in on the secret per Tobias's order—an order he'd given us on a night that now remains at the forefront of all our minds.

Months ago, Tobias summoned us to his spot the same way he had before leaving for France. As we all crowded around the bonfire, half a decade after the first, the tension rolling off T had clued us all in that the meeting was going to be far different in nature. And it was, especially when Tobias unveiled his game plan for Roman.

"We're going to go basic with our strategy," Tobias declares, staring into the flames, a faraway look in his eyes. His timbre was laced with ire because of his unintentional run-in with Roman earlier that day while picking Dom up from the library.

"Meaning?" I ask, ears perked due to his grave, imparting tone.

"We've got to play this just right. The only way to defeat a man like Roman is to play sleeping giant," he relays as an inkling charges through the air between the four of us.

"Think Helen of Troy," Dom clarifies, already receptive to his brother.

There was an edge to the words spoken that night that I felt to my bones—an indescribable stillness before, one by one, we spoke our parts to play aloud, me being the first.

"I'm going to be a third-generation Marine. It's a given, and if there's one thing I know how to do—it's build an army."

From there, the conversation flowed, though the words seemed redundant as if it had been decided before any of us uttered a single one. It was only after, when I watched Dom approach Tobias just outside our circle, asking about the source of the war, and the mythological Helen behind it, that I tuned in, catching the ass end of their hushed exchange.

"*What about Helen?*" *Dom had asked, his back to me where they stood feet away, as Tobias scanned the construction site of Roman's nearby fortress.*

My ears had perked further due to the long pause just after.

"*We're leaving Helen out of it,*" *T answers definitively.*

Both a declaration and rule I silently but wholeheartedly agreed with before dismissing myself and stalking through the woods toward the ongoing war ensuing in my own home. They'd all given me shit that night, assuming I was strung out on a *she*. I was too irritated to even explain how complex the truth was—that my worry was divided between two women.

One of them being Regina Jennings and what my father might be subjecting her to that night.

The other was a woman I'd recently gathered from her kitchen floor before tucking her safely into bed. A woman who's slowly starting to invade my thoughts since our run-in in her living room a little over a month ago.

"Come on, what's up with you and Amy?" Sean prods, roping me back into the van, away from the silver-gray return stare I haven't been able to shake.

"Jesus, man, we're just talking, that's all," I sigh as Dom glances over to me, not bothering to hide his grin. "Is that all you think about?" I ask Sean's rearview reflection, the question rhetorical.

"What's with keeping it a secret?" Sean counters.

"Maybe because I didn't want to get interrogated," I retort dryly. Ever since Sean got his first taste, he's become a little obsessed with the fairer sex. Though I can't exactly say I'm any less guilty. Though it's more the *act* of sex that I use to escape when granted the chance.

"Don't play the gentleman, Tyler. Word is you are far from a gentleman."

Dom raises a brow at me, and I crack my neck in annoyance.

"Miller is fucking hot," Sean carries on, "but what I want to know is how in the hell you managed it. She's had a stick up her ass since middle school, and she's *older*."

I remain silent, ready to rid myself of the fly buzzing between my and Dom's seats.

"I have a theory," Sean continues, "future high and tight likes 'em *experienced* and *mean*."

"You're an idiot," I sigh.

"I heard no denial, did you, Dom?"

Dom smirks but remains quiet, sensing my mood.

"Hey, there's nothing wrong with being a gentleman," Sean tosses in, "I treat my girls very well. You'll hear no complaints."

"From all *one* of them?" Dom jests.

"Don't hate," Sean says as I turn off Main and stiffen, fingers tightening on the wheel when I spot my dad's F-150. Sean remains oblivious as Dom reads my posture and follows my line of sight to where Dad's truck is parked. Sean can be just as attuned when he wants to be. That thought is only confirmed when silent seconds pass before he finally reads the room.

"What just happened?" he asks, and Dom jerks his chin in response to shut him up.

"No, man," Sean protests, "shit just got tense in here. Talk to me."

"He doesn't want to share the details of his hookups, asshole, let it go," Dom covers for me. If there's one thing I've learned, it's that I can get very little past Dom these days. The good part about it is that he won't force me to address anything I don't want to, whereas Sean believes group sharing is an entitlement.

Typically, I would come clean to both, along with Tobias, but this is different. Lately, I've been sharing a lot less, not telling them about catching Dad cheating or the strange headspace that had me chanting breath count in Dom's living room afterward. For some reason, I've kept it all to my chest.

Probably because it's too close to a very raw fucking nerve. One I decide I can no longer ignore as I silently pull up to Sean's house to drop him off first.

"Fine," Sean spouts resentfully, grabbing the duffle packed with his football gear, "but you guys are dicks for not telling me." Sliding open the van door, he thinks better of his parting words and stares between us, all animation gone. "You good, Tyler?"

"Yeah, man, I'm good. I'll hit you up later."

"All right," he says, palming my shoulder before he and Dom exchange a look I don't bother to gauge or decipher.

Both know it's been hell on earth for Mom and me at home, and neither has pressed me too much for details, but the heaviness is there.

Once out of Sean's driveway, I pull to a stop sign and click the signal, though no one is behind me. Dom doesn't say a word as I sit for a full minute, maybe two, while he patiently waits for me. "Can I ask a favor?"

He nods without hesitation or asking what the nature of the favor is. One I don't give him before turning in the opposite direction of my signal.

Minutes later, I'm pulling up just outside the hole-in-the-wall at the end of the shopping center. Putting the van in park, I scan the building and mostly vacant parking lot before glancing back over to him. "Only step in if you have to."

Dom nods, needing little else in the way of information, as I slam my way out of the van and stalk toward the entrance.

Lynyrd Skynyrd's "Gimme Three Steps" blasts through the frigid air, filling my ears as I step through the tinted glass door. Once inside, I scan the bar, which is littered with dollar store Halloween decorations. Cheap, cardboard cutout jack-o'-lanterns collectively grin at me from where they're taped to every post supporting the drooping tiled ceiling of the hole-in-the-wall my dad's claimed as a second home. It takes seconds for me to spot him on his resident stool.

The difference between now and when I get the call to come and retrieve him is that the woman he's seeing is currently hanging all over him. It's as if there's any decency in making sure she's absent when I scrape him from his barstool. Fury lights a fire in me as I watch the man I once revered publicly cheat on my mother.

It's his smitten expression that has me crawling out of my skin as she practically grinds on his lap. Rounding the bar, I bide my time in a dark corner concealed behind some draped glittering black-and-orange tinsel, bristling in wait. My patience is rewarded when, not long after, she peels herself off him, heading toward the hall that leads to the restroom.

Circling the bar, I watch him down the last of his pint and signal for another. Seething, I stalk toward him, gaining momentum and advantage I utilize when his head snaps only an instant before impact. Slamming my palms into his chest, I shove him with every bit of the fury rolling through me, a sickening satisfaction flooding my veins when he lands flat on his back, the pleather stool rolling away from him.

Gasps and shocked murmurs sound around me as I kneel to where Dad landed just as a set of worn boots approaches inside my periphery.

"If you know what's good for you, you'll mind your business," I snap in warning to the interloper just as the bartender, Brian, speaks up on my behalf.

"Don't step in, man, that's Carter's son."

Within the next second, I'm dragging my laughing dad out of the glass door by his jacket and dropping his upper half on the frozen sidewalk. Snow dots the air as Dad slowly rises to his feet, stumbling a little before gaining his footing. His liquor-glazed eyes slowly lock and focus on me as he speaks through a smirk.

"So, tonight's the night, huh? You want to fight your old man, Son?"

Rage overtakes reason, and I step up, throwing a right that connects with his jaw, putting everything I have behind it. He absorbs the blow as I do. Feeling the gravity of what's just transpired blooming in my chest, I'm completely aware of how wrong it is—of how different our relationship will be from this moment forward.

"Not bad for a punk seventeen-year-old," he says with a sickening grin, smashing at the thin trail of blood lining his lips with his fingers. To our right, I see Dom's already out of the van, leaning against it, arms crossed.

"You're a disgrace—" I see the insult hit him, his armor somehow penetrable for the moment—"to your marriage, to the name you gave me, and to the uniform."

It's mom's anguished face I see when I step forward, landing another punch on his jaw. A punch he purposely doesn't react to, which surprises me.

"What, Dad?! No lessons to teach, no fucking tough love or lectures to bestow on being a man!?"

I pound my chest with a fist, hearing the crack in my voice, which echoes the fracture happening inside while willing the weakness out of me.

"You're a good son, Tyler," he says, seemingly sincere, his own voice shaking.

"Don't. Don't bother. You have no idea who the fuck I am. You haven't fucking seen me in years. Fucking years!"

"I know exactly who you are," he rasps, reticent and calm. "I'm staring at my reflection twenty years ago."

"Carter? Is everything okay?" a voice calls from the door behind me, and I can't bring myself to look back at the woman he's been cheating on my mother with for God knows how long.

"Get rid of her," I order as Dad holds up a palm.

"Go inside," Dad tells her, "I'll be in in a minute."

"But—"

"Grace, go!" She retreats inside as his guilty eyes flick back to me.

"Oh, the irony of a fucking name," I mock. "You're going to need all the *Grace* you can get because we're fucking done, Dad. Do you hear me? We're done with you as of this moment. You've destroyed our family, and you may be able to live with this, with what you're doing to her, but I can't. Tell Mom, or I will."

"She knows, Son," he says, his tone nothing but defeat.

"Bullshit." I shake my head vehemently. "Why couldn't you leave her? She knows everyone in this town. You're humiliating her. You're humiliating *me*. Our family. You're fucking disgusting."

"You're a good son," he repeats softly. "Truly, Tyler, you are, but what's happening between your mother and me is beyond your scope right now."

"You're going to pull this shit, really? Claim it's grown folks' business? You brought her into our fucking house!"

Dad has the sense to lower his eyes.

"I idolized you," I tell him. "I . . . and now, I'm ashamed. I'm ashamed to call you my father." I step forward, chin lifted, doing everything in my power not to shed the tears shimmering in my eyes. "All you have left is the woman you destroyed your family with. Hope she's worth it."

"Your mother won't leave me, Son." His voice is now just above a whisper.

"I'll make sure she does," I hiss. "I'll make goddamn sure she does. Tell her tonight."

"You're not hearing me, Regina knows."

"She knows, huh? She knows that you fuck Grace in her bed? I'm willing to bet she doesn't. You or me. Figure it out, fast," I snap, stepping off the curb and nodding towards Dom, who opens his passenger door as I pull my keys.

"She won't leave me because she won't fucking touch me anymore!" Dad shouts at my retreating back.

"Now *that's* adult business," I spout without a shred of sympathy.

Crowding me, he slams my driver's door shut. "But you've made it your business now, so you get to hear it."

When I reel on him, he steps back and glances toward the bar before scanning the parking lot. My confusion lasts only seconds as he shifts further into the light and lifts his shirt. My reaction is an audible release of air when I see the scar, or rather, the ocean of slick, burnt skin that runs the entire length of his right side.

"Your mother hasn't touched me in nearly two years... so yeah, Son, I went out and did what no married man should ever do because my wife finds me as disgusting as you do."

"Mom would never—"

"You sure about that?" he counters, chest heaving.

I shake my head, full-on denying she would be so cruel. "Couldn't be the fact that you're a full-blown alcoholic and temperamental bastard now, could it?"

"I'm not saying my behavior didn't have anything—"

"Yeah, that's what I thought."

"So fucking smug," he scoffs, "so arrogant and sure of yourself. Well, hold on tight to that confidence, Son, or just wait. They'll be happy to pump you full of it. But on the other side of that, you have no idea what coming home means. No fucking clue!"

"Well, you never took the time to tell me, did you? No, you drank that time away."

"You don't know what happens over there! You can't ever know because it's not fucking explainable!" He rips his shirt over his head, forcing me to look at the burns, to acknowledge they exist. I was just recovering from the fact that they did and probably have for years. How in the hell did I miss it?

"When?"

"Does it matter? It happened, and I deal with it."

I scoff. "Yeah, I've seen the way you deal."

"Son, when you grab your uniform, make sure you stand firm in your stance to be *nothing like me*."

"I won't," I declare confidently.

"No, because you'll do it better, right?" He shakes his head ironically. "You won't hurt your son, or fuck with his head, or belittle him like I swore I wouldn't. You won't disappear from your wife day by day like I swore I wouldn't. Go to war one man and come back another. You'll be the exception, the better soldier, husband, and father. You won't ever bring the war you carry on your back through your front door."

I weigh his words about staring at his reflection and shake my head, disbelieving what he's relaying. "You're telling me that Granddad—"

"Like I said, I'm staring at my reflection twenty years ago. It took me nearly ten of those to forgive him to the point of speaking to him and let him within a fucking mile of you. The man you know and the man that raised me are two entirely different men."

I stand there, shocked at his revelations and more stunned that my grandfather exhibited the same behavior.

"I'm a sunny Sunday in the park compared to what he was during the worst of it. So, yeah, your grandfather cracked, and your old man isn't weathering his own storm well, but you'll be the soldier to do it, right? Fuck"—he scrapes a hand down his jaw—"I hope for your sake that you are. But I'm telling you right now . . ." His eyes grip mine in warning. "Don't do it."

"What?"

"They'll break you down only to build you up, making you believe you're a god. They'll make you feel invincible, but you won't be. No man is. At the end of it, if you make it out alive, you'll come home with scars you can't hide, physical or otherwise, and the fact you can't hide them will eat you fucking alive. Then you'll remember what they told you versus what you actually fucking survived and see they don't quite match up. But the most damning lie is that you will have the *capability* to leave it over there when you get home. That you'll be able to find the fucking door. All this time, I'm still looking for the door to you and your mother, Son, because I've looked everywhere, and I can't get back to you." His voice breaks as I feel my resolve start to dismantle. "I can't get back to you and Regina."

I gape at him, nausea threatening. "You're seriously telling me not to enlist?"

"I'm telling you that things have changed. The military isn't the same as the one your granddad and I signed up for, and I don't want you to find that out by gambling with your life. I'm telling you that I'm sorry I failed you. That I know I lost my way . . . lost myself. That I know you and your mother deserve better . . . and I'll tell her. I'll leave if she wants me to."

The truth of what's happening starts to settle in on us both, and remorse threatens, but I bat it away due to the constant sight of my mother's tears.

"I love you and your mother, Son, with every fiber of my being. I know I was better off coming home in a box to both of you . . . or not at all, but I didn't want to let you go." He crumbles where he stands, as does my entire belief system. "But you both let me go a long time ago, didn't you?"

He piles his hands on his head, his voice cracking so wide that I don't recognize it.

"I chose the uniform too many times, and now I can't find the fucking door." He cries openly now. It's messy and horrific, and I recognize the man speaking to me as the dad I grew up with. And that he's not apologizing because he got caught but because he means it, but it's too late.

"You could have talked to her," I sling at him, hurt seeping through my anger. "Mom's a goddamned psychologist, Dad. She could have tried to help you find the fucking door."

He shakes his head, negating that as a possibility, and blows out a breath. "You're a good son," he whispers hoarsely. "I'm sorry."

He turns and starts walking toward the side of the bar, opposite the front door, as I shout at his retreating back.

"Hey, Master Sergeant Jennings!" He snaps to and holds my eyes. "If you truly mean that, get the fuck away from my mother!"

Inside the van, I spin tires as I race away from the bar, reeling with his revelations as my heart finalizes the slow shatter it started years ago. Overcome, I force myself to pull over and stalk away from the van as my emotions get the best of me. Chest heaving, I feel the largest part of myself breaking away from me—years of Dad's expectations evaporating as I look up at the night sky. Snow pours from it, seemingly from nothing but the gaping black space hovering above. Face upturned, I hit the frozen ground, unable to move in any direction as a guttural cry bursts out of me.

Dom's boots appear sometime later as I rip at the frozen grass, dirt collecting beneath my nails as I rehash my father's admissions.

"He's right," I sniff, hating he's seeing me in this state—this fucking raw—but if I'm going to get emotional, I would rather Dom lay witness than any other. Dom sits next to me for a few beats before his words break through my audible pants.

"I'm so fucking sorry, Tyler," he whispers hoarsely. It's then I realize I'm not the only one who's emotional. I don't dare look over as I grip my knees, my fingers white, nails somehow bloody.

"We'll figure this out, man. I swear we will. You don't have to enlist." His words come out mangled as he absorbs the blow alongside me. What most people aren't privy to is that my chosen brother lives by his feelings, primarily those of his gut. If there were a way for him to suppress or box his emotions, he wouldn't survive it. His heart is what fuels him, though he's an expert at masking that truth. It's in rationalizing that about him that an idea strikes me, a notion of a possible way.

"No," I rasp out in both declaration and vow. "I'm going to be the one that breaks the cycle."

I don't have to glance over to know he's nodding.

"Come to my house," he finally says. "Stay with me tonight. Sleep in Tobias's bed. Don't go home."

I can't help but chuckle. "Sorry, man, but did you ever once think that your house would be the place I'd seek refuge?"

"Fuck you," he spits, a smile lifting his lips. "Then again, no offense taken." Neither of us moves as he speaks up a few beats later.

"She's leveled out some, though, hasn't she?" No mystery to the *she* he's referring to.

"Yeah, I've noticed," I admit. Delphine's been trying to build some semblance of a relationship with Dom since Tobias left for France, and Dom's done nothing but cruelly dismiss her. I wipe some of the frozen grass off my jeans as I stand. "She's been trying since before T left, but I knew better than to point it out to you."

"Think I should give her a chance?"

"I think you want to, and I'm not telling you one way or another, but, Dom—" I frown, unsure if I should tell him.

"What?" he asks in subtle demand.

"I read a few of the letters in her cigar box some months back. From what I can tell, what her ex-husband put her through, fuck man, it was horrific. I know it was wrong to invade her privacy like that, but after scraping her off the floor so many times, I had to know."

"That bad?"

"Like I said, I only read a few of her letters, and what I did still fucks with me."

He cut off my hair to the scalp.
Last night, he made me sleep in the snow.

Those written words physically pained me to read. What fucks with me most, and what I find incomprehensible, is that the formidable woman I'm accustomed to is the same woman who wrote those letters.

"Heads up"—I look over at him—"your mom's return letters are in there, too, and are only marginally better. Abijah was no saint."

"I thought you said you only read two?"

"Of Delphine's," I admit, guilty of the accusation in his eyes.

He arches a brow. "If I decide to start a diary, are you going to read it?" he cracks to lighten things, though my heart now bears a weight I know I'll never be free of.

"Fuck off." I wipe my face clear as fatigue starts to set in. "Sorry I drug you into that."

His eyes snap to mine. "Don't ever apologize to me," he scolds. "I'm fucking glad I was there."

"Me too."

"Wish you would have confided in me sooner."

"We all have our shit," I relay on exhale.

"This is different, and I mean it," he continues in a rare, serious tone, "you don't have to enlist."

"I've got some time to decide."

"Yeah, you do, and whatever you do decide, we've got your back."

Pulling into his driveway, I sit idly behind the wheel, feeling more exhausted than I can ever remember being.

"Coming in?" Dom asks as he gets out and grips the passenger door.

"Yeah, I'm going to drop the van off, and I'll be back."

Nodding, he closes the door before heading toward the house. Halfway to the porch, he glances back, shooting a rare concerned look before I give him a reassuring nod through the windshield.

After dropping the van and sneaking the key onto the counter, I exit my house undetected and start the short walk back to Dom's. As I hit the street, I welcome the sting on my face in hopes that the biting cold will help clear my head while grappling with what had just transpired—along with Dad's admissions. My mother can't know he's cheating. She can't. She's too prideful. She loves him too fucking much. She would never be so callous and turn him away for a burn he endured in the line of duty. He's full of shit. He's got to be.

Rounding the corner to Dom's street, I spot Delphine exiting the front door, stopping just short of the iron railing enclosing the porch. The sight of her breaks up some of my inner turmoil as a spark ignites, the cherry burning at the end of her cigarette stoking the notion that struck me earlier. A spark that has me hastening my steps toward her and a possible solution. As she comes into view, I notice her attention is fixed on the falling snow.

Without overthinking it, I make a beeline toward her. As I pound up the snow-dusted steps and approach, I can visibly see when my presence jars her out of whatever memory she was just lost in as she flits her focus to me. Her expression bleak, seeming . . . mournful.

"I need you to teach me," I say as I reach her, towering over her as I did months ago.

The silver-gray eyes that have been haunting me since she brought me back that day slowly focus on mine as confusion sets in her expression. "Teach you *what*?"

"*Everything.*"

Chapter Eleven

Delphine

Sunlight streams through my bedroom window, further warming my burning skin as the skipping blades of my rusted fan drag me further into consciousness. Peeling the sweat-covered sheet from my body before readjusting it, I curse the fact that I didn't close my curtains last night in my stupor. Burying my face into my pillow to shield my eyes from the blinding sun, I grope for the pint on my nightstand. Lifting it, I can tell by the lack of weight that there is not a drop left, knowing I drained whatever my bottles held last night. The snow has come early this year, taunting me with Matis's pleas.

"Je suis vraiment désolé. Je suis vraiment désolé. Pardonne-moi." *I'm so sorry. I'm so sorry. Forgive me.*

His ancient whispers had me reaching for more drink — too much drink. The pounding in my head only confirms this as I release the empty pint, which smacks against my nightstand before clunking loudly on the floor.

"Merde," I grumble before a light chuckle sounds from feet away.

Cracking one eye open, I look over to see Tyler standing in my bedroom doorway. "What are you doing here?"

"Training day one. Your orders, *remember*?"

"Oui." A small lie. I had reached for more drink as soon as the drift began. Through my haze and Matis's distant whispers through the snowfall, I vaguely remember his request because of the haunted look in his eyes. That, and his determined expression when he approached me to ask for help.

Help to . . . teach him. "We were to start *after* school."

"It's almost four o'clock," he notes, turning the face of a watch on his wrist in my direction.

The pounding in my head protests my idiocy in agreeing as I dismiss him.

"Go, we . . ." My skull tightens. "W-we will start *tomorrow. Merci.*"

When he continues to linger in my doorway, I slit my eyes open again to see him still standing there, *expectantly*.

"What is it you do not understand? I told you, tomm—"

"I don't have until tomorrow, Delphine."

Both his delivery and tone are not those of a teenage boy but resolute and lined with desperation. His tone and disposition are familiar because of Ezekiel's own determination to grow from boy to man before his time, dismissing his childhood altogether to raise Jean Dominic as if he were his own.

And he did. At only eleven years old, Ezekiel did all he tasked himself with soon after Celine and Beau died.

A failure I will never allow myself to forgive, nor the image and finality of the two coffins suspended over his parents' waiting plots. That, and the vision of the two orphans who loomed at the edge of the hallowed earth dressed in different sizes of the same suit. Both with hair black as midnight, one with his father's fire-laced eyes, the other's eyes like my own. Eyes that searched his older brother's that day as he continued to beg for the impossible.

"*Can we open them?*" *Jean Dominic asks of the caskets.*

"*No,*" *Ezekiel replies, no longer resembling the boy with the tiny hands I gripped while he guided me around Celine's kitchen the day before I left France—a memory that now seems a lifetime ago. Ezekiel's eyes now dimmed, lacking the light they once held in his mother's presence.*

"I want to see Maman," Dom whines, "why can't we open them? Can I see Papa?"

"Dom," Ezekiel scolds in a strict whisper, "be quiet. The preacher is speaking."

"I just want to see them!" Dominic shrieks before crumbling into hysterical tears. Some of those gathered turn to watch the scene Jean Dominic makes, my eyes catching and holding onto the woman standing adjacent to Celine's sons—a woman tracing their exchange carefully, eyes filled with shimmering tears and unmistakable guilt.

A woman whom I trusted with many of my secrets. The sight of her guilt-stricken face a testament to never again give all my hidden truths to one person—to allow anyone such power over me. Some of the last advice Matis left me with.

Diane stands alone at the side of the caskets as I batter her with my glare, her own eyes glued to my nephews. Refusing to let up, I bide my time, holding my accusatory glare until her shame-filled, fearful eyes finally lift to mine.

She knows.

Roman Horner's whore knows exactly what transpired the night of that explosion. Though she denied any knowledge of what happened when I confronted her, it was her gaunt complexion, wandering eyes, and shaking hands that had been enough to convince me.

The same expression she holds now as she peers back at me. Guilt. Unmistakable guilt. For withholding the truth of what happened to the last of my family. Her return stare erases all doubt as I curse my stupidity in trusting her.

Hatred filled me in those moments as I followed Matis's rule to trail every enemy until they've disappeared out of sight. In doing so, I watched Diane crumble into herself halfway down the small hill. Her shaking body and the palms covering her mouth to stifle her sobs confirming my suspicions. She didn't know Celine and Beau well enough to grieve in such a way.

To this day, I remain haunted that I practically handed

Celine and Beau to her because I believed her enough to share my knowledge about Roman's corruption. Encouraged her often to speak to him and told her I was not alone in knowing of his true nature.

In revealing that I wasn't the only one aware of her lover's theft, Roman could have looked up Celine's past, unveiled her activist history in France, and decided she and Beau were real threats.

Their *accidental* deaths a perfect way to silence them while sending a message to the rest of us.

It was a glimpse of her rounding belly months later—when I spotted her in passing on the street—which gave motive of why she would protect Roman so fiercely. And likely the reason she never tried again to reveal her secret to me. Her pregnancy.

I vowed that day to avenge them, to bide my time for retribution. I swore as I followed her to her battered car and watched her drive away to never again trust any outsider or to trust at all. She knew and, to this day, *still knows* as I do that confiding in her may be the very reason they died.

My cross to bear, its weight dissolved into my skin and bones, into my soul, which now barely recognizes its host.

The remembrance of that day I blurred last night and the night before, as I have since their deaths. Proof of that is the drink seeping from my every pore, gliding down the sweat on my back. Proof that I've lived to carry that weight another day. The last lingering image forever haunting me as I stood graveside, beseeching Celine with a question I have asked myself all these years later.

"How could you leave me to raise what I despise?"

"Delphine?" Tyler prompts, his voice distant as the scrape of the fan continues to fill my ears, the throbbing in my head increasing as I turn back on my side and study Tyler.

"Are you okay?"

He's being kind. Always so kind. Even, and especially when he helps me to bed after a long night of too many sips. Too many 'one more's. Never condemning me with a cross remark like Jean Dominic so often does. Which for Tyler surprises me, considering his father, too, numbs with drink.

It was through concerned whispers between Sean and Jean Dominic across the hall that I discovered this truth, which is maybe what compelled me to agree to help him.

Or maybe it was the fucking drink.

Either way, I selfishly regret offering, and know he must see that regret before I roll on my back, studying the sagging patch of ceiling above my bed.

"You're young," *have no cross* to bear, "and have many, many tomorrows ahead of you," I manage through dry lips, the increasing throb at my temples blurring my view of the brown-splotched stain hovering above.

Instead of responding, Tyler stalks into my room as if he has the right to do so and goes straight for the box of powders on my dresser. I sit up suddenly, holding my blanket to my chest, unsure of what I'm wearing beneath it. "What in the hell are you doing?"

It's then I realize he has a sports drink in his hand. He grabs a packet from the box and thrusts both packet and drink to me as if ready for my excuse.

"I'll start some coffee and meet you in the kitchen," he adds. A subtle but commanding *order*. Something which should take more time to master so efficiently than his short years.

"Tyler, I do not know what you think you can learn from me."

"Yes, you do," he replies vehemently, lingering briefly as if to say more, but he doesn't, instead turning and leaving my room.

After pulling on my robe, washing my face, and brushing my teeth, I find him sitting at the kitchen table. Next to him sits a steaming cup of coffee and a ready Smirnoff pint. I pause at the sight of the insult and assumption.

"I *do not* drink in the day," I snap, pushing the bottle aside for the steaming mug. "I have a fucking job."

"Sorry, I"—he angles his head, considering me—"I just thought you might want a little hair of the dog."

"Hair of the *what*?" I snap, leashing my tongue when his posture draws up in defense before he lowers his eyes to the forgotten wildflower-covered suitcase dangling from my hand.

"Hair of the dog is when you drink a little of what you had the night before to take the edge off any headaches." He delivers this carefully as if he knows what precise tone to use while diverting the conversation to lessen any offense.

An artful tactic he might have mastered because of his drink-dependent father, which tells me he's already wary of me. Shame threatens, with the knowledge that I should spare him my company and take back my offer. I lower my gaze from the boy's prying eyes and glance back toward my bedroom in desperate need of retreat. Of my bath, of my cleansing.

"What's in the case?" he asks, clearly sensing I'm weighing my decision. I have no business teaching this boy anything. My past record is every indication that I will fail again.

"Come on, show me, please?" he prompts softly, his expression sympathetic without a hint of the insult it can carry.

Or maybe he's sincere, Delphine, and you are being insufferable.

Sighing, I place the suitcase on the table before him, brushing my finger over the loose buckle. The sight of it pains me as I carefully unlatch it to reveal the case's contents.

Tyler curiously stares at what lies inside. "Books?"

"Not just books, your"—I search for the English word—"curricum."

"Curriculum?" he corrects, holding his laugh successfully, though I see it in his eyes.

I slam the case closed. "I don't need one more teenage boy making me feel a fucking fool in my own house!"

He stands so abruptly that I shuffle back.

"I meant no offense. I'm sorry, really sorry." He bites

his lip, palms open. "Shit, I'm sorry," he repeats again. "I'm taking this seriously, I swear to you."

He's just a boy, Delphine.

Unsettled by the stillness in the air about my tongue lashing and aching for my bath, I quickly dole out my order. "You must read, comprehend, and *memorize* each book before we can truly begin."

"Memorize . . ." he repeats softly, apprehension filling his expression.

"Not all of the books, but the wisdom of each strategist and the battle formations . . . unless you have changed your mind." I shrug, lifting and unscrewing the pint before pouring some dog's hair into my coffee.

"No, no, I'm good with that," he relays as the weight of my task clouds his eyes—that and disappointment.

"What did you think this would be, a physical fitness trial for trophy?" I flash him a smile I know is unkind. "You can become a brute in your own time, but in our time, you will gain the most important aspect of being a soldier, and it is mentality. But to satisfy you, I will add two miles of running a day to start strengthening your stamina, which is also key."

"I'll take them," he accepts instantly. "I'll take all of it."

After stirring my coffee, I glance over and study him, sensing the fortitude building inside him as he considers a few of the books. As if one of them may hold the answer he seeks.

"Give me two weeks," he states confidently.

I scoff. "Ten books in two weeks?"

"I read a book a day, like Dom. Sean's the only one still flipping comics," he jokes, and I don't share his smile. "Two weeks should do it."

He declares this again, his rich brown eyes burning with an intensity I've seen in few. He considers me now just as he did the books, but I know all too well any answer he's in need of isn't where his eyes now linger with curiosity.

"You don't think I can do it," he disputes, "I'm going to prove you wrong."

"Arrogance and soldiering do not align well, Tyler. The necessary *confidence* you will need only comes with *education*."

"But we've just started, so . . ." A dimple dents his jaw with his smile. "Care to make a *bet*?"

I stiffen at his words, taking a long drink of my coffee before I reply. "I do not *make* or take *bets*."

"Fair enough," he says, pulling another of the books out of the case before I start back to my bedroom.

"I'm going to shower."

"Two weeks," he calls out in reminder as I roll my eyes and stalk toward my bathroom.

Sure, kid.

After dressing, I run a brush through my wet hair before I lotion my arms and hands to buy more time. Out of excuses, I pause at my bedroom door, unsure of why a teenage boy's audience—other than Dom's—is keeping me idle. Annoyed by that, I tear open my door only to find myself thankful when I hear the snap and close of the screen door.

Relieved, I approach the table to see every one of the books is gone, my empty suitcase remaining. He must have sensed its significance to me.

From just our short time this morning, I've gathered he's highly observant and has the promising tongue of a mediator, if not a negotiator. All skills needed to play his part in Ezekiel's design but with unreasonable ambition.

"Foolish boy," I mumble, unsure of why it took him so long to simply collect the books and leave. It's when I go to buckle the case that I realize the frail metal is no longer loose. Glancing toward the storm door, I catch Tyler's eyes focused on where my finger lingers on the buckle. Arms cradling the books, I glimpse a whisper of his satisfied smile before he turns, taking the porch steps down to the driveway before jogging across the street.

Chapter Twelve

Tyler

Hit me up, cousin.

After shooting off a text to Barrett, I gather the menu from the four-top the hostess seated me at to scan it, side-eyeing my phone in hopes he'll finally return it. Barrett's been dodging me since the Apple Festival last month.

Before my and Dad's confrontation last week, Carter Jennings had already done his fucking worst to desecrate all remaining relationships with everyone Jennings. Having eradicated his place in the annual family tradition at our festival stand to represent our farm on Labor Day weekend. Which only further justified the two swings I landed even as I continue to grapple with the fact it happened.

That I struck my father. Twice.

Though I wasn't there, small-town news traveled fast that Barrett was seething mad when Dad showed up shit-faced and on a war path.

Barrett had taken it most personally since his future consists of taking over the family farm. Since that day, a large majority of the Jennings crew have been slow to answer and harder to reach by Mom and me, making us accomplices by association and blackening our wool. We've now been made to feel like outcasts from everyone aside from Uncle Gray and Granddad, who both check in every week or so. Though, at this point, I think it's more out of obligation to Dad.

An obligation I've also ignored since I faced off with my father in that parking lot. Since then, I've spent every minute that I'm not sleeping outside the doors of the Jennings house. Some of those days with Dom at the library, using his place of refuge as my own while inhaling and memorizing Delphine's curriculum.

But today, I found myself in need of a different type of distraction and decided to seek it out the same way I have the last few times we've hooked up.

Sensing her stare, I glance up to see Kayley eyeing me as she takes an order while I sweep her costume. Thigh-high stockings showcase her long legs, an inches-above-appropriate pleated skirt hanging from her curvy hips. Combined with the white collared button top, it's no big mystery what look she is going for. For me, it's a fucking summons, one I savor every inch of. My thorough sweep of her is slow and deliberate until I lift my eyes to hold her light blue return stare.

My invitation's receipt comes by way of a subtle lift of glossy pink, lush lips. Lips I spent last summer obsessing over, stretching them with the thrust of my cock every chance Kayley gave me. Though my attention is a bit more divided now than it was last year or the year before, it's the divide itself—a pair of silver eyes—that has me seeking this hookup and reality check.

Satisfied I've extended the invite and unable to think of a better way to spend Halloween than playing principal, I glance back down at the menu.

"I don't know why you even bother when you always order the same thing." This voice comes from my left as I look up to greet Sean's latest obsession. An obsession who's hustling shifts between Horner Tech and Sean's parents' restaurant to earn her way through cosmetology school.

"Sup, Layla," I greet as she peers down at me, wearing

jeans and a form-fitting long-sleeve Pitt Stop shirt, her gorgeous blonde mane secured in a messy bun. "Didn't feel like dressing up?"

"I'm too boring these days and work too damned much," she says with a sigh. "I swear, if I didn't know everyone in this town, I'd rob Triple Savings and Loan."

"I might help you," I joke, "restoring my truck might cost me an internal organ." I glance around the bustling restaurant. "Looks like business is pretty good."

"Yeah, today. But the last two shifts, I only had a few tables. I was better off saving the gas money."

"Sorry to hear it. How close are you now?"

"To getting my cosmetology license?" She frowns. "Not much longer, and believe me, I can't wait. Between sweating in that fucking factory during the summers"—she lowers her voice—"and dealing with some of the old-timing assholes here that think tipping pocket change is enough, I'm about to go batshit."

"It'll pay off," I tell her, tucking this conversation away to suggest her as a possible recruit on Tobias's next trip home. Layla is good people and trustworthy, and despite T's misogynistic hangup, it wouldn't hurt us to have a lady bird within our ranks.

"Well, tell you what, if you'll have me, I'll be one of the first in your chair."

"I'd be honored to get my hands on that beautiful head of hair before the United States Marines lop it all off," she says, playfully running her fingers through it. It's easy to see why she's Sean's current obsession, but unclear to him at the moment is that she's in a league of her own and way out of his wheelhouse.

"You really on the menu for something else?" she drawls suggestively, which gives me a little pause.

"Not a bad idea to switch it up sometimes," I shrug.

"I agree, but"—she glances behind her, biting her full bottom lip—"from the daggers Kayley is shooting our way, it could get tricky for you."

"Nah." I grin. "Kayley knows you don't fuck with High School."

"As if she could judge," she muses. "But you're right, I don't, so relay that to your idiot starting quarterback, would you?"

She nods toward the kitchen where Sean's currently flipping burgers on the line.

"Yeah, he's a bit slow on the uptake in that respect, but he does throw a mean spiral."

"He does, especially for a junior." She cocks her hip. "Though, aren't you a *senior* this year?"

"Yeah, I've got Dom and Sean beat in age by a few months shy of a year, which they both hate, and Mom started me in kindergarten when I was four. Probably because she knew I was smarter than that paste eater." I toss a thumb toward the cut-out between the kitchen and dining room.

Timing impeccable, Sean looks up from where he's helping man the grill, eyes flicking between the two of us as we share a laugh.

"Well, I don't disagree with her." Layla sweeps me appreciatively. "The maturity shows."

"Wouldn't be so obvious if he didn't act like an overheated stray dog," I chuckle as Sean narrows his eyes on me. "So, do yourself a favor and don't give him any kibble, and he'll eventually find another porch to stalk."

"Got to give him credit." She grins as she eyes him, "He's persistent."

"You've got a boyfriend, though, right?" I ask her.

"In between. The last one was an asshole, just like the one before him." She shakes her head. "I think I might have developed an unhealthy weakness for bad boys."

"Do me a favor and don't mention that to Sean. I have a feeling it would not bode well for any of us." I extend my menu toward her. "I'll take my usual, please."

Grabbing the menu, she gives me a wink. "On it, and don't forget you promised me that first haircut."

"It's a date," I say, just as Sean snaps an "order up!"

"I think you're being summoned," I draw out, unable to help my grin.

"Which is idiotic"—she elevates her voice for Sean—"considering that's not at all how we do it here!" She rolls her eyes. "I'll be back."

My cell rings just as I spot Kayley approaching in my peripheral. Lifting it, I see Mom's calling just as Kayley makes it to my table. I lift a finger to keep her idle as I answer.

"Hey, Mom." I roll my eyes suggestively down Kayley as she not so subtly brushes her bare thigh against my arm. "I'm kind of in the middle of some—"

"Tyler," Mom croaks. At the sound of it, I go rigid, and Kayley's brows draw, sensing the shift in me.

"What's wrong?"

"I . . . your father and I have been in an accident."

Already on my feet, I place some cash on the table, shooting Kayley an apologetic look before hauling ass out the door and onto Main Street. Bypassing a few trick-or-treaters with bags and buckets in hand, I round the corner of the red-brick building, plugging my open ear. "What happened?"

"We were out running errands, and your father lost control of the wheel."

"Are you okay?"

"I'm a little banged up, but I'm okay. The doctor is releasing me now."

"Is Dad—"

"Tyler," she interjects as dread settles low in my gut. A gust of freezing air hits me as I run my palm down my face.

"What, Mom, what?" I ask, seeing the anguish in his expression when we faced off before shooting up a fast prayer that it's not the last memory I'll have of him—with him.

"He's in jail," she relays tearfully as my fear immediately morphs into fury. "No one else got hurt," she adds quickly.

But it's what she's not saying and the implications of it that has my mind racing as the full weight of what's happening settles in.

"Why was he driving in the first place?" The question

feels like lead coming off my tongue as lividity fills me. Whatever explanation she gives is drowned out by the blood that starts to pulse in my ears. Any excuse won't be good enough. Only the truth that my dad was drunk and got arrested for DUI.

The rest of the unspoken fear in her voice is due to what the more damning consequences could be aside from the legal mess and possible jail time. Her genuine fear is that this isn't or won't be Dad's rock bottom.

No, this is just the heads-up that it's coming, and we both know why.

Chances are Carter Jennings's most recent fuckup just ended his twenty-year career as a US Marine.

"I'm on my way home."

***

Mom sits in a chair in the living room, silent tears trickling down her bruised cheek. A goose egg now sits fully formed at her right temple, *both* of her wrists taped. Sitting on the couch opposite her, I take in every detail, my rage festering and threatening to take over as I bristle across from her in wait. Uncle Gray had called in a favor with one of his cop buddies—the favor allowing him to post bail before Dad had to serve the required time in the drunk tank. They're due any minute, but I can't help but address my mom as the seconds tick down.

"Mom—"

"I know what you're about to say," she sniffs, gently blotting away her tears, "and I'm asking you not to."

"Please, Mom. Please just leave him. He's not going to get any better. Things are just going to get worse."

Pushing the ottoman sitting at the foot of her chair to the side, I take a knee before her and gently grip her hands in mine.

"I'll help pay the bills." A sob bursts from her with my offer. "I'll do whatever you need me to. It's been you and me for so long anyway." I squeeze her hands. "We can make it work without him. At least until you get on your feet."

"Enough," she clips, her return gaze flaring in warning.

My own temper flares at the sight of it. "Jesus Christ, Mom. Look in the mirror. He could have killed you!"

"Stop," she whispers, "just stop."

Releasing her hands, I shake my head in aggravation.

"Why are you taking it easy on him?" I shout. "The man has condemned everyone in this house for the slightest fuckup. We got no mercy, did we? Why should he get away with this? With any of it."

"Tyler stop!"

"No, you deserve better. He's a piece of fucking shit for cheating on you—"

Mom raises her hand to strike me, and I visibly flinch, gaping at her ready hand, her brown eyes piercing me as venom spews from her mouth.

"Don't you *ever* talk about your father like that again. My marriage is none of your goddamn business, do you hear me? Stay out of it!"

In that moment, as I study my mother's poised hand, ready to strike her son because she doesn't want to hear the truth come out of his mouth, I decide that, in the future, when it comes to matters of the heart, I'll never make anyone else's relationship my fucking business.

"Tyler." Uncle Grayson's voice sounds from the entryway before we both turn to see Dad and Uncle Gray standing feet away. Front door still open, their collective expressions tell us they didn't miss a word of our exchange.

"So, this is how it is, huh?" Palming the ottoman, I slowly stand, sharing my glare between my parents. Silent, damning seconds pass as Dad slowly sweeps Mom, missing none of it—not the bruises, bandage, or the tears streaming down her cheeks before his eyes lower.

"You want me to stay out of it, Mom? Consider it done," I clip out bitterly, "I'm completely fucking done."

Mom gasps my name, and I scowl down at her, betrayal coating my voice. "He's all yours, *Mrs. Jennings* . . . and you fucking deserve each other."

Mom cups her mouth as I barrel out of the living room, slamming the garage door on my way out, feeling the finality of it.

Pressing past all threatening emotions, instead, I shift my focus to my future, on my brothers, and our game plan. It's all I have left and all that matters.

Once outside the garage, I start at a dead run, speeding toward a future that's beginning to take shape, the edges of the map becoming more defined with each step. I race toward it by order of the host of the silver-gray eyes that inexplicably have been calling to me like a beacon. A beacon that fills my chest with a slight glimmer of something that feels a little like hope.

Chapter Thirteen

DELPHINE

"*Two days* EARLY," Tyler reports, short of breath, chest heaving, sweat pouring from him as he lifts several plastic bags for my inspection. Dressed in a long-sleeved shirt, jeans, and sneakers, his dark brown hair lays scattered and plastered to his crown.

"And where are my books?" I eye him speculatively while taking the haul I ordered him to bring once he was finished with his curriculum.

"Still on loan, for now, okay?" He scrapes his bottom lip with his teeth, a flicker of something passing in his brown eyes, too brief to decipher.

"Fine, you may be early, but did you shower *in your clothes* before coming here?"

Tyler opens his mouth just as Dom stalks into the kitchen, an empty coffee mug in hand, his inquiry the same as he scours Tyler's disheveled appearance. "The fuck happened to you?"

"I ran to the store and back," Tyler reports to us both before glancing at me. "Only a mile and a half, but I'm getting there."

Dom pours his coffee, looking between us, his typical unimpressed expression encompassing his face. His obvious disdain for me much too ingrained to pose the question budding in his eyes as I dump the bags' contents on the table and address him. "Drinking too much of that may stunt your growth," I warn.

I glance over as he pointedly eyes the pint of vodka on the table while obnoxiously slurping his coffee.

"You have school tomorrow," I remind him.

He poses his question to Tyler instead. "What is this?"

"You know what it is," I retort while pulling the toy soldiers from their packaging. "I played with Ezekiel many times before he left for France."

"Bullshit," Dom clips out, eyeing the soldiers. "*When?*"

I hesitate in answering as I search my memory and can't recall a single time Dominic was present when we played. My mind forever failing me.

"Maybe . . . it was when you were still dirtying all your clothes by hanging from the trees with Sean," I joke.

"Your memory is lacking *as usual*, Tatie," he drawls out, "I've never had *good clothes*."

"But they do still hang from the trees," Tyler inserts, an obvious attempt to cut the tension—a tactic Sean also often uses when Dom is in one of his moods. Moods he refuses to allow anyone to overlook, especially me.

"While this looks *riveting*," Dom spouts, "I'll leave you to it." He turns to Tyler. "Give me a ride to the library?"

"Sorry, man, Mom's using the van tonight," Tyler replies, lowering his eyes, his lie detectable even as he checks his watch. "Library's closing soon anyway—" Tyler cuts himself off, and I glance over to see it's because of Dom's hostile return expression.

I hold my eye roll and unpackage more soldiers as they silently communicate behind my back as if I'm dense enough not to know the library is not Dom's true destination.

This is only confirmed when Dom opens a cabinet and grabs a box of cereal bars and a large bag of chips. I say nothing about the fact that he's packing groceries and haven't since Dom unleashed his wrath on me not long after Ezekiel left.

"Just because you eat the minimum piece of toast at 2 a.m. to make sure you don't dull too much of your buzz doesn't mean no one else in the house needs to fucking eat!"

He slammed his bedroom door in my face just after, his venom-filled *"selfish bitch"* carrying through the barrier before he clicked on his stereo to mute any reply I might have.

Since that night, I have not allowed the cabinets to go bare, making sure there is something for him to easily cook and eat. The hours I spent in the bath with my bottle that night were some of my worst. My biased memory refuses to allow me to forget that night or any other in which I am reminded of my failure with my nephews.

"I hate her."

"Shh, Dom, she'll hear you," Tobias scolds.

"I don't care. I hate her. I hope she dies."

Their hushed whispers from years ago fill my ears as I watch Dom gather and pack more food. Where he brings his small bounties to or to whom remains a mystery.

"I could drive you," I offer, just as he turns to reply to Tyler.

"All good. See you tomorrow, man."

"It's no trouble for me to drive you," I call after him as he stalks toward the front door.

"Play with your little plastic soldiers, Tatie," he scoffs, "I'd rather not have the fucking town drunk chauffeuring me."

His insult reaches me just as he slams the storm door behind him so hard that both Tyler and I flinch.

Fury fills me as I take a step toward the front door and still myself, fighting both my will and tongue not to go after him. The same battle I've been in for years since his brother's departure. It's Ezekiel's parting words before he left for France that continually stop me.

"Treat him well. He's immune to you now. Things won't change overnight, but if you remain the same, he'll fall in line. Do this, and you will have earned my trust."

Five long years later, I still have not managed to gain an inch of ground to stand on where Jean Dominic is concerned. That truth more evident than ever as his contemptuous parting words linger in the house.

"I *never drive* when I drink," I tell Tyler, who's staring at the ground between us, his posture tense. "That is a lie, Tyler," I insist.

Tyler's eyes shoot to mine in search as if he wants to believe my words as mortification heats my neck and cheeks.

"Turn on some music," I order Tyler to divert his probing gaze as the burning increases. "Classical only." I nod toward the radio sitting on the kitchen counter next to my canisters.

"On it," Tyler says, walking into the kitchen as I turn back to the table full of soldiers. Humiliation continues to batter me and has me calling out another order as Tyler shuffles through a few radio stations.

"Divide each of our battalions into *three hundred*," I instruct, snatching my bottle from the counter. "I will be back."

"Will do," he replies, keeping his eyes lowered.

"Prepare yourself, private. You are going to war," I call over my shoulder with false bravado, racing toward my bedroom. Bracing myself against the closed door, I bite into my forearm, releasing my idle tears, the relief slight and fleeting as I muffle my cries while focusing on the pain.

After several paralyzing minutes, I decide on a quick scrub to attempt to take some of the lingering sting away.

Turning on the faucet, I set the water temperature to as hot as I can tolerate and unscrew my bottle, taking several mouthfuls of drink. With my focus fixed on the flow of water from the jagged faucet, mixed whispers traverse back to me.

"*I wish she would die.*"
"*Selfish bitch.*"
"*I hate her.*"

Unzipping my robe, I submerse myself into the steaming

water as the images and voices collide in their punishing, perpetual blur.

The boiling water further heats my skin, sweat gathering at my temples as I run my palms over the top of the steaming surface, Matis's words seeping into me as I begin my soak.

"Cleanliness draws God's attention. You must keep your body free of filth to allow God to cleanse your mind and heart so he will wash you of your sins."

Scrubbing my skin, I send up my ritual prayer as my eyes catch on a sagging patch of ceiling. I stare and stare, zeroing in on the brown tint, the same hue as the polished wood grain on Celine's coffin.

Staring at the twin graves before me, I pull at the loose thread at the hip of my dress and wind it around my finger, stopping the flow of blood until it numbs. Wishing I had brought my bottle, the task ahead fills me with terror.

A task written in the spilled blood of Celine and Beau King—to raise their sons from boys to men.

The haze then reveals a memory of a night not long after their funeral—of an exchange that continues to plague me daily.

"I don't want to be a mother," I whisper to eleven-year-old Ezekiel before his firelit eyes condemn me.

"Then don't. I'll feed him. I'll bathe him. I'll walk him to school. You don't touch him, don't yell at him. I'll do it all."

And I let him.

Failing my sister.
Failing her husband.
Failing their sons.
Failing. Failing. Failing.

"Delphine," Ormand whispers at my back just as I grip Jean Dominic and Ezekiel's hands to start to usher them out of the cemetery. "Please don't shut me out," he croaks.

Stilling, I feel Ezekiel's eyes on me as I keep mine forward, focused on the swaying line of trees ahead of us.

"Tatie, your hand is shaking," Dominic squeaks from

beneath me before Tobias shushes him, and Ormand's plea reaches me.

"Delphine, please—"

"Go back to France, Ormand. I have nothing left to give you."

The strangled noise he made when I cruelly dismissed him still haunts and confuses me. Confusion for the disdain and hostility I felt for him when I woke in that hospital bed.

Ormand, whom I trusted over all Alain's men. Who was a friend and support—whose pain remains with me after I cast him out of my life, unsure of why his presence no longer held any comfort but instead repulsed me. Ormand, who waited for me in hopes of more for the entire length of my marriage, only to be exiled from my life and heart as Beau's and Celine's coffins lowered. The loss of him feeling like another death to mourn.

Discarding my washcloth, I sink beneath the surface of the water. The world beneath no different than the world above. Words just as muffled and the faces just as blurry as I lose time, days, and minutes as I have since I woke that night, mere months before Beau and Celine were murdered.

In need of breath, I surface just before a sharp knock jerks me to sit, reminding me I'm not alone in the house. Focusing on the knob, I jump when Tyler's voice sounds from the other side of it.

"Delphine?" Tyler knocks again. "I'm ready for you."

How long have I been in the bath?

Lifting my hands, my pruned fingers tell me some time has passed.

Time, which many claim is a healer, has been anything but for me. My underwater mind refusing me of all forward progress while making a goddamned fool of me.

It's the haze that works against me, blurring my days and weeks. The haze which muddles my memories, bringing me back and to, confusing me, paralyzing me. Even as I cleanse myself over and over for God, seeking His attention, my prayers for clarity are never heard—refused. My sins too many to cleanse, to garner His attention.

"Delphine? You okay in there?"

"I need . . ."

Eyeing my bedroom doorknob from the tub, I squint to see it start to turn. Capping my bottle, I rise slowly from the water, grabbing my towel and palming it over my chest. "Tyler, do not come in!"

"I'm not . . . I-I wouldn't." His confusion has me blinking to realize the knob has not turned by a fraction.

Get it together, Delphine, and get rid of the boy!

Because that's all he is, a boy. A harmless boy.

It's my fear that sneaks its way in as I keep focused on the knob.

Boys turn into men.

"How could you leave me to raise what I despise?"

The hem of my towel soaks as it dances along the top of the water as I remain paralyzed by fear in the corner of the tub. My eyes transfixed on the cheap brass knob with the worthless lock.

"Delphine?"

"I need five minutes!"

"Sounds good," Tyler calls back as I rip my eyes from the knob and sip the bottle until the fear starts to slither away, coiling itself back into the darkest part of my water-drenched mind—readying itself for the next time.

Unplugging the drain, I retrieve what's left of my bottle, capping it before redressing in my robe. Tugging down my sleeves, I clear my eyes before walking out to dismiss Tyler. I cannot possibly help him and am in no position to do so. Whatever this foolish boy seeks or sees in me is delusion.

Opening my mouth to send him home, the words are muted when I see Tyler has aligned our individual armies perfectly on opposite sides of the table. The sight of it sparks a distant excitement inside me—a flicker of a simpler time.

Of a time when I was brave. Before the haze and blur. A welcome feeling in exchange for fear and confusion. It's when I take in the expression of the wide-eyed boy, eyes patient and imploring, which seek my approval, that I falter, unable to deny him.

"This is very good," I compliment as I lift one of the soldiers, brushing my fingers over it.

"I think I see where you're going with this, *Yoda*," he jokes enthusiastically in an effort to appease me. Kind. Always so kind.

"Do you?" I reply, hearing the lingering shake in my voice, willing the burning inside my chest to subside as the numb starts to take hold, relieving me.

"It's a game I have played since I was very young . . . Bataille," I whisper.

"Battle," Tyler translates easily as he scans the soldiers. "If I would have known *this* is what I was prepping for, I would have cut off a few more days."

I roll my eyes at his arrogance. "You will not be so smug when I take your army down, *private*."

My threat does not deter him as he lifts one of his soldiers. "So, who taught you?"

"Matis." I slide into the chair opposite of him.

"Matis?"

"My father," I clarify, to which he gives me a forlorn nod. Tyler ran here tonight, and by the look of him, it seems he did not plan to come. As I scrutinize him, that truth becomes more obvious. He has not yet memorized the books but came to seek refuge from his life at home.

Stupid boy. What refuge could he possibly see in me?

In needing and seeking my own escape, I decide not to reject him.

"What?" He peers over at me, realizing how closely I'm watching him.

"Study your opponent," I instruct. "Memorize them. In every exchange, look for tells, for lies, and most important, for weakness."

He nods quickly—too quickly—and I'm unsure if he heeds my warning.

"So, T played this?" he asks, positioning his men, his question because of his affection and bond with Ezekiel.

"Yes, and he was *very, very* good."

"Challenge accepted," he draws out. "Did he ever beat *you*?"

"Never," I relay with a grin, pushing up my sleeves so as not to knock any of my soldiers over. It's when Tyler stills that I look up to see his gaze locked on my forearm. I follow his focus to see the angry red teeth marks and the surrounding swollen skin before quickly pulling my sleeves back down.

"Ezekiel was a very skilled," I continue, "very wise opponent," I manage without shake before unscrewing the cap of my bottle.

"Well, this"—his tone lifts to match mine—"right here is *my task* to *master*," he informs me with no shortage of ambition. One I don't dismiss easily this time.

Instead, I nod in silent confirmation, fully aware of Ezekiel's plans.

Plans my oldest nephew is now putting into motion with Ormand's help—the first contact I gave him when he landed in France. My intention for making that connection is to help aid Ezekiel in his quest to do what I didn't—avenge Celine and Beau.

Another of my failures that Ezekiel took upon himself to rectify. More weight that lays heavily on my soul, but weight I'm thankful for.

"Delphine?" Tyler drawls. "Where did you go?"

"Shh," I whisper, "know your enemy."

I focus on my new and willing opponent as he does the same. An opponent that, in truth, is an ally, eager to take on a part of Ezekiel and Dominic's quest. Tyler seems to catch on as he stares right back at me, raising his chin, unflinching.

It's in Tyler's unwavering gaze that I allow myself to

think mentoring him could be another chance to do my part—to honor Celine. A chance for vengeance that the haze denied me. A chance that Dominic continues to refuse me. Maybe with true effort, Tyler will grant me the ability to right some of my wrongs. A start that I've attempted for years while fighting through the haze and numbing with drink.

To try.

"Let's begin."

Chapter Fourteen

Tyler

Stalking down the mostly vacant hall to meet Dom—who summoned me by text—I catch the heated whispers as they escalate, pinpointing exactly who's exchanging them as I round the corner.

"Fucking snitch," Sean spits venomously just before throwing his mid-evil right hook. In an instant, I'm at Dom's side as Sean takes one of his own defensive linemen to the floor. Their beef having started in middle school over some stupid bullshit. This means that given any reason or chance Blake Spellman gives Sean to keep the feud going, Sean takes it.

Sean and Blake's brawl starts to escalate, their sneakers squeaking loudly while their collective grunts intensify. The sound of their scuffle muting Mrs. Hill's English lit lecture just outside her classroom door.

It's when a few lingering students take notice and start to walk in our direction to watch the spectacle that Dom gives Sean the heads-up.

"Wrap it up, or the only balls you'll be playing with Friday are your own," Dom snarks, arms crossed, his menacing grin in place as we watch Sean dominate the fight, throwing punch after punch, already the victor.

"What's this one about?" I ask, wincing at the shot

Sean just took to his ribs, knowing it's going to sting like a bitch later.

In lieu of an answer, Dom steps forward or rather stomps forward, his step subtle but purposeful as he slowly inches the rest of himself toward his idle boot. The sight of it has me perking as I gauge the satisfied look in Dom's eyes.

Something's up.

"You're good, bro. I think he got the message," Dom says, as I roll my eyes, knowing better, before pulling Sean off Blake. Spellman jumps from the ancient, overly polished white tile, glancing around to see who witnessed his ass whooping. Pride battered, Blake wipes his mouth, spitting venom at Sean through blood-laced teeth.

"The fuck, Roberts? The fuck are you talking about, snitch?"

"Rat me out to Coach again, I fucking dare you," Sean barks in warning before Mrs. Hill's door opens, and the small group of students that gathered to watch the fight start to scatter. A second later, she nails Dom with a ready glare.

"Do we have a problem here, Mr. King?" She shifts her focus to me. "Mr. Jennings? Mr. Roberts, do the three of you not have somewhere to be?"

"Yes, ma'am," I state as Dom keeps planted firmly in place.

"Mr. Spellman," she calls after Blake's retreating back. "Do we need to take this conversation elsewhere?"

Blake waves his hand, not bothering to turn around. "All good."

Mrs. Hill gives each of us a pointed look as she speaks. "I suggest you three get back to class before I find both a problem and a place for you all to be."

"Yes, ma'am," Sean says, giving her a flirtatious grin and salute before righting his vintage Batman T-shirt. It's when Dom nods in agreement instead of popping off that I know something is definitely up.

It's confirmed a second later when Mrs. Hill snaps her door shut, and Dom drops, retrieving and carefully cupping the prize under his boot before disposing of it in Sean's waiting hand. A hand he promptly closes into a tight fist as Dom barks his order. "Hit the shop and get it back to me before sixth period."

"On it." Sean shoots me a wink before sauntering off in the direction Spellman went, calling after Blake in taunt. "Come back, snitchy. Daddy needs a word."

"The hell?" I ask as Dom strides off, a smug smile blooming on his face at my confusion when I fall in step next to him.

"Can you borrow your mom's van tonight?" He asks.

"Probably, yeah."

"Good. Pick us up at midnight."

I pause my footing. "That's past curfew."

"Then get grounded," he calls back to me, "it'll be worth it."

Sighing, I decide it's better for now not to ask, especially since Dom's in a theatrical mood. Not long after the clock strikes twelve, the three of us are creeping to the other side of town in Mom's minivan. Cam'ron's "Killa Cam" plays in the background before I cut it off and park where Dom instructs. When the three of us sit idle for a few long seconds, blocks away from an open-gated industrial complex that houses three buildings, I finally demand my explanation.

"Speak," I state before Dom rips his gaze from one of the buildings and turns to me.

"We're going shopping," he states matter-of-factly.

"For?" I ask as Dom gets out, grabbing the packed duffle he brought. Sean and I follow suit, shivering at the change in temp, as Dom bends, unzipping the bag at our collective feet.

"Love to your mom and all," Dom starts, pulling out three ski masks.

"*So much love* for Regina," Sean interjects, palming his

heart before sliding it down to cup his junk. I waste no time thumping his ear as hard as possible. His features pinch in pain before they disappear behind his ski mask when he pulls it down, cocking his head. "Was that absolutely necessary?"

"Yes," I state, pulling my own mask on along with the gloves Dom supplies next.

"Your mom is lava fucking hot, bro," Sean quips as he pulls on a glove, "deal with it. God knows *I want to*."

"Like I was saying," Dom snaps to shut Sean up, grabbing a few more masks and pairs of gloves from the open duffle before tossing it back into the van and closing the door. "Love to Mom for the loan, but I'm growing tired of the minivan." He turns to Sean. "Got it?"

Sean produces a key from his jeans and hands it to Dom.

"That's all I'm getting?" I ask as the three of us start to creep toward the complex, a shiver running up my spine. This fall has been unseasonably cold, with a few nights of early snowfall, some dropping below dead of winter temperatures. This proves to be an advantage for us—at least for tonight. The frigid cold no doubt responsible for the lack of life at the complex and surrounding neighborhood.

"So, this plan is sound?" I ask Dom, eyeing the extra masks and gloves in his hands.

"As it can be, though I enlisted help."

As if aware of my question of who, a distant "ca-*caw*" sounds from blocks away, and Dom chuckles in response.

"Really fucking discreet," I snap, knowing it could only be Russell. I'm proven right when, minutes later, he appears, dressed in black like the rest of us as instructed, and he's not alone.

"The fuck is going on?" I ask, hackles rising as Russell sidles up to us with ease, with a guy who looks around our age, brown hair and eyes, average build, wearing a dopey smile.

"Tyler, this is Jeremy," Russell introduces. "This is the recruit I've been telling you about, remember?"

"Probably not. Tyler's been distracted playing with little plastic soldiers on school nights," Dom supplies as I glare at the side of his head before scouring Jeremy.

"Sup, man," Jeremy greets me, his tone tentative.

"Hey, man," I say, feeling awkward as fuck about the impromptu meeting while becoming more ill at ease at the fact I'm clueless as to what's going on.

"We can finish the meet and greet later." Dom jumps in, sensing my apprehension. "Russell, Jeremy, you two head over first and try the lock," Dom commands, as if he's been doing this his whole life. Extending the masks and gloves to them, he then lifts the key for Russell. "We'll watch your six."

"Six?" Jeremy mimics in clear confusion as he pulls his mask down.

"It means to watch your back," Russell supplies, taking the key after gloving up.

"Shit, sorry, *dumbass*," Jeremy says through a self-deprecating chuckle. It's clear he's nervous, which makes me even more so. It's my trust in Dom that curbs some of the edge I'm feeling.

Dom, Sean, and I stay back, scanning the complex and surrounding streets as I front them out while Jeremy and Russell creep toward one of the buildings.

"The fuck? You planned this without me?" I hiss.

"Not really," Dom says, completely at ease. "Think of it more as an early Christmas present."

"You know damn well I'm not the one to move on shit *without knowing the plan*."

Dom palms my shoulder. "This is impromptu, brother. We didn't know if we would be able to get the key."

It strikes me then how we're gaining access to the building and why. The key I now know belongs to Blake Spellman. The why is because he works for his dad, who provides car parts—many custom—for garages and shops in and out of Triple Falls.

"You had him start a fucking fight to pocket that key," I surmise.

"If I had started it," Dom spouts, "it wouldn't be believable, and that key ring is now tucked safely back in Blake's pocket thanks to some unexpected consoling from Ginger after school. Nothing heavy."

Ginger is Dom's on-again, off-again hookup and has been since middle school.

"Fight was happening anyway because *he did* rat me out to Coach," Sean pipes as the door opens, and Russell and Jeremy wave us over.

"We lucked out he had the key on him," Sean adds as the three of us sprint through the darkest part of the path to get to the door. My adrenaline spikes as Dom locks it, and the three of us begin to scout the office for security cameras, relieved when we come up empty.

"All clear," Dom sounds out before opening the door, which leads to the larger part of the building. The space is the size of a small warehouse, which Russell and Jeremy are already scouring.

"This is the warehouse Spellman's dad uses to keep the *vintage parts* he sells for mad money online. Merry fucking Christmas." Dom grins, holding the door open for Sean, who slaps Dom's chest in celebration as he passes.

"Fucking genius, bro." Sean beams, stopping just past the door as I follow him. "And totally worth the loose molar," he adds, eyes sparkling as he tightens his gloves with his fingers in anticipation. "Now, if you'll excuse me, boys, I'm going to collect my winnings before I go grab a good night kiss from Tyler's mommy."

Sean barely dodges my swing before jogging over to join Russell and Jeremy. I watch the three of them for a few seconds as Dom walks back into the office, gazing out the window to make sure we got in undetected.

"So, Jeremy?" I prompt as Dom thumbs through a few papers on a nearby desk.

"Transplant," he says, "checked out of Raleigh a few months back."

"Checked out?"

"Boys home," Dom says, stalking over to join me at the door. "He's no mechanic, but he's really good with his hands." He pitches his voice into the warehouse. "Isn't that right, Jeremy?"

Jeremy nods, his mask already lifted to his forehead before he reaches into his jeans and lifts a wallet.

My fucking wallet.

"The fuck?" I say, palming my back pocket in shock as Jeremy saunters over, giving me a sheepish grin.

"Sorry, man"—he nods towards Dom—"his idea. It's all still there." He pats my shoulder. "Thanks for letting me in on this."

Before I can tell him I had nothing to do with it, he runs back over to help Russell.

"Shit," I whisper, utterly shocked at how he managed to pickpocket me. "I didn't feel a thing. How the fuck did he even get close enough?"

"Talent," Dom quips with a pleased grin before he lowers his voice, canting his head toward me. "He's been surfing from dumpsters to sidewalks, sleeping in any hole he can climb into, and robbing only when he has to, to try and keep from getting picked up again. He'll do anything to avoid being tossed back into the system. He came to the garage a month ago asking Russell if we needed help, but has no experience. Russell's been talking to him since, and he's been hanging around King's for a few weeks now."

Dom crosses his arms, leaning against the door before turning to me.

"I've checked him out, bro. I swear I vetted him thoroughly. He's had it rough"—he stares back at Jeremy—"really fucking rough, but he's willing to put in the time to learn to be a mechanic. I thought"—he shrugs—"if it works out, we could consider putting him on payroll. We need another full-timer anyway, and he can work every day. What do you think?"

I eye Jeremy. "Yeah, I mean, I want to talk to him first, feel him out myself, but yeah, I trust your judgment."

"It's time to build our nest, and what better way to induct him than have him incriminating himself with us?" Dom chuckles.

Sensing our conversation, Jeremy lifts his eyes, volleying them back and forth between the two of us with what I know is guarded hope. It's then that I feel the inclination to speak up. "Didn't Sean just put an old couch in the commercial bay for his hookups?"

Dom turns to me. "Yeah, I was thinking the same thing. Didn't know if it was too soon."

I lean over, eyeing Jeremy. "It might balance the scales, right? Maybe enough so Santa won't cross us off his list before Christmas Eve."

"Fuck Santa," Dom snarks, walking backward into the warehouse, his silver eyes dancing, "we're going to make him look like a stingy, irrelevant fuck."

I can't help but chuckle as I trail him to join the rest of our growing nest. Ironically, that night, after committing my first punishable offense and after a thorough tongue-lashing from Mom for breaking curfew—which seemed laughable in contrast—I slept like the dead. But I woke up with a smile, spending my shower replaying the events of last night in detail, realizing Dom made our induction to a life of criminality utterly painless.

Chapter Fifteen

Tyler

WINTER 2004

"TYLER!" DAD BARKS from the front door, the jingle of the merry little bundle of bells Mom has hanging on the knob distorted in delivery as he slams it.

In the weeks since both our confrontations, my parents have been avoiding me more and more. Probably because when they do meet my eyes, I never let them forget what they're doing to each other and to me, refusing to live their lie.

It's their decision to live with and my punishment to bear witness to the slow, painful desecration of their ideas of one another.

"Tyler!" the man I once knew as my father hollers as he smacks into the wall next to my door before his heavy footfalls resume on the hardwoods. His mud-covered boots come into view before he stumbles inside my bedroom, tripping on nothing but alcoholism and bitterness.

As feared, Dad's DUI had him discharged from the Corps—though honorably, in consideration of his decades of service. Now seen as a liability, they cut him loose. I wasn't given any more details than that because I didn't ask. As far as I'm concerned, there's no conversation to have. Unapologetically back to his old habits mere weeks after his latest and most detrimental fuckup, he's more unbearable than ever.

Closing my book, I passively stare up at him, feigning confusion while knowing he's spoiling for the fight he couldn't find at the bar. Chances are Brian threw him out after I failed to retrieve him—a call I purposefully ignored.

"Why the fuck didn't you pick me up?"

"Mom spent half the morning cleaning the floors," I divert as he charges in further, failing to get the flinch he so desperately wants from me.

"Yeah? Good on her. And what the fuck did *you do* today that was productive?" His delivery is a mix of spit and slur as he sizes me up.

"I attended school, which is age appropriate considering I'm a senior in high school, and worked my shift at the garage after. *You?*"

Tension and fury radiate from him as he leers at me from only a foot away.

"Maybe I'll take the fucking truck away," he threatens.

"That would be pointless because it's not running yet, and you can't take what you don't own."

"Yeah? Well, I own the fucking roof currently over your head!"

I don't mince words. "Are you kicking me out?"

"Did I fucking say I was?"

Mom predictably comes to my aid, appearing in the doorframe, shoulders slumped when she sees the state of her floor before her eyes frantically dart between us. I firmly shake my head at her just as she opens her mouth to speak. It's a cliché situation, and sadly, the solution for me lies in enlisting the second I turn eighteen. A large part of me wishes I could leave now, but it would only shift his focus and wrath on her. With his rapid spiral, I refuse to do it—not even to spare myself. Though, she hasn't extended the same courtesy. Swallowing the litany of insults I want to hurl at him, and in seeing Mom's state, I go diplomatic.

"I'm sorry, Dad. I'll pick you up next time. I grilled tonight and left a plate for you on the counter."

Dad's lips peel back as he glares at my books. "You won't be no fancy college boy. We can't afford it."

"I have no plans of attending Harvard."

I just have to test well enough to enlist. A subject I'll no longer broach with him, nor any other, since he endangered my mother's life.

"If you do go, you're going *state* because Uncle Sam is gonna pay. He fucking owes me."

Annoyed that his belligerent ass isn't understanding that I'm not arguing with him, I nod. "Hungry? Let's get you fed."

Grabbing my new cell phone from my dresser—another early Christmas present from Tobias—Dad tosses it on the book in my lap, failing, yet again, to get his wanted flinch. One which would require a modicum of respect and fear I no longer have when it comes to him. Instead, I lift my chin in defiance as he does his worst to best me while making sure he fucking fails.

"The next time I fucking call you, you answer. Do you hear me?"

"I'm sorry, sir. I'll do better," I utter in a lifeless, rehearsed tone.

"Don't fucking *patronize me*," he snaps, lifting a finger less than an inch from my nose. Fury begins to build inside me as I take a few cleansing breaths. The only upside to his nightly tirades, in which he now targets me, is the practice of controlling my rage with Delphine's breathing techniques.

"I'll do better, *be better*," I recite. "I'll be a man you can be proud of, *sir.*"

He weighs my words, knowing I no longer mean them. Glancing over his shoulder at Mom, he turns his back to me.

"Look at what you raised, Regina. Arrogant, disrespectful, and smug. Aren't you fucking proud?"

Tears brim in Mom's eyes as he crashes past her before they focus on mine, shining with an unspoken apology for subjecting us both to his slow, toxic implosion.

The minute Dad passes out, I text Dom, push into my sneakers, and grab the bag from my dresser on my way out. Stalking through the house, I'm stopped short by the sight of Mom putting the last of the glittering decorations on the tree. Her attempt in resurrecting the familiar décor tonight an obvious Hail Mary. Her underlying hope to spark some nostalgia while knowing she has no semblance of family left to host.

Trying to slip out undetected, I fail when Mom spots me sneaking through the kitchen toward the garage, calling my name in summons. As I approach, she reaches into a shoe box before thrusting a familiar decoration toward me.

"First grade," she boasts, as I eye the ancient artwork I constructed with craft paper and cotton balls. "Come on," she drawls, nudging me, "you always put it on the tree."

"That was then," I say, refusing to buy into the charade as I turn and stalk toward the front door.

"Tyler," she calls after me.

"I'll be home before curfew," I utter before shutting the door, hoping I'll catch Delphine before she hits her own wall. The irony not lost on me that I'm seeking comfort in exchanging one alcoholic's company for another's.

These last weeks have passed by in a blur. Delphine's company being the one I crave most. Between Dom's brooding about Tobias's extended absences, working his share of shifts at the garage, and holing up in his room on the net, he's been scarcer. Sean's been tied up as well, working between the Pitt stop and King's, finishing the football season, and building his little black book.

As always, we still band together, inseparable and on each other's heels in the halls at school, even if we split after the last bell to do our own thing.

Me, I've been running every morning and night like my ass is on fire to reach a timed *three*-mile mark with easy strides. Also working my share of shifts at the garage while spending almost every night with a French fireball who keeps me on my toes. Most of those nights are spent becoming overtly attuned to her.

Eyeing the gift bag as I walk up the drive, I second-guess my decision to deliver it tonight, but it's her companionship that's saving me from dwelling on the war zone in my house.

Knocking lightly on the storm door before I can reconsider, I peer through the frosted glass only to lock eyes with Delphine, who's standing on the other side of the counter. Cracking the door open to gauge my welcome and her mood, she gives me an easy nod, and I walk over to greet her.

Tonight, she's dressed in a thinner robe than her typical blue. Unable to ignore the knot holding it together is coming loose, I manage to glimpse a side view and curve of one of her perfect breasts. The rest of the groan-inducing view is obstructed by the silky dark braid resting atop it as she unfolds a packet of powdered painkillers. Pouring it on her tongue, she follows it with a sip of water before finally addressing me.

Her constant indication that I'm no one of importance only further encourages me to stop the ridiculous fucking fixation that began months ago. One I'm fueling with every look I steal.

"No game tonight," she states, her temperament hard to gauge with her delivery as I allow my eyes to sweep the perfection of her profile. Her features alone are utterly fucking surreal, having no less effect on me than they did yesterday or the day before.

No chance in hell, Jennings.

These last weeks have been a mix of heaven and hell. In giving me the education I practically begged her for, I've become completely cognizant of just how much of her beauty I was formerly blind to. Every day, I resign and align myself to the fact that my attraction for her is not only dangerous but utterly idiotic. That logic thwarted the instant I again catch sight of her.

At this point, I can't even lie to myself that it's training alone that keeps me coming back. Day by day, she consumes me a little more with her mystery while giving me bits and pieces of herself—her intelligence, her humor. She even has a warmth anyone who respects her enough and treats her well enough can easily draw upon. A warmth that's smothered by the hostility and resentment that surrounds her—namely Dom's.

"Evening, and I'm not here to play," I say, my tone threatening to betray me in how my seconds-long assessment of her affects me. She'd probably find my lingering gaze endearing and childish if she noticed at all. But she never lets on for a second that she's aware of my growing fixation because I don't, at all, let her see it. I do my best to make sure she can't *feel* it, either.

Looks can be felt, and I know this from playing the game myself with my hookups, so I don't go there with her. Ever.

I would chalk it up to nothing more than a crush, but ironically, her lack of acknowledgment is the only thing currently crushing me.

Because you're seventeen, you fucking idiot!

And because this simmering attraction growing between us is entirely my own, I've been tossing my mental hard-on aside in lieu of the invaluable knowledge she's bestowing upon me. So far, I've been presented with a mind-blowing arsenal of shit I've never considered before.

"He's in his room." Delphine dismisses me, interrupting my inner musings while pointing in the direction of the hall that leads to all three of their bedrooms. Instead, I draw closer to a fire I have no business warming up to, let alone attempting to play with. Opting to stay near it, I take a few steps closer while leaving myself on the opposite side of the counter, which serves as a partition separating the kitchen from the living room.

A safe distance from her to shield my growing delusion

and prolonged humiliation. Knowing good and well that if I ever give her the slightest hint of my growing attraction, I will lose her company.

Though, when I look at Delphine, I don't see Dom's aunt or our age difference—not since the day I got my first real look at her. If anything, I see a twenty-something who's wearing her grandmother's wardrobe. Her skin fucking glows with youth, her onyx hair silky in look.

In noticing that, I've acquired a healthy suspicion that she purposefully tries to mask both her body and beauty.

"You off to work soon?" I ask in a shitty attempt at conversation. Her latest job is working the graveyard shift at a boxing company—one of the only other factories in Triple Falls, aside from Horner Tech, which she quit when Celine and Beau died.

"Non, I'm off tonight."

I eye the clock on the stove. "So, why are you drinking coffee?"

"Why the questions?"

"Because maybe I want some, and it was my polite way of hinting around to what you *haven't* offered," I jest, "with your impeccable *lack* of hosting skills. So, how about it?"

"No," she replies sharply, barely sparing me a glance. "From this moment forward, you will eat only things which grow from the earth and lean protein. Water to drink. Only water. No drinking or drugs."

"All right, so no more experimenting with crack. Got it," I state pointlessly, which earns me a barely perceptible lift of full lips. "Though I can't help but think this is punishment because I'm winning, General."

"Non, you are not," she relays, "we're still very much at war."

"I leveled over half your companies last night," I counter.

"I was waiting for you to *watch me* make my next move," she says, walking over to the table, where our battalions are on opposite sides of the line, engaged in our first long-term war. I study the board to see not a soldier out of place and give her a nod. Coffee in one hand, she flicks her fingers with the other.

"Airstrike. Airstrike," she laughs maniacally while shooting my soldiers to the kitchen floor.

"The hell?" I balk.

"*Uh*-oh, *sniper*," she sing-songs, flicking several more soldiers before glancing over to me with a shrug. "And now you have no soldiers in your right flank."

"We've never done an airstrike. That's cheating."

She quirks a dark brow. "And what's the name of our new game, Tyler?"

The slight purr she uses to draw out my name rolls through me briefly, making me forget the question for a beat. My reaction only further letting me know I need to hook up with Kayley, and soon, so I can again respect myself. The notion of us is ridiculous, even to me.

"Mmm?" Delphine prompts as I search for both the question and answer before squeezing my eyes shut.

"1911. *Fuck*. The first air strikes happened in 1911, the Italo-Turk war."

"And you know this why?" she presses.

Her books, my curriculum. "Point taken."

"Not yet. We might have moved on from BC wars, but I gave you all you needed in the name. You did not prepare," she taunts as I glance down to see her advantage. It takes me seconds to assess how it will play out.

"Shit, I've already lost this war," I state, sinking where I stand. "Haven't I?"

"Maybe next time," she laughs as I narrow my eyes.

"I demand a rematch." My battered pride speaks.

"You will have it, but before you get one, you need to know all available weaponry during that time. It's time to"—she frowns, searching for the right expression, and I don't dare hand it to her—"*up to* your game."

Good enough, I decide, as she batters another metaphor. A translation trait I find fucking adorable.

"Oh, I'll bring my game up," I say, wanting to dissolve into the floor.

Go home, Jennings, and jerk this out of your system!

"I will start a new war soon. I don't want to ruin your Christmas."

"Oh, I think you do, which is not very Christian. So, what's the name of this one?"

She gifts me a rare, full smile. "You have to wait and see."

"Looking forward to it."

On a few occasions, I've peeked through the sliding glass back door after lights-out to see her latest setup and have spent entire days at school coming up with the right tactics to counter her. Then spending the rest of that time mangling pen caps while recalling new details that have nothing to do with our game.

Never going to happen, Jennings. Stop fixating.

"And"—she sips her coffee—"add two miles to your current run."

"Shit," I grumble. "Do you have *any* good news? Am I at least promoted to private first class?"

"After only weeks? No chance," she replies, not budging an inch. "How is your breathing?"

"Good, I'm getting there. It's been hard to concentrate lately."

When we're not playing, she spends our time teaching me the ins and outs of what I now know is flat space—temporary emotional suppression. A state I've since coined *pocketing*.

The state is temporary because I have no intention of shelving my emotions entirely or trying to forget any part of my experiences. I know better, and doing so could make me a prime candidate for PTSD. Because of that, I've declared my own mind a testing lab. It might be an unrealistic ambition, but then again, the education I'm drawing from Mom's psychology books has convinced me that the mind is a fucking magical thing.

"One sip," she says, offering the coffee she thinks I'm eyeing, thankful she has no idea I'm fixed on the divot at her throat.

She doesn't bother to hide her smirk when I sip the black tar I accepted, stifling a gag as I swallow it down. "This is fucking terrible."

"Dom likes it strong."

"Strong is one thing. This tastes like . . . God, aren't the French known for having the best coffee?"

"*That* is a luxury," she quips, lifting her free hand to indicate the state of the house. "Does it look like I can afford such luxuries?"

I deposit her cup on the counter. "So, then change your circumstances."

"So easy," she scoffs, silver-glazed eyes flaring with warning. "You're arrogant."

"Yeah, maybe it's my youth talking," I declare dryly while staring back just as intently.

She 'hmm's in agreement, her eyes laser-focused on mine for the second time in minutes as I hope, in vain, for once she doesn't see the naïve, round-eyed kid she met years ago. Or even the boy she started drilling into recently, though I know it's a lost cause.

"I got you this." I lift the gift bag.

"Today is not Christmas."

"I'm aware. Think of it as a thank you . . . for helping me."

She eyes the bag as if it's shit before a flicker of something crosses her expression. "What is it?"

"Kind of the point of the gift-giving part and the packaging."

The slight lift of her lips brightens the dismal yellow kitchen bulb lighting the space. She grabs the bag and lifts the tissue paper before pulling the tin and shrink-wrapped movies out.

"Didn't know if you'd seen them, but since Dom got a DVD player, I thought . . ." I shrug, having no idea where I was going with it.

She frowns at the movies as if figuring out a puzzle,

her mouth opening and moving as if she's about to read aloud before her eyes bulge. "Star Wars?"

"Yeah, these are the first two. They are prequels to the original three movies."

"Prequels?"

"They take place before Luke and Leia. It's the story of Darth Vader."

Her eyes light up with intrigue as she eyes the movies, and I take in her expression as a reward.

"Have you watched?" she asks, taken aback by her gift, which further warms my insides while gutting me. She clearly hasn't been given much in her life, which becomes more painfully apparent by the way she's reacting to such a small gesture.

"Yeah, but I'll watch them with you if you want."

"Peanut brittle," she whispers, studying the tin before lifting her spoon-colored eyes to mine. "How did you know?"

"You used to have a tin of it next to your coffee pot. I took a guess."

"You *guessed* well," she says softly, her expression just as tender, "it's my favorite treat." She cradles the movies and tin to her chest, her whisper sincere. "Merci, Tyler."

"Welcome," I say before tossing a thumb over my shoulder. "I'm going to . . ."

She waves a hand in dismissal but gifts me a rare smile as she does this. And fuck how that small reception feels like a big one inside of me. Thankful that went better than I hoped, it's when I'm a few strides away that I get the inkling to look back at her. For the first time in our time together, I see her curiously staring after me. When her eyes immediately drop, I bite back a smile and continue down the hall, refusing to read anything into it.

At Dom's bedroom door, a single knock with my knuckles has me opening it to catch a glimpse of Dom . . . enthusiastically pounding into Ginger. Upon discovery, my presence is acknowledged by her screech when she catches sight of me as a smug grin stretches across Dom's face. He shields her with his body as I swiftly slam myself back on the other side.

"You fucking idiot," I scold, keeping my voice low, "you could have told me you were tied up when I texted."

"We're saving the rope for next time," Dom grunts, his words meant for the girl he shamelessly hasn't stopped driving into. "Aren't we, baby?"

As of late, and with our collective home lives a wreck, fucking seems to be the most prominent thing on all our minds. Sex that would probably be more of an escape for me if my fantasies weren't quickly becoming riddled by an off-limits woman twelve years my senior.

"I'll meet you at the garage. One hour," I snap, "or I'm leaving."

My reply is a faint moan *from Ginger* before I stalk back down the hall, meeting Delphine at the end of it.

"Might want to spare yourself," I say, heat creeping up my neck due to the fucked position my brother just put me in. "Dom's not alone."

"I'm aware," she says, moving to push past me.

I lightly clamp her arm to stop her. "Delphine, you really don't want to go back there right now. They're not studying for Dom's next spelling bee."

"*Oh*," she says softly, indecision in her expression as she stares at the closed door just as Cypress Hill starts to bump through the entire house.

Classy, Dom.

"He's growing up, Delphine. We all are," I reiterate, a little too emphatically, knowing it's pointless. Even as I try to drill that truth in, my discipline slips slightly as I take her in up close. Which proves to be a mistake. At this distance, she's positively radiant. Even dressed in an outdated robe, with no makeup and her onyx hair twisted in a simple braid, all I can seem to do is fucking want.

Kick rocks, Jennings. She's off-limits.

So, like yesterday and the day before, I chalk it up to

curiosity and one-sided physical attraction. To wanting what I can't and, more importantly, shouldn't have.

Even if there was a slight curiosity in her gaze minutes ago, it's a scarcity I'll likely never glimpse again, and it sure as hell wasn't sexual in nature. She's never, not once, looked at me like that and won't.

But as I stare back at her at the foot of the hallway—as Dom serenades Ginger with Cypress Hill—thrust in the most inappropriate and uncomfortable fucking situation imaginable, my thoughts start to go just as incongruous.

"He's not stupid, not in that respect," she credits Dom.

"You know, it might mean something if you gave him that backhanded compliment directly."

"Backhand compliment?"

I grin. "A sarcastic compliment."

"Oh," she says, her full lips lifting slightly even as her eyes dim. "He stopped listening to me when Ezekiel left."

"I see you trying, Delphine." I shift to face her, crossing my arms and leaning against the wall as she takes a distancing step back. "He's noticed. He's just got a lot to get over."

She gives me the slightest dip of her chin, her expression dimming further.

"I'm not saying this to guilt you, but he has noticed."

This seems to pique her interest, adding a glimmer of hope to her eyes. "You have talked to him about this?"

"Very briefly, but yes. Thing is, you don't or really shouldn't try to lecture Dom about anything," I tell her. "He gets that enough from Tobias. If you truly want his audience, question him, ask for his opinion. He'll likely speak up then."

She scrutinizes me. "Have you always been so observant of people?"

"Not until"—I briefly drop my gaze—"let's just say I got a wake-up call from one of the closest people to me when I found out I didn't know them at all."

"Your father," she supplies, not at all a question, but I nod anyway.

"It's unfortunate that we have this in common, Tyler."

She holds her words briefly as if deciding whether the disclosure is worth it. "But this gift of observation will get you far with your soldiering. Though, I'm sorry for this for you, I, too, observe people and hear things in passing."

"Because *you both look and listen* for them," I counter, calling her out. It's one of the traits I've learned is practiced by those who suffer from trauma. They are often the ones to analyze people closest to them, forever looking for and *expecting* bad things to happen. It's a trait we share—another commonality that I don't put a voice to. *Can't* put a voice to because she's unaware I'm privy to some of the trauma caused by her ex-husband. "Tell you a secret?"

She nods.

"I *look and listen*, too."

She tilts her head, examining me. That look again—as if she's considering me, her eyes searching. I stare right back for an entirely different reason.

Get the fuck out before you embarrass yourself, Jennings.

I repeat this to myself as I slip past her, whispering a quick "I'm going to take off. Night, Delphine."

She nods.

Exiting the house, I bounce off my sneakers to start my nightly run toward the garage while trying to shake off the self-sabotaging thoughts invading me, knowing full well she's not going to give me a second thought tonight. That I'm utterly alone with the want starting to fester inside me. And so, I do my best to burn it off as I speed straight into the freezing wind.

Chapter Sixteen

Delphine

Eyeing my bottle, I opt out of uncapping it to continue to arrange my soldiers from where I stand at the end of the kitchen table. It's when I do that I realize I've only sipped three-quarters of the pint tonight!

The low amount of drink encouraging me since I started mentoring Tyler—sometimes, forgetting to sip for the needed concentration. The anticipation of our matches often has me getting lost in strategy, distracted from the haze, and helps to keep my head above water.

The haze is always there but less stifling with Tyler's lessons, forcing me to stay present and focused during our matches. Much like it did in the past when I hosted meetings or when I played with Ezekiel. Again, having something to look forward to.

Trying is working!

The excitement of my next match with Tyler has me situating my battalion carefully as the sliding glass door opens behind me.

"You have no chance tonight, private," I warn through a laugh.

When I get no answer, I glance over to see Dom approaching before he tosses a small box onto the kitchen table, which knocks down a few of my soldiers. This earns him my glare. "I just spent an hour moving those soldiers into position."

"Oops," he mutters without apology as I eye the box. "What is it?"

"Open it," he says, "or rather, *look* at the pretty picture like you so often do."

His insult strikes where he intended, but I wave it off as I do the box.

"I don't need this."

"Everyone is or has switched to cell phones, Tatie," he sighs with impatience. "It's only a matter of time before landlines cease to exist."

"Landlines you still use for your internet," I point out, picking up my fallen soldiers.

"For now." He shakes his head with impatience. "We're years into the twenty-first century, and while I couldn't give a fuck less if you want to remain in the stone age, this gift isn't from me."

"I'm *twenty-nine*," I snap, "far from the relic you accuse me of being." I pick up the box, considering the gift. "From Ezekiel?"

"He wants us all wired and connected, so you at least need to learn the basics."

"Fine," I say, unpackaging the box before examining the cell phone in confusion. Dom sighs before flipping the screen.

"This is . . . a keyboard, not a cell phone," I tell him.

"Jesus. The board is meant for texting." He points exaggeratedly to the large letters on the box. Embarrassment threatening, I blink at the words, doing my best not to move my mouth.

"It's a Sidekick Two," he enunciates as if I'm imbecilic, "the latest model."

I can't help but smile.

"What?" he demands, reading my pleased expression.

"That is what I called Ezekiel when he was a boy. My

acolyte, err, sidekick. I wonder if he remembers and it's why he got me *this* model."

"Doubt it. He bought us all the same one," he supplies, eliminating that possibility.

Smile fading, I swallow that truth and nod. "Will you show me how to use it?"

"There's an instruction book inside."

"Is there a French translation—"

"Probably, but you can read English," he snaps, "I know you can, and you've been here in the States, what, *half* your life now?"

"I have not mastered my English," I snap defensively, biting the rest of the truth away as Dom impatiently snatches the phone and powers it on.

"What is a text?" I ask.

"You're killing me," Dominic sighs. "Tobias was just as clueless not that long ago. Text means you can send a message to someone instead of calling."

"Oh," I say, swallowing before putting the phone aside to sort my army.

"What, Tatie? *You can* read English. You used to read to me."

I blink at him in surprise. "You remember this?"

This confuses him. "You don't?"

"I don't remember which books. I can learn to text later."

"Right." He pauses at my side and, to my surprise, takes a seat at the table next to me. Pulling out his phone, I watch carefully as he programs each number in, adding Tyler's number last. I avert my eyes as he does this, knowing our new mentor relationship both puzzles and aggravates him.

"It would be good if you joined our games, Dominic. You have much to—"

"You don't even know what a fucking text is," he states, slapping the phone on the table. "What in the hell could I possibly have to learn from you?"

"You're right. You have too much arrogance, and I doubt you could win," I clip out, eyeing my bottle but refusing to sip more.

My lash-out seems to satisfy him, earning me a menacing smile.

"Yeah, thought so. I'm not buying this *new you* bullshit."

"I never claimed *new me*. I'm only trying—" I shake my head, knowing he will never understand, never try to understand.

"To what?" he prompts.

"There is little point talking to you. You will only criticize me."

"Yeah, well, you're borrowing my friends, so let them listen to your drivel."

"Not drivel. I'm helping Tyler with tactics he will need. That you all will need. Ezekiel did not balk at me as you do, and I can see Sean and Tyler's potential and appreciate it in a way you—"

"Don't even fucking go there preaching to me about my fucking friends."

"I don't presume to—"

"Save it." He stands, "I get enough lectures from Tobias."

"For good reason, Dom, your anger—"

"*My* anger?" He scoffs, an indication that he deems me a hypocrite.

"Fine," I say, exhaling as I drop the subject seconds before he slams his bedroom door.

Standing, I unscrew my bottle, taking a long drink before swatting my soldiers to the floor.

***

Tyler

privit I laern to tetx to mess to yuo.

"The fuck?" I chuckle, reading Delphine's text as Mom

snores lightly in her recliner. Her comatose noise rivaling Jim Carrey as he stutters out "the-the-the-the Grinch!" to Cindy Lou on the screen feet away.

Tonight, I caved and gave in to participating in our Christmas Eve tradition of watching our favorite holiday flicks, suffering through Mom's choice of *It's a Wonderful Life* before we got to mine.

Though unspoken, Mom glanced at the front door every few minutes in wait for her husband before eyeing the phone for his nightly pickup—a duty I've been relieved of permanently after missing one too many calls.

Mom and I still aren't talking much, but I've recently realized that freezing her out isn't something I'm completely capable of. That only hits further home as I pull one of our quilts off the loveseat and cover her with it. Before I pull my hands away, she grips one and squeezes before opening her rapidly watering eyes.

"Merry Christmas, my beautiful son."

"Merry Christmas, Mom."

She turns and nestles into the recliner as a tear glides down her temple. The lump in my throat at the sight of it only fuels the paving of another brick in the wall I'm reinforcing with Carter on the other side.

Glancing back down at my phone as I head to my room, I frown at the compilation of Delphine's text. One I must have missed while watching the movies. Though it's not hard to decipher, it's sloppy as hell. My smile disappears when I realize she must be drunk. Has to be.

Minutes later, I'm peering through her sliding glass door to gauge our board and frown when I see the soldiers have been knocked off and are scattered on the kitchen floor. It's then that I spot tiny feet and inch along the glass door until Delphine comes into view, slumped against the cabinets beneath her kitchen sink. In seeing her, I waste no time stepping into the house and into the kitchen, noting every surface littered with flour, sugar, and other baking ingredients. Delphine sits on the floor, cradling measuring spoons in her hands, eyes glossy. She barely acknowledges me as I slowly kneel in front of her. But the second her eyes focus on me, her face lights up. "Tyler! Can you help me?"

Her expression and tone have me eagerly agreeing. "Sure."

"Will you read it out loud?" she asks, producing a tattered brown index card from the mess on the counter before thrusting it toward me. "There is English translation on the back."

"Sure." I read off the first line, which is hell to make out.

"Say it again, one cup?" she prompts.

"No, two cups, and I think, two teaspoons. The writing is messy."

"It's Celine's. She writes good English."

"I beg to differ."

She frowns back at me. "You beg for what?"

"It's an expression that means I have a different opinion." I thrust the card toward her. "Because *this* isn't legible."

"Non, you read it. *Out loud*," she insists again, pushing my hand away.

"All right, two cups of flour and I think . . . two teaspoons of baking soda."

"Okay." She takes a steadying breath as if readying herself for much more than baking. "Two cups," she says, measuring the flour, biting her lip in concentration before sorting through the spoons. Putting the spoon down, she lifts the cup again. "This?"

"No"—I grin—"two teaspoons of the powder now." I frown at the writing. "I think this means teaspoon." Thumbing the card, I flip it toward her. "Delphine, it's right here. Just read it."

"I want you to read it!" she snaps, and I jerk back in surprise, seeing her immediate regret.

"It's okay," I tell her with pinched brows, "don't get frustrated. We'll figure it out."

"Celine made these cookies for Dominic. He loved

them," she explains a little manically as she sorts the spoons for the right one. As she rattles feet away from me, I can both see and *feel* her desperate need to get it right before she turns back, reads my expression, and deflates.

"It doesn't matter." Her voice shakes as she relays this before tossing the spoons into the sink and stalking off, my eyes catching on the empty pint of Smirnoff at the top of the trash. She's drunk, but it's clear something or someone has triggered her.

"Delphine," I call at her retreating back as she rounds the counter, lifting her hand. "It's fine, Tyler. I'll play Battle with you tomorrow."

"If you'll wait, I'll help."

"It's late," she says more forcefully as I scour the kitchen. "It doesn't matter, will not matter to him." I catch her faint whisper as she retreats down the hall.

"Merry Christmas," I utter, not even sure she's aware of it, and knowing the him she's referring to is Dom. Evidence he was here by the sight of her new cell phone, which is covered in flour—as if she's been texting with coated fingers for hours. Picking it up, I frown when I see she only sent one text—to me. That truth ignites my chest. After cleaning the crust off the letters and wiping the screen, I leave it on the table where I found it. Staring in the direction she fled, I hear running water start between the walls, which means hours of disappearance—if she reappears at all.

Wanting to finish the recipe for her, I scrutinize the worn-out card until my vision doubles, and I'm forced to raise my own white flag. Sliding the door closed behind me shortly after, I eye the fallen soldiers as an ill feeling snakes its way into me. Some internal warnings going off in both head and chest. And I'm right because it's the last time I see her for weeks.

Chapter Seventeen

Delphine

Snow accumulates on the cheap iron table on our squared cement back porch as I run my finger over the scar at the back of my head. A scar I can remember. Scissors. A permanent reminder of the night Alain had cut my hair to the scalp after accusing me, for the first time, of infidelity. I light a cigarette as I refuse that memory and its clarity, opting to concentrate on the murkier, much more difficult memories to summon.

At my back, behind the door, the house roars with testosterone, mixed voices chattering around the kitchen table as I do all I can to avoid it. The sounds and feel of it similar, familiar—so familiar it brings me back to a different time. To an image of Ormand and Alain at the same table when I first arrived in the States, both animated and in good spirits. It was the beginning. Years before the haze, before I began my life underwater. My last memories and perception of both men now far different. Alain's forever tarnished.

Ormand's memory now plagued by the way he cried the night I woke in that hospital bed. That memory of him haunting me most. It was the nature of the way he grieved. As if filled with remorse.

The rest of the night is nothing but a hazy mix of images that refuse true clarity—the dim, pale peach light coming from somewhere behind the hospital bed. Mixed, muted voices drowned out by the pounding in my temple. The crackling fuzz surrounding my view of the slow drip of the IV, the itch of the fabric of my gown as I searched and searched my mind for the hours before I regained consciousness. As I have year after year.

The only true knowledge I have of what happened after I woke in that bed is the permanent absence of something vital. As if something that was inside me no longer exists. Not my heart, which still beats true, but something more substantial. Something far, far out of reach as my vision doubles, and I blink to clear it as the haze returns. The fog I gained—which now replaces what was stolen—is merciless, refusing to free me all these years later, to allow me to see what was taken.

It's as the silent snow falls that I pitch forward, willing my mind to cooperate, to press past that memory the night I woke to the next—to any day after that. Bowing my head as the flakes whirl around me, I again plead with God.

Please, please let it play.

Miraculously, the details of that night began to come to me.

Ormand's hand grips mine, his features twisted in agony as a blurry Beau stands behind his chair opposite the doctor, who scratches another page on his clipboard.

"... *several contusions on the spine, three broken ribs* ..."

Loud laughter from inside the house disrupts any more recollection as my eyes burn with frustration. Hands shaking, I uncap the bottle and sip to try and calm my nerves. Desperate to get back to it, I close my eyes as the muddled sounds ring true while the images never fully take shape.

"Please," I whisper. "Please let me see."

My prayer remains unanswered as only the doctor's voice rings through. As it has so many times before.

"... *fractured wrist and ulna. Significant damage to her windpipe. The bite marks*—"

"*Will heal,*" I speak aloud with the memory of that voice while living the contradiction to his prognosis.

Another burst of loud laughter sounds from behind the sliding door. One of those laughs now familiar, coming from my budding soldier. My chest stretches at the sound of it. Happy for him that he can feel such joy despite what he endures.

His progress during our short time together is astounding. Of all the men currently inside the house—and aside from Ezekiel—Tyler is the only one who takes anything I say into himself. When I began to train him, I had hope for the first time in *years*. That was until the blanket came back, surrounding me in its bitter embrace, setting the ache into my bones, refusing to allow me any more clarity.

Before the biting cold came back to steal what peace I had, my skin had started to become far more sufferable to live in than the year before. And the year before that. All because of the beautiful boy and his desire to learn. To be the best soldier he can be.

Tipping the bottle back, I mourn the loss of that temporary peace as the snowdrift summons me, and Matis's words whisper back to me through the snow, through time.

"*Je t'aime petite fleur . . . Je suis vraiment désolé. Je suis vraiment désolé. Pardonne-moi.*" *I love you little flower . . . I'm so sorry. I'm so sorry. Forgive me.*

It's days like this when I cannot control the haze, fear, or shake—that I loathe my inability to stop any of it and the numbing consumption that follows.

Failing. Failing. Failing.

Again.

Every day, failing to recognize the girl who flew to America so young, fearless, and ready to fight—to live her dream.

The glass door slides open, and I don't bother looking over my shoulder, knowing it's Tyler. The strong scent of marijuana fills my nose, and to my surprise, black boots come into view next to where I sit.

"You have the whole of the house," I grumble, knowing no good will come of this interaction because my fear has stolen all my patience today. Breathing deeply, I summon what I can. "Can you not allow me space out here?"

"That maternal instinct inside you is something to behold," Dominic slings in insult. His latest sarcastic remark ringing true. It's no surprise when I look up to see him staring at me speculatively, armed and ready to spar. To punish. Though as brilliant as Jean Dominic is, I seem to be the one person he hasn't fully figured out yet.

"I'm sorry to keep disappointing you," I reply truthfully, though my tone indicates otherwise, my heart not in the fight.

Silence fills the space, and I rub my trembling hands together to keep him from noticing. Something I'm sure he'll attribute to the drink. When more loud laughter bursts from behind the door, it's all I can do to keep from flinching. Needing the distraction, I look up at him from my chair and eye him just as speculatively. "Do you despise me, Jean Dominic?"

So tall now, so angry. Much more than Ezekiel was. So ready to hurt the world that hurt him—to hurt me. Celine's face crosses my mind as I stare at her youngest son. In it, I see the care she gave me, the tenderness forever there. Always patiently reaching out to embrace whatever side of me was visible. I know it as a truth that the same capability resides in both of her sons. Though when he doesn't answer, I take his silence as confirmation I have earned his hate.

"Rest well knowing Celine would be disappointed in me much like you because she was so very kind, Dominic. So selfless."

He stands idly by for a long moment.

"You never talk about them," he finally says. It's then I spot the red wings drifting through the snow as the image fills my mind.

The same bird . . .

I stretch forward, leaning into the memory as the cardinal lands on the fence in front of us.

"Beau! Beau, look!" Celine exclaims next to me as Jean Dominic stands again for his second attempt to walk. Nearby, Beau smiles down at his son as he shakily stands in the yard, surrounded by bright green grass. Jean looks up to Beau as I hold out my hands to encourage him forward.

"Come to me, Jean Dominic!" I urge the beautiful baby as he inches toward me.

"Alain, look!" I call over to him, where he sits with Ezekiel, helping him assemble a toy from Dominic's recent birthday party. Alain lifts his eyes, watching Jean Dominic take his first step, landing into my arms before Celine greedily takes him from me, beaming with pride.

"He did it!"

"Maybe he would have taken another if you hadn't stopped him," Beau jokes, his red hair glinting in the sun as his eyes, too, glitter with pride on Jean Dominic.

Shifting my focus back to Alain, I find him looking at me much the way he did when we first began as a couple in France. We've been together now for some time, but only mere weeks of our marriage have truly been good. Since Beau and Celine joined us in America—not long after I arrived—Alain's been much less violent. My suspicion is that Beau has something to do with it. But it's Alain's return stare now which gives me hope. Maybe this year, maybe . . .

"Do you believe in fate, Dominic?" I whisper hoarsely as that sunny day beams through the drifting snow before shuttering out, my eyes misting with the gift of the memory.

Thank you, God. Thank you!

"Really?" he jabs. "*That's* what you're leading with?"

"With good reason. The day you took your first steps was in the backyard of *this house*. There, right next to the fence." The image fresh in my mind, I point toward a brown patch of grass being rapidly dusted with snow. "Just after, a cardinal landed, and I remember your parents walking you over to it."

When he further steps into view, I watch him eye the bird without much interest before he speaks. "And that constitutes your tears?"

"Must you humiliate me every fucking day, Dominic?" I whisper before taking a long sip of drink. "You may think me a silly woman for my sentiments. But it was a rare good day. I still miss your mother. Very much."

And I remembered, I remembered!

An old memory made new, one I pray stays with me. Tears of happiness sting my eyes as I push the emotion down to speak.

"No one ever spoke about my parents or grandparents either," I offer him. "I wasn't sure if you wanted that."

He pinches his brows. "What were they like? My grandparents?"

Ezekiel knows I'm not his true aunt, but I've never told Jean Dominic. Ezekiel knows that I don't want my past shared with his brother yet but insists it will help our relationship. But because of Jean Dominic's constant verbal contempt, I have yet to do so. His resentment is still too strong for him to consider me for any understanding. For Celine, I'll keep trying. For myself, too, and for the affection I harbor for the boy I taught with my own behavior to hate me.

"As you know, your mother no longer contacted them once she got here because of Abijah."

He nods.

"Your grandparents were good people. Francis was kind. Hardworking. Considerate. Marine was strict but attentive. Your mother was very close to her. They were good enough to take me in when I was separated from my father."

Dominic's eyes widen in surprise at my admission. "What. The. Actual. *Fuck?*"

"Your mother was not my true sister."

"I'm getting that," he snaps. "Does Tobias know?"

"Yes," I say, speaking quickly to temper his shock, "but we are close related family, Dominic. You have my hair color and eyes, for God's sake. My papa's eyes. Celine's eyes. Celine and I were not sisters—as much as your mother wanted to believe it so—but my experience is much the same as yours. My mother left me when I was young, and I was separated from my papa not long after. My father, Matis, was uncle to Celine's father, your grandfather, Francis."

He remains silent, but I know he wants to hear more.

"The explanation for this is long, but what is important to know is that you came from a good family. Your mother was a good woman, the best I have ever known. Caring, generous, happy. Your father also had a good heart and was patient enough, but when he was angry, he could scare a room into silence. He was an authority—" I frown, summoning the right word. ". . . authorities man. A man to respect and not to cross. When he spoke, people listened. Both you and Ezekiel possess this."

I see in his expression this pleases him, and so I continue.

"You have his temper, I assure you. From what Celine said, he got into many fights in school. It was a miracle they didn't expel him. In some ways, he was unpredictable, but his heart was so very loyal, and he loved your mother and his sons, you and Ezekiel, with the whole of it. Your mother loved me the same. That is why Beau tolerated me . . . and protected me."

"From?"

"Life." I drag my cigarette. "I was not there when they met, but I witnessed their love after they came from France while your mother was growing you in her belly, and they were so very in love. Watching them with you and Ezekiel gave me so much hope for my own marriage, and I envied their connection"—I exhale as I speak—"everyone did."

Dom remains silent, his gaze on the snow and his demeanor the same, but I know he's listening raptly.

"You were created during the best part of their love.

Love of the purest kind by two people who cared deeply for other people. Who truly wanted to give you a good life and championed as hard as they could to do it before they were killed."

"Why are you talking like that's your last bottle?" he asks without a hint of emotion before taking a hit from his joint. "And what happened to your marriage?"

"Dom." Tyler speaks up, and we both turn to see the door open. He scans me, nodding over his shoulder. "They're looking for you."

Tyler shifts his assessing gaze back to me, missing nothing. His disappointment clear as he eyes my dwindling bottle before he greets me.

"Hey, Delphine."

I nod, meeting Tyler's soft brown eyes despite wanting to keep mine lowered. The last time I saw Tyler, he found me passed out on the kitchen floor. He'd lifted me from the pile of broken mini-bottles surrounding me. It was another failed attempt to cut the amount of drink—to measure my consumption. Though upset about our missed game, he'd been gentle when placing me in bed and stood at my door waiting for endless minutes, our eyes locked until mine closed. Though, during those tense seconds, I could practically hear every word that died on his tongue as he weighed his decision on whether to try to reprimand me. More judgment from another boy who is playing a man. Several of which my house is currently full of.

Though, I can't help marveling at the fact that I'm now surrounded by mirror images of a younger me. Children growing up too soon, and their ideology driving them to believe they can make a difference. To change this world and become soldiers with purpose.

One of which I've spent months with recently, knowing my drinking affects him more than most. When he's nearby, I find myself trying to hide each sip from him more and more. The fact that it bothers me now only has me lifting the bottle to take a defiant mouthful. I have no place giving weight to the opinion of a boy, and with one hearty sip, I decide to take away any power I might have given to him to condemn me.

Plagued by what's transpired in mere minutes by simply sitting at a fucking table, I lift the bottle continually, sipping it while wanting to both shatter and savor it. Tears blur my vision when I finally drop it with a loud clank on the table as my conflicting emotions take over.

"Delphine," a voice whispers in summons, and I realize Dominic has disappeared into the house. Tyler kneels in front of me now, eyeing my bottle like it's his enemy, as I realize I just lost myself again in the haze.

"Where are you right now? What's happening?"

Gazing down at him, I shake my head. "I'm nowhere, and I cannot get anywhere," I croak as he grips my hands in his.

"You're shaking so badly," he states, "tell me what has that expression on your face . . . that look in your eyes. Please."

Loud music blasts from inside the house, and this time, I can't help but flinch.

"Jesus, please tell me what's happening right now," Tyler prods and I blink more tears away to see his own eyes drowning with concern.

"It's snowing," I reply.

His brows pinch together as he takes in my state while aware of my ploy to try and divert his attention. This beautiful, sad, brilliant boy. "Is the noise bothering you, too?"

"Do you like the snow?" I redirect again, and he closes his eyes briefly in frustration before answering.

"Doesn't really affect me one way or another." He holds out his bare palm to catch some of the drift before prodding again. "But I know you don't."

Lifting the bottle, I unscrew the cap, and he places his warm hand on mine to stop me. "It's empty, Delphine. Tell me, what about the snow bothers you?"

I shake my head. Though Tyler is young, he's not untouched by women. That much is evident in his healthy confidence. His hurt stems from disappointment by those he has faith in, not by romantic love. Any days he had of trusting without fear are already far behind him—something that I can easily recognize.

Sometimes, I want to ask him what causes his fugue states. What could have possibly happened to him to have him seeking darkness and remaining there? But now, as I seek refuge in my own reflective darkness, I want him nowhere near me. I stay silent as he stares up at me while rubbing each of my hands vigorously through his to warm them.

"Your hands are freezing. Come inside. Let me take you to lay down."

Shaking my head, I pull my hands from his grip. "I'm okay right here."

"No, you're not—"

"I don't want"—I swallow—"to e-mb-barrass Jean Dominic." A sob bursts out of me with my admission as I fail to rein any more emotion in. "T-Tyler, p-please leave me."

His eyes go distant as he shakes his head, his frustration clear as I make the same request.

"P-please go," I beg.

As he stands, I see his resignation. "Let me get you some gloves at least."

"Leave me, Tyler," I scold. "I'm *not* in need of help."

"No? Well, let's give it a fucking minute," he clips sarcastically before he shoves his clenching fists in his jeans, clearly angry he has no authority over me. "I'm sorry," he offers quickly in a soft whisper of apology. "I'm sorry, Delphine. I didn't mean that."

"Yes, you did," I sniff as another tear rolls down my cheek. "I know what you all think of me. I can *feel it* before any of you say a word."

"You have no fucking idea what I think of you," he whispers vehemently.

"Tyler, leave me, please."

"Fuck . . . fine, but I'm getting you a goddamned blanket."

I nearly laugh at his outburst as he mumbles his frustration and enters the house. As I become lost in the flurries surrounding me, the numb I so desperately need starts to set in before I'm covered by a thick wool blanket. Just after cloaking me with it, Tyler again kneels at my feet, his brown eyes flickering with warmth as he looks up at me imploringly.

"I'm not trying to upset you. I just want to know you," he relays softly.

"I no longer know myself, Tyler," I admit, pulling another cigarette from my pack as he grabs my lighter.

"What do you mean?" He frowns while lighting my cigarette.

"It's not important," I say on exhale, "what matters right now is that when I look at you, I see so much. There is so much good in you, Tyler. Your potential is limitless. I should have told you before now, but I want you to know this."

"Then stop disappearing on me," he implores with a hint of agitation. "You've been avoiding me for weeks."

"I'm not in a good place."

"Neither am I," he retorts instantly. "And I know you know that, but we were doing good until you checked out, weren't we?"

I nod, my eyes filling again, agitating me further. My overwhelming emotions keeping me helpless to the blanket threatening to pull me back under. It's the look in his eyes that keeps me from succumbing.

"So, fuck it. Have bad days, but don't withdraw from me, and let me try to be there for you."

"I'm not a good person to mentor you." I shake my head. "I'm not good in my mind. Mentally." It's the first time I've admitted it out loud—to anyone.

"Well, you are good in *my mind*," he says forcefully.

I shake my head as he wipes a tear from my chin. "Tyler... I have very bad problems with my memory, and I often get aggravated and lash out. I don't want to do more harm than I have. I have no business shaping your mind."

"Listen to me," he says sharply, commanding my eyes. "I already knew what you just admitted, and I can handle it. But I also know how much you helped Tobias before he left. I've learned so much from you already, and as selfish as it may be to ask, I need this. I *need* your help, Delphine. Help me, and I swear to you right now, no matter what happens, I won't hold it against you. Ever. So please stop avoiding me. I have bad days, too. Very bad days. Trust me."

"I know you do," I tell him. "I know because there is another side to you that no one sees. Not even them." I point toward the door. "It's dangerous for you because you don't know what it is or will become."

He bites his lip as if trying to decipher whether to confirm it before nodding his head. "I need help with that, too."

I palm his cheek, and his features twist in anguish as he presses into my palm, seeming desperate for the touch. It's then I again find myself unable to refuse him. "Do not be ashamed. I can help you with this."

"So you'll help me?"

Shivering in the blanket, I withdraw my hand and nod. "I will try, but you must trust me. Can you trust me?"

"I already do," he whispers.

"Maybe"—I bite the tear that lines my lips—"if I tell you one day why I hate the snow, you will talk to me about who you become when you step into the shadows at night and stare into my window."

He nods.

"Then I will try."

Chapter Eighteen

TYLER

SPRING 2005

THE FIRST HINTS of spring perfume the air as I stalk toward Dom's driveway, cooling down from my latest run. Inhaling deeply, I fill my nose as Delphine spots me walking up the drive.

"Tyler, come!" Approaching, I find her rooting around in the trunk of her open sedan, which is brimming with baskets of flowers and porch plants.

"Look!" Delphine turns back to me, dressed in a thin-strapped dark red sundress. Her long onyx hair styled in her usual braid over one of her shoulders. It's the sight of her dressed in something other than her robe, along with the genuine smile she flashes toward me, that has me stopping short of reaching her.

It seems the last few months have been a little transformative for us both. After a grueling winter in which we spent a lot of time animatedly playing Battalion on her good days, we've managed to find a way to work together around the bad. Sometimes, in amicable, oddly comfortable silence. Each of us sorting through our own individual shit.

Even during the weeks the clouds refused to part, Delphine became more and more participatory—more of a presence in the house rather than hiding in the shadows with her bottle. Only taking long absences after a bad day.

Thinking on it now as I watch her dig through her trunk, I can't remember the last time any of us have scraped her from any surface of the house or lawn to usher her to bed.

Though forever volatile and no less dependent on vodka than when we started, she seems to be slowly blooming along with the season. The changes in her so far have been subtle but are starting to add up as I study her. Having traded in her dingy robe and winter staple, it's easy to see she's added a little healthy weight, which only enhances her curves.

Now, in the bright light of day, under the sun's rays, she's fucking flawless. Today, she made a real effort in her appearance, which is impossible to ignore. So much so, I force myself to rip my eyes away from her dark, wine-painted lips.

"Need some help?" I ask, my recovery too slow in execution as a slight tension fills the open air between us, and her eyes drop. It's then I know I've done it again. After months of one-on-one sessions at her kitchen table, it's clear to me by now that she hates any lingering attention from *any* male eye—especially if it's appreciative in nature.

The problem is, as of late, I can't fucking stop taking in her details. Dozens of chewed pen caps during class are a testament to the little things I've memorized so far. Her metal gray eyes are the most startling in contrast with her dark lashes and olive skin, which is already starting to tint from exposure to the sun.

"I got all of this on sale," she pipes before producing a ripe watermelon from the trunk and thrusting it toward me. "Fresh melon! I thought it would be a good treat!"

I can't help but grin at her ancient verbiage delivery choice or her excitement. Her expression is so fucking endearing as she searches my own for approval.

"Love fresh melon," I say as she turns back to sort

her haul, while I take the few steps toward her that separate us.

"Me too!" she shouts as I hover mere inches behind her, thankful she can't see my answering grin. There's an innocence about her that I swear to Christ no one sees. Truth is, no one is looking due to her flip-switch behavior and tantrums.

At this point, I can't really blame Dom for not looking after years of witnessing and enduring her self-sabotage. If we hadn't just spent the last seven months in each other's company, I might have missed it too.

"The plants are beautiful, non?" she asks, gathering another melon in her arms as I quickly divert my attention to it.

"Yeah," I agree, finding it utterly ironic that ripe fruit and plants bring her so much joy. She's such tough company to impress otherwise. Following her up the drive to the porch, I muse at her animation as she talks a mile a minute about her short expedition to the farmer's market.

It's when we both spot Dom in the kitchen, mug in hand and reading the paper, that I feel the instant shift in the air and Delphine's brief hesitation—as if we just entered a room with *her parent* inside.

Her eyes do a quick, indecisive sweep over Dom before she speaks up, mustering some of her enthusiasm.

"Dom," she calls, presenting the watermelon, "I found this at the farmer's market. Look!"

Dom doesn't so much as spare a glance at her prized fruit. "Kudos, Tatie, you found *produce* at the *market*. Will you be as excited if you find *cars* in a *parking lot*?"

That snub is felt by both of us as she turns and silently washes the melon before pulling out a knife to slice it. Her eyes are cast down as she addresses me.

"Tyler, will you put the rest of the plants on the porch?" Her tone is now void of the life it had seconds before, and I inwardly curse as I glare at Dom's profile.

"Sure," I agree easily, just as Dom looks up, giving me an eye roll. One I don't acknowledge. He wants me to condone his inhumane treatment of her, but as of late, it's starting to grate on me. He's only vaguely aware that her ex-husband brutally terrorized her in this very fucking house, and only because I told him.

Memories I'm sure she often needs to clear her mind of. The shake in her hands and certain sounds jarring her at times, telling me when she's triggered. I'm just not sure exactly by what, yet, having only snuck in a handful of the letters between her and Celine.

Her triggers are so fucking textbook that I'm surprised Dom hasn't taken notice while at the same time knowing exactly why—resentment. This makes me a bit of a hypocrite because I refuse to acknowledge any effort Dad makes on his rare good days. But unlike Dad, Delphine doesn't falsify reality on her good days the way Carter Jennings does, pretending like he isn't the source of the tension in our house. While my dad now expects acknowledgment for completing old responsibilities he previously ignored, Delphine merely tries to make up for her wrongs, hoping for forgiveness and some semblance of a relationship—not demanding it.

"Come help me," I tell Dom, sidling up to him where he's perched at the counter.

"Busy." He lifts the paper, shutting down a conversation between us that he knows will end with a reprimand from me.

"Two wrongs don't make things right, asshole," I interject anyway, bumping his shoulder before I head to her car.

"Neither does your little hard-on," he relays cooly before snapping his paper. A quip I ignore because it's bullshit, and he knows it. Despite me taking notice of how beautiful his aunt is, there's nothing remotely inappropriate happening between us, and he's aware of that. Especially when we encourage him to join us during every game of Battle, and I invite him on my runs.

It's when I step back into the house that I see the full crack in Delphine's exterior as she unscrews her pint *two hours* before her usual first drink of the night.

At the sight of it, and for the first time since Dom and I became friends, I resent his fuck-all disposition and fail to find the humor in his brutal delivery.

Not your business, Jennings.

Not long after, Dom leaves for the library. It's as I sit at the table to contemplate my next move that Delphine approaches, hesitating with what looks to be a sketchbook in her hand.

"More to memorize?" I ask, grinning up at her. "You're relentless, General."

"Not exactly."

"What's got you so nervous?" I frown at her finger-whitening grip on the book.

"I'm not nervous," she snaps defensively, and I catch the instant flash of regret in her eyes due to her harsh delivery. "Non," she dismisses, a slight blush ghosting her cheeks and neck, "some other time."

"Come on," I prompt, stopping her with my hand on the book, careful not to touch her. "Let me see."

Biting her plump lower lip, she studies me for sincere interest before setting the book in front of me. Opening it, I start to flip through the pages.

"The true genius of any strategist," she relays, "lies within the *surprise*."

"These are yours?" I ask, running my finger over one of the drawings.

"Hmm." She nods, a little pride-filled smile playing on her lips as I scan the penciled, heavily shaded artwork.

"Delphine, this is *really, really fucking* good," I tell her honestly.

She shrugs.

"It is just . . ." She pauses, searching for the words, which she does often. "Rough." She nods. "Rough draftings."

I don't correct her, other than her downplaying her effort.

"You put real time into these." I examine some of her battle formations. "And a hell of a lot of thought." I point to a few on the page. "It shows."

In the last few weeks, we've gone forward and backward on the battles fought by expert strategists and legends, namely Alexander the Great and Napoleon, including the details of their private lives. Delphine is adamant that all aspects of an enemy—including knowing the ins and outs of how they conduct themselves personally—will give some advantage.

I don't disagree, which is why I continue to educate myself with my mom's psychology books.

Despite Dom's best efforts to destroy her mood today, her optimism slowly starts to shift back as I flip through the book. From the way she speaks to me, it's as if she's been waiting for years to tell me these things. The more we talk, the more attentive and receptive I am, the more animated she becomes, and I don't credit her swallows of Smirnoff for it. Her enthusiasm for this isn't at all vodka-fabricated, and it's evident the more we discuss each page.

"How long have you been doing these?" I ask, noting that a few pages are less defined and sloppier in execution, as are her notes next to them—the handwriting like night and day. The deterioration, I suspect, is due to her drinking. Guilt threatens at the thought just before she confirms it.

"For many years," she relays, avoiding my eyes, "since before I came from France."

"And when was that?" I flip another page.

"When I was young. Younger than you are now."

I haven't probed into her past yet. It always felt like those questions were off the table, but I can't help but ask one.

"Why did you leave France?" I ask, knowing the answer.

"Why all come to the States."

"The American Dream," I utter, my tone indicative that I'm not buying it as I table it figuratively and literally for a different time.

"You know," I tell her as she glances over to me. "I've

never met a woman—even those in my military family—who is so fascinated by all facets of war and, more notably, the brazen and brave acts of historical figures."

"True history is too often ignored, Tyler. Far more stories than those selected for history books. Tales of unsinged heroes who deserve recognition."

I hold my smirk at her misspoken verbiage.

"There was a woman who was part of the French resistance in World War Two who was instrumental in helping to keep the Germans from reclaiming a stronghold in Paris. She's barely mentioned, and her efforts were many. Her acts those of a very brave, fed-up street soldier. It's soldiers like that who I admire most and respect." She smiles. "This is the type of soldier Ezekiel is and that you, Sean, and Dom will become."

"I hope so," I say.

"No need to hope. When Ezekiel left, I saw it in his eyes. The determination to do, not say. I see it in Jean Dominic. I also see it in you."

"You know they don't go by their birth names, right?"

She smiles. "That's why I use them."

"To piss them off?"

"No, because *I* named them."

"What?" I ask, shocked by the disclosure.

She nods. "I named them both. It was my"—she pauses—"my privilege Celine gave for being aunt."

"Do they know this?"

"No, I don't want to give them more of a reason not to use their names . . . Ezekiel means 'strength of God,' and Jean means 'God's grace.'"

We stare off for a long second before collectively bursting into laughter.

"Dom's namesake doesn't quite suit," I cackle.

"He will grow into it." She beams back at me. "He's still young but very much has his mother's heart."

My chuckle slows as a flicker passes over her features, one I know is thanks to the subject himself. It's her expression that has me fighting myself to keep my oath—that other's personal relationships are none of my fucking business. Something I know will serve me well.

"He'll grow out of that, too," I assure her, and she waves her hand, ending the discussion. Within a matter of minutes, we're back studying the tactics of Alexander the Great.

As she speaks, I can't help but marvel at her. So much of what's inside this woman's head astounds me, and more so that all of this time, I sought my father's advice when I had her intelligence within reach. Tobias has been stressing to Dom, Sean, and me that Delphine's wisdom knows no bounds and that all three of us could benefit from her, but thus far, I'm still the only one paying attention.

The fact that she is so fucking smart, not to mention capable, and daily chooses to drink that value away, abusing herself by the bottle, both saddens and frustrates me. In those times, I remember my place and never push her too hard.

"Mindset and stamina are key, private," she continues, as the soft skin of her arm brushes my bicep before a light, musky scent fills my nose. It's rich but not too overpowering, and I find myself inhaling it again when she brushes against me to point out part of an old sketch. That slight brush has my spine tightening with awareness—one I've done my best to ignore for months.

Though I'm positive *she's* nothing I should want. If she, for one second, entertained a small amount of the attraction I have brewing for her, she might one—toy with me, two—outright reject me. Either way, fucking with my head and heart in a way I know I won't be easily resilient to. Even so, I'm quickly finding all parts of me wanting all parts of her—especially the broken ones.

But my psyche—who's currently tossing out red flags—doesn't give a damn about any of these forming opinions or observations. My cock doesn't either. This is only confirmed a second later when my mind goes blank because I'm hard.

Rock fucking hard.

Chapter Nineteen

Tyler

"Shhh," I whisper, flattening my palms on the back of my bedroom door as I thrust into Kayley's wet mouth, where she kneels beneath me.

Keeping one hand firmly planted on the door—though it's locked—I cup her cheek, running my thumb from the excess length she can't fit into her mouth to her stretched top lip, reveling in the obscene sight of it. Trying to ease more of it in, I earn the narrow of light blue eyes when I gag her.

Hiding my grin, I scrape my lower lip with my teeth before licking its length, an unspoken promise of a pleasurable payback.

"Relax your throat, baby, just a little more," I coax, drinking in the sight of her on her knees, shirt open, bra unclasped, her nipples peaked as she does my bidding. A girl not so easily swayed to please but doing her best for me, which only turns me on more.

Slowing my hips, I savor the last of the rush as everything starts to draw tight, and I manage to inch in a bit further. It's the stretch that always unravels me, tipping me over.

"Fuck beautiful, the view you're giving me," I grit out, picking up my pace as she deep-throats me. I'm seconds from coming when a sharp knock sounds on the other side of my bedroom door.

Kayley freezes, eyes bulging as I cup the back of her head to keep her there, refusing her withdrawal as Mom speaks up.

"Tyler, dinner will be ready in an hour... Kayley staying?"

Turning my head, I pitch my voice toward the other side of my room. "No, Kayley has to get home soon."

A pause on the other side of the door has me looking back down at Kayley. Encouraging her to stay put, I stroke her chin as she glares at me with watering eyes. At the sight of them, I thrust in further, sending tears streaming down her cheeks. Satisfaction fills me at the sight of the running mascara.

You're a fucking asshole, Jennings.

The silence stretches a little too long before Mom finally stalks off. Once in the clear, Kayley starts to pull away, and I fist her hair to stop her while uttering my warning.

"I'm going to come, with or without your help, and if I come alone, you do too. But if you're good to me"—I pump my hips a little—"I'm going to be really fucking good to you," I promise.

Shortly after delivering on said promise, I walk Kayley to my front door, kissing her chastely without any guarantee of a call. One she's never required, and I don't intend on making. She flashes me a bold grin that I share before I close the door. Only partially satiated, I'm halfway back to my room when a sharp order is emitted from the kitchen.

"In here, Son. *Now.*"

I walk in to see Mom rolling out pie crust, for what I know is homemade chicken pot pie—my favorite. She eyes me warily as I take the stool on the opposite side of the counter.

"Don't you ever fucking do that again when I'm in the house," she barks, "it's a disgusting lack of disrespect."

"Don't I know it," I sigh.

"And what's that supposed to mean?"

"It won't happen again. We done?"

"No, we're not done," she says with a heavy exhale. "Next time, be a normal teenage kid and at least try to hide it, or"—her eyes drill mine—"tell me, Son, was that some blatant F U to me?"

"No, Mom, it had nothing to do with you," and everything to do with another—*you can't have her*—needed reality check.

She scrutinizes me. "How old is that girl?"

"My age," I lie, for Kayley's sake, and she's not local, which is one of the main reasons I continue to hook up with her.

"Are you using—"

"Protection, seriously?" I hold up my palm. "Isn't this a script for a father to use and way overdue?"

"He should be home any minute. Want me to take it up with him?" she threatens.

I roll my eyes at it, knowing it's empty. "Yeah, I'm using protection. I have no plans of *fathering anyone*."

Her brows rise. "Ever?"

"Not really enthusiastic about the family dynamic lately." I pop a chopped, raw carrot into my mouth as she stills briefly at my barb before continuing to roll out her crust. We've been in the same silent standoff for months, only talking about the surface shit—something I find completely ironic, seeing how it's her everyday job to get to the root of other people's problems.

She's become an expert at avoidance since Christmas. Though looking at her now, I scan her contemplatively. My friends forever giving me shit about how beautiful my mom is. Though their remarks repulse me, I can't disagree. Regina Jennings *is* beautiful and looks younger than most of my friends' parents, except for one whose technical title is *Aunt*. Though I inherited my face and build from my dad, as I study my mom, I wonder what inherited traits and other attributes I garnered from her.

"What, Son?" Mom asks without looking up.

Observant. That's one. But a given and necessary considering her profession as a psychologist.

"Just wondering why you're going through all this trouble to cook when you know he's leaving for the bar soon."

Her shoulders deflate as she brings her eyes to mine. "Maybe I'm interested in feeding my son since he's intent on leaving me." A pause. "You graduate in a few weeks and turn eighteen a few months after. When do you plan to enlist?"

I shrug. "Not sure. I'm thinking about prolonging enlisting until after Sean and Dom graduate next May. It all depends."

"Really?" Her eyes light with hope. "On what?"

"A lot of things," I tell her, a flash of silver-gray eyes flitting through my mind along with the devilish grin that lights the rest of the fire. Prolonging leaving Delphine wouldn't be the only benefit.

By staying, I could help ensure the club is on a more solid foundation before I start my time in the Corps. We're nowhere near ready yet, not by a long shot. Not that I don't plan on visiting home as often as Tobias if I'm capable. It's our task list, which is growing by the day with everyone the French bastard visits, that's become daunting.

It's the idea of prolonging my stint in this fucking house that has me rethinking it all. However, leaving Mom means leaving her alone to defend herself.

"I've already met with my recruiter," I tell her. "I'm taking my ASVAB test after graduation and might go ahead and schedule my physical."

She stops her rolling pin. "Tyler, seriously?"

"What?" I shrug.

"You didn't think to discuss that with me?"

"You know I'm not changing my mind."

"If your father finds out—"

"He'll what, Mom? He'll what? Like he has any say in the matter."

"Jesus, if I would have known you were going to take off right after you turned eighteen, I wouldn't have started you in kindergarten so early."

"You had no choice because you were a single parent and needed help with childcare," I tell her. "Still are."

Her eyes roll down my face. "That's not true."

"Sure it's not, by the way, your baby boy ate at the Pitt Stop after school."

"Perfect." She discards the dough in a messy heap before slapping her flour-coated hand on the counter and giving me a stern look.

"What is this? Why such blatant callousness toward me lately?" Her eyes water. "Do you think I don't want things to get better? That I'm ignoring what's happening around here?"

"I don't know what you want anymore, Mom. You barely look at me."

"Because I'm ashamed, Tyler," she croaks, holding my gaze.

I drop my own eyes, hating myself a little for the tears I'm causing.

"Look at me," she snaps, "you wanted to hurt me, so look at it and be satisfied."

I do, and the guilt intensifies.

"Feel better?" she asks.

"No, Mom, shit." I palm my jaw. "I'm sorry, I'm sorry," I repeat, barely above a whisper. "I'm just in a messed-up place lately."

"And I don't blame you for it, but I promise you that I'm not immune to it, and I didn't think this needed explaining because *you are* worlds above average in deciphering things like this. So, I didn't see the point in spelling it out."

Perceptive, that's another.

"I just don't understand why you won't divorce him and give yourself a second chance at a better life."

"He *is my life*, as are you. The life I chose and won't quit during hard times and time is what he needs. What may heal him and the amount is subjective. This can't be rushed."

"You truly believe that?"

"Yes, but do you really want me to give up on him?"

"I want you to put *yourself* first," I grit out. Wishing to give some of the same brand of brutal truth to the woman who's starting to destroy my willpower.

"When he's spent the majority of his life putting others first? Especially us?" she counters.

"I don't see it that way."

"Because you don't want to. When he wasn't deployed and before that godforsaken career got the best of him, he was present for you. Deny it all you want, but that doesn't make it true. That's why this is hurting you so much." She sighs. "I refuse to forget that and the husband he was to me. You don't just leave someone you've spent half your life with because they're going through a dark period. That's not what you do. At least, that's not what I'm going to do."

She holds up a defensive palm, cutting me off. "But I also know I'm tolerating too much. I'm at the end of my rope, but I'm hanging on for him. Before his last deployment, I asked for one thing—for him to come back alive. Not to be the man I married, just to come home, and I swore to myself that I would help him through the worst of it. He fulfilled his end, and so I'm going to see my end of that deal through."

Ignorance for want. Loyalty to a fault. This is getting fucking scary.

"He's done nothing but cause you pain. Carter is gone, Mom," I say for the last time, knowing this argument—like our last—is pointless.

"No, baby, he's not. He just needs more time."

Slamming my own palms on the counter, I shake my head. "I can't do this."

Temper—definitely from Dad.

"I assumed as much, and that's why I won't talk to you about it. You're too angry to see the pain he's in, let alone anything else."

"I don't care about the pain he's in!" I rebuke. "I care about yours."

Chest rising and falling, she turns and stills before pumping some soap and rinsing her hands in the sink.

"Is it true?" I ask her back, knowing that I could never pose this question face to face. "Did you stop being intimate with him . . . because he got burned?"

"How did you . . ." She turns to gape at me before wiping her hands on a towel. "It's not that simple."

"It never is. Explain it to me."

"That's private."

"No topic is off the table. Your words. That's what you *instilled* in me since I was a kid."

"Maybe, but that's too personal and for your father and me to work out," she bites defensively, "but do you want to know why I won't give up?"

"Enlighten me."

"Happy to if you stop with the tone," she snaps and inhales deeply, shaking her head. "It's because your father was dead set on winning me. So much so that he spent *three straight years* chasing me. A year of that showering me with a kind of love I didn't think existed in anything but movies and books, and I *was not* an easy shell to crack. I was terrified. A gorgeous man like that, capable of getting any girl he wanted, and dead set on *me*? But he waited, and he was faithful to me when I wasn't even his to be faithful to. He spent every day, for three straight years, proving his love for me until I gave in."

"He's not faithful anymore."

Her eyes water. "I'm waiting for him, Tyler, for as long as it takes, and if that's three more years, I'll wait three more years. I'm not condoning *any* of his behavior, and my resentment is building, so our marriage might not make it. But you have to love the light and the dark in a human being for longevity in any relationship. All of that person, that's what true commitment is."

"Even if he's cheating?"

"Tyler," she snaps, "you don't have to keep reminding me of your father's infidelity, which is unusually cruel of *you*. And you're missing my point. I'm in it and waiting for the best friend I have made a life and raised a son with. I'm still in this for a man I love far beyond our physical relationship, and I'm not leaving my best friend at his worst until I know he's safe. At least from himself. Only then will I confront what's left of our marriage. I'm not in denial, Son. I'm waiting. He needs help, but he needs to want it. It's the only way."

Shaking my head, I push off from the counter. "Whatever you say, Mom."

Flouring her hands, she grabs the dough and resumes pounding it with her fist. "You know, if you don't want honest answers to hard questions," she spits bitterly, "don't ask them."

"Can I take the van?" I counter, done with the conversation.

"Fine," she sighs in disappointment, "just be home by curfew."

Grabbing the keys from our ancient Gone Fishin' dish, I crack the garage door and am rounding the back of the van when the whisper reaches me, and I freeze.

". . . I must master it as I must master my life. My rifle, without me, is useless. Without my rifle, I am useless."

Chapter Twenty

Tyler

"I must master it as I must master my life. My rifle, without me, is useless. Without my rifle, I am useless."

Terror grips me as I will my feet forward, and he comes into view. Sitting on his weight bench, a plastic card table sits in front of him as he continues his chant.

". . . I must master it as I must master my life. My rifle, without me, is useless. Without my rifle, I am useless."

Eyes glazed, his hands blur in motion on the table in front of him as he loads and unloads his rifle. Fear is etched on his features as he stares blankly in front of him—through me.

"Dad?" I croak, terror and dread overwhelming every inch of me. Nausea threatens as my stomach roils as he continues his chant, dismantling his rifle before assembling it again in a blur of well-rehearsed motion.

I jump back when he lifts it and aims straight in front of him at the closed garage door before dismantling it again, the chant pouring from his lips. ". . . IS. My. Life. I m-m-must master it as I must m-master my life. My rifle, without me, is useless. Without my rifle, *I am* useless."

Paralyzed, I watch him doing this in rapid succession, softly calling his name as tears start to pour out of his eyes, his voice barely a whisper.

". . . without my rifle, I am useless."

"Mom," I croak, the fear of leaving him to get her help crippling me in place. I don't move. I don't so much as blink as I watch him repeat his lightning-fast movements again and again, slight spittle dripping from his lips as his whispers grow more urgent.

Hitting my knees, fear rips from my throat as I close my eyes.

The crack of the garage door sounds before a swish of air brushes against me as Mom passes. I *feel* it the second she sees him.

"Carter? . . . Baby?"

Keeping my eyes closed, even as my fear for her sets in, I can't open them because the man sitting feet away looks every bit like my father while at the same time holding no resemblance to Carter Jennings.

Dread grips me tightly, muffling the world around me before Mom's pleas break through.

". . . Son, please, Son, call your Uncle Grayson right now. Tyler? Please go. Carter," Mom orders calmly before turning back to him. "Carter, baby, look at me, put the gun down. Carter, please put the gun down."

Time blurs as do faces before I come to, the neighbors crowding our yard as Dad is strapped into a gurney, his eyes glossy, mouth moving almost imperceptibly, no sound coming out—though I can still hear the chant as clear as day.

"*My rifle, without me, is useless. Without my rifle, I am useless.*"

My father is living that chant right now—believing it. Believing he's nothing without the uniform. Institutionalized in his thinking.

I feel that truth in the depths of my soul. Lost would not be the word I would use to describe what I saw. It's the utter fear and devastation in his expression that guts me again and again. A blunt knife to the stomach continually stabbing into me as the gurney bangs loudly against the edge of the ambulance bed before they secure him inside.

I'd been balls deep in Kayley and arguing with my mother about his worth while my dad was . . . unraveling. He's been at war, in his mind, inside himself this whole time. But I pathetically had to *see it* to finally understand just what that hell looked like, let alone imagine what it felt like.

"I still can't find the front door."

But I've seen that hell in another face—the same haunted expression, the same unmistakable pain, in a woman who fights it daily to help me, to shape me.

"Such a shame," our neighbor Carrie whispers to another, just feet away. "He just hasn't been the same since he came back . . . Regina!" She pitches her voice. "Honey, let us know if there's anything we can do."

I turn on her then, fury lighting up my veins as I stalk toward her, and her eyes widen. "How about stop talking about him like he's useless cattle being sent out to fucking pasture!"

"Tyler!" Uncle Gray snaps, striding toward me with the cops on his heels as the medics slam the back of the ambulance closed. And with it, I feel my own snap.

"He's a human fucking being!" I shout as rage swallows me—blinds me. "A human being who put his life on the line for two decades so no one can dictate what comes off your waggling fucking tongue!"

Mom calls my name, the sound of it distant as Uncle Gray clamps his arms around me, whispering fast in my ear, but it's too late.

BLINK. *BLACK.*

"Seventy-two hours under observation." Uncle Gray's muffled voice brings me to where I sit in Dad's recliner. Shifting slightly, I can feel my T-shirt stuck to my sweat-dried back as his voice filters in, clarity in his words. ". . . and then we're going to transfer him into rehab."

"They can't afford it," Aunt Rhonda whispers back to him from where she scrubs Mom's counters in the kitchen.

"They're paying," Uncle Gray states.

"They fucking better," Rhonda counters with unmistakable animosity. I don't have to hear more to know she's relieved Uncle Gray got out of the Corps when he did.

Thoughts heavy, nausea threatening at the ingrained sight of Dad at that table, I stand and excuse myself.

Uncle Grayson eyes me as I give him a nod, a lying gesture that tells him I'm good before stalking out of the house and making the call.

Twenty minutes later, I'm standing in the woods, staring at the full moon between two trees in the night sky, when I feel him approach. Not long ago, we gathered in this exact spot to map our plan. A blueprint Tobias had no idea that Sean, Dom, and I desperately needed, grappling with our current, directionless lives. Plans I cling to now with an alteration in mind—my own purpose.

"I have a stake in this," I tell him, chest still pumping from the long run to get here.

"I'm listening," Tobias says. "But first, tell me what's happened, brother."

Ignoring the shake that he can clearly see in my posture as hot tears line my jaw, I muster the words. "It's my dad, I . . . I think I caught him in the nick of time tonight. I'm not sure, but he was . . . I barely even recognized him. He's under observation now and going to rehab after."

"Jesus Christ, Tyler, I'm—"

"Don't," I say, finding the resolve I've been searching for as the very last tear I'll shed evaporates on my skin. "Don't tell me you're sorry, T."

I turn to see him looking well put together in one of his suits. A look he's adopted in recent years, and I can't help but admire him, knowing that whatever he's doing, he too is taking steps to alter his mindset to become whatever version he's created of himself for the future. Even though he's often present, he's still become something of an enigma to us. Dom has hinted here and there that he's involved in something overseas, but I've never pressed him for what. He's too used to being big brother to all of us. That has to change between us tonight in order for my own plan to work.

"I don't want your sympathy. I want you to tell me you'll back me up on this. I want you to tell me you'll do whatever it is within your power to help me see this through—to the very fucking end. But before we start, this secret, until I decide otherwise, stays solely between us."

"I swear it."

"Then you need to come clean with me. I need to know every facet of what's going on, of the totality of your plans, not just what you pick and choose to let us in on, and that, too, will be our secret."

He crosses his arms, his eyes trailing down me curiously. "Why the need to know?"

"If I'm to build our army and oversee its integrity, then I need the full picture, and that's half of what my stake is in this. With what I have in mind, I'm going to be the one you rely on most. You and I, we can't keep any secrets between us if it's going to work. If you want my allegiance, my fealty, my loyalty, then give me this, and you'll have it."

"And what is your plan?"

"To take on the US military."

An hour later, I'm in the know, more so than Dom and Sean, and make peace with it while standing across the street from my best friend's house, peering into the living room. My throat burns as I gaze upon Delphine in her recliner. The ache and need to go to her intensifying as I recall the details of the last few letters I read.

He blames me for the baby and tells me God knew I would be a horrible mother . . .

He's raping me now, Celine . . .

Last night, he forced me to sleep on the porch in the snow . . .

I am poison to the men I love . . .

As she fills her glass, like my father, I know that she's mentally in a place I can't get to. Everything inside me wants to be who she reaches for now as my heart fills with the truth.

I'm falling for her, and chances are I'll never openly be able to express it. It's likely I'll never get the fucking chance to try to become the man she reaches for. Or be able to battle the poison that numbs the wounds inside her that continue to fester. Wounds that keep her in the vicious cycle of slow self-implosion, right along with my dad. Love can't heal those deep-etched scars away.

Or can it?

Thanks to my idiotic fucking heart and its fixation, I may never get the luxury of finding out. But I can be there for her. Even if it leads to some personal detriment.

But it's the broken areas where we share our most common ground, and it's there that maybe we'll find a place—together. It's then my mom's earlier words about timing resonate the most, and I make peace with it.

"Mindset and stamina," I mumble before turning on my heels and pressing off against the concrete. I run a mile, then two, reaching ten and pushing forward. The ache not abating a single second as I envision a man capable of taking on that battle, setting my sights on a man with an iron will and unbreakable resolve. Who backs his promises and camouflages his own pain. A man that will break the cycle, break the fucking mold.

A man to reach for.

To entrust.

A man that will be me.

And the only fucking man for her.

Chapter Twenty-One

Delphine

After making my move, I glance over at Tyler, who stares *through* his dwindling battalion, showing no signs of animation. Typically capable of concealing any despair, I can't help but recognize the thinly veiled sting in the beautiful soul sitting across from me. Unable to handle any more of his radiating, silent pain, I force him to speak.

"Soldier," I whisper in a slight scold, "you just lost four men and are about to lose more."

His lifeless eyes snap to mine. "Shit, yeah." He exhales heavily, glancing down at his newly weakened formation. "Sorry."

When he makes a counter move, I make my own. "You just lost twelve more men with your absence of mind. Apologize to *them* and to the families that will mourn them."

"I . . ." He shifts in his seat. "My head's not in it today."

"No need to point obvious to me." His lips lift slightly, letting me know I misspoke another metaphor. "You must realize this is the whole point?" I ask. "To put aside all else. This will not be a convenience you have in any battle or on any day in your Marines. That is"—I position a soldier while giving him a pointed look—"if you're still imbecile enough to sign up for *another man's* army."

"Counting down the days." He lifelessly returns fire, unwilling to spar with me in our ongoing fight. It's been our only real battle thus far—one I am determined to win. But seeing the defeat in him today, I decide against making his distracting pain any more of a teaching moment.

"Fine, we can resume our game later," I relay as my eyes catch on the filtering rays that start to cascade through the living room window. A notion strikes as I glance back over to Tyler, who stares intently at one of his soldiers, seeming to search the plastic figure for what answers he seeks.

"The day is still very young. Maybe—" I again glance toward the brightening window before making my request. "Will you maybe consider . . . taking me to fish?"

His face animates instantly in confusion at my suggestion, and I chortle at his reaction. "Sean and Dom say your family has land and that you fish there."

"Not so much lately, but yeah, there's a catfish pond."

"Which you never told me of." He cocks his head curiously as if disbelieving of my interest. "I wish to see it."

He furrows his brows. "You *like* fishing?"

"You don't know your opponent very well," I scold in jest.

"Because honestly, it's kind of shocking." He considers me. "You truly want to go?"

"Do you have poles and bait?"

"Hell yeah, I do." He stands from the table, the severity of his posture visibly relaxing by a fraction.

"Then I wish to go," I tell him, rising from my chair.

"It's an apple orchard, to be more specific," he relays.

"Is there privacy?"

"Two hundred acres enough?"

My eyes bulge. "You say your family is mostly military?"

"Most of them." He nods. "Why?"

"Then bring guns and ammunition too." I stand as he gawks at me.

"Seriously, you want to *fish* and *shoot guns*?"

"You truly don't know much of your opponent, private. It's disappointing."

"Not for lack of trying, *Fort Knox*," he jokes. "You're

not planning on *shooting the fish*, are you? Because that's not how we do it around here."

"So funny. Ha-ha." I roll my eyes. "I'm going to change."

Once dressed, he follows me out of the front door, holding the screen as I lock it. The twist of the key has me recalling the night I first took notice of Ezekiel's compulsion—a nervous compulsion that started not long after Celine and Beau were killed. Three times. Always three times.

"Hey, where did you go?" Tyler asks, preventing me from getting lost in the sting the memory causes. An act he practices often and effectively, which only stokes my intent to return the favor.

"Is this okay?" I point to the tank shirt, overall shorts, and brown boots I found in my closet before I quickly braided my hair.

He scratches his head, the motion seeming unnatural as he scans my dress and nods. "You're perfect," he utters, the words coming out strained. "So, if we're taking a field trip," he adds quickly, does this mean I've advanced to private first class?"

"Not by a *fraction*."

"Jesus, General," he sighs, "your army is fucking *brutal*."

"As it should be." I shrug. "No soldier advances in my army without justcation."

"Justification," he corrects.

"Right." I nod.

At the top of the porch steps, Tyler animates, reporting that he doesn't fish as much anymore because his previous 'fishin' buddy,' and cousin, Barrett, has become 'distracted by the ladies.' It's then I know his mind has drifted back from the place he was lost in, and his heart now beats lighter. As if reading my thoughts, he pauses his footing at the bottom step and turns to look up at me. Gripping my arm lightly, his sincere whisper and rich brown eyes cover me in their warmth. "Thank you."

"You deserve a day of RR, *private*." I extend my car keys. "Today, you are the boss," I declare.

"Good with that." He takes the offering and rounds the car, forced to adjust it to accommodate his height before he can get into the driver's seat. "Jeez, you're a half-pint."

"Five foot five is not that short," I defend.

"It is when you exaggerate your height by an inch or *three*," he says with a wink before turning the ignition and pausing. "So, is this enthusiasm to fish," he asks in afterthought, "was it just bullshit to get me out of my head, or—"

"Imbecile," I utter playfully. "You won't be asking this when I *catch and cook* your dinner."

Tyler stops by his house, gathering several supplies and a cooler, which I help load into my car. Though his home is far more inviting in appearance, I know its look is deceiving by the weight he sometimes carries. As he buckles his belt, he turns to me.

"My mom is already at the orchard planting vegetables with my aunt Rhonda and a few others, so we're going to lay low to try to avoid them." He bulges his eyes. "I'm already putting a strategy together."

I frown at his words. "But having much family is good, non?"

His chest pumps ironically. "Depends on which family you're talking about."

"This I understand," I tell him.

"I know you do. I'm just not in the mood to deal with them today," he explains. I nod again before glancing toward the packed back seat, taking in the plethora of supplies he gathered.

"You are too kind to me, Tyler," I admit in a soft whisper. "You didn't have to go to all this trouble. I'm happy just to fish."

"I could say the same. You've done a lot for me the past six months, and it's not something I'll ever forget."

"As you have done for me, soldier," I relay honestly. "It's

been a relief to mentor you. It helps to keep me out of here." I point to my temple. "Which can be a very dangerous place."

"Seems like we're pretty good for each other," he whispers affectionately before leaning over and nudging my shoulder with his. "You've kinda become my new best friend, you know?"

My heart stutters at this admission. "This you believe?"

"Hell yeah, I do," he draws out before frowning. "Am I not yours?"

"I don't have any friends," I joke.

"Thanks a lot," he retorts sarcastically as he grips the seat rest behind my head and glances back to exit the driveway. As he does, I take in the changes in him—so much more confidence from the shadow-ridden boy who approached me for help last fall. My chest squeezes at his admission that I might have had something to do with this.

"What, General?" His lips lift slightly as he senses my speculative stare. "What are you thinking?"

"I'm excited to fish." A half-truth. The other half is that I believe this admission about our friendship. In the months I've mentored him, I have spent fewer days lost in my mind—in the haze—while trying to sort my past in the bath and consuming slightly less drink.

As we pull off, I can't help my excitement in believing again—trying is *working*.

Several minutes into the drive to the other side of town and after stopping for fresh worms, Tyler turns onto a winding road. The sudden shift in the atmosphere is jarring as I take in our new surroundings. Outside our windows, endless evergreens give way to rapidly blooming terrain. Just ahead, water trickles over two-toned, jagged cliff rock, and a cloudless, neon blue sky hovers above.

"It's a beautiful day," I utter, my voice coated by my captivation.

"Very," Tyler agrees easily next to me. "This was a great idea."

One last turn has us emerging through a vast opening

that gives way to a blindingly beautiful stretch of massive, sprawling green hills. To either side of us sits endless rows of crooked-branched trees, their blossoms solid white. The rest of the grounds are blanketed in a colorful array of various blooming bushes and mixed grasses. The sun lights much of the bright lime-green hillsides, those still shaded in contrast next to them, making the view even more spectacular.

"Mon Dieu!" *My God.* "Tyler! *Is this* the land, your family's land?"

His widening smile pops his dimple. "Yeah, and I actually know a guy who's about to inherit some of it, but he's kind of an asshole."

I frown. "Why is he asshole?"

Smile dimming, he takes his arresting, warm brown eyes from the road and gently rolls them over my face. "Because he didn't realize his new best friend loves to fish."

"Tyler! You will *own* some of this land?" I exclaim, stunned by both our surroundings and his admission.

"Yeah, fifty acres will be signed over to me when I turn eighteen at the end of the summer."

Utterly enthralled, I get lost in the misty sunrays beaming down upon his family's orchard as if in blessing. "It is a dream here!"

"Ah, so she's a sucker for scenery."

"I suck for what?" I ask in mild confusion as he chuckles at my expense, and I narrow my eyes.

"Don't raise your sword just yet, General. It means you love nature's view."

"More than you could *ever* imagine," I tell him honestly.

"I think I'm getting a pretty good idea, but I'll show you what I'm to inherit on our next fishing trip. I want to bait the hooks while the fish are biting."

I nod as Tyler takes a turn on a long gravel road, slowing the sedan as we pass some stacked crates. I inaudibly sound out the name Jennings & Sons, which is printed on the side of each. My eyes feast on it all as questions start to pour from me. He patiently answers each of my inquiries, a constant smile playing on his lips due to my enthusiasm until he parks next to a large, white, two-story farmhouse. A house that is situated perfectly amongst the land for the best imaginable view.

Stepping out of my car, mixed scents start to fill my nose. Feeling transported, I inhale deeply as I turn to him. "I cannot imagine waking up to such a view! I would *never* stop smiling! Though I do not think I would stay indoors if I lived here . . . *What*?" I ask, of his return expression. "What is this look?"

He shakes his head, a clear *something* in his eyes even as he answers, "Nothing."

"Where will we fish here?" I ask, scouring the florescent green grounds, the rolling hills, and endless rows of apple trees, seeing no pond.

"We're not. This is my granddad's house. We're just here to switch modes of transportation." He points to a utility vehicle parked just a few feet away, and my smile only grows.

"So much history here," I gawk, grabbing the poles from the back seat as he goes to gather the cooler. "You must be so very proud!"

"Of the history part and of most of my family, yeah, I am. All military, most serving before quietly retiring here."

I still, knowing that he can't possibly know that his privilege is my life's dream. Instead of the bitterness I thought I would feel at this, I find myself happy for him.

"That is your plan?" I ask. "To soldier and one day live on this land?"

"Absolutely, and not one I have any intention of messing with. If it ain't broke, don't fix it, right?"

"Oui"—I wrinkle my nose—"no . . . fix what?"

He again chuckles at my expense, but it doesn't irritate me like it does when Dom does the same. Tyler's intent is never meant to humiliate me.

"It's an expression that means if it works for someone, there's no reason to change it."

"Ah," I say as we continue to unload the back of my car. "Ain't," I laugh, "what a stupid word."

"It's not really a proper word," he relays. "More a Southern thing."

"Yes, I know what you mean."

The sun beams down on him as he lifts the cooler and leads me toward the vehicle as I haul the poles and tackle box behind him.

"Did you know *land* has been a main reason for many wars?"

His dimple appears. "And here I thought I had the day off."

"It's just conversation. Your America has participated in over one hundred sixty wars, only just over two hundred years old."

"So, what you're saying is we're nosy bastards," he declares.

"Oui, but you've also been very powerful allies."

"It's your America, too, you know," he points out.

"I'm French. I will die a French immigrant because I don't align wholly with all American values, but I'm happy to borrow your land. Your reason to fight." I trail off and feel his stare on my profile. "This is a very good reason to fight, Tyler. To protect this land, *I would fight*."

"Agreed, they don't call it God's country for no reason."

I look over to him. "That's what it is called?"

"Yeah," he whispers, just as taken briefly by our view.

"It's the perfect name for this land. There is so much peace here."

A mischievous glint flashes in his eyes. "Peaceful, huh?"

"Very peaceful." I narrow my eyes. "Why?"

"Just hold that thought."

***

"Mon Dieu!" I roar, a hysterical laugh leaving me because of Tyler's erratic driving. "Imbecile! You're going to kill us!" I shout over the engine as he speeds down a very steep slope, never letting off the gas.

"You sound *really* terrified," he muses sarcastically as the vehicle takes every bit of his abuse. My eyes bulge as I notice a deep gap between some hills feet ahead and screech his name in warning. When Tyler does not deter, I brace myself for impact, shrieking with fear as he laughs at my reaction. Peeking through my fingers, I'm shocked as he steers right for a fallen tree limb before turning back to see we glided right over it.

"Wow, fuck!" I exclaim, thoroughly impressed with the vehicle's capabilities.

"Right?" Tyler chuckles.

"It performs very, very well."

"I know."

I glance over to where he steers, the breeze in the open cabin lifting his sunlit brown hair. "You're still an imbecile!"

My poke does not faze him, his smile telling. "I consider it a term of endearment coming from you." He eyes me. "Don't forget I heard you unleash on the mailman last week."

I frown. "Because he knocked over my plant with his carelessness. *Connard*." *Jerk.*

"And that's why I'm sure he's reconsidering his career choice," he jokes as we glide effortlessly over another gaping hole. I whip my head back in disbelief. "It's all-terrain," he calls over the whirring between us. "That means—"

"I know what that means," I scold in irritation while still smiling. "What is this vehicle called?"

"A Polaris Ranger."

"If ain't broke, don't fix it!" I shout.

"Not *exactly* how it's used, but you'll get there." He shoots me a confident wink, and I burst into more laughter as he rounds a hillside, the two of us riding vertically while holding onto the frame of the Ranger. Nervous, excited laughter continues to pour out of me with the knowledge that if my door weren't firmly shut, I'd be rolling down the side of a hilltop.

My enthusiasm only grows when the pond comes into view. Tall mixed grasses surround it, encompassing all sides of the water. Moss covers part of the surface next to the outstretched dock, which stops halfway into the length of the pond. The only sign of life is small ringlets of tiny waves breaking over the surface of the otherwise calm water. A peace washes over me as we unpack the car and sit next to one another on the dock, feet dangling. We spend a few quiet minutes baiting and casting our lines before he speaks up.

"What were you like in school?"

His question catches me off guard, but I answer honestly. "Bored"—I shrug—"and mostly annoyed."

"Sounds about right," he chuckles.

"I started in school very late because of my father and was behind in their curriculum, and in learning English. This caused me many conflicts with the girls. I did not like them because they were boring, and they *did not* like me because I kissed all the boys," I tell him. "I was a salope—" I search for the English word. ". . . tramp."

Tossing his head back, he howls with laughter at my admission.

"A *kissing* tramp," I correct. "I did not *fuck* the boys." His eyes widen as he chokes slightly on his receding laugh, and I shrug. "It's the truth."

"Well, thanks for the honesty," he says with a humorous shake of his head.

"*What?*" I counter. "I never understand why so many people polite dance around the truth so much. It annoys me."

"I'm learning that. It's just that your delivery is just a bit . . ." He trails off.

"You won't offend me, but I know what you're not wanting to say. That I talk like a *bitch*."

His eyes bulge. "Not a bitch, just bold with your word choice, more like . . . *brash*," he says.

"Brash. I like that. I am *brash*."

"Unapologetically," he confirms before biting his lip and nailing me with his soul-filled stare, "but you should know that's why you're often misunderstood."

"I don't care if they understand," I declare defiantly.

"That's admirable," he says, and I sense his curious stare but glance over to see his eyes on his bobber.

"Not admirable. My brash honesty has cost me much, but I still see no point of being so *overly careful* around the truth."

"Trust me, I'm annoyed myself. Both my parents have been tap dancing like fucking professionals around the truth for years now."

"You can talk to me about it, Tyler. I, too, struggle *very much* with forgiving my own papa for unforgivable sins he committed. I won't be brash to you about this."

"Hey." He commands my attention. "Don't ever tap dance around the truth with me, Delphine. I would fucking hate it."

I nod.

"So, these unforgivable sins he committed, you mean you and Celine's dad?"

When I shake my head, Tyler's eyes widen in shock.

"Celine was not my true sister. Her father was my father Matis's *nephew*."

"So, that means Dom and T aren't really your nephews, but your *cousins*?"

I nod.

"Holy shit . . ." His mouth gapes as he stares at me in shock. "Do *they* know?"

"I told Dom that day in the snow." He nods. "And I told Ezekiel some of my past before he left for school in France, but this is a secret I share with you, *only you*. A new best friend secret."

"I won't tell a soul, Delphine. I promise."

"Merci." I inhale deeply as I scour the grounds. "Relation doesn't matter anyway, Tyler. Celine became a sister to me in my heart." I palm my chest. "She accepted me as I am. The filthy, brash orphan dumped on her parent's doorstep. She loved me as I was, and in return, I loved her the same, so we had the sister relationship she wanted us to have. I care for my nephews the same way, and relation will never matter."

"I get it . . . but you just said orphan?" I tense at this. "Can I ask what happened with Matis and to your mother?"

I bite my lip, and he nudges me. "Hey, some other time, then. We're here to fish today and get out of our heads, so let's do that, deal?"

"Deal," I say, turning my face up to the sun. "Deal, private."

Not long after, my bobber goes under. We spend most of our day fishing, and to my delight, when the fish don't bite for Tyler, he reports the catfish have turned lazy, preferring the cold water of the bottom, no longer trying for the worm. To him, I report he's a terrible, lazy fisherman, which earns me a scowl. Just after, he takes me on the Ranger to explore some of the orchards. Our plan is to cast lines again after sundown when it has cooled enough in temperature.

For some of the day, we shoot what guns he could gather, and I surprise him by taking the tops off several plastic bottles he lined up yards away.

"Shit," he says, "remind me not to piss you off." He bulges his eyes, which has me laughing before I again take aim and fire.

"It would be good for you to try for marksman certification," I tell him between shots.

"Are you?" he asks curiously.

"I was never a real soldier, so I never tested."

"Well, you have a terrifyingly accurate aim." He swallows in intimidation as I take another top off before shooting holes through the water-filled bottle and blasting it off a fence post. "You're a fucking headhunter," he gawks.

"Like riding a bike," I boast proudly, and he nods in approval of my use of the metaphor.

Just before sundown, Tyler starts a small fire on the top

of a grassy hillside. Kneeling, he adds some of our collected kindling as the sun begins to slowly sink past his shoulder. Its descent merges the blue sky with a dazzling melody of pink, orange, red, and gold. The fire chases the slight chill now seeping over the land, the grass cooling under my bare thighs. I run my palms over my arms at its arrival.

"Cold?" he asks. "I can head down the hill and find a blanket."

"I'm far too happy to be uncomfortable. This land . . . this place has a magic kind of peace. This has been the perfect day, Tyler. Merci," I whisper, hearing the slight shake in my voice. My spoken happiness clear in my words.

He stills at this briefly before responding. "My pleasure. We can make this a weekly thing if you want."

I perk at his proposal. "I would be your new fishin' buddy?"

He nods. "Slot is all yours if you want it."

"I want it," I tell him honestly. "For so long, I have wanted—" I stop myself as he tilts his head, his chocolate eyes prodding mine.

"What?"

"This land, *this life*. Your future was my dream for myself for so long. To soldier and then to settle in a place like your God's country. To fish and hunt, to watch the sunset every single day as seasons change." I sigh, palming the grass behind me as I inhale deeply. "I am truly happy for you, Tyler. For you to have this dream to make your future reality." I feel the weight of his stare and shake my head in slight embarrassment. "I must seem like a simple woman to you."

"Simple? Shit," he chuckles. "That's not a word to describe you—the opposite of the word to describe you, Delphine. And you loving to fish and hunt. Well, that description is pretty alluring for a lot of the men around here. Trust me."

"I don't at all care about that," I tell him sharply, too sharply. Too brash.

"Sorry." He shrugs. "I'm just saying you're not simple, that's all."

"I know..." I bite my lip, and he tosses some kindling at me.

"Stop pausing," he scolds gently. "Best friends don't pause when they talk. That's a rule."

I nod. "I say that I don't care, that is mostly the truth, but I know I make it hard for people to like me."

"*I like you*," he says softly, tossing the last of the kindling on the fire. "And *fuck anyone* who doesn't. Like I said, you're misunderstood. That much I know, so if they don't want to take the time to figure that out about you, it's their loss."

I can tell he wants to say more, but I change the subject. "How will we fish in the dark?"

He grins. "I've got us covered. Electric lanterns."

"Smart," I give in compliment.

"Yeah, well, some tiny French lady—who gives me a lot of hellacious orders—is always on my ass to stay prepared."

"It's good advice," I boast as the sun starts to slowly disappear between the hills. "Soldier, do you prefer sunrise or sunset?"

"Sunset," he answers quickly. "*You?*"

"Sunset." I give him honesty. "Because it means I have made it another day." A day fighting through the haze and farther from my past.

"I get that," he tells me.

"You so often understand what I say, Tyler, and there is meaning behind it. Some people simply pretend. Dom is lucky to have you as a friend."

"I'm your friend, too," he reminds me.

"Then I am also lucky," I tell him.

"Me too, General Brash." He winks, the breeze lifting his dark hair as he glances over at me. It's then I notice his rich brown eyes are crowded by thick, naturally curled lashes—it is probably why I find them so beautiful.

As the sun sinks a little deeper and the fire begins to glow a little brighter, I perk at the sound that starts to surround us.

"I know that calculating look," he says, "what's going on in that beautiful brain?"

"Does your watch have a timer?"

"Yeah"—he angles his head—"why?"

"I want you to time fifteen seconds when I say and count the cricket chirps when you start it."

"Okay." He clicks his watch a few times and nods when the allotted time passes. "Done."

"How many chirps?" I ask.

"Twenty-three," he replies.

"If the crickets chirp twenty-three times in fifteen seconds, you add forty to that, and it gives the current temperature in American degrees. Or very close to."

"Huh," he says, glancing down at his watch and pressing a button to light it to see the screen, which I assume gives him both time and temperature. "Shit, you're right, it's close, sixty-two degrees. That's a pretty cool trick."

"If you tune into the crickets and remain aware, the *absence* of chirp can alert you to the presence of predators and help you gauge the direction the danger is coming from."

"Unreal," he whispers, staring at me over the low-lit fire.

"What?" I smile.

"Leave it to you to find a teaching moment out of nothing."

"You knew about crickets' chirps to tell the temperature," I confront in a dry tone.

His jaw drops slightly. "How did you know that?"

"I can detect lies, Tyler. I'm *very good* at it."

"Then you must teach me this, General Yoda. And I didn't lie. I just didn't want to impress you too much," he jokes.

"Ha, you caught *no fish*, and if you want to impress me, disappear into the wild with nothing but a knife for two weeks."

He gapes at me. "Seriously?"

"It's a true test of man's abilities, a test you are not yet ready for," I declare as I stand, scouring the cliffside adjacent to us. "Ah, Tyler, come."

Without hesitation, he follows me as I walk over to the clay ridge at the side of the mountaintop and stop when I see what I'm looking for.

"You know, I grew up here," he says, "but I have a feeling you're about to embarrass the shit out of me."

"You're young," I state, bending to the protruding foliage, urging him closer. "So don't be so hard on yourself. God may provide, but we still need education from mentors of what to look for. See?" I point to a branch protruding from the cliff rock. "Count the leaves. See the pattern?"

He nods, hovering just behind me. "Yeah."

I gently pull one of the roots from the rock, making sure to keep it intact. "Smell," I encourage, lifting the root to him, "take a small bite."

He does, and the genuine surprise in his face is my reward. "Licorice . . . no wait, root beer?"

"Sassafras," I tell him, dropping the root and wiping my hands, "which does make root beer, but you can make tea with it. It has nutritious value, vitamins, antoxidants, and is used in many medicines."

He shakes his head in astonishment. "And once again, my general summons a lesson out of nothing."

"Not nothing, never nothing. God provides," I say, soaking in the peace surrounding us. "He gave us everything we need. He mapped this earth with hints and clues, colored nutritious food. He marked snakes and other animals for danger. God gave us *so much* to guide us."

"Let me guess, Matis taught you that?"

I nod, scanning my sucker scenery view as the last of the sun sinks behind the hills. "My papa . . . Matis was so smart, Tyler," I relay, my whisper strained.

"So is his daughter," he relays in a rough whisper of his own, gripping my hand and lifting it slowly to his lips. My chest stutters at the look in his eyes. A look he maintains as he presses and holds his warm lips to my hand before lowering it, spreading his thumbs across where the kiss lingers as if to push it further into my skin.

Ripping my hand away, I ignore his flinch, playing blind to it as I turn and begin to walk toward the dock. Equally and purposely deafening myself to the "I'm sorry," which carries on the wind behind me as he quickly snuffs the fire out by kicking dirt over it with his boots.

Not long after, those boots sound on the wood planks of the dock before Tyler slowly takes a seat next to me, lighting the space between us with the soft glow of the lanterns. We sit for many uncomfortable minutes, casting our lines as my anxiety continues to build from our exchange on the hilltop. Cursing my stupidity, I turn to him to ask him to take me home when he speaks up.

"I didn't forget," he utters softly, opening the cooler before lifting a flask toward me.

Shame fills me at the sight of it, and I bite my lip and nod in silent thank you. Taking several numbing sips, I mull over the nature of our unconventional friendship, of my influence, and the unfriendly kiss and discomfort now between us because of it. Disheartened, I'm just about to speak when he nudges me.

"Come on, fishin' buddy, cast your line. I need to catch at least one before we go home, or my man card might get revoked."

Nodding, I cast my line before slowly easing back into the peace surrounding us, the cicadas calling loudly on the chilly breeze as night sets in. "Tyler?"

"Hmm?"

"What is man card?"

***

General Half-Pint: Tyler is Delphne questn for sodler

I know who it is, General. Sure, what's your question?

General Half-Pint: Can fish todya

Sorry, I can't fish today. I'm in class and have errands to run for my mom after. How about tomorrow after class? I get out at noon.

General Half-Pint: Oui m erci pleas e vry muc h want to fish with solder

I want to fish with you again, too, General. I'm looking forward to it.

General Half-Pint: one more queston for solder

Anything.

General Half-Pint: Be honets wiht me

Of course, I'll be honest. No tap dancing around the truth. Promise.

General Half-Pint: Jean domicn humulate   tell me my tex t is so bad d

I will not lie. Your texting is rough. You get letters backward, use space when you shouldn't, and often misspell by a letter or two. No punctuation either.

General Half-Pint: Merde I knw Jean not li e

General Half-Pint: Merde is shit in French

I know what it means. And you didn't misspell that. Ha Ha!

General Half-Pint: ha ha funy I resad and wri et so bettr before haze

You read and wrote better before the haze?

General Half-Pint: oui now embarees taks me very logn time to make tetx and read text kyesboard very har d to deciph er Frech esier

I'm sure it is easier. French is your first language, BUT I promise I understand your texts just fine. I promise. I'll be patient and wait for any text you want to send me.

General Half-Pint: nerci fish bud dy

How about we text every day to practice?

General Half-Pint: merci doo not think I stupd wo man I am not stupd i

I could never think you're stupid. You're fucking brilliant. You speak English fine. More than fine. You just misfire a few verbs here and there and still need a little Americanization and help with metaphors. Which I can help with. I'm sorry I poke fun at you. I won't be an asshole about it anymore.

General Half-Pint: non solder k eep poke me asshle

Ha ha, there's my brash General.

General Half-Pint: Donot want fee sorry for me don want fsel like imbelcile when tex t poeple

You're anything but an imbecile. Take your time. I'll wait for every text you send. Don't feel bad. It's no big deal. Dom's a dick for making you feel bad about it.

General Half-Pint: You are go od best frend solider merci ha ve much happy in heart for yuo

Severed Heart

I'm happy in my heart about it, too, General. I've got your back, always, Delphine.

General Half-Pint: I knw this mea ns

Good, because that's the truth. I'll always look out for you. Please don't let Dom hurt your feelings over this anymore.

General Half-Pint: Oui goodnigt privite

Night, General.

Chapter Twenty-Two

Delphine

Tyler knocks before bursting through the storm door, and I jump back in surprise as he stalks toward me—a light dancing in his eyes as he issues his order. "Get dressed, General."

"I am dressed," I utter, tightening my robe, not budging an inch.

"Then change, and before you ask, it's a surprise," he says. "Come on, or we'll be late."

I eye the pint on the counter, and his own eyes follow. "Bring it. Just stick it in your purse."

I shake my head. "I don't like not knowing where I go."

"Trust me on this. You'll like it. *A lot.* Wear something simple. Jeans and a T-shirt is fine, but bring a sweater in case it gets cold."

"Why would I be cold?" I stall as he stares over at me. It's then I notice he is dressed well, and his hair is neatly combed.

"No more questions, and I know you don't have to work tonight"—his demanding tone rips my eyes from his styled hair—"so stop trying to come up with excuses."

"We can finish our battle," I propose, nodding toward our table of soldiers in play.

"Not tonight," he insists, his expression resigned.

"Fine," I sigh, "but if—"

"If you don't like it, we'll leave," he finishes, "I promise."

Forty-five minutes later, Tyler and I glance around the parking lot as hordes of people exit their cars to enter the Asheville shopping mall. I turn to him where he sits in my driver's seat.

"This is terrible surprise, Soldier. You still don't know your opponent well. I am not enthusiastic to shop. Take me home."

He laughs as he pulls out his wallet before lifting two papers from it and thrusting them toward me. "Still want to go home?"

I push his wrist away, and his expression pinches in remorse now that he's aware of my issue with reading and writing.

"Shit, sorry"—he lifts his voice—"these right here are *tickets* to Revenge of the Sith," he boasts, "Star Wars—"

"EPISODE THREE! TYLER!" I clap excitedly as he cracks his door open with a dimple-filled smile.

"Still want to go home?"

I shake my head.

"Then come on, little Yoda," he urges, getting out and rounding the car to meet me at my door before lifting his elbow. I stare down at it as he extends his offered arm further toward me. "It could get hairy in there," he warns.

"How could a movie be hairy?" I wrinkle my nose.

"No, the theater, hairy means busy."

"That is just a stupid expression," I say. "Why not just say busy? I suspect you use the worst possible metaphors just to confuse and tease me."

"I absolutely fucking do," he admits with a chuckle as I take his offered arm.

"Not as nice of a boy as you make yourself to be," I harrumph.

"Oh, I can be very naughty," he teases, "and it will be busy in there because it's opening weekend. I don't want to lose track of you, General Half-Pint, so don't let go."

"Okay." Beaming, I tighten my hand around his bicep,

unable to stop smiling even after the attendant takes our tickets and tears them, handing me the stubs.

Just after, Tyler gently ushers me to the concession counter as an anxious, sweat-covered teenager steps up, eyeing the growing line behind us with apprehension before posing his question to me.

"What will you have?"

"I don't care," I mutter, glancing around the crowded theater complex.

"What she *meant to say* is," Tyler speaks up on my behalf, amused by my brash as he scans the brightly lit menu hovering behind the attendant. "We'll take a large popcorn with extra butter, layered, and two large Cokes, *please*," he adds before turning to me, eyes dancing with mirth as he gently shakes his head. "You are something else."

"What else could I be?" I shrug.

"Exactly," he laughs as I roll my eyes at his constant poking, which I am thankful for over any pity. Minutes later, after gathering our pile of snacks from the counter, Tyler guides me down the hall toward our designated theater. I whip my head back and forth to take it all in while tightly gripping the huge, ridiculously expensive Cokes in my hands, being careful not to spill them—which he doesn't miss—biting his smile away.

"What? They are *so* expensive."

"Always are," he retorts, guiding me into the dimly lit theater. Glancing around the hushed room, I follow him down the aisle between a sea of large red seats, many of them occupied.

"Do you have a preference?" Tyler asks me over his shoulder.

"For what?"

"Where do you want to sit? You an up close to the action kinda gal or"—he waggles his brows—"more into the action at the back of the house?"

"I don't know."

"What? The *kissing tramp* doesn't know?" he pokes.

"I have never been to a movie," I whisper my admission.

"You're shittin' me," he utters without an ounce of humor in his tone as he runs gentle eyes over my face.

"Non, not shittin' you. Which is also a terrible expression, but this is my first time, so merci beaucoup, Tyler."

"My pleasure," he whispers sweetly. "Follow me," he says, cradling the popcorn in one arm, his other hand gripping several boxes of candy as he scans the aisles.

"Why such *big* drinks?" I ask as he leads us down a row in the middle.

"You won't be asking after a couple handfuls of popcorn," he says, politely navigating us past a few of those already sitting in our aisle.

As we take our seats, I inhale a mouthwatering whiff of cologne and freeze when I realize it's wafting from the boy next to me.

He's wearing cologne?

As he adjusts himself in his seat, and after I put the drinks into the holders—*very convenient*—it strikes me then just how nicely he's dressed. As he settles in and grabs a mouthful of popcorn from the tub now in my lap, I catch a glint of his watch. This one shiny silver, not the typical plastic sports watch he wears.

My excitement dims with that realization as I sink into the large seat, *so very comfortable*, and glance around the theater, noticing many couples surround us. A few rows down, a group of teenagers toss popcorn back and forth while talking loudly. Unease starts to sneak in as I turn to question Tyler. "No one else wanted to come? Not Dom or Sean?"

"They're at the garage installing a part on Sean's Nova. And they aren't really into Star Wars like we are." He shrugs. "They'll probably wait for the DVD to come out."

With his easy delivery of this, I try to relax. It's when a couple a row down begins to kiss that I realize why he mentioned the kissing tramp, and I avert my eyes as more unease settles over me. Of course, I know that it is tradition for couples to kiss at the movies, but we are not a couple. Tyler doesn't want to kiss me. He is my fishin' buddy. I'm his mentor. Nothing more. Sensing the tension in me, the polished-up boy in the seat next to me speaks up. "Hey." He gently nudges my arm on the rest. "You okay? Do you want to go?"

The lights dim just as I open my mouth to speak, and the large screen bursts to life, deafening sound surrounding us. Startled, I spill some of the bucket of popcorn. Tyler chuckles as I flick some of the kernels from my jeans, my cheeks heating for looking so simple.

"I am the imbecile tonight." I roll my eyes at him.

"No, Delphine, you're not. You could never be that," he whispers so sincerely that I look over at him. "I'm glad I get to share this first time with you."

I give him a smile I know is kind. A smile I feel. "Me too."

I am safe. Tyler is safe.

I remind myself of this as my nerves start to fray because, in truth, I do feel safe with Tyler and relay this as best as possible as I turn to him. "This was a wonderful surprise and treat, private. Thank you."

"Welcome," he says, leaning over for more popcorn, his inviting scent invading my senses, pulling me in slightly. Trying to push any ill feelings the sensation causes to the side, I blindly reach for my purse on the floor to retrieve my bottle.

Just a sip.

"Delphine," Tyler whispers when I take two sips instead. "If you're uncomfortable, we can leave. I won't be upset."

"No, no, I want to watch," I insist, keeping my eyes on the screen. As the movie starts, I take one more sip and another. But even after I get lost in the movie, the unease refuses to leave me fully. By the time the movie ends, I have few sips left.

***

"You're awfully quiet," Tyler says several minutes into our drive home.

"Why is that awful?" I ask, pulling my eyes from the passing traffic.

"Another expression," he grins, a devilish sparkle in his eyes as the air vents blow his cologne through the cabin of the car, and it again surrounds me. "You haven't said much since we left the theater."

"I am just thinking about the movie."

"And?" he asks, exiting the highway to enter Triple Falls.

"So many parallels to our true world. Man's greed and struggle for power. For one side to reign, as another fights for independence, for freedom of such strict rule. The same story for so many wars, and still we never learn."

"Agreed."

"It was tragic," I say. "Anakin's descent... loss of himself to his darkness, to become Darth Vader. You know it will happen, but you are sad when it does. It's painful to know what remains behind his mask, his future cross to bear."

"It's grim, but that's the story."

"Sadly, yes, the true nature of the struggle within everyone." I turn to him as the streetlights run over his profile. "Everyone wears a mask," I point out with a sigh.

"Think so?"

"You know this, Tyler. Don't play ignorance."

"I'm not. What's my mask?" he asks.

"You know that too."

"Tell me anyway."

"Your mask is reliable, Tyler, with the sad, soulful eyes who thinks opinions he does not dare speak. Tyler, who cares for his mother, loyal to his friends." I unscrew my bottle and sip the last of my pint. "Tyler, who caters to his best friend's drunk aunt."

"Whoa," he says, pulling to a stoplight before giving me

a hard stare. "You're no charity case. I hang with you because I fucking want to."

"See"—I point toward him, dropping my empty bottle in my purse—"you're using your mask right now because you're afraid to offend me, but I often see what you refuse to say. But what happens when Tyler, who is not so okay all the time, gets irrationally angry and releases those words? Reveals his true thoughts in those moments and dark parts of himself. What will happen?"

He presses the gas, his jaw tightening. "I don't know, but I sure as shit don't want to go around being some out-of-control, frothing-at-the-mouth, unhinged asshole who acts on his anger only to fuck up my relationships and possibly my life."

"Hmm, like me?"

His head whips toward me. "No, that's not what I'm saying . . . Jesus, I'm not insulting you. Why are you trying to start an argument?"

"I'm not, but that is what you think. If you are brash like me, you know it will not bode well for you. I'm a good example of what not to do."

"Stop twisting it."

"There is no twisting this truth, Tyler. I know what my mouth does to people. I make them uncomfortable. I say things that do real damage that I cannot take back. You stop yourself. I chose not to in my past. Now, I try not to be so brash. Cause less damage."

"Is that why you isolate so much? Is this what you think about in your long baths?"

I slowly nod as he glances over, knowing my opponent has studied me far more closely than I thought, as the unease spikes again.

"I sabotage myself and make many unforgivable mistakes. My cross to bear as the maskless woman."

"So, stop doing it," he says as if the task is simple.

"Do not be so naïve. It's against my true nature."

"I know you can. You're trying every day."

"You have a fool's faith," I warn. "Too much faith in me."

"You do, too. I'm no fucking angel. I do drop my mask," he asserts. Maybe not in a way that damns me, yet, but I do," he confesses. "And it's far from innocent."

"Show me," I challenge.

"What?"

"Show me," I prompt. "Speak to me as Tyler without his mask."

"It's not that simple."

"Because you refuse to," I counter.

"It's different . . . it's a different atmosphere, a different circumstance on the occasions I do." He pauses. "Honestly, I don't think of it as a mask."

"It is as is for everyone."

"It's not like I'm hiding a whole other personality. It's just anger," he explains, "emotion overload."

"Of this, you are sure?"

"No," he spouts in aggravation. "I don't fucking know." His jaw hardens a fraction. "This is a weird conversation."

"It is *uncomfortable* conversation because you fear maskless Tyler. Welcome to the dark side of the force, Luke," I joke. "Do you have bad thoughts when you go dark?"

"They're blackouts, so I don't know."

"Then you need to tap into them and find out."

"How in the hell can I do that?" He balks. "It's absence of consciousness. I can't just flip a switch to get to that headspace."

"Why not?"

"Because . . . that's not possible. This isn't fucking Star Wars, there is no force to tap into," he scoffs.

"It is possible. If you can breathe your way out, why can you not breathe your way in? May not be nonsense like Jedi force, but our minds are very powerful."

"I'm aware." He bites his lip as he considers my words. "So, you mean, like, blink to black?"

"Exactly." I nod.

"Seems unrealistic," he dismisses.

"Tyler, do you believe that people who carry out orders to kill feel happy mental space before every mission?"

"No, but—"

"Sociopaths and bloodthirst killers maybe, but made weapons, like a sniper, do much psychological training to do their job and after to remain humane."

"How in the hell am I going to do that? You know of a sniper school around here?"

"I told you I can help you with this. We can start anytime. I'm waiting on you, but you are resisting this. Purposely stalling."

"Because this whole conversation is fucking . . ." He glances over at me and grins to help to lighten the tension. "Let me get this straight. You're trying to lure me to the dark side of the force?"

"No, this conversation is nonsense to you because you are making it nonsense. I'm pointing out truth. You need to look inside and see what is there. Maybe you do not believe me or hear me because you think me weak for not defending myself to Dominic."

He gapes at me. "Where is this coming from? I never said that."

"You don't have to. I can *feel* your annoyance when I do not defend myself to him, but your mask won't let you say it."

"It's not my business, but yeah, it bothers me to see you hurt."

"Don't let it, and do not let it interfere with your relationship with Dominic. In taking a look inside, I know my lack of mask allowed me to behave horrible toward *two* scared little boys, and I failed them because I'm not a maternal woman."

"There's nothing wrong with that. The maternal part, anyway."

"There is when you have to raise two grieving young

boys. It was a problem I could not solve in the haze, and I hurt them for it."

"You had been through something. You had just lost your sister."

I shake my head. "Try again."

"Fine." His posture grows taut. "Because you're an asshole?"

I nod. "Frothing at mouth asshole."

"But you care, you love." He pleads for me. "You said so yourself. You loved Celine."

"I care, I have loved, but I have a cruel nature that I not only embrace often but used to do damage I cannot rectify." I sigh. "My baths are to cleanse myself so God will better hear my prayers and help with my regret."

"Cleanliness is next to godliness and all that shit?"

"Not shit," I defend. "I don't tell you what to believe, so do not condemn mine."

"Got it," he sighs out. "Sorry." At the next light, he stays silent for a long moment. "That's such a bleak fucking existence, Delphine. You could just apologize."

"You cannot apologize for that sort of thing. Those apologies do not get accepted, Tyler. Dom's anger is my fault. Look at me," I implore, and he does, his expression a mask of refusal even as I tell him otherwise.

"I am a villain, not victim, not a damsel in stress. I made selfish choices and spoke horrible things, many of them were purposeful. Believe my truth and not what you want to see in me."

"I don't share your opinion."

"That is funny because a villain is the only thing I am sure I am anymore, but in mentoring you, I see the chance to maybe redeem myself."

"So, that's what this friendship is for you," he says, running a finger along the bottom of the wheel at the stoplight as the air grows thick with his anger. "I'm your shot at redemption with Dom and Tobias. Got it. All right."

Fury lights his expression before he gives me another hard stare.

"I'm not drunk," I declare. "But think it anyway, so you can say to yourself, 'she didn't mean any of her brash last night. It was the vodka talking for her.' So you can forgive me and forget this conversation, and we can be like normal tomorrow. Masks on."

"You are being an asshole," he declares bitterly as he stomps on the gas, his face lit by the green light as we pass. "How about that?"

"Oh, mean, tough guy," I laugh and shake my head. "That is being defensive, Tyler, not dropping your mask."

"What got you so pissed at me tonight? I thought we were having a good time."

"I'm not mad at you, Tyler. I'm reflecting on my past decisions, my cross, and maybe I'm the asshole to you for it. I'm sorry to upset you with my brash truth."

"Only because you flat out admitted you're using me because you can't get to Dom."

"Maybe it was part of the truth at the beginning, but it's not truth anymore. You have become my very good friend, but you should not be spending your free time with me. You should be spending time with your friends, Dom and Sean, with people of your age."

His face pinches in anger. "I do. I do every single day, and you know that."

"But you end most of them with me."

"What's fucking wrong with that?" he retorts with edge in his voice.

"Why did you hide us from your family when we fish?" I ask, speaking quickly, as not to allow whatever excuse he may come up with to pass his lips. "Because you know they would not approve of friendship with a woman of my age."

"We're not doing anything wrong," he utters in weak argument.

"We know that, but we also know outsiders won't understand."

I turn to see the hurt etched on his face and quickly dart my eyes away.

"You know I speak the truth, and yes, we do have a very good friendship. You are a beautiful boy," I tell him, "who should also be distracted by the ladies like cousin Barrett."

"Trust me, I'm fucking covered there." His short laugh is menacing as his stare hardens further. "Unlike you, I am *not just a kissing tramp and do fuck* the girls." His chest pumps with a silent laugh as he shakes his head ironically. "Jesus, I just wanted to take you to the fucking movies."

"Tyler—"

He whips his head toward me, pinning me silent with a withering stare. "Mask off, huh?" he chides, his eyes sweeping me in condescension.

"You want to know what I've learned these last few years about so-called fucking adults?" he delivers with a voice full of venom. "That adults are just a bunch of petrified *kids*, running around, fucking up their lives. Acting like toddlers while making bigger mistakes than any kid my age could and numbing themselves fucking *stupid after*, all the while claiming undeserved moral high ground. While in truth, a majority of them are masking *who they really are* and what they want from the rest of the world. So, excuse me if I take my confidence, arrogance, and lingering youth over being the next in line to live the adult *lie* any day."

His bite stings me briefly mute, but I manage my reply. "Maybe this is the truth, but I am not your answer."

"No, maybe you're not," he relays bitterly, "but you're only a dozen years older than me. So, you can drop the bullshit pretense you think fits our unconventional *friendship*." He spits the word as if it annoys him. "You're *no one* of authority over me who has to act any certain way in my company. Not that you've ever bothered too much *before*."

During the rest of the ride back to my house, I keep my eyes focused forward, only catching glimpses of his hands tightening on the steering wheel, along with the increasing rigidity in his shoulders. His affections—for whatever they may be—are misplaced, and I can't allow him to get any closer. Can't allow that look I sometimes catch whispers of in his eyes to deepen any further. Knowing that if I entertain any of it for a single second, it could be detrimental to our friendship. One I had hoped so much to keep but feel slipping through my hands with his offense. When he parks in my driveway and angrily opens the passenger door for my exit, I catch his wary gaze and will him to understand.

I am poison, beautiful boy. I am poison.

"Tyler, please understand I didn't mean to—"

"It's fine. I'm sorry, I lashed out," he says, cupping the back of his head. No lingering warmth to be found when he lifts my keys to take. "I guess I misunderstood our friendship. Thanks for setting me straight. Night, Delphine."

The look of dejection he leaves me with follows me as I speed to my freezer to open a new pint.

***

I'm sorry, General. I didn't mean it. I was a frothing-at-the-mouth asshole.

General, it's been a week. It's hard to apologize when you won't let me.

General Half-Pint: Is fine I workin g

It's not fine. I'm sorry. Want to go fishing tomorrow so I can make it up to you?

General Half-Pint: Non I bsy wrk many shifs solder keep run miles

Severed Heart

No issue there. I'm up to six a day.

Hey General. I graduated today!

General Half-Pint: very hap py for this privaet for accompihsl this

Up for a game tonight to help celebrate?

General Half-Pint: Non I wo rk you shuold celbrate with Dom and Seen

Maybe this weekend? Bet the fish are biting.

Chapter Twenty-Three

Tyler

SUMMER 2005

I FUCKED UP.
 I let my guard down. Despite my best attempts to conceal them, Delphine glimpsed my attraction and sensed my feelings when I pitched a bitch, and I'm now paying hell for it. Since our movie night, she's withdrawn almost completely from me. Dismissing our game nights only to send me on fool's errands by way of physical training. She's checked out, and after months of embarrassing brush-off texts, my battered pride is letting her.

While resentment brews for the ease in which she's dismissed me, my ache and missing of her only grows. Whether it be the resentment for the space she's purposely putting between us, or the gnawing of her absence, I raided the entirety of Delphine's cigar box when she and Dom were working their shifts this past weekend.

I spent hours discovering what haunts her—one of them in which I arranged the letters by what postmarked envelopes remained. The postmark itself timestamping their correspondence lasted only months before Celine and Beau fled to the States. Celine's and Delphine's escalating situations leading to multiple letters sent by one or both per week. It was the last few letters that kept a stinging ball lodged in my throat as some understanding of what triggers Delphine started clicking into place.

When I lock myself in the bedroom, he uses a butterknife to release it. To get to me.

A sting which only increased as I arranged the letters back in the way I found them—not that they're ever hidden. Delphine's foolproof safe, at least where I'm concerned, is in thinking there's a language barrier. A barrier I've spent months eradicating—my intent to surprise her—but have now used instead to wrong her by invading her privacy in a way I can't take back or fucking forget. Not for a second.

He's raping me now, Celine.

That backfire becoming increasingly painful as her translated words scrape my insides daily. Continually driving me back to the patch of blacked-out cement between streetlights after my nightly runs to peer into her living room. A ritual I haven't stopped, even after she called me out for it last winter. In truth, her haunts have become mine since the night I read the first letter last fall.

I am poison to the men I love.

Riddled with guilt and rage, I ran for endless miles after repacking her cigar box, utterly gutted by what she'd suffered—or rather survived at the hands of her ex-husband. With every single step, I battled to temper an anger I'd never experienced. One I was barely able to control in the days that followed. The lingering guilt from invading her privacy is only curbed now by the mystery of what transpired after Celine and Beau joined Delphine and Alain in Triple Falls—though Celine and Beau's fate is no mystery. It's Delphine's missing pieces of what happened in the years before Alain left and why that I'm starting to grow desperate for.

Not that I have any ground with her to get answers. She was as close to happy as I've ever seen her before she slammed up her defenses. As of now, I can't, for the life of me, seem to regain that ground in getting our easy dynamic back. Somehow she fucking saw it—my infatuation—and I let her. And I knew better. I fucking knew better.

My frustration grows as I tighten a bolt on Dom's newly delivered part, feigning focus. Doing what I have for months—camouflaging my ache and shortening temper while obsessing over an unattainable woman.

"Getting there," I mutter to Dom to show a sign of life when his weighted stare lingers on my profile as he works with me to get his part installed. Russell—now completely in the know—had taken off after supervising us for a few minutes before hauling ass home, summoned by his overbearing and highly demanding mother. Russell's sentence seemingly passed right along with his father's, who is still serving hard time for tax evasion.

So far, Dom's restoration is taking the longest. Not because we can't get it done at a quicker pace but because he is obsessed with perfection—not to mention the cost. I can't blame him in the least, being just as anal and adamant about my own. As of now, we're running low on cash, and all of us are getting frustrated with the snail's pace and the idleness of our current lives. Sean especially, acting out more than usual—especially since the paint dried on his Nova.

A Nova which roars with his arrival as Dom and I collectively glance out of the bay to see Sean coming in hot. The heavy repeat of his engine rumbles through the garage as he expertly dodges the cars lined up for service to round the side of the building. Just after, a lone police siren sounds, its increasing wail telling that it's headed straight fucking for us.

"The hell," Dom utters as Sean bursts through the side door, chest heaving while hauling ass toward the open hood of the Dodge Ram sitting in the last bay. Pulling a tool from his box, Sean hedges our inquisitive stares as he makes his request. "If anyone asks, I've been here *all night*."

Before we're able to utter a single question, the crunch of gravel sounds as the cruiser appears, scattering rocks. A few of them thwack against the shop door, the rest shedding like a wave into the bay as it comes to a threatening stop.

The officer behind the wheel scans the garage, and even from where I stand, I can clearly see the wrath of hell in the livid cop's eyes.

"You stupid motherfucker," Dom grits out. "Please tell me you didn't . . ."

"Didn't what?" I bite out as the cruiser door cracks open, mentally trying to prepare myself for whatever's coming.

"Jesus, you did," Dom seethes next to me, and I know it's because he just spared a glance at our red-handed brother.

"Did *what*?" I repeat through clenched teeth, dread settling in my chest as we both prompt Sean, who refuses to meet our hostile stares behind the open hoods.

"Fuck the sheriff's daughter," Dom supplies in a muted tone just as the cruiser door closes. Dom and I both snap to, ready to defend our brother even as our fury grows.

The recently elected sheriff—whom one Roman Horner heavily endorsed—fixes his ready glare on Dom and me when we both round the hood of his Camaro. Though unspoken, I know we're both banking that the cop is unaware Sean's in the garage. Our relief is short-lived when he sounds up, asking as much. "Where is he?"

"Pardon, officer. Who?" I ask, wiping my hands on a soiled shop towel as Sean plays statue behind the hood of the Ram. From where he is in the bay, the sheriff would have to step in and physically search the garage to see him.

"You know good and damn well *who*," he spits, looking between Dom and me. The second his eyes linger on Dom, I see that this exchange could go further south, and fast.

"We have four employees here, Sheriff," I drop casually while helping to intercept him, "so you'll have to be more specific."

"Sean Roberts, red Nova, specific enough?"

"Afraid we haven't seen him yet tonight," Dom interjects, fucking us both as I mask my wince at the gamble we're now risking.

"Mind if I have a look around?" he asks.

"Actually," Dom drawls, straightening his spine, "we do mind. We're closing up shop, and business hours are long over. So, unless you have just cause, which you don't, or a warrant, Sheriff, a search would be illegal, wouldn't it?"

"Don't fuck with me," he snaps. "Where is he?"

"Well, he's around, bright red car, and his parents own a restaurant you frequent with your daughter. What's her name, again?"

Goddamnit, Dom!

"Lacey," he grits out.

"Right, *Lacey*," Dom taunts. "So, you're sure to catch up with him at some point."

"I prefer we converse now." The sheriff digs his heels in.

"As I said, we can't help you tonight, officer, and seeing how you're in uniform and haven't stated anything of a *business* nature, I'm thinking this is *personal*," Dom quips, taking a menacing step forward without closing any real space. When the cop's hand starts to inch toward his hip in response, I ready myself to shut this shit down. "But we can leave him a message," Dom offers as I decide exactly how *Sean's message* will play out.

Dom stares off with the sheriff for excruciatingly long seconds before the cop slowly shifts his gaze over to me. "You're Carter Jennings's boy."

I nod because it wasn't a question.

"He was a buddy of mine back when."

"Oh yeah, I think I remember you," I lie.

"Be a shame to waste your potential here," he mutters, scanning Dom, his implication clear.

"I plan to enlist soon." I play the game as fury lights inside me that I have to go diplomatic by letting the cop know I'm following suit to protect and serve. But unlike this piece of shit who just tried to diversify us with a loaded, overtly insinuating look, I plan on serving all people, not just those who will take contributions from a killer to win his next election.

"I think I'll deliver that message myself," the cop finally says, stepping back from the garage as I will Sean to dissolve into the floor until the cruiser clears our driveway.

"Have a good night, Sheriff," I manage cordially before he dips his chin, shooting Dom a withering look before finally taking the wheel. The second the police cruiser speeds out of sight, Dom and I collectively close all open bay doors and kick back in wait, arms crossed. Not long after, grease-stained boots appear, as does Sean, sporting the complexion of a ghost, which only pales further as he meets our furious stares. Dom and I bristle, ready to pounce, as Sean tries to shrug it off.

"All right, I'll admit it was not my best moment," he drawls. Dom and I close in as Sean starts to back away, palms up. "But think about it, what's the use of having a getaway car if it isn't used to *get away* with shit?"

✲✲✲

The Beastie Boys' "Sabotage" blares through the whipping air in the cabin of the Ranger between the three of us as I floor the gas, rocketing us over the hills surrounding the orchard. Sean roars with a mix of laughter and words of encouragement from where he sits behind me.

Even Dom—who's riding passenger—is failing to bite away his grin as he keeps a tight grip on the bars while I barrel us around the steep hills. After pushing the Ranger to its limits, I steer us in the direction of the faint trail's entrance, which is heavily canopied by dark green, low-hanging branches.

As I slow, bright rays peek through the gaps in the hovering trees, the air cooling dramatically beneath their cover while shielding us from the last of the fading season's sun. The further we travel along the path, the more it starts to feel like we're not headed toward any destination but back in time. It's memories of exploring with Barrett when we were kids that keep the land familiar and easy to navigate. Some of the mysteries of the generations-old acres revealing themselves as we go. Especially when an ancient, partially dilapidated house comes into view, perched on some cliff rock to our right. An eroded fuel tank sitting next to it.

"Holy shit, brother," Sean spouts in intrigue. "How old is that house?"

We all scrutinize the wood-constructed shack as I slow to a stop. "A hundred years easily, maybe more."

Dom cocks his head next to me, peering up at the house from where we're parked. The interior facing the path clearly visible after decades of exposure and erosion. An antique bed frame and mattress are easily seen from our vantage point, as well as other outdated furnishings.

"Early 1900s," Dom deduces.

"Agreed," I add, eyeballing the protruding frame of the vintage brass bed.

"Let's check it out," Sean says, hopping off the Ranger.

"Fuck no, man, it's too dangerous," I object in a warning that Sean completely ignores.

"I've got this," he says, hauling himself up the rocky terrain as easily as the Ranger would before making himself at home in the remains of the house. In a matter of seconds, Sean's pilfering through the contents as Dom and I exit, propping ourselves against the side of the Ranger, already on edge.

"Careful, dumbass," I shout as Sean rummages around the house like a bull in a china shop. "That damned thing could collapse any minute, and I don't fucking like you enough right now to go in after you."

Sean pops his head up before peering between us. "How many times do I have to apologize?"

"For fucking the sheriff's daughter and catching both

the attention and wrath of the Triple Falls police force?" I snap. "We're letting Tobias decide."

Sean visibly jerks back at this, which would be comical if we weren't still pissed. "You ratted me out?"

"Fuck that noise, you fucked up," Dom clues him in unapologetically. "If Tyler hadn't told him, I fucking would have."

"It was stupid and blatant, and you deserve whatever is fucking coming," I grit out.

"I'm not afraid of Tobias," Sean spouts with shit conviction.

"No?" I ask, shooting him a menacing smile. "I guess we'll see about that."

His fuckup could cost him his wings, and he's not taking it seriously enough. Dom seems to read my thoughts as he speaks up, his words for me.

"He's got the attention span of a gnat lately," Dom quips as a crash echoes back to us. Dom and I both tense, and I curse him in a heartbeat before Sean pops back into view with, "all good!"

"Motherfucker!" I bellow, relaxing slightly. "Seriously, brother, are you purposely trying to piss us off? Get the fuck out of there."

"Sorry, man, sorry. Jesus, you could use a little Lacey yourself," his rebuttal one of a petulant child speaking to an out-of-touch parent.

"He'll get bored soon enough," Dom cuts in, gauging exactly where my temper is while eyeing the duffle bag I loaded onto the Ranger. "So, what's with the impromptu field trip?"

"Because Sean's got the attention span of a fucking gnat"—I parrot his words—"and lately the sense of one. T might very well clip his wings."

"I know, and he would deserve it . . . but fuck, I don't *want to do this* without him." He shoots me a look full of rare vulnerability.

"Same. Let me handle this," I tell him, and he gives me

an easy nod, seemingly lost on how to remedy this. Unlike the two of us, Sean doesn't withdraw or brood much when shit gets tough. He just becomes fucking reckless. A habit we have to curb—if not cure him of—before we can go any further.

"Come on, idiot," Dom shouts with a bite, "I'm not digging you out of that shit if the roof collapses."

"Yes, you will," Sean spouts confidently, further convincing me that we did the right thing telling T.

"Holy shit, found something," he says, popping up, a leather-bound book in hand as he glides down the steep, jagged terrain with ease. The three of us stand perched against the Ranger, collectively scrutinizing the scribblings after Sean opens the book.

"It's nothing but a list of bank names," Sean says, looking at me. "Who owned this place?"

"Don't know," I tell him, and he drops his eyes back to the book so as not to press it, knowing that my dad's the historian of the family—one I no longer speak to. The last time was my graduation day months ago, a call he made from rehab apologizing for not being there to witness his only son walk. The conversation had been strained, and I all but tossed the cell phone back to Mom to free myself of it. Not even a month later, Carter flung himself off the wagon and back to the starting line—this time in rehab for a ninety-day stint. I haven't visited once and dread the day he's released despite my mission. I'm still heavily dedicated to investigating the military for myself. But for the dad I *had*, who now feels indefinitely lost to me.

"Bank robbers?" Sean asks between us. "Has to be. Who writes a list of nothing but bank names? Look, maybe these are the dates they planned to hit?"

"Or maybe it's a ledger of deposit dates, Nancy Drew," I quip with an eye roll.

"Not so far-fetched." Dom scans the dilapidated house. "Have to admit, it's the perfect place to hide out."

"It'd be ironic, huh" — Sean grins, nudging me — "if you came from a bloodline of farmers, Marines, *and* thieves." He glances back down at the book and stills. "Shit . . . no fucking way."

Dom and I frown as he lifts a heavily weathered page, his finger hooked on the top of the book next to some scribbled initials. "Tell me I'm full of shit but is that not a B and a C?"

Dom scrutinizes it. "Has to be a coincidence."

"I highly doubt this was a hideout of Bonnie and Clyde, bro," I agree.

"Well, I'm keeping it," Sean declares, tossing the leather-bound book into the Ranger. All three of us silently peer at the house for a few moments, no doubt curious as to what life was lived inside the shack, before loading up. I steer us out for a few more minutes onto the path before pulling to a stop.

Pulling out my cell phone, I managed to get enough signal and fire off a quick text, seeing the one I sent Delphine weeks ago has still gone unanswered. Ignoring the sting it brings, I jump off the Ranger and grab the duffle as Sean and Dom scan the land.

"What is this place?" Sean asks, glancing around. "Are we sparking one up here or—" His question is cut short as he turns to me, where I hold the barrel of my Glock an inch at most from his nose. His eyes widen before he stumbles back a few steps. I press in, closing the space as Sean continually shuffles away from me, his footing unstable, hands fruitlessly palming the air for leverage that isn't there, his sun-tinted skin rapidly paling. "The fuck, Tyler?"

"Disarm me," I challenge.

"What?" he croaks.

"You're already fucking dead," I snap, feeling Dom's heavy stare on me due to my extremes. Taking his silence as trust, I advance on Sean, cornering him with the gun alone as he continues to stare at the barrel, transfixed.

"What's wrong, Sean? Never had a gun pointed at you?"

He swallows and, to his credit, doesn't look over to Dom.

"You're right," I say, "this land holds a lot of secrets, and I'm pretty sure there's some unmarked graves around here somewhere. Bound to be more at some point. *Who'll be digging them remains subjective.*"

"Tyler." Sean looks just above the barrel now, as if he's never seen me before, but I hold the gun steady, though his expression pains me.

"See, we can go around talking shit, making plans, saying we're going to do this and that, but I'm afraid the few months of karate class you took only a handful of years after your foreskin was snipped isn't going to cut it."

"The fuck," Sean rasps out, his eyes frantically scanning my face for any sign of a bluff as I make sure he finds none. "Get the fucking gun out of my face."

"Make me," I taunt.

"You've made your fucking point," Sean hisses in a tone I've never heard. One that reeks of calm before the storm. I can hear the intrigue in Dom's voice as he recognizes it and speaks up, his comment for me.

"Goddamn, brother. I think you better sleep with one eye open tonight."

"Nah," I counter, "this clown poses no threat to anyone, and it's getting fucking embarrassing. Tell me, *clown*, what kind of gun is this?"

"It's a Glock," Sean spits, face reddening with fury.

"No points for the obvious, Roberts. What caliber?" I grit out, letting my own anger through. "How many rounds fit in the clip? Is the safety on? Is there one in the chamber? Where should I position my finger when I'm not using it?"

I take another menacing step toward him, knowing my expression reflects my wrath.

"The answer is you don't know and have done fuck all to remedy that. See, Dom's been spending endless nights researching how to invest the fruits of our upcoming labor, compiling a list of possible hits to add to our net value while earning us some side cash. A cash pool that you've drawn upon but don't often fucking contribute to. And *me*." I stretch the gun further in his direction, palming my chest with my free hand. "I've spent most nights learning tactics, others mastering weaponry, practicing hand-to-hand, and have gained ten pounds of muscle all the while working my King's shifts, *you*?"

Sensing his snap a nanosecond before it happens, Sean tackles me to the ground. I allow him to land his predictable but punishing right before easily tossing him off me. In an instant, we're both back on our feet, squaring off before I again lift my Glock.

"Uh-oh, dead again," I taunt. "What's your part in the club, Sean?"

His death glare lingers before it drops to the bag full of guns at our feet.

"Those, my friend, are loaded, as is this one." I offer him the handle of the Glock in my hand. "But the safety is on."

He eyes the offered gun but doesn't take it, a new grudge stinging in his eyes as he swallows the heavy blow I just dealt to his pride. But it's my fear for him that has me silencing any apology on my tongue and delivering the brutal truth instead. "Playtime is over, Sean, you need to wake the fuck up, or rather *grow up*."

"Fuck you," Sean rattles low, his tone lethal.

"No, fuck you," I counter. "We don't want to do this without you, man. You're the beating heart between us, but you're pissing your position away."

"I know what's at stake," he defends weakly.

"Then act like it!" I shout. "But our question for you is, do you even want to be in this? Because we haven't been inked yet, but it's coming. We haven't had guns pointed at us, but it's coming. Gunpowder coating your hands with a body on the other side is fucking coming,

Sean. One day, it won't be talk, and you have to want this. You have to do the work and put the time in to be ready. Either you don't want this, or you aren't sure what you want from this yet. Dom can answer the question in a heartbeat, and so can I. I have major skin in this game. So, I'm going to ask you again, what's your part and stake in this?"

His chest heaves as he finally starts to scatter his stare between Dom and me. "What is this? Some fucking intervention?"

"No, this is our way of begging you to stop sabotaging your place in our club and to actually fucking figure out what you want from it before we *take* both your place and choice away. If you haven't already lost it, and Sean, there is a *very good* fucking chance you have."

"When the fuck have I not shown up?" Sean spits, his posture drawn tight, still ready to brawl.

"That's not enough anymore. Loving your brothers enough to go to war—to become a fucking outlaw—is not enough. There's got to be something in it for you. And make no fucking mistake, you will be the most instrumental in knowing everything about this. As you're well fucking aware, Dom and I are leaving to do our parts, which means it'll be on you to bring them here. To teach them hand-to-hand and how to carry discreetly while making sure they don't shoot their dicks off. Their fucking lives will rest on your shoulders. Which includes leading by *example* as well as enforcing how to keep a goddamn secret. Your capabilities are nowhere close to being able to carry out that task. Last chance, Sean," I warn, "or I'm not going to bat for you with T."

"Me neither," Dom adds, "I've lost faith."

Sean's eyes sting with fresh betrayal as his mouth parts.

"This isn't a fucking bluff or some lame attempt at tough love," Dom relays gravely. "You might already be out, and you know you would fucking deserve it."

"Jesus." Sean cups his mouth, sliding his hand down

his throat as he looks between us. A few tense beats pass before he finally speaks. "I want my parents' restaurant to survive." He shakes his head. "Fuck that, I want them to *thrive*. Matter of fact, I don't want a single door from a struggling business owner in this town to close due to the corrupt and greedy fucks demanding so much of what they break their backs for."

"Modern-day John Dillinger?" Dom nods approvingly, speaking of one of his heroes. "I can get behind that."

Sean nods, his eyes watering as his anger dissipates and his fear thickens the air between the three of us.

"I heard my mom crying last night. They're terrified. They don't know how long they'll be able to keep Pitt's doors open. I don't want to live in that fear, and I don't want my children to feel it. I've seen what it can do." He eyes Dom, his voice cracking with his admission. Dom stiffens but allows it, his fear for Sean's place in our club overriding his pride.

"That's all part of it," Dom assures. "That's really all you want?"

"No, as much of a fuckup as you both think I might be, I want to do something important with my life. My other dreams are simple, but this isn't. I need this, and I do want it. I don't see any other future for myself."

"Then why the fuck are you sabotaging it?" I demand.

"Because I'm a fucking idiot," he states, "it was a cheap thrill, a distraction. It was reckless and stupid, and I get it, okay? I do. It won't happen again," Sean declares in a rare serious tone. "I'll figure my shit out, but please, don't let him take my wings." He piles his hands on his head as he does when he's really upset. "Fuck. I'm just . . . I'm sorry."

"Sorry won't ever cut it again," I state emphatically, "no matter your fucking headspace."

Sean slowly nods as I drop the Glock and step up to him before palming his shoulders.

"The days of your parents' struggles are numbered, I

swear to you, and I'll sweeten the deal and play fucking Friar when the time comes to pass out your blessings. That's if you still have a place with us."

"Don't let him take my wings," Sean croaks between us, "please—"

"I won't," Tobias interjects, emerging from the nearby trees where I messaged him we'd be. Dressed in jeans and a T-shirt, expression unforgiving, his wrath-filled fire-colored eyes are fixed on Sean, whose complexion is now ashen. "And it would do you some good to remember that your place in the club is not *up to them*," Tobias spits, kneeling before pulling an AK out of the bag, his gaze as unforgiving as his tone as he continues to level Sean with both. "So, consider this day one of a *very long* fucking *probation* and your first and last fucking warning from the *decision maker*. Brother or not, if you ever fuck up like that again, you're done."

Dom shakes his head at his brother's unexpected appearance, a broadening grin on his face. "You're really playing your part these days, ghost of fucking Triple past."

Tobias keeps his pointed stare on Sean a beat longer before embracing his brother in greeting. Glancing over, I see Sean bat away a few tears of relief.

"Thank fuck," I say on exhale, my shoulders sagging as Sean stares back at me in a way I know the fresh sting between us will take some time to fade.

"I've been waiting a very long time for this day," Tobias says between us, "but that day is finally here, and the true work starts *now*," he reiterates to Sean, who slowly dips his head in response.

Just after, Sean disappears between the trees for a beat, and I resist the urge to follow him, helping T and Dom unpack the duffle instead. My fear for Sean outweighing my need for us to be in good standing. Not long after, I know I made the right call when Sean emerges without a trace of animation in his expression. Eyes sharp, jaw set, and focused, he chooses his weapon and joins our lineup. It's then I start to feel it. A feeling similar to the day we stood outside the garage just after Dom signed for the key. The beginning . . . of something more. More meaningful. Our purpose.

It's on the silent ride back to my granddad's that I sense the last of the shift—the true end of summer. Of our lives as we once knew them.

The end of our innocence.

Chapter Twenty-Four

TYLER

FALL 2005

*S*he's on a fucking date.
Beer in hand, I stare into the bonfire feet away from me, doing my best to try to contain the inferno roaring inside as I consider *my own* date. Red cup in her own hand, Amy unknowingly chats amongst our group of made birds and the newer recruits present at our latest meetup.

Let her go, Jennings.

Sensing the weight of my stare, Amy turns and beams at me. I give her a wink of acknowledgment in return before scanning those crowded around the fire. But instead of seeing the group as they are in reality—drinking, laughing, smoking, and chatting enthusiastically—I see their individual positions on the board. All a part of the army I'm slowly cultivating.

Russell is a prime candidate for second-in-command, forever ready to step up when summoned. Daily, he makes it his mission to pay careful attention to every detail of the goings-on of the club. Jeremy, though naturally a clown, is a cunning one. Good at disarming people to get close enough for recon and any smoke-and-mirror theft if we're put in a tight spot. Between his criminal mind and Dom's, we'll never run out of creative heists.

Over the next few years, I have gaps and positions that need filling, and thanks to Delphine, I can see each so clearly. Ignoring the beer in my hand as I have all night, my mental plotting takes front and center, my eyes landing next on Layla, now heavily in on the secret.

Ironically, after my suggestion that Layla become a bird, she was brought organically into the fold by a recruit, Craig. A recruit she's currently delaying my introduction to as they maul each other in a camping chair a few feet away. After a few conversations with Tobias, Layla's suggested plans of her part to play will prove her worth. With close ties to damned near everyone in this town — and after opening her salon — she'll not only be helpful in adding to our revenue stream but also become our resident spy. Utilizing her salon chair to keep up with the gossip and goings-on of everyone in Triple Falls. Over time, if she proves herself, she will be our first lady bird.

The rest of the small but growing crowd of faces I picture so easily in my lineup. Mentally positioning them based on their strengths and weaknesses — the way my heartless general taught me. A general whose lighthearted greeting earlier tonight leveled me as she breezed into the living room dressed to kill in a long-sleeved sweaterdress, knee-high boots, onyx hair down and tousled. Her lush lips painted wine red. The sight of her dressed like that — and for another man — snatched my beating heart right out of my goddamned chest.

She might be on a date . . . but so are you.

Full of resentment and white-hot jealousy, I picked up Amy just after, determined to live within the parameters Delphine set with *girls my own age*. An attempt to press through the heartache I've been battling for too many fucking months and move on, trying to date a girl I might get somewhere with. Because, of course, girls my own age are interested in drawing parallels between Star Wars and our current society. Talking for hours about battles of the past and the private lives and actions of historical figures to determine tactics in psychological warfare. Oh, and love to fish and hunt.

While I'm certain there's a runner-up somewhere that might eventually fit the bill, I don't want any part of her.

That much became evident when I gave Amy a little something to remember me by earlier tonight before choking when the time came to fit the condom that was burning a hole in my pocket. Even as she begged for it, and even while I was on fucking fire for some touch.

But for her. Always for her.

Just after Delphine breezed in all smiles, our eyes met and held right before hers dropped, granting me access to feast. The image of her now ingrained, and tap dancing along my psyche, while keeping my heart raw.

That fucking dress hugged her every curve.

Focusing back on the girl who deserves it, I consider making good on it. To kick the stronghold in my head and chest, but it's that stronghold that tells me it's not happening tonight or ever.

You're in love with her.

In a desperate search for a silver lining, I catch the fresh gleam of my truck parked feet away. I'd picked up my denial date right after the tape was pulled off the immaculate paint job, deciding to debut my lime green antique pickup with a blacktop at our meetup. Lately, I've found a lot of satisfaction in working on cars, taking things apart, and figuring out their inner workings before making them whole again. The irony not lost on me that I wish it were as easy in life—for people. Though people aren't fixable, their mistakes can be camouflaged.

It's my newly discovered niche.

Another lining is that since our blowout this summer, Sean has stepped up in a major way, using his former schmoozing skills for his hookups to start networking.

The board is getting closer to where I need it to be for my departure into the Corps. But even with the table set, it's my fucking heart that keeps me continually running past my recruiter's office. At this point, I'm only a signature away from being sent to march. For months, I've been holding out hope but unable to take a fucking step in any direction personally.

Just leave, Jennings. She won't even notice.

That sting lingers as Amy sidles up to me, and I turn to her, unable to escape the grim ache leaching into me tonight. "Hey, you mind if we get out of here?"

"Sure." She gives me an easy nod as I turn to signal Dom, who gives me a chin lift, the mischievous glint in his silver-gray eyes filled with the assumption I'm about to have a good night. I'm fucking not. The never-ending longing in my chest is telling me as much and only fueling my frustration.

Fifteen minutes later, I'm met with Amy's frown as I palm the back of her head, giving her a slow kiss of apology. An attempt to find some spark.

"I didn't think you were taking me home," she says, slightly dazed as I pull away, my decision solidified.

"I'm sorry," I whisper. "As cliché as it sounds, it's not you and a thousand percent me. My mind isn't here tonight, and you deserve better."

"Tyler, I want to give you what you want. You know I'm into you," she admits as the guilt settles in.

"I'm an asshole," I admit. "I'm just not there right now. Head and heart. I'm sorry."

"So, it's over?" she asks in a shaky tone.

"I don't want to lead you on," I tell her. "Is that okay?"

"Guess it has to be," she sighs. "You're into someone else?"

I nod and give her sincerity. "I really am sorry. I feel like shit."

"I believe you are," she finally says after a long beat. "You were a surprise"—she winks—"a good one." She presses her forehead to mine, eyes watering. "Thanks for not being like the others."

She gets out of the truck, shooting me a smile through the passenger glass as I do the same. Neither one of us feeling it. Too restless to go home, I familiarize myself with the town I grew up in, knowing it might come in handy someday. Where most see roads now, I see Delphine's mental mapping techniques. Where most meet people and greet others with a handshake, I find myself taking in their details, gestures, word choice, and movements. Delphine's opened my mind to everything, including the feeling I can't shake.

You're in love with her, and that can't be camouflaged.

That truth rings clear in my mind and heart, plaguing me as my cell phone rattles in my pocket. Pulling it out, I see Dom's texted me a location. Confused but in need of distraction, I navigate to the address, which ends in an alleyway off Main, and catch movement. Headlights beaming on the darkened alley, I pull to a stop when I see two familiar heads pop above a patched quilt where they're huddled next to a large dumpster.

Exiting my truck, I call out to them. "Charlie? Tweety? What in the hell are you two doing out here?"

"Dammit, Dom," I hear Charlie grumble as I approach. "I knew he wouldn't let it go. Don't tell him," she snaps. "Don't you fucking dare."

"But it's Big Bird," Jane counters.

"I know who the hell it is."

"You should, Charlie," I interject, now standing directly in front of them, "because I licked your tonsils dry trying to learn how to French kiss." A short pause ensues before they slowly pull the blanket down, Jane grinning as Charlie gives me the evil eye.

"That's why I dumped you," Charlie delivers with ease before she deadpans.

I palm my chest and grimace. "Oof. Such a heart-breaker."

"Though . . ." She rolls her eyes down my frame. "I have to admit you're looking better now," Charlie spouts. "You've grown into your big-ass ears."

"Shots fired," I drawl, "and eat your heart out."

"And you can eat a dick." She beams at me with her delivery. "But the dimple is hot."

It's then I notice the bags stacked next to them, and my heart stutters at the sight.

"All right," I say, my protective streak taking over as I cross my arms. "Time to come clean. What the hell is going on?"

Jane's blue eyes water as Charlie maintains her notoriously stiff upper lip—though her expression is fear-filled. Jane ditches the quilt and steps up to me as I ask the obvious.

"You ran away?" I ask, and Tweety nods. It's no surprise, seeing as their parents are neglectful addicts.

Though we met years ago—barely out of diapers and daycare—we've gathered on many nights since, sharing food while commiserating. A sort of streetside potluck of misfits who didn't really have dinner to go home to or, like me, didn't want to be at the table—the reason Dom's constantly raiding the cabinets. Even though his bank account amount is gradually increasing, he still passes through often, especially because Charlie and Jane are his favorites and the reason for his text.

"We can't do it anymore, Tyler." Jane's eyes spill over. "They were going to pawn us off on some relative again to go on a bender. We just want to wait it out until she turns eighteen in a few months." She nods toward Charlie.

Racking my brain, I think of our garage and know that's no place for them to stay temporarily. My house is no place for guests for the moment, either, what with Dad's hellish mission to stay sober. At this point, Carter's home is the place where I bathe and sleep while practicing living in the shadows. Just after I dismiss those options, an idea comes to me, one I assume is why Dom texted, and I stalk over to Charlie, who now has tears in her own eyes.

"Charlie, you know damned well that you can trust me." Both Charlie and Jane are in the know about our club but opted out. Neither wanting to live an unpredictable life after what they've already endured.

"I know . . . I'm just embarrassed," Charlie says, a prideful tear sliding down her cheek. "We can't go back to them, Tyler. We just can't."

"I've got you. It's not the greatest place, but it has a roof and plumbing." I pick up a handful of their bags and walk them over to deposit them in my truck bed. "Come on, Tweety, let's get you to your new nest. It's freezing out here," I tell Jane as she runs over and enthusiastically grabs more bags.

"Where are we going?" Charlie asks skeptically as I load the last of them into my truck.

"You like apples?" I ask as we pull out of the alley.

"Love 'em," Jane says as Charlie shrugs in indifference.

An hour later, I have them set up and warming next to a firepit at one of our labor houses at the orchard, which won't be needed until early spring. If push comes to shove, I'll tell Uncle Gray. He won't like it, but he'll allow it once I relay the situation in detail. Thinking on that, I decide to shoot off a text to Barrett relaying the same. Our relationship is on a slow mend but still strained due to Dad's bullshit. With Barrett's quick reply, I feel a little better leaving them there, especially after he agrees to check in on them and report back since he lives close to the labor house.

It's when I still can't find a mental way to wind down as I drive back across town that I find myself parking my truck and walking along the edge of the neighborhood to get to their street. Stalking toward the patch of sidewalk across from her house, her written words drive me toward it—forever on the forefront of my mind.

I told him I would leave him and woke up with a knife to my throat.

Images of her written words shutter through my mind as a rogue thought sends an uneasy skitter up my spine. Who exactly is this asshole she decided to allow to court her? And why now? I was worried she might decline during our months apart, but maybe Delphine's made more progress, and I should be happy about it. Still, I can't help the unease that's been sneaking in all night at the thought of any man entering her life and their treatment toward her after what she's survived.

It's when I corner her street that my sudden ill-at-ease premonition is confirmed as Delphine's shriek reaches me.

Chapter Twenty-Five

Tyler

In a blink, I'm only a few houses away from her driveway as the source of her annoyance bursts out of the front door, half-dressed, shirt in hand while making a beeline for his car.

Ignoring the immediate sting of jealousy, I make it to her driveway in a blur, taking a mental snapshot of the license before meeting the asshole at the front bumper of his expensive sedan. Pulling his keys from his pocket, he barely acknowledges my murderous stare while issuing his warning.

"I wouldn't recommend going in there." He glances back at the house as he opens his driver's door muttering, "Crazy bitch."

Needing to get to her but tempted to make him swallow his fucking tongue, her cries reach me where I stand—deciding for me on which instinct to act on just before the asshole races out of her driveway.

Burning his plate into memory for safekeeping, I pound up the porch steps two at a time, and am stopped short outside the screen door by the sight of her.

Crouched in the middle of her living room floor, wearing nothing but fitted white cotton underwear, Delphine rocks back and forth, arms wrapped around her legs.

Without thinking, I stalk in and easily lift her from where

she sits and into my arms. Mixed mumbles pour from her lips, and I faintly make out a few of her whispered words as I search her for any signs he was aggressive with her.

"W-wrist and u-l-na..." she croaks in a delivery I can't decipher, "d-damage t-to... pipe... *will heal*." Her voice breaks on the last two words as if they're a lie before her face crumples and a guttural sob escapes her.

Panicked by her state, I desperately search her, satisfied when I come up empty for fresh injury. It's when I start walking with her that she seems to lift slightly from her stupor, relaxing in my hold only when she realizes who's carrying her.

"Tyler." She whispers my name in a dream-like lilt, which in any other circumstance would sound sublime coming from her perfect lips. She peers back at me with vodka-glazed eyes, a black smudge beneath one of them, her lipstick slightly smeared. My heart fractures at the image of her I've been replaying all night in contrast to her current state. Cradling her to me while trying to ignore the feel of her in my arms, I stare back at her, heart pounding, without any fucking idea of what to say.

As I take the hallway toward her room, she continues to keep her silver-gray gaze fixed on me, arms tightening around my neck as I walk her into her bedroom. Crimson threatens to snake into my vision as I eye the bed while crossing the threshold, finally getting my words out.

"Are you hurt?"

"Non... that is not possible," she declares defiantly, even in her weakened state. "Men cannot hurt me anymore." She shakes her head as if the notion is laughable. "No man in my life has been worth the conflict they cause," she spits icily. "Not one. Al—" She cuts herself off, refusing to say her ex-husband's name. But I know it. All too fucking well now. A name branded into my psyche as well as my hatred for him.

Alain.

"This whole charade between men and women,"

Delphine whispers, "this notion of true love," she expels with disgust, her tone gathering a bitter strength as I stand at the edge of her bed while idling with her securely in my arms, "makes those who believe in it weak, pathetic fucking fools."

"I can't, at all, disagree with you for the moment," the declaration spoken straight from said fool's mouth as I gently deposit my weakness on her bed.

"Non?" she asks, staring up at me, eyes sweeping back and forth.

"Yeah, for the moment, I'm with you on that," I say as she studies me closely. Forever searching, weighing words for truth. Trust issues seem a mild blanket statement in comparison to what she's battling. And fuck how I want the trust to seek the rest of those answers. At this point, she's become more than a person but rather a place I want to be, and I think that's what bothers me most about the space she's put between us.

Pulling the covers up to guard her modesty, I avert my eyes after glimpsing a peek of her quarter-sized, rose-colored nipples, holding my groan inward. Palming the sheet to her chest, she barks out a mocking laugh while pulling a cigarette out of a pack from her bedside table.

"You Americans and your modesty," she scoffs. "Men and women should have no issue stating their desires, showing both passion in their words and allowing dominance in their lovemaking without restraint."

"I'm also with you on that." Grabbing her lighter, I spark up her cigarette before she has a chance to. "I'm not really good at restraint in that particular area."

She takes a long drag, speaking on exhale, seeming unphased by my confession or simply lost in her rant. I glance around for her bottle to check the level and come up empty.

"The men I encounter always claim to be titans, forces to be reckoned with. Whispering ignorant promises. Every single time." She lets out a sarcastic laugh. "That connard

Severed Heart

probably could not please a woman if he had *two cocks*, let alone be half the man he declared himself to be," she sighs, seeming to truly see me before sobering considerably and dropping her gaze.

"Mon Dieu, Tyler, I'm sorry." She blows out a long breath. "This, I . . . no, that was not meant for you to see." She points toward the living room. "Or to hear or for us to discuss." She shakes her head, clear shame in her expression. "Forgive me. Sometimes, I forget you are so young."

How I fucking wish you would.

I don't bother to mention that naked women don't intimidate me in the least. It's her bare skin I can't allow myself to feast on because I can still feel the silk of her skin buzzing on my fingers.

"Not that young," I pointlessly remind her.

Briefly, I wonder what my moody, French version of Yoda would think if she knew I'm more Anakin inside than any pure-as-the-driven-snow, guileless, clueless Luke Skywalker. Laughably, and now ironically, in the same fucked predicament as Anakin—infatuated with an older woman who sees him as nothing more than a kid.

"Dom is not here." She bites her lip, keeping her eyes lowered. "I wouldn't have brought him home if—"

"I know, he's at the meetup, and you don't have to justify it to me." I hate the words, rebuke them altogether the second I release them as jealousy snakes its way back in. Because I want her to feel accountable to me. I want her making excuses for why she even fucking entertained another man tonight. And stupidly and hypocritically, even as I've done everything in my power to fuck her out of my headspace with my hookups, I now want her fidelity.

As she keeps her eyes lowered, I memorize what I can—the arc of her slender neck, olive skin, and contoured shoulders. Her hair down and still tousled, looking like black silk as it cascades in thick waves over each of her shoulders. Even when I look at her objectively to try to reason with myself, she only looks slightly older than the *girls my age*, with one exception—by comparison, she's a fucking bombshell with the insides to match.

"I didn't come to see Dom," I state, unable to hold the hint of underlying heat, which costs me fucking dearly when her eyes drift up and hold a beat. *Fuck.*

"Turn your head, Tyler."

Doing as I'm told, I hear the rustle of fabric. Not long after, she sighs her consent, and I turn back to find my view interrupted by the large T-shirt she procured from a nearby pile of laundry. Just next to it sits her infamous cigar box, her French translation bible never far from it.

She was triggered tonight, and the knowledge of why is never far from my psyche.

Eyeing the closest picture, I see who I now know is Alain with Delphine possessively in his grip, a sadistic fucking look in his eyes. The utter hate and territorial jealousy I feel for someone I've never met threatens as I palm the back of my neck, fighting the anger his presence—even in his permanent absence—evokes from me. "Can I . . . get you anything?"

"No," she answers sharply, too sharply as she does when she senses my eyes on her for too long.

Securing my mask tightly in place while pushing all desire-filled thoughts away, I flit through the number of questions I'm becoming more impatient to ask as she rattles below me. The one most burning. 'What was so special about Alain that you endured his abuse for so long?' Instead, I ask the only one that truly matters. "Are you okay, Delphine?"

The use of her name has her staring back at me, unflinching, despite the state I found her in. If anything, she seems to be filling with contempt. She retrieves her cigarette from the dirty ashtray on her nightstand, resting against her tattered wicker headboard while pulling the sheet up and over her crossed legs.

"How old are you now, Tyler?"

"I turned eighteen a few months ago," I relay, knowing it means fuck all to her.

She runs her thumb down the side of her cigarette. "Old enough to do yourself and the women in your life a service."

"Oh yeah? What's that?"

"Don't make promises to women you have no intention of keeping, in and out of the bedroom."

"I'll keep that in mind."

"Will you? I doubt it," she scoffs, exhaling a plume of smoke, her steady stare penetrating. Guard rising, a snake-like fog starts to cloud her eyes. Its arrival letting me know her alcohol-drenched brain is convincing her that I'm going from ally to enemy. There's nothing I can get her. There's no way to get to her, and it's time to go before she lashes out. "I'm going to head home."

"Why?" she asks with a venomous smirk that brings my irritation to its breaking point. "You don't like taking advice from a woman?"

"No, because your lecture is *unnecessary*, hence the shaking thighs of the girl I just drove home. I know very well how *to fuck*, Delphine, so I'm covered there. Sorry your date didn't work out as well," I grit out. "And as far as your advice, I'm *all ears for it whenever* Smirnoff isn't the one helping to cultivate it. Nor am I willing to tune into it when you've got a warped sense that I'm the enemy and a cruel, calculating fucking look in your eyes for me that we both know I don't deserve. So yeah, tonight, I'm going to pass."

When her lips part in clear surprise, a sick satisfaction thrums through me that I got any reaction from her at all.

"Sorry," I draw out dryly, my tone anything but apologetic, "I'm utilizing my mask a little less these days, General. Advice of yours I *chose* to take because I've aged into playing the fucking adult game now." I shake my head, speaking on exhale. "The fuck am I doing?"

Knowing better than to argue with alcohol, I bite out my parting words. "Take care. I guess I'll see you around."

She bites her lip and nods as I turn and stride toward her bedroom door. I'm a step outside of it when I hear her whispered confession.

"I miss fishin' buddy very much."

Freezing, I turn back to see the release of a tiny tear and go utterly still at the sight of it. She stares back at me in shock that I heard her barely audible confession as the ice around my heart instantly melts at her acknowledgment. The rest of it sliding off as I watch the tear I know belongs to me trailing down her cheek. A tear that has me stepping back toward her bed in demand of an explanation. When she sees my intent, her mouth opens and closes but I shake my head in warning, refuting her any ability to try and backtrack.

"You miss me?" I ask, point-blank, holding her gaze in demand of an answer. But it's the defeated look in her eyes that speaks volumes before her lips finally part.

"Oui," she whispers, "I miss you very much. You were my only friend."

"Then why in the fuck did you push me away?"

She bites her lip, and her eyes drop.

"Okay, we both know why, and I'll own that I behaved badly and probably acted exactly like you expected I would. That's on me. And trust me, I regret it. But I have always respected your boundaries, and you all but slammed the door in my face. So the way I see it, we're both assholes. But right now, you're being the bigger one."

"I am sorry, Soldier," she whispers. "You are right. I have no business giving advice." She nods. "I was a fucking fool to try to go on a date. Merci. Thank you for coming to help me, *again*." Her lips shake with her delivery. "Just forgive me and go." She nods toward the door. "You do not deserve this. My contempt, it's not for you. It's for me."

My heart fucking stutters as she waves me away. Again.

"Please, Tyler," she urges, "go, I am fine. I will be fine."

Refusing her order, I remain standing at her bedside, positive she's used to people dismissing her after she shoots her venom—leaving her in the state she's in. But what if, and maybe for the first time, someone stayed? Someone remained there to witness what happens after. Knowing I'm stepping on a landmine, I keep my footing steady.

"Or . . . you can cut the shit, stop tap dancing around the truth, realize I'm here *for you* and fucking talk to me." I double down by kneeling at her bedside. "Talk to me, damn it. Tell me why you're so upset. If it's not the asshole who just left, then what is it?"

"Tyler, this is not for you to deal with . . . or to decipher."

"The fuck it's not. You just said I'm your only friend, and I still want to be. I care very much about you, so let me in."

She stares at me for long seconds before her eyes drop to the letters flowing out of her cigar box. Her features pinch in anger as she grabs a fist full of them into her palm.

"This, *this*." She lifts the clenched paper eye level. "This is proof enough that *'love the fucking liar'* can make a fool of you. Make you weak, pathetic."

"So what is it about those letters that haunts you so much?" I ask, my investment in her pain obvious in my tone. "Is it regret?"

She takes another drag of her cigarette, considering me as she lowers the letters, the anger fog dispersing as she slowly exhales her answer. "So much regret, Tyler. So much."

"For?"

She bites her lip, her eyes blurring. "For trusting men who made me believe their own ideas of themselves and punishing me for reminding them of who they told me they were. For letting them punish me."

"And you can't come back from that?"

"Look at me," she challenges.

"I am," I state with an edge in her defense.

"I am what failure looks like," she admits hoarsely.

"Not to me," I whisper back, unable to help my question, eyeing the letters as a few heartbeats pass. "Delphine, what happened with your ex-husband?"

She pauses for a long moment, and for a few of those tense seconds, I think she won't answer before she finally speaks. "I woke one day, and *poof,* he was gone . . ." Her eyes cloud. "As if he never existed."

I frown, knowing that can't be the whole truth of it.

"You don't know where he went?"

"I don't know *anything.*" She shakes her head in frustration. "My fucking mind is a battlefield. Every day I wake up at war with it, fighting this fucking haze I cannot escape, and I do not remember any of it!" she croaks as she lowers her eyes and the letters on her lap. "Pieces, tiny, tiny pieces, but never a clear memory anymore, and I read . . ." She releases an anguished sob, and my heart flinches at the sound. "I read these fucking letters so many times, but the haze will not clear to let me understand what happened to me. To understand where the Delphine who came to America went and why. I spend so much time trying to remember, Tyler. So much time in the fucking bath, in the battle, and fail every time." She cries openly now, tears streaming down her cheeks.

"And *I hate* her," she sniffs, her voice filled with venom, "the pathetic girl who wrote these letters. I despise her. I want to erase her from existence because the girl cannot be me! I don't understand her." She voices my own questions aloud, seemingly having no idea of the answer. "I cannot forgive her. I refuse to forgive her." Her jaw shakes as her eyes turn murderous. "Every day, I fight to be *nothing* like her, to never again be deceived by *'love the fucking liar.'* Being a brash bitch is better. Anything is better than that fool." She nods toward the letters. "But even she fucks up her life and has become a failure."

Pushing the scattered papers off her lap, she sinks into bed. Head resting on her pillow, she turns toward me as my hands twitch to grab her—to pull her into me and shield her from herself, from her own abuse.

Instead, I slowly lift my hand to palm her crown, gently

sweeping my thumb along her hairline as she levels me with the despair in her voice.

"The truth of what happened to me, to my husband, died with Celine and Beau in that fire, and maybe . . . I died with them because I feel like a ghost to myself now." Her breath stutters as she bares herself to me, gutting me. "I am so tired of losing," she whispers hoarsely, "of failing. So very tired, Tyler."

"You're not losing, Delphine," I whisper back.

She shakes her head to rebuke my words as I press in.

"I'm not just saying that to make you feel better." Sliding my hand down, I cradle her face, tucking my fingers between her cheek and her pillow, running my thumb along her jaw.

"I heard you. I swear to God I heard every word you just said, and now I want you to listen to me," I urge. "For once, I want you to listen to me and try to take my words to heart. Will you try that for me?"

She nods, her eyes focused on me, no longer searching.

"All today was, was just another bad day. Nothing more. So don't give it any more power than that. The sunset you love so much is proof you fought bravely, so keep remembering that on your bad days . . . and remember that when the clock ticks past midnight, it's another chance to win. I've seen you on good days, and you have them. It's just that days like today are good at making you forget them. But you have them. I've been there. I've seen them. I've seen the bold, vibrant, life-filled, beautiful woman on days she's won that battle. So, don't believe the lie a bad day is telling you. And truth be told, you're winning every day you show up." I press in. "Fighting for yourself will *never be* failing."

I continue to run my thumb gently over her cheek as her breathing evens out, and her chest bounces slightly in the aftermath. "Do you want to tell me why you went on a date tonight?"

"I don't know," she whispers. "Many reasons."

A notion comes to me, but I bite the question away and ask another, keeping my thumb running lightly over her skin in a soothing motion as she further sinks into it, her eyes softening as her lids lower.

"Swear to me he didn't hurt you," I implore her.

"Non," she whispers, "non, I scared him." She laughs without humor.

"Well, you don't scare me," I whisper, stilling my palm on her cheek. "So, do you want to have one of those good days with me when you open your eyes, General? Because I miss my fishin' buddy and best friend too," I admit, praying it doesn't cost me but unable to hold it in any longer. "I miss her so fucking much."

Behind her fresh tears, I see a sliver of hope just before she nods, the fire in my chest going inferno because I know I've kept her trust.

"Good. Then get some sleep because this soldier is eagerly awaiting your next order, and regardless of what you think of yourself." I swallow and swallow again, allowing the love I feel for her into my voice. "This soldier is in fucking awe of the fighter you are."

I sit with her a minute longer, caressing her lightly, until her eyes start to lower.

"See you tomorrow?" I rasp, my heart thudding at the look of her under my touch before I gently pull my hand away.

She faintly nods again in reply. The soft look in her eyes, the way she's staring back at me, has my chest blazing. But I force myself to my feet and toward the door, every step fucking grueling as my heart pounds in protest to go back to her. Just as I get to the threshold, her whisper reaches me.

"Il a prédit que je détruirais ce qu'il y a de bon dans tout homme qui choisirait de m'aimer." *He predicted I would destroy the good in any man who chose to love me.*

I glance back to see her sliding her hand beneath her

pillow. Her eyes focused on me. "Malheureusement, je savais déjà que c'était vrai." *Sadly, I already knew it was true.* She holds my gaze intently for another beat.

"J'espère que l'amour est bien plus tendre avec toi, mon beau garçon." *I hope love is much more kind to you, my beautiful boy.*

I swallow as she nods toward the switch. "Please turn off the light."

I do and stand there until her eyes flutter closed and continue to darken her door before leaving her with a whisper, a hope of my own.

"Si seulement tu me laissais te montrer à quel point l'amour peut être bon, belle femme." *If only you would let me show you how kind love can be, beautiful woman.*

***

WINTER 2005

>General Half-Pint: Privit what doign this delpihne queston mark

>I always know who this is, General Half-Pint. ;)

>General Half-Pint: You mad e wink face. I make it ;/

>Not quite, but you'll get there.

>General Half-Pint: I ment to do mean face ha ha

>I had a feeling. Feeling a little feisty tonight, huh?

>General Half-Pint: Oui and yuo will looes next batile so bad

>Looking forward to your ass-whoopin'

General Half-Pint: You army gong be so broke so can not fixx it

Damn. Should I be scared?

General Half-Pint: Hmm mabye

See you later, General.

General Half-Pint: Not if see yuo first

You nailed that use of expression! I'll make an American metaphor master out of you yet, and damn, you've got a mouth on you today.

General Half-Pint: Is not mout h imbcile is txting

I'm aware we're texting, but I can hear you speaking every time you text.

General Half-Pint: Oh can hear this questin mark   I'm so kick yuo in your asshloe

In my asshole? That sounds painful and yet intriguing.

General Half-Pint: Shut muoth Hurr y up I talk ng to the floor os to come to me

Okay, that text I didn't understand. You're talking to the floor?

General Half-Pint: Sory privit I my haze bad tonigt you at me tomorw batle

Got it. I'm sorry the haze is bad tonight. I'll be there.

General Half-Pint: No wink fcae queston mar k

I always have a wink for you, General. How about two? ;) ;)

***

General Half-Pint: Solier Dom tell you came to my hosue an I wsa not here I sad

Yeah, I think I just missed you. You're sad?

General Half-Pint: I mis you to nigt

You miss me, General?

General Half-Pint: wht, you not say you miss me fish budy question mar k

I always miss you, General.

Every fucking minute of every day I'm not with you. You looked so beautiful riding passenger yesterday, that sweaterdress, your gorgeous hair blowing in the breeze as you flashed me that fucking smile of yours. I thought I was going to lose my shit.

Backspace. Backspace. Backspace. Delete. Hold.

I can come back.

General Half-Pint: Plse come me now tmrrow to far way for good da y

Tomorrow is too far away?

General Half-Pint: Oui for goo d day with m y solder

If tomorrow is too far away from a good day with your soldier, then your soldier is on his way.

***

General Half-Pint: Jean stil l say me txet so bad /; tel l not txet him agn

I'm sorry. Your texting is improving a little.

General Half-Pint: Non no top dace arond trut h solder

Okay, not dancing around the truth. It's still pretty bad. You still get your letters backward a lot and misspell a lot of words, but I understand every single text you send. So how about you only text me and call everyone else?

General Half-Pint: good battle plan

You just sent a perfect message, General. PERFECT.

General Half-Pint: Took sooooo lon g to write.

I'll wait as long as it takes for a text from you. Perfect or not. I don't care. Don't let it worry you, okay?

General Half-Pint: I read wroet english bteter before haze and now so bad

So you used to be better at it, doesn't mean you have to beat yourself up for it.

General Half-Pint: Jean ebarrses me

Please stop before I stage a very accurate swing on my best friend that will daze him so hard it will feel suspect.

Backspace. Backspace. Backspace. Delete. Hold.

I'm sorry. He can be such a dick.

General Half-Pint: Don t be maen dom abot me

I won't. I wasn't even thinking about being mean to Dom.

General Half-Pint: Solder is Liarrrr tongiht

You have got to teach me how to do that Jedi mind trick.

General Half-Pint: Dom somtim take my smile waay but my solder gve it b ack.

I'll give you back every fucking smile he steals from you, baby. I promise.

Backspace. Backspace. Backspace. Delete. Hold.

Don't worry about your asshole nephew. Dom's just mad because his boots fucking stink. ;)

General Half-Pint: The y stink so bad I love wehn you make win k face)

See, that text you just sent was almost perfect. And I know you love wink face, that's why I do it.

General Half-Pint: the haze maek lettrs hard to dicpher when mind asshleo

Delphine, when did the haze start?

Backspace. Backspace. Backspace. Delete. Hold.

I'm sorry your mind is being an asshole, and it's hard to make out the letters. We'll just keep practicing together.

General Half-Pint: Oui Is so harrd to readn wriet English now

I'll help you all I can.

General Half-Pint: merci solder you such good friend be txtin budyy

I'm your man.

General Half-Pint: Oui Fish bud y goodnigh t

※※※

General Half-Pint: asshole if cme hous do not tikcle me

Asshole, huh? Your insults are so often spelled correctly that it's suspicious, General.

General Half-Pint: Imbeicle

Spoke too soon, but now that I know how ticklish you are, you are screwed.

General Half-Pint: non no screw me

Don't I know it.

Backspace. Backspace. Backspace. Delete. Hold.

I didn't mean it like that.

General Half-Pint: I knw imbeciel was joke No tickl me if come to house asshole e

Severed Heart

You secretly like my tickling, so you're the lying asshole, but all right, no tickling tonight. This asshole is on his way.

General Half-Pint: K make wink face texte to mee

How about I wink in person?

General Half-Pint: maybe hurr up

***

General Half-Pint: Hve bad day soder is snow

I just ran in it, but it's late. I didn't know if you were up. I can come over. We can watch a Star Wars DVD.

General Half-Pint: I am not cry tonght solder wan t to try to face snow alone I stroger now

You are stronger, much stronger, but that doesn't mean you have to face the snow alone. Let me be there for you. Maybe you can tell me why you hate it so much.

General Half-Pint: Non merci, non tnight do not want tell tired of cry in bath strongre

Okay, no crying or baths tonight, and we don't have to talk about it, but you can stop texting.

General Half-Pint: you don t wan text me is to much tired soder questn mar

No, not because I'm tired, but because I'm jumping over the fence. ;)

***

General Half-Pint: thikin non bad day but mad day mad faec ;/

Thinking about what things? Why are you mad, baby?

Backspace. Backspace. Backspace. Backspace.

Thinking about what things? Why are you mad?

General Half-Pint: I hate job thin boss tr y fuck me

Your boss is trying to fuck you?

General Half-Pint: he say imbcile things digusgtng

Give me his address. I'll fix the problem with your disgusting imbecile of a fucking boss really fucking quick.

General Half-Pint: Not funn y ha hah

Well, I'm not fucking laughing, Delphine. We will be talking about this face-to-face.

General Half-Pint: Don be imbicile jealus man

You have no fucking idea.

Backspace. Backspace. Backspace. Delete. Hold.

We'll talk about it later.

General Half-Pint: non hate jealous non soldeir I am roll my ey es

No need to roll your eyes and I'm not jealous. He shouldn't be talking to you like that.

General Half-Pint: Oui I will smash bos s imbeclie cock

Smashing his cock could do it. But you know you can quit working now anyway. Your nephews are officially fucking rich.

General Half-Pint: Not take ezekil jean mone y I not ea rn it

Ezekiel didn't earn it either, a horse did. ;)

General Half-Pint: Ha I laugh merci it felt so go od to lagh

;)

General Half-Pint: I feel beter now you gave me wink face. NO one else ner text me are only frineds I go to frezer not for icecream

It's okay if I'm the only one. I'm the only friend you need, right? We can talk about why you go to the freezer and not for ice cream when you're ready. Want me to come over?

General Half-Pint: Is okya just bad work I okay don have to come to me

Too late, General, I'm already jumping the fence ;)

SPRING 2006

General Half-Pint: Tyler, you are the best friend I've ever had in my life. You are so warm and kind. It comes from your eyes. I love the way you speak to me and listen to me. I don't think a man has ever really listened to me before like you do. Maybe Ezekiel. You make me smile every day, even on bad days. You battle snow with me. You make my heart feel lighter. Free. I am so happy when

I'm with you. Thank you for being the friend you are to me. I can't say this to your face because of my brash, but I want you to know I care about you very much. I hope I make you happy too sometimes like you make me. I hope I am the same friend to you that you have been to me. I hope you take this text to your heart, my soldier, and know that you have changed my life in many good ways.

I'm so fucking in love with you. I'm trying so hard not to drop my wrench right now, fly to wherever you are and confess how much while trying to keep my shit together in front of the clowns surrounding me. I can't stop thinking about the way you looked at me before we last parted. I want you so fucking much, but I'll be as patient as you need me to be. I promise . . . but please look at me that way again. Even if you don't, I'll wait for you for a dozen more seasons just for the chance.

Backspace. Backspace. Backspace. Backspace. Backspace. Delete. Hold.

General . . . I'm blown away. That text was fucking perfect. How did you do that?

General Half-Pint: She asked me to text you for her. She really wanted to convey it right. Hi Tyler, I'm Michele.

Oh, hi.

General Half-Pint: Sorry, didn't mean to make this awkward, but you should see the look on this woman's face. She talked about you for a good ten minutes before asking me to text you for her. I don't know what you've done to her, but if you have a brother, send him to the ABC liquor store off Main. I'm giving her the phone back now. Just thought you should know. Please don't hurt her.

Never, and thanks.

General Half-Pint: Soldier is me delpine again I hope not embarses you qusetion mark

Fuck no. God no. Not embarrassed at all. That meant so much to me. But General, I'll take your words any day. Your words mean just as much. Even if they aren't perfectly typed, they are perfect to me. Okay?

General Half-Pint: Oui Is so much tex makee my brian exploed but I want you knw feel frmy my hart

We can't have your beautiful brain exploding, now can we? And your soldier got your heartfelt message loud and clear. Can I come over?

General Half-Pint: I go t go work soo n sad face

Well, I just really wanted to come over to say my own heartfelt words to you. But I'll just text you that I feel the same. You're the best friend I've ever had, too, General. You make me happier than you'll ever know. But shhh don't tell anyone, or feelings will get hurt. Sean is a crybaby, so shhhh ;)

General Half-Pint: non, no tell sean non be brash bitc h make cry wha ha ha

Ha ha! I like brash bitch very much. Please don't ever change, Delphine. ;)

General Half-Pint: Imbecile

Ah, yep, there's my girl. ;)

***

General Half-Pint: You so cath so mush fish today soilder WoWWWWW

But you cooked them. ;)

General Half-Pint: IT tasted so bad shitttt do not lie asshiole I saw you gaggle

Hey, hey, let's not be too brash. It was edible-ish.

General Half-Pint: Bullshiittng I threw up got throw all ovoer toliet

Ok, I'll be honest. I threw up, too. For like an hour. Maybe we shouldn't eat fish from the pond anymore.

General Half-Pint: Non agree not eat poson fish but we fish agan soon quest mrak

Very soon. I'll pick you up early. Night General Half-Pint.

General Half-Pint: Nigth solider of my heart. Maybe see yuo in dream

I have no idea how to fucking take these messages anymore, and I'm losing my fucking mind. Please ask your God to put me out of my misery. I'm leaving soon, and I know I might need to let the idea of us go, but I can't. Especially when you say things like this and look at me the way you're starting to. I know I can't risk losing you to hasten our season, either. I'm going blind with the need to touch you, to kiss the wrinkle between your brows away and bite the lip you hold when you concentrate. To grab your shaking hand and press my lips to it until it's shaking in a way that feels good. God, how I want to make you shake in a way that feels good.

"But I can't. I'll lose you, baby," I blow out through a breath of frustration. "So I'll keep deleting these confessions, but fuck how I'm tempted to let one slip through. To hit the send button and see how it lands. But you're worth waiting for, General. You're worth this hellacious ache. You're worth it."

Hitting the combination of back and delete buttons I've alternated for months, I compose a text that borders the truth, but I know won't endanger us.

This soldier of your heart wants to see you in his dreams, too, General. ;)

"Why does it have to be in our dreams, baby?" I rasp, gently sweeping my thumb over her words on the screen before flipping the phone to pass it over the slick Marine Corps sticker attached to the back of it.

A sticker my recruiter gifted me on my last visit to his office. Rotating my phone in my hand, I weigh the view of her text against the sight of the sticker, the act mirroring the crux of what's happening inside me. What was originally the plan is starting to feel more and more like a choice.

It was my first face-to-face with Preston—a birthday gift from Tobias months ago—that amped my long-term vision and is now keeping me torn. I want both the woman and the career, but I can't put off enlisting much longer.

Stilling the phone back on the screen side, I scroll all the way back up, getting lost in months of texting. Even with the feelings our back and forth evokes, the sinking suspicion that started weeks into our exchanges begins to blanket me.

Not an hour later, I close one of Mom's books, worrying my lip painfully in indecision as the gnawing continues.

The apprehension remains as I step into a scalding shower and stroke out some much-needed release. Palming the tile, I pump the top of my cock as I choke out her name to one of a hundred visions of her, too easily summoned. This one fresh, ingrained just days ago. The vision of her crystal, sitting on the dock in a pale blue sundress, one of the straps resting at the top of her arm, leaving her shoulder bare. Her olive skin ripe for my bite and soothing. Her mischievous silver stare slowly lifting to mine as her lush lips followed.

When the gnawing continues as I towel off and dress, it becomes more and more apparent that I won't get a second of sleep until I finally accept defeat and that I've gone as far as I can on my own.

Decision made, I grab my phone from the bed, the stinging ball lodged in my throat, increasing the burn as I exit my bedroom in search of my mom. Knowing that if I'm right about my suspicions, it will fucking annihilate me.

Searching the house, I bypass Dad, who's fast asleep in his recliner, as Mom busies herself in the kitchen, packing his lunch for tomorrow. As of late, Dad's been helping Uncle Gray at the farm to ease himself back into the workforce.

An effort that hasn't gone unnoticed but remains unacknowledged by me. He's only inside mere months of decent behavior outside of the hellish years he put us through. While my heart wants to forgive him—especially after witnessing his spiral in the garage—my memory refuses to allow it as I dodge his every attempt to bridge the gap between us. Even attempts at small talk.

Easily pushing thoughts of Dad away as my heart rattles in my chest, I tilt my head in a silent prompt when Mom spots me approaching the kitchen. Her light expression immediately morphs into one of maternal concern as she nods before silently following me into the garage. Once inside, she stares up at me, her eyes creasing with worry. "Shit, Son, you're scaring the hell out of me. What's wrong?"

"Mom," I croak, the fissure in my heart widening as her eyes do in alarm.

"Normally, I'd tap into my patience here," she says, raking my expression, "but I'm terrified, so spit it out."

"I need your help," I whisper, hearing the mournful timbre in my voice.

"Anything," she says, "anything. Talk to me."

"If I do, not a breath of this conversation is to make it an inch outside of the garage or to anyone else, and I mean *anyone*. Not ever."

"You have my word, please," she assures, the concern in her voice increasing tenfold. "What's going on? Did something happen?"

"This isn't about me," I assure her, choking on the ache in my chest as my eyes start to burn, "this is about the woman I'm in love with."

Chapter Twenty-Six

Delphine

"M<small>ON DIEU</small>!" *My God*, I exclaim as Tyler stalks into my bedroom with a toolbox and stepladder as water pours from my bathroom ceiling. "I'm sorry, Dom is at the library," I add hastily. "I maybe should have called a plumber—"

"No need to insult me." He gives me the wink I love. "I'm *the* problem solver and have been known to be pretty good with my hands," he emits in a low rumble, waggling his brows.

"Imbecile," I roll my eyes, unable to help my smile.

"Well, good afternoon to *you too*, General," he says, surveying the leak. "Hate to say I told you so—"

"You love telling me so," I scoff, "and a new roof is very expensive."

"Nothing a simple call to France couldn't remedy, but we can argue about that *later*," he says before setting his toolbox on the sink and opening his stepladder, his hair and T-shirt damp from the ongoing storm. After placing the ladder in the tub, he reaches the top just as the sagging ceiling gives way, instantly soaking him. Laughter bursts out of both of us as he comically steps right back down, his mirth-filled, warm brown eyes meeting mine. Dark brown hair drenched, water drips from his long lashes.

At the sight of it, a stirring hits me as my eyes continue to trace the droplets trailing down his jaw and Adam's apple.

When did it become this pronounced? And his lips . . . so full.

I've noticed the smaller changes in him in our time together, but they've started to add up dramatically in recent months. The beautiful boy who approached me years ago with shadows in his eyes is starting to look more and more like a beautiful *man*.

"Well, shit," Tyler says, jerking me from my thoughts while surveying his soaked clothes. Grinning, he shakes off the excess water like a wet dog as I scold him, jumping back.

"Real hand man," I joke, shaking my head. "I'll grab you a shirt from Dom's room."

"That's *handyman* . . . don't scowl at me. You told me to start correcting you," he chuckles. "And I never proclaimed to be a *professional*," he taunts as I turn and hurry across the hall, opening a few of Dom's drawers before pulling out a black T-shirt. When I return to the bathroom, I'm stopped short by the sight of a shirtless Tyler, his head now in the gaping hole in my bathroom ceiling. The view from my vantage point utterly paralyzing.

My eyes sweep him from his boots to the powerful thighs straining against the denim—which hangs threateningly low on his hips. He's utterly etched in muscle, with deep lines on either side of his abdomen. His trim waist creating a small gap at the button of his jeans. The ridges in his stomach are heavily defined, with pebbled sinew on either side, leading up to a broad chest that looks cut from stone.

So much difference in him.

Should I feel this much guilt to appreciate the beauty of my best friend? Shame provides the answer as quickly as it did when I began asking.

"Definitely a roof leak," Tyler shouts, jerking me out of my appreciation for his efforts as he calls out to me, thinking I'm out of the room. With that knowledge, I continue to allow myself to feast. Ancient stirrings fuel my thirsty eyes, reminding me of the days I felt such desire.

My thirst only grows as I imagine gaining access to explore his body, tracing every inch of his etched skin with my—

Delphine!

Briefly, I entertain retreating to Dom's room to scrub my eyes—*my mind*—of such thoughts of him. Instead, I'm slammed back into the moment as I become aware of a return stare. A very, very intent return stare. And in the eyes peering back at me . . .

Molten brown flames roar, blazing a path straight into me. The hellfire of desire inside them consuming and cleansing my insides with overwhelming ferocity as I inhale a sharp breath.

Mon Dieu!

Unsure of my own expression, I stumble forward, holding Dom's shirt out and shaking it for Tyler to take so I can release myself from our paralyzing connection. But it's Tyler's fire that refuses to free me, the look in them all too familiar—the predatory hunger inside naming me prey. And I feel it, weakening me as I begin to shake with the force of it, willing myself to speak, to snap his debilitating hold even as my body responds.

Stop this now, Delphine!

"What is the issue?" I ask, my tone betraying my stupor. Stupor and shock that he's capable of such a look—a look he maintains as he slowly, so slowly takes the offered shirt.

"Will it be expensive to fix?" I ask in a telling squeak. The intensity flowing between us increases substantially as he takes a few heart-rending beats to answer.

"It's a roof leak," he emits in a low whisper, exhaling a harsh breath and clearing his eyes before looking back up at the ceiling. "I can't really get to it until the storm passes, but I can patch up the roof and ceiling once it dries out. We're lucky the leak will be isolated over the tub until I can get to the repair."

"Okay, Merci." I nod at his every word like a fool. "Let me . . . get you a clean towel before you put the shirt on," I offer. "You are soaked. What was I thinking?" I joke to break some of the lingering tension.

"Yes, General," he drawls, the command in his tone stopping me short from my retreat as his eyes roam from my face to my feet and back up. "What *were* you thinking?"

I turn and flee to my bed, pulling a towel from a clean laundry pile. Taking my time to steady my mind and breathe, I make my way back to Tyler, handing the towel over and placing a few others on the floor to soak up some of the water. As I mop up what I can, I reason with myself that I'm only curious after spending so much time with him. We've talked of everything in recent months but never broached anything about personal relationships. During those months, I found myself wanting and hoping to change some of his perceptions of me. But it's not his perception that has me fixated as I lift my eyes to watch him wipe the water from the expanse of muscle along his torso and stomach—swallowing when his eyes catch and hold my lingering stare. *Again.*

"So much change I see in you," I rasp out like an utter fool. Desire clear in my voice as his rich brown eyes flare.

"Likewise," he rasps back, his timbre smooth and full of insinuation, which covers me in goose bumps. "Changes for the better?" he asks, his own eyes taking liberties he has been careful to avoid before today as I give him the truth.

"*Very good,* you have taken your physical training *very seriously*, Soldier."

His lips lift slightly in amusement due to the apparent fool I have become in these tense moments. The amusement disappearing just as quickly as Tyler runs his teeth over his bottom lip, and I follow the movement carefully before he replies.

"That I have, General." I barely manage to conceal the shiver his tone elicits while willing myself to *stop* staring back. Tyler utters something low, and when I'm certain I hear 'tap dancing' as part of his whisper, I tense.

How did this become so difficult? It's been *nothing but easy* between us these past months together. Just yesterday, it was easy. Why is there such a difference today? Searching for a way back from this uncomfortable shift in atmosphere between us, a notion comes to me.

"Oh!" I practically shout, startling us both. "I have a graduation present for you!"

He frowns. "I graduated last year, General."

"No, this is a *soldier* graduation present. Come." I pull at his hand, and he follows me to my nightstand.

"Soldier graduation present?" he asks, brows rising in surprise.

"Oui." Reaching into my drawer, I grab my offering and place it in his palm. Staring down at it, he slowly brushes his thumb down the detailed etching carved into the handle as I explain. "This brought much luck to the soldier who owned it, and I want you to have that luck."

He widens his eyes in surprise. "This belonged to Matis?" Tyler shakes his head gently, his reluctance evident. "General, I can't take this." He lifts the pocketknife in his open palm. "I know how much this means to you."

"It's the last thing I have of my papa," I relay, "but remains wasted in my possession. I want it in the hands of someone who will use it. Of someone worthy, and Tyler, you are *so very worthy*. Please take it," I urge, closing his fingers around it.

"Okay, I will," he whispers as the tension builds again, this time in my chest. "This means a lot to me," he relays softly, his words heartfelt as he pockets the knife, his eyes holding mine. "I'll keep it safe."

I nod. "I know you will."

Eyes lighting, he flashes me a half smile, making his dimple pop. "So, is this the part where the Jedi disappears into the swamp alone, only to come out later kicking ass?"

"Oui," I sniff as his smile disappears. "Gah, I'm sorry." I shake my head in embarrassment. "I've been fighting these stupid emotions all week and thought I was capable today, but now I feel like imbecile."

"What? What emotions, what's wrong, bab—" He swallows when my eyes widen at his near-whispered term of endearment and rephrases his question. "What's wrong?"

"Nothing is wrong . . . I'm a little melancholy for this admission, but it's due." I press a tear away as his gentle eyes follow every movement carefully. I blow out a breath to try and steady myself as he inches closer.

"What? What is it?" he coaxes gently.

"The truth is, I have now taught you everything I know," I relay with a clear shake in my voice, but press through for the words he deserves. "You have worked so very hard all these months, Tyler. As you know, I do not give commendations lightly, but I am so happy to report you have surpassed my every expectation. Your stamina is close to inhuman. Your mentality is very, very strong. Your confidence is still irritating"—we share a smile—"but now justified by *education*, and you know you have mastered battalion," I state with a clear grudge and an eye roll.

"Beat you five times *in a row*," he boasts, buffing his nails on his shirt, which earns him my dead stare. "And oh," he draws out playfully before he begins to tickle my sides, "how you *hate that* because you definitely didn't let me win."

"Stop tickling me, asshole." I jump out of his reach, my scorn playful.

He chuckles at my retreat before giving me a bewildered shake of his head, eyes searching mine. "I'm really done?"

"Oui. Somehow, you moved up the ranks straight from private to general, but this is proof I did a good job, non?"

"Very good." He steps forward, grabbing my hands and shaking them lightly. "Thank you, Delphine." His whisper is so heartfelt it fully warms my insides. "I don't think"—he glances down at our connected hands, his thick, curled lashes flitting over his sculpted cheeks—"no, I fucking know I wouldn't have survived these past few years without you."

I balk at this. "Has so much time passed, Soldier?"

"We're a few months shy of it, but getting close."

"Wow," I say. "Well, maybe have trained you well, but you clearly failed because I am still a brash bitch." I buff my own nails on my shirt.

"Thank God." He grins. "But seriously, have you looked in the mirror lately, General? You're fucking glowing."

I harrumph as I turn to exit my bedroom.

"Deny it all you want, *kissing tramp*," he taunts, trailing me, "but you've become a slightly more tolerable and, dare I say, mildly happier human."

"Shut up before I kick your balls," I call over my shoulder as we head toward the kitchen.

"That's my girl," he chuckles, "and I mean, you could give it your best shot, but I doubt your little legs could kick so high," he teases as I pour him a glass of water from the faucet and hand it over.

"Ha-ha, so funny," I retort dryly before drawing my own glass as we stand side by side at the sink, watching the rain trickle down the windowpane as the storm wind batters the trees.

"Is it okay to say I'm proud of you, too?" he asks, his eyes imploring.

I swallow and nod. "It's okay, I know you aren't being condescending."

"Good because I am. So fucking proud. It's been beautiful to watch." His eyes gently roll over me. "So . . ."

He tugs at the loop on my shorts playfully. "You really setting me free? *Done* with me?"

"Non." His question brings me some relief. "Still and always will be a best friend and fishin' buddy, but your soldiering now depends all on you. And your ability to master blink to black." His eyes lower at the mention, which is telling, but I decide not to press him on it.

"Well," he says, "as newly appointed general, I have a mission for you."

"Oh?" I grin. "I don't remember agreeing to take your orders."

"Then how about a request?" He drops his eyes briefly.

"Hmm, now I am intrigued, General Jennings, spit out this request."

"Oof, say it again," he teases, "I love the sound of it coming off your tongue."

"Your request, imbecile," I counter dryly.

"Fine. I'm hoping you'll draw me a map"—he poses his question with hope in his eyes—"several maps. As many as you'll make me of Triple Falls."

I draw up my face in confusion. "Soldier, there are already many maps of Triple Falls. Professional maps."

"I'm aware, but I need an *expert strategist's* maps, with a few key variations. Including the underground hangout you told me about, that spot teenagers frequented during the sixties, remember?"

"Oui, because I was the one that told you," I retort sarcastically.

"Right, smartass." He shakes his head. "Well, first, I want an aerial map with coordinates. Then a detailed street map, and then a map with highlighted details of any other locations just like that underground spot."

I glance up and over at him as he keeps his eyes on the rain—another of his tells that he's hiding something behind this request.

"For what purpose?" I ask.

"I'll tell you when the time comes," he offers with promise.

"Planning to start a war already?"

"Maybe." He sips his water. "So will you do it?"

"This is a mysterious request."

"I'm a mysterious guy," he boasts, which earns him another of my eye rolls. "I'll make it worth your while." He gives me a slow wink.

"So I don't get to know why *or* what the payment is? That is much trust."

"Well, then." He refills his glass. "It's a good thing you trust me, and when I get back, we can—"

My stomach drops. "Get back from where?"

He glances over at me in confusion. "You know where. I'm enlisting at the end of summer."

The shatter of glass barely registers between us.

Chapter Twenty-Seven

Delphine

Tyler frowns down at my shattered water glass in the sink as I turn to face him fully. "*What?*"

"I'm enlisting at the end of summer," he repeats as I gape at him.

"You're not serious... Soldier, are you fucking joking?"

"What the . . . of course I'm serious." He cocks his head. "*Are you joking?*"

"You haven't said anything in months and months!" I shout, my tone and reaction surprising me. Bile climbs my throat, my anxiety spiking as I drop my eyes. I was already in fear of losing his constant company due to the end of our training.

"I know it's a sore subject for you, so I never bring it up," he admonishes, alarmed by the sudden shift in me.

"I t-thought you had reconsidered." Panic continues to rise as I clamp my mouth shut while dread thoroughly seizes me. When I start to pick up the broken glass in the sink, he nudges me aside to do it, but I refuse him— needing the task, any task to keep myself together.

"Delphine," he whispers in a consoling tone as I continue to carefully retrieve the shards. "Those plans we made together are for the future *after* I serve."

"News to me now. Then what are you waiting for? What

have you been waiting for? Go, Marine. I have no more to teach you anyway. You have what you need from me."

"Well, *hello bullshit*, are we multitasking today by lying *while we tap dance?*" he bites out with edge.

Refusing to acknowledge his statement, I keep my eyes on the glass as I continue to pick at the dozens of tiny shards.

"Delphine," he exhales, "I told you this when we started—"

"You were barely seventeen," I argue, cradling the glass in my hand, "you *were* confused—"

"I've never been confused about enlisting," he states, taking my wrist and dumping the glass I gathered from my palm into his to protect me, as if I'm a child, before disposing it into my nearby trashcan.

"I don't understand why you're giving me hell about this," he says, gripping the side of the sink as I start to gather more of the broken pieces. "This reaction is ridiculous."

"Do not call me ridiculous!" I snap, unable to justify a single word or reaction bursting out of me. Unable to stand another second of the unease, I head for the freezer.

"Stop," he snaps, rounding me to make me face him, "don't. Not yet. Talk to me."

I push at his chest, and he doesn't budge. "You talk *to me*, Soldier. Explain *to me* why you plan to enlist in a controlled army, carrying out others' orders. Orders of corrupt puppeteers. I taught you how to *lead*, to *build and run your own army*, not to fight in someone else's wars!"

"Tobias is—"

"Has no idea what he is asking his biggest asset!" I screech. "I work with you for your future with Ezekiel and Jean Dominic, not the fucking US military."

"Look, I agree it's flawed, but that's why I'm—"

"Flawed?!" I gawk as my hands begin to tremble. I haven't raised my voice *like this* to a man in years with such concern. I steady myself on the counter as that truth sinks in. Seeing my sudden shift, Tyler covers my shaking hands with his own. I bite my lip as I stare down at them.

Who will steady my hands when he leaves?

Selfish. I'm being selfish, and my selfish mouth speaks again. "What are *you thinking*, Soldier?"

"I'm thinking you can't write the whole bushel off for a few bad apples. There are thousands and thousands of good men and women who sign up with the best of intentions. So, what I'm thinking is that I'm doing this for them, for the dad I had, and for my Uncle Gray, whose hands sometimes shake like yours. What I'm also thinking is that I have to have the fucking resume to protect any higher-up in government. If we get Preston into office, think of what we can do and the changes we can make."

"If, Tyler, *if*," I say, as my entire upper body begins to tremble.

"Don't be afraid," he utters softly. So close, he's so close. His smell surrounds me, bringing me comfort in one heartbeat while searing me the next. "Speak your mind, yell at me. I can take anything but you being afraid of me."

"I'm not afraid of you, Tyler," I exhale, "I'm afraid *for* you."

"Do you honestly have so little faith in me?"

"All the faith in the world!" I admonish, chest heaving as the anxiety builds and builds, and my eyes start to water. "All of the faith I am capable of resides inside *you*, Tyler, and my nephews. You have all my respect, you have my hopes, and you have my—" I stop myself as realization sets in that I'm squaring off with not any man but this man, and it's becoming more and more clear why.

He runs his thumbs soothingly over the back of my hands, his eyes dipping to the movement as I study him up close. So beautiful, my best friend, and he's leaving. He's leaving.

"Glad you think so," he whispers, bringing his pleading, rich brown eyes to mine, "but this is my fight. This is my stake in this club. This is my chance to try to make a difference."

"Tyler." I take a deep inhale. "You are needed here. *Here*, in Triple Falls, I did not spend all this time . . ." I bite my lip, disbelieving of my selfishness. "All this time."

I pull my hands away before stalking over to the freezer for my pint. He's at my back in an instant, crowding me against it. He cradles me with his body as my selfish tears start to fall.

"*Who* needs me here, Delphine?" he asks, his voice telling in that he's aware of his answer as his warm breath tickles my ear. "I'll come back. You know I will. I can't go a single day now without talking to or seeing my best friend."

The feel of him has me opening my freezer door, and he slaps it shut just as quickly, inching in and cradling me with his body, his warmth enveloping me. "Please don't. Please talk to me."

"No point," I croak weakly. "I know you well enough to know you have made up your imbecilic mind."

"*Who* needs me here, Delphine?" he repeats, as he grips my hip with a warm, calloused palm while burying his nose in my hair. He's steel behind me, solid man, and briefly, I get lost in the feel of him, sinking into his hold and comfort. "God dammit . . . *now*?" he whispers, running his forehead back and forth along my shoulder.

I stiffen in understanding of his meaning as he slowly turns me to face him, caging me in his arms against my refrigerator. Edging in, his eyes implore mine, the tension in the air thickening, his perfect, full lips so close.

"You are too valuable to be someone else's soldier," I utter hoarsely.

Grabbing my hand, he presses my palm to his chest. "I'll never be anyone else's soldier, and I think you just realized that."

"My soldier would stay," I whisper as he lifts his hand to stroke my cheek with gentle fingers. He's so close now that we're sharing breath, our foreheads touching.

"Soldiers don't stay, General," he whispers, "but your soldier will come back to you. Every fucking time you order him to."

"Then I order you not to go." I lick at a tear as it reaches my lip, and he follows the movement.

Licking his own lips, he slowly lifts my bleeding thumb to his mouth before wrapping his lips around it and gently sucking. The added feel of his tongue tracing the tiny cut has my eyes fluttering.

Entranced, I watch as he continues to suck my thumb, and a soft whimper I can't hold escapes me. His eyes fire as it leaves my parted lips. The need to flee fills me, the desire running rampant between us with no way to contain it. It's too prominent now, too present and threatening. As my breaths increase, I realize this attraction has gone on longer than I've allowed myself to acknowledge. The look in his eyes confirming as much, as well as my response to him. When did I let this happen?

"I'm here now," he whispers in a way that heats every inch of me.

I drop my eyes. "Tyler, we—"

"Look at me, Delphine."

I do, as the blaze from minutes ago reignites fully in his eyes. So easily summoned that my entire body draws tight in response, and a pulse between my thighs begins to pound, demanding relief.

"You're the most beautiful goddamned woman I've ever laid eyes on," he states emphatically. "I'm sorry you don't like that to be noticed, but just so you're aware, for me, it's fucking impossible not to."

When I try to escape his caging embrace, he keeps me loosely trapped between his swollen biceps, his palms on the freezer. Eyes drilling into mine, breath becomes hard to hold at the intensity residing inside them. "Tell me why I can't say it. Tell me why I'm not allowed to take notice of it or compliment you, even if only to do that."

"You know why." I swallow. "Men's attention has brought me nothing but misery."

"Because of Alain?"

The casual drop of his name unnerves me further. "This is not for us to discuss."

"Do you ever *feel* beautiful?" he demands.

"Let me go."

"No, I'm sorry, not this time," he offers, "this conversation is past overdue. I'm done tap dancing around this, Delphine. We can't even go a few minutes anymore without fucking each other with our eyes, and I don't want to, I fucking refuse to ignore it anymore." He pins me with his fire. "I want you so fucking much, it's eating me alive, and I'm done playing ignorant to the fact that you want me too."

I gape at him. "You don't know what you are saying. So much can change in a short time, Tyler . . . within a single blink."

"You think I don't know that? My whole life has imploded in blinks the last few years, but this isn't a blink type of thing. I want to give you all of them."

In his eyes, I see his resignation to continue to confront the feelings between us. To deny me the retreat to put us back in our place in an effort to keep his precious friendship.

"I'm pushing nineteen now, Delphine, and you know—"

"*Nineteen*," I scoff. "Do you hear yourself, Soldier? Let me go."

"Fuck no," he snaps. "No, we're doing this."

"I watched you grow up," I swallow.

"I could say the same, but we both know that's bullshit. We never really or truly saw each other until that day in the living room. Even then, I'm positive I was the first to notice, and you're all I've seen since."

"Tyler," I groan, every hair on my body raising on its end as his mouthwatering smell surrounds me, making this fight so much harder.

"Nearly two fucking years we've spent together, and you know everything about me," he says adamantly. "You know me inside and out, my every weakness, about my parents, about my darkest thoughts, and I know almost as much about you, aside from one fucking elephant that's constantly in the room and is now in our way." He hesitates only briefly before stating his demand. "It's time to tell me about Alain."

"How do you even know his name? I'm positive I have never spoken it to you once. I never speak it to anyone. Ever. Drunk or not."

His eyes drop. "Do you want me to lie?"

It's then I see the truth of what I've suspected for some time. Since I saw his eyes roaming over highlighted passages of my French translation bible when he thought I wasn't looking. His eyes moved *with ease* because he was *reading*. "You are fluent."

He nods slowly.

"You read my letters."

He keeps unapologetic eyes on mine. "Yeah, I fucking did," he counters as humiliation stings me as well as his easy admission.

"Get out," I say, ducking from beneath him as he grips my arm and pulls me flush to him.

"I know it was wrong, and trust me, I felt that guilt, but I had to know," he whispers roughly, his voice weak with torment as he cups my face, sliding his thumb over my cheek. Even as fury and embarrassment threaten, I see the pain in his eyes. "I had to know," he rasps out, "what or who hurt you so severely that you numb yourself."

"It was not your fucking place to know," I snap, as tears of humiliation sting my eyes. "Not your place!"

"Why not me?" He continues to gently sweep his thumb across my cheek as if I am what is most precious to him, and I feel the sincerity. Have felt it. "Why isn't it my place? Why can't it be? I'm the fucking man who's been scraping you from every surface your pain leaves you lying on. Talking you down on your worst days, facing your fears with you before tucking you in at night. I don't have a right to know?"

"I've never asked you for any—"

"Oh, the fuck you didn't. You asked us all to because of the way you've treated and punished yourself, but I'm the one who *wanted* to know. You've left those letters and pictures out in plain fucking sight for years for anyone to see. Didn't you ever once stop to think I might get curious?"

We stare off for long, tense seconds. Seconds in which I'm too mortified to speak as he carefully weighs my reaction.

"I think deep down you wanted me to know, and that's why you're not as angry as you want to be right now. So, I'm not going to let you make me feel like shit for giving a fuck about the woman who has literally *saved me* from some of my darkest hours over the last two years. Who has strengthened me during the worst time of my life while suffering every day in her own fucking skin. I cared, I still care, so fucking much, and so I read them because I had to know." He swallows. "Now that I do, I can't for the fucking life of me understand how any man could look at you, get the best parts of you, look into your eyes, touch your beautiful body, and fucking hurt you like that."

He swallows again, and I feel the pain in his words, his eyes. I can feel it from him, as I always have. I've felt it through our shared looks in the dark—through our whispered confessions. I recognize now we've been more to each other than teacher and student for some time, and our relationship shifted well before today, though I can't pinpoint when. But he's been taking on my pain while confronting his own for much longer. From the beginning. Right up to the first day when he fixed that buckle on my suitcase because he knew it meant something to me. My eyes spill over in defeat as he forces me to realize and confront what I've known for some time now—that he's managed the impossible and now resides as part of the beat in my chest.

"Delphine, if I apologize to you right now for prying into what hurt you, it won't fucking be sincere because I had to know. Had to . . . and I hope, someday, that you'll trust me enough to tell me the whole story." I lower my eyes, and he tips my chin, leaning in so close his lips nearly touch mine. "But until you do, I'll be staring into your goddamn house every night that I'm capable. To make sure you know that I won't let anyone hurt you like that ever again. With the hope that your soldier makes you feel safe because that's all he wants. Well, not all he wants," he whispers roughly, "but now he's made that clear, too."

He tracks the tears trailing down my cheeks and considers them before gently brushing them away.

Shame fills me as he inches even closer, and I stiffen in recognition that I want it—that I want him closer. That I, too have been thinking about him differently. Never with this much attraction before, but enough to shame myself. That I search my window every night for him, feeling safer when I see his silhouette across the street. That I feel beautiful and cared for by the way he listens to me. That I have felt more myself with him than any other since Celine. But whatever this attraction is, I won't allow it to destroy the peace I have with him. Or his peace.

"I will not risk our friendship for this. Whatever you think you feel—"

"Oh no, you fucking don't," he snaps. I meet his eyes only to see rejection and hurt shining in them. "If I don't get to say anything more aloud, you sure as fuck don't get to dismiss and deny what hasn't even been spoken but is so fucking obvious between us. At least in the bright light of fucking day, right? Because we both know what happens between us in the dark, the looks we share before you close your eyes haven't all been innocent. At least not in the last few months."

"Get out," I barely manage to say.

"No, whatever *I think I feel*," he scoffs, "you feel it too, and it's been worth every minute of the wait to see you recognize it."

"Wait for what?"

"For our season," he declares.

"What season? You are leaving."

"You can't be serious. You're going to use the one thing you fucking *trained me to do* to try and push me away?"

"No soldier of mine would ever be so fucking foolish."

"Me becoming a Marine is not what we're talking about anymore."

"Yes, it is." I can't stop the shake, I can't stop it, and I lash out as he notices it with his prodding beautiful eyes. "If you are going, go now. I won't help you with this any longer. I will not—" I shake my head. "This is a mistake."

"All right," he snaps as a fire lights in his eyes, "if we're lying about the nature of this fucking argument, then I can't agree with you. I'm sorry. I'll always be the soldier you made me first and foremost, but we will have that future," he declares with arrogant confidence. "The one we planned."

"You lie to us both," I declare back, ducking out from under him. "Get out."

He remains steadfast, tone unflinching. "Love may have lied to you in the past, but I'm not them, Delphine. You know I'm not. You trust me. This is just your fear talking."

"Please leave," I order weakly, my weakness for him leaking from my every pore. "Please, Tyler. I need space."

Perplexed, he stares over at me, chest heaving for long seconds as I cower.

"God dammit!" he barks, and I jump in response before he stalks out of the kitchen. Snatching my pint, I jump again when he slams out of the front door. Reeling, I sink against the refrigerator, letting my selfish tears fall, hating myself for what I've done to him and for what I feel.

For what I want.

For the truth that now beats clear in my chest. For the truth he spoke aloud, one that I avoided the second the whispers started in both my head and my heart. The whispers that told me that he not only brought back a trust I believed myself incapable of ever having again, but also other emotions and feelings I had long declared myself immune to.

Happiness.
Contentment.
Adoration.
Longing.
Desire.
So much desire.

Shame threatens to consume me for the last as I nurse the pint until I'm numb to it all. Sometime later, I feel myself being lifted, warm lips pressing to my temple as I'm deposited into bed. Pulled under from too much drink, I feel the gentle brush of his fingertips along my profile just before his whisper of promise surrounds me. "I'm coming back. I swear to God, Delphine, I'm coming back to you."

"Soldier," I finally croak, willing myself to rouse, to open my eyes. But when I finally manage to, he's gone.

Chapter Twenty-Eight

Tyler

"Slippin'" by DMX croons from a nearby speaker playing background to Sean's latest philosophical rant. One I've tuned out of from where I sit in a child-sized bean bag on Dom's bedroom floor.

"You're missing my point, man," Sean argues while pinching the joint between his fingers. Ankles crossed, his dirty boots hang over the edge of Dom's decades-old twin mattress. Perched against the wall at the head of it, Dom flips the page of the book in his lap.

"I don't think you have a point," I grumble, peering through the gap of Dom's bedroom door to the vacant room across the hall. Tobias's recent extended absences are more notable since he gambled his way into becoming a millionaire and forming Exodus. That power play starting a pendulum swing, its underside serving as the chopping blade now gradually lowering toward Roman.

With Sean stepping up and my current army positioned, I'm as comfortable as I can be leaving. Aside from the guttural ache for the woman somewhere in this house, that has me mentally pushing back the departure date further and further away. I've exhausted myself in the days since our fight to give her space. Continually running past my recruiter's office to avoid the signature, pulling extra shifts at the garage, upping my workouts, as well as wearing my fucking wrist out in the shower—*the usual.*

Growing more and more anxious to get to her with every hourly chirp of my watch, my hope rides on that if we can work things out, I'll be stationed close. Luckily enough, there are plenty of bases within driving distance, so I can keep a close watch on the club while lengthening our growing roster. Hopefully, while still earning the woman I'm growing desperate to claim.

That is *if* I can get her to give in. Aside from the physical, it's been surreal to get so close to her. If the attraction wasn't so fucking brutally apparent now, I might've been able to settle for our friendship alone. Now that it's out there, I can't let it go. The torture is evident in my obvious agitation in these last few days and only made more apparent when Sean brings his Zippo to the end of his newly rolled joint.

"Don't light that shit while I'm in this room," I snap.

Dom flips another page without looking up. "Don't be a dick. You know his piss has to sparkle."

"Is secondhand smoke a myth?" Sean quips with the click of his Zippo, running the flame teasingly along the joint. "Shall we find out?"

"Fuck you." I stand to make a quick exit while giving him a withering look. Closing his book, Dom, too, glares at Sean, no added words necessary.

"Jesus, I wasn't going to light it," Sean says, ducking under our wrath-filled stares. "I was just fucking around."

"Remember the last time you fucked around and ended up with a piss puddle in your panties?" Dom clips, rubbing salt in the long-healing wound between Sean and me, his brand of brash far worse than his aunt's.

"Jesus, Dom," I expel on exhale, shooting him a cutting look.

"Sorry, man," Sean clips toward me, eyes lowering.

"It's cool, brother," I assure, after noting his long swallow. "I'm just in a shit head space tonight."

His stinging eyes lift at my tone, holding mine for a beat before he nods.

"I think I'll go for a run," I give in an excuse to make my exit.

"Don't stray too far," Sean says, "we shouldn't be long."

Their mission tonight is to do recon for their upcoming heist. One I had a major hand in devising but am not allowed in any way to participate in. An order doled out by *both* King brothers because of how close I am to marching.

"I'm good. I'll just catch up with y'all tomorrow." As I start to make my exit, I spot the plastic-wrapped cap and gown hanging on the back of Dom's bedroom door and glance at him. "Tobias coming?"

Dom lifts a shoulder without looking up. "Wouldn't know. You talk to him more than me these days."

Sean catches my gaze, giving me a subtle shake of his head that the subject of Tobias is off-limits. While Tobias might skip the ceremony to keep a low profile, I know he'll be here to celebrate after in some way.

Closing the door of Dom's room as they spark up, I stalk through the house, following the drift of French music to spot Delphine's boom box on the ledge of the open kitchen window—a tape playing, pouring a melody through the open screen.

As I approach the sliding glass door, I spot dozens of drafts of the maps I requested on the table. The sight of what looks like endless hour's worth of effort has my insides rattling. Confirmation that she's been thinking of me since the night I scooped her from the kitchen floor for the first time in months. Gutted that *I* was the reason for her overindulgence that night as I tucked her in and whispered my promise. Knowing she heard me, her eventual return whisper saying as much as she called my name in summons just after I reached her bedroom door. It was all I could do to continue to give her the space she asked for. It was both brutal and beautiful to watch her realize her feelings for me. So much so it's been a different kind of fucking hell delaying whatever decision waits for me on the other side of the glass door.

A door I'm stopped just outside of by the view that greets me. The tiny soldier that's utterly captured me—mind and heart—sways in the middle of her yard, arms wrapped around her as if she's self-soothing. Hands gripping her hips, her head is tilted skyward, and I quickly burn the vision of her into memory as I have so many others.

All images of the formidable, temperamental woman I knew now erased by the sight of her running off the pond dock and jumping into the water while plugging her nose like an eight-year-old.

Another image of her drip drying on the dock, just after, hand propping her head as my eyes traced the curves of her body a second before she turned back and beamed at me. The animation on her face as she watched her first movie in a theater. Telling stories across the firelight at the orchard. Playing Battle. Sharing snow cones while watching the sunset on my tailgate. Filling our days with simple things and enjoying simple pleasures as our feelings became anything but.

Years of memories between us now. Years together where we went from mentor and pupil to friends and to whatever she decides we are now.

Following her line of sight, I take in her view. Lightning flashes in the distance, defining the silhouette of the trees hovering over the wooden fence. A faint littering of stars twinkles just next to a looming storm cloud. Just below, a luminous half-moon sits nestled between the branches of a large oak. Thunder rumbles the ground for a few lingering seconds, and Delphine doesn't so much as flinch. Lost in thought or some memory, she continues to sway, hugging herself in the middle of the yard.

The wind kicks up slightly as I, in turn, get swept away by the sight of her. And fuck, how I love the look of every inch of her. My attraction only amplified by the darkness she camouflages, which, to me, feels like a jagged turnkey, a key that lines up perfectly with my inner lock.

A turnkey who's harnessed everything that resides inside me, which, by the second, feels on the brink of coming undone.

Leaning against the brick to the side of the door, I fall further with every sharp inhale of want, contented enough by simply watching her as the tips of her dark hair dance across the expanse of her small back. She's dressed in white shorts and a tube top—both her shoulders and feet bare.

Even as I decide laying eyes on her is enough for now, I both *feel* and *see* it the second she senses me and looks over her naked shoulder.

"Tyler, it's the perfect night!" she declares, subtly wiping her eyes, her voice tearful, which has my chest cracking wide open, confirming what I already know. It's me she's thinking of, and my imminent departure causing her tears. Certain of it, I also know it'll be hell in making her admit it.

"Come, dance with me," she urges.

"It's about to storm," I point out uselessly. She waves away my objection, but I stay where I am, knowing how dangerously close I am to my breaking point.

"Come," she whispers. "Come dance with me, Soldier," she urges, reaching out for me. Blowing out a breath of defeat, I push off my heels, head and chest buzzing with the feelings already bouncing between us.

"I'm not much of a dancer," I admit, gripping her offered hand and halting her movement by pulling her into me. The impact of her hits me harder than I expected as I allow her to decide where my free hand will go. As she situates us, her hand grips mine before she rests our now threaded fingers against my chest and draws the other to rest on the small of her exposed back. When she begins to sway, I mimic her movement, inhaling her light musk, which catapults my thirst into overdrive.

Kicking myself in the ass for indulging her, I shadow her lead as light rain starts to fall. It's the sight of Dom's bedroom light going dark, and the rumble of his Camaro seconds after that permits me to get lost in her. The feel of her in my arms negates all fucks I have left to give in that respect as she hums, her light, airy voice vibrating along my chest. My entire body ignites as I press my splayed fingers into her silken bare skin and pull her tighter to me, stroking my thumb lightly down her spine.

"What is this music?"

Her sigh is breezy before she speaks. "A song I used to dance to with my papa. In the wildflowers."

"It's catchy," I tell her, "I like it."

She laughs lightly. "No, you don't."

"I'm listening. I'm trying to understand what the fuss is about."

"It was a different time," she utters as I pull her closer, taking liberties because while she might be buzzed, I'm already drunk on her. It's while listening that my chest bounces at the irony. I lean down and begin to whisper in her ear.

"Oh, she was so beautiful, I dared not to love her. Oh, she was so beautiful, I cannot forget her."

It takes a few seconds for me to realize she's stopped dancing and is gaping at me. "You truly are fluent."

"I have two French best friends." I shrug. "So it made sense to opt for French instead of Spanish." Though I don't mention, I'm fluent in both and adding German by the day.

"It's humiliating you can speak *my language* so fluently after such a short education while I'm still trying very hard to master yours," she admits sheepishly.

"You're succeeding."

"Maybe verbally, but my texting is still terrible," she whispers.

"It's perfect to me," I murmur, dropping my eyes so she can't read what I'm hiding. Of what I'm becoming more certain of, especially after talking to my mom about what her ailments are, where they might stem from, and how. It's a serious discussion we need to have, but the *when* of relaying this is tricky—along with her responsiveness to the conversation.

The moon sinks further between the branches of the oak as I glance away briefly to try to regain my bearings. The wind kicks up slightly, and the rain is still light, more of a drizzle lining our skin with droplets.

"Well, maybe one day, when you forgive me, you'll let me practice my French with you."

"I told you I will never forgive you," she counters. "When are you leaving?"

"That hasn't changed since our fight." I grip her tighter. "The end of summer. Which is still months away, General. We have time to fish, swim, play Battle, and watch movies. Anything you want."

"Imbecile," she spouts, hurling the insult without giving a damn whether it hits or not. "Why, Tyler?"

"Stop. You understand why," I scold, cutting the bullshit, and her eyes drop with that win. "You couldn't possibly be reviving this argument because you're going to miss me?" I ask, point-blank. One last stretch of my hand, of my fucking heart.

"Hmm, one less mouth to feed," she jabs, her eyes lifting to mine as a soft smile tilts her lips. A smile that guts me. Another dismissal.

"As if you cook," I jibe back, my tone lacking life before I press our tethered fingers into my chest. "Tu vas me manquer." *I'll miss you.*

She stills briefly, but I don't miss it—the hesitation. We continue to sway until the song ends, and another begins to play. "So, what's got you in the dancing mood tonight?"

"I don't know," she lies, "what puts *you* in a mood?"

"Lots of things," I answer just as vaguely.

"You're doing this on purpose," she reproaches as we continue to hold each other like the world is fucking ending while making small talk. She's lying about her mood, her eyes reflective of that as the need to confront her summons all the willpower I have left.

"Doing what?" I counter in a tone of clear condescension.

She looks up at me through thick black lashes. "Mimics . . . mimicking me."

"Ah, well, you're currently doling out bullshit like a Pez dispenser, so I didn't think you would mind."

She wrinkles her perfect nose, and the light smattering of freckles is more pronounced due to her short length of time in the spring sun—with me.

"What is a Pez?"

"A sweet candy that comes in small doses." I widen my eyes. "Kind of like your good moods."

"And you're ruining it with your smart mouth," she quips.

"Liar," I rasp out. "You love my smart mouth. You love that I spar with you."

A few beats pass as we stare on at one another, fully absorbed before she speaks, her tone clearly affected. "Maybe."

"Maybe?"

"Maybe I'll miss my soldier." Her voice shakes with the delivery, as does the last of my patience.

Unable to handle another second, I grip the back of her head and tilt her face up to mine. "How much?"

Her eyes search mine frantically, and I see a hint of fear before she tries to pull away from me.

"Tyler—"

"Tell me I'm imagining what's been happening between us, and I'll call you out on that lie."

"You are."

"God dammit, stop it," I scratch out, gripping her tighter, *"enough."*

She immediately starts spouting out some reasoning I know is contrived. "We've been spending much time together and have a very strong friendship and care for one another deeply. There can be nothing more. Don't be an imbecile. You're a young boy."

I take her blow and rebound just as quickly.

"I'm both a *man* and the soldier you helped to create, and you've done an incredible job of ignoring it these last few weeks, fucking months, but I'm not alone in this anymore, even if you don't want it to be true."

"You're doing exactly what I told you not to do that night," she says adamantly, still trying to loosen herself from my grip.

"What night?" I ask, knowing exactly what night things started to shift and perking up at her mention of it. "And what was it you told me?"

"Not to make promises that you won't keep. Saying things—"

"You *heard* me." Her eyes instantly drop, confirming she heard the whisper I left her with the night of her date. Fire lights in my veins at the truth of it. "Nice try, General, but your most important lesson about being a watcher, an observer is pinpointing *motive*. If you ignore that you heard it, you don't have to acknowledge it happened. You fucking heard me whisper those words to you and know I meant them," I declare, cupping her face with my palm while bending eye level. "Are you drunk?"

"Why?"

"Are. You. Drunk?"

"Tyler, I—"

"Like I'd fucking care if you were." I force whatever words she starts to convey away as I crush her mouth with mine, my kiss anything but gentle. Gripping her hip, I pull her fully into me, and she gasps against my lips, feeling just how fucking hard I am—*everywhere*—for her. Her return kiss is hesitant as I rebuke any resistance with the swipe of my tongue demanding entry, and she slowly, so slowly, opens for me.

Groaning due to the permission, I thrust in and feel her breath catch as I taste and explore, licking the roof of her mouth. Delving into every corner, I savor the feel of it, relieved by the fact she's kissing me back.

She's kissing me back.

Our tentative kiss turns wildfire as I dive in fully, my lust in overdrive.

Her moan vibrates my tongue as I groan in response, my body lit, every muscle coiling as I let myself go—fusing every thought, every fantasy, every single memory of her I can conjure into my kiss. Palming her ass, I lift her as she clasps her hands behind my neck, curling into me as I roll her against my length so she can feel what she does to me.

Rain begins to pelt the iron table feet away, the storm intensifying around us, mirroring the culmination of emotions inside me as I devour her, fusing them into the contact. Inhaling every one of her moans as fuel, I keep the connection, keeping the kiss going while refusing to let up.

Now that I'm positive it's mutual, I'm not fucking letting it go. As if she senses that decision, she pulls back abruptly.

"Mon Dieu," she pants against my lips before glancing around us frantically, "what am I doing? Tyler, put me down."

"We're alone, Delphine." I blow out a harsh breath, not loosening my arms one bit. "Don't pull away from me. Damn you," I whisper hoarsely. "We *both want this*."

"Are you crazy? Put me down right now," she orders, more insistently, even as her eyes linger on my lips.

Seizing the moment once more, I capture her mouth, and her whimpered protest brings my cock to a raging status. The kiss cut far too short when she again rips herself away.

"Tyler," she croaks, in a way I know her protest is hard won, "let me down." Reluctantly, I release her slowly—keeping her close as possible as I do—so she can feel just how fucking much I want her. Her fast intake of breath my only consolation. Once on her feet, she turns abruptly to head back toward the house. Bending from the impact, I palm my thighs with a low "fuck" before she turns back to me on a dime.

"This never happened." Her voice carries on the increasing wind surrounding us.

"Oh, it happened," I snap, stalking toward her as she retreats, backing her against the brick of the house next to the open door. "We're not breaking any fucking laws, and before you go spouting off about age and what's appropriate, save your breath. I'm not listening to that bullshit."

Chest heaving, her nipples spike through her dampening tube top as her body naturally draws up against me. The dim yellow porch light illuminating us enough to clearly see one another as I stand my ground.

"Denying it won't make it true," I whisper forcefully. "That kiss said differently, and you're not going to convince me otherwise."

She shakes her head incredulously. "You expect me to take this . . . *you* seriously?"

"Yes, and when I get back from—"

"Never." She jerks her chin. "I don't wait for men."

"Then I'll be your first because I'm worth waiting for."

She gapes at me. "Confessions of a boy with misplaced affection."

"Declarations of a fucking *man* who's already matured beyond his years. I haven't been a boy in a long time because my life and the people in it made it that way. And you know it, you fucking know it. Ask me in a year how I feel about you, and I'll say the same, and the year after that."

"You *don't know* what you're saying," she dismisses.

"I haven't even begun because you've refused to let me, so why don't you hear me out before you turn me down." I swallow. The need inside to convince her to believe me has every word coming out raw and unrehearsed, never truly thinking I'd get the chance to utter any of them.

"There will be no other women for me because there is no other woman meant for me. I'm certain there is no other woman alive who will hear these types of promises from me because you're all I want."

She pauses, her eyes glazing over as she shakes her head in disbelief.

"Wait for me, and I'll give you any life you can dream up."

"One kiss and you think you have some say in my future and expect me to stay faithful?" She harrumphs. "You must be joking."

"Look at me," I snap. She does, her eyes searching, forever searching.

"Jesus, how you're fucking tap dancing right now." I hold her gaze. "We both know this isn't just about the kiss, and this"—I gesture between us—"runs far deeper than physical. Trust me with your heart, trust me with that much. When I get back—"

"Non," she clips. "I won't entertain this, *you*, another second. You're a boy, and I'm—"

"Call me a *boy* one. More. Fucking. Time," I grit out in warning as irritation attempts to take the reins, but it's my heart that grips it before firmly pressing it back under. "We both know I'm more of a man than any other fucking sorry excuse you've dragged into this house the last few years. And I only say *a few* because that's how long I've been paying attention. Since the first time I truly saw you for who you really are, not what you hide behind or your cruelty and attention-seeking tantrums."

Her body tenses with the insult as I press in.

"You were right. There is a side to me that exists that most don't and won't see." I rake my lower lip as her eyes flare in surprise. "One I've been biding my time to introduce you to, but only *if* you finally saw me for the man I am. And you did, you have, maybe for longer than you're admitting to yourself, but it happened."

"Tyler," she counters, as if reasoning with me, "you *are* a boy—"

Within a heartbeat, I've got her plastered to the side of the house, facing the brick. "I warned you," I hiss, holding her in position with one palm while running the other along her smooth stomach as I dip to deliver another. "*Mask off, Delphine.*"

Rain ticks loudly on the overhang above us as I wrap her hair in my fist, gently pulling it to the side while I bite into her shoulder. Her answering moan spurs me on as I inhale her scent, flirting the pads of my fingers along the top of her shorts to make my intent known.

"Une si belle femme." *So beautiful.*

Heart sputtering wildly as she sags against me, I force myself to further test the waters, unbuttoning her shorts and pausing to give her another chance to object. Her answering whimper has me sliding my palm into her shorts, my fingertips gliding into the silky top of her underwear and straight through her soaked slit. I don't bother to hold my groan when I find her drenched and needy. Fast pants start to leave her as she arches her back, sliding her arm up to hook my neck while gripping my hair. To pull me *closer.*

Closer.

Permission.

Every single cell in my body ignites, white-hot fire roaring in my chest as I fight my instincts to go feral and devour her. Whispering my lips against the curve of her neck, I bide my time, calming myself to the point I can effectively speak.

"Every day," I relay roughly, rimming her pussy before thrusting a finger into her. She buckles against me as I keep her upright. "For fucking years." I bring the slick pad up to her clit, whispering it in tease before driving it back into her. "I've imagined touching you like this." I bite into her shoulder a second time as she arches further against me in offering. "Kissing you." I flick my tongue along the shell of her ear, palming her mouth to muffle her escalating moans to ensure she hears me. "Fucking you, making you come. Just the thought of stretching your pussy with my cock is enough to get me off." Her moan vibrates my palm as she bucks her hips, and I massage her with my fingertips before plunging back into her insanely tight, wet heat.

"The idea of *us* coming together this way." Lust coats every word of my admissions as she soaks my fingers, sinking against me, gasping against my palm. "It's everything. *You* are all I want."

Freedom zings through me as I start to kiss her neck, running my fingers back and forth, bringing her close until I know she's agitated. Until her hips start to frantically buck for more friction. As I pull my palm away, unchecked, choppy moans begin to leave her as I escalate the workings of my fingers. Purposely stirring her up as my cock strains in my jeans, begging for some relief, for her. Denying us both but satisfied as she continues to writhe against me, I pull my soaked fingers out of her, cutting off her protest by pushing them through her parted lips.

"A *boy* couldn't get you this wet. You won't be fantasizing about what this *man* would've done to you had you shut the hell up."

Stiff in surprise, she hesitates a beat before closing her mouth around my fingers and sucking with abandon. I curse, eyes fluttering when she adds her tongue. The swirl of it around the tips of my fingers has my control slipping briefly as I run my raging cock along her back. As she starts to shake in want, I pull my fingers out of her mouth.

Slowly turning her against the brick, I command her eyes, willing her to face the man doing this to her. Chest heaving, eyes wide, pupils dilating with desire, she gapes up at me. Into the wildfire that I'm sure reflects in my eyes as I suck on my fingers to savor what's left. Once I've taken my taste, I palm the brick beside her head and bend so we're eye level.

"I don't live like a *boy*, think, act, or *fuck* like a boy. So, it's probably best that you brush up on that definition before you ever think about applying it to me again."

Gripping her hip, I yank her bottom half flush to me, flipping up her tube top and exposing her breasts before running my calloused palm over them—stroking her pebbled nipple deftly before roaming to the other. With my open hand, I run back and forth between her perfect tits and peaked nipples, getting lost in the sight of her silken skin. In the look of her, submissive and wanton beneath my touch as her eyes hood into silver slits.

As close to naked as I can get her where we are, I put enough space between us to slide my hand into her shorts before flipping my wrist to thrust my fingers into her soaked pussy. Adding my thumb, I start to slowly massage her clit as she shakes under my touch.

"Ah, mon Dieu," she cries out, her back arched against the brick, body drawn taut, arms dangling lifelessly at her sides. Keeping my fingers going, I dip and pull one of her pebbled nipples into my mouth, sucking feverishly before lapping at it with my tongue.

Gasping, she clutches my head to her chest as I slowly fuck her with my hand, biting lightly at her nipple before soothing it with both lips. I work her just enough to keep her on edge and wanting. Enough to keep her focused on my touch but aching for more. Aching for *me*.

When I pull away, leaving both of her perfect tits soaked with my kiss, I stare down at her with every bit of pent-up desire I've been shielding for far too fucking long. Her silver-gray stare remains latched to mine, feeding the lightning buzz now ricocheting between us.

Free hand roaming, I greedily cover every inch of her exposed skin. Running my fingers along her throat, palming her shoulders, her breasts, her torso, and her stomach.

"Do you feel beautiful, Delphine?" I whisper as she arches into my every touch, responding eagerly to every single movement, body drawn just as tight as her pussy is around my fingers. Lips swollen from our kiss, she watches me lick my own for remnants of her taste.

Dying to sink to my knees for more, I'm too entranced by her response to give up a second of it. Slowing my fingers, I again palm the brick next to her, leaning in as she writhes under my touch.

"Look at me, baby," I murmur with every ounce of the love I feel. "Look into your soldier's eyes, listen to his voice, and you'll see just how beautiful you are to him. You'll understand what touching you like this does to him,"

I order as her body hums against mine with need for release. "You'll realize to him you are *anything but* poison."

Her eyes eagerly soak in my expression as I slow my touch as she chases it with her body. In and out, I stroke her intimately with my fingers as I beg her to see what's in my eyes, my heart.

"Can you sense what's happening inside me? How good this feels for me because of how beautiful you are inside and out? *Answer me*," I order, rimming her again, tracing her soaked entrance before extending my finger as far as it can go. I'm rewarded with an entire body shiver. "Tell me, can you see how beautiful you are when you look at me?"

"Oui," she croaks. "I see, Tyler," she rasps out, her eyes watering as I hesitantly withdraw my fingers. She mewls in protest as I slowly lean in, brushing her lips lightly as I unbutton my jeans. Her eyes drop as I take one of her idle hands and cover my heart while taking her other and guiding it into my boxers to wrap it around my cock.

"Yours," I declare. "This"—I cover the hand on my heart—"is yours, and this"—I squeeze the hand now holding my cock and thrust it a few times into her firm grip—"also belongs to you."

Her silver eyes shine brighter before she releases her fearful tears while I do all I can to quiet them, banish them.

"Utterly and entirely *yours*," I whisper in offering as she stares up at me, her lips parted, her return expression granting me my answer before I ask the question. "Tell me, beautiful," I ask her, as tears spill over her cheeks, "is love lying to you right now?"

Her answer comes out in a croak. "Non."

Our pull magnetic, I dip just as she lifts, and our lips meet in a soul-rending kiss. We take our time exploring, discovering, and feeding, our tongues dueling in a perfect mix until we're gasping, and our hands are eagerly mapping the other. When I pull back, I don't stray far, our foreheads touching. Chests still heaving, I lower her top and refasten her shorts while feeling her watchful eyes on my profile. Meeting them, I rebuke the guilt I see starting to threaten.

"All you should feel, or that I hope you feel right now, is *safe*," I murmur, "*worshipped* and *beautiful*. I want to give that to you and so much fucking more." I press my forehead gently into hers. "What's happening here, what's happening between us, started pure and remains pure." I stroke her cheek with my thumb. "It happened gradually and naturally. Neither of us forced this. Just . . . wait for me. I can't be here for you while I'm gone, but I'll come right back to you."

She refutes my words. "I'm not your problem, Soldier."

"No, what you are, is my fucking *reason*," I declare, pulling back slightly to command her eyes. "My reason to *fight* and my reason to come home. You are home. Haven't you figured that out yet?"

"You say these things, but you don't know what your life will become."

"I know what I want it to be," I utter. "And I'm standing here telling you that whatever happens outside of *us* will revolve around the *two of us*, not the other way around if you let this, *us*, happen."

She shakes her head adamantly. "You're going to become something you cannot deny or push aside for something as silly as a woman. Tyler, your future is so big—"

"You're not just any woman, never have been or will be for me, and I know fucking well what promises I can and will keep, especially when it comes to you. Don't presume to tell me how to think anymore. You've done enough of that. Not when it comes to *this*, anyway. This is where I prove to you that a man can be worth waiting for. I know a part of you believes me. Trust that part because I know you trust me."

Dipping, I press one more kiss to her lips and look her right in the eyes with a soul-deep declaration. "*Your* soldier. *Loyally* and *faithfully* yours."

She softens against me, even as she gives an incredulous slight shake of her head. "Tyler—"

Kissing her one last time to quiet what I can of her fears, I pull away and fasten my jeans, slowly inching backward to the fence as my entire being lights with fury that I'm no longer touching her. But I can't have her the way I want to tonight. I've come on too strong already, and I want to let the idea settle. I want it to be her decision if we get more physical. Our eyes remain locked like magnets, even as I land on the other side of the fence. I revel in the fact that she's staring after me in the way I've been praying for while considering my words, considering *us*. So, when she opens her mouth to speak, I beat her to it.

"It's already done," I declare vehemently. "It's done, Delphine."

Tearing my eyes from her, I turn and stalk home, my chest alight with that truth.

Chapter Twenty-Nine

TYLER

Bass rattles the bay doors courtesy of Mobb Deep, "Amerikaz Nightmare," as Dom secures a clip into his Glock. Pride thrums through me, that the act and ease in which he does it now is first nature as he addresses my anxiety. "Don't think about it."

"Like that's fucking possible," I counter, eyeing the discarded cap and gown lying on the couch behind him in the bay. Dom had rid himself of them not long after crossing the stage today, as did Sean. As he took those steps toward his diploma, I felt his pause before he scanned the crowd. Physically *felt* his hope in that moment that Tobias was somewhere amongst the families in the small stadium. Delphine, the only blood relative that did show up for Dom, had kept her distance, sitting on the other side of the entirety of the Roberts crew.

Distance I let her maintain once everyone scattered outside the high school to take pictures. Though she looked beautiful, she was nervous enough, and it was visible. But it was her disappointment when Dom barely acknowledged her presence that broke my fucking heart.

My residual anger and resentment towards the brother standing in front of me now morphing into concern as I watch him strap up.

"I need to be there," I stress as Sean pulls a clean T-shirt from a nearby package after discarding his button-up. While most of the recently graduated are readying themselves for tonight's parties after their rite of passage, my brothers are strapping up to commit a robbery. With the police busy with the task of answering calls for said parties, we decided it was the perfect time to strike. However, I can't help shaking my head at the irony of it while real fear sets in.

"If you carry it out just like we planned, a single shell shouldn't touch ground," I remind them both, the need to go with them overwhelming as my heart thuds steadily. We've pulled a lot off in the last year, but this is by far the fucking riskiest. The fact that I planned this particular grab doesn't sit well at all. Though the plan is simple enough. Between the crew we've assembled and each's specific skill set—which I assessed and assigned—it *should be* a cakewalk. It's the risk of being discovered by *who* we're stealing from that has me on edge—*the Town of Triple Falls*. The chamber's funds and treasury. Our take— eighteen grand. A few thousand less than Roman's last contribution so as not to make it too obvious. A contribution in which we've decided to reallocate where the money goes.

It's our first real test, and I would think it idiotic if the cash grab—thanks to Roman's boasting—wasn't close to foolproof. Even so, I can't help the unease skittering up and down my spine.

"Fuck this," I say, grabbing a vest to suit up. Dom chuckles and jerks it from my grip.

"We get caught," Dom says, tossing it to the floor, "you don't get the high and tight haircut, and I'm not missing that. Go find something to distract yourself with."

I glance around the garage at cars I won't be focused enough to fix properly. "Not fucking likely."

"And not our problem," Dom clips, his tone playful, his eyes the opposite. "You're too valuable to risk."

"And you're not?"

"We've been over this," Sean sighs, drawing a cigarette

from his pack and lighting it with the flick of his Zippo. "I have a good feeling about tonight."

"Well, you're a fucking nauseating optimist, so that eases none of my worries," I snap sarcastically.

"Between you two broody assholes, someone has to keep things light. Face it, I'm the yang to your yings, baby," Sean says, wrapping the Velcro around his chest before double-checking his stash of guns. His own movements now those of an expert in weaponry. A part of his impressive growing skill set.

"It's the control freak in you"—Dom speaks up—"that's fretting for *nothing*. Handle that shit," he orders me. "We're going to be doing a lot of this kind of shit solo while you're doing pushups for Uncle Sam, so get used to it."

I open my mouth again to protest, and Dom cuts me off with his stare, his eyes just as calculating as his aunt's. They're so much alike it's uncanny, and no doubt why they barely get along.

"You're about to make the biggest sacrifice of the three of us," Dom points out in an attempt to put me at ease.

"It isn't a sacrifice," I say. "It's the plan."

"It's your *freedom*," Sean reminds me. "What about that?" he asks through a plume of smoke. "The US government is about to *own your ass* for four long years, at the least, and we can't ever repay you for that. Not in any capacity."

Jeremy and Russell honk from the van they secured outside as Sean takes one last drag of his cigarette before crushing it under his boot and tousling my hair. "You be a good boy and sit tight. Mommy and Daddy will be right back."

"Fuck off."

"Love you too, brother," Sean says through a chuckle. "If, by some bad luck, I don't return, I'll miss you most of all."

"I'm hurt," Dom says without an ounce of emotion. "Meet you back at my house after," he tells me.

"I'll be there," I assure him.

As they exit the bay, I give them both a solemn nod, making as much peace as I can with it as I close up the garage. Minutes later, I'm sitting outside a gas station, and just as I'm about to get out, my phone rings.

"Hey T, I was just about to call."

"Where is your head?" he asks, sensing my state.

"Confident in the party but fucking hating I'm not going," I say, exiting the truck and walking into the gas station.

"You know, technically, you'll be the first partygoer," he gives in a rare compliment.

"That's not exactly true now, is it? How's France?" I ask, pulling a soda from the cooler.

"Too much of the same."

"I thought you'd be here today." I weigh whether or not to tell him about Dom's disappointment as he replies.

"I'm boarding now."

It's my first genuine smile since I left Delphine on the porch.

"He's going to be stoked, Sean too."

"Are they ready?"

"More than," I assure him, knowing his brother is most of the reason his heart beats. Sean and I are the reason for the rest of them. What I've come to realize is that after slowly losing my own family these last few years, I'm with my brothers in totality. Aside from Barrett, who's been unexpectedly keeping himself occupied with Charlie since the first day he checked on her and Jane in the labor house. Rumor is that Charlie is giving him chase. According to Barrett, not a lot of chase, but he's declared he's in it for the long haul. Time will tell. My own long-haul chase is still up in the air as my clock starts to continually tick out. I stare into the cooler as Tobias jars me by speaking up.

"Where did you go?" T prompts.

"Sorry, just thinking of a way to distract myself until the cavalry comes home." *A way that doesn't include racing to your childhood home and burying myself in your aunt.*

In that sense, this situation is a little fucked, but worth it for her. My predicament now is that I was attempting to give Delphine space and time to come to me, but with Dom's order to meet him at his house, that timer's been set. The feeling in my chest was not at all one of protest with an excuse to show up. I have to face her and whatever decisions she's made. However, the fact that my cell phone hasn't rumbled since that night isn't a good sign.

"Keep me updated," he spouts, and not as a request.

"Will do," I say, "see you soon."

"Tyler."

"Yeah, T?"

"Are you telling me everything?"

"I don't talk personal shit," I tell him, grabbing a bag of chips and jerky off an end cap.

"Yes, brother, you've made yourself very clear on that. But I'm here."

"I know." I run my hand through the top of my hair after setting the drink and snacks down on the counter. The cashier stands from where he was perched, reading a paperback on a nearby stool.

"If I'm honest right now, I'm not looking forward to the haircut."

A deep chuckle sounds over the line. "The payoff, though," Tobias reminds me.

"Yeah, the fucking payoff." I half grin, half grimace, knowing that this step will set so many of our plans into motion. "See you soon, brother." I cut the call a second before a toddler barrels into me.

"Whoa, buddy, where's the fire?" I ask through a chuckle, bending down to see the little guy's mouth smeared with ketchup, his tiny fingers covered in it as well as he chews.

"What're you eating?"

"Shicken nuggets," the little boy replies, his dark brown eyes wide.

"Oh, yeah? Love chicken nuggets," I tell him.

"Sorry about that, man," the cashier says.

"It's fine," I say, taking in the little guy's features as a woman races down the aisles toward us, calling his name.

"That you? You Zach?" I ask.

"I, Zach." He presses a tiny ketchup-coated finger to his chest.

"Oh my God, I'm sorry," the woman says breathlessly as she approaches. "So sorry," she admonishes, scooping the toddler in her arms as we both stand before she shoots the cashier a glacial side-eye. "I told you I was doing inventory and to watch him."

"It's fine," I tell her, "he's adorable."

"That'll be five fifty-two," the cashier says.

I hand him a bill as I keep my eyes on the kid who's reaching for me.

"Hole me," Zach demands.

"Can't tonight, buddy, but maybe some other time," I tell him, ruffling his hair.

"He likes you," the woman says with a laugh, her eyes meeting mine and roaming over me briefly before she freezes. I frown at her rapidly shifting reaction to me as she opens her mouth and closes it just as quickly, her eyes darting from me to the cashier. A second later, she nods toward the aisle she just raced down as Zach continually reaches for me, wiggling in her arms to get to me.

"Hole me!"

"So, I'm just going to take him back now," she adds as if she owes me more of an excuse. "I'm really sorry about that," she says with a pleading look in her eyes. Perplexed, I give her a slow nod in reply before she turns and flees toward the open door at the back of the gas station.

The fuck?

Utterly puzzled by her fast retreat, I turn to the cashier as he deposits my change in my open palm. "Is that your wife?"

He nods. "Yeah."

I glance back in the direction she fled. "She looks familiar."

"You go to First Baptist? She sings in the choir."

"No . . . huh, must be from here."

"Yeah, she works here most days." He looks down at the empty silver rungs just next to the register before shouting, "Grace!"

Every hair on my body stands on end, a clear vision filtering in of a bar on one of the worst nights of my life.

"What?" Grace calls from the back.

The night I lost my hero.

"We're out of plastic bags up front!" he shouts.

The night I lost all sense of security.

"Tim, I'm a little busy back here!"

"I don't need a bag," I hear myself say as my veins start to boil. Swiping my haul from the counter, I barely register Tim's parting wish for me to have a good night. Just before I clear the door, I glance back across the top of the aisles to meet the terrified eyes of the woman standing in the doorway of the back room. Her own eyes already trained on me as she holds her son. A son with the same color hair and eyes as mine and those of my father. The guilt and fear marring her expression due to her part in helping destroy my family. By having an affair with my father and fucking him in my mother's bed.

My father's *Grace*, but the destruction of my own.

***

Minutes later, I pull up curbside at Delphine's to see an unfamiliar truck in the driveway. Blinking at the sight of it, crimson threatens to steal my vision. Vision I just spent long minutes clearing in an effort to get back from the state I was in—to get back to her. Eyeing the storm door, I feel the jealousy snapping me into motion as my heart stutters with the notion of what it could mean.

She wouldn't.

No, please, no.

Fuck no.

Heart thundering, I barrel out of my truck and make it up the steps just as a man—who looks to be in his late twenties—steps out of the front door. In an instant, I'm gripping his neck, lifting him to his toes as I size him up. Within a second, I recognize just how easy it would be to snap his neck and dispose of him. Easily assessing within the same length of time just how little I would feel if I committed the act. Loosening my grip slightly as his face starts to redden, he instantly starts stuttering as I scan him from head to foot. "Hey man, I don't know what—"

Regripping his neck, I plaster him to the side of the house, my hand making it clear I don't want any excuse from him. Instead, I deliver a threat I have every intention of carrying out if he doesn't heed the warning.

"Leave without another word, or you'll cease to fucking exist." When he opens his mouth, I jerk my chin in final warning, knowing there is murder in my eyes. "Just get in your fucking truck"—I drop my eyes to the name stitched on his shirt—"Eric, and drive away."

He must see his imminent death in my gaze because he manages to keep from so much as brushing me when I release him before scrambling to his truck. Gripping the storm door handle as adrenaline does its thing, I do my best to counteract it, even as her warning months ago reaches my ears and snakes its way into my psyche.

"Look at me. I am a villain."

Just outside the door, I take long, calming breaths to ease my way out of my fury fog. When I feel I've evened out enough, I stalk into the house, the breathing having done absolutely shit to ease the hellfire happening in my chest. Ears perked, I hear the water running. My heart thunders with my footfalls as I stalk down the hall toward her bedroom.

"I sabotage myself and make many unforgivable mistakes."

Bursting through the bedroom door, I hear a tell-tale slosh of water, knowing I've scared her as I scour her bed. The sight of it does nothing to ease the burning, forever the same unmade mess it always is. Inhaling deeply for a few long seconds, when I finally flit my focus to the bathroom, I see Delphine leaning back into her tub, her eyes now closed—a bottle of Smirnoff on the floor next to her.

How long was I breathing?

Taking the few steps over, I glare at her from the doorway as she keeps her eyes closed, purposefully ignoring me. It's all I can do to keep from jerking her from the tub as I scour the milky water concealing most of her, the tops of her breasts the only thing protruding above the steaming surface. Her silky dark hair is already soaked, droplets of water line her lashes as her lush lips slowly start to curve up and into her signature smirk. "Are you going to keep staring or—"

"Did you fuck him?" I can hear the anguish in my voice and decide I don't give a fuck if my vulnerability is showing. If this was her attempt to thwart us, she delivered exactly where I am my weakest. She knows her opponent and precisely how to destroy me.

Her shoulders go rigid at my question, and very long seconds pass before her metal eyes open. Inside them resides a glare I haven't been the recipient of in a very long time.

A look that names me her enemy.

"Tyler," she sighs as if in disappointment, "I told you—"

"Did. You. Fuck. Him?"

She shakes her head, not as an answer, but in annoyance.

"I told you last week, and I'll tell you now, no man will ever have claim over me again."

"Alain," I state her ex's name, "never owned you. He just manipulated you, and you let him."

She lifts and uncaps the waiting vodka bottle, taking a long pull as if I didn't speak a word. "You don't know what the hell you're speaking."

"I think I do."

"He was a phase," she sighs, "a very dangerous phase like I am for you."

"That's where you don't know what you're speaking," I snap, mocking her.

"You're right. I'll never master my English. Maybe I should go back to France. My job is done," she whispers.

"You actually think you raised him?"

"Ah hello maskless, Tyler." She smirks. "There you finally are . . . but save yourself the trouble and your insults, Soldier. They mean nothing to me." Even as she expels it, her voice shakes with the delivery. "I gave you nothing," she sighs. "Since the very first time I saw that look in your eyes. Where did I go wrong?"

Her words infuriate me. I should have known she saw it. Always saw it. "Because you fucking looked back," I say, the shake of rage in my voice clear.

"Haven't you figured it out yet? You're so intelligent, Soldier, but these feelings are making you less so. Maybe this is the one thing I have left to teach you." Her lifeless eyes roll over to me before she stares at the opposite side of the tub. "Love is *not kind*, is never worth it, and is not worth waiting for."

I'm already at her side as she finishes.

"Yeah, let's drink to that." I snatch her bottle, taking a few long pulls until I know I'm going to feel it.

Now perched on the side of the tub so I'm sitting adjacent to her, I allow myself to feast, the water becoming clearer by the second. In size, she's tiny. Toned legs, luscious, curvy hips, perfectly full breasts, and mouthwatering dark rose-colored nipples. The sight of her naked in my state is blisteringly painful. It's my first real eyeful of the body beneath, and despite the fact I want to drown her, I want to drown in her far more.

"Thinking about putting my head underwater?" she prods as I set her bottle out of reach.

"That was one brutal move, General, but this isn't a fucking game for me, so make up your mind," I snap.

"Am I still worthy of the love you seek from me?"

"I don't have to search for the truth when it comes to you. That's *your* confusion, not mine. I know who you are beneath your little veil of bullshit." I run my palm along the top of the water and cut my eyes at her. "Answer me."

She remains mute, staring back at me without expression, her eyes void of all warmth.

"Jesus." I shake my head. "You really do play your part so fucking well."

"I don't act," she snaps. "Not for you, not for anyone."

"Maybe not. Your self-destruction and sabotage is far too fucking messy to be rehearsed. Did. You. Fuck. Him?"

"Go home, Tyler. I should never have entertained this."

"*I am fucking home* and just in time to clean up another mess," I hiss. Leaning in, I slowly grip her neck, sliding my thumb to her pulse point as it pounds at a steady rate—not the accelerated beat of someone who just actively had sex and is coming down from any type of high. Even so, her expression remains calm and defiant as her void, lying eyes roll over me.

"My mess, Tyler, not yours."

"We'll see about that."

She grips my hand and squeezes it, cutting off her own breath. "You don't have it inside you."

I cut off her air altogether. "You're sadly mistaken, but I would never fucking hurt you. You know that. You fucking know that. Physically or otherwise. Not in the ways you've been hurt. Not in the same ways he hurt you. But unlike that piece of shit you married, I *will fight* for you, Delphine. I'll fight you with everything I have to make you mine and to keep you mine. To keep you smiling and happy. To keep your beautiful face free of fear. To keep you protected and feeling safe for as long as there is breath in me."

She stares off with me, unflinching as I relax my grip enough for her to breathe and she laughs in my face. "Isn't it past your bed—"

In an instant, I'm jerking her soaked body out of the tub and pulling her onto my waiting lap. Her back to my chest, she thrashes in my hold as I steady her and keep her in my steel grip.

"Let me go."

"Such a weak protest, you don't want that. You're fighting a man who only wants to show you differently... did you fuck him?" I can hear the crack in my voice in the delivery.

"Did he make you come?" I ask, spreading her legs before hooking each one over my knees. She doesn't at all struggle when I palm her stomach and rest a beat, careful not to cross the fine line I'm walking. When she remains mute, I lower my palm and slide a finger through her pussy, revulsed at the thought of someone else having just touched her.

My chest goes inferno as I force myself to forge on, unsure if I can forgive her, but in the next breath, I do. Knowing I'll probably have to a thousand more times before this war is over.

"Did he come inside you?" I croak, my heart threatening to give out.

She remains mute, her body pliant as her silence slices into me.

"Did you let him use you to punish yourself for kissing me? For wanting me back?" I push another finger inside her as she starts to writhe in my hold. "Did you imagine it was *me* as he fucked you?"

"Non," she snaps, as I widen my thighs to widen her own as she soaks me through my jeans and T-shirt.

"Did he make you *feel anything*? Because I know *I do*. That's what you're fighting. It's not me."

She moans when I add another finger, and I feel her begin to shake in my arms as I glide them in and out. In and out.

"Nah, you're not capable of that, right? You feel nothing. Just an empty shell, only meant for abuse, or whatever cock you decide on."

It's then she snaps, lashing out, clawing at the arms encasing her as I continue to fuck her with my fingers, opening her up, giving just enough pressure on her clit to get her agitated. Stilling her head with my own, I put my lips to her ear.

"What's wrong, Delphine? You want the fucking conclusions drawn but just don't want anyone to put a voice to it? It's the decision you make, over and over, and you expect someone to view you differently? To see you differently. You want to be viewed as *more,* but act this way."

Ripping her head from mine, she turns and looks me right in the eyes. "I will *never* love you."

"You're already starting to," I declare confidently, even as that burn has its way with me. "And you're fighting it. Have been. That's why you're punishing us both. Did you stage this or see it through? That's where I'm stuck. Guess what? You've done your worst, and my feelings haven't changed. There's not a fucking thing on earth you could ever do to me to change them. So your little show was all for nothing."

"I never should have trained you," she snaps. "I never saw you as anything more. You're lying to yourself."

"Now on that, we agree, until it happened, it's still happening. See, we're both hungry, but *you're the one starving.* Fuck how you need it and how much I'm desperate to give it to you." I press my fingers in and flick the tips over her G as she bucks her hips against me. "And not just for my touch, but for what's inside me."

Her head falls back on my shoulder when I begin to touch her like I want to, caressing her clit with tenderness as I slow my fingers and run them across her swollen flesh, my cock past full mast beneath her. "Should I feed that starving woman?"

"Please . . . s-stop," she begs, and I instantly do. I withdraw my hand, and she goes limp in my arms.

"I'm sorry," I rasp out roughly, my heart speaking for me as the rest of me makes the decision that I can't care what her answer is. Lifting her to stand, I tip her chin up to bring her reinforced steel eyes to mine. "I don't deserve this. I've been nothing but good to you. Please, Delphine,"

Severed Heart

my stretched, bleeding heart asks, begs her, "tell me. Did you fuck him?"

When she doesn't answer, I gently push her away from me before stalking toward the bathroom door and stopping.

"I only lied about one thing tonight," I say, glancing back at her as I bat the burning tear from my jaw. "If you meant to hurt me, well played. I'm bleeding freely, and for you, I will continue to as much as you need me to. I'll take everything you have to throw at me. Everything. I'll eat their sins, I'll bathe in their wrongs, I'll pay for the way they hurt you. I'll take it all—for you. I'll take it all just for the chance to be with you."

Even if I can forgive her, I can't move forward with anything I want to give her tonight, the searing in my chest too raw. As I clear the door, she answers. It's faint, but I hear her soft whisper. "Non."

I keep idle, my back still to her as breaths start to come easier for the first time since I pulled up. This woman will be the end of me. She already fucking is. I've been patient because I've had no choice. I turn to face her, my eyes roaming over her dripping body. So goddamn beautiful and so dangerous. Need sieges me, but I go for words over actions.

"Tell me you'll wait."

"Non," she says, clutching a towel to her chest.

"Give me *something*."

"It would be a mistake."

"I wholeheartedly disagree, but since you're so good and apologetic about making those, make one with me, and I'll prove you otherwise."

"Tyler," she whispers. The curl of my name on her tongue has me snatching the towel and tossing it before yanking her flush to me and staring down at her with everything I feel.

A second later, we're locked in an explosive kiss, tongues dueling as she greedily kisses me back. Palming her bare ass, I lift her from the floor, her feet dangling. She cradles my head in her arms, fingers digging into my hair as she furiously sucks my tongue. I feed just as greedily, not letting up as needy, urgent moans rumble her throat. Only then do I deposit her on the carpet in front of her mattress.

Taking a step away, I fist my hands at my sides as the last of my control threatens to buckle.

"Get on the bed, spread your legs, leave your hands on your thighs, and don't take your eyes off mine."

Chapter Thirty

Tyler

"Get on the bed, spread your legs, leave your hands on your thighs, and don't take your eyes off mine."

Her eyes flare with a mix of defiance and heat as I let her see my intent.

"Get on the bed, Delphine, or tell me to leave. I can't last much longer."

She bites her lip, her frailty where it always is, just beneath the surface of her hostility. Stepping back, I heel off my sneakers, fisting my shirt and tossing it on the floor. As I unbuckle my belt to loosen my raging cock from its confines, her desire-filled gaze rolls over me in a thorough sweep. It's everything I've been begging life for for nearly two years, and I rejoice in the sight of it as I push off my jeans, leaving my boxers on.

Silver eyes blazing, she slowly lowers herself to the bed, propping herself on her elbow while holding my gaze. The air thickens with our humming connection as I dip into my boxers and strangle my raging cock to keep what control I have left in check.

She adjusts back on the mattress, lifting her closed legs at the knees before slowly, so slowly, spreading herself for me. She rests her shaking hands on her thighs as I follow the droplets of water dripping down her skin and allow my thirst to grow unbearably as I take in the sight of her.

Naked, open, willing, and submissive, the look in her eyes is filled with a mix of lust and permission.

I may just fucking die right now.

"Don't move," I order as I commit the breathing fantasy lying beneath me to memory. Everything about her is perfection—every single inch.

Eyes greedily roaming, I take in her drawn rose nipples, toned stomach and lower them to her glistening pussy, which is still swollen from my touch. I stalk to the end of the bed and reach over, slowly pulling her ass down to rest at the edge of it. Mirror-colored eyes remain fixed on mine as I take both knees before pulling her straight to my mouth.

Her back arches instantly, a cry leaving her lips as I suck the whole of her pussy feverishly. The sound both obnoxious and intoxicating as I eagerly taste before spearing her apart with my fingers and tongue.

Her musky flavor serves as a lightning rod straight to my cock. A cock currently weeping with joy while raging with the buildup of daydreams and fantasies concocted on my nightly runs. Every single fantasy, every lingering look, all leading to this moment.

Eyes locked, I lick her with precision as her raspy moans fill the room, and she begins to shake under my explorative tongue. Too soon, way too soon, she clamps her thighs around my head and bucks. Determined to draw it out, I pull away, commanding control while slowing my movements. I left her starving days ago, and it's evident in the way she's responding now.

"Open for me," I demand, and she instantly widens her legs further before I hook her knees on my shoulders. Lifting my pointer, I slowly push it in, rimming her pussy and taunting the fleshy pad just inside, and her hips buck in fast response. So fucking responsive. It's too good. Too fucking good.

Palming her abdomen, I press down before sucking her clit into my mouth and thrusting my finger in to stimulate her G spot. Pressing just past it, I move my finger with precision along the whole of her wall, priming her while flicking my tongue rapidly along her clit. Her moans start to escalate, along with the heated sound of my name, as she begins to shake from the stimulation.

"Tyler," she gasps in slight fear and question, unsure of the sensation happening inside her. In response, I hasten my finger, knowing I've got her close to where I want her while engulfed in a haze of pure lust.

"Mon Dieu," she heaves out dramatically. Too turned on to laugh, I continue to run my finger along her swelling wall, stimulating the entirety of it while hammering the tiny ball at the tip of her clit to maximize the build. Thighs shaking, I palm her mouth just in time to muffle her scream against it as I summon the orgasm. As it peaks, she bucks furiously, her body shuddering with the onslaught as she grips the sheets, completely unraveling.

I pull my finger from her just as she detonates, her clit spasming in strong waves against my tongue as she comes and comes, soaking her thighs and sheets until she goes limp.

Bending again, I resume my workings as she fights me briefly due to sensitivity as I adamantly lick her through another orgasm—targeting my finger in the places to stoke it along. As I lift to watch her glow, I revel in the sheen of sweat covering her skin and the way it glistens in aftermath. Chest pumping, her lips continually part in surprise as she stares up at me in wide-eyed wonder. Likely because of the way I just manipulated her body with ease, more likely by the amount of pleasure I just summoned at will.

Inside, I revel in the fact that it's just the beginning of the things I'm capable of making her feel physically. I can see the questions in her eyes but shake my head as I push off my boxers, baring myself to her fully. Her eyes widen further as she gauges my size, giving her a visual of why I've made fucking sure I've mastered the art of prep work.

Knowing I've readied her as much as I can, I secure her shaking legs around my hips. Palming the mattress next to her head, I give her one last chance to object as my eyes track every inch of her beautiful face.

She stares back up at me, her soaked onyx hair splayed over the mattress as my eyes glitter down on her. As surreal as this feels, it also feels natural—destined—and I can't help saying as much.

"Nothing about this, us, is wrong," I murmur as I line us up, running my tip along her slit as she tentatively raises her shaking hands and begins running them along my chest. Her silent touch permission enough. Gripping my cock between us, I tease her opening with my head, dragging it up and down her soaked slit again and again until she widens her legs a little further for me, her eyes hooding. More permission.

Hell-bent on seizing her in one claiming thrust, I push in to do just that when I'm met by a strangling, unmistakable resistance that can only mean one thing. In feeling it, I jerk back to look down at her and see her eyes shining with tears. Her features pinch in pain even as she grips my shoulders, keeping me close to her.

"What the hell?" I whisper hoarsely as it dawns on me that she is, in fact, giving me something. Something substantial. Something she hasn't trusted another man with in a very, very long time—access to her body.

"Don't stop, Tyler, please," she whispers, her hand roaming my chest, her eyes staring up at me in wonder and need.

"Are you hurt?" I rasp out hoarsely, tempted to pull out.

She shakes her head furiously as I gape at her, bewildered by the fact that I'd gotten it all wrong, so fucking wrong. Feeling like a total bastard as that truth surrounds me, I force myself to move, too afraid of how that truth will alter me. Elbows bent, I cradle her face as I gently push in, inch by inch, as her lips continually part.

"I'm sorry, baby, I'm so sorry," I whisper as she lets out a feral moan, scratching at my skin, blunting her nails down my arms and back as I stretch her until I finally manage to seat myself. The feel of it has us both gasping. It's too good, too fucking perfect.

Especially when she locks her legs around me.

Gently fisting her hair, I pull it back to expose her throat, licking along it before whispering kisses along her neck and chest. I slowly thrust in and out, greedily feeding her every inch of my raging cock, easing in and out of her as gently as I can. When her whimpers start to morph into drawn-out moans and her hands become more urgent, I finally close my eyes and allow myself to feel all of it.

After gently thrusting into her a few times, I open my eyes and lift to gaze down at her, refusing to let her take the opportunity away from me.

"I love you," I declare before rearing back and burying myself inside her. "I fucking love you," I stamp out again with my thrust, refusing to let her ignore my declaration as my heart rings that truth for the first time in my life. She stares up at me, mouth parted, watching me unravel internally as I physically start to lose myself in the connection, fucking her at a furious pace. Claiming her body is just her wake-up call, but far from my goal. I want all of it, and the fact that she feels so fucking perfect, that our connection amplifies the growing feelings between us, only cements what I've always known.

I'm hers, been hers, and it's time she knows just how far I'll go to make sure it's the case for us both.

Opening her thighs further, moans pour from her as she slowly starts to meet my thrusts, calling out to me between pants.

It's the sweetest victory I've ever known after tortuous months of battling myself. It's when she reaches for me, wanting me closer, wanting my kiss, that I know I've cracked her just enough to snake some of the way in.

Though I press worshipful kisses along her skin, I deny her my mouth and any more tenderness. Even with the power-rendering love I feel, I can feel our underlying darkness start to merge—the lock and key—and feed on it, thrusting into her deeply a few times. Her eyes flare in recognition before she opens up to me further in permission. It's then I press past pleasure a little into pain. Each depravity-filled thrust indicates this is just the beginning. She shrieks out my name as she meets and accepts each one, and I exhale a breath of relief. Of her acceptance of it, of our compatibility, as anticipation thrums through me.

"Like that?" I grit out, dragging my tongue up her neck as I palm her thigh, driving deeper into her, knowing the force behind it is painful, but that I've primed her for this very purpose as I drag my cock along the spot I know will set her off. I feel it the second I do as she clamps down, her shrieks deafening as she explodes around me, tears of pleasure and pain rolling down her temples as I snatch them up greedily with my tongue. Her orgasm lasting as I pump my hips lightning fast to stoke the rest out of her. She comes for long, intense seconds as I watch her shake with the gravity of it.

"Oh, my God," she whispers as her thighs continue to tremble, her body following suit. "T-Tyler, m-m-y G-God," she repeats, her jaw involuntarily chattering with her stuttered whimper as she stares up at me in shock. Dipping, I draw her perfect lips into a slow kiss before uttering my warning.

"Hold onto me, baby," I murmur, "it's about to get a whole lot better."

Readjusting, I begin pumping into her with deft precision, running my cock along her clit to wring out as much pleasure as possible. Proof of that as praise-filled murmurs pour from her lips. She cries out to me in surprise with every little death I give her, bringing her to the brink over and over her again, fucking her ruthlessly, mercilessly until I'm covered in sweat.

Even then, I continue to have my way with her. Rolling her onto her side and lifting her leg, I piston inside her, snatching another orgasm before gripping a fistful of her hair and riding her from behind. After claiming another orgasm, I continue to position her in half a dozen ways, leaving her coming in every single one until I'm certain I've pushed her into a different headspace. A headspace where only Tyler and Delphine exist and are all that matters. The feel of our two bodies connecting as our hearts sync up and beat together. Until we've got nothing but each other in the dark—it's there, in that space, that I feel her with me. It's in her every movement. In her eyes, in her raspy tone, in the way she continues to reach for me to bring me closer.

Giving into it, unable to last a second longer, I finally groan out my own release and milk it out by thrusting into her as I come, remaining inside her as I come down. When I do allow myself a breath of recovery, I root into her further before gently collapsing atop her. The fire in my heart stoked further as she pulls me tightly to her chest, wrapping her legs around me.

It's unexplainable how she makes me feel, and I don't care if I can't ever put words to it as long as I can continue to feel it—with her. All of what's left, of what her cruel life has made of her, I want for myself.

She runs her hands through my soaked hair for several silent seconds until I finally lift to gaze down at her. She stares right back at me, equally as unguarded, just as immersed in the feelings bouncing between our heaving chests. I wait her out, knowing she's weighing the decision on whether or not to deny us. To break our connection and scurry away to nurse a bottle while condemning us both. As I mentally prepare for that, she pulls me flusher to her, our hearts syncing up. Pulling my head down, she starts to kiss me heatedly, and I deny her, lifting again to keep her gaze.

She lifts again, pressing her heaving breasts into my chest, an attempt at seduction, a way to sweep any emotion under the rug and call this sex. Sex is what I initially gave her. What I truly want comes next. If I was a praying man, I would beg God that she let me have it.

When her lips brush mine to claim a kiss, I deny her one last time, and her eyes flare in frustration.

"Tyler," she draws out in aggravation.

"No," I grit out, growing hard inside her. At the feel of me, she bucks her hips, and I pin her to the mattress with my weight, stilling her movement. Hovering above the most beautiful woman I've ever seen, known, or touched, the need to move inside her threatens to consume me as I bat it away in lieu of the one thing I want more.

"You gave me something. Tell me what you gave me."

"You know," she whispers, tentatively reaching up to palm my jaw.

"*Tell* me."

"You are the only one. Since Alain."

The only one.

The truth of that lights a fire in me that will never fade, never flicker out, and never fucking die. My eyes search hers, and I allow her to see the shift in them, the love I feel for her, giving her everything I just deprived her of. Everything I will continue to do if she opens a little further for me.

"I love you," I repeat softly, not expecting a reply. I said it for me all three times because I know she won't entertain it yet.

In reply, she grips my neck and slowly pulls me back down. Tentatively, she brushes my lips with hers, her kiss gentle, a painful, defeated noise in her throat as she releases herself to stake her claim. No longer asking but demanding my kiss in return, the emotion behind it undeniable. She wants the connection back, and that's all I need to free us both.

Relieved, I bask in her surrender, all my restraint, all fight leaving me as I win the battle and shift to begin the long war. The war to fight with her as long as I have to so we can revisit this place whenever we need refuge. A comfort we discovered and found in each other. A home within one another. A safe place for us both. Inside and with her, I've forged a new threshold, forsaking all others. A true home. It's only with her that I feel that place is again possible.

Dipping, I thrust that notion wordlessly into her with my tongue, with my lips. She kisses me back with just as much emotion behind it. Carnal desire thrust on the back burner, we slide our tongues against one another's unhurried until we're both utterly consumed by our emotional connection. The shift surreal as I'm forced to break away for breath. Rock hard inside her as she begins to writhe at the feel.

It's only when she brings her unguarded eyes to mine, allowing me to see the emotion inside them, that I begin to slowly move, cradling her head with one hand, brushing her temple with my thumb while drawing one of her legs tightly around my waist. Keeping her thigh cradled in my palm, I roll my hips gently, stroking her sweetly, pouring all I feel into every slow thrust. Her breath leaves her in a whoosh against my lips as she begins to build. The panic in her eyes lighting fire to every part of me as I tell her what she means to me, solidifying the truth and speaking aloud of the refuge I found in her heart.

"J'ai besoin de toi . . . *I need you* . . . Vous êtes la porte d'entrée. *You're my front door.* Tu es mon seul moyen de rentrer chez moi. *You're my only way home.*"

She begins to caress my skin with her fingers, exploring my body with her hands. Wordlessly, she presses worshipful kisses to my biceps and my pecs, her hands never stopping, her whimpers, moans, and fast breaths fueling me along with the look in her eyes. Releasing every bit of discipline I held close, I let go, heart unguarded as I make love to her, but more so, she makes love to me.

When she pushes at my chest in silent demand, I roll instantly to my back, watching raptly as she lifts to position herself above me—noting the fire that's now lit inside her as she sinks down on me. I soak in the look of her taking control as her demeanor shifts with the power she's taking as she begins to buck against me, taking from me, even as her eyes give.

"Tyler," she whispers, tears of freedom trailing down her cheeks as I grip the back of her neck and lift, soaking them up with my lips, reveling in their arrival. Knowing these are tears of relief. Healing tears. The good type of emotion driving them out of her as I grip her hips and pump into her gently while letting her control the pace.

It's the best I've ever felt in my life watching the woman I love draw her power back from me.

Her gasps and whispered French fuel me to hold out as long as possible as she takes and takes until she's utterly wrung out and clenching around me with a sweet release.

Only after she buckles against me do I flip her on her back, keeping her gaze as the rush takes me, filtering through my limbs as I pump into her, threading our fingers as I pour inside her.

Minutes later, hands tethered, a peace I've never known washes over me as I will the aftermath to last. Both of us mute, we lie for long minutes in a mess of sweaty, tangled limbs.

Elated at the feeling of having her so close but wanting her closer, I situate her so that she's lying on top of me. Her exhaled breaths hit the divot in my neck as I trail my fingers along her spine. She strokes me back, nestled perfectly atop me as she tenderly runs an explorative palm over my chest and biceps, down my arms, and back up again, tightening her hold on me every few seconds as if to make sure I'm still with her.

"You're beautiful too, Soldier. So beautiful," she whispers low before pressing a kiss to my chest, just above where my heart lies.

It's enough for now, maybe forever. She's so terrified of love, of men, of the idea of coupling that even with her earned trust, access to her body, and what residence I know I have in her heart, it would be a miracle if the affection was ever voiced aloud. I make peace with never hearing her voice it, and never asking her to.

Once we've both recovered and knowing I've probably scared her with the multitude of declarations, I attempt to ease what fears I can. Lifting her chin, I see her eyes settled on mine.

"I know what love and trust have done to you in the past," I whisper before kissing her forehead. "But in time, if you let me, I will prove it." I kiss her nose and both of her cheeks. "That this is real for me, and my feelings for you will never change."

My phone rumbles on the floor in my jeans as I curse the fucking timing, and she tenses in my arms, the unspoken reason evident.

"We are none of anyone's fucking business, and we're going to keep it that way until *we* decide otherwise," I assure her without gauging her reaction as I gently ease away from her.

Turning on her side, hand beneath her pillow, she mutely watches me dress. I stare right back as her eyes start to lower before they finally flutter closed. By the time I'm lacing my sneakers, she's asleep. Kneeling on the mattress, I bend and press one more kiss to her lips.

Already pulled under, she barely registers and returns my kiss. Feeling lighter than I have in years, I race home to shower and change. To ready myself for whatever battle I'm likely to face when she opens her eyes.

Chapter Thirty-One

TYLER

I RELIVE EVERY HEAVENLY second of the last few hours with Delphine as I shower and pull on my briefs. Every one of those moments blissful in recollection. Our physical coupling so incredibly natural from the onslaught. The feel of her bare, a first for me, was utter fucking perfection. The discussion of protection unnecessary since I chauffeured her to her OB one afternoon before we went fishing to get her birth control shot. An appointment she said she hasn't missed since she was a teenager.

The conversation even less pressing for now as my chest thuds steadily at the fact I'm the only one. Not her first, but with the solidified ambition to be her last. Heart alight that our season has finally come, I'm towel drying my hair when I exit my bathroom, stopping short when I see my dad waiting for me.

Perched at the end of my bed, he stares at me expectantly as the anger I tempered last night threatens to rush me. Instead of entertaining it—or him—I continue dressing around the elephant in my room as if he's not there. Getting back to Delphine and sorting us out is the only thing I'm concerning myself with today. That and a celebration with my brothers—my true family. Especially with Tobias due to pop up at the house anytime this morning.

Tension grows thick as I pull on my jeans, certain my

dad's about to spill some bullshit about Grace. Excuses that, at this point, I don't give enough of a fuck about to hear, though he surprises me when he finally speaks. "Your recruiter came by last night," he grinds out. "Says you've been visiting him for *over a year.*"

"Don't be too hard on yourself," I quip absently, pulling down a T-shirt and grabbing my sneakers, "you've been busy, right?"

"I haven't fucking slept, Tyler." I look over to see his eyes are red-rimmed, and his hair is thoroughly picked through. "When were you planning on telling me?"

The rage I managed to suppress since I left that gas station last night starts to filter back in with his demanding delivery and confrontational tone.

"Tyler, when were you going to tell me?" he presses.

Walking over to my nightstand, I feel the weight of his expectant stare on me as I plug my cell in to charge before pocketing my wallet and keys.

"I deserve an answer," he growls as I make my way toward my bedroom door, and he grips my forearm to stop me from passing him.

"Tyler, damn it. Talk to me."

Ripping my arm from his grip, my chest bounces with my sardonic laugh as the anger slams into me full force. "You really want to force this, huh, to have a discussion about my future?"

His features twist in confusion at the amount of hostility coming from me. I cross my arms inches from his face, which turns indignant as he bites out his words. "I get that you're pissed at me, but you need to right your tone and your posture, Son. I raised you better than that."

"Let's be honest, *my mother* raised me, and your fucking demand for respect at this point is laughable, *Carter.*"

His face reddens. "I've had just about enough of you treating me like I'm fucking beneath you. I know I've made some mistakes—"

"*Mistakes,*" I scoff at his audacity. "All right, Dad, I'll grant you your demanded *father-son* chat to talk about my future, but before we do, how about you answer a question for me first?"

He nods, his anxious eyes weighing my every move.

"So, I had a little run-in with your *mistress* last night."

His expression immediately screws up into one of guilt as he emits a low, "I ended that a long time ago."

"Yeah, good on you. But what was news to me is that her *husband* owns a gas station I frequent, and she sings in the choir at First Baptist. Things I'm sure you know, but what really surprised me was the *toddler* on her hip."

"Like I said, I ended that a long time ago."

"Doesn't answer my question. That toddler has *our eyes,* Dad. Looks a lot like *he could be fathered* by a Jennings."

"What?" His reddening face immediately starts to lose color.

"That's what you couldn't forgive Mom for, right? That's her only unforgivable sin toward you. So, did you even the score? Is Zach yours? Sure looks like he could be yours."

"Of course fucking not. Jesus Christ, Son, no." He scrubs his face with his palm. "Is that what you think of me?"

"I don't know, *Carter*." I bend, palms on my knees, as I look him right in the eyes. "But wouldn't you agree that the nature of this fucking conversation alone and the fact that these are the questions *your only son* is asking you disqualifies you from parenting him or having *any current say* in his life or future?"

"The hell?" he grits out. "You don't mean that."

"Yeah, I absolutely fucking do. I *meant* it a long time ago. I'm done, been done." I glance around my childhood bedroom as resignation sets in. "And I think it's past time I start living that decision."

Stalking over to my closet, I grab a duffle and begin packing it.

"What?" Dad stands as I start to stuff what I can into the bag. "What the fuck does that mean? What the hell are you doing? Tyler, stop."

"I'm leaving, exiting stage left because I'm done playing part of the doting, loyal, loving son in the fucking farce you and Mom are still calling a family. This ceased to be my home a long time ago."

"Stop," he snaps in a harsh whisper. "Tyler, I'm doing all I can to make things right." He grips the bag in protest. "Talk to me, Son. Don't do this." He glances out of my open door to the closed door across the hall, where Mom still sleeps. Eyes filling with trepidation, he looks back at me. "She'll never forgive me."

"Guess it doesn't matter that I won't either."

"Of course it fucking matters. I'm trying," he releases in exasperation, keeping his hand on my packed bag. We enter a brief fucking idiotic tug of war before I release it, and he stumbles back with the bag at his chest.

"Jesus, fucking keep it," I drawl with an ironic shake of my head. "I no longer want or need shit from you, and I can't handle another second of the liability that comes with being your son." I glare over at him. "Do you have any idea what it felt like looking at that kid and thinking that he might be . . ." The admission burns me, and I allow that burn to lace my resignation. "So yeah, I mean it. I'm fucking done with you."

"Tyler," he utters, tears shining in his eyes. "I swear to God, that's not the truth."

"Maybe, but here's my truth. I can't forgive you, Dad. I've tried so hard. But every time I start to, something like this happens, reminding me of how far you went and selfishly dragged us down with you." Biting my lip, I dart my eyes outside my open door at the family photo hanging between our bedrooms and turn back to him, giving him brutal honesty. "You brought her *here*," I whisper for my mother's sake, "into our *home*—"

"Son—" he starts, voice strangled as he drops the bag.

"I *heard you fucking her*," I admit hoarsely. "I *heard you* destroying our family. You didn't protect me from *that*, and it's probably the one and only time I've ever needed your protection in the *years* you *weren't* here. Until you became the one I needed protection from."

His eyes spill over as he lowers them. "I'm so—"

"Even if I can forgive that, you didn't protect *her*. Purposely insisting you drive the fucking truck that day and endangering her life."

He slowly lifts his shame-filled eyes back to mine.

"It's true then . . ." I bite my lip and nod, "I suspected it, but you just confirmed it because I know you. I spent most of my life trying to become your replica, but I've spent the last year undoing that. I think I can forgive the way you tortured us day in and day out with your bullshit because of your pain. I can forgive you for a lot, but what I can't make peace with or forgive you for is that you almost took my mother away when you already took my father . . . so for that, I'm leaving. And for that, you're going to *let me* go."

We stand for long seconds on opposite sides of his mistakes, the ache between us unbearable, before he finally bends and zips the duffle. Lifting it, he offers the handle to me as silent tears start to pour from his eyes.

"Okay, S-Son," he croaks, "you take it and whatever else you n-need." His whisper is guttural as I slowly lift my hand and take the duffle. "Do you n-need money?" His voice shakes as he scrambles to pull out his wallet before pinching the entirety of the stack of bills inside—the sight of his desperation gutting me.

"No, Dad, *stop*." I grimace as the pain lancing through me becomes harder to manage. "You don't get to make me feel guilty for this," I declare to us both.

"I k-know." His features pinch. "But I-I'll b-be here." He falters, his face crumbling as his voice continually cracks on every word. "I-if you decide that you can try to forgive me." He swallows, his tears flowing with his apologies. "I'm sorry," he expels. "I'm so sorry. I love you, and no matter what, y-you're my son, and I'm s-sorry." He falters again, and I watch the visible shatter in him as his worry for me surfaces.

"P-please be safe," he begs, "p-please c-call us, ca-call your mother," he bargains, his fear painfully evident. The sting in my throat increases, leaving me unable to do anything but nod as my eyes start to burn. Though I can feel the break I'm causing in the man standing feet away, I can't heal my own, let alone his. It's too deep. The finality of what's happening shatters something inside. Something buried. As I stare at my father, I realize it's most likely what hope I had remaining.

"Just tell Mom I'll call her later," I manage as I take a step for the door.

"Please don't leave like this," he sobs, dropping his wallet at his feet before covering his eyes with his fists. His face twists in devastation and I crack wide open at the sight of it, my eyes spilling over as I give him all I can—my truth.

"I can't live under this roof with you any longer with the way I feel about you, but if you truly want my forgiveness," I relay before he slowly lowers his fists and searches my face, eyes earnest. "Love and treat her the way she deserves." I swallow as I harden my stare. "But if you can't love her like that anymore, if you're no longer capable, let her fucking go."

He nods, drops his gaze, and steps back in defeat, openly crying as I grip the strap at my shoulder, letting out a pain-fueled exhale.

Turning, I take a few steps toward the door and force myself to stop at the threshold, knowing I won't be able to live with myself if I leave without saying it. "I love you too, Dad."

A harsh breath leaves him, his muffled cries following me as I stalk out of my room. I feel his eyes on my back as I slip out the front door and softly close it behind me. And with that act, I free myself from the slow suffocation of living under the same roof as the man who almost destroyed me. Heart seizing with every step, I'm reminded I've made another home inside the woman I love and begin the march toward my future.

***

Minutes later, I'm stuffing my duffle into my truck, still parked curbside at Delphine's, feeling Dom's weighted gaze on me from where he sits on the porch in the lone rusted spring chair. His question sounds from over the rail as I make my way to the porch to see him rolling a joint.

"Going somewhere?" he asks.

"Not yet, but it looks like you're about to," I joke as he seals it closed.

"What's with the duffle?" he asks.

"It's a story for another time. I don't really want to get into it." He stands as I palm the handle of the storm door. "Let's just say I won't be heading home for the holidays any year soon—if ever."

His eyes snap to my profile before I pass through the door, and he trails me into the kitchen. His prodding gaze remains unrelenting as I pour each of us a cup of freshly brewed coffee and hand his over.

"It was a long time coming, Dom," I finally say after taking a sip. "Sorry to ask already, but I'm going to need my cut from last night to hole up somewhere temporarily until I'm off to march."

"You can stay here," he offers without missing a beat.

"Nah," I say, "thanks, but I'll figure it out."

"You'll have it tonight, but brother, if you—"

"I'm good, man, swear," I say, ending the Q & A. Feeling his inner struggle just after, in one of his rare efforts to mute himself, I divert. "I got your text, but how did it go?"

"Exactly like you mapped it," he says, finding a grin, "and it feels fucking good." He runs a hand down his face. "But fuck, I'm wiped."

"You haven't slept yet?" I ask, knowing the answer

while trying to convince him I don't. He expected me here until he came home, so my truck parked at the curb doesn't require explanation. My alibi sadly aided by the baggage I brought with me and my new predicament.

"I've been covering up our tracks for a few hours."

"And?" I ask.

"We're golden," he says, refilling his coffee before thinking better of it. "Fuck, I'm too drained to even attempt this day without sleep."

"I think I'm going to go for a quick run," I say, far too restless to stay idle as I ditch my coffee cup and head toward the sliding glass door. Dom follows me out back, sparking up his joint as he scans our surroundings, which are slowly starting to tint and brighten with the sunrise.

"I'm going to smoke this, log on for a few, and then crash," he relays as I jump the fence. "Wake me up when he gets here."

No question who *he* is as I grin over at him. "You knew he was coming?"

His smirk turns into a full smile. "I know a lot, but I pick and choose when I want to let anyone else in on it." He gives me a pointed look.

"You got something particular in mind you want to disclose?" I ask, point-blank.

"Not at the moment, *you*?" he counters.

"Nothing in particular, except that you're a dick," I supply, stretching my hamstrings.

"Old news. You should probably rest up, too. I'm thinking that French bastard is going to keep us busy."

"You're French too, you know," I say, starting my run as his reply follows me.

"Prove it," he calls to my back.

Racing with the sun as it lights the day, I manage to reach my mileage goal despite my exhaustion. I'm cooling down when Dom's bleeding speakers reach me as I hit the driveway. The volume becoming obnoxiously louder with every step I take toward the house. Once inside, I glance down the hallway to see his door is closed. Though I can't help but think he's purposely doing it to torture his only roommate.

Shortly after, said roommate appears looking pissed and doesn't even glance my way after stalking down the hall. It's the sight of the pint in the pocket of her robe that has dread seeping into me. Batting all ill feelings away—knowing Dom's early morning serenade is most likely the reason for her current mood—I trail her into the kitchen as she pours her coffee.

"He's such a dick. Whether you refuse to spar with him or not, you have the divine right to raise hell to anyone blasting fucking music at seven in the damned morning."

She doesn't so much as acknowledge me as she tightens her robe. Dread courses through me at the sight of the gesture as I trace her every movement. After dispersing her ritual powdered pain reliever on her tongue, she uncharacteristically washes it down with vodka.

"Hey," I whisper, "you don't drink in the mornings and have nothing to feel guilty for. Come on, don't start today this way. Talk to me."

As if in contempt, she unscrews her bottle and takes an overly numbing sip, not bothering to spare me a glance before I rip it away. She doesn't react at all when some of the liquor spills between us before she turns and pours some coffee. Snatching the bottle from the counter where I just deposited it, she free-pours it in.

"Damn it, stop numbing and talk to me."

When she refuses to look at me, my patience starts to wear thin.

"All right, fuck, so if you're going to try to do this, you're going to look me in the eye and fucking do it *sober*."

Nostrils flaring, she finally lifts her eyes to mine. Void, vacant, no emotion to be found. By the glazed look, it seems she's already well over a few drinks in.

Fuck.

Hold steady, Jennings—first battle of many.

Her words come out low and laced with ire. "You insult me so *gravely* last night and have the nerve to behave as if you are insulted?"

"What?" I furrow my brows.

Coffee in one hand, she opens the junk drawer next to her and pulls out a piece of paper before thrusting it toward me. I take it to see that it's an invoice for the ceiling repair. I sink where I stand as the guilt for my assumption resurfaces.

"I'm—"

"He forgot to leave the invoice after patching my ceiling. I was already in my robe, ready to take a bath, when he knocked." It's then that dread covers me as her glare turns accusatory. "But what do you assume when you see a man in my driveway? You assumed I *fucked a* repair man just to prove a point to you?"

"Delphine, I'm sorry, I am. I—"

"I give you my trust and friendship, and you drew that conclusion so easily with your jealous fucking love."

"Jesus." I palm the counter, ducking to keep her eyes when she lowers them. "I thought we were okay."

"You thought wrong, Soldier. Did you once offer a *real* apology?"

"No." I palm the back of my neck. "But I'll beg for your forgiveness now. I was in a really bad state last night. A fucked headspace before I got here. I had just run into my dad's mistress—"

"Sounds familiar." She tilts her head.

"Don't," I snap in warning. "Don't compare me to him."

"Why not? This is a pattern I know very well. That is how it started with Alain. First, it was a declaration of devotion to win my heart and trust. Of how he loved me. That his dreams were my own. It was a living dream until he started to get in his moods." She opens the drawer next to her. "He was in a bad place mentally, too, when he slammed my hand in this drawer for palming Ormand's shoulder when he made me laugh."

"Fuck," I whisper, taking a step toward her, reading

just how volatile the situation is as she holds up a damning palm to stop me, lifting her chin while eyeing the table feet away. "He raped me after, on that table we play Battle on every night. Many times out of jealousy."

"Jesus Christ," I utter, my whole being tensing with the pain her admission causes as she casually sips her coffee.

"Do you know why I stay in this fucking house of horrors? Why I don't fix the roof, scrub the floors, or make any effort to paint the walls blue to make it more like a true home? Because it's not a home for me but a reminder that *love is a fucking liar*, a reminder to never believe that lie again."

"Delphine, please." I take another step forward, the need to surround her eating my insides.

"You ask me if I ever feel beautiful. Oui, Tyler, when my best friend purposely chooses to spend his free time with me. When he reaches for me in any way other than physical. When he listens, when he takes my words for value without *fucking me* with his eyes. But you ruined that friendship with your demand for more. So, you are right. There is no going back. Our friendship is over."

"Please don't do this. We can work this out. I didn't mean any of it. We were just okay—at least I thought we were, what the fuck happened?"

"Men have been looking at me the way you are since I was a *fucking child.* This fucking face, this body, whatever men see, I have paid for it every day since I was a fucking baby. Matis saw it. The way they looked at me."

I prepare myself for whatever is coming as dread fills me head to toe. She glances out of the window, speaking as if we're chatting about the weather, even as she drops bombs.

"So, my own papa decided that my virtue—*that my* worth—was worth a spoon of heroin."

"Jesus Christ," I utter, cupping my jaw.

"My consolation is that they killed him for not getting to collect his *bet.*" She points to herself. "I'm a bad bet, Soldier."

Both rage and devastation war within me as I step forward, and she steps back twice as far.

Fuck. Fuck. Fuck!

"I can still hear Matis's pathetic fucking cries as his old army friend ripped me from my papa's arms to save me from being his sacrifice. I can hear *love the fucking liar* begging me, so clearly, to forgive him," she whispers, holding up her shaking hand. "Reaching for me in the snow."

Her eyes mist, and I visibly see her getting lost in that day as she speaks again, her next whisper barely audible. *"Open your eyes, little flower. Please don't break my heart."*

"Baby, *please*," I croak, my insides bottoming out. "Please listen to me, I swear I didn't mean anything I said in anger. I swear to God. I was in a really bad place. Fuck, I know that's not an excuse, but it's the truth." The need to pull her to me becomes unbearable as her eyes flash briefly with vulnerability.

She's in there, Jennings. Hold steady.

"That doesn't change the fact you believe me capable of using a tactic so callous to give you an answer instead of simply speaking one. So, I will make it simple for you. I don't want your jealous fucking love, Tyler. I don't want *any man's love* for that very reason."

"You don't mean that."

"I do," she delivers with metal eyes in an emotionless tone. "It's a ridiculous dream you have."

"You know I would never hurt you."

"Do I? Just after that insult, did you not use words to try and hurt me in ways you discovered during our friendship? Preying on my weaknesses?"

"I'll do anything to make it up to you," I whisper. "I'm so fucking sorry."

She approaches and stops just next to me, staring down at the counter, her delivery slightly less icy. "I believe that *you believe* the words you spoke to me about your affection, but those are your words, your desires, *not mine*."

That blow strikes hard, despite how well I was prepped for it and whatever else she decides to deliver.

"We were okay when I left. What happened? Where did your mind go?"

It's when she slowly lifts her resolute gaze up to mine that I know I underestimated just how not okay we were when I left.

"What happened? You happened." She shakes her head in refusal. "Or maybe I remembered that I come with a high price, Soldier, and you have the look in your eyes of a *buyer*."

"Fine." I swallow. "You don't think I was already ready to pay for Matis and Alain? Think again. You couldn't be more fucking wrong. I'll pay any price you ask because you're worth it for me."

"Any price," she repeats with a sharp nod.

I swallow, knowing I just fucked up.

"Then I ask for a promise."

"No."

"Oui. Forget your foolish idea of us. Treat me as if this never happened."

"Never. Delphine. Never, it's far too fucking late for that," I snap. My hackles rise as her darkness begins to fill the room, and her silver eyes dare me to look inside. I face it—her—head-on.

"Then love has made a liar of you already," she scoffs. "Have you even considered what I want?"

"You want me. You want us. This is bullshit, and I'm not buying it."

"*Fool*," she condemns me. "What I truly want is for you to promise me you will take that look in your eyes, never to bring it back to this house or me. If last night did not satisfy the rest of your curiosity, then your imagination will have to do. It will never happen again."

"Don't do this," I grit out. "You weren't drunk."

"I am drunk *every night*. I do things I regret every day. You are my regret today."

"You're lying."

"*Love* is the fucking liar, Soldier, and the sooner you learn that, the better soldier you will be." She swallows, and I can feel her hesitation before she speaks and levels me with her gaze. "Love is lying to you right now. Telling you things are so simple between us, but they are not. The truth you don't want to hear is that you are an eighteen-year-old *boy*."

"You already love me," I grit out. "Soldier of your heart, *your words*," I remind her.

"I love my *nephews* with what heart remains, and they are all I have left. I won't be the *disgusting* aunt who ruined their childhood and humiliated them by fucking their friends. I won't be the laughingstock of this town who looks so desperate she has to fuck a *teenage boy*. Go. Do not come back to this house until that look is gone. Go, soldier. This is the last order I will give you."

"I'm not your—"

"Ah, so then you are not my soldier?" she fires next, crossing her arms. "Your words to me. 'Your soldier, *loyally and faithfully yours*' was another lie?"

I slam my palm on the counter. "This is a truly fucking genius twist, but I'm not that simple-minded, Delphine. You're being predictable. That's not the way I fucking meant those words, and you know it."

"It is the only way those words will ever mean anything to me. Promise me it never happened."

"Don't do this." I bite my lip as I realize just how much power she has over me. How much power I gave her.

She sighs again, snatching the vodka from the counter and unscrewing the cap as I brace myself for the worst.

"Take your crush and go. It's not welcome here, and if you cannot be adult enough to leave it at home, do not come back."

"You done?" I ask as her eyes flare.

"You're right, I've been a horrible . . . aunt," she exhales through swollen lips. Lips I spent hours kissing. Lips which kissed me back just as frenzied, just as tenderly. Lips that are currently spewing lies, anything to distance us.

"I didn't mean it—"

"As strained as it may be," she continues, "the relationship I have with my nephews now is far different than years ago. I won't risk that progress for this little affair you have in your head. I've brought enough shame to myself, to my family, to Celine's memory."

"Liar, you fucking liar," I snap. "You were there," I say, resentment clear as I lower my voice, "in every sense of the word. You felt it. You kissed me back. You pulled me closer. That was you, Delphine. You can't fucking fake that."

"It's a delusion, Tyler. What you want to believe about us is not the truth *for me*. If you love me as you say you do," she interjects, her insistent ice eyes steel resolve, "make the promise I am asking for. Forget this ever happened. Treat it—*treat me*—as if it never did, or my nephews will read the heartbreak on you and have something else to hate me for. They are all I have left."

"They don't even fucking see you—" I bite my tongue, knowing I'm playing into her if I strike back with any more insult. Staring back at her, I raise my sword once more.

"I just spent the last two years of my life showering you with every bit of the love I have, proving how kind love can be."

"And I let you *fuck me* for it. Do you feel compensated enough"—she tilts her head menacingly—"or entitled to more?"

I gape at her. That blow far too hard-hitting. Unable to swallow, I find myself unable to react, to say a single fucking word in response. To back up any promise I made to her or myself. Instead of fighting, I feel every goddamn word she's spoken to my core. In truth, she *is* showing up for battle. For two men. Men that aren't me but might very well take what residence she has left in her heart.

I knew an excuse was coming, and I knew it would be good, but this... I expected to be able to barter with myself

Severed Heart

and make allowances, to duel with her on anything. But it's the severity of her dismissal and the fact that I'm guilty of everything she's accused me of that has me gridlocked.

The way I acted last night, bursting in in a jealous rage, insulting her, and then touching her before pressing her for more physically. It sinks in then that I might have let the wants of my heart rule my head far too much. That I might have misjudged and taken one hellacious overstep assuming she felt the same way. Thinking back, she's never once said a single word in agreement with me—of a future between us. The words of love and devotion, of a future, were all *mine*. My heart starts a freefall as I gaze back at her, unable to absorb the blow.

"If I *ever* made you feel like that," I rasp out as tears I couldn't hold if my fucking life depended on it streak my face, "like you owed me, then I have failed you." I swallow in defeat.

It's then I see a tiny sliver of remorse snaking through her ice-coated eyes. For the briefest of moments, I glimpse the woman I fell in love with, even as her next words decimate me.

"You didn't force me, Soldier, and I won't allow you to think that, but it was *a mistake*. So I'm asking you now, please, Tyler, never look at me the way you are now again. Push this idea out of your mind and forget it happened. I'm a drunk—"

"Stop," I wheeze as my heart finally hits the asphalt, the shatter reaching every corner of me, far too many pieces to ever be put back right.

She's made her decision, and it isn't me.

A car door sounds, and our eyes snap toward the door and then back to each other as the clock ticks out.

"*Promise me, Tyler.* If you truly love me as you say you do, promise me you will never come back to this house with that look in your eyes for me." Her eyes implore mine, desperation seeping from her every pore. "*Please*, Soldier, promise me."

"It never happened," I hear myself say while wishing wholeheartedly it was the truth. Not if this is the payoff of giving so much of yourself to another human being. Of loving them to the point their wants overshadow your own—of loving another more than yourself. Ripping my eyes away, within my next breath, I'm closing the sliding door just as Tobias enters through the front. I catch their muffled greetings before I jump the fence and start at a dead run. As my feet start to pound the asphalt, I feel the silence in my chest pumping while my mind tries to temper the implosion happening throughout the rest of me, forcing my thinking into a one-eighty. Into thinking I don't need a single thing that I thought I couldn't live without mere seconds ago—my mind's way of protecting me as I embrace the lifeline.

Delphine once told me the true genius of a strategist lies within the surprise, and hers was far too damning and honest to be completely contrived.

She chose Tobias and Dom when I never even knew I had that competition, that there would be a choice to make between us. I'm not her decision and will never be. My legs fuel me as the roar in my chest intensifies, a lot of that ache feeling like betrayal and broken faith.

The same faith and trust I had in my father. It's then I realize I foolishly fused it and projected it all into Delphine. I had given her all I had left, and she destroyed me in the same heartless goddamned way. Made me her world like my father had for a time, just to discard as easily.

Cast out.

Not enough.

For either of them.

A mistake. A mistake. A mistake. The word alone holds more power than almost any other she spoke, and it's no mystery why. I've been paying for mistakes *dearly* for years, ironically so few of them my own.

Agony races on my heels, threatening to catch up as I pound the asphalt, my empty heartbeat pulsing in my ears. Even as it happens, I begin to shed the weight of their mistakes, brick by brick. A wall made up of the load I've been carrying for people who've never shown up to do the same for me, for too fucking long.

Weight created by their selfishness and missteps. My every attempt to help them with their burdens thwarted or overlooked. So, as I shed their collective sins, their burdens, I materialize a wall between myself and their fucking decisions, becoming lighter with every step.

Resigned to let their burdens be their own. To let them lie in their beds, weighed down as they battle their own fucking demons, haunts, and the consequences of their missteps.

Faults I can't camouflage or fix, and I am losing all desire to with every step that distances me from them, growing lighter and lighter as I go.

As I shed the final brick on one side and lay it on the other, I press through the pain, intent on becoming the man I envisioned—my mission the same.

My mission the only thing within my sights. The only thing that matters.

Now, a homeless soldier, but a soldier just the same.

A soldier with a purpose.

Just after I fix my sight, a mental clarity kicks in before a tunnel envelops me, surrounding my view until I'm hyper-focused. Racing toward a pinprick I can so clearly see. It's then I reach the precipice I've been close to reaching for months and finally press past it, finding my freedom with the slow sweep of my eyes.

BLINK. *BLACK.*

An hour later, I'm a Marine.

PART 2

"He who makes a beast of himself gets rid of the pain of being a man." —Samuel Johnson

Chapter Thirty-Two

Tyler

US PRESIDENT: BARACK OBAMA | 2009–2017
SPRING 2010
Camp Lejeune, North Carolina
Four years later

Blink.

"Nineteen! Twenty! Twenty-one! Fuck you, Jennings!" Beekman's voice booms through the crowd surrounding me as I lift my chin past the bar. More catcalls ring out as I summon the last of my willpower and hit a record twenty-five pull-ups before landing on my boots. Celebratory cheers ringing out from all sides as I finish my final physical test of my four-year active stint as a Marine.

"He ran 17:39 on the three mile this morning," Beekman boasts while landing an exaggerated clap on my shoulder "Eat that, fuckers!"

I hadn't meant to make a show of it, but as I take in the commotion surrounding me, I can't help the swell of pride for adding to my cutting score. Though I've been training for years—readying myself for this—I've surpassed my own expectations. The long runs for endurance are paying off in spades, as well as knowing exactly what efforts will get me promoted within the ranks. I set my sights early on my goal before enlisting, hell-bent on a position in Security

Forces, before doing an eighteen-month stint overseas. After completing my MCIs and all other needed curriculum, I've got enough points to gain promotion if offered—possibly before starting my reserves.

There's a lot that factors into it, but I'll rest easy tonight knowing I've done all I can to rank sergeant.

It's taken years of sweat, focus, and dedication, but the prep work I put in before joining has been heavily on my side. I keep myself well-fed, work out a ridiculous number of hours, staying sharp and mentally engaged as long as I'm conscious. The only unbearable hours are the rare few I allow myself between lights-out and the early wake-up call. It's then I see her face and hear her voice—*and mine*. Mostly the haunting echo of my promises to her. Promises unfulfilled. Promises that will remain that way, save *one*.

Because it never happened.

It's during those long hours of silence that force reflection when I recall a life that feels so distant now—having exchanged every comfort I once knew for life in the Corps. After that morning, as I mentally forged myself anew while racing toward my recruiter, I enlisted as a heartbroken, pissed-off kid with his father's chip on his shoulder.

Since then, I've exhausted that kid's conflicting emotions and baptized him by hellfire with the help of the Corps. But no matter how much distance or how many months and years I've put between that morning and this moment, the ache for her remains. Even without her aware of it, my heart kept its promise.

"Ask me in a year how I feel about you, and I'll say the same."

That I've loved her every second, turned minutes into hours, becoming weeks, months, and years since I started inhaling militant breaths and exhaling my way through this mission. Engrossed in this life that I signed up for in an effort to become both the man and soldier I envisioned.

"Where did you go?" Beekman asks as we exit the complex.

"Just thinking about what's next." I shrug, glancing around to ensure we're out of earshot. "Have you heard anything?"

"No, but keep your ringer on," he says, cupping the back of his neck, the bold raven ink pattern on his arm mirroring mine. Though his tattoo is fresh, and over time, Beekman proved himself—becoming my first recruit—he's far from my last. Over a dozen of America's finest are steadily earning their ink by the day.

"Sadly, they don't give a shit about timing for our *convenience*," he states, his harsh exhale an indication that he's just as on edge about not yet getting a call.

Like me, Beekman is set to start his time in the reserves soon, but his future plans include joining the alphabet mafia. His ambitions high for a spot in the bureau. Luckily for us both, he already has some connections in central intelligence. Connections which gave him the ability to make contact for the two of us to be considered as part of a loophole. One that will allow us to serve both our country and our wings on a far higher level—a level that will further my mission for education *beyond* the scope of ninety-nine percent of others who serve.

"The silence is getting pretty damning, man," I tell him, my anxiety ramping up that if we don't get called up, my homecoming to Triple Falls is imminent. Dom is still finishing up at MIT, thinking of going for his master's after possibly taking a semester or two off, which will delay our mutual homecoming. A grenade he pulled the pin on during my last visit to Triple—which I always keep brief. The upside is that in a few weeks, I'll grab my rank promotion—if offered—having fulfilled my part in the Jennings legacy. Even if my father didn't want me to have that part in it, he sent a letter every month in an effort to mend our fractured relationship.

A year into my time in the service, I sent my first return letter. While our relationship will never be what it once was, we aren't nowhere, which is where it was when I left.

Keeping tabs on home is easy by way of my fly-throughs whenever I can get off base and by my mother, who faithfully reports all things Jennings. A mother who refuses to let *any* extended period of time pass without contact. Her threats heard in the communications tent more than once during my first year. Something the guys in my company still give me shit about to this day. That and the fact that once they saw her on screen, they started voicing that they wouldn't mind their own personal visits from Regina Jennings.

Fuckers.

"Fuck it, right? We knew it was a long shot." Beekman flashes me a reassuring half-smile. "I'm going to grab a shower and some chow. We'll just keep the faith, man, but in the meantime, I could use my wingman tonight and—"

"No," I snap. "Immediately fucking no. I told you I'm never drinking with you again, and I meant it." I cut my eyes at him in warning. "*Ever.*"

Beekman and I are the few in our inner circle presently unattached, and he's never once been in genuine need of a wingman. His personal record being ten minutes in securing a hookup, whether it be male or female. His all-American look is deceiving as hell, as the devil residing within him reminds me of both Dom and Sean—especially with his *nighttime antics*. But I both love and trust him like one of my brothers, and I'm looking forward to making the introduction when the time comes.

"Aww baby, that night was just a mix-up," he coos before reading my expression and lifts his palms. "All right, but seriously, if neither of us gets the call, maybe I'll fly home with you, and we can set up shop for a while."

I give him a nod. "Yeah, that might work."

"Catch up with you in a few," he says, walking backward, exaggerating his swagger though his expression rings sincere, "but know this, Corporal Jennings, they'd be fucking *idiots* not to dial *you.*"

"Thanks, man," I tell him, mustering a grin as he turns and saunters away, leaving me feeling uneasy about his suggestion to move back to Triple Falls full-time. Some part of me feels my time in the service is unfinished. Like I'm not yet ready for phase two, which once included setting myself up on the orchard.

Plans Barrett beat me to, already having set up house and home on the Jennings farm with Charlie, their son due any day. Both are actively living the dream I once pictured for myself, in a different life, and with a woman who had the same dream—just not with me.

But where my younger cousin is planting roots, I feel as if I've spread my wings—constantly shifting directions and forging a different path for my future with my brothers, both in arms and ink. My attention and efforts are now dedicated to their flight patterns, which now take priority over any significant shift of my own.

Even when they piss me off, they remain my forever constants. At times my heroes—other times annoying as fuck. But in letting go of everyone else's mistakes and simply allowing the people closest to me to be who they are without running interference, I've liberated myself from the weight of their burdens. Forever trying to tame my inner hypocrite who judges too harshly for not acting or reacting like I would in their own situations. More importantly, showing up when they need me most to camouflage their mistakes. For them, and even from afar, I've become the problem solver. A role I take seriously to protect them at all costs while keeping my resolve that if it's personal for them, it's none of my fucking business.

For the near handful of years I've been gone, I've been trying to forgive both my father and Delphine for the hurt they've caused themselves in sorting their lives and how personally *I* took it. I no longer regret the son I tried to be or loving Delphine with the whole of my heart and soul—even if she broke it.

So, while it's liberating, there's still a lingering soul-deep ache when I allow myself a glimpse at the rearview. Because even if I've resigned myself to that way of thinking, and even if it's serving me well daily, I still feel as if something is missing. Something that still won't be there when I eventually return to Triple Falls.

And so, I live in time measured by the slow sweep of my eyes, blinking from one day to the next through any aches that arise because of the gnawing that has yet to leave me. All the while keeping my promise, no matter how bad it burns—it never happened.

***

Triple Falls Police Department
One Week Later

BLINK.

"Wakey wakey . . . eggs and bakey."

Peter's eyes bug open from where he lays on the bunk bed as Reggie—who owes me half a dozen more favors—closes the jail cell behind me before pocketing the litter of keys on his ring. When Peter jerks to sit, I manage to pin him to the inch-thick mattress in time to muffle his cry with a firm hand.

"Already breaking rule number one, man. Shhhh," I whisper as I gauge the look of him—pale, malnourished. Like me, he's already jaded by life's cruelly dealt hand at only seventeen.

"Robin Peter Morgan?" I muse. "Seriously? Your parents did you dirty."

When Peter narrows his eyes at my barb, I can't help chuckling. There's a spark of a fighter and an anger inside him that he hasn't managed to harness yet. One I'm all too familiar with.

"Not to worry, man. Half of our crew uses their middle names in their everyday because their parents cursed them the same way. So, I think I'll take it as a good sign where you're concerned."

Confusion pinches his features as he does what he can to scan the marine dressed in civvies who's currently confining him to his mattress in a jail cell. Fear wins as he struggles again, and I keep him pinned.

"Ah, ah, calm down, kitten. We don't have much time. I was owed a favor, and I came to collect. Don't you want to know why?"

Peter slackens slightly when I press in, and I decide to cut the theatrics when Reggie clears his throat to alert me that time is scarce.

"I can't help but to think your namesake was a prelude to your literal future of Robin' Peter to pay Paul. You're a devious little shit, aren't you? Everything from five-fingering the church offering plate to selling Grandma's Fabergé egg on the internet to landing yourself here for another count of petty theft. You've been a busy, busy boy. Your rap sheet is getting a bit thick, considering your balls have barely dropped, and by my count, you're running out of strikes, so let me reiterate—*amateur*."

His eyes widen slightly as my words sink in.

"Yeah, we've had our eye on you for some time but don't get any ideas. You're not my type."

I glance around the cell. "So, they locked you in here to scare you straight." I smirk. "Are you *scared*, Robin?"

He glares up at me.

"Didn't think so. My guess is the only thing cooking in that head of yours right now is who to borrow from the second you get out of here."

He relaxes a little under my hold, his curiosity getting the better of him.

"But what you need to think about now is *what if* . . . what if things were different . . . what if you didn't have to steal because your dad left you concussed on the floor of that trailer." I tap the pink scar over his left eyebrow.

"And living hand-to-mouth to feed your mother and infant sister?"

Peter stares up at me, and I know I've gained his attention by reciting the details of his life—details I've made it my business to know.

"What if you could get rid of Paul altogether, and *you* were the one collecting payment? Think about how satisfying it would feel to have a fat roll of green in your pocket just for doing what you were born to do."

I ease my grip, and he stays idle, his attention fully mine as he considers my words.

"It's crazy where a day can take you"—I widen my eyes—"trust me on this. Now, I'm going to pull my hand away and see if you can keep a secret, and if you can, we'll be in touch."

Chapter Thirty-Three

Tyler

SUMMER 2010
Camp Lejeune, North Carolina

Blink.

"Jennings," I answer my cell, rolling my neck due to the fatigue of my latest workout, one hand on the wheel as I pull to a stoplight.

"Turn around."

"Pardon?" I ask, pulling the phone away from my ear and gaining no clue who's calling, only the time ticking on the otherwise blank screen. The hair rises on the back of my neck as recognition kicks in on who it might be.

"You just left base," he clips, "turn around."

"And?"

"Meet me in the parking lot of the Waffle House. Black F-150."

"And you are?"

"The guy you asked to speak to."

The line goes dead as I search for and find a way to make a quick U-turn. I have five minutes at most to cement a decision that will alter the course of my life. In a way that only a select few have. I make my decision in less than a minute after forcing thoughts of her away from being a reason to move forward. Shifting my mindset on what lies ahead, I scramble to dial his new burner number.

"Good to hear from you, Sergeant Jennings," Tobias greets with pride on the second ring.

"Hey, T." I swallow and swallow again, rare emotion clogging my throat. The reason being that this might be the last time we ever speak. He senses my struggle immediately with hesitation on the line, and I beat his inquiry to the punch. "Just want to let you know I'll be delayed coming home."

A short but loaded silence ensues. "By how long?"

"There's a chance I won't be home this Christmas or next," I relay, wiping the summer heat from my forehead.

"Fuck," Tobias exhales, knowing precisely what I'm telling him. We've discussed this possibility in detail, but I can sense his own emotion surfacing as the reality and implications set in. "Christ, brother. You don't know how to fail, do you?"

"I made it happen."

"And this is truly what you want?" he prompts.

A future I can't have flits before my eyes. Our hands clasped as we walk along rows of apple trees, talking for hours before swaying in a hammock for two. Eyes meeting across a fire as we exchange long glances, peace in our hearts. Making love to her in the tall mixed grasses surrounding the pond. The two of us perched on the hillside with her nestled in my arms, watching endless sunsets as the seasons change. I don't want that life without her. I can't picture it without her, and so I don't want to fucking bother attempting to live it.

I press those illusions down, down, down, into a faraway, unreachable place until the sting starts to dissipate.

It's over. Has to be over.

Needs to fucking be over. Especially after four long years without a word between us. A disconnect that has starved my dream to the point that it's already starting to fade along with what youth remains in my heart. And as soon as I hit that parking lot, *I'll* technically be over. Voluntarily ceasing to exist for as long as I decide to.

Tyler Carter Jennings's wants and needs will be useless. With this one move, I'll become both a vessel of protection and revenge—for my brothers, for my father, and for my country.

"My decision is made," I finally speak, "and I hope it makes my family proud." The implication is clear on which family I'm referring to.

"Your family could not be more fucking proud," Tobias declares in a pained tone, "and will be waiting anxiously for your return."

"Where are you?" I ask, fighting the last of my starving hope.

"I'm home."

He's there, and possibly with her. With one last mile between me and my future, I briefly wonder if Delphine's nearby. If they're sitting at her kitchen table or outside on the porch. If she can hear my voice. If she wants to hear it. I stall a beat before speaking precious words I don't have enough time to thoughtfully put together.

"Tell my brothers . . . my family, in the off chance I don't make it back anytime soon," *or ever*. Emotion clogs my throat as he waits patiently before I finally get them out. "That whatever happens, it was worth it for me. Okay?"

"I will. Take care, brother. Come home when you can . . . and Tyler?"

"Yeah?"

"I need you to come home," Tobias whispers roughly. Another pause. "We *all* do."

She's there, and maybe she's listening, but I tamp down the idea his words were in any way specific to her. His order isn't hers. She made her decision, and I'm living it. Making peace as I pull into the parking lot, I swallow down the fact that even if Tobias's request included her, it's not enough.

"Fuck," he exhales, "all I can see right now is that lanky kid mowing my lawn," he croaks hoarsely. When I let out a chuckle at that, and he doesn't, the mutual sting increases over the line.

"Come back to us," he finally says, "that *is* a fucking order."

"Love you too, brother."

Neither of us hangs up, holding onto the seconds we have left as they start to tick out.

I told him that if I got the call, I would have to keep my distance from the club indefinitely to ensure my new bosses don't pick up on my extracurriculars. This means my involvement in the club ceases entirely until I'm sure I'm not being watched outside of it. We never told Sean or Dom that I would be seeking this invitation because of the likelihood it wouldn't come. But now that it's here, the surreal reality is that in doing this, living this decision means there will be stints, some of them long, where I lose all ties and ability to protect *her*, protect them all.

When the line finally goes dead, I exhale a long breath. As of this moment, and for the foreseeable future, I'm completely on my own.

Here we fucking go.

***

FALL 2011
Syrian Border
Thirteen Months Later

BLINK.

Scanning the terrain in the pitch dark with night vision, my inkling pays off the second I spot the first few of multiple, heavily armed bodies creeping in our direction.

Snapping to as my adrenaline ramps up, I address everyone on the wire. "Eyes! Wake up! We've got company."

Shultz and Ramirez, both from my branch along with Stuart, are the first to respond, their surprise sounding over the line. Just as I thought and voiced, we fucked up by stopping for the night to get a few needed hours of shut-eye. The majority won against my protests to put more distance between ourselves and the aftermath we left hours ago. Outvoted, I positioned us on the defensive, opting to keep watch while feeling ill at ease the entire time. It's a fine line between trying to stay sharp while sleep-deprived, no matter how well-trained we are. This has been our longest stint so far in the field due to difficulties in initially reaching our target, and our tanks are running dangerously low.

Armstrong, a seasoned Army Ranger, crawls over to me, reaching me in seconds, his goggles lifted as he sounds out his count. "We've got twenty, fuck, twenty-*three* coming straight for us, two with fucking RPGs in hand. Stuart!" Armstrong summons.

Positioned a half click ahead and to our right with several of our able bodies at his disposal, Stuart clips out his own count. "We're made. We're fucking made, my count is the same. Two clicks and closing."

"Then it's a fair fight," I bark over the line, "don't give me that defeated tone, Stuart, and don't forget who we fucking are. You'll just have to get your beauty rest later."

Armstrong shoots me a blinding white grin that would be visible without night goggles. He's been my favorite to work with so far out of the teams built in my time with the Global Response Staff. Stuart, whom I met days ago when we landed for this mission, is fast becoming my least. It's clear that during his short stint here he's realized he was better off taking security detail and escort jobs for US diplomats rather than participating in field missions. As far as I'm concerned, he's dead weight. But as team leader, Stuart's fate is in my hands, as well as the others currently unaccounted for to our left.

"Hey assholes, wake up, or are you too busy bouncing beach balls on your noses?" I bark over the line.

"Fuck you, Jennings, we've got the same count on both sides." McCormick claps back, a highly decorated Navy Seal who came into the mission wheels hot a mere nine hours ago. Company I'm thankful for because he doesn't fucking miss once he's got a target in his crosshairs. Ever.

"What's your position?" I ask.

"Where you put us three hours ago, dick. Two clicks and closing," he rings out in reminder.

"By my count, that's six sexy Seals, two romp-ready Rangers, and at least *three* well-endowed Marines—*sorry, Stuart*," Armstrong quips. "And I'm going to have to agree with Jennings. I happen to like our fucking odds," he says, lifting his rifle to keep his scope on our approaching company.

"Fuck you, Armstrong. Jennings?" Stuart prompts, his panic evident.

"Clear the line," I snap. "I'm thinking."

"Mind speeding that up a bit?" Shultz clips before McCormick sounds up.

"We've got a sniper joining the party."

"That means we did our job," I clap back. "You have him?"

"Yep," McCormick fires back, and I know he's curling his finger on the trigger with his spoken threat already in his crosshairs.

"Thompson, you getting this? We're going to need some love from above."

"Roger," home confirms over the line. "I've got your position. I need ten minutes."

Fuck.

"Might want to make haste and do better or prepare yourself to explain the high count of body bags of America's finest to the boss."

"On it," Thompson replies tersely, seemingly unaffected, though I know he's in a panic.

"Being hunted is a compliment, boys," I declare, "they don't like that we silenced their boss and shorted their paychecks. When the first ping flies, fucking *peel it* and get to high ground if you can. We'll send messengers with goodie bags wherever you land."

Our odds are jacked, but I press past any threatening panic and spend precious seconds deep breathing to clear my headspace instead. Pulse steady in my ears, I hear her speaking to me as if she were standing beside me in the dirt, whispering into my ear. Once armed with an idea, I push off the rock wall we were camping against and glance over to Armstrong, who gives me a lift of his chin.

"I know that look," Armstong says, his grin amping, "and I love it."

"Shall we make them think twice about paying us compliments?" I ask.

"Fuck yeah," Armstrong counters before I address everyone over the wire.

"Home, hold off, but leave the lights on. I have an idea."

BLINK. *BLACK.*

***

SPRING 2012
NEW YORK CITY, NEW YORK
Six months later

BLINK.

"Jennings," Phillip barks, summoning me from the black plastic bucket chair I've been waiting in while watching the goings-on of the shipping warehouse. Rolling my neck, I stand and stretch a little before following him into a shoe-box-sized office. Though fatigued, I don't bother taking a seat as he opens a file I'm intimately familiar with.

Phillip, who I gauge is somewhere in his mid-forties, wipes his nose with a fresh Kleenex—one he always seems to keep on hand. Some of his ruddy complexion no doubt due to his raging allergies. An affliction I suspect, along with his sickly, fragile build, that has kept him from being an active participant in any field work. A prime example of those that can't do—*teaching*, or in Phillip's case, *doling* out missions. Orders already passed and carried out as he sifts through the details of a dozen or more in the file on his desk. All of which I completed after I was unlisted as a Marine and joined the Global Response Staff, AKA the GRS.

A thankless job with high pay but zero credit, which I give fuck all about. A job that includes missions unlikely to earn an explanation letter postmarked to my family if one goes awry. High-risk orders that are tasked to a select few by the CIA, which include diplomatic tape blind expeditions. Expeditions carried out by the world's most finely tuned and experienced vets for the best interest of our country.

By joining the GRS, I gained the ability to decipher and validate the nature of such missions, furthering my investigation of the military to the next level. All the while honing my skills in the field. It's the deal I made in the parking lot after serving my listed four years, which led me to the handler sitting at the desk opposite me. "Phillip," no last name ever mentioned, had recruited me for himself and, for the most part, has been my task master in doling out said missions. Over the last nineteen months, our rapport has mostly been filled with mutual respect along with a brewing friendship.

"What you've accomplished at this point," Phillip utters, glancing up from my file, "is beyond my comprehension."

I muster a nod because exhaustion is finally taking hold. The last of my adrenaline was spent getting out of a sticky situation in the African desert that we were extracted from eighteen hours ago before being flown back to the States.

In the last nineteen months, I've come close to depleting myself and my reserves, taking successive missions in lieu of going back to Triple Falls. My reasoning for that is entirely selfish. No home, no future. No reason other than the club, and it's thriving without me. With the army that I put together during my listed time and Dom in school, things have run smoothly since. It's as if I planted roots, and they're sprouting deep and wide on their own.

Phillip scrutinizes me carefully from where he sits, seeming to have aged some since our last face-to-face—a little grayer at his temples. Judging from our last few phone calls, he's grown a lot less patient. Though, he always seems to muster some for me during our conversations, making it clear that I've earned his respect.

"There's no fucking way you should have survived two of these. I'm thinking you're aware of which?"

I bite my lip and nod.

"You're cutting it close, Jennings. Any particular reason why you haven't sipped an umbrella drink or taken any leave since you started?"

"I'm ambitious."

"Or *suicidal*," he counters, scouring my person.

"Frankly, sir, if I wanted that fate, we wouldn't be talking."

He opens the file and points to a mission name that I glance at—Adobe. "How in the fuck did you get out of this?"

"You want a play-by-play?" I ask with zero condescension in my tone.

"Actually, I would," he replies, brows drawing further into a V, which I consider a compliment, knowing the intrinsic, highly complicated nature of the orders he doles out to the others in the GRS. "Have a seat."

I toss my ball cap on the edge of his desk and take the offered chair as I scan our surroundings. Though my interest is becoming piqued, I know better than to question why he's chosen a temporary office in a shipping warehouse in downtown New York. Much like my own club, theirs is just as tight-lipped in providing answers.

"The long and the short of it is," I start, and damn near laugh at my explanation, "have you ever heard of Anvil and Hammer?"

"Get the fuck out of here," he says, scrutinizing the paper in front of him.

"With twenty-four coming in arrogant and overconfident, I already had our teams split into right and left flank positions to crowd them. So, we let them gain some ground before cutting their number in half and rushing them before we dropped it."

"Jesus Christ, Jennings." He gapes at me. "Are you fucking telling me you used a tactic from *before Christ* to survive this?"

I shrug. "Worked for Alexander the Great."

"How in the fuck did you think of that?"

A French mastermind. One I'm getting more desperate to thank personally after each completed mission. It takes me a few seconds to answer, but I manage to get through his extensive questions while leaving said mastermind out of it. I want to tell her myself. Some day. Maybe a day in the near future because the more missions I carry out, the more it becomes obvious that she's owed, at the very least, a thank you.

"Look," he finally says, "as helpful as you've been, we're starting to close shops all over due to the increasing risk. At this point, we have a growing need to utilize minds just like yours in station."

I blink at his suggestion. "You mean re-enlist?"

"Reserves, but with a specific job in mind. I can guarantee your time card will be punched for the stint you've put in with me, and"—he pauses for emphasis—"it will count, Jennings. You'll go in high on the scoreboard as gunnery sergeant with the deserved pay increase."

Home. He wants to send me home. Or at least, back to—"North Carolina?" I ask.

"Greensboro. Any objections to that? You will work with outside intelligence via satellite while attending to your responsibilities on base. In addition, your reserve contract will be drawn up on your terms."

Home. Or closer to home, and after months of minimum

contact, I have no idea what's happening there. Even between jobs, I've rarely checked in with Mom. Mostly to keep hard-wired in my missions in lieu of what's happening, which would only distract me. Now I have that chance. The thought of seeing it through—of going home—has my pulse pounding. For one reason alone—to *thank* her and selfishly lay eyes on her.

It's as I stare back at Phillip, his offer lingering in the air, I realize I've done all I need to. I've been postponing the inevitable. I've done my service and beyond. I can quit now, walk away, and consider my time well spent, or take him up on his offer and again exceed my own expectations with a higher clearance to finish my investigation. It's too good to pass up.

"Before you make your decision," Phillip interjects with caution, "I'm going to add the caveat of a favor. One of a more personal nature."

"Of course you are." I blow out a long breath.

"You'll get to cherry-pick your team. But if you carry this out for me—successfully—I will owe you."

"Owe me what?"

"A significant favor. No questions asked. If it's within my power, I will get it done, and as you're aware, there's very little I can deny you."

"Make it *two* favors," I say, "no questions asked. And I need a little desk help on something I've been working on that has nothing to do with either significant favor you'll owe me."

I give him a pointed look. In return, I'm granted his unimpressed stare. "Quite the barterer."

"That's what my father tells me."

"Done," he says.

"I've got my own caveat," I add.

"Of course you do," he replies, his smirk growing.

I nod toward his desk. "You destroy that file, and anything else with my name attached, the second I complete this last mission."

"That's not even necessary," he states, "you know we protect our—"

"Sure you do, but it's necessary for *me*. Not a trace, Phillip."

Gazes locked because our relationship just shifted, a pregnant pause ensues before he finally speaks.

"Understood."

I nod. "Where am I going?"

His dimming expression tells me all I need to know.

BLINK.

Armstrong's eyes start to glaze over from where he lays propped in my lap as the medics' glove-covered, splayed palms hover over him for a few weighted seconds. Shoulders inching down in defeat, he finally withdraws, sitting back and giving me a grim nod, the verdict clear in his eyes. I subtly nod back just as the chopper shifts direction, putting more safe space between us and our extraction point.

"Tell me something . . . Jennings," Armstrong rasps out as dawn begins to light the skies, the steady *thwomp, thwomp, thwomp* of the hawk's blades muting his words before I lean in to catch every last one. The truth of that has the sting increasing in my chest.

"What's that?"

"Where do you go?" he asks as I stretch my upper half a little further to fully meet his eyes.

"This is what you want to talk about right now?" I ask, our hands fisted together atop his chest, several safe inches above the mortal shot he took to the gut.

"Yeah . . . seven missions together, and I never could bring myself to ask, but I want to know." He coughs. Hearing the telling rattle inside it, I curse the fact that I couldn't get to him while guilt starts to set in.

"Eight," I correct. "Stop talking, save your strength. You've got a lot of recovery ahead of you."

"The only place I'm go-ing today, brother, is h-heaven," he wheezes, and I hesitate briefly before nodding in resignation. Armstrong's always been an unapologetic man of faith, kissing his dog tags and praying before our boots touch the ground. We've spent many idle hours in wait perched together in varying terrain, at times talking about all things religion, philosophy, and the world. Sharing beers after hellish days and endless close calls. The truth of how close we've become hits hard, along with a painful wave of awareness that I'm the reason he's speaking his last words—taking his last breaths. Because I'm the one who summoned him for this mission.

"Do you have any messages for me?" I ask.

"When you love the people in your life the way you're supposed to, no messages are necessary."

"As if you're such a saint." I wink. "Smug bastard."

"Smug bastard I may be, but I rest easy knowing I did right by them. They know," he wheezes again. "Fuck."

"I'm sorry, man." I grip his hand tightly. "Please try to hold on."

"Hell no, I'm running to that better place. You all can have this one," he coughs again, and I can tell he's fading. He has a minute at most. "Tell me, brother," he prompts, "where do you go?"

I stare down at him as he gives me his 'no bullshit' return stare and says as much. "You know what the hell I'm asking. You look, move, and dole out orders *like you*, but you aren't really *there*. It's in *your eyes*. They're like a wall of metal when you check out."

I furrow my brows, uncomfortable with the question, as he squeezes my hand, a sign that he's running out of time and wants the answer. Staring down at him, I try to muster a way to describe my mentality when I blink to black.

"It's more like *checking in* while detaching from all emotional decision-making." I concentrate hard on what sticks out most. "Keeping the notion of right or wrong while dialing in on the most basic survival instincts to complete the mission by any means necessary." It's a state of clarity that's nearly impossible to describe, but for my friend, I try. "I become hyperaware of sight and sound. All of my senses magnify tenfold, as well as my adrenaline."

"You moved like fucking lightning to try and get to me . . . I saw it."

"Not fast enough," I grit out, the apology evident in my voice.

"Don't take this on yourself," he orders adamantly, his blood-coated lips lifting, his whispers becoming forced and less audible. "I know you have a crush on me."

"Fuck, and I tried so hard to hide it," I reply, as a burn starts to take hold in place of the sting.

"Every man . . ." he struggles, "in this fucking bird knows you just saved them. Whether they thank you or not." Feeling their eyes on me, I shake my head as Armstrong grips my hand harder, commanding my attention. "I'm glad it's you with me," he whispers as the hellfire sets in.

"Me too," I reply, the selfish urge to blink out the moment coming on strong, but I bat it away because he deserves my presence, and I need to feel it.

". . . See you, brother," he utters brokenly, his arms seizing involuntarily for a few seconds at his sides before his body relaxes. I keep my grip tight as the sun invades the chopper's interior, lighting up his face.

"See you," I utter, gripping his hand harder just as he releases mine.

Chapter Thirty-Four

TYLER

SUMMER 2012
Fourth of July
Triple Falls, North Carolina

BLINK.
 Bone-deep exhaustion keeps every step heavy as a scream ascends into the sky at my back, the pop and sizzle following shortly after. Keeping my eyes on my boots, I push through every step until I get to the familiar crack in the cement. Gripping my dog tags, I run them back and forth along the ridges of the metal chain. With a shuddered exhale, I will my boots to turn, surprised when my body obeys.

Eyes and throat dry, the night's heat relentlessly batters me as another shriek rips across the sky above, the sound ricocheting *through* my entirety, threatening to transport me to a different place and time. Places and times that my whole being has been desperately seeking refuge from for months. The collection of hellacious days fueling the notion that the cement I'm taking residence on might give me that refuge, that long-lost sense of belonging—of home.

With the gradual lift of my head, my hungry eyes take in the bungalow-style house I spent years of my youth treating as such a sanctuary. The potted plants on the porch are a welcome sight, though now hanging limply outside the terracotta housing them. The roof is still missing the same shingles, the dwelling forever in a perpetual state of disrepair. Delphine's reasoning for that echoes back to me through space and time—from the morning I left.

Space and time that seem so fucking vast now, playing barrier. Though, for the most part, the view looks the same, stoking some of the low-lit hope in my chest even as it refuses to fuel so much as a whisper towards the flame.

"Please," I grit out. "*Please*," I beg, unsure of what or whom I'm bargaining with.

The sight of her ancient sedan in the driveway promises an added spark of familiarity, a flash of the memory of the first day I drove it. Our matching smiles across the cabin and the wonder in her expression the first time I took her to the orchard.

Swallowing the memory and pain that recollection stirs, I finally shift my gaze to the large four-squared windowpane that gives an uninterrupted view into her living room. The view provided from where I linger in the shadows is similar to what it was for so many consecutive nights in my last lifetime.

She's there. In the same chair. Still there, and against all odds, now within reach—never seeming anything close to that in my mind. Even with my consistent trips back to Triple Falls, she was always a world away, a lifetime away. This street, this house, remaining foreign soil to me, crossed off the map. Abandoned in head and heart, and yet, it still exists. Behind her sedan sits Dom's Camaro, another barrier created by both of us, by her order and my promise. One I've maintained to this day. One that keeps me idle now and peering through her window. The only light in the living room is provided by the TV, outlining what little view I have of her in dull color.

Sweat gathers at my temple as I watch her sip from her glass as old hurts start to seep in.

Six years.

For six fucking years, I've been absent from this spot,

at least to the naked eye. From a distance, nothing at all seems to have changed. The truth is that upon closer inspection, I know life has altered us both in different ways. What remains of me now feels foreign, even to me.

Is she still the same? Would she recognize me, or any part of the boy I was? Inside, I feel that boy with me, begging me not to move, breathe, or exist as the battle begins between us.

Her battles and mine differing.

Her current battle?

Life was kind enough to gift her a curveball by way of *cancer.*

She was diagnosed just after I got called up to join the response team and began long stints without contact. Tobias told me of her diagnosis when I finally felt safe enough to allow myself back on the Raven radar and fully back in the know. Though relieved by her recent prognosis, she's been deathly ill, and I haven't seen her *once* or spoken a word to her. Maybe as far as she knows, I've been aware the whole time she's been battling and chose no contact, but that isn't the whole truth. It only became the truth when I was made aware she was sick, and I still maintained my distance. I chose to stay away, until now. Even now, in seeing her so fucking close, the paved street continually stretches in front of me, my boots weighing me down as my inner battle ensues. Getting to this cement from my truck felt like wading through an unforgiving current—through the sands of time. A hellish, slow-motion descent into the battle happening in my mind. Soaking in the view I've been fucking frantic for, it does absolutely nothing to calm the conflict between boy and man.

This was supposed to feel different.

But as I take in the sight that I've been desperately telling myself I need, it brings none of the relief I thought it would—not after so much time. Eyes burning with frustration, my chest starts to scream with ancient aches as I scour the house, willing myself to cross the fucking street.

It's my limbs that refuse my order. It's my tired, aching, depleted, battered soldier's heart that wants inside that fucking house, even if there's no relief in the view. The vision of her just yards away, *right there*, across the street, is too surreal to believe. As explosions continually sound at my back, sweat begins to pour from my temple.

Dropping my gaze to my worn boots, I will the eighteen-year-old inside me who can't forget that morning to recognize the *man* that now hosts him. Willing him to identify how far we've come and how many steps we've taken *without* her.

Just a little further, I tell him and get no response.

I swallow and swallow again as I peer through the window at her, tracing her profile as carefully as I can in the dim light.

I've marched endless miles, crawled, crept, ran, carried others on my back in the worst imaginable conditions, but I can't seem to fucking manage fifty steps, give or take, to cross the fucking street?

Freedom explodes across the night sky as if mocking me, while my father's stifling words choose this moment to haunt me.

"I still can't find the fucking door."

His tearful confession batters me as the burning in my chest amplifies with that truth. A shriek pierces the midnight-cloaked sky before the deafening boom follows, and another so loud it reaches my bones, rattling them with memory, willing the images to flood me.

Any relief I could have felt at laying eyes on her is trampled and stripped completely as my pulse spikes with memory-induced adrenaline—my body's way of reminding me of just how many steps I've taken since her. Of the battles fought and the blood spilled to get back to this cement. It's then a notion strikes me that if I would've come to her before I left for the GRS, I could have crossed this fucking street. Maybe not with ease, but I could have done it—would have done it. A large part of me, before I joined, was still the boy who ran from her that morning and is taking shelter beneath the rubble of the aftermath now, unwilling to budge.

Every pop and screech at my back confirms I've practically erased that starry-eyed kid's idea of what being a soldier is versus the reality.

Have I erased her now, too?

The escalating pain at the sight before me tells me that's not the case and that she's not the cause. It's me. My decision to continue to march—to take on another mission—that initiated the change. The realization sets in that I understand my father's blind decision now, in that he probably has no idea which battle it was in which he lost himself, just that he did.

"Go to her, you fucking bastard," I grit out breaths coming hard. "She deserves a thank you," I gasp out as I will my feet forward. Even as I scream at my psyche, I can't and don't manage a single step.

The need to protect her outweighs any selfish other because if I do manage to cross the street, I'll bring it all with me—the visions, the adrenaline, the anger, the night sweats, the blood on my hands, as well as my current body count.

"They'll break you down only to build you up, making you believe you're a god. They'll make you feel invincible, but you won't be. No man is. At the end of it, if you make it out alive, you'll come home with scars you can't hide, physical or otherwise, and the fact you can't hide them will eat you fucking alive."

Except it wasn't the Marines who made me believe I was different—I did that all on my own, thinking myself some exception. I trusted it was the truth, up until this very moment as the door disappears from my vision, and I become blinded by my father's view—no door. There's no door.

"No," I rebuke as my chest cracks wide. "Not you," I condemn both boy and man. "You're different," I grunt as failure thrums through me. "You made yourself a different fucking soldier . . . God dammit!"

Cupping my jaw, I run my palm down my face as defeat lodges in my throat, the ache now screaming in my skin, embedded deep in my bones. The longing for the home I swore I saw in her eyes, the shelter I made inside her heart. And now, no matter how hard I try to visualize it, there's no longer a door. I erased it. She erased it.

Blinking rapidly to clear my eyes, without a single weapon, the hardest battle I've ever fought plays out on the cement beneath my feet.

"Please, Tyler, please cross the fucking street, look into her eyes, and t-thank her."

Just as the words leave my lips—as if she can hear my struggle—she turns in her chair as if searching for my shadow. A second later, I know she sees me when she stands so abruptly that she stumbles back a step.

My starving eyes desperately search her, an unbearable ache detonating when I'm only able to clearly make out her silhouette, nothing more. But I feel it, the connection in the way she's standing stock still and staring back, as the whisper of home I thought I had in her begins to beckon me. A relieved breath leaves my lips as she begins to walk toward the storm door, just as I finally take a step toward her. In the next instant, our connection is lost as Dom interrupts our connection, stalking into the kitchen and turning on the light. My view of her now blocked altogether, this time by the barrier of a promise—a promise I can't keep if I take another step toward her.

Searing, white-hot pain shoots through me as I realize I might not ever be able to walk back into that house again. To look into her eyes without any of the affection I felt and still feel.

I still love her and am in love with her, and my thundering heart is telling me now that I always will. But my soldier's heart is weary, and it needs its sanctuary. It needs her. I need my front fucking door.

Severed Heart

"I will never love you."

I never believed that—never believed her—but maybe I should. Even with evidence of her surprise through that window, it's her silence in my absence that prevents me from believing anything else.

Swiping my face free of the debris of any foolish delusions of a homecoming, I turn and stalk away from that cement, from the deceiving view, and retreat toward refuge from the unforgiving sky. Once inside the cab of my truck, I slam my fist into my wheel as the guttural pain I've been curbing for six years crashes through me like a tidal wave.

You're her soldier. She made you! She saved you! Turn around and thank her!

Chest heaving, the battle allows no escape as color explodes across my windshield, the smoke slowly tracing its path just after, as if savoring the victory. Shackled to her promise not to ever darken her door with a hint of what I feel for her, I allow myself to hate her for it in that moment—for forcing me to utter those words. With that promise, she took away any chance I had of a homecoming. Putting my truck in gear, I press the gas and don't let up on it until I'm well past the county line. Speeding toward my reality—now convinced of what was solidified the day I left Triple Falls—that I am now and forever a homeless soldier.

Chapter Thirty-Five

TYLER

SUMMER 2014
Fourth of July
Charlotte, North Carolina

BLINK.
Sporadic, colorful blasts of light streak across my windshield, thrusting me briefly back into the battle I lost on that sidewalk two years ago. Pushing any lingering ache of the recollection of that night aside, I gas it toward downtown Charlotte in one of multiple nondescript vehicles on the same mission. Ravens currently spreading in all directions for the very same purpose—to protect Dom at all costs.

My current mental state is the same as it was this morning. Stuck in a mind-blowing mix of terror, fury, and fucking awe to try to cover up the fact that my brother went rogue this morning by halting a mass murderer's plans. Plans eradicated in the dead stare of Joshua Brown—the kid Dom stopped *point-blank* outside that stadium. A stadium that was set to be filled to the brim tonight with unsuspecting families to watch fireworks. But with Dom's act of bravery comes the toll that goes with the tough call he made to prevent *another* massacre. The nature and likes of similar killing sprees are becoming far too fucking common in our country. And it's the corrupt fucks like the military officials we've been investigating and plotting against for weeks, who put guns meant for soldiers into the hands of sick kids like Joshua Brown. Officials rerouting crates of arms meant to be safeguarded on military bases back to US soil and into the streets, sold indiscriminately to the highest bidder, no matter their intent of use.

Making officials and others like them enemy number one for me—outside of Roman.

Another shot of adrenaline shoots up my spine as I press a little harder on the gas with the overwhelming need to protect Dom from further detriment. Other than the moral battle I'm certain is currently warring inside him, his words from this morning gutting me while ringing true.

"When we wait for someone to do something, no one ever fucking shows up."

Determined to not only show up but do everything within my power to shield him, I lift my cell phone while shouting back in the van full of birds to cut out some of their rushed chatter. Dialing a number I created with my last mission, specifically for times such as these, I'm thankful when Phillip answers on the second ring.

"I was wondering when and if I would hear from you," Phillip greets.

"I'm calling to collect my first favor," I manage to convey over the cocking of guns behind me as Russell stirs to attention where he rides passenger. Impossibly, Russell's become even more invaluable during my time away. Successfully networking with Sean to further cement and implement club rules. As my first and most trusted recruit, I've been considering promoting Russell as my second-in-command, especially since I plan on taking extended leave if and when Preston gets elected.

"I'm listening," Phillip speaks as I will every bit of fatigue to drain from my body, confident Sean and his most trusted are doing their part—to shield Dom by any means fucking necessary.

"There was an incident in North Carolina this morning."

A brief pause. "I'm aware," Phillip finally replies.

"I'm working on rearranging the details surrounding it. What happened was a *solo* act *preventative in nature*."

"No second?" he asks, speaking of the 'second suspected gunman' currently being reported by news channels as armed and dangerous across every news station while Dom is simultaneously being hunted by authorities statewide.

"He doesn't exist," I clip, "and never did, *that's* the favor. If anything solid comes up indicating otherwise, it *disappears*."

"I see . . . then consider it done, and I'll do you one better," Phillip states, as I hold up my fist to Russell to get the squawking idiots behind me to quiet down. A heartbeat later, all chatter ceases.

"What's that?" I prompt Phillip.

"In taking your word for it, this one is on the house," he relays as I exhale my first breath of relief since I faced off with Dom in our junkyard hours ago. A confrontation in which I finally glimpsed the haunted look in his eyes that he's been shielding us from for months. The look of a heavily weighed down, highly fatigued soldier who's close to his breaking point. A feeling I'm all too fucking familiar with.

No matter how hard I've tried in recent months to get him to open up, Dom's dodged and hedged my every attempt, just as determined to protect me from similar evils that I've already gone toe to toe with. His knowledge of my time in the GRS is extremely limited due to the mental struggles I'm still dealing with. So, along with my worry for Dom's mental state comes the added dilemma of relaying this situation to his brother and the *when*. Another to add to our list of crimes against Tobias that started with our mutual homecoming.

A long-awaited homecoming for Dom and me that was

kicked off by the sudden appearance and invasion of one Cecelia Leann Horner. Since then, it's been a free-for-all shit show in bad *personal decisions* and hell on earth in keeping them none of my fucking business due to their effect on the club.

With Cecelia now heavily in the mix, involved with both my brothers, and now teetering on the knife point of indecision in joining—an invitation I'm not even sure could be honored *if* accepted—it's been a three-ring circus juggling act. The task list is stacking up with pacifying Dom's bristling need to free himself of Tobias's unrelenting hold, our mounting tensions with Miami, as well as discovering crates of guns *while* kickstarting our revenge plans against Roman. Scribbling in the addition of investigating the crates' origins and backstory involving dirty military, and I'm close to running out of mental ink. Daily, I feel like I'm watching multiple explosive-filled cargo trains speeding toward one another on a rapidly appearing track, with little to no way to stop them.

I've been tackling the insurmountable list of shit piling up as best I can, thankful for the hustle to keep time from drifting by, from revisiting daydreams I should have long forgotten. But I am most definitely *not thankful* for the number of fucking trains I'm trying to reroute or altogether derail. As much as my stance hasn't changed on getting involved in the personal, Dom, Sean, and Cecelia's ménage has become *the* runaway train likely to be most caustic.

"Jennings?" Phillip prompts, jarring me back into my most pressing worry.

"I'm here, just keep me updated."

"I'm on it now, and it will be done," he declares.

"Appreciate it."

"Sometime soon, you're going to have to give me some insight into what you're up to these days," Phillip relays. Something I've considered since I ended my time in the GRS, knowing Phillip's involvement would be advantageous for the club on so many levels.

"I've been thinking the same, and we'll have that conversation once you come through. Heads up, you'll have some help from a little birdie, so keep your ringer on. He'll be in touch in a few, and so will I." I swallow. "I really need this—"

"Say no more. It's done," Phillip assures before cutting the call.

Easing off the gas when my radar alerts me there are cops ahead, I dread the fact that of all the fucking days that Dom decided to go rogue, this particular is one of a few in the calendar year that the number of cops on patrol increases significantly, making our collective task tonight a lot riskier. Holding up my cell in the dim light to dial, I can't help but lash out.

"Shut the fuck up!" I bark toward the back, cursing the fact that I've been so short of time since this shit happened that I've been stalled in making the two most important phone calls.

"Want me to drive?" Russell asks, and I shake my head, adamant. Resigned to my mission—nothing fucking happens to Dom.

Another lone firework explodes, sliding across my windshield. The strays lit by individual residents to celebrate since shows have been canceled all across North Carolina due to the threat today. As it bursts in a cloud of glittering gold, I curse the geniuses who decided to honor freedom in any way by dedicating an entire night to plaguing vets who might not be able to handle hearing mock war in the sky. Some probably cowering from the inescapable nationwide celebration. Vets like my father, who just celebrated his latest sobriety chip two years in now, sadly falling off a second time in the years since he started rehab. A fall I didn't and won't condemn him for. Dialing the next number as I watched purple streak the sky, I'm thankful when Beekman also picks up on ring two.

"Hey motherfucker, I was just thinking about you," he greets.

"Change of plans," I clip, "no time to chat about the why. I need you on, now."

"Done," Beekman's voice instantly morphs into all business, "talk to me."

"I'm dropping off the *finger paints* the kids made in your jurisdiction within the hour."

"I thought we were—"

"Like I said, change of plans, couldn't be helped," I reiterate, knowing Beekman is already doing what he can without flagging himself inside the Bureau to start to build his case against the dirty officials.

"Nail these motherfuckers," I bite out with emphasis, "and make it look convincing, bro. They get *no grace*. Make their downfall a spectacle."

"I'll do my fucking worst," Beekman assures.

"I feel the need to stress at this point that this can't fall into anyone else's hands but yours," I relay, tightening my hand on the wheel, thankful as hell that Beekman set up shop in the last twelve months in a branch in the North Carolina sector of the FBI. His involvement is one of the reasons that Miami is so bent out of shape in wanting access to Beekman and any others like him. Access we fucking denied.

But with my favor being called in and Beekman being our inside bird to build the case, we'll be close to out of the woods. As long as the trail on the 'second suspected gunman' goes ice cold, and the takedown of the military officials is enough to steal Dom's current media spotlight.

"Don't lose an ounce of sleep over this," Beekman speaks up, sensing my state. In his imparting tone, I can practically hear his heavily bolded wings twitching to life. "I'll snatch this shit from local as soon as I'm able. Just make sure you get it over state lines to make it federal."

"Already on it," I tell him. "Thanks, man."

"Oh, it's *my fucking pleasure*," he declares, equally as offended for our military brethren. "Make sure to keep a few copies in your pocket in case *they* have someone on the inside to cover for them."

"Fuck," I snap, that possible oversight stinging me. "I didn't even think of that. Will do."

"Well, you can't be Superman *every day*," he jibes. "Rest easy, I've fucking been ready for this for too long," he assures again. I can't help the shared pride that this is precisely the kind of situation we've been breaking our fucking backs for years to position ourselves for.

"Not happy about the circumstances, but yeah," I agree. "I'll call you in a few."

"Before you go, you need to know I have a few anxious friends waiting to meet you."

"Good to know. We'll catch up after my meeting, which is going down in *twenty*. I called in a favor," I state. Though Beekman never got the call-up for the GRS, he's spent his time wisely by obtaining his status in the FBI. "I'm sending you a number to the helping hand I mentioned who's now chipping in on this bill. He's waiting for your call. Gentle reminder, he's ink *free*."

"Say no more," he clips before ending the call.

Holding my phone out to Russell, I give him my order. "Message the number I called first to the number I just hung up with."

"On it . . . and fucking genius, bro," Russell compliments, in the know about Phillip and Beekman as I glance back in my rearview at my other most trusted. Sean and I had decided to divide and conquer. My team consists of Denny, Jeremy, Russell, and *Peter*—whose earned ink is still fresh. All strapped and ready to do whatever it takes to protect our brother.

"Who's got the prints?" I ask.

"I do." Denny speaks up about the prints we extracted from the officials' houses and transferred on some of the bullets for this purpose. With the victimless crimes we're about to commit in addition to Dom's this morning, it should be just enough to get our feathered fed the green light to yank it from local police's hands. Our dilemma in bringing it to Beekman's level was solved by Dom's stunt this morning. Something Dom *knew* was necessary to further our plan—the *brave, brilliant* motherfucker.

"Keep a few in plastic for *insurance*," I emphasize, and Denny nods.

"Listen up," I snap as I slow to a stop outside the abandoned warehouse. "In and out, empty every fucking clip you've got, and straight back to the van. No variation," I state as they crack open the back doors, and I turn in my seat to face them. "Keep sharp. Every second counts, and we're going to be at this all fucking night. You with me?"

I get collective nods and small grunts of confirmation, all of them perked up and ready.

"Go," I order as Russell leans over with a clap on my shoulder.

"Hang in, man, we've got him," Russell assures in a show of solidarity as the weight tries to settle between my shoulders. Just as quickly, I bat the notion of failure away. I've been prepping for this for ten years, and I'll be fucked if we go out like this.

As I watch Dom's brothers covertly approach the warehouse, their training evident in their movements—a swell of pride thrums through me. More crashing into me as their collective gunfire lights the building up, making a pathetic mockery out of what's happening in the sky. Just as quickly, they're back in the van, the evidence planted for Beekman, as we speed away toward our next stop.

It strikes me then that it's *Delphine's army* marching tonight. Our strategy playing out so flawlessly because of the way she molded her soldier's mind. To think and act as a shield to the street soldiers she predestined we would become. Her faith in my competence to guard them unwavering, even in the beginning. Which continues to ring true in my head and heart throughout the night as we fly through our mission in synchronized motion.

It's when the sun starts to light up the horizon long hours later, and as her exhausted soldiers file out of the van, that the need to go to her starts to overwhelm me. It's only when I'm behind my own wheel that I allow my eyes to burn with the sting reflecting in my chest.

Running my finger along the ridges of my wheel, I fight myself once more to keep from racing to her door. From telling her that we became the synchronized birds we are now because once upon a time, she took in a lost, mind-fucked teenager beneath her wing and nurtured the soldier within him.

Because of her.

All because of her.

Chapter Thirty-Six

TYLER

B LINK.
 The screen door slaps behind me, delivering another brutal nostalgia hit as my eyes easily find and fix on the woman who's been haunting me for nearly a decade. I blink and blink again at the surrealness of this moment in addition to the soul-searing moments before it—at the reality that it wasn't Delphine or me that initiated our collision today.

No, the utterly paralyzing face-to-face that took place hours ago was due to the act of a clueless girl with a selfless heart. A girl who, in mere minutes, ripped my mental barrier away, unknowingly forcing me to confront what I've been battling for eight long years.

What seems like just a short collection of minutes ago, I was contentedly rolling a shopping cart, with Cecelia teetering on the end as we debated our favorite Kevin Smith movies. The two of us perusing the cleaning aisles as Cecelia dodged my increasingly inquisitive stares.

"*Clerks.*" *I offer my choice as Cecelia lifts and weighs a big and small bottle of Windex in her hands. Making the decision for her, I grab the big bottle, tossing it amongst the growing mix of cleaners she's already collected in preparation for an errand. One she specifically summoned me for but has yet to clue me in on.*

"*Of course, you'd choose Clerks,*" she snarks as I roll us a few feet, halting me with a jerk of her chin. A movement very Dominic King in nature, and I can't help but grin at the arrival of it.

"So, what's yours? *Mallrats?*"

"No way, *Chasing Amy*," she delivers as if it should be obvious while scanning the wall of products.

"That's because you're a die-hard romantic," I quip with an eye roll.

"Proud of it, and toss in a young Ben Affleck to boot," she fans her face as she coos, "yes, please."

I quirk a brow, keeping my voice low and free of any condemnation, knowing the topic is still settling within her. "You are aware you have two boyfriends, right, Cee?"

She waggles her brows. "*Ain't it cool?*"

"*Pulp Fiction,*" I retort confidently, continuing our ongoing quote game for all movies nineties, a game we're evenly matched in with Adam Sandler lines.

"*Two points to the Marine.*" She winks. As she tosses in more supplies, I study the former bookworm and good girl who has been in a rapid state of metamorphosis since she invaded Triple Falls along with my brothers' hearts. In discovering the nature of her heart, I've recognized why they would risk so much. In living in the townhouse Dom, Sean, and I share, I've been forced to witness the three of them falling, in every stage, since day one. At first, I was raging against their coupling in fear for all three of them, despite my stance on the personal, but for the sake of the club.

At this point, there's no fighting about her presence in any of our lives any longer or denying that Cecelia's heart is remarkable in a way that few are. Because of that, every bird in our close-knit circle is now smitten with her. Over the course of the summer, Cecelia and I have created a sincere friendship, and I've already made the decision to shield her in the future. Whether she chooses the ink or not, I'm grandfathering her under my wing like I have Jane *and Charlie. Because, like them, Cecelia is the best of people, admirably having made the most of the shit hand life has dealt her while blindly trusting with her heart.*

Which is why protecting her both for and from my brothers is becoming a high priority. Tobias's imminent homecoming guarantees she'll need it. It's the tectonic plates shifting beneath her blind footing—dangerous ground she's not aware of, that has me keeping close watch.

As I study the girl who's completely altered our world for better and worse by simply trying to survive her life and the circumstances created by the people in it—something I identify with—she senses my weighted stare. Grinning adorably over at me, she tilts her head with a "What?"

"What?" I parrot, glancing down at the cart loaded with cleaners and TV dinners. "Either you're prepping for the end of times in the most spotless underground cave, or . . . ?"

"Or?" she prompts.

"Cee . . . it's time to fess up," I coax gently, "what are we doing today?"

"Before you say no"—she holds up a palm in an ask to hear her out—"just know that I chose you specifically for this because I know you'll get my reasoning." She lowers her beautiful navy blues. "At least, I hope so."

"All right." I stop the cart, crossing my arms and giving her a pointed stare. "Out with it."

"I want to clean Delphine's house," she blurts as my heart stutters to a full fucking stop.

"Come again?" I blink, my whole being lighting with awareness.

"She's so, so sick, Tyler." Cecelia's eyes water with concern. "And so thin. So thin. She looks like death, and it's fucking terrifying. She can barely walk from one room to the other. I don't know if she's going to live much longer or if I'm just seeing things grimly, but she's all alone—"

Cecelia's voice faded after her delivery as I blinked into autopilot while my heart went fucking hummingbird with fear. Everything slowed as I swiped my card at the checkout, mustering words for a mock argument with Cecelia about paying and, after, somehow summoning return conversation on the drive to Delphine's house. Coming apart at the seams as I loaded the bags and followed her up to the porch steps to the door, a door Cecelia forced me to see still existed.

A blink later, coming face to face with a woman I'd spent endless days and nights believing was utterly out of my reach. Until, with the swing of her front door, Delphine was merely an arm's length away as our eyes collided and held. Shock was evident in our expressions until devastation took its place within me at the state of her.

Every agonizing second after was a surreal blur, up to the one where I knelt in front of Delphine's chair and truly took her in. Our mouths moving in a heavily camouflaged exchange with Cecelia close by, tuning into the tension our collision was creating as our eyes carried a different conversation altogether. Both of us greedily drinking the sight of one another in as I searched for any sign of my fighter and glimpsed only a pathetic *trace*. A majority of Delphine's words were predictable, as if she, too, had partially flipped to autopilot. Only her return gaze told a different story, one that she didn't verbalize.

Her soft whispered "thank you" to us back at her door, ringing sincere but defeated before she unexpectedly snatched me into a hug. An embrace Delphine held for long seconds that felt every bit like a goodbye—as if she was stealing the time for us before she forced herself to let me go. Those seconds in her embrace ignited a hellfire in my chest before I was released, and the door was again snapped closed, with Delphine behind it. That snap ending any real chance at an honest exchange or confrontation.

Reeling and disbelieving once we were back in my truck, I confessed the true nature of our relationship to Cecelia, though I heavily camouflaged some of the surrounding details. I was left reeling when Cecelia left me with a hug back in the shopping center parking lot . . . until anger kicked in.

Anger, which had me driving straight back to Delphine's fucking door in search of an answer to one question.

I break the speed limit before exiting my truck and pounding back up the steps. Ripping open a door I can now so clearly fucking see. A door I stand just a step inside of now as my pulse kicks heavy with fury. Fury which roars inside the man hosting the kid who fled this house. A man who takes the fucking wheel now, who is hell-bent on seeing this through and getting his answer.

"My first crush?" I scoff as seconds continually tick by while Delphine doesn't so much as look at me, eyes lowered as she sips her *glass* of vodka. "Is that what we're calling it, Delphine?"

Cecelia might have unknowingly destroyed my mental barrier today with her insistence on coming here, her abundant heart ignorant of what it was asking of mine. But those cumulative years full of repressed heartache are being replaced with resentment as I glance around the tomb encasing Delphine, as the question burns a hole through my brain. The question of *why?*

If her decision didn't include a *life* with *me*, fine. But *this* is what she chose instead—eight years stuck back in her starting position? Regressing a thousand steps back from the state in which I left her?

Why?

She doesn't so much as look up as she lifts and pours more vodka into her glass, her French translation bible sitting open in her lap. Probably due to Cecelia's impromptu study with her, in which I dismissed myself to clean the other two rooms. In truth, I'd locked myself in Tobias's room before sitting on the edge of his bed, utterly wrecked and trying to get my shit together from the look of her. The fucking *loss* of her.

All that trepidation is obliterated now as I glare over at her where she sits in her recliner, mind-numbing TV the only background noise to the war brewing inside me as I sweep her thoroughly and unabashedly.

As Cecelia described, she's terrifyingly thin and so sickly—it's gutting. A description that neither of my brothers included in their short updates. Maybe because they assumed I would or *should* know.

Of course, I expected her to be sick, *to look sick*, but *this*? The state of her indicates she's committing nothing short of slow, purposeful suicide.

Deep etched half-moons look like stains beneath her eyes. Her typically poised, perfect posture sagging—more evidence of defeat and the poisonous cells multiplying inside her, weighing her down. Or a side effect of the poison chasing those cells to rob them of their job. One she *purposefully* thwarts now, pouring even more fucking poison in her glass—her mission clear. But it was the defeat in her eyes when I knelt in front of her, so little left of her in her silver return stare, that had my heart remembering who broke it.

A fighter.

A fighter that's imperceptible now. One I'm actively deciding to pick a fucking *war with* the longer I stare at her. She was embarrassed when she locked eyes with me initially at her door, but she's flat-out refusing now. It's because she knows exactly what I'm piecing together because she's *guilty*. Rage replaces all anger as I do what I can to temper myself.

"Back so soon?" she finally drawls in pure condescension as she tops her glass to the brim, the sight nauseating, the amount indicative she's well past numbing sips and measuring her pints.

"Why this sudden hostility, Delphine? Wasn't that *you* who just hugged me goodbye?"

She lifts and drops a shoulder. "The last time you left, you were gone for a very long time."

"If recollection serves, you fucking asked me to," I spit in contempt that I don't bother to mask.

Severed Heart

"Ah, I see. Well, Soldier, over the years, I've come to believe we have a different opinion on the nature of your promise."

"Is that so?" I shove my fists into my jeans. "Well, by all means, clue me in, General," I bite out, cutting all bullshit, not missing the slight but visceral reaction to her spoken nickname—one which still glides easily off my tongue.

"You *know* very well what I'm speaking," she states. "Why are you here, Tyler?"

"I'm afraid not only do I *not know*, Delphine, I have no fucking idea. So, I'm afraid cryptic replies won't do. What do you mean we have a different opinion on the nature of my promise? And you might need to refresh my memory," I lie, "because I've done a lot of living since that day . . . seems like I'm the *only one*."

"So many words coming from you, but you haven't answered my question," she says above a whisper, knowing I can hear it.

"I'm here for *her*," I state, cutting through the bullshit pretense we used for almost the entirety of the time Cecelia and I were here.

"For the woman I first laid true eyes on when I was sixteen *after* she helped me breathe through taking one of the hardest hits of my life. The woman I befriended when I was seventeen who challenged me, taught me about necessary evils, and how to soldier. The woman who, despite our age difference, somehow became my best friend at eighteen. Who I trusted with my darkest secrets. The woman who broke my fucking heart when I was a blink away from nineteen because she thought it was the right thing to do. I'm here for her, and I want to spend time with her before she dies—*if* she dies—and that's still a *very big if*, according to your oncologist."

"That woman . . . is no longer here," Delphine delivers on exhale, lifting more poison to her lips. "And by the way you refuse to spare me from your disappointment and continue to condemn me with your eyes and tongue—you are very aware that's the truth of it."

"How would you know? You haven't looked at me once since I walked through the fucking door," I snap, taking a step in to engage the long-awaited battle awakening inside me. "And she's fucking here," I declare, taking another menacing step toward her chair, "and I want her back."

"Hmm." She makes a mockery out of my words with that trite jab, and it's all I can do to keep from smashing the bottle she's continually draining with my fist.

"You better enjoy that bottle," I snap, "because it's your fucking last."

She takes a long sip, hesitating briefly before putting the glass down.

"This seems familiar, Soldier," she relays cooly, "an appearance and another demand."

"I know what I did. I did exactly what you expected me to do. What they've all done to you, but you knew just what to say and how to get me to leave you, though I realized that not long after I left."

"But you didn't return," she states, her purposeful lack of eye contact infuriating.

"I've since made it a healthy habit of taking people for their word when I'm not wanted, preferring to be in the company of those who do."

"I see . . . well, that was long ago, Tyler, so there is no point in arguing or bringing up the past," she counters.

"That's rich," I snark, "since you live in a fucking shrine to your own past. From the looks of it, you haven't bothered to—"

"Let's not fight. Come. Sit, tell me how you are," she prompts.

"I'm quite comfortable staring down at you, making you *uncomfortable*. Seems like no one has managed to successfully do that in years. But what I do know, Delphine, is that as of right now—and because of what you've fucking done to *her*, to the woman I came for—my tap shoes have fucking ceased to exist. So, I'm afraid I'm not up for tap dancing around the truth today."

It's then she finally lifts her gorgeous gray eyes to me to reveal why she's been avoiding contact. Because they're not only fully bloodshot but severely swollen. I take a few more steps closer to see her face is heavily splotched, indicating she hasn't just been crying since we left—she's been *sobbing*. My heart cracks instantly at the sight, and that I was dead on in interpreting what that hug meant. She has no plans of surviving or trying to. None. That hug was goodbye.

Hold steady, Jennings.

"Why did you come back?" she asks, her voice shaking, even as her eyes ice over in preparation. "To further humiliate me? To gloat? You have no audience this time."

"You've made that all too easy, whether intentional or not. And I just fucking told you why." I stand my ground unapologetically.

"Because you still care for me?" she scoffs. "Still *love* me?"

"Yes," I reply simply as her lips part slightly in surprise as I take another step toward her chair. "I've just been doing it from a distance as *ordered*."

"My order remains the same," she states, turning her head away from me. "Leave me, Tyler. You are obviously *thriving* and... very happy. You only came here because you were forced. That girl," Delphine sighs, "has a naïve heart, and as much as it annoyed me today, it's *her heart* that brought you here, my lost soldier, *not yours*," she condemns.

"Oh, is that the truth of it?" I shake my head in annoyance.

"You'll be a fool to try and convince me otherwise. So"—she waves me away—"take your fucking pity and condemnation with you when you go. And whatever obligation you might feel you have"—she turns her head and pins me with her glare—"allow me to relieve you of it."

"Love might be the only thing I have left for you, and it's not romantic in nature." Her eyes dull as if that's not news as I continue to lie through my fucking teeth while blurting the rest of the truth. "Respect, *gone*. Admiration, *gone*. Everything that once attracted me to you, *gone,* and it has little to nothing to do with the way you fucking look but what you've done to the woman I knew. For that, *you will* fucking answer to me."

"You have no right to me," she utters in lifeless defense, "or to speak to me this way."

"I have every right because you're fucking killing yourself!"

"I'm taking treatment—"

"To pacify your nephews, but I see right through it. Do you really think you can fucking hide this from me?!"

"Tyler," she sighs in annoyance, as if I'm a fly refusing to be batted away, "I am not worth this effort. Go find a woman—"

"Worthy?" Another step. "Yeah, you're definitely *not that*, either. But my fucking heart remains here, as it always has, loyal to you, faithful to you, as much as I hate it, so here we fucking are. But *again*, I'm not here for *that*. My promise remains intact. Look at me."

She lifts her eyes to mine as I keep the mask she's forced me to sport for eight years firmly in place, knowing I'll be forced to keep it there indefinitely in order to win this war. "Do you see any sign of a lovesick teenager?"

Her gaze instantly drops.

"Yeah, didn't think so. So now that I've held up my end, I'm going to have to ask for my fucking general back."

"That is a very tall order, Soldier. One I regret I cannot fulfill."

She takes a large sip of her drink, and it's all I can do to keep from snatching it from her.

"In case you haven't noticed, Delphine, there's no one left. They left you to live their lives while you've continually suffocated in this fucking prison you built." The brief pain my statement causes in her eyes is dismissed a second after it appears.

"As did you," she admonishes with surprising pride. "You left to live your life, and look at you, Tyler. Mon Dieu, look at you." Her eyes roam me greedily, softening as they did briefly when I was here.

She's in there, Jennings. She's just buried.

"You have finally become what you've hoped to be, non?"

"And you didn't. Why?" I utter, looking around. "Jesus, you're wealthy, have been for *years*, why are you fucking living this way?"

"It would be money wasted."

"I made sure—" Her eyes snap to mine, but I don't bother to deny the accusation there. "*We all* made sure you didn't have to fucking live this way. Why haven't you moved? Jesus, do you still need a daily reminder to keep men at bay? Because we both know you're more than capable of that feat without continuing to dwell in this shithole."

I stalk over, snatch the bible from her lap, and snap it closed as she keeps her gaze lowered, her voice resigned. "You have continually insulted me from the second you walked into my door with no remorse. I had hoped to have a conversation, but I understand now that's not possible. Please keep our friendship in your memory, and please be well, Soldier. I want nothing but happiness for you, always. I truly mean that."

"I'm sure you do, General. Thanks for your blessing and send-off, but I'm an adult now and not so easily swayed or intimidated anymore. Where I come and go remains my fucking decision. And if I'm unapologetic, it's because the shell you're dwelling in is resigned to *fucking kill* my best friend. So, I think it's pretty important I don't tap dance around that. Why are you killing her?"

"I'm taking treatment," she whispers.

"That's not what I fucking asked you." I take another step, my posture as demanding as my eyes. "Answer me, Delphine."

She licks her lips, keeping her eyes lowered. "Why can we not just keep this civil? Tell me of your life—"

"You need someone to confess to?" I cut in, refuting her diversion and tapping the leather spine of her bible to my chest. "Confess to *me*. Keep your relationship with *Him*, but He's going to let you die if that's His will, right? But, you see, General, I'm going to be the man to witness it, so I deserve your fucking confessions as well."

A small part of her exterior cracks at my words, and her lips begin to tremble. I make peace with the fact that might be the most of what I get from her—if anything.

"It's a pointless choice to stay here. Your faith in me is—"

"Scarce at most because you've lost twenty years grieving the fictional life you wanted and are still mourning while your real life might be *ending* with the help of your own fucking hand."

"It's a little early for this."

"It's too goddamn late!" I roar.

She doesn't so much as flinch. Her reaction the same as if I'd whispered it to her. She seems to have hardened herself to me. Just another man who swore he loved her and abandoned her. To others, she's a junkyard dog everyone believes should be put down. But wounded animals—especially when cornered—are their most vicious because of hurts others can't see. I'm so intimate with her wounds at this point—they're my own, a part of me.

"Tell me where the guilt still is," I demand, "and who is it for?"

She remains quiet, her gray eyes steadily boring into mine, all pretenses between us gone.

"You hate yourself, and that's evident. Jesus Christ, Delphine. Why? For being a victim?"

"I am *not* a *victim*," she states emphatically.

"The fuck you aren't," I counter. "That's all you've ever been. First, by the men who wronged you and then by your own maliciousness. I'm not sure who won in that fucking battle, but Jesus, have you tried to outdo them since I left."

"Just leave, Tyler," she says in a whisper. "Spare yourself this pointless argument."

"Don't waste your breath by repeating that again. I'm not leaving. I was cut short of finishing our argument years ago, and that's my biggest regret in the eight years since you ripped my heart out and sent me packing with it."

I've explored psychology for over half my life for several reasons—to better understand the actions and decisions of those I'm close to, as well as my opponents. An education that has served me well and that I desperately need now as I try to decipher what's happening inside her—why she's made the decision to stop fighting. Looking at her from a psychological standpoint, there's nothing I can do for her but enable her if I want to keep things civil. Fuck that.

"What did you do, Delphine, that you can't live with?"

"I'm tired, Tyler."

"Neither of us is moving an inch until you fucking answer me."

"And who are you really?" she snaps icily. "Who are you to me now?" She shrugs. "A boy I spent a few years with when you were younger to teach, to train." She shakes her head in exasperation. "What do you think you can mean to me, Tyler, after all this time away?"

"Then why the red-rimmed eyes, Delphine? Who the fuck were you crying for when we left? I'm pretty sure it wasn't because of Cecelia's gesture."

"Get out."

"Truth?" I shrug. "My reasons for being here are more selfish than anything at this point."

It took me the anger-filled drive back here to face the fact that if I make this my sole mission and fail, it will haunt me until my fucking dying day. That if I fail, she dies in this state, and as I stare down at her, I decide I can't live with that any more than I can live with the failure of trying. In loving her, I'm already haunted enough.

My head screams for me to run—that she chose her fate over and over again for close to two decades—it's my masochistic fucking heart that still wants to be with her in any way I can. As of right now, she's just as much of an obstacle for me in living my own life as she is for herself.

"More truth? This *delusional man* is the only person on earth who will grieve you long past your death. Who wants and cares about your confessions." I hold her gaze. "The only man who's ever truly loved you, despite the fucking mess you've made and continue to make of yourself."

"I tried!" she booms in a sudden outburst, and I damn near jerk back at the sight of it. "I have tried! Many times!"

"When?" I cross my arms. "When have you fucking tried?"

"Many times, I—" She shakes her head. "I tried after Celine died, before Tobias left for France, before *you*. I tried when we were friends and only drank during the night. When I only drank pint. I tried many times in the years since you left, so that when—" She clamps her mouth closed.

"So that when what?"

Her eyes spill over as she shakes her head. "Oh, fuck you! Fuck you, Tyler! You know *nothing*. You've been absent for nearly a decade, and here you are, coming back with your condemnation. I don't need your fucking judgment and—"

"No, no, you need another fucking drink!" I take the bottle and pour its contents until it floods the glass on the table, the liquid soaking the surface and trailing onto the carpet beneath. "You need to continue to live the very definition of insanity, right?"

She watches raptly as I continue to pour the vodka until it's running in rivulets off the table.

"Take a good look at your life," I grit out. "Isn't it *beautiful*? Every single one of your memories, they all look the same."

"Stop." The word comes out faint as I empty most of the bottle, saving a few drinks for myself. Tapping her glass harshly, I motion toward her to lift her glass as I lift the bottle to my lips.

"Stop, why? You've never pussy footed around how you thought I was wasting my potential. Allow me to do the same, or better yet, lift that glass, Delphine. Let's toast to your wasted fucking life."

I toss the vodka back, the burn only fueling my anger. Fully expecting defiance, instead, she bows her head, her hands visibly shaking as she folds them in her lap. No fight. None. It's utterly gone.

"What future do you see for me?" she utters softly. "Even if I battle the drink, I might not survive."

"Years ago, you told me you didn't know who you were, but we both know who you are beyond your past, what life you want. What future you've longed for. That future is so fucking easily attainable, Delphine, it's laughable. You beat the alcohol, and you're already halfway there. You want to be a soldier? I know of a club that could use your expertise."

She stares at me, her gaze solid.

"You want to fish and hunt? Well, it's in your backyard. You want to watch sunsets in every season? There's a show every night. You want a place to do that at? I happen to know a place you fucking love."

She whips her head up where I now tower over her. "So easy," she scoffs.

"Absolutely not. At this point, you're close to institutionalized in your thinking. The bottle is step one. Step two is sorting your past and finally putting it behind you. Step three will be you actually living your dream. I know exactly what life you want, and I'm offering it to you right now. You once told me that it's the tests in life that make or break you. You can do this, Delphine," I state. "You could have all along. My only condition is this, as long as you try, really try, and even if you fail, I won't fucking leave you."

"You can't make that promise," she whispers.

"I just did," I declare with certainty.

"You have so much—"

"I know what I have. I'll do what I need to do. If I can make this happen, then you can too. Show me, Delphine. Show me you want it, and I'll move heaven and earth to be there for you, to help you succeed, and won't ask for a damn thing in return."

She bites her lip, eyeing the glass before lifting it, her eyes meeting mine in challenge.

"We both know it's not the drink we're up against," I state emphatically. "It's not the fucking drink."

Doubling down, I pull out the last of my armor and decide to fight dirty. To forcibly try to create that shred of hope and pull out my arsenal. An arsenal I've been building in the years since I left her.

"You turned down life with me for what? For this?" I fist my hands at my sides. "Well, that's fucking insulting, but again, I'm not here to win your heart. I'm here to fight for what life you have left. Long or short, I want you to have it because it's clear you're no longer fighting at all for yourself and haven't since the night Alain tried to kill you."

Chapter Thirty-Seven

TYLER

SHE GAPES UP at me in shock as I stare down at her, resigned to finally see this through.

"As for who you were, your name is Delphine Moreau Baptiste." I spit Alain's last name like the dagger it feels like. "Your father, Matis Moreau, was a highly decorated soldier who served in the French army, which is why he was recruited to be an informant for a *new* and highly classified intelligence branch within. His expertise quickly led him down a rabbit hole to infiltrate a group of very dangerous men. Men he consorted with regularly to build his case. But in an effort to guard his young wife and infant daughter, he tucked them in a hideaway in Levallois-Perret until he could see his mission through."

Her mouth continually parts as she stares at me, bewildered.

"Your mother, Nicole Dubos, met Matis while he was on leave while serving when he was twenty-nine and she was only nineteen. Promising himself to her, he courted her for a year before they married. Shortly after, they became pregnant. Their relationship was volatile from the start and took a turn for the worse when Matis fell victim to heroin, which the thugs he was investigating happily supplied him with. During that time, your mother became well known for taking marriage lightly and having embarrassing public affairs, which further fueled Matis's growing addiction. Nicole's frequent affairs led her to eventually fall in love with a French writer, and for him, she left Matis and you when you were five years old."

"Tyler," Delphine croaks. "How do—"

"With that writer," I continue, "she fled Levallois-Perret but was only with him a year when she drowned while on holiday off the French coast. A death your father had no knowledge of during the short years he raised you alone. Up until the day Matis died, he tried to shield you from his biggest mistake, one of which was thinking his government would protect you both. This perspective gifted from a very old, very cranky British man by the name of Frederick Bell, whom Matis called upon to rescue you the night the thugs came to collect you. Bell, who worked for British intelligence at the time, was stationed in France. Though he served with your father, he refuted the possibility of your father's legitimate assignment because of his spiral and addiction. Bell, now mostly retired, lives in St. Albans, twenty minutes outside of London, and still works from time to time in intelligence. He sends his regards and has *deep remorse* for how he relayed the reasoning behind your father's debt to you. That and the fact that he didn't believe Matis. A confession he probably still regrets due to the lingering sting of the severely bruised jaw he suffered after clearing his conscience to *me.*"

She stills fully, almost unblinking, as I recall the details of the rest of that meeting.

"After Bell admittedly ripped you from your screaming father's arms, he deposited you on Matis's nephew's porch. Where Francis Moreau and his wife, Marine, immediately took you into their custody. Francis, an aristocrat by day, remained an activist by night, keeping his involvements hidden well, especially from his wife, Marine, whom he divorced a year after their only daughter, Celine, disappeared."

Delphine cups her mouth.

"Francis imparted this tearfully to me after learning of his daughter's untimely death and your own fate. He would very much like to talk to you. I have his number."

She gasps behind her palm as I take a knee in front of her.

"Marine passed two years ago from complications of gallbladder surgery. Francis has been happily remarried for fifteen years and has a son set to start HEC prep next fall. Which means you still have family in France, Delphine."

"Tyler," she expels, her croak muffled as tears continually pour from her eyes.

"Your second cousin, Celine Moreau, nearly nine years your senior when you landed, heartbroken and traumatized, on her doorstep, was instantly taken with you. Her affection for you eventually bonded you more as *sisters* than cousins. And it was Celine's involvement with her first husband, Abijah Baran, Tobias's birth father, that led you to an introduction to Alain Baptiste when you were just barely twelve years old. Baptiste was raised in a severely impoverished and volatile family which scattered to ashes after his father was killed in a bombing. Alain, ambitious to become an activist in the wake of his father's death, hopped on a train to the nearest city to seek out others like him. It was on those streets that he came across Abijah Baran, who took Alain under his wing until Alain's ambitions warped him to the point that he went against Abijah's orders and bombed a police station. Just after, Abijah washed his hands of him, and Alain fled France with the closest in his circle—including his childhood best friend and confident, Ormand Anouilh. Ormand, whom you must have had lingering trust for since you sent Tobias to him, deeming Ormand your nephew's first to contact when he landed in France. Ormand, who, to this day, remains one of Tobias's most trusted French business partners."

Delphine presses her palm more firmly to her mouth, muting herself from any noise, her body visibly trembling as she hangs onto my every word.

"Ormand did not take part in the bombing, which

severely wounded twelve officers, but killed *two*, a crime which has kept Alain on the most wanted list to *this day*. But before Alain fled both police and Abijah's wrath, he courted you, promising to send for you once he settled in America. Infatuated with Alain's idea of himself and blind to his sadistic ways, when he sent you an aisle-seat ticket as promised, you fled Francis's home and boarded that plane. You left the only family you had with Celine, with hopes of becoming an independent street soldier—to become a part of something bigger than yourself. But mere weeks after you got to Triple Falls, you quickly found yourself a victim of Alain's manipulations and horrific abuse."

She visibly shakes as I continue to speak of the information I've spent years collecting, the last of it with Phillip's help in locating Bell during my last trip to France.

"After months of nonstop domestic abuse, many accounts written by your own hand in letters to Celine, urging her to leave Abijah, who was rapidly deteriorating due to schizophrenia, Celine took you up on your invitation. She managed to secure a safe escape from Abijah with the help of a man she'd fallen in love with—a man by the name of Beau King. It was with Beau that Celine and her five-year-old son Tobias joined you and Alain here in North Carolina. Finally reunited with your sister—no doubt hopeful things would take a turn for the better—you realized far too late that would never be the case when you woke up in the hospital in critical condition after having suffered multiple injuries dealt by the hands of the sadistic fuck. One who lured you to America only to have you support him and endure his abuse. Even with Celine and Beau here, and the fast addition of Dominic King once they arrived stateside, Alain continued to habitually terrorize you for *years* up to the night he tried to kill you, the very night he *disappeared*," I state, my heart growing heavier as she stares back at me, in utter disbelief. Unblinking now as her tears continue to fall, one by one, her grief evident, her shock more so.

"Mere months after you woke up in that hospital, your sister and her husband—the two people whom you've long convinced yourself remained your only true family—Celine and Beau, the only witnesses to what transpired the night of Alain's disappearance, were murdered in a plant fire, leaving you none the wiser of what happened the night you were hospitalized. Their sudden and tragic deaths left you to raise their two orphaned boys. Abijah's son, Ezekiel, and Dominic, fathered by Beau."

"How did you—"

"Terrified, you took on the responsibility of raising two young boys while still recovering from injuries you sustained months before at your husband's unforgiving hands. Already alcohol dependent and afflicted with seasonal depression, thanks to your father and that fateful day in the snow, you attempted to begin to support Celine and Beau's orphan boys. You were triggered daily due to PTSD after years of verbal and physical abuse from Alain, including *habitual sexual assault*. A responsibility that terrified you because you were still trying to gain your bearings *and heal* from an endless list of injuries that Alain left you with the night he tried to end your life, the most damning—a *traumatic brain injury* to your *left temporal lobe*. An injury you've desperately tried to heal from *without* the doctor's recommended rehabilitation."

I grip her hands.

"All of these things collectively adding up, keeping you confused and terrified. Feeling utterly alone, you turned to the bottle again and again to help you both quiet the fears and numb the pain of the betrayal thanks to the men in your life."

I lower my propped knee, leaving myself on both in front of her.

"You've been fighting a very long war *alone* to try and put the pieces together, as well as quiet your mind enough to heal. But you've been kicked while down one too many fucking times and plagued daily with reminders of the horror you endured. Prideful but too ashamed, you've refused to seek help, guilting yourself for the last twenty years for the mistakes of *others* due to the decisions you made when you were just a *young girl.*"

A sob erupts from her as I hold steady.

"Mistakes made due to the pain and loss of surviving the trauma you went through because of the horrific crimes the men in your life committed against you. From those you trusted most from a very young age until the day your own husband tried to end your life. Blaming yourself for other people's failures. Blaming yourself over and over for not being able to recover from an injury that *cannot be healed*. Could never be healed because the damage is *permanent.*"

I bite my lip, agony lacing my words. "It's a traumatic brain injury, Delphine," I deliver against her muffled cries, intent on having her hear me. Sobs wrack her tiny body as she stares over at me, completely exposed, as I lean in and palm her cheek. "This can cause *hazy vision*, both short- and long-term *memory loss, severe mood swings*, bouts of anxiety and *depression*, as well as problems with *writing and reading* comprehension, and can also affect speech. An injury you suffered at the hands of your ex-husband, *which makes you a victim.*"

Taking her shaking hands, I squeeze them lightly while keeping command of her eyes.

"So, all this guilt and shame you've piled upon yourself for not being able to piece together what happened, of not being able to repair yourself, and Alain's lingering reign of fucking terror, ends today—ends right now if you want it to," I relay, the sting in my chest intensifying tenfold at the sight of the woman rapidly unraveling in front of me, her composure crumbling.

"You're not going to find the peace you seek in a bottle or that book. You know that by now. You've tried to do it alone every day since you woke up in that hospital, but you don't have to. You don't have to do it alone anymore, and there's nothing wrong with that, but it's not the drink we're up against, Delphine."

My heart speaks now as I allow my own pain to ring through.

"The only way you're going to find peace is by being brave enough to live again." Her cries multiply as I soften my gaze and keep her hands in mine, rubbing my thumbs soothingly along the back of them.

"You're right, you don't owe me anything, but I'm *begging* you for this. I'm begging you that if you want any part of that future, let me help you get to it. But it's not the fucking bottle we're up against, Delphine. Never has been. It's just how you numb it. And aside from sorting what happened and putting that son of a bitch behind you, he doesn't get to have *any more of you* or a second past these few of *your future*."

Her face twists in agony as shuddered cries erupt from her.

"Because I want those seconds. I want as many of them as I can get. I *need* them because I need my goddamned general back." I falter slightly along with my delivery as her hands tighten around mine. "I know I told you once that soldiers don't stay, General, but they don't fight wars such as these alone. If you want to finally end this battle, I swear to God, we'll go in and do it together."

She visibly fractures before launching herself at me, wrapping herself around me as her cries surround me.

"Soldierrrr," she expels as if it's being ripped from her, her cry so guttural that I collapse on my heels and cage her as she breaks against me. The anguish-filled lilt behind her call I know I'll never forget as long as my fucking heart beats. Decades of pain and confusion inside of it, thanks to the monster who not only tried to rob her of her life but damaged her in a near irreparable way. In knowing that, I bring her shaking hand to my heart while keeping her nestled firmly to my chest as I make what promises I know I will keep. But only if she'll allow me.

"Tell me you want it," I whisper.

"I w-want it," she cries. "I w-want it s-so much."

"Then I will not leave you. You know my promise is real. You know I meant every word I just said. It scares you, just like it scared you then. Let yourself fucking feel it all, Delphine," I whisper. "Stop numbing and let me be here when it comes. I want this for you, always have, but you have to want it too, or it won't work."

"I want it," she repeats as her tears soak my neck while setting my heart alight with hope. She's clutching me back so tightly that I think it might hurt her. "P-please, Tyler, I w-want it," she whispers brokenly, shattered in my arms, her hurt seeping out of her like the rivulets still pouring from the table. "I'm s-so scared," she croaks, her chest bouncing involuntarily as her breaths become shuddered.

"I know you are, but I swear, Delphine, you have nothing or no one to be afraid of because as you were fighting your war, you created a soldier who made it his first mission to keep you safe, and to this day will never allow any threat within an inch of you. He's been on watch of you since he was sixteen years old, and there's absolutely nothing on earth he wouldn't do for you. Because being with you created him and helped make him the man he is for better or worse, so he's going to tell you one of the secrets he's been hiding from everyone since he left, and you're the only soul on earth he'll confess it to." She pulls away, her eyes anxiously tracing my face, my every feature.

"Your soldier needs you just as badly right now," I declare, that truth filtering down my cheeks. "He's not the same without you. He's been missing a very large piece of himself for eight long fucking years."

Her lips tremble as my voice shakes with my admission.

"I've loved you for nearly eleven years of my goddamned life, Delphine, and only had your body *one night*. It was never about sex for me and never will be, but *I need you*. I need to heal, and you're the only one who might be able to help me do it, so please let me be your friend again, General. That's all I want, I promise."

"Oui. I want that so much." She nestles back into me, her head on my chest as she nods into my neck. "My f-fishin' b-buddy, my b-best friend. I missed you s-so much."

"I won't let go this time. I swear this to you, I won't fucking let go, no matter what, and I won't leave you," I tell her as she continually nods into my neck. "I fucking promise on all that I am, this war we fight together."

Time be damned, disease be damned, illness be damned, I'll defy it all and keep my promise. To make the most of every fucking second she gives me. But most importantly, make the most of *hers*.

I cage her in my embrace in the silent moments we spend in her decision, guarding her from the shame and humiliation that plagues her.

Even if I never have her love in return, I have her for the time being, for as long as it takes for her to heal— maybe for *us both* to heal as I speak my last truth. "We healed each other before, Delphine, and we're going to do it again," I vow. "We're going to do it again."

Chapter Thirty-Eight

TYLER

UTTER. FUCKING. HELL.
It's the only way to describe watching twenty years of alcoholism drain from Delphine before my eyes. Fists at my sides at the end of her bed, I watch as she vomits, or rather, dry heaves, hovering over the plastic tub the nurse holds at her bedside. Delphine's hair and face are soaked in sweat, as is the sheet plastered to her body. Each of her accompanying groans relentlessly replacing hope with fear that she might not survive the night. Though I told her I would be by her side every second, I signed up for a hellacious journey of laying witness to each one. Though I was assured Delphine could handle detoxing at home with the proper medical supervision, as each agony-filled second passes, I second-guess my decision not to have hospitalized her. After another thirty minutes of watching her endure the worst of her first battle, I reach my breaking point.

"Sedate her again," I grit out in an order to the nurse, Kerri, who's currently fucking *knitting* now in a kitchen chair that I moved to Delphine's bedside.

"She's almost through the worst of it," she offers blandly.

"She doesn't and *shouldn't fucking have to* suffer through it all, sedate her."

"Mr. Jennings, I'm simply—"

"I don't give a fuck!" I roar. "Sedate her or get the fuck out!" I stalk toward Delphine's dresser, which is now lined with medical supplies, in search. The specialized nurse—who came highly recommended for high-risk detox—finally shoots her useless ass up from her chair and grabs a ready syringe. Glaring at her, I take a knee next to Delphine's bedside and grab her hand as she looks over to me.

"You're not b-behaving like a s-soldier," she challenges in an attempt to joke as I run my fingers through her soaked hair, trying to hide my worry. The only reason I'm keeping her here is because she hasn't had a seizure—I know this because I haven't slept in the last thirty-six hours. But it's the third and fourth day she's most at risk, and I'm coming apart at the idea that it could happen any time.

"Give us the room," I order Kerri, who immediately takes her leave under my glare.

"You know, technically," I whisper to Delphine, "I'm a Marine now. I've even got a fancy title."

"What is it?" she asks, shaking so badly that I fight for breath.

"Gunnery sergeant." I flash her a grin I don't feel. "But I'll always be your soldier"—I wink—"and you know that. How you doing, General?"

"I c-could use a drink," she manages, her eyes latched to mine, her face clammy, her body soaked with sweat.

"I'm kind of with you on that. I could use one myself." I peer back at her, curious as to when she started day drinking. The knowledge battering me that years ago, when she limited her intake, this wouldn't have been nearly as dangerous—that and the fact that this really could kill her.

"I d-don't want to fail you." She shivers as I stand and bend, unlacing my boots while never dropping eye contact.

"Then don't," I tell her, fisting off my shirt.

"I don't w-want to fail *me*," she admits in a whisper while taking a curious eyeful of the tattoo on my right pec.

"Even better," I commend just as her face twists in

discomfort, her jaw shaking involuntarily. "We're going in together this round, General. Are you ready?"

Delphine nods, keeping her eyes locked with mine, and in seconds, I'm stripped into nothing but my boxers before I slip into bed and turn on my side. Propped on my hand, I stare down at her where she lays on her back beneath me. "I have a few more secrets to tell you," I confess as Delphine gazes up at me, slick hair plastered to her scalp, her lips tinged blue. "Want to hear them?"

"Oui." She nods for emphasis.

"Before your soldier left for the Marines, he gave himself two missions to see through in the sixteen days he had before he was to board his bus. The first was that he spent *twelve* days alone in the woods with the pocketknife you gave him."

She winces at her failed effort to get closer, and I palm her hip, adjusting her so she's as flush to me as possible.

"Better?" She nods as she gazes up at me with pride in her eyes.

"You r-really did it?"

"I admit it was no picnic, but yeah. I did it." I wink. "So, you impressed?"

She musters a tiny smile. "I am imp-pressed"—she shivers—"and proud."

"You're scared," I murmur, and her eyes instantly water. Still propped on my hand, I palm the top of her head, brushing my thumb along her hairline the very same way I did so many years ago. Her long exhale hits my neck as she sinks into the sweep of my touch. "I'm not scared, and do you know why?"

"Why?"

"Because after you win this battle, there's nothing and no one to be afraid of anymore. Which brings me to my second mission. Do you want to hear it?"

"O-oui, t-tell me." Her jaw slows the involuntary shake as I continue to caress her hairline, and her lids start to lower. Staring down at her, I bite my lip, hesitating briefly before deciding to see it through.

"In seeking an answer to a question that had been plaguing your soldier for years, I made it my mission to get that answer before I left. As close as we were, Delphine, I wasn't sure if you would tell me if I asked." She frowns but remains silent.

"So, three days before your soldier got on that bus to train as a Marine, I got that answer. The question being... if some of his general's guilt might stem from the fact that her ex-husband might not have simply *disappeared*."

Her gasp is audible. "Tyler, non, I did not kill him—"

"*I know*, General," I whisper, cupping her cheek. "Want to know how I know?" Her eyes widen even as her body starts to go lax due to the sedative. "Because *I did*."

She gapes at me as I continually sweep my thumb along her profile.

"Because your soldier hunted him down, only to find him wasting away in a dilapidated trailer in Georgia. Living in utter fucking filth."

Her exhales cease against my neck as the intensity of her gaze increases tenfold.

"That night, Alain suffered the most brutal of deaths," I admit unapologetically. "His injuries were *extensive, injuries* you're *familiar* with."

I sweep my finger along her cheek while recounting the list of injuries she'd stuttered through the night I found her rocking on her living room floor in her underwear.

"*Several contusions on the spine . . . three broken ribs . . .* a fractured wrist and ulna . . . significant damage to the windpipe, *bite marks*," I whisper, capturing the tear streaming down her temple with the pad of my thumb. "But what *ended* his life," I whisper low, "was a brutal blow to his *left temporal lobe*"—her eyes spill over—"a blow his wife *survived*, but that your soldier made sure *Alain didn't*."

Leaning in, I press a slow kiss to her temple, just above

the surface of the injury that lay beneath. Pulling back, I see her gaping up at me in utter shock. In those tense seconds, I completely lower my mask, allowing her to take in the expression of a man with zero regrets. Who summoned his darkness within the length of a long, deep inhale and a blink. A shift made a second before he turned the knob on that battered, yellowing trailer door. Mask off, I allow her to view the man who stepped through her ex-husband's doorway, both filled and fueled by the need for retribution. A man void of all empathy and compassion. Void of anything but the hate that had been festering inside him for years and the dire need for vengeance for the woman he loved. I allow her to see the extent of the capabilities within the soldier she helped to shape and the assassin he molded within himself before and while in her absence. And she does, she sees it all within that length of time as he speaks.

"What can I say, General? Of all the things you said that morning, you were absolutely right about one thing . . ." I lean down and stroke her cheek. "I'm a jealous fucking man."

***

Hours later, I rouse as Kerri exchanges Delphine's IV bag. Glancing down, I see Delphine sleeping soundly. Gazing down at her freely, I take in the changes. Of the natural signs of aging, the unnatural ruddiness in her complexion, and the tiny broken vessels in her cheeks due to years of drinking. Knowing that some of it will clear up and the circles will possibly fade with the end of her treatment. Even so, I can clearly make out the same surreal mix of features that I memorized for endless hours when I was a teenager. Her beauty is not so far gone that it's no longer noticeable. Just veiled behind years of self-abuse and illness. With time and some focus on her health, she'll regain some of her vibrance. Not that I give a shit, much preferring her animation back over anything. The ache remains that I still love her so fucking much, *romantically*. The lie I told her was completely necessary and one I will uphold like I did my promise. Because all these years of fighting it have taught me that I don't want to live without her. So, if it means lying, then I can live with that, just not *without her* in any capacity. Holding her, being this close to her again after so many years apart, is fucking everything—even if it's temporary.

"Is she out of the woods for seizures?" I ask Kerri after she exchanges the bag while still gazing down at Delphine.

"For the most part, yes," she replies.

I nod, satisfied. "Then you are dismissed."

"I'm happy to stay," she offers, "she really does need supervision."

"That's what I'm here for," I tell her. "I'm sorry about the way I spoke to you"—I let the words linger—"but not at all sorry for my reaction." I glance over to see offense in her expression, as expected, but I don't let it deter me. "As many times as you've seen this, I'm sure it's hard to muster empathy. Especially with your amount of experience, but fucking *knitting while* someone is *writhing in pain* right next to you?"

She has the good sense to look ashamed.

"I'm sure you've heard it all, Kerri, seen it all, and have reached a wall for the sympathy you have left for people who choose this life path. But *this woman*." I gaze down at Delphine. "I assure you. You've never heard a story quite like hers. She's more than worthy of your empathy, and so is any other human being *brave enough* to seek your *help* and expertise."

We stare off for a silent beat before she speaks.

"I apologize, Mr. Jennings," she replies sincerely. "It's obvious you love her very much."

I nod.

"I really don't mind staying," Kerri offers, remorse clear in her tone.

"No, I've got her."

Sometime later, the feel of fingers running through my hair has me easing back from my slip out of consciousness. As I rouse, I absorb as much as I can of Delphine's gentle touch, surprised by the nature of it considering my confession. My smile precedes the opening of my eyes as I take her in. In a short assessment, she seems to have regained slight color, a step up from ghastly pale. Her eyes, though filled with sleep, hold some of the disbelief they harbored before she closed them.

"Did I dream that, Soldier?" she whispers, still stroking my hair.

"No," I emit low, but unflinching.

She glances around the room.

"We're alone. I dismissed the nurse," I relay. "Don't be afraid of me."

"I'm not," she replies instantly. "I'm not afraid, Tyler. Never of you, but you . . . found him. You truly found Alain?"

"*Hunted* would be the more appropriate word, but yes."

"And you . . . killed him?"

"Yes," I state unapologetically. "He suffered every wound he gave you that night in that exact order."

"Why?"

I readjust my pillow, facing her. "Because I couldn't live with the fact that he was still breathing. Because I knew the first time I took a life, it would alter me, change me as it does for every man. So, I controlled that decision, and in doing so, it was utterly fucking painless."

"Painless . . . but, Tyler, you're—"

"Yes, I am, and *you know* I am," I state emphatically as her eyes roam my face. "You knew long ago that my blood can run very, very cold. You saw it when I was a kid. You suspected I was capable. I didn't want to talk about it because I *knew* I was. But because I faced it, I've got control of it, not the other way around." I let out a long exhale. "But let me be clear, I can only speak with *ease* about it *to you and only with you*. Don't think I didn't battle the weight of what it means, mind and soul, because I did for some time."

She nods and continues running her fingers over my brow, eyes heavy with the need for sleep as questions lie inside them.

"One step at a time, and this isn't the time yet. Do you trust me?"

"With my life, but... you"—she shakes her head—"discovered so much."

"This is a trauma you need to work through, *build up to*, and it's going to take time. I want us to be as armed as possible when we go into that battle, but we're not ready yet. I can't promise it will be easy, but you will have your answers."

"Okay, Soldier, I will trust you." She palms my jaw, and I close my eyes at the feel of it. "I have missed you... imbecile," she jokes weakly, "very much."

I can't help but smile even as the melancholy hits. "Me too, General."

By the time I open by eyes, her fingers have stilled, and she's drifted back to sleep.

Chapter Thirty-Nine

Delphine

Opening my eyes due to the sun rays heating my back through the blinds and the screaming of my bladder, I'm met by the sight of Tyler, who sleeps soundly facing me.

Aside from the dog tags hanging limply from his neck, he's bare from the waist up, the sheet draped along his hip. Inching my head back on my pillow to gain more view, I do my best not to disturb the light grip of his palm on my hip—one that indicates he must have reached for me in the night. As awful as I feel, I can't help but appreciate and soak in every detail of the man lying next to me.

My beautiful boy, my soldier, came back all man. A man with very few signs of the boy who left. One of those signs being very faint freckles on the bridge of his nose ending at the edge of each of his cheeks. His ridiculously long, curled lashes grab several seconds of my admiration, thick dark brows complimenting his complexion and bone structure. The dimple in his jaw now seems etched, especially now that it's covered in light stubble and stays present without animation. His slightly parted, full lips, which are taking shallow breaths, are tinted dark pink. The look of them is so soft. The remembrance of their touch is so powerful that I can easily recall the *physical* feel of them—

the feel of *all* of him. A night even my treacherous mind refuses to let me forget. It wasn't at all a boy who took my body that night. It was a preview of the man lying in front of me now, utterly captivating me.

From the waist up, his sun-tinted skin is covered in nothing but deeply defined muscle. His brown hair looks darker now, neatly trimmed on the sides. Only a few inches long, the top trimmed off, just where there used to be a slight curl. I loved that curl.

Tyler, as a boy, was so beautiful, but the man who took his place has done nothing but continually take my breath away since he appeared at my door. My fingers itch to palm his jaw, to touch any part of him, though I no longer have any right to take such liberties.

It's then that his words from days ago still my itching, eager fingers. His declaration of what love remains for me is limited to that of friends—something I will have to accept as much as it pains me. But for any time with him, I will force myself to try to understand. His declaration that he needed me would have to hold me. His healing will be my priority, as he has made mine his. My screaming bladder doesn't allow me to contemplate anything further as it reminds me of why I woke.

It's as I come further to consciousness that I remember his confession and barely manage to keep myself still as the shock again filters in.

He killed Alain.

Hunted him—something I can't fathom processing now. So, I don't, and instead, concentrate on soaking in as much of my soldier as I can as he sleeps. Even as my bladder demands relief, I sweep him thoroughly, my eyes catching on the tattoo etched into his heavily defined pectoral—a tattoo I first caught a glimpse of when he lifted his shirt to wipe his brow while cleaning my kitchen. One I had assumed was Marine in nature, but it does not look so much now upon closer inspection. Circular in shape, a very menacing-looking skull with only the top jaw lies atop crossbones, surrounded by a perfectly symmetrical cross, but not quite a cross. All four extensions are the same length, the edges of each ending in a T-shape—the top of the skull surrounded by a half circle made up of six stars. The lower part of the half-circle consisting of three sets of Roman numerals. The more I examine it, the more I realize nothing about this tattoo looks Marine.

Where has my soldier been? As if sensing my question, he stirs.

"Morning, General," he rumbles in a sleep-filled voice before opening his gorgeous brown eyes, "what do you need?"

"I have to pee," I admit with a wince. "Very badly."

"Okay, let's go," he says, standing bedside within a blink. The act of simply standing daunts me, hair damp and clumped in sweaty heaps. In short, I feel disgusting. Inside just as bad. Temporarily ignoring the strange feeling of sobriety that I haven't experienced fully in years, the lingering sedatives are not enough to hold my building insecurity as I voice my next concern.

"Soldier, I need to pee and *shower*."

He nods, brows drawing as I give him wide eyes. "So, can we maybe call the nurse back?"

"I'm your nurse," he declares, and I give him a pleading look.

"What? You prefer blondes?" He winks, and I grimace in return.

"I prefer a woman," I tell him honestly. "I don't want you to see me—"

"Pee?" he spouts through thick lips. "Seriously?"

"Yes, seriously."

"I can call her back, but I don't want to. Can we try it my way?" He gives me stupid adorable puppy eyes with his request, his lashes so damned long it enhances his beg. "Just for today?"

Bladder screaming, I have no choice but to nod. In an instant, he sweeps me into his arms, and I yelp in surprise before he deposits both me and my IV in front of the toilet with ease before closing the door behind him. I stand stunned at the efficiency with which he did it as my bladder says time's up. Just as I go to lower my pajama pants, the door pops open, and I jerk back as his hand appears, blindly searching for the faucet before he twists the knob on the sink so that the water flows as he speaks. "In case you get stage fright and need some help finding your flow."

Laughter erupts from me before the door closes again—crazy, stupid, beautiful boy, but not a boy. Surprising myself, I manage to do my business easily and flush the toilet. Just after, Tyler knocks twice before popping open the door as I pull up my pants. "No, no, I'm going to shower now."

"Delphine, you're too weak to do it alone."

"I'm not," I lie.

"Liar," he spouts, opening the door a little wider, his eyes holding mine in a demand to help. The look inside them is more intent and . . . indifferent? Maybe a look I deserve, but one that stings. Familiar guilt starts to eat at me as he steps in to stand in front of me.

"There's got to be a way, *alone*," I say, my brain proving useless as I try to find a solution and come up empty.

"Yeah, it's called I've been *inside* you and licked every inch of your body." He shrugs. "So, since when did you become a French monk?"

My eyes bulge at his candor. "This is—"

"You're sick. You're too thin. You're coming down from twenty years of alcoholism. You're embarrassed. I get it, and I can admit I'm scared of fucking this up, so . . . let's just be *human and honest* about it, all right?"

His blunt delivery puts me somewhat at ease, and I nod.

"I'm going to take your pants and panties down," he relays.

"I can take my pants—"

He keeps his gaze on mine and slides my pants and panties down, and I instantly cover my naked crotch with my hand as my neck heats. "God, I know I stink."

"You do," he chuckles. "Actually, you reek."

"Connard," I mumble, feeling shaky on my legs, fatigued already as sweat gathers at my temple.

"Talk to me, General," he coaxes, sensing the change in me as he unbuttons my pajama top.

"Just, very weak. How long has it been?"

"Five days."

"*Five* days?" I repeat, having lost count of them somewhere.

"It's going to take a while longer, maybe a few more weeks, to feel somewhat normal, but I think it's safe to say at this point you did it," he says, gently getting my top free from my IV. Now utterly bare, he keeps his eyes on mine, turning and placing my hands on his shoulders for support before turning to start the shower.

"How do you feel?" he asks.

"Like I look," I counter.

"I mean inside," he whispers as he palms the water to test the temperature as my eyes roll down the perfection in front of me.

"I'm—" My words die as I continue to feast on him. Before me stands a man in his prime, every part of him cut muscle and tanned flesh. His rippling skin is heaven beneath my palms. So virile and alive, I can't help but voice it.

"Tyler," I rasp out, "you are so beautiful." I caress his shoulders as he turns back to me, his expression pinched as his long exhale tickles my nose and chin.

"Appreciate the compliment, but that's not how you *feel*," he drawls.

"I feel so much right now, but I'm so very happy you are here," I admit honestly.

"Me too," he utters before palming my naked hips and sighing. "In the spirit of keeping things honest, I can't help what might or might not happen down below, okay? So, if you get an accidental cock salute, General, we're going to ignore it."

I bite my smile and nod, the fatigue already setting in

as he gently guides me over the top of the tub and under the shower without tangling my IV.

"Tell me if at any second you feel faint," he orders.

I nod again, feeling useless, as he places my palms on his shoulders and quickly begins to lather my hair. We both stand beneath the stream for long seconds, the feel of his fingers heaven as the coconut scent fills the air.

"I'm not going to make you talk to me," he finally speaks, keeping his eyes intent on his task, "but I've got both ears open for whatever you feel up to discussing."

I train my eyes between his pronounced pectoral muscles and the deeply inked tattoo etched into one before lowering my palm over it.

"I was looking at this when I woke. What does this stand for?" I ask, tracing the skull and Roman numerals. "I thought it was a Marine tattoo, but it does not look Marine."

"You truly don't know?" he asks, genuinely surprised as he scrubs my scalp.

"I'm not as up to date as I once was."

"*You?*" He quirks a skeptical brow.

I shake my head.

"Huh . . . well, it stands for Global Response Staff or the GRS. The numerals represent each letter's numeric place in the alphabet." He grips my pointer, bringing it to the first set of Roman numerals. "G," then moves it to the second, "R." I glance up at him as he moves it to the third set. "S."

He releases my finger as I keep my palm on the tattoo, running my hand over it. His eyes keep and hold mine as a few seconds tick by before he grabs the loofah hanging from my plastic shelf.

"Soap?" he asks, sorting through the bottles behind me.

"Gold and white bottle," I answer absently, entranced while gently tracing his tattoo before his eyes dip to mine. The look in them reading dull? Bored? Irritated? As his nostrils flare in . . . annoyance? Anger? "So, not a Marine tattoo?"

"The opposite actually," he says, wetting and roughing the loofah with soap to make suds, "it's a lot like my raven tattoo. This"—he covers my palm briefly with his—"doesn't exist."

"Tell me."

"It's an alphabet operation outside of our government that uses experienced vets, the best of each branch of the military, to carry out missions that also don't exist. I've done a hell of a lot of marching, General."

My eyes widen. "You have faced so many battles, Soldier?"

"One too many," he exhales, keeping my eyes as he drops the loofah and grabs my shampoo.

"So, you weren't in the Marines all this time?"

"Yes and no. According to the United States, I've been a Marine for eight consecutive years and counting. Truth? I served my first four years in the Marines, two years and change in the GRS, and the rest in the reserves. No one knows the extent of it but Tobias, who I thought might have told you."

"You didn't tell Dom and Sean?"

"Jesus, we have a lot to talk about." He massages my scalp with his fingers as he answers. "Yes and no. I gave them enough to hold them because there were long periods that I couldn't contact home. And when I did, I kept it to a bare minimum because I didn't want my boss at the time—who was in the CIA—catching wind of the club."

"Tyler," I gawk. "You worked for the CIA?"

"No, I worked for *me*," he says, gently ushering me under the shower head to rinse, "as a contractor, under the *guise* that I was working for them. I was investigating the military, like I told you I would. I didn't want our club on their radar, so while I was in, I didn't come home and made very few calls. I've spent the last few years before this summer on a base in Greensboro. Now I'm here until I can secure an invitation to the secret service"—he resumes with my loofah—"or join Preston's security detail, depending on which invite comes first."

"You've been back *many times* to Triple Falls?"

"*Many times*," he delivers like a blow. I bite my lip and nod, the anger just beneath his words muting any more questions as I drop my gaze.

"Hey," he says, pulling my eyes back to his with his timbre alone.

"Let's not start on a shitty note. I have so much to tell you, that is if you want to hear it," he whispers, running the loofah gently over my back.

"I want to hear it all," I say, catching his eyes trailing a little lower before he darts them to the side of the shower stall, all the while gently massaging the sponge along my body.

"I don't know how to thank you, Soldier," I whisper. "I don't know how to thank you for doing this for me. For the lengths you have gone to, for . . ." My eyes fill. "I'm . . . I can't believe all you have done for me after—"

His eyes pierce me deep, cutting the words I can't yet summon but am determined to *find*. "I told you I don't want anything in return, but if you really want to, then thank me by stealing your life back. By *taking* your future in your hands and *living* it the way you've always wanted to," he says, gently scrubbing my skin. "And winning this fucking war, General."

I nod in determination despite my fatigue. "I will fight hard, I promise. For you, and for me, Soldier. I will fucking fight *so hard*."

His lips lift slightly. "I knew you were still in there."

"I will admit I've been an imbecile for some time with my health, Soldier, but cancer is a fucking asshole. It is merciless."

"Do you feel any better today?"

"I am tired and aching in places I forgot existed," I sigh. "To be honest, it feels *very strange* right now to be sober."

"When did you start day drinking?" he asks, gently scrubbing my stomach.

"Two years ago," I admit. "It was a very bad time. Very bad. I was fed up with doctors and needles. With all of it, I had—" I shake my head. "I got tired of hoping."

"Before you gave up?" he prods, and I bite my lips before I nod in a truthful reply.

"I was not ready to die but no longer wanted to fight. I no longer felt any reason to. I did not see or feel capable of whatever fight you saw in me when you came."

He lifts my chin with his finger. "I've always seen it—*you*, Delphine."

My eyes spill over. "I had not seen you in so long, Soldier, I forgot myself. I forgot the way you saw me, the way I was starting to see myself before you left. It's my fault, I know, but it's the truth."

He stops his movements, anger radiating just beneath his skin, and in his return stare before he hands me the sponge. I take it as he turns his back, palming the tile in front of him so that I can comfortably clean myself intimately. Making quick work of it, I scour every inch of his insane build as I do. Once done, I drop the loofah and tentatively place my palms on his back, feeling him tense instantly before I press my forehead between his bulging blades.

"Soldier," I rasp softly, running my hands from his shoulders, over the swollen curves of his biceps, and down to his muscular forearms. He emits a low curse when I slowly and appreciatively run my hands back up his arms, keeping them on his shoulders before I lean in, pressing a kiss to his skin before I speak. "Tyler, I—"

"Let's get you out," he clips before turning abruptly and staring down at me with barely concealed contempt as both of us ignore the very obvious cock salute in his boxers. "You ready?"

Stinging and desperate for a numbing sip, I nod.

Short minutes later, he's pulling a clean T-shirt from his duffle over my head. The scent of fabric softener surrounds me as he sits me at the edge of my bed and starts to run a brush through my towel-dried hair. Exhausted, I'm barely able to keep upright. My limbs shaking with effort to remain where I am—to take in his gentle touch and tender brush strokes.

"I did not miss this fucking house," he states. Glancing back, I watch his expression harden as he sweeps my bedroom until our gazes again meet and hold. He breaks contact, continuing to brush my hair. I briefly trail the water still running from his skin to the towel now wrapped around his waist.

"You must be so tired," I utter, comforted by the feel of his hands.

"I'm fine," he assures.

"I've done nothing but sleep and can't even think."

"You don't have to think," he states as I glance back at him. "In fact, you're relieved of thinking until further notice."

I latch my eyes to his as he continues.

"I'm going to tell you what to do, what to eat, and when to sleep. Don't scowl at me." His lips lift at my expression. "It's simply to establish a new routine. One you know you need. You and me, we're going to keep *very busy*. And tomorrow, you're going to talk to someone."

I tense as he turns my head gently to face forward and continues brushing. "You know my mother is a psychologist."

"You can't be serious," I admonish as he keeps me facing forward.

"Dead serious, she's the only one I trust," he relays, continually running the brush.

"And *you're the only one* I trust," I tell him.

"Same, but this is different, Delphine."

"You truly want me to tell *your mother* about myself? My life? My past and secrets, Tyler?"

"Why not?"

"Because she'll know." I bulge my eyes back at him.

"That you've been horribly wronged by life and shitty

circumstances like every other human? Yes, she'll know," he says, easily straightening my head again as anxiety thrums through me.

"Tyler, this is not a good idea."

"You said you trust me," he reminds me with a sharp edge.

"I do, but therapy with your mother?" I shake my head. "My past is no one's business."

"Well, your way hasn't worked in twenty years, so we're going to try it my way . . . Just," he sighs, "just talk to her, try to talk about what you hold so close. Besides, if you're worried about anonymity, she's required, *by law*, never to tell another soul."

"Really?" I ask.

"Really," he assures. "Not even me."

I blow out a breath as his eyes beckon me to agree. "Fine. I'll try." I puff my cheeks with breath. "God, I fucking hate feeling so weak."

"Right now, you're *anything but* weak, Delphine. I swear to you." He stops the brush. "Come on, let's get you back in bed."

"Pathetic," I utter at the relief I feel once resting on the mattress, "that a *shower* took so much effort and energy."

"You'll get it back," he assures, pulling some clothes from his duffle. "Will you be all right if I go change?"

I nod, watching as he retreats into Dom's room. As he starts to close the door, my eyes begin to slip shut, but not before meeting his gaze briefly before he drops it. The truth becoming more evident that I've hurt my soldier in a way he may never forgive me for.

***

"Wake up, sleepyhead," Tyler whispers, running a finger along my cheek. Managing a smile despite the bone-deep ache and sweat on my brow, I open my eyes to see him sitting next to me on the mattress, fully dressed. The smell wafting from him is heavenly. He gestures for me to sit, and I lift to perch against my headboard. Tyler adjusts a pillow behind me for my comfort before handing me a steaming cup of broth. I thank him before glancing toward the blinds and realize it's dark outside.

"I missed the sunset," I utter mournfully.

"We'll catch it tomorrow," he assures as I sip the broth.

Behind his shoulder, I see a new TV set up on my tall dresser, and he follows my curious stare.

"I dug out your old DVD player. Star Wars is ready to play," he says, lifting the remote from my nightstand to lay it within reach.

"You're leaving?" I ask, hating how pathetic I sound.

"I should be back before the credits roll, but you can call me if you need me before I do." He lifts my Sidekick from the nightstand. "Seriously?" He spouts incredulously that I haven't replaced my phone.

"It still works," I tell him.

He rolls his eyes as he programs his new number in under "Soldier"—which makes me smile even as he condemns me. "Jesus, you're cheap."

"Not cheap," I defend, "it works fine, so no need to waste money."

"Hit play," he says with a slight head shake, "and I'll be right back."

"Yes, yes, Soldier, I'm fine. Go."

"Again, if you need me, call me from your dinosaur phone that's being replaced as soon as possible."

"A different battle for a different day, Soldier." I raise a brow, to which he gives me a wink.

"I have missed that wink," I say as he lingers in my doorway. "I have missed your winky face texts so much."

It's then I feel the mountain of words we haven't spoken as his eyes drill into mine because of my sentiment and my part in the loss of them.

"I am so curious about your life," I confess. "I've heard things, *listened* for them, but Dom left not long after you, and they only say so much when they do come or call."

"Which is not often, I'm guessing." He eyes me with concern.

"Dom takes me to and from treatment. He still checks in."

"And T?"

"He calls every few weeks. But yes, I'm an obligation, Tyler."

"They care," he assures me.

"Not like you," I whisper.

"No one cares like me," he draws out, "but you've got to let other people in for that. This is the stuff my mom will help you work out. Okay?"

I nod, unable to help my question. "Are you sleeping here tonight?"

"Yeah, I'll take Dom's bed," he states.

I nod quickly to mask my disappointment. Surely he has women to warm his bed, and knowing that, I can't help but ask my question. "Do you have a girl?"

He lifts his brows, faint amusement tickling his lips where he remains in my doorway. "A girl?"

"You know what I'm asking. A girlfriend. Someone you see?"

"Well, it's definitely not *Cecelia I'm fucking*," he counters of my jealous slip the day he and Cecelia came to clean.

"I see," I say, pulling the sheet up tightly to me and grabbing the remote. "Will she be very upset you are helping me?"

"Not sure," he drawls playfully.

"This is serious. If I was your woman, the shower would make me very upset, Soldier. *Very*, very upset."

He crosses his arms, leaning against the doorjamb. "Hmm. Maybe I shouldn't tell her."

I shake my head adamantly. "You should probably not tell her, no." I wince. "And maybe don't tell her we fucked . . . before."

"Welcome back, General *Brash*," he chuckles, his dimple popping. "Let me get this straight. Are you telling me to lie to my woman?"

"Yes. She'll be suspicious because of that, even if it was long ago, and it will only incite more suspicion. I want to respect her ... but maybe keep her from that knowledge." I widen my eyes. "Trust me, she will not understand."

"I don't know, I really like to be honest with my women," he says playfully. "Any other advice?"

"Don't be a connard," I snap, tilting my head, knowing he's enjoying this too much at my expense. "I'm fine." I wave him off. "You can go. Spend the night with her if she needs the assurance," I say, hating every word. "I don't need you to babysit me."

"Do you want a drink?"

"Yes," I tell him instantly if only to numb the burn of my own jealousy.

"Then I'll stop babysitting when you don't."

I nod. "Are you going to her tonight?"

"Not tonight," he says, "no."

"Tyler, do not ruin whatever you have for me."

"I couldn't," he assures.

"Oh," I say, darting my gaze around, wishing I hadn't asked so many questions. "Well ... that's good."

"Delphine," he sighs.

"Hm?" I ask, slowly bringing my eyes back to his.

"I'm single."

"Oh."

"I don't do girlfriends," he says, palming the frame above him, biceps bulging.

"Okay," I exhale in a shaky rush as I scour the look of him standing at my door, all too alluring. He looks *so fucking good* in simple jeans and a white fitted T-shirt. Such simple dress, but so mouthwatering. His tags somehow add so much to his appeal. He's not only gorgeous, but he's ... fucking sexy. So fucking sexy.

"I've been in love once in my life," he states, dumping cold water on my thoughts. "Didn't work out."

"Tyler—" I falter at his delivery.

"She said she would never love me back," he delivers

with such ease that I physically flinch. It takes me almost a full ten seconds to speak.

"And so, you left her for eight long years without a word," I utter mournfully, hearing every second of those years in my voice as a tense silence follows before he breaks it.

"I'll be back," he says, releasing the jamb before rapping it lightly with his knuckles.

"Soldier," I call after him just as he steps out of sight. He reappears a second later, the frozen screen lighting up his profile. "You have much to tell me?" I ask, and he slowly nods. "Will you tell me when you get back?"

"Not yet," he whispers through the space.

"Then I will wait," I tell him. "I am eager to hear it . . . when you are ready. But I want you to know I will always regret the words I—"

"I need to go, Delphine," he says, cutting my apology abruptly. It's then I know that no matter how close he gets, I'm very far from certain types of honesty. Honesty he's so easily pulling from me, but honesty he seems to no longer want. Words I want so much to say die in my throat at his dismissal, but I give him some truth anyway.

"I hope you know I tried for you, *too*, Tyler," I tell him. "Very hard. I did not drink during the day. At night, I would go longer and longer before I would sip—"

"Until you were triggered," he finishes for me. "I know, Delphine."

"I just want you to know that you knew me *sober*."

"I do know," he relays across the space, feeling as if it's starting to widen from how intimate we were last night and this morning.

"Okay, I'm sorry to keep you. Go to your errand."

"Do me a favor," he asks.

"Anything," I blurt like a lovesick fool.

"Try to *watch* the movie. You can start sorting out whatever you need to tomorrow morning, okay? Stay out of that dangerous place"—he taps his temple—"for a little while longer."

"I will try," I promise as he takes his leave, and I start the movie, knowing I will do *anything* he asks of me. It's my heart that might not be agreeable to the distance he's intent on keeping from his. This truth is evident as it pounds in the direction of his footfalls, following him out of the snap of the storm door and into his truck as it sparks to life, trailing him long after the rumble fades with his departure. Both pounding and aching *heavily* reminding me of the loss of his presence, of what that ache feels like as it has for eight unforgiving years.

Chapter Forty

Tyler

BLINK.

Stalking toward the pin Russell sent, it's the location adjacent to it that has dread coursing through me as I hasten my steps. I'm already on edge about the fact that Dom picked Delphine up tonight from one of the last of the treatments she has left. That and how Delphine's body might respond so soon after detox. Some of my anxiety stems from the fact that the start of Delphine's therapy has been rough on her. My mom came through in a major way for us both, giving me a hug before delivering a light tongue-lashing about visiting home, which I now deem *Carter's* house. Just after, she'd postured up like the professional she is.

Though technically, having my mother treat her might be a conflict of interest, I meant what I told Delphine. Regina Jennings is the only one I trust with her. And seeing as how they've never met before that day and that we're not currently romantically involved, Mom is confident she can treat her objectively.

Not only did Regina Jennings take the edge off what I thought would be an awkward introduction to Delphine, but within half an hour, Mom made it to where Delphine felt comfortable enough to send me packing so they could begin their first session.

Therapy has seemed a good start, despite the rough days

that have followed. I've spent every night of them with her, sleeping across the hall in Dom's bed, tossing and turning right along with her. Before tonight, some of my anxiety has been from second-guessing if I did the right thing getting her to sort through the trauma that she's already relived for two fucking decades. But Mom assures me Delphine needs new coping mechanisms along with some much-needed altered perception of thinking about what was done to her. In believing the same, I'm trusting that Mom truly knows best.

Anxious to get back to Delphine but growing even more so as I draw closer to the pin, I switch my focus, stalking toward the shadow standing next to the tree. Dread fills me as I approach and glimpse Russell's expression and the fact that we're tucked away in the woods across the street from Peter's house.

"Tell me right fucking now that he's okay," I demand, my soft spot for Peter evident amongst our birds since I recruited him from that jail cell. More obvious now as I scan his pitch-black house with my heart in my throat.

"Physically, yeah, mentally, not good," Russell says, scanning the house with me.

"What happened?"

"His dad has been coming around the last few weeks. Apparently, one of Peter's cousins jacked his jaws about how well he was doing and about buying the house and his mom a car. So, of course, out of the fucking gutter comes dear old, drug-addicted Dad, who's been stalking Peter and his mom collectively ever since. He started by harassing his mom for money at the gas station she works at and claiming rights to see Annabelle. Since then, he's gotten more aggressive and has been pounding on their door during late hours, demanding money."

"The fuck?" I grit out. "Why didn't he come to us?"

"I think he didn't want to weigh us down with all the shit we have going on. He didn't even tell *me*," he exhales heavily. "He probably assumed his dad would crawl back into the hole he came out of when he got nothing from his threats. But tonight, he fucking busted in the door."

I don't need Russell to put a voice to it, knowing precisely what happened next. "Please tell me Annabelle wasn't here."

"No, thank God, she's still with the babysitter, and his mom is working the night shift at the gas station."

"Were the neighbors home?" With Peter's house sitting at the end of the last street inside the small subdivision, and the woods we're standing in facing the front of his house, his only nearby neighbors are to his right.

"Not at the time. They pulled in ten minutes ago."

"All right, no one was called, no blue lights?"

"No. We've already made sure a call wasn't put in to anyone. It's likely no one heard it. It was storming pretty hard earlier tonight, which was probably our saving grace." Russell's expression dims, his hesitancy earning him an impatient glare from me.

"Stop with the fucking suspense-filled pauses," I snap. "Lay it all out, *now*."

"Sorry, man. It's just that his dad was rushing him, so it ended up being a point-blank shot that took him down, and it's extremely fucking messy in that house. I pinged you *here* to keep traffic to a minimum until we figure out a plan."

"You made the right call." I palm his back, and he nods.

"We can access the house by the alley," he relays.

I scan the quiet street—a street Peter has gone to great lengths to get to from the dilapidated trailer he lived in with a hole the size of a bowling ball in the floor. A hole his father had beaten him unconscious in front of the day he bailed on them. The amount of pride in Peter's eyes the day he bought his house is one of the reasons I recruited him. A milestone and home that is now and forever tainted by a memory that can't and won't be erased. Anxious to get to him, I turn to Russell. "Where is he?"

"Inside," he sighs, "we tried, man, but he can't stop staring at him. He's refusing to leave his side."

"Fuck." I palm my neck. "Get Denny out here to clean

up, and tell him to bring his strongest mix," I order. Layla's fiancé is our most trusted—and now our go-to—when it comes to precisely *this type* of situation. An expertise of Denny's that I discovered on a very hard night that I happened to be in town for years back.

"I did. He's already on his way," Russell replies, the fear in his tone for Peter amping my own. I press the side button on my G-SHOCK to give me the dimly lit time and keep our cover.

"How long until Mom's shift ends?"

"Midnight."

I nod. "Four hours. Plenty of time to make it happen if all birds are on deck. Round up our most discreet, most capable, and delegate. Renovate floor to ceiling and take it out of our piggy bank. I don't care how it's done, but *get it done*. I'll get him out of there and coach him through how to handle this as we pick up Annabelle."

"Done." Russell takes off like a shot armed with our strategy. Minutes later, I step through the back door via the alley. The streetlight adjacent to the backyard streams through the thick kitchen blinds, lighting Peter up in divided, measured shadows where he sits feet away from his father's lifeless body. The house utterly and eerily silent.

"Give me the room," I order Jeremy, who's standing in the kitchen next to the counter, arms crossed, his expression riddled with concern. A heartbeat later, and with one last lingering glance, Jeremy wordlessly slips through the back door as I carefully bypass the pool of coagulating blood before crouching down and palming Peter's shoulder. Even in the dim light, I can see how pale he is, his expression haunted.

"Look at me, brother," I whisper, hating the lasting effect this will have on him and knowing the nature of this expression all too well—his first kill. Peter's tear-filled eyes float over to mine, the agony there unmistakable. It's then that my instincts about him are confirmed. It's my job to know the limits of each of our Ravens, and though I had done my best to keep Peter closer to my wing—to shield him from this part of it—I could never truly save him from this fate. Even so, this isn't in any way an ideal introduction. Peter's part in our club is that of a criminal mastermind in helping Dom with recon and the planning and execution of heists, not human waste disposal. With that in mind, I keep my gaze steady, my voice just as level. "Look at me, Peter."

It takes a few seconds for his eyes to focus.

"Tyler," he croaks, "I'm so sorry, I, am I . . . a am I out?"

"Keep your eyes on me *and hear me*. You had no choice. Even if you got him out tonight, he was *never* going to leave you alone. The first time you gave in and gave him a taste, he would have escalated it. You protected yourself and your family from a threat that was not going to go away. Rest easy. I won't let you go down for this."

"Maybe I should," he croaks, "I killed my own dad." He swallows as a tear glides along his jaw. "Who does that?"

"A son and brother who will do anything to protect their family. We'll get through this. I swear to you, brother. We'll do it together. Let's go."

***

Two hours later—confident we've camouflaged Peter's secret—I walk through Delphine's door, bundled wildflowers twined together atop a pizza I picked up before Russell's ping. Unease sneaks in when I don't feel Delphine anywhere close by. Though her car is in the driveway, she doesn't answer when I call her name. On edge, I walk into the kitchen and glance around. Setting the pizza and flowers on the table, I freeze when I see a small, familiar, empty brown bag on the counter.

Fuck.

Defeat tries to snake its way in, but I bat it away. I knew there was a chance she'd have a setback during her initial battle and curse the fact that the club keeps me from being a more constant sober companion. But I'm not giving up, and I'm sure as fuck not letting her slip be the last of our war. It's then I detect the low music playing just outside the sliding glass door. Walking to it, I spot her sitting at the table, her back to me as she runs the end of an unlit cigarette along an ashtray. Leaving the porch light off gives me little view of her, though her slumped posture screams defeat.

Staving off the disappointment so she can't see it, I accept the temporary setback as just that, *a setback* and nothing more. Sliding open the door, I stalk toward her, knowing she senses me there even as the soft music and screaming cicadas mute some of my approach.

"It's okay, General. It was just a bad day," I whisper, running a palm down her back, "just tell me how much you've had."

She drops her chin and instantly starts to cry as I kneel at her side, eyeing the pint sitting in the middle of the table, unable to see the level.

"Hey, hey, it's *one day*, General," I relay in a soothing tone. "We armor up and start again tomorrow."

She turns and grips my hand before slowly pulling it to her lips and pressing a reverent kiss to it while lifting her silver eyes to mine. "You would forgive me so . . . *too, easily*, Soldier. My God, I do not deserve you"—she lowers her eyes—"and I never have."

"Not true," I whisper as she releases my hand and begins to clear her face of tears, seeming annoyed by them.

"It is true, Soldier. It's so true," she sniffs. "I want no lies between us. Not ever again. I will never lie to you again, Tyler."

"Glad to hear it," I say, brushing the last tear from her cheek. "Talk to me. Tell me what happened," I coax gently as I eye the bottle again, cursing the fact that it might be empty.

"When Dom picked me up from my treatment, I asked him to take me to a sunset, and I made my confession, my apology after all these years, as Regina suggested."

"And it didn't go well?" Fire starts to lace my veins at the thought Dom might have triggered her.

"No," she sniffs. "Well, *yes*, it went very well. He took me to the most beautiful place for a sunset and told me the most wonderful story. He seemed to accept my apology. Until we got home, and I confessed how I had wronged Cecelia in the past. It is my greatest evil, Tyler. One that I want to confess to you," she exhales and turns her face toward the moonless sky. "I think he will forgive me with time. He was just outraged because he is just . . . in love. He's so very in love with her, Tyler. I have so much happiness for him for that."

"Okay." My shoulders inch down slightly. "So what has you so upset?"

"It's happiness, its sadness, it's regret, so much regret. Regret for you," she says. "For so many things, and I feel it, Tyler. All of it," she whispers between us. "I feel," she shakes her head. "Remember when you told me to stop numbing and let it all come?" She croaks, "it has come."

I nod in understanding, scooping her into a firm hold against me and walking her through the door. Just as I start to close it, she begins to wiggle out of my hold, and I release her in confusion.

"No, Tyler, no." She doubles back and snatches the bottle from the table as dread fills me. "This fucking shit," she hisses as she sweeps past me, grabbing my hand in the process.

"It was just a slip-up," I assure her, on her heels as she stalks us over to the sink. It's then she cracks the bottle, and I gape at her in realization.

"No one *slips up* for twenty fucking years, Tyler," she says, uncapping it, and without hesitation, begins pouring it into the sink. My heart explodes into rhythm as she looks over at me, her gray eyes resolute.

"No more fucking excuses. No more hiding behind this house, my past, or myself. I choose me," she declares, "I choose my nephews—though it may be too late—and I choose *you*." The liquid continues to pour from the bottle as she watches it with wrath before looking over to me.

"I choose our *precious friendship* that I have missed every fucking day because it matters far more than numbing any discomfort, but this," she presses her palm to her chest where her heart lies. "This is," she shakes her head. "It's full of *so much feeling* I have numbed for so long, Tyler. So many regrets for my decisions and actions. It's all coming at once. But I am thankful to finally say it. To speak of what Alain did to me. That *motherfucker*," she hisses before blowing out a breath. "As much as I hate speaking it to Regina, it's time. It's time because I *choose* now to *live*." She tosses the drained bottle into the sink with finality as she moves to stand in front of me and grips my hands.

"I have many regrets, but this is the decision I will never regret and make again and again for *me*. Because I want my future, Tyler, and I want you in it so much. I'm *fucking done* with the drink," she declares. "Done."

Explosions detonate in my chest as every fiber of my being lights at her confession, and I pull her to me, clutching her as tightly as I can without hurting her. "I'm so proud of you, General."

She cries for a few seconds before her muffled voice fills my ears. "Do you believe," she asks, pulling away to look up at me, "that I can still be redeemed?"

"You already are," I assure her, wiping her tears. "For yourself, that's most important."

"I don't want to hide anymore," she relays low.

"You can't, not from me."

"Tyler," she croaks, and I see it then—the fear, the emotions crashing into her, the weight she's holding, and the levee threatening to break. She palms my face, her eyes glistening with fresh tears.

"So much to say to you, Soldier, but I want you to know I understand why you didn't text me or come back."

I frown at her words but let her speak, her chest shuddering as her tears start to flow rapidly. "I understand why you were angry with me. You bravely let me see all of you, and I gave you so little. I d-do not blame you for deciding to stay away. But I am ready to confess to you now. All that I can." She pulls me to her and grips me tightly. "I want to tell you of my past."

"I'm right here." Feeling the bloodletting happening inside her, along with her fear, my chest stretches as I utter the only words I know she needs to hear. "I'm here, Delphine, and I'm listening."

She leads me to the table where we've spent years mutely sharing our pain before finally putting a voice to what her pain consists of and where it stemmed from. Starting at the beginning with what she remembers of her mother, and of her fondest memories with Matis. Ending with her first-hand account of that fateful day in the snow. Recounting the night she met Alain, and the 'favors' she did for him at only twelve and thirteen years old. Of flying to America alone to become his child bride, sole supporter, and ultimately, his victim. Exhausting herself with all that she can recall. Relaying fondly some of her most beloved memories with her chosen sister, Celine. Whose loss fueled her spiral and the retribution-filled act she committed against Diane and Roman by way of Cecelia. An act she deems her darkest and most damning by putting a loaded gun in Cecelia's crib.

I sit, utterly in awe, devastated by the events of her life as she lays herself bare for me, begging me not to think the worst of her as she unveils her demons. As she does this, another storm rolls in, and we weather it as it rages, both outside the house and within her.

Near dawn and exhausted, while simultaneously renewed, we share cold cheese pizza while playing a game of Battle. Our eyes meeting and holding continuously as we flash each other grins between moves.

Just as the sun starts to light the sky, we walk out of the backdoor to greet another day. Hand in hand on the small patio, the feel of this dawn, this day, is distinctly *different*. In knowing one of her biggest battles has been fought and won. That sentiment shared but unspoken as I glance over her, just as she looks over to me, the sun lighting both our faces as she speaks.

"Thank you for coming back, soldier of my heart," she whispers, full of emotion, lighting me up before turning back to scan the morning sky. "I'm so thankful you came home."

"I am too," I whisper, unable to rip my eyes away, realizing how far she's come already in such a short time. Only ten days sober, I realize she's already kicked open the door to her own cage.

My fighter, my survivor, my general, and the love of my fucking life.

In awe of her for the first time in years, her first enormous feat reminds me of why I fell for her in the first place. Her ability to appreciate the beauty of a world that has done nothing but hurt her. The battered heart which steadily beats inside her chest despite the horrific scars made by those who abused it. For her boundless love of the simplest pleasures despite her complicated existence. Maybe I forced her the day I stormed in less than two weeks ago, demanding she fight for herself. Declaring a war she should have, but it's evident now that she's taking over. Especially as she grips my hand tightly, her head continually lifting to the sun as its beam strengthens on her face. As if it's fueling her.

As we reach the orchard later that morning, both exhausted from lack of sleep and the emotional toll, I feel her resilience taking hold. Glancing over as she scans the grounds, a smile budding on her lips, it's then that a certainty starts to settle into me. The certainty that someday, in the future, when the right moment presents itself, she's going to spread her wings and take flight.

And I'm going to be the one to watch her do it.

Chapter Forty-One

Tyler

B LINK.
Ringing his number, it's answered on the second trill.

"Evening, brother," I greet, beating him to the punch, my heart lighter with the news on the tip of my tongue, but forcing myself mute so as not to deny Delphine what she's rightfully earned to share herself. Mere days from her victory, her spirits are high despite her grueling daily therapy. It's then I continually repeat his name for long seconds of the connected call despite hearing his breath clearly on the other end of the line.

"T?" I prompt again, hearing a barrage of background noise, which sounds like a bar, as I steer my truck into a nearby parking lot. Checking my signal, a second later, I hear a French prompt. "En voudriez-vous un autre?" *Would you like another?*

"T? I think we've got a bad connection. I'm going to ring you back."

Hanging up, I dial his number again. This time it's answered on the *first* ring as confusion sets in. It's as the seconds of silence tick by that the smile I've been sporting for days begins to fade with realization. Realization that there's nothing wrong with our phone connection, but it's our bond as brother's that's rapidly fissuring across the line because of my treachery.

A full minute of silence ticks by as I grapple with what I could possibly fucking say because he's waiting for the start of a *confession*. It's then I *physically* start to sense the rage coming from the man at the end of the line as the noise around him ceases as if he's entered a room. Anxiety ramping, I palm my forehead and let out a harsh exhale, knowing I'm fucking damned no matter what words I choose. "I'm so fucking sorry, brother—"

Before I get a full sentence out, he's gone.

Pulling up to the garage minutes later, I pass Russell, Jeremy, and Peter—who we haven't let isolate since the night of our latest secret—taking off in one of our FLEET vans on a new mission. They sound a horn in greeting as I pull in, and they speed away. With their absence, I'm thankful when I catch Sean working alone in a bay, a lit cigarette dangling from his lips. He glances over at me as he secures a part, his eyes lighting up as he greets me.

"Hey there, *stranger*, I paid your part of the light bill, not that your light is *ever on* these days."

Tossing his smoke, Sean grinds it out with his boot and finally looks over to me, a smile on his face. A contented smile. One I've spotted on both my brothers' faces in recent months. However, their expressions are a continual mix of both contentment and fear when we're behind closed doors and away from Cecelia because of one reason—their deception to their brother.

It's the look of happiness on Sean's face now, of being in love and knowing what it feels like. Like this fucked up world finally makes more sense. Like there's purpose and meaning. A feeling of belonging that's fucking indescribable with the right woman. Which is exactly how I feel when I'm with Delphine. It's when Sean gauges my return expression that I rip every bit of that contentment and happiness away.

"He knows," Sean deduces, lowering his eyes for long seconds before chucking the tool in his hand. It clangs loudly on the bay floor as he begins to pace, lighting up again. "Do you know how he found out?"

"If you're in any way suggesting—" I grit out, taking fast offense, and he cuts me off mid-sentence.

"I'm not, brother. Hand to God. I know you didn't tell him, and for your own sake, you should have. Question is, who the fuck did?"

"He's not a fucking idiot, Sean. He's actually quite brilliant. In fact, him being distracted while a continent away, along with his collective trust in the three of us, was your only shot at keeping an upper hand."

"What did he say?" he asks before taking a massive pull on his cigarette.

"Nothing. Just *long, tense* seconds of damning fucking silence, and trust me, that's enough." Sean pauses his footing and stops, really looking at me with remorse-filled eyes.

"I'm sorry, Tyler. I really am. The situation we put you in is fucked."

I nod, knowing that not only will I have to face the fucking hell coming my way for my silence, but in breaking the oath Tobias and I made years ago, I lost a level of trust I may never earn back.

"What do we do?" Sean asks.

"*We*? I'm not in this. In fact, I'm ten steps removed. You and Dom work it out. I'll deal with mending my relationship with T *my way.*"

He swallows and nods.

"Where are they?" I ask.

"On a date," Sean sighs.

"Dom . . . on a date." I shake my head at the irony. "Hell really has frozen over."

"He loves her," he states emphatically, forever having Dom's back. "*I* fucking love her, Tyler. *She's it for me*, brother," he admits hoarsely.

"I know." His eyes fill with more trepidation as he resumes pacing. "But Tobias is not going to hear it, Sean.

This went too far beyond any rectifiable time frame, so you need to expect the fucking worst."

"And that would be?" Sean stops, dread evident in his posture.

"That you're both out," I state.

"Best case?" he asks with pleading eyes.

"Truth? A punishment fitting of the crime in addition to months or years mending the bridge back to his trust. I can't fucking imagine what he's feeling right now." I grimace. "And honestly don't want to."

"Would you be so hard on us?" Sean prods.

"Putting myself in his shoes, if I didn't know what it was like to be in love . . . yeah, I would. But this isn't about me. I just get to share the fucking punishment."

"I'll make this right with you," he vows. "One day. I swear to you, Tyler."

"Don't worry about that right now. I've *got me*. But you best call Dom and know this heads-up is the last thing you're getting from me." I turn to stalk back toward my truck and stop to glance back at him. "And if *France* finds out it was me who warned you, I'll *never* have your fucking back again."

"Understood," he says, my implication clear, "where are you going?"

"I'll be back when you really need me," I say.

"That won't be long," he utters, devastation filling his timbre, which has me hesitating in leaving him. Because I've felt what he's feeling. Not in the same way, but enough to ache for him. The crack happening in my brother's massive heart is palpable from feet away. "Forgive me, brother," he pleads, "I was selfish to ask this of you. I just . . . wanted to be happy a little longer, you know?"

"Unfortunately, man, I really fucking do," I admit honestly. "So count on me to be there when you really do need me, but Sean . . . choose your next moves very *wisely*."

"I will . . . thank you, Tyler," he relays, already lost in the panic filling him as he pulls his burner from his jeans.

***

Back aching, I pull up to Delphine's and stare into the house. Anticipation brews in my veins as I continue to block out the panic I've been tamping down for hours, thanks to T's discovery. Scraping some of the residue from my thumbnail, I scour Delphine's prison, hating every fucking bit of brick and mortar that makes up her cage. My contempt for the house almost as powerful as my contempt for Alain. She had a long session with Mom today, who reported by text earlier that she was in decent spirits when she left.

In knowing that my general might be up for an escape with me—and after burning my candle at both ends since the beginning of summer—I can't think of a better time to finally see if my efforts might pay off.

Cracking my neck, I haul myself up the steps, feeling every bit of the residual effort I made this morning as I stalk toward the door. Much to my delight, my refuge meets me at it. Hand on the knob, she sports a smile as she ushers me in, wearing a thin white robe which is covered in light blue flowers.

Her frame is slightly healthier now, and her coloring is better, too—though the chemo robs her of progress in the days following treatment. And fuck am I thankful she has so few left to go. She's battling so much at once and taking it all on the chin for the most part. Though some of her visits with Mom set her back emotionally, it seems today's session didn't, as she eagerly ushers me in, beaming at me as she does.

"Soldier, I thought you would *never* get here!" It's on the tip of my tongue to tell her of the shit show about to go down, but in gauging her mood, I decide to keep the peace with a white lie. "Sorry, General. It was a busy day, which threatened to turn into a busy night."

"No, no, it's okay. I just . . . I have a present for you," she admonishes breathlessly, her silver eyes lit with anticipation.

"Oh, yeah?" I ask, as she nods enthusiastically and takes my hand, leading me toward the kitchen table where our latest game of Battle awaits.

"Oui!" she says, anxiously pulling me through the living room. In the short time we've been together, we've fallen easily into our old groove. We spent a night watching Star Wars when she was fatigued and managed a few games of Battle. My ask tonight might push her out of her comfort zone, so as she rattles in anticipation, I do too. It's when I spot the flowers that I got mere days ago already wilting in a mason jar on the divider counter that I speak up.

"You need to toss those, or they'll stink up the house."

"I can't bring myself to part with them yet," she spouts.

"Why not?" I frown at the length they lasted as she, too, eyes the limp flowers.

"Because my soldier bought them for me," she finally says. "They remind me he's coming back the next day." I pause my footing at her admission, and, in turn, stop her from guiding me toward the table.

"Delphine," I say, jiggling our clasped hands. "I'm coming back every day," I whisper as her eyes drop. "Look at me," I order, and her eyes instantly dart to mine. "I'm coming back every day. I sleep here *every night*."

"I know," she nods. "I will throw them away, Soldier. Maybe tomorrow."

"*Do* you know?" I ask. The temptation to cup her face is strong, but I resist it. I don't want her to mistake it as intimate, and for me, it would be. My renewed attraction for her is stifled daily, as I purposely refuse to pick apart or decipher any return looks she grants me for my own wants. The eighteen-year-old me standing firmly with me in that stance.

"I believe you," she whispers, tugging at my hand. Before I get a chance to poke further into her worry, she leads me to the end of the table. On it sits a thick book, twice the size of a bible—its cover a light, thick blue plastic with no title. It looks to be filled with laminated pages which are bound together with plastic rings. A book that looks fit for a presentation and was put together at a place like Kinko's or Office Depot.

"Are we having some sort of orientation tonight, General?" I joke.

"What?" she asks, her accompanying smile making me feel like an asshole for making one.

"Nothing," I say, noting she's nervous even as she speaks up, revealing as much.

"Okay, sit down," she orders, "or you can stand," she says, shaking her head. "No, sit down, Tyler," she says, fondly rolling her gaze over me. "Yes, sit down."

"All right, now I'm intrigued." I take a seat at the end of the table.

"Okay." She splays her hands excitedly. "*Open it.*"

Grinning, I flip open the plastic top to see . . . maps. Not one or two, but what looks like . . . hundreds of detailed maps of Triple Falls. As I continue to flip, utter shock filters through me.

"Holy . . . fucking shit, General," I rasp out as I go through every page, my mind fucking blown at the amount of detail she put into every single one.

"There is a table of contents," she spills excitedly as she points out the ins and outs of the book while I stare down at it in astonishment. Shaken by the amount of work I'm positive she must have done.

"The woman who made it," Delphine explains, "well, helped me put it together, made sure it was perfect because my writing is still not so good. She helped me label the streets correctly and spell them." She widens her eyes. "So you weren't on Elmbs Street, instead of Elm." She laughs before turning to me, her eyes misted with clear emotion. "She did a good job, non?"

"*She* did a good job?" I gape up at her to see proud tears multiplying in her eyes as she reads my answering expression. I keep a tight hold of her with my free hand as I flip through, the ball lodged in my throat swelling rapidly. "General . . . how *long*." I swallow and swallow again, the need to know the answer to my question more than the need for my next breath. "How long did it take you to draw these?" I hear the guttural ache in my voice while lifting my eyes to hers.

"Oh, Tyler, no." She shakes her head adamantly as the emotion I can't tame fills my expression. "Please do not be sad." She lifts my palm and softly kisses it. "It was no trouble at all. I was *so very happy* to do it for my soldier," she insists.

I tug our clasped hands to pull her closer to me.

"That's not what I asked," I rasp out, rubbing my thumb over the back of her hand as she stares down at the bulging book, tears shimmering in her eyes.

"How long, Delphine?" I manage to get past the rapidly swelling lump. A long silence passes as I start to grow impatient before she answers.

"Six years," she finally admits, as I watch twin tears slowly glide down her cheeks, her eyes purposefully fixed on a laminated page as she speaks again. "For six long years, I prayed my soldier would come back for his maps," she relays shakily, her voice filled with mourning, which mirrors the ache I feel.

"Six years," I repeat as she nods, tears flowing as she holds a shaky smile. "Why six, Delphine?" I ask, anger and a dozen other emotions filtering through me as I stare between her and the book.

She shrugs, which only fuels my upset and stokes my suspicion of exactly what day she gave up.

"I got . . . was very sick then."

"Delphine—"

"Soldier, can I *please* tell you another time?" she pleads, "I am happy and don't *want to want* a drink," she rambles nervously.

"Okay." I blow out a breath before inhaling some patience. "Do you like it?"

"Like it?" I utter, stupefied as I twist my lips around

the fucking boulder lodged in my throat and the seizing in my chest. "*Like* is far too *weak* of a word." I stare down at the book. "It's fucking incredible."

"I realize why you did it, why you asked me for these maps." She slowly kneels at my boots, pulling my hand to her face before staring up at me earnestly. "You told me to trust you on *why*, but I realize why. It's because you knew." She shakes her head in embarrassment. "You knew about my brain injury and that it would be good to help with my rehabilitation, non?"

Biting my lip, I nod.

"My soldier," she whispers, her tears lining the hand palming her cheek, "still trying to save me, even in his absence," she relays. "I will find a way to deserve you."

Paralyzed by the sight of her at my feet, by her gesture, I fight for control to pull her to me, to crush her lips, knowing it's only going to get harder with the road ahead.

"I know you're still angry with me and don't want to hear my apology, but will you please, please, let me say I'm sorry? Tyler, I regret so badly that morning. The way I made you feel." She looks up to me, her eyes scanning my face as she ripples with anxiety. "And that I still regret it every day and always will."

I nod as more of her tears spill over—these are different in nature. These are tears of the healing kind as my chest continues seizing with a need for her.

"I thought maybe if you . . ." Her chest bounces as she tries her best to rein them in. "I thought that if you saw this book, you would see that all my time was not wasted . . . and maybe you won't think so little of me?"

I grip the back of her neck, brushing her tears away, adding my other hand to firmly grip her face so she can see the truth in my eyes. "Do you see anything in my face that says any part of you is wasted?"

"Always saying the right things," she tries to pull away, "I'm so sorry for—"

"Shhh," I whisper, the need to fucking kiss her overwhelming as she scans my face. In an effort to shield it, I release her in an instant, standing. "I have a surprise for you, too."

"You do?" she asks, a look of . . . *dejection* . . . turning into one of surprise. Am I reading her right? Or is this just my hope blooming?

The notion strikes that these are probably my wants.

But . . . does she *want* intimacy? Her kiss in the shower said so, but she was weak at the time—at her *weakest*, and I don't ever want her accusations from that morning anywhere fucking near us haunting our friendship now. Though she admitted she wanted to be intimate that night we had sex, even the morning after *while* she obliterated me, I won't even let that play a factor in us *now*. Resigning myself back to dedication to our friendship—which keeps me safely in her life—I decide not to mull over it or let it fuck with my head another second. Unsure if I could ever handle going there with her again, even as my heart begs for it. The fucker begged me last time too.

"But hear me," I palm the book on the table. "Before we get to what I hope is *your surprise*, *this*," I run my hand over the cover, "has just become my most prized possession, fucking *ever*."

"Then it was worth every minute," she whispers as she stands. "I made you happy, Soldier?"

"So fucking happy," I tell her. "So, in the spirit of that, are you up for a trip?"

"Tonight?" she asks, glancing out of the living room window.

"Yes, go pack a bag," I tell her, lifting her to her feet. "We're not going far."

"Really? A bag? To *stay* somewhere?"

"Yeah, for a night or longer, so bring your toothbrush, pajamas, and a few day clothes."

"Okay," she whispers, "I'm so excited." She stalls. "You won't tell me?"

"Non," I state with a wink.

"Okay, I'll be fast."

"You don't have to be fast. I'm not going anywhere, Delphine."

She nods and stops halfway down the hall, turning back to me with a breathtaking smile on her face. "Tyler! For the first time in *so long*, I don't have to worry to bring my fucking bottle! It's stupid to mention, I know—"

"The fuck it is, it's a victory," I tell her. "And we're taking every single one. Big and small. That's a big one."

"Right, yes, it's a victory," she says, pumping her fist with a giggle before she disappears. Stupefied, I stare after her for long seconds before glancing back at the book as a sinking suspicion sneaks in.

Six years.

Six years. If I'm right about the day she gave up—and my seizing chest is telling me I am—it will fucking alter me in a way I might not be able to hide. I decide not to press it tonight as I run my palm over the book, her words circling back to me. *"For six long years, I prayed my soldier would come back for his maps."*

Forty minutes later, I've done my best to put her admission aside, my anticipation spiking as I pull up the long gravel drive before she turns to me. "I know where we are, Tyler," she draws out, "we are on *your land*."

"I knew you would," I say, slowing to a stop at the foot of the house. The newly installed porch light illuminating a good portion of the single-story white farmhouse with light blue shutters. The porch—also newly rebuilt—houses a single step to the door and is painted the same shade of blue. Long planter boxes sit bolted beneath the windows facing us. To the right of the light blue front door sits a large window, which gives a view of a spacious living room. To the left of the door sits a slightly smaller bedroom window outlined by the same classic shutters. The totality of the interior currently lit with newly installed ceiling fans and updated light fixtures.

"I love it." She claps. "We get to stay *here* tonight?"

"Yeah, we do," I say, dipping into my jeans pocket and pulling out the key.

"Oh!" she exclaims, eyes lighting as she grabs it and springs from the truck straight to the porch. Easing out of the seat to follow her, I'm at her back by the time she opens it. The smell of fresh paint hits us both as she takes it in. Each one painted in varying shades of light and dark blue.

"Tyler," she admonishes as she walks in, stops at the hall, and does a one-eighty to stare into the kitchen before walking back to where I stand in the empty living room.

"This house is so beautiful, but," she laughs nervously, "there is no furniture here."

"Well, that's because the owner hasn't furnished it yet."

"Oh, but . . . where will we sleep?"

"Let's ask the owner?" I give her a pointed look.

"Okay," she stalls, weighing my expression before it starts to sink in. "Wait, what is this, Soldier?"

"*This* is *your house*, Delphine," I whisper. "So you wake up every day smiling."

She jerks back a few feet before scanning the kitchen with the newly installed baby blue old-school Frigidaire, matching new gas stove, and other appliances. Whipping her head in every direction, her gorgeous silver eyes dart to an old-fashioned iron wood stove fireplace, to the large living room window, which gives the best imaginable view of the orchard—a view she hasn't yet seen, hence the reason for our trip. I wanted to see her wake up to it. That is if she accepts the house.

"Soldier, you're joking," she says, her eyes shimmering with tears.

"I'm not joking," I tell her. "It's yours."

"No!" she booms. "No, it's really . . . mine? This house is *mine*?"

"You kicked the bottle," I tell her, "so you get to live the dream."

"Tyler," she exhales so harshly, I know there's no breath

left in her, "you are my best friend, but if you are bullshitting to me, I will kick your balls *so fucking hard*."

"Well shit," I chuckle, "I was hoping to room with you for a while, but now I'm just scared."

"This is really my house, and you will live here too?" She searches my face frantically.

"Well, when you put it like that, I was hoping to. I can't handle living in that townhouse a day longer, and I thought I'd room with you for a while anyway to be your sober companion."

"Oh," she says, lowering her eyes. "I would love that so much, but, Soldier," she shakes her head, bewildered. "A *whole house*?"

"It's a *tiny* house," I say, "for a tiny general. But it's got three bedrooms."

"This can't be right." She cups her mouth, her eyes spilling over. "This can't be mine!" Her face erupts, and she begins to cry, to rebuke it all as she keeps a hand on her mouth, and I crowd her, knowing these tears are utter happiness. "No." She pushes my chest again and again as I watch her unravel in front of me.

"It's your dream, Delphine. I saw it the minute we drove here before you even spoke a word. You deserve it, and I want you to have it."

She sniffles, keeping her mouth covered, her lashes soaked. "Tyler, who did this house belong to?"

"To me," I tell her honestly. "It was my granddad's starter home and came with the land I inherited.

"Then it's yours," she says, holding out the key.

"I don't want to live alone out here." I bulge my eyes. "Who will protect me from the crickets?"

"Shut the fuck up!" she bursts into a heap of emotion again, crying as she turns in circles again and again.

"You shut the fuck up," I chuckle as she melts onto the refinished hardwoods and cries for solid minutes, slumped in an adorable weepy heap, her legs in a V on the floor as

I crouch down and grin at her. "This is not very general of you."

"Oh, Soldier, I don't care, I can die now. This can't be real life."

Her reaction makes the aches worth it, every single one. "You haven't seen the rest of the house yet."

"I don't care," she says before her eyes bulge. "I mean, I do, of course, but I don't. I'm so happy. I don't care if the rest is a shack. These two rooms alone. So beautiful." She palms my jaw. "You painted it blue *for me*? You did all this for me?"

"I started renovations when I got back at the beginning of summer. But if I'm completely honest, I always had you in mind to live here. It made choosing the paint easy. In my mind, this has always been your house, Delphine. I've always pictured you living here. Even back then."

"Tyler," she palms her heart. "This is all I have ever wanted. To live on land so beautiful," she sniffs as I pull her up from the floor, "but I did not *earn this*."

"There are about three dozen soldiers or more who owe their lives to you that would say otherwise," I tell her.

"What? What do you mean?" she asks.

"I'll tell you another time." I pause a beat as she shakes her head, bewildered. "So, you don't think you'll have an issue moving?"

"Moving here? Are you fucking joking?" She palms my chest. "I know what you mean," she taps her finger to her head, "mentally, and the answer is no. No issue. I told your mother *yesterday* I want out of that fucking house. And knowing I can live here with my soldier, I don't *ever* want to go back," she states emphatically.

"Then you never have to go back," I say as her sentiment sets my chest pumping. "I'll get your stuff boxed and here for you tomorrow."

"No, no, leave it. I don't want a single part of my past to touch my future. I will get what I have to from it later."

She lifts her chin. "I will make this all new. A new life, Tyler." Her eyes sparkle. "My future."

She brings her watery gaze to mine, gripping my hands, hers shaking. "Soldier, this is the best day of my life, and *you* gave it to me."

"No, it's *not*," I tell her as she beams at me. "I promise you it's not."

Chapter Forty-Two

DELPHINE

Ezekiel groans from where he lays on my old couch, swatting at his forehead where a fly landed, his action severely delayed due to his state. Not long after, he turns his agony-twisted expression toward me where I sit inches away—perched at the edge of the coffee table while trying *very hard* to hold my laughter. My typically immaculately dressed and formidable nephew looks an utter mess in his disheveled suit, gin leaking from his every pore. Even with my hope that he never abuses the drink as I have, I manage to find the humor in this situation. Especially as he groans in his stupor at the headache I'm sure is brewing behind his eyes.

"I do *not* miss this part, *at all*," I whisper to Tyler, where he stands behind me, also in wait. Armed with one of my headache powders, a dog's hair of my nephew's preferred gin sits in the glass next to me, as well as one of Tyler's sports drinks.

After another handful of seconds, Ezekiel groans, and I can't help the soft, nervous laugh that escapes me when he loudly smacks his parched lips. At the sound of my chuckle, Ezekiel's eyes finally slit open. The unmistakable color of his father's, he looks over and blinks a few times before he focuses on me.

Just after, he lifts his fire-colored gaze over my shoulder and narrows it on the man standing behind me. My oldest nephew had crash-landed last night after weeks of purposeful silence. His refusal to speak to his brothers a punishment after discovering Jean Dominic and Sean's betrayal in their involvement with Cecelia. Tyler reported Ezekiel was so angry upon arrival that he got black-out drunk and passed out just after doling out the rest of their punishment. Which forced Tyler to somehow get him here and drag him to the couch.

Tyler called me just after and asked if it was okay that he stay with him until he woke. I happily stayed home, unafraid, after three *blissful* weeks in the new house. The change of location alone during these weeks having transported me into a much better headspace—a healing space. But despite my hatred for this house, I came to see my nephew and possibly sort through what contents here that I might consider bringing to my new home.

"The fuck are you two doing?" Ezekiel finally asks as he lifts to sit and then stand, taking off his jacket due to the stifling August heat and the shit air conditioning in this house. Something else I do not miss. Making me question how I lived here for so long with so little comfort?

In a drunken, numb blur. *That's how.*

Picking up the gin and powder, I offer it to Ezekiel, and he takes it, his glare remaining on Tyler.

"Hello to you too," I say through another laugh. "*I am here* to pick up some things and came to see you," I tell him as he has sense enough to open the powder, but only *after* gulping down his gin. After lining his tongue with the medicine, he downs half the sports drink as I chuckle. My laughter earns me a nasty side-eye from Tobias before he poses his question to Tyler. "And you?"

"I'm the guy who got you to safety last night after you went comatose, *remember*?" Tyler utters as the tension between them starts to brew.

Sighing, Ezekiel resumes his seat in front of me, and I

grab his hand in an effort to regain his attention. Celine's son has become such a strong, intimidating, powerful, brilliant, and handsome man. Just after I softly say his name, Ezekiel finally lowers his wrathful gaze to me and stares back at me. A few long seconds pass before his stare lightens by a fraction. "You look . . . *well*, Tatie."

"Thank you," I smile, "I feel well, and you look like *shit*," I laugh.

"Thanks," he clips, rolling his eyes before addressing me, "and your treatments are done?" he prods, ignoring Tyler entirely as he scans me, starting to sense the change.

"Yes, all done, thank fuck," I answer with a happy sigh as he continues to stare back at me curiously.

"You've put on some weight. Your complexion is . . ." He pauses the sports drink at his lips. "Wait . . ." his eyes roll over me for long speculative seconds. "Tatie, are you . . . *sober*?"

I nod several times, smiling with pride-filled tears in my eyes. "*Thirty-four* days *today*, Ezekiel."

His jaw goes slack, and his eyes immediately lift to Tyler before they narrow.

"It's not like I could fucking tell you with you avoiding me," Tyler defends, "you were MIA for three fucking weeks before you popped up last night, *brother*."

"Yeah well, as it seems, *we're all full* of surprises," he snaps with contempt before Ezekiel's eyes slowly float back down to me. "Tatie, how? I mean—"

"Tyler got me an at-home nurse to detox here," I say, reaching for Tyler's hand as it lands on my shoulder. Ezekiel eyes the contact, but I don't release it, holding each of their hands.

"I'm in therapy now if you can believe it. Every day." I bulge my eyes as I squeeze his hand. "I came here today to make you a promise. That I will never drink again, Ezekiel. I'm sorry it's taken me so long, and it may be far too late for this apology, but I swear to you I will never take another sip."

Shock registers everywhere in his face as he tilts his head, still a bit disbelieving.

"You don't have to . . . promise me, Tatie, but it's, fuck, it's good to hear," he winces, his hangover visibly increasing as he takes his hand back to unbutton and roll the sleeves of his linen shirt up his forearms. "But," he shakes his head a little, his expression sincere. "I'm proud of you . . . which is not something I can fucking say about anyone else at the moment."

"Don't let our shit take this from her," Tyler snaps, "she's been bursting at the fucking seams to tell you."

Ezekiel shakes his head sarcastically. "I'm gone for mere months, and where the fuck do I land?" he sighs, "in an alternate reality."

"You can't control people, T, or their emotions," Tyler states with an edge. "That's what I've learned the hard way over time and why I don't do *personal*. You and I need to have a conversation. I owe you an apology that I truly want to give along with an explanation," he sighs, "but it's clear you're not going to hear it today. So, I'll be waiting for you when you're ready to talk, but," Tyler grips me around my middle before pulling me off the table. Squealing in surprise, he hoists me to his side, propping me next to him and smiling down at me.

"She's having a good day that she worked really fucking hard to get to, and neither of us nor our shit needs to ruin it for her. So how about you let her clear the doorway before you take a swing at me? Or better yet, when you decide you'll hear me out, give me a call."

Ezekiel stands suddenly, wrath clear on his face.

"Don't hold your fucking breath for that call," he snaps. "I won't be dialing it, and you think I haven't fucking known you've been in love with her since you were seventeen?" He scoffs. "You're *all fucking delusional*, but don't think for one second I'll be viewing you as some stand-in *stepdaddy*." Ezekiel tilts his head menacingly. "Or maybe that's why your thinking is fucking warped right now, and you believe you have some right to call the shots on this."

Ezekiel's comment sucks all oxygen from the space as Tyler releases me. I feel the dangerous tension start to fill the room before Tyler speaks, his warning lethal in delivery. "You get one, *one* fucking below-the-belt shot, and *that* was it. *One*," he spits with a venom I've never heard, "or maybe I stop answering your calls *altogether*."

"You say that as if it would be a bad thing," Ezekiel snaps back instantly. "And you have some fucking audacity thinking that's a threat for me."

"Careful, asshole," Tyler warns, the anger rolling off both men palpable. "You've already written off *two* of your brothers. Do you want to go for *three*?"

"Do I *have* brothers left?" Ezekiel scoffs. "Seems to me that they've all decided to start substituting their dicks for their goddamned brains."

Tyler turns to me, a fire lit in his eyes. "Go grab whatever you need to from the bedroom, okay?"

"I can wait," I whisper, the violence rolling off him, sparking a dangerous air in the room. The air surrounding Ezekiel alone enough to stifle me.

Tyler shakes his head, his expression reassuring even as his body starts to coil. "You said you wanted to get some things?"

I nod, fear filtering in as both men look upon one another as if ready to draw blood.

"Please don't fight," I whisper to Tyler before addressing my nephew. "Ezekiel, please try to see reason. I know you are hurt, and I understand, but please try."

"I can't right now, Tatie," he utters, an equally dangerous edge in his timbre, "and you know well why. Stay out of this."

"Go," Tyler urges, facing off with Ezekiel, chin lifted. "Grab what you want. I'll load it up in a little bit."

Ten long minutes later, Tyler and Ezekiel are practically screaming in the living room, and I wince at the sound of their blistering back-and-forth.

"... you destroyed my fucking trust! Why in the fuck should I listen to a word you say?" Ezekiel argues.

"... sending them away when we've just started to set things in motion? We've been separated for fucking *years* already, Tobias!"

"And you don't think it's just punishment?"

"Yes," Tyler responds as I dig into the back of my closet for the first time in decades. "I do. Honestly, I do, T, but then again, you have no fucking idea what fielding the shit that's gone down this summer has been like! No fucking clue because I've protected you from it! I've literally killed myself, and so has Dom, as well as every inked bird to keep you from the brunt of the weight of it! ... Look, I can't imagine how you're feeling right now, and it's warranted. I'm not denying that, but it's your reaction now, *this behavior*, is exactly why you weren't fucking told or trusted with it!"

"Don't you dare fucking preach to me about morality. Are you fucking my aunt?"

I wince at Ezekiel's blunt question as Tyler instantly explodes with his reply. "That's not and will never be your goddamned business!"

"No," Ezekiel counters, "because you don't do personal, right brother?"

"No, I fucking don't and never will because of this fucking situation right here. This shit always gets messy. But they didn't do this to hurt you, and I'm positive you fucking saw that last night in their faces as I have for *months*! Drunk or not, I know you *saw* it, and I'm willing to bet *my own ink* it's why you let them keep theirs ... Jesus, I'm sorry, and I'm sorry I covered for them, but I would do the fucking same for you if the circumstances were reversed."

"No secrets between us, your words, *your fucking oath to me*!" Ezekiel roars.

"That's right, *my oath*, not theirs. This is different, T. They didn't expect to fall in love with her."

"And because you're just as fucked in the head, that makes it okay?"

"Being in love or caring for someone is not being fucked in the head, you blind fucking bastard, but I'm done throwing pearls in front of swine today. I'm done talking *at you* another fucking minute. Come find me when your anger isn't the sole basis for your judgment, and you've reached a place where you can speak like a reasonable adult."

"Who do the fuck do you think you are talking to me like this? You forget your place."

"My place?!" Tyler roars. "My fucking place is whatever and wherever I want it to be, you arrogant fuck, and by choice! We might have decided together there is a pecking order, but it's always been our decision to honor it. We aren't fucking bound to you by anything else but loyalty. And you might want to remember that when and *if* they *willingly* get on that fucking plane as ordered . . . and you know what, asshole? While you're at it—and since you deem us all unfit to handle your club—deal with it *yourself* for a while, and let's see how you fucking fare without our help!"

"Fine with me, motherfucker!" Ezekiel snaps before they both explode in more heated back-and-forth. Filled to the brim with anxiety, when I lift an old sheet set, I come across a box. The sight of it has every hair on my body standing on end before I'm pulled straight under.

"*—what are these?*"

"*—you found—*"

An image of Alain standing next to the kitchen table, eyes littered with rage, fills my vision as mixed voices continually surround me.

"*—don't worry, I got them cheap.*"

"*—when I find you, I will fucking kill you!*"

"Delphine," Tyler whispers as I come to, seeing that he's on his knees in front of me in the closet. Ezekiel stands behind him, peering at me where I'm cowering, with my hands covering my chest and head as Tyler frantically scans my face.

"What is it?" Tyler asks, scouring the closet before gently

palming and lowering the protective hands I have lifted. "Please," Tyler prods, "please talk to me."

I blink several times before I finally croak. "What happened?"

"You started screaming," Ezekiel rasps out behind him, his admission haunted, as are both their expressions.

"I want to go," I whisper low, "I want *nothing here*. Soldier, please get me out of here," I whimper before a fear-filled cry bursts out of me. For the first time in a decade or more, I crack in front of Ezekiel, who gapes at my outburst as Tyler clutches me to him, holding me for several seconds to his chest.

"Jesus Christ, you're shaking so badly," Tyler whispers. "I've got you, let's go."

Tyler sweeps me to my feet before we walk past Ezekiel, who carefully trails the two of us, watching our every move. Tyler guides me down the hall, stopping at the end of it before glancing back at my baffled nephew.

"Like I said, brother. You have no fucking idea what's been happening here, and if you want to talk, we can have a conversation later."

Ezekiel ignores him completely, his eyes bolted to me.

"Tatie . . . are you okay?" His confusion tugs my heart as he tries to understand what just happened while I grapple with the emotions pummeling me. Normally, I would retreat, isolate, and sip to numb, to stifle it. To protect him from seeing me in such a state, but I have no such luxury anymore. The one true price of my sobriety. A price I want to solely pay.

"I will be fine. I just need to get out of this fucking house," I tell him, and he draws his brows in confusion. "I don't live here anymore," I clarify in a rush. "I want to talk to you," I tell him, "but maybe not today, okay?"

He lingers in my doorway before glancing inside my closet, and I know he's looking for the source of my distress as I address him.

"Ezekiel, *leave it*," I command in a tone he knows well,

a firm order. "Close the door . . . this is *my mess* to sort, and I will when I am ready. This is not for you. I have . . ." *protected you from this for too long.* "Close the door."

He nods, pulling the door closed as I asked, confused by what's happening as he speaks again. "You don't *live* here?"

"No. I've freed myself of all poisons," I blow out a breath. "Please be careful to do the same. Anger is a very dangerous poison. I know you are hurt, but please try to remember that with Jean Dominic and Sean."

"How long have you *not lived* here?" he asks, deaf to my reason, the pain leaking from him clear as he stands looking like a man lost. My need to go to him strengthens, but I know I have to gather myself for that.

"That's what happens when you don't answer your phone for almost a fucking month," Tyler snaps.

"Stop it, Soldier," I scold gently before looking back to my nephew. For a brief second, I see a glimpse of the boy who waved me off at Celine's feet the day before I left France.

"*Au revoir, Tatie!*"

"*Au revoir, Ézéchiel.*"

"I will come to you. We will talk soon, okay?"

Ezekiel gives me a slow nod, utterly perplexed by what's transpired. Just after, Tyler ushers me out of the house and into the cab of his truck.

"I saw Alain," I confess in a rush as Tyler turns the ignition, and I look over to see him eagerly searching me. "I saw him clearly. *That night*. I saw him coming toward me," I start to shake again. "I saw his rage. I saw my death in his eyes."

Tyler swallows and nods. "I'll call Mom and have her meet us at the house," he whispers before palming my hip and sliding me flush to him in the seat. "Hold onto me, General, and don't let go."

Face planted to his chest and inhaling his comforting smell, I don't let go the whole ride back to the orchard.

Chapter Forty-Three

Delphine

The birds sing their morning songs through the open windows as I unbox the last pillow, adding it to the set on the couch before glancing around the house with pride. Not only have I pried open my wallet recently, but I've also spent a fortune decorating. Never in my dreams did I think of myself as a decorator of any sort. But as I look around at the furnishings that Charlie—Barrett's girlfriend—helped me to carefully choose, I can't help but feel excited. Even with her four-year-old son, Elijah, constantly attached to her hip, we set the house up in record time.

Just five weeks in, and it's done. The house itself and the view it provides from every single room is one I could only summon in my wildest dreams. A view that has had me smiling every day since Tyler and I had camped on the front lawn the night he gifted it to me. I had awoken the next morning living in my future, and the view of the land was only outdone by my soldier's breathtaking smile. It was all I could do to keep from confessing my feelings for him as the sun rose. Instead, I tasked myself to make this a real home for us both with every imaginable comfort.

The house—built at the bottom of a valley—gives spectacular views of the surrounding hills and much of the orchard. Though it is small, and the bedrooms are tiny, it suits us perfectly, housing Tyler and me very comfortably.

The kitchen Tyler designed is a dream for me. It mirrors one of the nineteen-fifties, with the fridge and stove reminiscent of the era, both colored light blue. The dark aqua couch I chose and tan chairs are perfect with the designer pops of red throw pillows and other décor, keeping the look old-fashioned with modern comfort. My bedroom—which is the largest of the three—Tyler painted a dark navy blue. With it, I chose gold and solid white accents.

For our beds, I chose only the finest linens so that we feel like we are sleeping on clouds every night. It's only in these recent weeks that I've felt the dire need to combine our clouds. At night, I stare into the open door across the hall and into his bedroom, where he sleeps in nothing but black boxer briefs—many nights atop his sheets. On those nights, I ache for him, tossing and turning while trying so hard not to remember the looks he gave me the night he fucked me to within an inch of my life. Continually gazing at my gorgeous soldier in hopes that just once, he would open his eyes and that those eyes would host the long-lost fire they once held for me.

It's when Tyler's tractor nears and cuts abruptly that I thrum with anticipation, rushing to open the cabinet I recently lined with red pinstriped paper to grab him a glass. Setting it on the counter, a light breeze streams in through the kitchen window, the fleeting summer heat intermixed with a hint of autumn, which is fast approaching, flitting over my face.

Seconds later, my soldier appears on the porch through the storm door, shirtless and covered in a sheen of sweat, dressed in nothing but his light camouflage pants and Marine boots. When the door opens, his dog tags catch a glint of sun as he greets me with the pop of his dimple. I can't help but feel the flush of desire that follows as I drink in every drop of his skin, which has darkened from his long days in the sun and efforts to cultivate the grounds surrounding the property. A feat he's worked at tirelessly when not running endless errands for Ezekiel. Ezekiel who now seems to be purposefully running Tyler into the ground as punishment. One I have been closed-lipped about so far.

Though it pains me that the punishment time for Dom and Sean starts today, Ezekiel's hurt and anger are evident in his adamance to carry it out. Like Tyler, I've resigned myself to let them resolve this on their own without interference. Instead, I spend my time repairing myself and pouring my efforts into my new life so I can be capable of helping my nephews if needed at some point in the future.

Tyler stalks in as I pour his favorite drink—heavily sweetened iced tea—and thrust it toward him as he meets me in the kitchen.

"It looks fucking awesome in here, General," he says, scouring the living room and kitchen as he takes the glass.

"Thank you. I think I am close to done," I say, hands on my hips. "Not much to do, now."

"Plenty to do." He winks before drinking his tea in long gulps. I fill his glass again as I soak him in from head to foot. "I think I might have tackled a majority of the grass—"

"Soldier, will you want to fuck girls here in this house?" I blurt the question that has been heavy on my mind in the weeks since we moved in.

Tyler's mouth parts slightly before he lets out a long whistle, staring at the ice in his tea. "Well, this is not a conversation I thought we'd be having at eight in the morning." He shakes his head. "Leave it to you, General Brash."

"It's a fair question." I shrug, not feeling any part of the gesture as dread settles low in my belly. "You are man." I swallow. "A very good-looking man, who must want to have . . ." I wave my hand so that he gets my insinuation.

"Have what?" He quirks a brow in challenge.

"Oh, stop, Soldier . . . *pussy*," I deliver bluntly, which earns me the wicked curl of his mouth. He takes another long drink before he runs his tongue along his bottom lip, and my eyes follow.

"What's got you thinking about *my need for pussy*, Delphine?"

"I am curious. Can't I be curious?" I lie. "You are living here. I expect you will want to bring girls here at some point. Should we do a rule or something?"

"I'm pretty boring these days." He again grins into his glass before sipping it. "And considering I just escaped a fucking frat house that included a built-in soundtrack of a *porno* for *months*, I'm not really into the freaky roommate thing or becoming one just yet. So, should we establish a rule for if you want to go out hunting some *dick*?" His words carry an edge that's hard to identify. "I guess if you get lucky . . . make sure to leave a sock on the door," he chuckles.

"For?"

He frowns. "It's a sign to let your roommate know you're getting laid."

"This is the truth?" I frown. "A sock on the door. Why not just say it?"

"It's a covert signal." He winks. "Ever heard the saying '*sock it to me*'?"

"You're fucking with me," I snap. "I'm trying to have a serious discussion."

"About pussy?" He laughs again. "And no, I'm not fucking with you." He holds up a palm in defense. "I'm serious. It's a thing."

"Fine." I sigh. "I will look for a sock on your door and then know." I swallow. "You're getting laid."

"Well, rest easy, I'm a gentleman. I don't really talk about this stuff nor display it for others to know."

"Okay." I palm the counter briefly for strength as I speak, keeping my eyes down. "But maybe, if you want to fuck a girl, just tell me." I blow out a harsh breath.

"I'll be sure to let you know," he drawls as he sips his glass beside me. I turn to see him lowering his eyes, shaking his head with a smile, his gorgeous, curled lashes flitting along his gorgeous fucking cheeks as his gorgeous fucking smirk mocks me.

Even as I want to slap him for being so smug, it's the

gnawing damned lust that fills me. Though my frustration and desire grow as I come further and further back into myself, I take a step over and wrap my arms around him. His arms flare out in surprise as I grip him tightly to me, my cheek warming on his sun-tinted skin.

"Whoa, General," he whispers, setting his glass down on the counter before hugging me back, "that was one hell of a sneak attack."

"I'm sorry, it's just. You've changed my life. This house, this dream." I fight the stupid tears I frequently have to battle, mostly these days of *gratitude* rather than any other emotion. "You're an incredible man, Tyler."

Pulling back, I press a lingering kiss over his skin where his heart lies and feel him tense as I mourn the fact that once it was mine. I might have some place inside but may never get the place I once had back, even as my heart *begs me* to try to reclaim that place now. Maybe this part of my dream will go unrealized. In trying to accept it, I brave a look up and see the friendship, the love, but no sign of desire before I pull away and drop my eyes.

"I have to go," I tell him. "I have an appointment."

He nods, seeming confused by my behavior, but I'm starting to suspect more and more that it's contrived. I've been giving him lingering looks, suggestions with my eyes, everything I can think of to ask him for that look back. Gestures I'm coming to believe he's purposefully ignoring because he no longer reciprocates the desire. His cock salute in the shower weeks ago might have just been the result of a touch of a woman—not *this* woman. Every day that he ignores my tells, I find myself more desperate to find the kindling to create some of the fire we once had—for any fucking sign of a spark that I might get my true dream.

A dream I wasn't allowed to have before. To think or to speak. A dream I felt shame for having. And now that I could, if my affections were returned, I'd feel alone in it. At the same time, I wonder why my soldier would make this much effort.

Why go to all this trouble . . . for only a friend?

However, I must admit to myself that this might be the case because of the man Tyler is. But I *feel* his love. He touches me every single day. Though, I'm finding myself more and more disappointed by only the whisper of a finger against my cheek or his reassuring palm on my back. Of the hand holding, but no more. His distance even more apparent since Tobias spoke about us weeks ago, which may be why his touches are becoming briefer.

"After I finish the grass"—Tyler interrupts my thoughts, picking his glass up from the counter—"I'm going to stop by the Apple Festival for a few minutes before I meet the movers with Dom and Sean at the townhouse to clear it out." He shakes his head, his voice full of ache. "They're leaving today."

I nod. "I know. I said my goodbyes yesterday. I'm sorry, Soldier. Dom is not doing well," I report.

"Yeah, I know," he agrees as we share a lingering look, neither of us happy with Ezekiel's decision.

"I need to go." I shoulder my purse. "I will see you later."

"See you, roomie," he calls at my back as if in taunt as I head for the door. "Make sure to grab some socks while you're out," he chuckles as I shut the door hard to cut his laugh.

Because for me, it's not funny. Not even a little. Just like our first conversation about girls wasn't amusing, but he seemed to draw pleasure out of it. Some smug satisfaction as if he knows my true feelings, which he's refused me to voice. It's then I *know* he must have sensed, *seen* my desire for him by now, and can't help but wonder if it's punishment.

I feel punished now, thoroughly. I should be satisfied. More than satisfied with the lengths he's taken for me to live this dream. He's done so much for me. To demand those looks back isn't possible. To ask for his heart back might be impossible and selfish. Walking to my sedan, I drop my purse in my seat through my open car window. Glancing back at the house, I meet Tyler's eyes just as he pulls a ball cap down, which only sharpens his sleek features and the cut of his jaw.

Fuck. Merde. Fuck. God help me.

"Buckle up, see you in a bit." He winks, and I damn near fan my face at the sight of him as he saunters toward his tractor.

Some woman is going to come along soon and try to claim the man I'm going blind with the need to touch, to have, to love, and the thought of it fills me with dread.

As I watch him mount the tractor, my resolve fills me to try and somehow gain a fraction of that heated look he once had for me back. To get *something* from him telling me I'm not completely alone in this longing or if I need to let go of the rest of my dream altogether—that reality devastating. Straightening my shoulders and determined to do everything I can to have him *see me* again, I get into my sedan and turn my ignition over. As he takes off on his tractor, I decide *this battle* is the most important I have to fight because the future I truly want very much includes having *all* of my soldier.

With a fucking sock forever on *our* bedroom door.

***

A loud bell jingles as I walk through the door and freeze, all eyes drifting from the women in the shop, who begin scanning me curiously.

What was I thinking?

The need to flee takes over as I hesitate at the door.

"Delphine!" Layla exclaims, poking her head through a doorway in the back of the shop.

Merde.

Even as I entertain leaving, Layla takes long strides toward me—such a beautiful girl. Tall and tan from the summer sun, she's wearing a halter dress that hugs her curves, accentuated by the sash fastened around her *Beauty Mark* smock. Her long, light blonde hair cascading in beautiful waves down her shoulders. I take all of this in as she approaches.

"Ignore them," she whispers, gently taking my elbow

to usher me toward her station. "I have to admit," she says, snapping out a plastic cape before fastening it around my neck, "I was surprised when I saw your name in the appointment calendar but in a *good* way."

Her eyes command mine in the mirror as I speak, trying to fight my anxiety. "I was told this is your second shop. You must be very proud."

"Hell yeah, I am. We opened this Main Street location a few weeks ago, and as you can see, business is booming." I glance through the streetside glass at the foot traffic on Main Street because of the Apple Festival happening just outside of it as she speaks up. "Don't let the traffic out there or in here scare you—or their bug eyes," she lifts her voice to the women surrounding us. "They'll be clucking like hens about some bullshit in no time."

Nodding, I dart my eyes to my reflection. Noting the gray hairs as well as my complexion as Layla perches in front of the small counter at her station and crosses her arms.

"So, what are we doing today?"

"Everything," I relay as she quirks a brow. "I want to get the gray out."

"Okay, so definitely a color. How about a cut to make it a little healthier."

I mull over my request as humiliation threatens. "Fuck it," I finally spout with a shrug. "Can you help my face to not look *so old*?"

"Not a mincer of words. I love it," she laughs before leaning in. "Honey, I've got a girl on speed dial with tiny magic needles full of youth that can not only get the wrinkles out but plump your face up a bit to take years away, and it's practically *painless*."

"Good." I nod. "I want everything we can do but . . . still look like *me*."

"I've got you." She winks as she starts to stroke my hair. "No duck lips."

"Non." I shake my head adamantly. "Non. No lips like a duck."

"You know, I do it." She points to her face as I scrutinize her. "I keep it natural."

"Oh, then, oui." I nod enthusiastically. "Like you do. Please."

"I'll call her right now. She's only a few doors down. I'm just going to run to the back and whip us up some color."

I grip her arm lightly as she starts to walk away, and she glances down at me in concern as the words die on my tongue. She seems to sense them, her expression softening. "You want to feel and look beautiful, right? Well, look around," she urges, and I do, very briefly. "Every woman in this salon wants the very same thing, I promise you. This is what I do, and *I'm living for this with you*, so will you try your best to trust me?"

I blow out a breath as the stupid fucking tears threaten, and I nod. "Oui. Yes. Please, anything you can do to help."

"Oh, honey. This salon is full service, so I can do a lot." She gives me an assuring wink. "I'll be right back."

A few hours later, I've been moisturized, scrubbed, and then moisturized again with a steamer to my face that looked like a vacuum. After I was waxed—around my lip and chin, brows, and what Layla called my 'lady bits,' I was poked several times with the magic needles. Needles that were not exactly painless but far less painful than the devil wax. A wax job that Layla swore to me could guide in a seven-forty-seven plane. We both laughed like hyenas in the back room of the salon as she explained the metaphor about my new landing strip. Though I feel like I've been through several battles, Layla's gentle massage of my scalp and second moisture gloss treatment is the best consolation I could hope for.

"I know you're a private woman, Delphine," she whispers, as the woman in surrounding chairs *do* cluck very much like hens around us. "But can I ask what made you come in today?"

I mull over the reasons and give her part of the truth. "A few reasons. The first is I have not taken care of myself in a *very* long time," I tell her. "I—" I falter in my delivery, and her whispers soothe me.

"A man in your past did you dirty?" she asks.

"Oui. My ex-husband, Alain. He was a very manipulative, abusive *narcissist*." I use Regina's words. "He almost killed me."

"Jesus," she whispers, her touch at my scalp becoming more gentle. "I'm so sorry you went through that."

"After, I didn't want to be beautiful. I didn't dress to get attention. I did everything I could to keep men away. But now." I think of Tyler, of the way he once looked at me, and my eyes water with the want to get that look back. "I-I want to." I swallow as emotion threatens. "I'm sorry. I have been very emotional since I started therapy and stop drinking."

"It's okay, honey, you don't have to talk about it," she consoles me.

"Non, I've been quiet for so many years, Layla—*too many* years. I'm doing so many things that make me uncomfortable now," I explain. "Therapy is very, very uncomfortable for me, but it has helped me to talk more. I want to tell you, I just need time to do it without so much emotion."

"Well, how about I make it a little easier for you?" she offers, and I nod. "So, before Denny, I dated this asshole I thought was the one. He was gorgeous and brilliant, and I really loved him. He had it rough when he was young, like most of us. He really wanted to be a better man, but he lost the battle with his demons and started treating me like shit. He got into drugs, I caught him cheating, it was a total shit show, and I put up with it *for far too long*." She runs the water close to my scalp as my shoulders relax, her touch tender. "He left scars both visible and invisible," she continues, pausing her fingers as if lost in her memories. "But then Denny came along and kind of loved me back to health. He swears I did the same for him. We're a little co-dependent. You know what that means?"

I nod.

"Well." Her magical fingers continue to massage my scalp. "They say it's not healthy in a relationship, but—"

"You look *very, very* healthy, Layla."

"Exactly." she smiles. "I'm thriving and happier than I've ever been. And though my fiancé is a moody asshole most days, he treats *me* like gold. He's fiercely protective of me, ridiculously jealous, and at times, it drives me crazy. But after what I went through, it makes me feel safe that he's possessive. So, frankly, I don't give a rat's ass that we need each other so much."

"Rat's ass," I laugh, and she grins. "I like that." I bite my lip. "So . . . how do you know Denny won't hurt you the same?"

"I don't," she answers easily. "I don't know." She pauses, staring down at me where my head remains in the shampoo bowl. "We don't get to know, Delphine. We just have to trust ourselves to know better, and that's the scary part. But it's been a long time, and I've forgiven the younger me for putting up with those hard years of abuse. The younger Layla just wanted to be loved."

"This is what I try to do every day in therapy. Forgive younger Delphine."

"This is a very good step in helping to do that—taking care of her again emotionally and physically. I'm glad you're doing it. But if I may say." She leans down, her voice barely above a whisper. "I think you already know that Tyler is the very best of men, and you're as safe as you can get."

My eyes bulge at her admission.

"Sorry, honey, but I'm a mother hen, and I make it a point to be aware of every bird's personal business, whether they like it or not. I'm just as protective of them as they are of me. But I didn't get this information from anyone inked. I saw you two together one day years back. You were at a snow cone stand. I had just pulled into the parking lot when I spotted you both in line. I saw the way he looked at you when you turned your head. I had known Tyler for years already and had never seen that look. So, I kept watching," she admits sheepishly. "Not long after, I saw the way *you looked back at him*. I could *see so clearly* that you two were in love."

She shrugs as I wince that we were so obvious.

"Unfortunately, it's one of the costs of living in such a small town, but it was the sight of you two that really made a lasting impression on me. You especially. You looked so beautiful and happy. I even remember you were wearing a light blue sundress with tiny straps."

My eyes water at her admission. "I do not look like that, like her anymore." I blow out a long breath. "For so long, I never wanted to be the beautiful woman people told me I was. Ironic now. All I want is to look a little like her again. So"—I wince, shaking my head and palming my face—"I'm an imbecile."

"No, honey, you're not," she whispers, gently pulling my hand away. "You want it back, for yourself and maybe from him?" she prompts.

I nod, my neck heating. "Very much."

She gives me a wink. "You're nowhere near as far gone as you think you are. Keep coming to me, put a little more weight on between visits, and I promise that you will see the difference. Okay?"

"Okay," I agree, hope lighting in my chest.

She scans my face. "But you and I both know Tyler doesn't love with his eyes, Delphine."

"Oui. I know."

Stopping the water, Layla draws a towel from the cabinet behind the sink above me, wiping her hands dry before taking a few steps to stand in front of me. Shielding me with her body from prying eyes, she grips both my hands.

"You're still very beautiful, Delphine. It will take a few weeks to show the full effect, but I can tell already it's kicking in a bit." Her smile grows as her eyes light up. "After we're done here, we're going to walk down to Retro Stitch, a little dress shop my friend Tessa owns. She owes me for her last color, and so we're going to find you another blue dress. Then you and I are going to get a pedicure—*together*—because I could use a little tender loving care myself.

"That's too much," I say. "Too much effort—"

"Honey, it's not enough. Girls like you and me owe *it to ourselves* to take our power back in any way we deem necessary. That's what you're doing today. Like I said, I *live for* stuff like this, so let's go a little crazy together. Make a day of it? I promise it will be just as much for me as it is for you."

I nod, feeling self-conscious about my emotions as my tears fall.

"I'm going to take these tears as a good sign," she says, brushing them from beneath my eyes before pulling me to stand and guiding me back to her station.

"Yes, they are the very good kind." I sniff and smile as I take the seat.

"I'm so excited." She gives me a wink as my own excitement builds, and I admit as much.

"You are making me very excited, too," I tell her.

"Good, then it's a date," she continues, cradling my dripping hair with a towel and gently pressing it to my head to soak up the water before pulling it away. As she does this, I gape at my reflection as her eyes light.

"Mon Dieu," *My God*, I say, disbelieving of the differences of the slight effect of the facial, wax, and hair color.

"Told you," she boasts proudly. "The miracle of modern cosmetology, and we're nowhere near done," she assures as she starts brushing out my newly black hair. A mischievous glint twinkles in her eyes as she lowers her head next to mine in the mirror, her chin an inch above my shoulder. "Oh, to be a fly on the wall when he sees you tonight."

Chapter Forty-Four

Tyler

Dom and Sean stand idly by in the driveway, exhaling mixed smokes while eating up some of their last few hours stateside as the movers latch the back of the truck before they pull off.

"You'll watch over her," Sean prompts for the umpteenth time, inhaling an exaggerated drag of his cigarette as I sigh and nod.

Dom remains wordless, burning down his joint just as excessively while wearing every bit of his brother's wrath in his worn frame. Some part of me is hoping alongside them that T will pop up—possibly changing his mind and orders at the last minute. Then again, after personally enduring Tobias's birdside manner the past few weeks that he gave Dom and Sean to prepare for their exile, I know better.

"I may be going along with this shit, but I won't let her out of my sight. Not for a single fucking day." Dom looks over to me then. "You have my word," I declare to them both.

"Do you think he'll forgive us?" Sean prompts.

"The best thing you can do is not miss that plane. That's all I really know right now, man."

Dom flicks his joint, his words for us both as he stalks

past. "I'm going to do one last sweep and take a piss. I'll be right back."

"Hurry up," Sean calls after him, "we need to hit the garage before we go." Sean turns to me. "Thanks for getting our shit somewhere in the meantime."

"I'll put the boxes Dom marked back at Delphine's and stick the rest in storage. You'll both have a fresh start of your choosing when you get back."

He nods, the worry in his eyes one I recognize, but he doesn't speak it aloud, having spent the last two weeks making peace with it. Sean pulls me into him and claps my back. "Love you, brother."

"Hang in there, man. It's just another hurdle," I tell him, "and she's worth it."

"Yeah, she is," he agrees easily. "So fucking worth it."

"Then go." I nod toward his Nova. "The sooner you leave, the sooner you can get back to her."

His nod is solemn, and I feel for him as he looks over at me.

"All of this is on me. I'm sorry, Tyler. I am, but I can't bring myself to regret it other than hurting him, and that's fucking hell to live with too . . . *fuck*." He glides his hand again through his thoroughly jacked hair.

"I know," I say, "head down but chin up. You'd be surprised how much you can endure for a woman who's worth it."

"Says the man who's been to hell and back for his own," he utters low as I go stock still. "I'm pulling for you."

I remain mute as Sean eyes the townhouse, no doubt to make sure Dom's out of range as he nudges me. "Come on, man. Ever wonder why I've asked about your hookups but never once asked you if you've been in love? It's because I knew that answer."

"When?" I ask, barely above a whisper.

"I spotted you looking over at her across that kitchen table one day and fucking knew. It was clear as day, and fuck how you hid it so well—almost too well. Well enough to make me doubt it, but that look you gave beat the guise hand over fist. To anyone who wasn't looking, they might never have noticed, but I'm a man who fucking loves his brothers enough to notice."

"Me too." I blow out a harsh exhale, realizing just how horribly I've hidden my affection for Delphine over the years. Apparently, *everyone* fucking knew.

"Ten months, fuck." He pulls me into a longer bro-hug before he stalks to his driver's door, taking one last look at the townhouse before entering and revving up his Nova. For a brief moment, I resent T and his fucked punishment, already missing them both despite the nightmare roommate situation. We've been apart for years already, and our fucking planning is just paying off. But even for and to me, this punishment *is* fitting of the crime, so I try to let it go.

Dom exits the house shortly after, a small box in his hand as he stalks up and holds it out to me. "Found this in the hall closet."

"Not mine," I say, frowning down at it.

"It's yours," he insists before palming my shoulder, his version of a hug. "Think your mom dropped it off when we first moved in, and you never really unpacked."

Grabbing the box, I peer over at him.

"I've got her," I assure, sensing his ache as he keeps his eyes lowered. "Look at me, Dom," I prompt, and he does, the unguarded pain in his expression enough to have me pissed at Tobias again. "I've got her."

He nods before glancing briefly at the townhouse and surprisingly pulling me into him for something closer to resembling a hug. "Thanks, brother. I owe you."

"Sure you don't want me to tell him?" I ask about the day he literally became a hero last month, but Dom's insistent that he doesn't want said heroics to play any part in this. He's worried that his actions might give Tobias more cause to leash him. Dom shakes his head, indicating as much. I decide it's one more secret I'll keep from T for a while longer. Because as of right now, today, fuck him, and he wasn't in on the secret.

His rules.

"Fine," I sigh. "Just hurry the fuck up," I say as he releases me, taking the passenger seat, before I watch the two of them pull out. Sean's motor hums in their wake well after they race out of sight.

Chest aching due to their departure, I head back inside and set the box on the kitchen counter before opening it. Inside sits a pair of sneakers I wore out with my runs, a few of my high school yearbooks, and other small hits of nostalgia. Especially when I pull out one of the battalion soldiers I kept from the first game I won against Delphine.

Besides my old phone, the rest of the contents are mostly junk, but the sight of my Sidekick jars me a little. I'd left it charging on my nightstand the morning I confronted my dad and left home for good. I never bothered to retrieve it after my sabbatical in the woods just after enlisting, or after my trip to Georgia before I got on that bus. I grin as I unwrap the charging cord and plug it in for kicks. Heading upstairs, I eye the small litter of trash on the living room floor of the otherwise empty townhouse. Melancholic—but thankful this hellacious summer is fucking over—I pack what's left and tape the boxes. Hours later, when I come down with the last of my shit, I click off the lights of the townhouse before retrieving my ancient phone from the counter. Freezing when I see I have fourteen missed calls and dozens of unread text messages.

I swallow as I open the feed up from Delphine and damn near hit my knees when I see what's on screen.

General Half-Pint: I di d not mean it solder

General Half-Pint: Plse come back

Severed Heart

I curse the fact that I don't know what date she sent them, but I know for certain it was after I left, especially when I read the next one.

General Half-Pint: Plese dp not stop be frien d to me.

General Half-Pint: does soldeir not miss fish buddy

General Half-Pint: I cna stop cr y for y ou come bak to me sodler

General Half-Pint: I was wrnog so sorry please txet me bac k

General Half-Pint: You go marines no say bye to me question mar k

General Half-Pint: Plesa don t leave wihtiou say bye to me sodier of my heart

General Half-Pint: Plesse sodker I was scaerd so scard I am sorry ever y day

General Half-Pint: I so sad ans sorrry since you left I cry evey day I cannt breathe solder

General Half-Pint: I geuss you li e to me quest mar

Furious tears line my jaw as I stare at her last text.

General Half-Pint: I will wait

***

Knowing I've put some serious wear and tear on my engine with my erratic driving, I furiously blaze a path down the driveway, rocks battering my truck as I battle my conflicting emotions. Fury burning through me as reminders fly at me of what she's already been through. It's the need to confront her that outweighs those reminders. What *I've* fucking been through in the aftermath of that morning that overrules everything else.

Jesus, has she really been waiting all this time?

The truth of that rings true as her words from weeks ago slam into me. "*I understand why you didn't text me or come back.*"

"Jesus Christ," I rasp out hoarsely, relieved when I see her ancient sedan parked in the driveway as I pull up. The porch light illuminating her other carefully laid out lanterns and plants. The same soft light glowing from the kitchen beckoning me that my answers are there as my heart thrashes in my chest.

Far too gone in my anger and utterly wasted on the texts I got nearly a *decade* late, I waste no more time exiting my truck. Stalking over the porch, through the front door, and into the kitchen . . . I'm stopped dead at the threshold by the sight that greets me.

Delphine stands at the refrigerator with the freezer door open. A pitcher of iced tea on the counter. But it's the sight of her, hair back to onyx-black, laying in silky waves over her shoulders, standing in a light blue sundress, feet bare, toenails painted, her skin glowing, full lips tinted, that sends me fucking reeling.

"Hi, Soldier," she whispers as she lifts her gorgeous silver eyes to mine, and I swear I see her cheeks heat.

"You look . . ."

"Not the same as I once did, I know, but I fixed my hair," she relays as if she's not knocking the breath out of me with a sledgehammer.

"So . . . fucking beautiful," I rasp out, swallowing and swallowing again as her eyes hold mine, searching for long seconds before they light with some satisfaction.

"It's so ironic," she utters. "You know I hated men

noticing me for so long. Hated being their idea of beautiful and today paid lots of money to resemble a fraction of that woman." Her eyes bulge. "It was so expensive, but Layla is my new friend, and I'm excited we are going to have *'lady dates.'* I learned so much today. It's so strange, but I have poison in my face!" She smiles, pointing to her cheeks. "And"—she extends her foot—"do you like my toes?"

Pulling the phone from my jeans as my heart thrashes toward the woman rattling feet away—looking like the dream I once worshipped with my eyes, lips, and cock—I lift my old Sidekick, and she stares at it like it's nothing to be concerned about.

"You will use your old phone again?" She frowns. "Okay, I will maybe need the number."

"Not exactly, Delphine." I take a menacing step forward as she searches my expression, seeming confused by the hostility radiating from me. "No, *today*, I finally got your missed calls and *messages*. Eight fucking years later."

She stares back at me, her eyes dropping. "Oh."

"*Oh*, she says." I shake my head in disbelief. "*Oh*? That's all you have to say."

She blows out a loaded breath as long seconds tick by, the night breeze lifting the kitchen curtains as she finally speaks. "What do you want me to say, Soldier?"

"I will wait," I grit out. "Wait, *how?*"

She remains mute as she visibly starts to shake.

"Look at me, goddamn you," I snap. When she does, she brings watering eyes to mine. "Wait, how, Delphine? Answer me!"

"How you asked me to."

"How I *asked you to*," I deliver with so much venom that she flinches. "How I *asked you to*? You mean as the woman I wanted to build a life with and around? The woman I wanted to love and trust with every part of me? Surrender my heart to? Make love to and fuck every chance I got? Be with in every way a man can be with a woman for the rest of my fucking life? In *that* way?"

"Yes," she answers, her silver eyes holding mine as they shed silent tears. "But I was not sure of that, Tyler, not as much then as I am now. You know it was very complicated."

"Complicated," I scoff. "Well, you sure didn't fucking help *uncomplicate that once*, did you? Not. Fucking. Once!"

"Soldier—"

"Did it ever once fucking occur to you that I switched phones or that maybe I was so hurt by what happened that I didn't bother to retrieve my phone before I left for the Marines?"

"I—but you have your phone," she points out.

"Because my *mother* put it in a box with other things she thought I might want to keep. Because my *mother* knew our text exchanges were on this phone because I showed them to her when we were trying to diagnose you."

"You showed her my messages?"

"I think you're missing the point, Delphine!"

"I'm not, Soldier. Do you want some iced tea?" she asks, voice shaking.

"Delphine!"

Another tear slips down her cheek.

"All this time, all this fucking time." I glare at her. "You wanted it too."

"I know this is serious, Soldier, but I had a really good day. I don't want it to turn into a bad day."

"Do you know how many fucking *bad days* I had because I didn't get these goddamned messages? Eight fucking years of bad days, Delphine. Eight fucking years!"

She nods. "I am sorry. All this time, I thought you purposely ignored them."

"Well, that's just fucking . . ." I shake my head. "Eight years, eight fucking years, and you didn't even try to talk to me!"

"But I did, Soldier. I called, and I messaged you. You see that. I took your silence as your decision. You did not call. Did not come back."

"Yeah, well, I was trying to be done with you, and do you know why?"

"You didn't see the calls or messages." Her voice cracks as the pain becomes palpable between us. Years of loss—of time passed. Years we could have had together if she'd once been fucking brave enough to tell me she was—

"You waited for me?" I rasp out, anger overruling my need to console her, instead wanting to shake her, to fucking eviscerate her. "All this time?"

She bites her lip, eyes flowing.

"Answer me," I snap, and she jumps again. The sight of it has my heart skyrocketing.

"Oui."

"Oui," I repeat, disbelieving of her calm—fucking hating it. Hating the sight of her altogether. "I can't," I say, shaking my head. "I can't fucking believe you let so much time pass. Even *now*, you haven't said shit!"

"You say you don't have those feelings for me anymore when you came to my house."

"Yeah, well, guess what, General," I drawl sarcastically. "*Love lied to you that fucking day* and has been lying *every day* since he came back so he could get you back and keep you in his life again!"

I rake her with my stare, unable to help myself as I eat up the sight of her. She's still too thin, but she looks fucking gorgeous, very much resembling the woman I worshipped when we were together.

Her eyes light with hope at my admission as I bite back words I know will hurt her. Because I know she wants this, and I've been batting every longing look away, knowing what she's capable of doing to me. Every part of me wants to obliterate that hope for her, wants *so fucking badly* to. Tension fills the air as she swallows, and the truth doesn't set me free—at all. If anything, it feels like it's strangling me.

"That morning," I say, voice laced with fury even as I whisper, "you said '*love is lying to you right now.*' You were flat out fucking telling me you were lying."

She bites her lip and nods. "Oui. But please, Soldier, please understand all of my reasons for it. I knew I was not good for you, Tyler. It was part lie but *so much truth*. I was twelve years older and the laughingstock of my family—an alcoholic with *many emotional* problems. I did not want to corrupt your future. I didn't want to hold you back."

"Well, guess what, Delphine," I deliver with clear lividity, "we're together again, messages *received* or *none*, so what does that fucking tell you?"

"Love never lied to me," she whispers, pressing a tear away. "I knew that, Tyler. In my heart." She palms her chest. "I knew I was the liar that day." Her eyes plead with mine for understanding that I'm incapable of right now due to the pain thrumming through me. "But we are together now, in this dream you created. You took a path meant for you to become a soldier, and I had to take my own to get here, in this place, mentally." She points to her temple. "And I am here now, and I want to share this dream with you." She takes a step forward. "I want so much to be with you in every way," she whispers, love and hope fueling her expression.

"Yeah, well, if you're this much of a *fucking coward*, why should I ever trust you with my fucking heart ever again?!" I snap before turning and smashing the phone against the kitchen wall. Her sobs follow me as I stalk out of the house, ignoring her desperate call of my name as I enter the cab of my truck. I turn the ignition over and look up to see her sobbing on the porch. She screams my name as I kick rocks up and race away, my heart cracking with the truth I've been suspecting since I came back. That she gave up the day I lost that battle and didn't fucking cross the street. But even so, she's been waiting for me this whole fucking time.

***

The patter of little feet sounds on the creaking hardwoods as I stare up at the ceiling of my room, my chest still pumping after endless hours of driving aimless miles. The fucking heart in my chest refusing any more distance as I drove every single one. Finally, turning around so it would stop battering me, continually ramming me in demand to get back to its owner. Glutton for more punishment for being in love with the most infuriating woman in existence since it made its fucking decision.

In a blink, she stands at the edge of my bed, but I don't look at her. I can't. If she's coming to me, then I need her to have the strength to continue to be the one to do it. And she does, tentatively brushing her fingers along my arm before straddling me and lowering herself to cover me. Her weight settles into me, a perfect fit, her naked breasts brushing my skin as she lays flush against me, resting her head beneath my chin. I can feel the heat from her core on my stomach through her thin silk panties as desire threatens to blind me. Softly, she whispers my name, and the curl of her tongue around it has my eyes fluttering closed.

Her silky hair glides along my bicep as she presses a kiss to my chest, where my heart lies, before gently stroking my pec, tracing my tattoo. Her apology is everywhere in how she's plastering herself against me in a silent plea. Inhaling her clean scent, I fist my hands at my sides to keep from touching her as I sink into the surreal feel of her—utterly bare to me in every way. Tamping down the raging lust now thrumming through me, I opt to speak, hearing the need in my voice as I do.

"Do you want to know why I really came back to you that day?" I ask, and she nods her head gently into my chest as she begins to trace the Roman numerals of my tattoo.

"Because the first time I noticed you, really saw you, I began to feel this innate need to stay near you. And when you confessed to me just after that you were hurt for the same reason, it only had me wanting to get closer. Both of us had been gutted and disappointed by our fathers. The men we trusted most with our hearts, who threw that trust away, threw our admiration, our *fucking love* away. That common bond explained my need to be with you because our scars matched and lined up so perfectly. But beyond that, it's because we both felt like we'd lost a sacred place, a safe haven we both needed because that's something we both need to feel whole."

A tear splashes against my chest as I give myself permission to run the pads of my fingers through her silky hair, nothing more.

"Back then, neither of us really put a voice to it, but we were still suffering together, silently sharing our pain and longing for that place. You were the only person who truly knew and understood what I was really going through, but you're the one who comforted me most. It shredded my heart that I couldn't be the same for you, but I wanted to, and I fucking tried so hard to be that for you."

"You did, you were, you did, Soldier. You know you did," she finally says. "I saw you."

"You saw a lost kid who reminded you of yourself, and I was, but that's not all it was. I know that now. Do you?"

She nods, continually tracing my tattoo.

"I fell in love with the woman you gave me glimpses of. The woman who still had life inside her, but I also fell in love with the woman who was in so much pain that she drowned herself inside it because I felt that same pain every day. My soul searching right along with yours."

Another tear splashes my chest.

"We might have come together because our scars matched, and we recognized we were missing the same thing, but we fell in love because we became the thing we both *needed for one another,* and that's a sense of security, of *home*." I swallow. "I knew you thought the worst of yourself for giving in that night. I was prepared to fight you on the morality of it all, especially after reading the letters, knowing you knew exactly what it was like with Alain. But when you pleaded with me to let go because you didn't want any more reason for them to hate you, I released you immediately because deep down, I did know they were your only true weakness. Dom especially."

I continually run my hands down her hair, which feels like heaven between my fingers.

"When I knelt in front of you weeks ago, all those years later, I saw you searching my eyes for the place we created. I saw that we were both lost because we'd lost the peace, security, and place we had found in each other when we parted that morning."

Another tear, and then another.

"I saw you recognize the boy you bonded with had become the man he hoped and promised you he would be, and then I saw your eyes dim because you didn't think that boy recognized home inside you anymore. But I did, Delphine. I saw it, and I still loved you. When I drove away from your house, I couldn't think of a reason for either of us to be without that peace anymore."

"You became that soldier, that man, Tyler."

"I became the soldier I swore I would be because it's all I've truly had since I lost that peace a second time. Even though I tried to make myself hate you for it, your voice helped me through some of the worst fucking days of my life. Even in your absence, you were still with me. You would find me in the black. I would hear you so fucking clearly." My voice breaks as the memory seeps in. The pop of bullets, the helplessness I felt, the sheer terror in the eyes looking to me for guidance.

Open your eyes, Tyler.
Breathe. One. Two. Three.
See it. Envision a way out. Do you see it?

"But you see, even if I got close to forgetting you, writing what we had off, and trying to put it in perspective, I couldn't. Because during the times I thought I escaped you—during my missions, through the worst of them, blood covering my hands, dirt beneath my fingernails, so fucking terrified, you were there. You were there with me, reminding me," I croak, "and you saved me, us, all of us, so many," I rasp hoarsely. "So many fucking times."

Finally wrapping my arms around her, I allow the truth to pour from me. "But I didn't come to you to *save you*, Delphine." I pull her tighter to me. "I came to *thank you*, to appreciate you, to *fucking love* you for the woman you are, not try and change you into some version of a woman I want you to be. I came back that day to spend time with the woman who recognized and embraced my darkness, as I did hers, and shaped me into her soldier. The woman who now and forever harbors the only place inside her that I will ever know that peace, home," I whisper in the otherwise silent room.

"But if you lift your mouth to mine. If you offer me whatever you have to give, I'm going to fucking take it, and I'm going to keep it and protect it. But I warn you now, if you do, there's not a thing on this fucking earth I'll allow between us ever again. Not even you—especially not you."

She instantly lifts her mouth to mine.

Chapter Forty-Five

Delphine

Tyler's lips capture mine in a kiss that steals my breath while setting my soul alight. Moaning my relief into his perfectly parted lips, I instantly open with the demanding swipe of his tongue. Inhaling his exhales, he thrusts it into my mouth. Years of excruciating longing and emotion meld together with every languid swipe as our flames reunite. Lost in the sensation, his consuming kiss frees me to roam, and I thrust my fingers into his hair just as he turns me on my back without losing any of our connection. The transition is so smooth that I only realize I'm wrapped around him when he pulls away. Our eyes lock as we wordlessly gaze at one another for several long seconds before his declaration hits my parted lips.

"This is it, Delphine, there's no going back," he declares with certainty. "There's *no going back*."

"Soldier, I don't ever want to," I affirm, taking his mouth more forcefully and sinking easily into the most erotic, most beautiful kiss of my life. Just after, emotion takes hold as elated tears glide down my temples. Pained exhales leave us both as we erase the years between us as he delves again and again. My return kiss is fueled with all I feel as I free myself to map every inch of his muscled skin, soaking it up with my fingers while worshipping with my palms as we feed incessantly. His touch is just as fevered as if we've both been starving all this time—the intensity of each kiss eradicating what space remains. When he finally pulls away, we continue to share breath, our lips so close, our eyes bolted.

"Tyler," I whisper as I stare straight into the molten desire and warmth that I've been begging God to restore. Though his room is dark, I can easily see it everywhere in his expression as I palm his jaw. "Soldier, God, how I've missed this look," I whisper. "How I prayed for it—prayed for *you*. Je suis désolé," *I'm sorry*, "*please*, forgive me. I was such a fool."

"Shh, not tonight." He shakes his head, negating all possibilities for arguments of the past as he recaptures my mouth. This kiss turning far more carnal as I start to squirm beneath him, pressing myself against him more urgently. Gripping my hair, he gently pulls, exposing my throat before covering it in tongued-filled kisses.

"Plus s'il vous plait," *more please*, I cry out, my entire body drawing as I lower my hand toward his briefs. Just as I near the waistband, he stops it, pulling my hand between our flush bodies to run his lips along my fingers.

"We," he exhales, halting all movement. "And . . . I can't fucking believe I'm saying this, but we can't go *there* tonight."

"It's only a *suggestion* to wait twenty-four hours after wax," I sigh, "now I wish I had not"—my neck heats—"I was not expecting *this*."

"Fucking hell," he groans, dropping his forehead between my breasts as he laces our fingers together, pinning them next to my head. "You're making things a lot worse," he whispers, his voice filled with desire. "But that's not the type of wait I'm talking about. It's just too soon to tax your body this way, and you know it. You're still struggling with fatigue day to day. And fair warning, if I so much as *glimpse* your freshly waxed pussy tonight, *we're both going to die*."

I can't help laughing. "But *I am okay*, Soldier. I assure you—"

He jerks his chin as I exhale a groan. "I want you more

than . . . fucking anything, but your immune system is in reset mode, and we need to let that happen. Just a little more time." He captures my lips in a reassuring kiss before again taking my eyes hostage. "It's been over *three thousand days* since I've fucked you, made love to you, and I can and *will* wait a little longer for you."

"I felt every one of those days, Tyler. Every single one," I whisper. "They hurt so much."

"Jesus, me too, believe me," he whispers before giving me a wicked grin that makes my toes curl. "But silver linings, at least for me, is that prolonging this gives me the advantage of payback for the *hell* you've put me through."

I glower at him, and he chuckles, stilling my wandering hand and pinning it in the same way as the other, leaving me helpless beneath him as he lightly brushes his erection along my thin panties, where he's now nestled between my thighs. His next brush elicits an aggravated mewl from me, and his eyes fire in delight before he speaks.

"Besides, I'm pretty sure you've been trying to kill me for years." He dips, drawing upon my nipple before noisily releasing it. "So, turnabout is fair play, and I'm building one hell of a strategy right now, baby. Many punishments included," he vows, his eyes intent.

"Punishment?" I utter weakly. "This does not seem just. I have not *once* tried to kill you. You're speaking imbecile."

"Au contraire, mon general," *on the contrary, my general,* "sassafras was stopped in use of the manufacturing of root beer because it's filled with *carcinogens* and considered *toxic,* so there's your *first* assassination attempt."

"What?" I gawk at him. "Merde," *shit*. I bulge my eyes. "Soldier, I had *no idea.*"

"Uh-huh, sure you didn't," he utters in a playful tone before he ticks off my list of offenses. "And then there's the months you denied our attraction before our recent eight years of torture," he whispers as I palm his jaw, "and counting—" He sucks a nipple into his mouth and flicks it with rapid licks as my panties flood with need.

"Tyler." I lift my upper half to try to get closer as his eyes twinkle with future retribution. "You saw my want of you, I know you did, and if—"

"Oh, *I saw it*, she-devil. But as you well know"—he blows on my peaked nipple—"I'm a pretty patient man—kind of *had to be* after falling in love with you." He laves at the taut peak before roaming to the next. "To the point that I've become a man who *can easily bide* his time," he declares before biting my nipple lightly and then soothing it with an exaggerated swipe of his tongue.

"Please," I beg unabashedly, "I feel fine."

"You know, I can wait *as long* as it takes." He licks along my bottom lip as I chase it for a kiss, still pinned by his body and his hands. "*You, however*, will not be able to go longer than a few blinks without recounting the details of the tortuous nights ahead of you."

"Tyler." I hear my pathetic whine. "I don't want to wait anymore. I am desperate for you."

He pauses his torture briefly, his fiery eyes drilling into mine. "Fuck . . . how long I've waited, *hoped* to hear words like that come from your lips."

"You already won this battle so long ago. It was *me* who refused to surrender, but I give it to you now." I bite my lip, tears filling my eyes.

"Baby," he murmurs, "all playing aside, I would be inside you right now if I thought it wouldn't hurt you, and you know that. But there are plenty of things we can do until you can make it up a hillside without losing breath. And for what I have in mind for us, and the thousands of ways I plan on fucking you, making love to you, once you've fully regained your strength, you're going to *need* to start training—tomorrow." He draws upon my lips. "But yeah, sorry, you're not getting away with doling out the torture I've endured. I will be seeking my satisfaction, along with." He gently bites my nipple, and I gasp, "A pound or twenty of *flesh*."

I can't help but smile despite the promise of torture.

"This sounds very, a-h, ah," I moan as he again draws upon one nipple, then the other, "serious."

"Oh, how the tables have turned, General Yoda. And now *it's my turn* to *get you* into shape."

"The pupil becomes the master," I croak breathlessly.

"*Exactly*, and man, am I going to enjoy this." His eyes roam over my bare skin. "You look so incredibly beautiful." His words cover me as he dips to kiss my torso and then my belly, covering what he's not kissing with his palms.

"Tyler, please," I cry, arching against his roaming lips as he lowers further and further.

"Damn," he groans, "my fucking name coming off that tongue of yours. I'm going to have to make you come tonight." He flicks my drawn nipple painfully, and I gasp. "Not that you really deserve it."

"Then let *me touch you*, Soldier. Let me *make you* come."

"Jesus, this is"—he shakes his head bewildered—"I never thought . . . I never thought *this day* would come."

"I want you so much," I admit. "So many nights I've touched myself in remembrance of that night."

"Now you're just fucking fighting dirty." He nails me with his expression. "Nice try, but I wouldn't try to top me in bed, General," he warns. "There's absolutely no fucking way you'll ever win *that flag*."

"I w-want"—my jaw starts shaking due to my abundance of desire, his dog tags tickling my skin as he places sporadic tongue-filled kisses along my body—"to touch you, so much to put my mouth on you."

"This is quite the dilemma we're in, General. Guess it's a good thing we're both strategists." He runs his swollen cock gently, so gently along my center. "And just because I told you what turns me on doesn't mean I'm going to let you bait me."

"This isn't a game for me." I shudder beneath him. "I need to feel you."

"It's never been a game for me," he counters so seriously that we both stop moving. "*I love you.* There's no game inside that truth, I promise, but *there is* foreplay." His dimple pops, and I groan at the sight. "And at that, General, I *excel.*"

"Please, Tyler, I feel fine, ah," I cry as he lowers his head between my legs, locking one over his muscular shoulder before he slowly dips, licking me wholly with a long swipe of his skilled tongue over my panties. Gripping the fingers I have twisted in his hair, he lowers them to the sides of the silk he's licking along before giving his rough order.

"Spread yourself for me, baby, and I'll make it quick. I don't want to hurt you." His fast exhales set my sensitive skin alight even through the material. "Do it," he orders, just before I pull myself apart for him, the only barrier the slip of silk. The instant I obey, he runs a sure finger up my slit, easily finding my clit a second before he furiously begins to lick it, exactly where I'm pulsing and needy. The sensation of his intense licks is so overwhelming that I clamp my legs around his head. His rough chuckle hits my thighs, his light stubble brushing against them before he palms my legs open, holding them easily. "Open for me," he commands roughly.

The second I do, I'm instantly pulled under.

"Tyler," I draw out, my mewl fueling him as he begins to rapidly dart his tongue against the throbbing ache. Within mere breaths, my chest is heaving, desire running rampant. Just as the rush begins, he pulls my throbbing clit into his mouth *through* my panties, sucking feverishly until I explode. Wave upon wave of pleasure crashes into me, through me, as I come utterly undone beneath him. He palms my thighs wider, prolonging my orgasm by sucking lightly until I become a shuddering puddle beneath him.

Lifting, he instantly moves to my side, kissing me and restoking my need before pulling back and gazing down at me. "You're so beautiful to me, you know that, right? You didn't have to spend a single dollar to showcase what I can so easily see."

"I wanted to," I manage to relay as my body shakes and hums in the aftermath. "It was just as much for me. It's been too long since I've cared for myself."

He nods in understanding as I palm his jaw.

"My God, how I wanted that look for me in your eyes, the look you have now. Every night, I have been tempted to cross that hall, to kiss your skin until you wake." Gliding my palm down his stomach, I dip into his briefs and grip his cock as the fantasy I started and have been fueling since I began gaining strength takes hold. "To taste you. And . . . I'm no longer asking. As you said, Soldier, turnabout is fair play."

"Fuck, baby," he grunts as I jerk his massive length, "just . . . easy," he utters with concern before I clamp his mouth with my palm, kissing the expanse of his chest as he chuckles against it. His groan vibrates against my hand as I flick his nipple and lower my kiss, running my tongue along every muscle, and his enormous cock pulses in my tight grip in response. I lower my kiss as I continually pump the silky skin, anticipation running through me like wildfire.

"So many nights I've thought of you," I murmur as he tracks my every move with molten brown eyes. "Of how you fucked me, made love to me, of how it felt between us."

"Turnabout is fucking right because if you keep touching me and talking like this, this is going to get embarrassing for me," he says, threading his hand into my hair before running his thumb along my jaw.

"So many days after—*years after*—I wondered how it was possible to crave a man *so much* and obsess over every touch. I thought I had lost more of my mind," I tell him honestly, paving a path with my lips while lightly pumping his cock in my hand. An instant later, he goes utterly still to restrain himself, releasing a frustrated groan.

"Would you reconsider?" I ask, hoping he'll change his mind.

"No," he answers instantly, "but not because I don't want to, because I do. A lot. In our future." He whispers his finger along my cheek, and I capture it, sucking the pad of it into my mouth. "Jesus, you are fighting so fucking dirty . . . but I'm willing to negotiate."

I can't help my victorious grin. "What are your terms?"

"Gain *five more* pounds and walk up the hillside next to our house *without getting winded*, and I'll give you as much of this as you want." He pumps his cock into my tight fist before lifting his lips into a deviant smirk. "Probably more than you can handle."

"That sounded more like an order, and who told you smug was so fucking sexy?" I grumble.

"*You did* this morning while you were goading me about other women, and we talked door socks while you fucked me with your eyes."

"You *have noticed everything* these past few weeks," I hiss in frustration, climbing back up briefly to sink my teeth into his lip.

"Ouwch, shibt," he groans, his cock growing impossibly harder in my hand as I suck his newly bitten lip before issuing my warning.

"I accept your challenge," I issue in a warning of my own. "You will soon discover that I, *too*, have an appetite, Soldier," I utter, biting into his jaw as he chuckles. It's when I run my thumb along his fat crown that his laughter stops altogether. As my kiss lowers, he keeps his fingers in my hair, massaging my scalp, his voice covering me with every word.

"Fuck . . . you feel so good," he mumbles as I lick every place I've imagined on his chest, along every ridge of his abdomen, and further down until I've reached the light trail of hair leading to his briefs. Unable to help myself at the sight of his perfect dick as I unveil it at the top of his waistband, I immediately inhale the engorged head to feast.

"Jesus," he grits out as I start vigorously pumping him with my hand, swirling my tongue around his tip, tracing it again and again, moaning my need for him as I do it.

"Fuck, fuck, fuck," he hisses, my hair growing tighter in his fist as I relax my throat to take in what I can. His cock is impossibly large. So much so, I'm only able to fit a fraction of him into my mouth, gagging on him as I do. Determined, I soak his shaft as much as possible while pumping his ridiculous girth in my unrelenting grip.

"Goddamn," he groans as he gently starts to thrust in. I pop him out of my mouth and, with the victorious lift of my lips, issue my order.

"Stop flirting and *fuck* my mouth."

"Delphine." His eyes flare, even as he voices his concern.

"Do it," I command, "I'm not made of glass, Soldier."

Surrounding him again, I strangle the base of his dick, and he instantly starts pumping more aggressively. After a few thrusts, I pop him out with my next order, sensing he's close.

"Come in my mouth," I tell him, taking in as much as I can as I claw his stomach and swallow him down. He thrusts a few times and stills my head until he's spent himself. His groan as he releases only fueling the rekindled fire between my legs. I'm nowhere near satiated with giving so little to him, even as he sinks into the bed as he comes down. Even so, I feel the familiar fatigue settling into me and hate it.

"Merde," *shit*, I whimper, as light sweat covers my skin. "We've waited so long, for so little," I utter as he drags me to straddle him, his chuckle ironic.

"We have time. To be honest, I'm surprised you're up for it this early on."

"Oh, I'm up for it," I mutter dryly. "And do you know why, my soldier? Because my memory, my mind—as much of a traitor as it is—has been kind enough to remind me every single damned day just *how well* you know how to use *this cock*." I grip him again, and he jerks due to the sensitivity, but I keep my grip firm to fight dirty. "Because you *weren't* just a kissing *tramp* and *fucked all the girls*."

A tense silence follows as I release him and sigh.

"I'm sorry I ever put that in your head," he whispers through the quiet room. "As much as I like to point the finger, I've said some shitty things to you in anger. I'm no saint, General, and I know that." He tenderly strokes my back with his fingers while pulling me closer. "I'll do my best to erase the words that hurt you."

"Non," I lift to speak what words I have for him, "what's done is done, and there is nothing you will ever say or do that could ever turn me away from you. You have given me the ability to trust again, Tyler, and this trust is *yours*." He stares up at me, emotion swirling in his eyes. "I know you are worried, but I am not. I want to be in the same bedroom. I want to share this life with you. Will you maybe consider it?"

"I think we have a miscommunication issue," he says.

"No, we don't. We have lingering hurts between us. I *hurt* you and wronged you, and you can't trust my words yet. It's *my turn* to prove love isn't a liar, and I want so much to make you happy."

"Then there's no miscommunication," he says, pulling me back to his chest, to where I fit so naturally, my head beneath his chin.

"Tyler," I whisper, "you truly have still wanted me this *whole* time? Even when you came to my door that day?"

"Since the first time I truly saw you, God, yes. Any way I can get you, always, Delphine. Always." He wraps both his arms around me firmly. Our mouths find each other again and again for long minutes until finally, we're facing each other an inch away on our own pillows. Hands clasped, legs tangled, we gaze upon one another, a new kind of beginning in each other's reflection. One that started long ago and that time revealed was the best thing to ever happen to me—a bond which I speak aloud.

"Re-bonjour mon meilleur ami." *Hello again, my best friend.*

Chapter Forty-Six

Delphine

Eyes closed but sensing his absence, I blindly palm Tyler's side of the bed and instantly feel the residual moisture where he lay next to me hours before. Of the handfuls of nights we've shared a bed, there have been a few where I've awoken soaked by *his* sweat-saturated body.

Sensing his distress, I quickly pull on my robe and slippers.

Knowing he's not in the house, it's confirmed a minute later when I look toward the front door to see it open, the screen door unlocked and slightly ajar behind it. Stalking through it in search of him, I'm thankful my path is lit by the moon, which blazes three-quarters full, as I begin my search through endless rows of apple trees. Rapidly coloring leaves flutter on all sides of me, a few breaking loose and flying past me on my path as I inhale the crisp air. After several minutes of a fruitless search, it's my worry for him that carries me through the threatening fatigue.

I'm only able to release a long, relieved breath when I finally spot him. That relief is short-lived at the sight of him standing utterly still between a line of trees, his posture rigid, hands clenched at his sides.

"Go back inside, Delphine," he clips when I'm ten feet away, his tone lacking life while at the same time intentionally casual and *lifelike*. So much so, if I didn't know the animation that typically resides inside it, I would never know the difference. Very aware of the distortion of the man standing feet away from me but not of what haunts him, I can visibly see the sheen of sweat still covering his naked upper half despite the cold. Though the air around him is alarming and ominous, his beauty is astonishing by comparison. It's my heart that refuses to take heed to his warning, but the second I lift my foot to inch forward, he speaks again. "*Don't*, Delphine." This order comes just as clipped and void of animation. "Go back to bed. I'll be back in a little while."

Refusing to move but heeding his words, I idle for long minutes as he stands so still—so utterly and terrifyingly still—my heart breaks at the sight of it.

"Tyler," I finally say, "turn to me."

"Damn it, Delphine, go back to the house!" he snaps, this voice very much belonging to the man I know. He's coming into himself because I'm refusing his order, but I can't allow whatever he's reliving to harm him any longer tonight.

"Please, Soldier. Please turn to me," I urge. It takes another minute until his shoulders relax a fraction, and he rolls his neck slightly. It's then I see his upper body visibly expanding and collapsing as he takes precisely measured breaths. A frigid breeze kicks up when he finally turns, and the sight of solid metal eyes greets me. The sight is jarring, but one I've seen before—the first time I found him in the living room. The second sighting was the night he stormed into my house, furious at the thought I had been with another man before he breathed through it and blinked his metal gaze away. "Where are you, Soldier?"

"Standing ten feet in front of you," he retorts sarcastically. "Couldn't you do what I asked?"

"Non, not if it pains you this much." I finally take a step forward. "Are you afraid you'll hurt me in your state?"

"No," he bites in offense, "and it's questions like the one you just asked me that have me wanting you to keep your fucking distance." Exhaling, he closes his eyes once more and runs a hand through his soaked hair, his irritation with me evident. "I'm completely aware of *everything* in *any fucking state* I'm in, Delphine."

"Then you are ashamed?" I prod.

"Partly, but mostly, right now, it should be apparent I'm annoyed," he bites out. "I asked you to leave me be. Couldn't you do that *one thing* for me?"

"I'm sorry, Soldier," I whisper. "I will do as you ask."

As he lifts his head skyward, I notice his expression is turning pained because of his need to protect me from himself and what haunts him. As I take one last lingering look at him, a strong breeze cloaks us both, and my involuntary shiver doesn't go unnoticed.

"Come on," he sighs, "it's cold." He walks over to me, palming my back to guide me forward. Feeling his restlessness, I remain mute on our walk back. When we reach the porch, he stops me when I lay a hand on the door, sliding his arm around my waist and pulling me back into him. "I'm sorry, baby"—he exhales a long breath—"but *you know* why I asked you to leave."

"Because you don't want me to witness it."

"Of course not," he murmurs, "you're going through enough."

"I'm stronger than I have been in *two decades*," I declare honestly. "So no, Soldier. I will not accept that. I have not forgotten these past weeks where you have spent all your focus *on me*, to heal me, that you confessed your own need to heal." I turn in his arms and gaze up at him. "So now I *need* to know. Where were you?"

"Not tonight, okay?" he replies with more tenderness in his voice.

"Oui, tonight, and *right now*. You get to demand my pain, to help me, and have probed to learn *my past*. Should I not get the same respect, the same privilege?"

He stares back at me, unflinching. "Yes, and you will, just not tonight."

"Give me *something*, Soldier."

He blows out a long breath. "I was allowing myself to try and process some things in an attempt to put them into perspective."

"And so, what? You think you are capable of what I am not without Regina's help?"

"I didn't say that," he defends, "but maybe I claim that because I've been researching this half my life for this very purpose."

"I'm not judging you." I palm his chest. "But can I not be just as adamant about your health? About the dangerous places *you* go?"

"Come on, it's cold," he says, ushering me back to bed like I'm a child as he slips in next to me, his eyes losing the rest of their brass glaze as he gently whispers his palm over the top of my head. I grip his hand and toss it away, refusing his coaxing touch as he exhales a groan of frustration.

"Well, I got a *three-for-one deal* on the French *pains in the ass* in my life when I befriended Dom, didn't I?" he coos with the pop of his dimple as I avoid his touch a second time. "Oof, baby," he admonishes, "I'm so looking forward to our *real* fights."

"Careful what you wish for, imbecile, and don't make me state the obvious," I finally bite.

"I think I will," he says with a slight edge.

"I care for you just as much, and I will refuse you to hide what hurts you by numbing with stupid fucking jokes to deter me."

"I flat out told you I'm trying to heal myself, Delphine. I'm not hiding that."

"And this is how you need me, Soldier? To witness you suffer and remain silent? *Non*."

"For now, *yes*," he states adamantly, "but only because I'm aware of the catalog of ways to help process PTSD, including grounding techniques, cognitive interventions, exposure techniques, and psychotherapy—otherwise known as *talk therapy*. And since I'm hell-bent on trying to stay off meds unless it worsens, I'm going through what I can on my own by using what I know. So, without sounding like more of an asshole than I'm acting like right now, I'm only reconfirming what I know any qualified psychotherapist, psychologist, or counselor would tell me. Spending money and time to gain an education I already have would be an utter waste. I feel confident enough on my own because I am fairing and functioning enough *for now*," he states before refusing the personal space I've forced between us by easily pulling me to lay beneath him. Bending, he takes my lips in a kiss so ravenous that I sink into it, glaring at his victorious smile when he pulls away. "Damn." One side of his mouth lifts. "you're sexy when you're pissed."

"Tyler—"

"When I'm ready to talk it out, you'll be *the first* I start talking to," he relays in a soft whisper.

"Promise me, Soldier," I prompt, palming his jaw as his fatigue becomes more present in his eyes.

"I swear it." He kisses my hand. "This is one of the reasons my parents used to fight, and I refuse to follow suit in that respect. But this was a minor episode. They come and go and always will. If I'm honest, they were becoming less frequent until this utter fucking *shit show* of a summer, which was therapy-inducing in and of itself. But it's the job and purpose I chose and will continue to."

"What happened this summer?"

"Jesus, you're a pushy little thing tonight." His eyes shimmer with love as I give him an adamant shrug. "Aren't you tired?"

"Non. *Tell me.*"

"Well . . . let's see." He shakes his head in slight disbelief before pinning me with an arduous stare. "And this is just to name the most significant."

I nod.

"I've had to help Dom reroute our vendetta strategy thanks to Cecelia's crash landing. While watching the slow-motion and dangerous descent of Sean and Dom collectively falling for her, I kept and continue to keep vigilant eyes on her to ensure no harm comes her way. This is while carrying out our plan to bring down our competitors—to be the first to get to Roman. In doing that, stumbling upon a nightmare by way of a warehouse inspection with contents so fucking dangerous that lifting them could have brought major heat to the club, with the potential to expose us before taking us *all down.*" He blows out a loaded breath. "During this time, dealing with Miami's possible defection, especially after Dom blew his lid after a street race, where we're almost positive it was a purposeful attempt to take Sean out. This is while we're in the midst of orchestrating and framing two higher-ups in the military because of what we found in that warehouse, with the help of our birds in higher places . . . Oh, add raiding an apartment full of drug addicts—also *Dom* initiated—before we left them screaming naked on the highway. Then, tack on investigating one of our local birds, Clint, and weighing the decision to erase him as a liability or get him rehabilitation. And the most recent nightmare, fucking covering Dom's tracks, yet again, by going on a tri-state crime spree. Finish it off with my daily responsibilities for the club, including passing out blessings and checking in for my mandatory Marine reserve duties, all the while trying to figure out the best way to deal with Tobias's incoming wrath."

My eyes are bulging out of my head as he finishes this list.

"So yeah," he sighs before affectionately brushing my cheek, "it's been a rough couple of months. And no offense to my brothers—and though I hate the fact that they're gone—I could use some downtime. Because as much as your nephews like to pride themselves on not being *drama queens,* those two are neck and neck in earning the crown."

"Mon Dieu, Tyler!" I rasp out, palming his chest as his

grin widens at whatever expression I'm wearing. "How did you . . . manage all that?"

"Well enough to fight another day," he murmurs, "but the best part, General of my heart," he whispers with affection, "is that it all comes back to *you*. And I'll give you every single detail of how, I promise. But I have to go see one of your drama queens in a few hours, so please let me get what sleep I can."

"Yes, of course, but"—I shake my head in astonishment—"I will now say you are faring very, *very well* considering."

"It's because of you, Delphine," he insists as I shake my head in refusal. "Shake your head all you want," he drawls, "but you've been with me the whole time. And when I tell you how I managed the summer from hell, and escaped so many sticky situations in the GRS, you will believe me."

"I can't wait to hear this, Soldier," I trace his tattoo. "I don't know how I will sleep, but rest, yes please," I order, reeling.

Ten minutes later, I'm still peering at my soldier in astonishment, and sensing it, a beautiful and knowing grin lifts his full lips as he keeps his eyes closed.

"Soldier, I'm so sorry, and I want you to get rest, but can I ask one thing—"

"Merde," *shit*, he exhales through a sleep-filled chuckle before he quiets all questions with his kiss.

Chapter Forty-Seven

TYLER

Exiting the elevator, I stalk toward the glass door leading to Exodus's reception area. Even all these years later, I'm still in awe that my brother owns a high rise. More so of what he's accomplished, as well as the man he's become. Even if I don't entirely agree with all the manufactured parts of him. Of the decisions he's made for himself in certain areas of his life. Nodding toward Shelly—Tobias's *everything* assistant who forever has her phone glued to her ear—she gives me a wink of permission to head in.

A heartbeat later, I'm closing his office door and turn to see him peering out of his floor-to-ceiling windows at the Charlotte skyline. Though he's immaculately dressed, his posture fitting of the mogul he's become, I know the true state of him.

After our blowout, the Triple crew all but snubbed him when T attempted to get back into the day-to-day of the club. Which only added more insult to his catastrophic injury. Sensing it within days, I took back some of the reins to alleviate some of his burden. In silently watching him for a few seconds, I decide to cut straight to the hurt I know he's feeling.

"You outgrew that role when you were sixteen, T," I offer, hoping he takes my words to heart. "And you know it."

"Here to gloat?" he counters, his words filled with an earned edge.

"Just the opposite. I'm here to give you the apology you deserve," I say, taking a few strides in. "I'm sorry if I seemed flippant that day at the house. You deserved better. I'm not going to ask for your forgiveness because that's up to you, but I want it. Though I need to have your trust back in the most basic sense for us to keep going, I know I'll have to earn the rest."

He keeps his back to me when he finally speaks. "Is this even my fucking club anymore, Tyler?"

"T," I exhale. "I know this feels like fucking shit, but there is no club without you. We'd all been living separate lives for *years* before we came back in, so the transition hasn't been easy on *any of us*." I instantly see the rejection of my statement in his slight shift of demeanor. "But far before Cecelia, and even after she came, we never made a single fucking move without you in mind. Ever. If you don't believe anything else that's coming from me, believe that."

"I don't know what you expect," he releases in exasperation as he turns to me, his fatigue evident even as he maintains his rigid posture.

"Nothing *today*, and maybe for months to come. I can only apologize so many times . . . though I would do it again."

Eyes flaring in warning, he nods toward the door so I can see myself out.

"You weren't there, Tobias, and it all comes down to that, but I'm not here to fight you or to glove up for them. They made their bed, and you reacted, and you're stuck in yours. I'm trying to get comfortable in mine and know I never will if things stay as they are, but I'd be lying if I said this isn't gnawing at me every waking fucking hour. I feel the disconnect you do, not on your level, but it fucking stings, brother."

He rolls his neck and takes a seat behind his keyboard, dismissing the conversation as he speaks. "Anything on Miami?"

"We're stalking their every move, but it's quiet, and you know I don't trust quiet."

"I'm getting back to closing in on Roman," he states. "It seems I've lost sight of a lot recently, so do what you will *there*, but remember their ties and why we can't simply *eliminate* the problem."

"Understood, but I'm not done," I say, stepping forward. "Tobias," I prompt as he lifts his unforgiving gaze to meet mine. "I'm fucking sorry."

"I heard you, Tyler. I'm—"

"What you're doing is leaving for Paris out of Charlotte in two hours." I stalk up to his desk and palm it. "Within an hour of landing, I will have tracked Abijah down, and you will come face to face with your birth father—*today*. You have my word, brother. I'll send you his exact location when you land. He won't be approached, but he'll be followed until you reach him."

This has him animating. "And how the fuck will you do that?"

"I called in a favor," I supply. "One of a very precious few I have, and I know this won't make up for it, but you and I have got to start communicating again. I've been digging tunnels that you need to be aware of for some time now. So, I'm not asking if we're good, T, because I know that will take time, but I am asking you to stop penalizing me with clipped orders so our club doesn't suffer. I'll give Shelly the details."

Turning to do that, he speaks to my retreating back.

"I don't know how to forgive this, Tyler."

I stop just short of the door, glancing at him over my shoulder. The brother I know personally finally making an appearance since he iced me out. "I don't know how you will, and honestly, I don't think I could so easily either.

But I do hope you figure out a way because we're all stinging pretty fucking badly."

"I know my aunt," he says as I grip the door handle and stiffen. "I know her because I took the time to discover what I could, what history she would reveal to me. I have a lot of the same education you got from her because we made peace well before I left for France . . . but she didn't reveal all to me, did she?"

I remain mute, which is confirmation enough for him, and he audibly sighs before I look back at him once more.

"All this time, I thought she mourned her ex-husband, but she suffered horribly at his hands," he deduces before his chest bounces without sound. "Jesus Christ, do we ever really know people?"

"Only the people we care enough about to pour our efforts into, exploring inside and out, but even then, they change."

"I have more fond memories of her than my brother." He slowly flips a burner phone on his sleek desk, seeming lost in thought. "Or maybe he's playing immune to any fond memory of her, but I remember well when she acted more a doting aunt than the woman who took us in."

"Dom remembers that too, and they've been working on getting somewhere in recent months," I relay, "but maybe you should let her know that someday. I know she'd be glad to hear it."

He gives me a slow, assessing nod.

"Safe trip," I expel, as the sting increases while I address him. "I'll text you the minute you land . . . and T?" I pause as he stares back at me, searching my person as if through a new lens. "I hope you get the answers you seek or whatever peace you're looking for with him, brother," I relay sincerely, identifying with his struggle to understand the nature and actions of the man that fathered him more than he could fathom. We stare off a few seconds in that bond before I turn and snap the door closed behind me.

Chapter Forty-Eight

Delphine

Soldier I have gained six pounds! Scans and blood are done and the Doctor says I'm clear to fuck ;)

    Laughing at the nature of my text, I add a picture of myself at the top of the hillside and send both off the way my soldier taught me on my new smartphone. Forever thankful Tyler alerted me to predictive text to save myself the frustration. Studying the picture as I trek back down the hill, I recognize the most noticeable changes. Not just in my face, which has plumped and is smoothing drastically because of the magic needles, but of the life inside my smile. That now resides in my eyes.
    More and more with each day, I come closer to resembling the woman I was before he left. A woman who harbors hope as well as a renewed sense of dignity. It's the shame that fills me of how it came to be that I have yet to press past. The truth that I didn't get to this place on my own.
    My frequent therapy with Regina is, at times, so brutal that some days, it threatens to keep me in dangerous places. Craving numbing sips so badly that during that time, I fear I will break my sobriety. As Tyler predicted, and I knew well, all has not been cured since I stopped numbing. In fact, the battles have become harder. I'm not always such a happy woman. I have days I'm intolerable, especially to

myself. But Regina told me there's no storybook life for even those most well-adjusted. That it's simply the nature of living, which I knew already as truth.

It's the man who stares at me with love in his eyes—no matter my state—over the kitchen table every morning and across our pillows at night who makes all days worth fighting for.

My want for Tyler's constant company no less now than it was all those years ago. My desire to make him happy taking priority over my own when I'm able. Now, instead of feeling shame for it and pushing him away, I cling to him as he does me. Finally deciding not to fault myself further for it, and possibly not by giving a rat's ass about it if I become so co-dependent *happy* like Layla.

At this point, it's the relentless sexual torture Tyler has made very good on delivering that now threatens to drive me to an early grave. Never in my life believing I would have to work so fucking hard to get a man in my bed. The irony has laughter erupting from me as I walk back down the hillside. Musing over the fact that the man I'm so desperate for, the only one I've felt such desire for, is putting me through so much just to get a fucking sock on our door.

Filling my watering can at the kitchen sink, I bask in the view just outside the window. The days still warm enough for lighter dress, while the leaves continue to drastically change, enhancing the land in a multitude of colors.

Stepping onto the front porch, I begin to water the plants as delicious anticipation races through me of what tonight might bring. Our most recent session of his torturous foreplay taking over my thoughts.

"This kitchen is a dream, Soldier!" I call to where he is in our bathroom while whipping eggs with a whisk. "Even a woman most resistant to cooking could not ignore its allure! I'm determined to master it now!"

"Oh yeah?" he calls back from the bedroom as he dresses.

"Oui, I have never in my life woke and thought, 'I'm

excited to make eggs,' but here I am, making fucking eggs for my"—I frown—"boyfriend?" I utter low, testing the word.

"You're what?" he calls back.

"Soldier, I think maybe I'm too old to call a man a boyfriend." Firing up the stove, I toss a pat of butter into my new frying pan. "And we both know lover is just . . . not true," I grumble aggravatedly. "Connard."

"Connard, huh?" Tyler chuckles as I jump out of my skin.

"FUCK!" I turn and push at his chest where he stands directly behind me. "How did you get so close? I didn't even sense you!"

"Careful, baby, or you'll be cooking your hair first," he says, reaching behind me to turn off the gas burner. "And I've been doing that trick for years."

I narrow my eyes. "What trick?"

"Getting this close to you without you aware of it," he muses, popping a chopped grape from the bowl of fruit I just cut into his mouth.

"Getting close when, like at night, in my room?" I ask, eyes wide.

"No, you assuming asshole, like in the bright light of day," he whispers, his eyes softening. "And every fucking chance I got."

"What would you do?"

"Get close enough to get a good whiff of that light musk you wore," he whispers, his eyes drilling into mine as he slowly lifts me onto the counter.

"I'm cooking," I remind him, in awe of the ease with which he lifts me.

"What was that?" he asks.

"What?" I utter, distracted by how gorgeous he looks freshly showered, his lashes and hair still damp, darker.

"The perfume you wore."

"Oh, I don't remember," I say honestly. "An old roll-on I think I had in my nightstand from AVON." I widen my eyes. "An old lady perfume."

"You're being a little ageist today. Why can't you call me your boyfriend?"

"It feels . . . juvenile, non?"

"Maybe it would be juvenile if I were twice your age, and it's better than connard," he murmurs. Tucking his fingers into my pajama bottoms and panties, he presses a hot kiss to the bared shoulder that my thin, long-sleeved pajama top hangs from.

"Non, Soldier, do not start this. You will be late for work."

"It's a good thing I'm my own boss." He rakes his lower lip with his teeth as his rapidly heating gaze roams over me. "And it's a shame about the perfume because it drove me fucking crazy."

"I'm cooking your breakfast." I lightly push at his chest as he begins to stroke the sensitive skin he has leveraged into my pajama bottoms and panties.

"I can see that. What's in there?" He nods toward a bowl.

"Lemon crème," I utter, getting lost in the length of his lashes. "It's for your fruit."

"Can I have a taste?"

"Hmm," I say, reaching back to put a little on my finger before holding it up to his lips. He sucks it off seductively, closing his eyes just after.

"Not just saying this, it's really good, baby."

"I know." I smile. "This recipe I remember." I tap my temple. "It's simple."

"Yeah?" he murmurs, his eyes smoldering as he surrounds me. "What else is on the menu?"

"Non." I shake my head. "Not me today. You aren't torturing me before you leave for work. I won't endure that again."

"You won't, huh?"

"Non, so don't waste your effort," I say, waving him away.

"After getting a good whiff," he continues, ignoring my dismissal while running his fingers along my skin in an intoxicating sweep.

"Soldierrrr," I draw out as a pulse begins to beat between my legs.

Ignoring me, his eyes light fire, captivating me as he easily tugs my pants and panties down before tossing them and leaving me half-naked on the counter.

"Tyler—"

"And with a nose full of you, I'd go home," he confesses, palming my knees apart before standing between them.

"And then what?" I whisper, my voice coated with my building arousal. The look in his rich brown eyes enough to set me alight as I trace the path of the tongue he drags along his full bottom lip. Just the sight of him, the stroke of his fingers, and the path of his tongue has me becoming acutely aware of everything else. His strategy for that intentional and never failing. It's the added look of him in his T-shirt and jeans, the curve of his biceps, and the fresh, mixed scents wafting from him that start to undo me.

"Then I'd take my cock in my hand . . . and fuck my fist," he murmurs, gently running his fingers up my thighs as he dips and places a kiss in the divot of my throat. "Thinking about this"—he kisses the divot again—"and this." He licks along the column of it as I tangle my fingers in his damp hair.

"You are going to be late," I remind him, my protest pathetic.

"Give me some more of that cream," he orders, and I do, taking a dollop onto my finger and playfully dotting his nose with it. He cuts his eyes at me as I laugh, and a second later, I'm flattened against the counter as he runs his cream-covered nose through my center.

"Soldier, I can't take this anymore," I utter. "I can't. Okay? I surrender, and since I've learned that means nothing to you, just take out your gun and shoot me."

A chuckle erupts as I glare down at him where he hovers above my bare pussy.

"Days and days of fingers and tongues," I release through a groan, "nothing but fingers and tongues and—ah," I cry *as he flattens his tongue on my clit before flicking it rapidly. I'm already battered into submission when he pulls away.*

"Don't like my tongue?" *he prompts, and I tighten my fingers in his hair before gently clawing his scalp. Keeping my gaze, he begins to leisurely lick me. At this point, I know better than to look away because the second I do, he stops.*

"Soldier, please," *I whimper as he brings me close, only to pull away, thrusting a finger inside me before expertly teasing me with it.*

"Please, what?"

"Do whatever is in your eyes."

"I am." *He adds another finger and begins to pump them into me.* "So fucking tight."

Bending over me, he feeds me his tongue first, his kiss a mix of lemon, my own taste, and mint from his toothbrush. Grappling with the strength of his kiss, I clutch and claw as he seduces me with his wicked mouth. "Fuck, baby," *he whispers directly into my ear,* "you're so wet."

"Please . . . can do just, ah," *I climb as his fingers hasten,* "do a little," *I whisper as he deposits wet kisses along my neck.*

"Just a little what?"

"A little," *I whisper.*

"You mean, just the tip?" *He chuckles.*

"Why is that so fucking funny?" *I growl.*

"Oof, baby, someone is getting frustrated."

"I'm not," *I lie.*

"Liar."

"We could fuck a little. Just a little," *I say.* "You love stretching my mouth." *I drop my eyes suggestively.*

His eyes narrow, and I hold my victorious smirk, having discovered his weakness early in our game with the way he constantly traces my lips.

"Brutal," *he utters, onto my ploy,* "but I promise you, you'll be the one who can't handle just a little."

"We will see," *I challenge, unfastening his jeans before unveiling and gripping his gorgeous, thick dick. As I do this, he keeps his lust-filled gaze on me as I pump him vigorously in my hand, the way he likes it. In turn, he pulls me to the edge of the counter, which conveniently matches his height. Taking a dollop of cream, he lowers my thin sweater and covers both my nipples, sucking it off noisily before pulling himself free of my hand.*

"*Just a little. No hands or tongue,*" *I order.*

"*Hmm.*" *He considers this and nods.* "*All right.*"

Gripping his massive erection, he slowly runs his thumb around the engorged, mouthwatering head as I watch on, entranced.

"*Sure?*" *He drawls as I lick my lips and nod. In turn, he dips, tracing a path with the tip of his tongue along both my lips while running his head through my center. Drawing himself up, he massages my pulsing clit with it. I instantly begin to gyrate, and he stills me.*

"*Easy, baby.*" *Cradling me with his arm, he begins to push, and we drop our gazes to where we connect. A moan rips from me as he pulls out, drawing his tip up to massage my clit with it once more. He alternates this pattern for long seconds as I grip and claw, my agitation and thirst growing unbearable.*

"*Tyler,*" *I whimper, the pulse now a pounding between my thighs.* "*This can't last.*"

"*Oh, but it can,*" *he assures, a wicked smile curving his lips.* "*This can last all day.*"

"*Soldier,*" *I moan, seeing his restraint in the corded muscles of his neck and shoulders as his eyes hood. He pushes in again, dropping his gaze before he starts to fuck me with just the tip of his cock.*

"*Ah,*" *I whimper, thrusting my hips forward, his firm grip keeping me from gaining any more of him.*

"*Still want only this?*" *he taunts, thrusting in and out, in and out, as my body draws up with need.*

Within seconds, I'm climbing but without enough friction—without enough of him. When my impatience gets the best of me, I angle my hips and buck, managing to gain an inch more. Though we both groan at the feel of it, he pulls away.

"Tyler," I snap. "Enough. Just fuck me."

"Just fuck you," he repeats, circling his head at my aching entrance, seemingly lost in the act, raw desire coating his voice. "There's no just fucking you, baby. Never has been . . . Jesus, just being able to fucking touch you after all these years is enough for me," he whispers in admission. "Especially when I think of how many times I denied myself. Fingers itching at my sides, my chest on fire with what I felt for you." His confessions have me soaking in the love in his eyes, his every word.

"So many times I would look over at you, get lost in the look of you. Praying for the look in your eyes now. Back then, I would have given anything, fucking anything, just to touch you the way I am now." Lifting my shirt, he runs his palms over the expanse of my stomach as he continually pumps his hips. The movement itself so sexy, the curve of his perfect ass slightly visible as he keeps his rhythm steady but measured. Maddeningly so. In and out. In and out. The ache for more increasing as he covers me in his fiery gaze, his molten touch, and his heated voice. Cupping a breast, he runs his thumb over my nipple reverently as he gently pumps his hips.

In and out.

In and out. But it's the look and feel of him, his words, which covers me. As if he's already inside me. Feeling worshipped, I gaze up at him, the words idling on the tip of my tongue as he speaks first.

"When I finally press into you again for the first time, it'll be, will mean forever," he murmurs as I start to climb. After licking his thumb, he presses it to my clit and begins to massage me in mesmerizing circles—

Tyler's engine sounds, pulling me out of my daydream stupor where I clutch my empty watering can to my chest. In the next second, his truck appears as he flies down the gravel as if he might come straight *through* our house. Just after, he skids to a stop feet away from the porch. Within a heartbeat, our eyes bolt through his windshield. I swallow at the predatory look inside them before tossing my can and stalking toward him.

Heart pounding, his gaze tracks me as I circle his truck, desire from my reminiscent daydream fueling each step as he keeps his fire-filled brown eyes on mine.

Before I make it to him, he's out of the truck and standing next to the open door. His eyes sweep my face and trail down to my peasant top and shorts. There's a dangerous energy rolling from him, and though I can tell he's in a . . . mood and not at all up for conversation, I speak first.

"Did you leave work? It's the middle of the da—"

I don't get another syllable out as he lifts me off my feet and turns us so I'm sitting next to the wheel of the truck, facing him.

In the next instant, he hooks his finger into my peasant top, lowering it to free a breast before inhaling it. My body shudders as he sucks as much of it as he can fit into his mouth. I clutch his head, gasping at the fast flicks of his tongue on my nipple as I speak. "Tyler, if Barrett comes—"

"I don't give a fuck," he growls, lifting my lower half and ridding me of my shorts and panties in seconds. Eyes filled with hunger, and without any hesitation or restraint, he bends and sucks the whole of my pussy into his demanding mouth.

"Jesus!" I shriek, his pulls hard as he draws even more intensity to the pulsing between my thighs. The sensation is so overwhelming that I squirm against his mouth. "T-T-Tyler," I stutter, "s-so strong, ah," I gasp as the pain quickly starts to mix with pleasure as he feeds and feeds, alternating the thrust of his tongue inside with fast targeted licks to my clit. His predator's gaze muting me as he keeps me captive with the blaze in his eyes and skilled mouth. The intention that lay behind his stare welcome even as a tinge of trepidation sneaks in.

It's not fear but the sight of his loss of control. One he's finally allowing now as he ravages my pussy, drawing on it again and again.

"Tyler," I screech as he lowers and presses his tongue inside, thrusting as far as it will go. It's then I go boneless, far too weak against the mixed sensations to fight a single one. It's when he lifts, his wet lips hovering over my clit as he dips a finger in, that I slowly start to lose my mind. The look in his eyes, the desire and heat are like nothing I've ever seen, and as he starts to glide a skilled finger along my insides, my vision blurs.

"Look at me," he demands, voice coarse, and I do. I watch as he continues to draw his finger in and out of me, my body swelling in reaction. Every part of me pulsing as he continues to target the same spot over and over. Over and over. Over and over.

"What are you . . . oh, God," I moan as my abdomen begins to coil. "Tylerrrr," I call as his eyes close briefly in relief as if it's the very reason he's here. Needing the release, I begin to buck my hips against his finger just as he removes it.

"What, *no!*" I protest as he cups the back of my head and lifts me to sit half-naked, running his tongue over my lips before drawing me into a ravenous kiss. I cling to him as he molds our mouths, thrusting my tongue against his just as hungrily as he dizzies me before pulling me away.

"Lay down," he says, pushing me gently back onto his bench seat, "hands beneath your ass, baby, and lift your hips as much as you can," he orders gruffly while unhooking his belt and unbuttoning his jeans. Doing as I'm told, I gape at him as he stares down at me, a man on fire, before releasing his engorged cock. The sight of it in the bright light of day has me swallowing even while anticipation peaks.

"I won't hurt you," he assures as I keep my hands beneath my bare ass, tilting up for him as ordered. As if memorizing the moment, he sweeps my heaving chest, branding it with his eyes before briefly pausing on my exposed pussy.

"You're a dream," he utters before my begging commences. I surrender utterly, knowing he's succeeded in every way to keep me under his wicked spell—to keep me wanton and full of desire. Every look, every touch, and every minute of the torturous days now marked with purpose as I realize just how ready my body is—physically and mentally. His preparations masterful. Calculated. Every molecule screaming for him as my lips utter my need.

"Now," I order, unable to take another second as he pushes my blouse up to my chin so that he's got an unobstructed view of my breasts. Stepping up on the metal rung hanging low beneath his truck door, he palms his dash with one hand and the top of his bench seat with the other. Eyes blazing down me, he rakes his lips in anticipation, his voice so rough, I barely recognize it when he speaks.

"I love you," he whispers, lining the fat head of his cock against my entrance as he hisses through his teeth before angling his hips down and slowly driving some of his length into me. Though ready, my body instantly reacts, my pussy tightening around him. Cursing, he pulls out and drives back in a little further as my mouth falls open at the stretch. Sensation consumes me, and I whimper his name as he eases into me partway.

"Fuck," he grunts as I shudder around him, tightening further as he pulls back, only to again drive in, going a little further each time. Angling his hips *just so*, he inches in again, feeding me his massive cock little by little. Barely shifting his hips, he purposefully drags his dick along my walls, precise, measured. The feel of it, of being so full of him, utter bliss.

Inside, I feel myself continually coiling at the pressure he's creating until I'm gasping his name. It builds and builds through blinding pleasure as his brown eyes hold me, hold our surreal connection which feels less hum, more lightning. Powerfully zig-zagging between our connected bodies as he claims me feet away from our front door.

Body tingling from head to foot, just as I'm about to tip over, he drives in fully, grinding against the swell he's caused.

At the feel of it, I clamp down around him and explode in sensation. My body shuddering uncontrollably as the rush seizes me with such intensity, that I lose my fucking mind. Grappling for *anything* to hold onto, endless waves of pleasure course through me. As I peak, a scream rips from my throat, cracking as I release it before I hoarsely call his name. The whole of me continually convulsing due to the strength of the most powerful orgasm of my life.

Lost in the pulse happening throughout my entire body, still unfurling, my breaths erratic, I continue to come apart until the wave recedes, leaving me shaking in aftermath. It's when Tyler pulls back—and I gain some small sense of reality—that I feel just how soaked I am where we're still connected.

"Look at me, baby. Watch me fuck you," he orders, his expression purely carnal as he rears back and thrusts in again and again.

And again.

And again.

Lost in a haze of disbelief, he brings me back to the point of combustion and pushes me over, drawing only a slightly less powerful release than the first until I'm a whimpering mess beneath him.

Seeming satisfied, he finally *touches* me. The added sensation of his hands has me losing any faculties I have remaining.

Threading our fingers together at the top of my thighs, he continues his relentless thrusts, his jaw going slack as his eyes soak every bit of it in, missing nothing.

As if triggered by the sight, he begins pumping more furiously into me, a growl ripping from his throat as he fucks me to within an inch of my life. I catch it the second he starts to succumb, his jaw tightening in the most delicious way. Eyes firing bright as he unleashes his sounds and pours into me, his chest straining beneath his T-shirt as he gasps and comes for long, intense seconds. His eyes remaining lit as he leans over and licks the tears from my face before collapsing on top of me.

Wrapping as much of myself around him, his labored breaths hit my bare chest as I drag my nails beneath his shirt, along his back, and all the rest of what heated skin I can reach.

I continue to shake beneath him as I try to make sense of what just happened, of how he knew how to fuck me in such a way.

When he finally lifts, his eyes sparkle with familiar warmth as he graces me with a dimple-popping grin. "So... I got your text."

We both burst into laughter as the sheen of sweat covering me starts to cool. Cradling my face in his hands, slowly, so slowly, he takes my mouth in the most tender of kisses. This one emotionally infused and lasting blissful, freeing seconds. Though far more leashed and controlled, it's no less perfect. When Tyler pulls away and stands, I lift from the seat to follow, and he shakes his head, gently palming my chest to keep me idle.

"No baby, stay here," he murmurs, running his finger down my profile. "I'll get something for us. Be right back."

"Tyler, I'm a mess," I protest with bulging eyes. "Your truck is a mess."

"Good, and don't you dare go shy on me. We're about to do that *again*." He grins as my cheeks heat. Standing at the door of his truck, covered in a sheen of sweat and looking lethally sexy, he imparts a devilish smile before his declaration. "All fucking night."

"Tyler," I whisper, my chest still pumping as I try to gather what wits remain. "What did you just do?"

Dipping, he kisses me until I'm breathless and pulls away. "I just fucked the woman I've been obsessing over for many years and made her come all over my cock."

"So dirty," I whisper.

"You don't know the half of it," he assures before his

warning. "Prepare yourself, that's not even a quarter of how fucking filthy it's about to get."

He pauses when he reads my expression.

"Baby, if you tell me you didn't like that, I'm going to have to call *bullshit*."

"Of course I liked it, I *loved* it, it's just . . ."

"Shit." He frowns. "Did I hurt you?"

"No, no, you're . . . you are *really good* at it," I widen my eyes.

"And that's a bad thing?"

I shake my head. "No, not bad."

He tips my chin, forcing my dropped gaze back to his before he sighs. "We can talk about it," he relays in response to my unspoken question, "but if we have this conversation, I warn you, it will most likely put me in a state you *don't want* me in."

"I've only had two men, *you included*," I say, hating my tone.

"Even knowing that," he expels with added edge, "I'm just as jealous of anyone who's ever touched you before me, Delphine, and took some sick satisfaction in ending his life for it." He shakes his head and curses, "I can't believe I just fucking admitted that, Jesus." He tosses his head back, closing his eyes, and I reach up and palm his jaw.

"Don't hide this from me," I command. "I will never fear you or whatever dark thoughts you have."

He opens his eyes and covers my comforting hand with his own before lowering them and lacing our fingers together.

"I'm glad for that, and I might joke around at times, but I know you don't like this about me. It's not something that will likely change. Not when it comes to you. So, I'd rather we not open this door. I've never been in love with any woman but you. I've never been in a real relationship with anyone but you. So, can we just not go there? At least not today?"

His eyes fill with warmth and easily recognizable devotion as he pulls me closer. "Right now, all I want to do is take my woman to our pond and fuck and make love to her until it's time to watch the sunset."

"Oui, yes, take me," I whisper. "*Take me*, Soldier."

Endless hours of his delivered promises later, we huddle together under a blanket just as the sun dips below the hills. Chest alight, body humming, I turn to my soldier with watering eyes. "Today is the best day of my life, Soldier."

He gazes back at me, his eyes filled with love and promise, his tone one of confidence. "No it's not, General, I promise you, it's not."

PART 3

"WHAT IS THE most *real* of what matters? . . . How about pain? Why pain? Try arguing it away . . . so if pain is the most fundamental reality, is there anything more fundamental than pain? . . .
Love.
Really.
So, if you're in pain . . . *love and truth*, that's what you got. And you know . . . if they're more powerful than pain, maybe they're the *most real things.*"

—Jordan Peterson

Chapter Forty-Nine

Delphine

FALL 2014

"T-TYLER, S-STOP!" I shout through my hysterical laugh as he pins me to the blanket, blowing on my stomach as I do my best to push him from me. And as usual, my efforts are futile because his strength is *astounding*.

"Non, stop, mercy, please!" I wail as he adds wiggling fingers to my sides, his villainous chuckle filling my ears as he increases the powerful vibration along my stomach.

"S-stop r-right now, you asshole!" I screech, pounding on his shoulders as agitated laughter erupts from me, and my head scrambles due to overstimulation. "Stop, p-please stop before I p-pee or fart! It's . . . is not sexy!"

Tyler instantly throws his head back, laughter bursting from his every pore as he peers down at me with twinkling eyes before it finally slows.

"So, it's true? Women fart? I thought that was a *myth* . . . and now I have to know!" He lowers and blows against my skin as I frantically slap his chest.

"Stop-p fruiting me right f-fucking n-now, or I swear to God, I will kick your balls *so hard* you can't fuck for a *month!*"

He pulls back, his face contorted as he chortles and snorts, barely getting his words through it. "F-f-fruiting you? Did you say stop fruiting you?" He runs his fingers up my sides as I slap his hands.

"O-o-oui, you d-damned imbecile," I manage, "that's w-what you called it, fruiting!"

Raucous laughter bursts from him, bellowing down the hillside we're perched upon as tears form in the corners of his eyes. I scowl up at him where he hovers above me, his outburst taking several seconds to tame until he can finally speak.

"B-baby—" he barks out another laugh before continuing, "It's called *b-blowing raspberries*, not *fruiting*."

When his amusement temporarily has him loosening his firm hold, I use it to my advantage, wiggling out of his grip before rolling out of reach. I'm nearly free of the blanket when he easily captures me by the ankle, pulling me back beneath him. As he gazes down at me, I refuse to meet his eyes, going utterly limp as I speak in defeat.

"No matter what it's called, I *hate it* now, and you will get nothing more from me today, Soldier. You are pissing me off!"

"Whoa,"—his eyes widen—"hey, hate is a strong word, General, but I'm sorry I went too far. No more fruiting today," he jokes.

"Well, I don't trust you," I counter.

"It stops now, I promise . . . but I'll get *no more from you today*, huh? You sure about that? That's a pretty strong declaration," he muses, running his warm palm under my sweater, over my belly, and up to the lace covering each of my breasts. Lace that I loaded my cart with on my last lady date with Layla. Lace that Tyler made very clear he loved, by words and demonstration. Unable to help myself as recent memories flit in, I stare back up at him, wrapping my hands around his neck.

"Fine, maybe I don't hate it, but you've given me no choice. I need a word of safety with you, *now*."

"A safe word, huh?" He grins.

"Oui," I say, catching my breath, "because you are a

brute with *even less manners* than me. I need to have a word that *saves me*. A word where you cease all *raspberries* assault and have mercy because it's evident 'no' and 'non' *do not work* with you"—I narrow my eyes at him—"imbecile."

"How about fruiting?" he suggests through a chuckle and an added dimple pop.

"Oh, *fuck you*." I roll my eyes.

"Oof." He frowns, his stinging eyes gripping mine as I sink at the sight of them.

"What, what is it?"

"I don't know . . . I guess 'fuck you' is pretty brutal even in jest," he says, "how about we save that particular brash for really nasty fights?" He whispers his finger along my cheek. "Maybe so I'll know just how badly I fucked up."

"I'm sorry." I palm his jaw. "I didn't know it would bother you this way."

"Me neither, and it's okay, beautiful, really. I can handle any brash you toss my way, and you know it." His grin returns. "But if I've aggravated you to the point of *'fuck you,'* I've obviously gone too far." His expression turns so sincere that my heart melts at the sight of it.

"But just so you know," he emits so softly it's barely above a whisper, "your laughter . . . does good things to me."

"What does it do?" I ask, utterly captivated, as the world blurs around him like it so often does now.

"So, we're fishin' for compliments, are we?" He winks.

"Ah, *finally*," I draw out, "a metaphor so easily interpreted"—I roll my eyes—"it only took you eight plus years to deliver."

"Yeah, maybe," he says, his voice mournful, his expression dimming, "but it took us so long to get here."

Just as he relays that, a rush of wind carries a flurry of foliage from the trees atop the hill along its wake, which rains briefly down on us. Cool leaves start to land on our faces and hands, covering some of our blanket. Taking our cue to take notice, we both scan the orchard, inhaling the crisp air and soaking in the deep green hillsides. Temporarily mute, we gaze upon the enchanted land as peace settles over us both.

"For me," he says after a few long minutes, pulling my focus back to him. "The wait has been worth it, Delphine," he adds before biting his lip thoughtfully.

"For me, too," I whisper. "So worth it . . . I just wish it wasn't so painful."

"If you want more honesty," he relays, tearing at some grass at the edge of the thick blue quilt he bought just for today, the low sun glinting off his lengthening brown hair. Hair which is long enough now to wrap around my fingers. The slight curl I love back. One I beg him not to cut, which he doesn't, just for me.

"I always want honest," I tell him, soaking in his every feature and expression.

He brings his eyes to mine. "Your laughter heals me."

"Tyler," I croak, tears threatening as I palm his jaw. "Then I don't hate it *at all*. You can *fruit* me anytime you want."

"You would endure that for me?" he jokes, but I don't smile as I speak from my heart.

"I would do absolutely *anything* for you, Soldier."

His return stare intensifies as he absorbs my words before he speaks again.

"You know I saw *this* for us years ago, before we ever touched each other, got intimate," he rasps out, eyes briefly losing focus. "I saw *this* in my mind. Days exactly like today, on this hillside, talking to you, making love to you on a blanket just like this one. Over the years, I've imagined dozens of similar moments, in *every kind* of weather"—he swallows—"the two of us together and happy."

"I did, too," I whisper. "I swear I *did, too*. Especially when you were gone," I admit. "I dreamed of this every day after you left."

"The mind is a powerful thing," he relays softly. "Such a fucking powerful thing. Our thoughts are so convincing that if we focus on one of them often enough, we eventually start gravitating to act on it. Taking actions consciously and subconsciously to make whatever that focus is and make it a reality. Manifesting is what most people call it, but it's not all magical." He tosses the grass. "It seems so simple, but in sorting and deciphering an average of *fifty thousand thoughts a day*, it can get dangerous and complicated. Fixating on the wrong thoughts can make it the *opposite* of simple," he relays with an ache in his voice.

"No, it's not simple"—I take his hand—"and I need you to realize I do know how hard I made it for us to get here. I don't expect you to, Soldier, but I do hope that one day you forgive me for that."

He stares back at me again for a long moment as he strokes my skin, always touching me, forever affectionate, and I can't get enough. Pulling back slightly, he lets out a long exhale before he speaks.

"As much as I've fucking fought it those years ago—insisting and practically demanding that you believe our age difference didn't mean shit—the truth is, it's the very thing that kept us apart, isn't it?"

"Not the only thing, but oui."

"I *was* a kid, a fucking *teenager* making promises to you that probably seemed over the top, but I swear I didn't feel that way. I didn't feel like a kid. I meant them. I wanted to mean them, keep them."

"I know, Soldier."

"But that's not why I'm at peace with it."

"You have made peace?" My heart lifts with hope.

"Yeah, baby . . . I think I just did in this moment, with you, and here's why in all its fucking painfully simple splendor—I *was eighteen*."

My eyes water, and I nod.

"And now that I'm around the age *you were* when we got started—I can see why you would doubt my words and fear for my future, thinking you would hold me back from whatever path you hoped and help to pave for me. As much as it pains me to admit that." He gently shakes his head. "Jesus, the distance in perspective from then to now. Of what's happened, of the amount of life I've lived during all those fucking blinks, Delphine."

"So, you forgive me?"

"For what? I'm the one who didn't keep my promise. I let you go without any real fight. You were right, you did reach out, and *I didn't*. Honestly, I should be seeking your forgiveness."

"There is nothing to forgive," I relay adamantly.

"That's not true though, is it?" He rakes his lower lip again as he stares over at me, trepidation littering his expression. "I don't know if I can handle this answer, but I have to fucking ask it."

"Please don't," I utter, knowing his question.

"So, it's true?" He swallows. "You gave up the night I didn't cross that fucking street."

"That is not so simple either, Tyler. Please—"

"Jesus." He shakes his head, his expression one of devastation. "If I would have come back that night. Or the next fucking day. Or any fucking day after, I would have found you waiting for me, wouldn't I?"

I bite my lip, refusing to answer but he sees it.

"I knew you were lying. I knew you were trying to protect me. Free me. I'm so sorry, baby. I'm so fucking sorry," he whispers hoarsely. "I'll forever regret I got in the way of us, too. I'll never forgive myself for the time we lost."

"No, no, please, you have to forgive young Tyler. Please forgive him. And maybe some part of you was relieved not to have to keep that promise?"

His eyes drop in confirmation as his entire being rattles with regret.

"How could I blame you for this? You were so young, and I was not a good woman to invest your precious future in."

When he opens his mouth to object, I shake my head.

"Please, please listen to me," I implore earnestly, and he nods, his eyes misted with guilt as he licks the corner of his mouth. The sight of it is so painful that I bring myself to kneel in front of him and grip his face.

"Soldier, I am begging you not to waste a second regretting it because it was never once your job to save me. It was *my job*." I palm my chest with my hand briefly. "It was my failure not to save myself. I have myself to forgive for that, not you. Please try to understand that and take that into your heart as the truth. But, there is more I need to say."

He nods, his eyes tracing my face so carefully, so reverently that I almost lose my words, but for him, I find them.

For him, *everything*.

"It's also my job to make *myself happy*." I recite what I've learned and taken as truth in therapy. "And I want very much to bring joy to your life, Tyler," I declare. "To care for, appreciate, and comfort you, and so much more."

"Then mission already accomplished, General," he whispers as he brushes my cheek sweetly with his thumb, before I dodge his kiss.

"Whoa, okay, this just got a lot heavier," he says, moving to sit across from me as I also adjust myself to sit. Facing each other fully, our bent knees touch as he palms the blanket and leans in, his face inches from mine.

"It is not easy for me to give words of affection. It never has been. Never. I have felt many things very intensely, but most of them have been left unspoken."

"I know that, baby," he assures, reaching out to gently stroke my cheek. "You don't have to expla—"

I palm his mouth to quiet him, and he chuckles against it before mumbling into it. "The floor is yours, my French menace."

The man of my life stares back at me, his warm brown depths softening as they do as I face him, hoping my own expression is full of all I feel for him. Pulling my palm from his mouth, I press it to my chest while summoning the strength to put words to the truth I've been numbing for two decades.

"I am a victim of severe child neglect from my father

and abandonment by my mother. I am a victim of domestic abuse, including rape and attempted murder. I am also a victim of the cruel mentality of strangers who wished harm against me *and acted* on it. A victim of their bullying."

His eyes widen slightly as I finally recite the truth I have long denied.

"I am also a victim of self-abuse, which robbed me of all dignity, to the extreme point that I helped sabotage my health with my illness so I could finally free myself of the embarrassment and shame." I blow out a breath. "You were right, I wanted to die. Ironically, I was scared to."

Tyler's eyes hold mine with strength as I summon my courage to voice the things I've held so close for most of my life. Speaking them aloud to acknowledge them for myself and for my soulmate to hear before I leave them as they happened—in my past. And for our future.

"With the heartbreak of Matis, my papa, who I do know and feel in my heart did love me but did not at all protect me in the ways a father should. To Alain, who terrorized me and manipulated me. Who beat and raped me when I became wise to his manipulations. And the strangers who taunted me and physically harmed me . . . for all these things, I gave up on myself, on life many times. But it was the haze and Celine's death that took all the fight I had left."

I swallow as he holds my gaze, fusing me with strength.

"After her death, I allowed myself to finally break for good. Selfishly, to the detriment of my nephews, whom I loved but could not take emotional care of because I was done taking care of myself." I swallow and swallow again. "I was so fucking intent on paying back life for what it gave to me that I did the minimum for Celine's sons, isolating every day, living in the haze, the numb, the hell I felt I deserved for giving up. That was my life, my cycle, every single day until you . . . and my God, *you.*" I allow my tears through, elated tears for being able to finally express this to him.

"But people are supposed to save themselves, Tyler. They

must, even if they need help, they have to *save themselves* with their actions. People are supposed to fight *for themselves*, to free themselves of the chains in their minds. I might have failed in doing that without you, but because you saw me and *loved me as I was*, without limit or condition, you ripped me from a place where I had no more belief in myself. You showed me those chains and gave me a way to unshackle them. With y-you . . ." I falter. "God, please help me say this," I croak. Tyler instantly cradles my face, eyes darting back and forth as he soaks in every word.

I stare back into the eyes of the one human being who refused to give up on me. Who refused my fate, who walked through the hellfire I helped create to drag me out—more than once—kicking and screaming as I tried to re-enter time and again. The gravity of that takes hold of me as I bare myself to him fully.

"What you have done for me, Tyler, is far, far beyond what most people would do for *anyone* they love when they so relentlessly abuse *themselves*. So, though we are not supposed to wait for some miracle to save us, you saved me. You are my *miracle*, Soldier. And here I am now, mere months free of that hell . . . and with you, I feel *safe*, *happy*, *content*, and *free*." I break on the word but continue. "I feel beautiful, so beautiful, and I *want* to be beautiful. With you, I feel cherished, adored, sexy, so sexy, respected, desired, *heard, and seen*. And for the first time in my life, loved. I feel truly and deeply *loved*."

He sits utterly still as I exhale and speak more from my heart. "From hell, you brought me into living in this *heaven* with you. A dream which became so much more in loving the man in front of me with all of my heart."

He instantly leans in, gently pressing his forehead to mine, eyes closing as his shuddered exhale hits my lips. I grip his neck, running my fingers through the hair at the back of it.

"Lift your eyes to me, Soldier, please," I beckon before he slowly lifts his watering eyes to mine. "Je t'aime, Tyler,

I've wanted for so long to tell you. For so, so very long. Before and after you left, and the second you came back, but felt it was so important to put actions before these words. Because actions are all you gave me for the years you denied yourself the words. But I felt it. I felt your love before you ever uttered the words, as I hope you have felt mine in our time here before I spoke it. That you know and feel with just as much confidence that I love you just as much, just as deeply. And that I am yours, loyally and faithfully yours."

His eyes spill over as we exhale into each other's mouths before he lays me beneath him. Hovering above me, he gazes down upon me with so much love before slowly dipping to rain unhurried, reverent kisses upon me. In turn, I deliver the same type of kiss. Along his jaw, his throat, everywhere I can until our mouths meet, our salted kisses mingling as we frantically shed what clothes we must to connect. Tyler wraps the blanket around us just as I sink onto him, palming his face with both hands as I begin to move.

Every second of our lovemaking excruciatingly beautiful as our hearts pound together, and we lose ourselves in the divine connection. Not a single movement is predetermined as he grips my hips, thrusting into me so deeply that I come undone around him. Utterly gone in my bliss as my love for him pours from me. I kiss every inch of his face, his cheeks, his jaw, and take his mouth as he comes inside me. The diminishing of our lost years mixing on our tongues as we banish them together before we finally part.

It's as we lay back, staring at one another for long minutes, caressing the other, that I realize I have one battle left to face. It's then I make the decision that for myself and my soldier, I'll endure this last battle to protect our paradise, our happiness, and the peace we've again reclaimed.

"It was you who was worth waiting for, Tyler," I whisper as he stares back at me. "Je t'aime, Soldier, creator of my newborn heart. Mon seul véritable amour." *My one true love.*

A harsh breath exits him as he pulls me back to him, gripping me so close as if he blinked, this dream would disappear. I clutch him to me just as tightly, preparing myself for what's to come—for what's left to face. The burden made more bearable and then forgotten as he takes me again on that hillside. Thrusting into me, harder and deeper each time, his eyes holding mine during every second, strengthening me as his long-ago spoken promises write themselves into my flesh. Branded permanently into my heart which pounds unguarded against his. He presses himself into me as he kisses away the tears he causes with his intense lovemaking and my release, some of it mental, much of it physical, while murmuring "forever" against my elated cries.

And then he takes me again.

And one last time on our merged clouds before we drift away together.

Chapter Fifty

Delphine

WINTER 2014

"Lean into it, Delphine," Regina encourages as my mind whispers along the memory while fear threatens to rob me of it.

"Lean in," she repeats evenly, "and tell me where you are."

"The kitchen," I relay as anxiety fills me.

Nerves firing, I take a numbing sip before putting the finishing touches on dinner as Alain showers. The shift in him this last week has me on edge.

"Delphine. Tell me what's happening right now."

"I'm cooking dinner. But something isn't right. Alain is not acting right."

Studying the notes from Alain's latest meeting where they lay on the kitchen table, I sense him behind me before stubbing my cigarette out in the marble ashtray. "Oh, good, dinner is almost ready."

Turning, I see Alain dressed, his hair still damp from the shower, but it's the box he's holding that has dread settling over me. Especially when he raises condemning eyes to mine.

"He found them."

"Found what?" Regina asks.

"What are these?" Alain asks as I eye the box I hid in the back of my closet a week ago. Lead coats my stomach as his eyes lower a fraction in speculation. A look I dread. A look I know far too well. Is this what his behavior has been about? Relieved that this may be the totality of his suspicions, I eye the box.

"Those are my new Doc Martens," I tell him simply.

"When did you buy them?"

"I didn't. They were given to me by a friend."

"What friend?"

"A friend from work, you know Diane," I relay passively just as a sharp knock sounds on the storm door.

"Ello," Ormand greets, walking in and shaking off the rain from the downpour outside. I fight not to close my eyes due to the weight of Alain's unrelenting stare as tension starts to roll off my husband. Tension which mounts as he turns to greet Ormand, who lowers his own eyes to the box in Alain's hands.

"Breathe, Delphine, tell me what is happening now," Regina prompts.

"Ormand is h-here. His . . . expression—he is gloating. Alain is going to know. I can see it in his eyes. He's fed up."

"Why is Ormand fed up, Delphine?"

"H-he wants me to l-leave Alain for him. He is going to tell Alain. I can feel it."

"Ah, Delphine," Ormand speaks, "so you finally showed him the boots I brought you. Don't worry, Alain," he assures with an overenthusiastic clap on my husband's back. One that makes me flinch. "I got them so cheap."

"Delphine, I'm right here," Regina whispers as I start to shake uncontrollably. "You are safe. Tell me what's happening."

My mind whispers back out of those tense moments as I lean in. Frustration threatens, but I breathe at Regina's command for long seconds before I'm granted a flash of myself in my bedroom. Twisting the coiled phone cord in my hand while staring at the lock on the bedroom door.

"What's happening, Delphine? Where are you now?"

"I'm in the bedroom, calling Celine to come because Ormand is leaving. The front door just closed. Alain is coming for me. He's coming."

"Delphine, breathe with me," Regina coaxes. "Inhale. Good. Exhale. Good. Where are you now?"

"I'm in the bedroom. I've locked the door and . . . I'm staring at the knob. There's no way out."

My entire body shudders as Alain bursts through the bedroom door, his expression . . . "He's going to kill me."

"Delphine, listen to me. You are home, in your home *with Tyler*. You are safe."

My mind races with images of Alain's fury as flashes of pain follow. Visions that refuse to be brought into focus, refusing to reveal themselves to me.

"Delphine, can you tell me where you are now? What's happening?"

"I don't know. I can't see anything." Just as I say it, I see myself gripping Alain's hands, clawing at them as the carpet burns my back, my scalp screaming.

"He is dragging me through the house, into the kitchen."

Screams, *my screams*, echo through my mind, filling my ears as Alain delivers one vicious blow after another, spittle dripping from his mouth and onto my face as sounds start to muddle, only a few ringing clear. The sound of ripping clothes . . . and pain. So much pain. Burning and tearing. Darkness follows briefly and my breath stops altogether . . . it's then the image I had weeks ago becomes clear. The sight of Alain standing at the kitchen table feet away. Death in his eyes, *my death*, clear and imminent from where I lay on the floor. Seething, he stares down at me with pure hatred and malice as he starts to reach for . . .

Darkness encompasses me, utter and complete darkness as only muddled sounds make it through. Awareness and then none. It's then I realize I'm going in and out of consciousness as the voices continue to cascade in sound. It's my sister's voice which rings through first. A voice that I cling to.

"Sister, can you hear me?"

"Celine . . ." *I wheeze, my voice broken.* "I can't see."

"Delphine, where are you?" Regina asks urgently.

"What," I croak. ". . . What happened?"

Beau's voice booms throughout the kitchen as my sister cradles my head in her lap, sobbing uncontrollably.

"It hurts so much, and I can't see anything."

"Where does it hurt?" Regina prods.

"Between my legs . . . my side, my hand, my throat, my head. I'm bleeding. I'm . . . naked below the waist. Beau is screaming so loud it hurts."

"What is he saying, Delphine?"

"*I will fucking kill you!*" Beau shouts. A loud thwack sounds against the glass of the sliding door before Alain screams out in pain.

"Beau, stop!" Celine cries out in panic. "You're going to kill him!"

Alain

Alain is what happened.

The boots. The fucking boots.

Darkness . . .

Ezekiel's voice sounds from somewhere at the front of the house as I come to. "Papa, what is happening? Why are you yelling at Alain?"

"Celine," I manage to croak, forcing the words out around the pain. Every syllable coming out cracked, broken, my voice foreign. "Do . . . not let Ezekiel see."

"Tobias, get your brother and get back in the car! Right now!" Celine shouts.

"Where is Tatie?" Ezekiel calls as the screen door creaks open.

"Tobias, go!" Beau booms. "Now!"

"I'm going!" Ezekiel shouts, and by his insolent tone, I know I'm shielded from his view. "Come on, Dom."

Darkness.

More struggle and grunts as I come to, and Celine presses a warm cloth to my eyes. "Hold on, Delphine," *she whispers.*

"Hold on, sister. Beau! Where is the goddamned ambulance?!"

Beau's rage fills my ears. "You better fucking run and far, Alain, because if the police don't catch you, I will hunt you down myself and fucking kill you!"

Darkness...

The sliding door sounds, along with the latch.

"He's gone," Beau tells Celine, his voice strained. It's then panic starts to rise inside me.

"Beau, p-please." Every word burns as I force them out. "Please, don't let"—my voice fractures again—"them see."

"Take them home," Beau orders Celine just after, his own voice hoarse and broken as a siren starts to wail in the distance. "Go, Celine. Take them home. They don't need to see this."

"I can't leave her!"

"Please, Celine," I croak.

"Okay," she cries, "okay, I'll come right back, I'll come right back as soon as I can." She leans down, her breath hitting my face, voice cracking. "I love you, sister."

"Celine, go," Beau orders more insistently.

All goes quiet when the storm door snaps closed with Celine's departure, and I open my eyes a fraction. When the light again blinds me, I clamp them closed. "Beau?"

"I'm here," he utters before I'm covered with a blanket. Darkness threatens to pull me back under, but it's fear which has me fighting to stay conscious. To warn him. As he tightens our clasped hands, I can feel the cuts and blood on his knuckles, apologies pouring from him. "I thought he had stopped, I'm so sorry. I'm so sorry."

"Beau... you have to go," I whisper. "You... Ezekiel—"

"Shh, I'm not leaving you... I thought he stopped. If I had known... I'm here, Delphine. I'm here," he croaks. "... I'm so sorry," he whispers as the wail of the siren draws closer. "He's gone, and he's never coming back. I'll never let him near you again... Jesus, why, Delphine, why, why did you stay with him?"

"It's my fault . . . I brought you here."
"What?"
". . . A-Abel," I whisper as Beau's breath catches. "If I left him . . . Alain was going to tell Abel where to find his grandson." I swallow the burn the words cause, my panic rising as I force my warning out. "Beau, Abel Baran cannot find Ezekiel—"

Beau's gasp is cut by darkness as it finally takes me under.

"It was Beau." Tears glide down my cheeks as I speak the truth aloud. What truth I'm able to speak. "It was Beau who chased Alain off."

"Okay, Delphine . . . follow my voice now. We're leaving that kitchen together. We're going to that hospital room, to the peach light. To Beau and the doctor."

For lingering seconds, my vision remains filled with the engrained images of that hospital room. From the peach light to the itchy gown. To the arrival of the haze and Beau's fuzzy outline. The doctor's voice. Focusing on those images, that memory as Regina guides me, I continue to narrow my vision to the edge of it as Ormand's sobs sound at my side. The days, weeks, and months after, all a blur of mixed memories, many unclear as the haze set in and my new life began. But it's enough. Enough of the memory of the night my husband tried to kill me.

"Breathe deeply . . . in and out . . . inhale . . . exhale. Good. So good. Breathe. Good . . . now, when you are ready, I want you to open your eyes."

A scream rips from me when I open my eyes and shoot straight up on the couch before racking sobs begin to pour from me.

"Delphine," Regina coaxes, "you are in the home you share with Tyler. Outside, the world is different. You are different. Do you understand? You are safe, Delphine. It's over. It's over," she whispers as my cries start to subside. After several long minutes, my vision begins to clear, and Regina's watering eyes finally come into view. "You are home and safe. Give me a nod if you can."

I nod as the final pieces click into place. Not a single memory I want to reclaim remains. None worth having. My life now full of only the memories I want to keep. With my soldier, in our heaven. Good days and bad. With Tyler.

"We will sort every emotion you are feeling, Delphine. I swear to you, but for now, we're going to give that beautiful brain of yours a little rest."

"I remembered," I finally say, "I remembered," I croak in disbelief, eyeing the shoebox I retrieved from my old house last night. After weeks of fruitless sessions, of drawing blanks. Weeks of believing my damaged brain would never allow me to see, I recovered the box from my closet in one last effort to try. Biting my lip, my eyes drift back to the woman I finally allow myself to truly view, to regard as Tyler's mother.

"Thank you, Regina." I swallow. "I will find a way to thank you."

"These circumstances are really unique, and so this request is purely selfish albeit unprofessional, but would you be okay if I hugged you?"

"Oui, yes," I say. With permission, she pulls me gently into her embrace, and I crumble in relief, holding her back just as tightly. The tears far more quietly shed than any others in our nearly ninety hours together as my body releases each one until an exhausted sleep claims me.

I wake up with strong arms surrounding me, lifting me, and look up to see Tyler gazing down at me. His expression is pained, though his posture is stoic. It's clear he's indecisive about what he needs to be for me right now as I palm his face to ease his anxiety. "I remembered," I whisper. "I remembered that night, Tyler," I croak, "and I am okay."

"I'm here, baby," he murmurs. "I'm right here if you want to talk about it." I glance around as he walks me toward our bedroom.

"Is it nighttime?"

"Yes, you've been out for a few hours. Are you hungry?"

he asks, depositing me on our bed and kneeling beside it, gripping my hand between his. "What can I do?"

"You've done enough," I whisper, running my fingers through his lengthening hair.

"Are you okay?" he croaks, real fear in his return gaze.

"You heard me scream?"

He nods.

"It was a scream of outrage, Soldier," I tell him honestly. "He gets no more of my fear . . ." I palm his jaw. "I'm glad you made him suffer, and I don't care what that makes me." I gently stroke his face as his eyes frantically search me. "I feel safe, I promise, and I love you."

"I love you, too, baby . . . *fuck*," he croaks, running a hand through his messy hair. It's then I recognize the true state of him.

"Tyler. I'm okay. I'm not lying to you. Look at me."

He does, his eyes roaming every inch before he finally nods, seeming satisfied. I turn on my pillow to fully face him, studying him carefully, astonished by the soldier I created. In utter awe of the secrets I suspect he's been guarding. "And though I am glad you made Alain suffer, you did not reveal all to me when you confessed about that night, did you?"

He slowly shakes his head. "I was going to tell you."

"You found out that night that you went to Alain why I stayed? You learned of his threat . . . about Abel?"

He nods again.

"And you never told Ezekiel?"

He blows out a long breath. "I can't and never will."

"And why is that, my soldier?"

"I had to," he whispers. "By the time I got there, Abel was already moving in on Tobias. They were playing chess in a park in France. I saw a window and used it to eliminate the threat to my brother." He swallows. "As far as Tobias knows, Abel died with no foul play. T attended his funeral."

"And you have kept this hidden from him all this time?"

He nods. "As much as I feel T should know what you endured to protect him, protect them all, you guarded this secret, so I did, too."

"I *endangered* them by urging them to come here. I just didn't realize it until they came to join me in the States. I wrote those letters before I discovered what Abijah was hiding. It was only after they got here that he started to threaten me." I sigh. "Over time, I realized there was only one thing Alain wanted more than anything else."

"You," he deduces easily.

"And I will never understand it."

"Sadly, I do," Tyler rasps out mournfully.

"Not like that. It's as if he became obsessed, and it was only my obedience that kept him quiet."

"Abel was . . . Jesus." He shakes his head, bewildered.

"The most evil of men." I nod. "You will one day find out that the longer you play this game, Soldier, how small this world truly is and how few real players there are. But, you've already discovered that, haven't you?"

Another dip of his chin as I sober my expression considerably.

"Tyler, listen to me, I never want Ezekiel to know of his grandfather's true nature. I never want him to know the evil that exists on his father's side, of the tainted blood that runs in his veins. Please, promise me you will keep this secret."

"I promise," he vows. "Baby, I swear it."

"And now Ezekiel is playing a dangerous game with Antoine?"

"He's winning," Tyler counters. "It's only a matter of time before it plays out in T's favor. Dom is already digging into it in France, and he's not going to let it go. You have to trust us."

"I will, I do. With everything, you have my trust. And now, sadly, you shoulder this burden with me. But some things are better left undiscovered by those we protect. This is a burden you will carry often in your position."

"I'm good with it," he swears, "and I've learned from the best," he relays with a sad smile. "But fuck baby, what you've gone through."

"It's nothing compared to what you will face. I'm sorry for this for you."

He gazes at me, his question evident.

"Ask me, Tyler."

"Why didn't you kill him, Delphine?"

"As much as I wanted to, as many times as I almost did, my gift is gathering information, deciphering intent, and strategy. So with Alain, that's what I did. I spent so many years in fear of Abel, finally realizing as each one passed that he was biding his time until Ezekiel grew. But of course, you eventually saved me from that fear, too."

"You suffered enough."

"I am tired, Soldier. I know you are curious, and we have much to discuss, but can we maybe talk of this another time?"

"Of course," he agrees easily.

"Will you stay with me until I sleep?"

He's instantly on his feet with my request, taking off his shirt while pushing off his boots. A heartbeat later he's pulling me to fit inside his arms. I run my fingertips along the space between the knuckles of the palm holding me to him as I speak.

"Hear me. I will never think less of you for protecting me or my nephews, Soldier. I will never see you as anything more than a man who saved me," I whisper. "And you truly have saved me, Tyler, in every way."

"It's only fair," he murmurs, emotion evident in his voice, "because you *saved me first*."

Chapter Fifty-One

Tyler

When Delphine has drifted into a sound enough sleep, I carefully unwrap myself from her to lock up the house so I can rejoin her and be there when she wakes. Reeling from what transpired today, my need to get back to her hastens my every step. It's when I reach our front door that I pause, spotting my mother sitting on the lone porch step.

"Mom?" I call softly, walking through the storm door and holding it so it doesn't snap closed before joining her where she sits. "I thought you left."

"I couldn't just yet," she admits in a tearful voice, wiping her eyes.

Glancing over at the woman who raised me, I track the splotches on her face, stinging at the sight of them while instantly running my palm down her back. "Shit, I'm sorry. I know that had to have taken a toll on you—"

"No, son." She looks over to me, knuckling more of her tears away. "Make *no mistake*," she sniffs. "These are tears of *pride*. Utter pride that I had a hand in raising a man so remarkable . . ." She shakes her head in incredulity, and I drop my gaze, which she instantly refuses.

"Look at me, Tyler," she demands adamantly until I do.

"A man so compassionate," she continues, "that he's a living, breathing example of empathy, who refuses to coax it gently both *from and for* the people he loves, but instead, *rages for their peace.*"

"You're giving me far too much credit," I tell her. "I'm capable of—"

"We all are, Tyler. We are all capable of bringing out whatever we fear from within ourselves, but what I'm speaking *to and of* right now is a huge part of who you are. You've been taking care of others so dutifully and selflessly your whole life . . . and though I'm naturally biased, I didn't say you were perfect." She shakes her head with a light laugh. "You're not *at all subtle*. You get furious and frustrated and lash out at those you devote yourself to for whatever solution you think might bring them that peace. You tend to give them *hell* if they don't recognize it the way you do," she imparts on a long exhale. "*But, it is still, very much, an expression of love.* And for that, I'm so very proud of the man you've become."

I swallow before I give her my admission. "I've been trying to kill my inner hypocrite for a long time."

"Self-awareness is half the battle, so don't give yourself too much hell. And as we get older, what seemed so simple when we were young, the solutions that seemed so damned easy become far more complex, don't they?"

"Understatement." I let out a long exhale. "I don't know how to thank you for this—for helping her."

"I'll take some credit, but *you are the one who* changed that woman's life. Sometimes, all it takes is *one person* to bring awareness to another in pain, to make them feel like they belong here on this earth and have their place. You *made* and *became that place for her*, and she did the rest. I'm so proud of you both, but *you* need to take some of that recognition for your part in that, Son. Okay?"

"I'll try . . . it's . . . she"—I shake my head—"she calls me her miracle."

"Biased as I may be, by choosing you, she's since developed *great taste* in men." She winks at me before scanning the orchard and night noise. "You both have built a beautiful life here."

"I want you to like her," I utter, "and I'm not asking for approval—"

"And you don't have to." She covers the hand on my knee as she holds my gaze. "Easily done, Son. I *love her* and my God, the way you look at one another. It's a beautiful thing. Of course, I feared your relationship with her early on, but with the trust you gave me and seeing what's become of it, I'm so thankful you entrusted me with this. I've never seen you so happy and honestly"—she nudges me—"I can't wait to get to know her on a more familial level . . . though we still have some things we need to work through." I nod as she stands, turning back to look down at me where I sit, giving me a pointed look too easy to decipher. "And one day, hopefully soon—"

"Mom—" I utter due to exhaustion, "can we not tonight?"

"*Please, Son. Please* try to find some of that empathy for the only human being who comes close to garnering the level of love you have for Delphine."

"That's not true," I counter.

She stares down at me for long seconds in a call of bullshit, her gaze unrelenting. "I'm fine being second to your father, always have been since you two bonded so deeply when you were young, but what I'm *not fine with* is getting *all the love* and attention you have for *both* of us."

I scrape my lip with my teeth as the distant ache becomes present. "I don't know why I can't let it go."

"Because he's the first great love of your life and broke your heart in a way you can't quite get over." She shivers as an icy breeze whispers over us. "But avoiding it isn't working, is it?"

"No," I admit grudgingly.

"So, just think about it, okay?"

I nod as she starts to walk toward her SUV and stops, turning back to me. "I heard the entire exchange with your father the morning you left home, Tyler. It was all I could do to keep from ripping open my bedroom door."

I gape up at her. "*All* of it?"

She nods solemnly. "You wanted to protect me from it, and so I wanted you to believe you did," she relays shakily, "and God, how I love you for it." She raises her hand as I go to speak. "Don't you dare apologize. It was me who should have better protected *you*, and I still fight at times to forgive myself for that. But I understood your reasons. Hell, I *sided* with you, which is why I let you go without a fight, as much as it damn near killed me. But you should know you left your mark, and I came so close to leaving him hours after you did. In hindsight . . . I'm so glad I stayed. It didn't happen overnight, not at all. It was hell, but eventually, your father lit fire to his mistakes and forgave himself. He earned *my* forgiveness and has since given me some of the best years of our marriage."

I stare back at her, trying to absorb her words as truth, and she nods in confirmation, sensing my doubt. "My best friend came back to me, Tyler. So don't thank me for *anything*."

Emotion swells my chest as I cup my jaw, heart heavy.

"Your father has done the work and is desperate for you to get to know who he is now," she releases a pained sigh. "He's never made peace with your absence and never will. He's waiting on you, but you need to know he's breaking a little more with your fly-throughs and overly polite exchanges. Please, my boy. I know she's your priority right now, but please consider talking to him soon. *Really* talking to him."

"I will, Mom," I manage through the burn in my throat. "I promise."

"Maybe you two could come to the house for Christmas?" she prompts, opening her SUV door.

"Let's not push it," I mutter in jest, which has us sharing a smile shortly after trading 'I love you's' before she drives away.

***

The morning sun beams on my back, its heat welcome due to the frigid cold. Tugging down my beanie, I prop the hood of my truck, needing the busywork to keep myself occupied. When I flip open my toolbox, Delphine's guttural scream again rings through my psyche, temporarily paralyzing me. A scream that's been on replay since I heard it yesterday.

The length of it alone, the way it morphed from one of fear to precisely what she spoke—outrage—damn near took me to my knees. I've been hovering and suspicious since Delphine left a few nights ago to 'run an errand she would explain later,' knowing that something was coming. It was when my mom suggested I stay close by before they started their session yesterday that those suspicions were confirmed.

But it was the gravity of what was happening behind our spare bedroom door, her eruption just after, feeling every bit like a physical and mental blow, that had me outside that fucking door within the same heartbeat. Pacing the hall outside of it, I tuned out what was happening to respect her privacy, preferring to hear it from the *source*. A trust I've broken in the past and knew I would have to earn back.

One she solidified I redeemed after she prompted my last confession. A confession I fully intended to give her but was hesitant to due to the picture it could've painted. Of a possible shift in her perception. My fears erased wholly by her reaction after. By the way she regarded me, thanked me. All secrets between us now shared. Even if it means continually deceiving my brother. Keeping him ignorant of the lengths we've both gone to and will continue to go to have his back. To keep him safe from evils unknown. Neither Delphine nor I blind to the sacrifices T's made for us thus far.

But as she suspected, I have learned the nature of the beast Delphine spoke of. Having committed the necessary evils while learning of my ability to do so, and with ease. Something that initially scared me, that I feared would repel her, which has now only brought us closer. Solidifying what I've always known. She is, and forever will be, the only woman to know me.

All of me.

In awe of her resilience, and though I know it will take more therapy to continue to incorporate coping mechanisms she will utilize for the day-to-day, I also know the fighter I fell in love with is far stronger than my mom might give her credit for.

Resisting the urge to check on her, to hover over her any more than I have, I'm relieved when the creak of the screen door sounds. Rounding my hood, I catch sight of Delphine emerging from the house in a black sweaterdress. Her hair styled in the gorgeous waves she often boasts that her new friend Layla taught her to make. Her feet covered in brand-new purple Doc Martens—boots I don't recognize ever seeing in our shared closet.

It's her expression that has me pausing, her silver eyes looking firelit. Dressed to kill, her mindset is evident in her face and posture. Looking ready for battle, I stand stunned, in awe of her, because Jesus, does she look incredible in the armor she chose. The sight of her in this state after what she endured yesterday nearly knocks me on my ass but only confirms my suspicions—she's already fighting again.

"I know that look"—I tilt my head, slowly making my way toward her—"or maybe I don't." Her expression remains stoic as the breeze lifts her hair, the sight of it fitting as I gaze at a woman utterly *on fire*.

It strikes me then what expression she's wearing—an utter *lack* of fear. In wonder of her, and though I'm growing more curious, I do my best to keep my comment casual. "Those are some pretty little boots you got on there, General."

Without acknowledging my comment, she lifts the cell phone in her hand. "I need to make a call, Tyler."

"Okay." I nod, a little confused by her statement. "Do you want some privacy?" I ask as I walk up to her, unable not to pay her the compliment.

"I would ask how you're feeling right now, but it's everywhere. You look fucking incredible, baby." I go to give her a chaste kiss and leave her to make her call. She palms my chest to stop me, leaving her hand there while lifting her fiery silver gaze to mine. Argent flames roaring inside them as she speaks.

"Merci," she says of my compliment. "*Stay for this,* Soldier," she whispers, her voice softening for me, even as her expression begins to morph into one of wrath. I nod as she keeps me idle with the palm on my chest. She initiates the call, putting it on speaker before the line trills, indicating it's overseas. Though confused, I stay mute.

"Ello?" A man answers a few rings in.

"Ormand," she whispers venomously, her voice curling around his name with pure ire. "This is Delphine."

A prolonged bout of silence follows.

"Ah, Delphine, how are yo—"

"I am wearing the boots you bought me twenty years ago," she cuts in. "*For the first time today* . . . and do *you* know why?"

Dead silence lingers on the other side of the line.

"Of course you fucking know why." Her voice rattles with ferocity as she continues. "It's why you were crying so hard the night I woke in that hospital bed and why I pushed you away that day and every fucking day after until I ordered you to go back to France."

I tense then, on edge about having dismissed Ormand as a suspect. Of having any part in wrongdoing toward her during my investigation due to his ties with Tobias. And the fact they're *still* overseas partners.

"So many times I wanted to tell you—" Ormand starts.

"You lying fucking coward," she hisses. "I could *never* understand why you took what happened upon yourself so gravely. Why you could not look me in the eyes for months after that night. And it was because you knew you had boasted your affection for me *in front of Alain*. Even after I *told you* the *cost to me*. But *that night, you decided* to tell him you gave me these fucking boots to assert and announce yourself as his *competition* while also letting me know your patience to wait for me to leave him for you was running out. Your way of staking claim on the woman you so desperately claimed to *love—*"

"Delphine—" Ormand croaks, confirming his guilt as my blood starts to boil.

"But you didn't stay after to watch what gloating over your gifted boots caused. Did not stay to watch your childhood friend brutally and repeatedly rape his wife as he viciously beat her until she was unable to move. Before he took a marble ashtray from the kitchen table and altered her life *forever*."

I swallow, my insides rattling with fury as Ormand begins to openly cry over the line.

"No, you did not stay for that ... did not stay to protect the woman you claimed to love. You only saw the *after*. And when I woke with no idea why my husband tried to kill me due to that damage, *you fucking knew*."

She relays this to us both as I match her stare, desperately trying to communicate what strength I can muster in my return gaze.

"Twenty fucking years," she bites out with undiluted venom, "all this time you left me to put the pieces of that night together. Knowing that now, and what a fucking snake you are, I suspect you convinced Celine and Beau that it was for the best for me not to know. I fucking dare you to deny this, Ormand."

"I will not," he admits as I mentally mark him for retribution.

Her eyes flare as he confirms it. "So *now*, I get to *know* why my husband tried to kill me. Why he did not stay to finish the job. Why he failed. It wasn't because the man who claimed to love me protected me. No, it was my sister's husband who ran him off."

"Delphine, I regret it every day," he offers weakly.

"You should have told me," she says to him as she keeps my gaze. "You could have eased my suffering greatly, but the truth is *you're just another fucking man who made love a liar* again," she condemns. I fall further in love with her with every word as she ends her war.

"I should hate you, Ormand. For so long, I could not understand my repulsion for you after—and even though my mind concealed this from me, my soul and heart *remembered* your betrayal."

"It is my biggest regret. Please believe me, Delphine," Ormand croaks.

"I do not give *a fuck* about *your regrets*. You had twenty years of chances to come to me, to right some of this wrong, but *you will hear* what I have to say."

A long silence ensues before Ormand gutturally replies, "I'm listening."

"Hating you takes too much energy from my life. A good life is what I have now." I cover the palm she still has on my chest. "All there is to do is forgive you, so it won't interrupt or steal that life. So I forgive you, Ormand. I forgive you for the part you played, even if it will never be deserved."

"I'm so sorry," he croaks. "I'll be sorry my whole life."

She ignores his comments as she keeps my gaze, her eyes softening.

"You should know I have found love from a man who is truthful with me. Who believes me *strong enough* to always know the truth. Who loves me with far more than his eyes. Not as a possession, but for who I am *inside*."

My chest lights fire at this as Ormand speaks.

"I am so happy you found this Delphine—"

"I don't need you to be happy for me," she cuts in as the conversation starts to shift from between them to the two of us. "I want *nothing* from you, Ormand, but your loyalty to Jean Dominic, who is currently under your watch, and Ezekiel as his partner. For you to look out for them both in France, to protect them *at all costs* because your price for this fucking betrayal is *your life for theirs.* If you in any way break your word, if either of my nephews meets any sort of harm there, no matter what the threat is, that is exactly how you will pay."

"You have my word. No harm will come to either of them here," he vows, "you have it."

"I have a man I love now," she declares as my soul lights fire. "Who has loved me wholly at my best and worst, beautiful or ugly, without any condition and would never hurt or betray me. A man who, for the first time in my life, made love a truth-teller. Because only the man who is right for you can make it so. And so I will never waste a second with him ever thinking of you again."

Ending the call, she drops the phone on the porch as I crush her to me. Her body shakes lightly as she begins to press kisses to my neck and jaw before capturing my lips in a kiss that has me soaring. When she closes it, I scoop her off her boots, which dangle at my shins as she beams down at me where I have her hoisted just above me. "You won your war, General," I rasp out, "I'm so fucking proud of you."

"Because of you, Soldier, because of you. Je t'aime, I love you, Tyler, my soldier, my one true love, my best friend, my miracle. My God, how I love you, and always will," she pledges, "forever."

No more words necessary, we collide, kissing for long minutes. When we pull away, her lips lift at my expression. "I know that look. I love this look, and oui, please s'il vous plaît, *fuck me senseless.*"

I'm already stalking us through the door before her order is doled out, headed straight for our bedroom, my heart thrashing against hers as they sync and pound between us. The energy bouncing between us surreal as we become impossibly *more* solidified.

"The day is young," she whispers as I lift her dress over her head, "but I have a request for after we watch our sunset."

"So do I, but mine is for right now."

"Oh? What is your request?" she asks through kiss-swollen lips.

"That you keep those pretty boots on," I grin, determined to erase their history, though she's already working on that herself. "Easy done, Soldier." She smiles as I ask.

"That's easily done," I correct.

"Merde," *shit*, "maybe I should just give up," she utters dryly. "I may never master English isms."

"But you won't, my *fighter*," I murmur, palming her skin, covering her perfect breasts as her eyes begin to hood with desire. Whispering kisses along her shoulder, my curiosity stoked, I pull back slightly to ask, "What are we doing after sunset?"

That spark of determination comes back in her eyes. "I want to make a big bonfire."

Inside that silver blaze, I see precisely what fuel she'll be using to stoke that fire, and personally, I can't wait to watch that fucking cigar box go up in flames.

Just after, and as I bury myself inside her again and again, a euphoria lights up in my veins. My whole being harmonizing with the completion of the mission I started long ago—by becoming a loyal man for her to entrust, the man she reaches for.

And *the only fucking man* for her.

Chapter Fifty-Two

Tyler

2015

BLINK. Barrett and I glance over the pesticide schedule on our phone screens as he nurses a beer.

"As it turns out, being alfalfa desperadoes is a lot more complex when it comes to maintenance," I jest, nudging him where we're perched against his Ranger. "Do you remember that day?"

"Yeah, *asshole,* in *vivid detail.*" Barrett speaks up instantly with a dead stare. "And do you know why, *'oldest cousin in charge'*? Because I was terrified my balls would *drop right off* my fucking body for nearly a year until I finally asked my dad," he spouts before we both burst into laughter.

"So yeah, I remember the day that you not only robbed my pockets and sanity, but I damn near cracked my neck thanks to your *'be a man and work your own land'* bullshit before your dad caught me."

Our conversation stalls, and so do our smiles, as it always does when Carter is mentioned. I continue to scroll my screen, stumped on the state of some of our low-die trees. I can feel Barrett's weighted stare on me as he takes another pull of his beer before he speaks. "I owe you an apology, cousin. One that's long overdue."

"Nah, man, it's not that kind of night," I say. "We're good."

"Sorry, I've got to get it off my chest," he says as I lift my eyes to his.

"I shouldn't have shut you out for his bullshit. You were going through enough. It was fucking selfish of me to hold his shit against you, so I'm sorry. And I owe you for introducing me to the love of my life after getting her off *the streets*." He takes another sip, his tone turning heavy. "And now that Charlie and I have our son"—he shakes his head—"and remembering who Carter was before, I can't imagine how you felt back then."

"I'll admit it stung, but we got through it. We're good, cousin."

"I'm glad you're back in our lives, that you're here," he states, "and that Elijah really knows you."

"Me too, man," I tell him. "He's my little buddy."

"You, uh, planning on having kids?" he asks carefully. "Can you?"

"No, we can't," I tell him honestly. "Which is fine. I'm happy with the way things are and always will be."

"So, really, no kids?"

"No. Even if we could, I wouldn't at this stage in my life, and you know why." I swallow. "Sometimes I think I should pack us up to protect yours."

"Hey," he snaps instantly, and I meet his gaze. "I might not have taken you up on your invitation to ink, but I've benefited because you've paid the tax bill without fail on the entire fucking farm for going on ten years. I can't tell you how that's saved us. I would have gone under by now. This place is your fucking home as much as it is mine. I know you would never intentionally jeopardize our family or put them in harm's way," he emphasizes. "Besides, it's common knowledge that if you cross into Jennings territory with any ill intent, you won't have enough time to wonder if you fucked around *as you fucking find out* . . . so if the time ever comes where you need us, I can guarantee you we'll all have your back." He glances down at the ink on my arm. "I'm proud of what you do, and I'm behind you."

"So then." I flash him a smile to lighten things up. "I can just borrow your kid when I need to scratch the daddy itch?"

"*Any. Time*," he states without humor. "I mean that. *Any. Fucking. Time.* Like tonight would be good." He breaks into a smile.

"Nah, I'm good having sex every night without a kid puking SpaghettiOs on me."

"I puked on you once, and you act like it was trauma," he snorts. "And fuck you, I get mine."

"Uh-huh," I say as the screen door slaps at our collective backs. At the sound of it, Barrett and I turn to see Delphine standing on the porch, *glaring* at me from feet away.

"Hey, General, what's up?" I ask, confused that not long ago—when we parted—that glare wasn't at all present. I wince as I try to remember if I put down the toilet seat. Having never lived with a woman before, I've been schooled by my general on a few things. And judging by her expression, she might have a lesson plan tonight. I bite away my smile at her open contempt as she addresses me.

"Tyler," she clips in the no-bullshit tone she uses when she's thoroughly aggravated, "I am *your woman* as you say."

"No question, baby." I can't help my answering chuckle.

"Oh, no question?" she counters sarcastically.

"None *at all*," I reply swiftly, glancing over at Barrett, who seems equally confused by her sudden hostility. "What's wrong? Where is this coming from?"

"Because I asked you to come to bed an *hour* ago, and you said you would be *right in*. And I lay in bed, waiting for you to *come and fuck me*, and where are you?"

Barrett immediately sprays the two of us with the beer in his mouth as I do my best to keep the threatening laughter from bursting out of me. Laughter that she can clearly see I'm fighting as she narrows her eyes even further, crossing her arms in a dare for me to release it.

God, how I fucking love her.

As predicted, fighting with her when we do, which is rare, is as fun as I thought it would be. The sex *always* fucking *fire, after or during.* Always fire, period. Maybe because, as it turns out, she's highly sexual and a little high-maintenance and has been since we got physical. A job I take great pleasure in taking seriously.

"And where are you now? Laughing like a hyena and talking with this *imbecile.*" She stops herself instantly, regret clear in her eyes at her lash out, and immediately addresses Barrett in a rush of *Regina Jennings's brand* of therapeutic apology. "I am sorry, Barrett, you are not an imbecile. I am angry with *Tyler* and should not take it out on you."

"No offense taken, sweetheart," Barrett immediately replies, doing his absolute best to maintain his composure as he begins to inch toward the driver's door of his Ranger. "I think we're good, cousin. I'm going to—" he thrusts a thumb over his shoulder. "It's getting late, so I'll be taking my leave now." He turns to me, his whisper low and goading. "You better, uh, get to tending to your woman."

I nod and turn back to my tiny, agitated, and apparently sexually frustrated terrorist, my love for her brimming as the fire brewing in her eyes ignites mine. Closing in on a year back in one another's lives, every day confirms what I've always known—she's my match, my soulmate.

A match who narrows her eyes at me, muttering under her breath low enough that she knows I can't hear it before she turns, and the storm door slaps closed behind her in her wake. Unable to hold my grin, I lift my chin to Barrett, who's full-on belly laughing now that she's safely out of earshot as he takes the driver's seat of his Ranger, shaking his head. "You're a lucky son of a bitch," he chuckles. "Always have been. God, what I wouldn't give to have Charlie coming out of our house *demanding dick* in front of *other* people."

"Eat your heart out, fucker," I taunt. "See you tomorrow."

Firing up, he gives me a salute as he takes off. I eagerly stalk toward her, managing to catch up with Delphine before she attempts to shut the door in my face. Unable to help it, I burst into laughter as I block it with my boot, and she all but growls at me. "Get out, imbecile. You have ruined my good mood."

"I have, huh?" I glance around to see candles lit on our dresser and nightstand and that she's recently changed the sheets—the room smelling clean, the ambiance purposefully romantic. It's then I truly take her in, recognizing she's wearing the silky white robe I got her for Christmas and suspecting the matching negligee beneath. "Shit baby, I'm sorry. I got distracted going over the spray schedule with Barrett and didn't realize what you were cooking up in here."

"Save your stupid metaphors," she snaps. "I don't like being ignored."

"That's obvious, but I assure you, you have my full attention now."

"Well, you get no more of *mine* tonight," she says. "I'm going to bed. You can go sleep with your stupid new horse."

Pressing my lips together to hold my smile, when the fucker breaks through, she instantly picks up a paperback and hurls it at my chest. It hits me square in the stomach as my cock hardens further and further at the sight of her. So full of fight. Olive skin tinted by the spring sun, curves full now that she's at a healthy weight and looking like every damned thing I've ever wanted. It's the strange energy coming from her that has my apology coming again. "I'm sorry, *really*. I didn't realize you were setting us up for *this kind* of night."

"No, you didn't because I wanted to surprise you and went to great trouble for you. I went to see Layla for a fresh wax yesterday, did my hair, painted my toes, and put on the lotion you like so much, only for you to ignore me."

"Your efforts weren't for nothing," I say, taking visual notes of everything she listed, "I assure you."

"Well . . . now I'm not in the mood."

"Liar."

"Get out, Tyler. Go back to Barrett. I am fine," she sighs.

"Not a fucking chance," I retort.

"I'm warning you, Tyler. I'm not in the mood for jokes at my expense."

"I can see that now, so I plan on kissing and making it better." I lift my chin in prompt. "Now, unhook that robe and show me what a fucking fool I am."

"Non," she replies instantly.

"Baby, I swear I just lost track of time and missed the signals. Can't you forgive me for that? I'm ready to make it up to you."

"It is obvious that . . ." She gestures between us and rolls her eyes up slightly, the shake in her voice unsettling. Her stunted silence telling me she's thinking of the right verbiage, which she confirms when she speaks up. "That period of time where everything is new . . . the phase is *over*."

"The honeymoon phase?"

"Yes. That's what it's called. Our *honeymoon phase* has ceased, and you don't desire me as much anymore."

"That's straight-up utter and complete bullshit," I say, pulling my belt off to ease some of the growing discomfort in my jeans, "but actions speak louder."

"Forget it." She shakes her head. "Like I want you to pity me and fuck me now." She rolls her eyes and begins turning her pillows the way she does as if readying herself to sleep.

"Hey, *best friend*," I clip firmly as her eyes dart to mine. "Remember when you told me to tell you when you're being a jerk? Well, you're being a jerk," I clip as her eyes lift and narrow. "Come here," I coax as we stand on opposite sides of the end of our bed.

"Non," she says, rattling with an energy that I don't like. It's then I decide to distract her from it, selfishly, too fucking hard for her to think about much else until I undo that robe.

"Just forget it."

"You sure?" I unbutton my jeans and free my cock, gripping it and stroking it a few times. "Because I promise there will be no pity in the way I plan on fucking you, and by the way you're acting, you're quickly tipping over into punishment fucking." Her silvery, blazing eyes glide down my frame as she watches me slowly stroke myself.

"Look at me," I say, heat licking up my spine. "I'm rock fucking hard for you, and let me be clear, nothing about us will ever be a fucking phase. Come here."

"Non," she whispers, her voice too obviously affected as she watches me stroke myself. I fight like hell to hold my grin as her breathing starts to pick up.

"Are your panties off?"

"You do not get to know," she taunts hoarsely.

"Pretty sure *I do know*," I tell her, loving this side of her. That, combined with the fight and the fact that she's openly admitting she's craving me—nothing has ever felt so good. All the longing for her paying off endlessly during our time together. There have been a lot of moments before this one, but this one in particular starts to undo me as my need for her takes over.

It's the shifting look in her eyes as she stares back at me that has me releasing my cock, certain there's more going on than I assumed.

"Delphine," I draw out in a more serious tone, "you have to trust me enough to tell me what's bothering you."

"I do trust you. I just don't like how much I want you right now." Her French lilt curls around the words as the caress of them seizes my heart in a vice grip. "It feels way too much like I need you now, and I don't think it's fucking funny. It scares me to be this co-dependent. I am *restless*. Every day, I can't wait for you to get home. Every day, I look for you to come up the driveway because I can't wait to talk to you. I can't wait for you to touch me. All of this feels too much."

Instantly tucking my raging junk back into my jeans, I stalk over to where she stands and snake my arms around her waist, inhaling her clean scent before plucking her off her feet honeymoon style. She buries her head in my chest, clearly embarrassed by her admission, as I nudge her chin with my nose to lift it. "Come on, look at me. We're so close now. We're past embarrassment," I order, not a trace of humor in my voice.

Even so, she cracks her eyes open to slits, her expression slightly sheepish. An expression I didn't think she was capable of, but it's there.

"Don't ever shy away from saying things like that to me. Not ever. I want it all, as raw as you'll give it to me, and I want you to hear me say this." I wait a few seconds to ensure I have every ounce of her attention.

"I *need you* just as much. I feel the exact same way. We're in love, Delphine, and so there's now a line between us flirting co-dependency. But, if the feeling is *mutual*, and no harm is happening to either of us, there's nothing to be ashamed of."

"I don't *want to give a rat's ass*, Soldier," she mumbles as I bite my lip so hard to keep from laughing that my eyes water. But I manage it because of her confession, which is still warming me from the inside out.

"Keep opening yourself to me this way so I can tell you I feel the same. And know that I race down that driveway to you every fucking night." I draw her lips into a long, slow, possessive kiss, and she immediately responds, moaning into my mouth. When I pull away, her eyes are lit with arousal and affection.

Placing her on her feet, I lower an inch of her robe over the skin of her shoulder. Biting down lightly, I slide my hand down the fabric of her robe beneath the matching camisole to find her bare. My smile at the discovery disappears when I see what remains in her expression.

"Delphine, you have got to help me out here."

"I don't know why my emotions are so *strong*, why I feel so much restless ache right now and . . . want to fuck *so much*."

"I have an inkling of what's happening," I tell her, said inkling growing when she claws the back of my neck when I pause my hands. "Do you know you're around the age you start to enter your sexual peak?"

"T-truly?" she replies as I savor the fact that I'm onto

something while tracking every bit of her reaction to my every touch.

"I wouldn't lie to you, especially when you're bothered this much, and oh, how I'm going to reap the benefits of this season in your life." I continue to stroke her over her negligee, loving the look of her under my touch.

"Tyler," she draws out in slight aggravation, further convincing me that I'm onto something.

"Think about it, baby, maybe your body has healed to the point you're in a hormonal state that you're actually *supposed to be* experiencing, and fuck does sexual frustration look good on you," I murmur.

"I feel this restlessness so often now," she whimpers, as my angry cock demands I take action, but I tamp it down to palm her cheek.

"Well, it could also be," I drawl, "that you are healthy," I whisper roughly, my lust starting to take over, "and cancer-free for the first time in half a decade, and settled here on the farm, so maybe you need something to sink your teeth into." I give her a wink. "Besides me."

"I have thought about a job much lately," she admits, "I don't want to be supported. Yes, I agree. I feel done being Betty Crock."

God help me. I screw my lips up as if in thought as I miraculously tamp more laughter down. "I have a job for you."

"The club?" she asks, pushing up the hem of my T-shirt as I pull it over my head. She instantly begins to palm my chest, her breaths intensifying as I continue to work her up.

"The timing couldn't be more perfect," I tell her honestly. "You already know everything there is to know."

I've spent the last few months relaying the ins and outs of the club, as well as recounting stories of my time in the GRS. In turn, she's given me more in-depth details of what she learned on the streets while running for Alain, as well as the backgrounds of the past and present players on the board in France.

"You know it's right. It feels right, but I'll sweeten the deal and keep your involvement between us until you're ready."

She nods, her eyes lit with the idea even as I palm one of her silk-covered breasts, then the other.

"I'll . . . take . . . the . . . job," she gasps, a sheen of sweat breaking over her skin as a needy moan escapes her.

"Okay," I chuckle darkly, "we'll talk benefits and 401k after I make you come because now"—I dip and sip on one of her dark nipples through the silk—"I'm fucking *starving*."

"Then, hurry up, Soldier," she whispers heatedly. "We have to get to work."

Sometime later, we're soaked in sweat, our connection deep as she cradles my back and neck with one arm, palming the mattress behind her with her opposite hand for support as she takes what she needs.

It's ecstasy fucking the woman I love—have loved for so long. My need never to be satiated. She's got it so wrong at the slightest notion I could ever tire of her. I do my best to show her as my chest goes raw, giving me no choice but to voice it.

"Forever," I whisper against her parted lips.

"Forever," she whispers back instantly.

I feel the truth of that vow everywhere because there's no honeymoon period when you find such a hypnotic and intoxicating connection with someone to the point that it feels spiritual. Even with as little experience as I have in relationships, I'm acutely aware of how lucky we are. Some part of me believes it's a reason for her restlessness as well. It's too good. Too perfect.

But just as I start to get lost in her, a haunting whisper in the back of my mind tries to work its way into my psyche, warning me there will be a price to pay for this perfection. Reminding myself that trauma has a way of haunting your present with these warnings, I bat it away and dismiss it for what it is—fear. Instead, embracing our surreal connection before utterly losing myself in her silk-covered love.

Chapter Fifty-Three

TYLER

SUMMER 2015

BLINK.
Standing idly in the woods between the clearing and Roman's house, I watch in real time as Cecelia enters the front door after bidding farewell to her date. Her first real attempt at moving on since Dom and Sean were exiled. It's evident in her disappointed expression and the lack of a kiss goodnight with Wesley—who I spent the morning vetting—that it didn't go well. I text Tobias this update, knowing it's mainly guilt-fueled. The message itself is one I'm certain he won't give two shits about. But as things stood twenty minutes ago, T and I were in a better place. As of now, and after the act I just fucking committed, we're sure to be at odds soon, *yet again.*

Even so, I stand in wait to see what reaction my gift might bring—if any—while resting in the knowledge that I did what was asked of me. Every one of my brothers is aware that I'm not the motherfucker to call to break protocol for personal reasons, and yet I can't seem to stop being dragged into these situations. But I've become quite the sloppy son of a bitch recently due to the increased, thriving beat in my own chest because of the woman who keeps it pounding—*steadily.*

It was my brother's desperate plea over the line—along with the love flowing freely inside me—that convinced me that for Cecelia, at the very least, it was the right thing to do. And so, I made the trip to that Asheville mall to our inked jeweler for both business and personal reasons.

Instincts aside, I did it as a friend and brother but also as a man deeply in love. Knowing all too painfully—by way of personal experience—just how fucking vitally important it is for Cecelia to get some sign, some acknowledgment that her own love and devotion for my brothers is not in vain. In no way personally could I hold a grudge against her decision to try and move on.

After spending too many years in a similar state, it was ultimately Cecelia's aching heart that made the decision for me to act on his request. After all, it was Cecelia who brought me back to the love of my life. And after vigilantly guarding her—while watching her suffer from a distance these past months—I felt it was the least I could do to try to ease her pain.

So, for me, the request wasn't as hard to carry out because she deserves to know that she'll soon be claimed and that her devotion is returned. She needs that hope to continue to carry on for just two more months. My gift tonight hopefully not only giving her that sign but also a way to keep my promise to have her back. To know that even though she feels most alone right now, she's anything but. It's when I pull up my phone to track my birds' current locations that any sense of relief I had in getting away with my latest move ceases to be. Trepidation snakes through me as I watch Tobias's locater dot—which is connected to the tracker on his Jag—heading straight fucking for me.

I've been made.

Fuck.

Though Tobias has access to the cameras, I made sure to make this as covert as fucking possible. Going so far as to drive a King's repair car from our lot here and parking it a quarter fucking mile away from Roman's property line.

A good distance from where we usually park next to the clearing before I practically crawled here to slip into Roman's house undetected. So, the question is, unless he was logged into the cameras at that exact moment... how?

Palming the back of my neck, more dread settles into me. As Tobias's Jag closes in, my mind starts to race. This can't be a coincidence—not with him. Even so, I rest in the fact that if I'm made, then he's coming for me, *not Cecelia*. Tobias won't go into that house and hasn't so much as sneezed in Cecelia's direction for the last eight months since his brothers left.

The relief in that knowledge is promptly stripped away when Cecelia's voice bellows as she bursts out of the back door of Roman's house—frantically calling Sean and Dom's names. A flashlight beam darting over the grass in front of her as she makes a beeline for the clearing.

Fuck. Fuck. Fuck!

I hadn't much thought about the false hope I would give her about them being *present* tonight as I hear her frantically covering ground while trying to summon them. A second later, Tobias's dot stops a mere fifty feet away. Not long after, I hear the faint but distinct clap of his car door.

This isn't fucking happening.

Was it the text I shot out that lured him here? If anything, he'd be relieved she was dating again. Wouldn't he? Seconds pass, and I remain idle, my vantage point declaring itself more so as the most epic of fucking backfires threatens to play out before my eyes. But as more time passes—and I don't sense T approaching me—I decide maybe I'm not made, and my secret might be safe for the moment.

But if it isn't me he's after, what the fuck is his motive for being here? Thinking on my toes, I consider calling him to deter him somehow but decide to opt out. If he's here, he must have good reason. Tobias is just as calculated as I am in every move he makes. As Cecelia finally enters the clearing, bellowing out their names, her voice filled with hope, my heart cracks for her as I inch back slightly to ensure I'm concealed, knowing their collision is imminent.

"Dom?! Sean?!" Cecelia summons, my heart aching for her and for my brothers. I simultaneously cringe at the announcement of herself to T, who I'm now certain is within earshot of her painful summons.

This is confirmed a heartbeat later when I see him breach the trees ahead, a mere fifteen feet away. From my vantage point, I can also clearly see Cecelia to his right as she scans the clearing frantically for any sign of Dom and Sean.

Tobias stops short of breaking through the cover surrounding him to observe her as she calls their names once more. The hope in her voice dwindling with every one that goes unanswered.

That is until my brother takes it upon himself to answer for both Dom and Sean, stepping through with his haughty greeting. "Sorry to disappoint you."

Cupping my neck, I shake my head in denial, knowing that I'm not getting away with *shit* tonight. Because even if their current collision is by some twist of fucking fate or coincidence, I feel it in my bones that the necklace I left on her pillow is somewhere on her person—if not already clasped around her *neck*.

Lifting my head heavenward, I decide then that life must be pissed at me for being happy because if Tobias so much as glimpses that all-too-familiar charm, he'll know immediately that it was *me* who left it.

Knowing it's pointless to try and stop what's already playing out, I edge in a little closer and watch. As they start to bicker, pride fills me as Cecelia holds her own, clapping back with expertise, as I simultaneously decide that I'll cop to it if asked, letting the chips fall where they may with T. It's when a commotion breaks out that I draw closer, tuning in fully to their back-and-forth and cursing as I carefully speed up my steps. I hear Cecelia's outraged screech as I near, seeing that Tobias has taken her down to the ground. I'm hauling ass toward them both, intent on breaking it up when they're back on their feet. I pause my footing, relieved, as they put space between them. Knowing Tobias would never physically hurt a woman, I rest in that as Cecelia screams at him.

"Why? Why? That was mine. He loves me!"

"Who . . . *who loves you*, Cecelia?" Tobias goads her.

"It's for me, for my protection! It's my promise!" Cecelia shouts, confirming Tobias not only *saw* the necklace but just fucking relieved her of it.

Perfect.

"Who do you need protection from?" Tobias muses, fucking with her.

"These are your laws! You're not allowed to fuck with that. He chose me!" Cecelia defends.

"You're pathetic," he taunts, "you think a trinket can protect you? It means nothing."

"It means something to me!" Cecelia croaks, shattered that he just stripped her hope away as my fists curl at my sides.

"You're a little girl with a crush."

"I'm a twenty-year-old woman, you ignorant bastard! And I belong to him." She holds her ground.

"Because he says so? You have no say. You're warped. And no, sweetheart, you don't. He's my brother."

Jesus Christ!

He just blew his own cover! A cover Sean, Dom, and I have endlessly kept since she arrived last year. He's not fucking thinking—not rationally, anyway. It's his emotions driving him tonight. From the shadows, I gauge the two of them facing off, literally now, and can feel the tension brewing unbearably as they spar without missing a beat. But this tension is palpable for me, even where I stand at a safe distance and concealed.

This is the opposite of how I hoped this would go, and no good can possibly come of this. But if I know Cecelia—and I do—she's a dog with a bone now, and she's not going to let it go. If Tobias keeps talking, soon enough, she'll discover just how much we all deceived her, and when that happens, she might lose hope altogether.

But there's something happening now between them that has inklings skittering up and down my spine. I know he resents her, but he's been vigilant of her innocence in this since she was a kid—purposefully protecting her from the war he's waged against Roman. Keeping her distanced, but as of now, of all fucking nights, he seems to be intentionally engaging her. As my hunch about his motive starts to take over, I know I need to take the cue and fucking step out. I have a woman at home, warming both my bed and my heart, and I'll be damned if I let more of my brothers' collective personal drama interfere with my first long stint of contentment.

This bullshit happening only reminds me of the blissful, peaceful months I've been gifted with the woman I love. Delphine and I worked so fucking hard to get to where we are now, and this situation has the potential to steal time from us. Fuck that. I won't let it. I refuse to. This life will continue to revolve around her even if I have to take a step back from it.

But a second after I decide to dip out, the levee breaks, and the two of them collide again, *physically* putting them back on the ground in the clearing. I'm a second from stepping forward and breaking it up when I realize what I'm witnessing . . . and with it, my entire body tenses.

Within the length of their kiss—one Cecelia *is participating in*—I watch in real-time as the rest of Tobias and his future relationship with his brothers implodes. And at the sight of it, and the knowledge that Cecelia is actively kissing him back—*I'm. Fucking. Out.*

However this plays from here on out is on them. Any further involvement makes me culpable.

Nope.

Walking away, I shake any sense of responsibility for what's taking place off my shoulders. Dom and Sean did their best to prepare Cecelia for our club, and so far, she has stepped up—even flying blind. It's past time she *sees* and has more knowledge of all the players involved. In doing so, this is either the end of her involvement or the beginning—a decision only she can make.

Stalking back to the car I borrowed from the King's lot, I pull up my smartphone to gauge my birds' locations to determine if I can call it a night. Spread out across the map, I see a few are currently huddled at the garage. As it is, Russell's working late at King's with Jeremy as well as Peter.

Layla and Denny are home. The rest of our Falls chapter is scattered throughout town, doing their thing. Besides the circus in the clearing, it looks to be a quiet night. It's that damn inkling that won't stop gnawing at me that clues me in that soon, quiet nights such as these might become scarce. Turning over the Kia, a picture of Delphine on that hilltop replaces my map on screen. In seeing it, seeing her victorious smile atop it, I instantly feel the relief it brings as I swipe to answer. "Hey, General," I greet, "what are you up to?"

"Soldier, hi!" she coos over the roaring motor of the Ranger I gifted her a few weeks ago in the background.

"You taking a late-night ride?"

"Yes, I love my Ranger so much!" she exclaims.

"I know you do. I can't keep you in the house at all anymore." I grin, forcing the anxiety of what just transpired out of me as I shift my focus on her.

"I cooked earlier and am waiting to eat with you, but no promises on taste, or if it's . . . merde," *shit*, "what is the word?"

"Edible?" I chuckle.

"Yes, that's it. *Edible.* You know how I am with measuring, and I tried to follow Charlie's recipe without help."

"I guess we'll see, and you know I'll eat it anyway."

"I know you will, soldier of my heart, but I made sure it was salt, not sugar, this time," she laughs, and I grin at the healing sound.

"How are things?" she asks, now fully in the know about

everything regarding the club, and every secret I'm privy to. Her involvement in the day-to-day has become the very thing she was growing restless for. It's proven to be beneficial for us both, keeping us close as we share the burdens and working together constantly to better up our game and delegate. I couldn't have asked for a better partner to help me, but in doing so, I spare her no truth.

"As of right now, things are kind of going to shit," I relay.

"Oh, no. How?"

"Well," I drawl, "as of minutes ago, you can start a fucking timer that in two months, things are going to get a lot worse, but I'm too fucking interested in getting back to you right now to give it much more attention tonight."

"How much worse, Soldier?"

"Enough to probably have *us both* in therapy," I chuckle.

"Putain," *fuck*, she says as she kills the engine of her Ranger.

"Don't panic, at least not yet. I'll explain when I get home. Promise."

"Then hurry up, Soldier," she murmurs.

"On my way, baby," I promise before I hang up, sitting back in the seat and rolling down the window, allowing the peaceful night noise in. The cicadas and crickets sound like heartbeats as the lush evergreens sway in a light breeze. Glancing in the direction of Roman's house, I decide to log into the security camera, managing to catch Cecelia walking past the pool and towards Roman's back door, her shoulders slumped. Pissed at T for taking what little happiness she was gifted away, I decide to take it as a good sign they went no further sexually, hoping it ended with that kiss.

Fucking hopefully.

If not, the temporary peace I've come to know is about to fucking end. An unsettling feeling that is the case washes over me as I pull onto the road. Racing toward my refuge, I start to soak up what peace remains, determined to bask in it and create more in the months to come, even as the mental timer I just set starts to tick.

Severed Heart

***

That kiss *wasn't* the end of it.

The truth of that painfully apparent mere days later as I finish my sweep of Roman's house. Tasked by Tobias this morning to recheck the cameras and mics Dom and I put in place last summer. Ironically, during none of our interactions in the last few days has T *once mentioned* the necklace, and it's becoming evident why. Especially with his sudden insistence that I sharpen my eagle eyes on Roman's house, in addition to upping the number of eyes on the man himself. That we scrutinize his every move more closely—until further notice. With that order, I know Tobias has made some decisions to change our game on Roman. A strategy T's altered with *Cecelia* in mind and has yet to share.

More unease snakes further into me after I enter the back door and head toward the kitchen, catching a muffled exchange before I'm stopped by the two of them facing off. Tobias stands in business dress, sleeves rolled up, at the counter where he appears to be *cooking*. Cecelia stands equally postured up, glaring at him from where she stands on the other side of the island. Feeling as though I've stepped on a landmine, I address my taskmaster first.

"All good," I tell T, and he dips his chin. Just after, I turn and focus on Cecelia, who looks freshly showered and gorgeous in a sundress. Deciding to utilize the moment to my advantage, I stalk toward her. "Look at you"—I flash her a grin—"you only get more beautiful."

Her lit expression at the sight of me dims considerably with hurt and anger as I near. Seeing it, I stop just short of her and speak the truth. "I've missed you, girl."

She crosses her arms in contempt. "Oh, *now I exist*. How convenient."

I blow out an exhale. "I know you're angry—"

"Angry," she huffs, "that's putting it mildly."

"Cee," I draw out, hoping she hears the regret in my voice as she shakes her head to refute it.

"Don't bother. What are you doing here?"

"Errands," I admit regretfully, feeling T watching our exchange curiously from feet away as Cecelia turns to glare at him. It's when I feel the energy bouncing between them that I start to confirm my suspicions. There's pure contempt emanating from them both, but there's also some undeniable chemistry as well. Deciding that I will be fucking exiting stage left to spare myself from laying witness to whatever's happening, I toss a thumb over my shoulder. "I guess . . . I guess I'll head out."

Tobias speaks up. "I'll get with you later."

"All right, man," I say before looking back at Cee, hesitant to leave her. We got close in our short time together last summer, and I've felt the burn of her absence since we were forced apart. As I stand idle, I marvel at the difference in both our lives from then to now. Mine especially. Just once, I wish I could fucking relay the secret I've been forced to keep. That I haven't missed a day of her pain. That I've been with her every day of it, even if she couldn't see or feel me. It's one of the most fucked costs of being in my position. Of being a watcher.

Opting to relay what I safely can, I give her useless words that I mean. "It was good to see you, Cee."

Turning due to the resentment I feel, every step increases the sting of leaving her this way as she calls after me, increasing it with her question.

"Was it you?" I look back to see her glaring at Tobias, whose jaw ticks before she shifts her focus back to me. "You promised to be there for me, to have my back. I considered you a friend."

"I do have your back," I relay instantly. "Always will."

It's the evident pain in her ocean blues that makes the decision for me.

Fuck this.

Stalking back toward her, I take her hand, ignoring the blazing amber eyes drilling into my profile from feet away. "And I am your friend," I assure her, glancing toward

Tobias and relaying in that brief exchange what an asshole he is before I turn back to give her more truth. "No, Cee, it wasn't me, and *trust me*, I'm paying for it."

It's when her eyes soften substantially that I know she takes my words as truth. "I know it wasn't," she relays shakily. "I'm so fucking mad at you."

"I know, *so is he*." I jerk my chin toward T, knowing he's weighing every word of our exchange as I lean in and press a kiss to her cheek. "I'm sorry," I utter sincerely before giving her words I've longed to since last summer. "And I just wanted to say *thank you*."

Turning so she can't question me why, more so because I don't want T to know Cecelia's responsible for uniting me with Delphine, I stalk out.

Heaviness and dread cloak me, shadowing my every step as the mental timer I set days ago starts to tick louder. The sinking feeling staying with me long after I exit Roman's house, softly closing the back door.

Chapter Fifty-Four

Tyler

BLINK. Delphine and I sway in the free-standing hammock I put together today at the side of the house, which grants the most optimal view of the hillside next to it. As we settle in for our nightly show and the sun starts its descent, I hold her a little tighter than usual. It's been a little over a week since her scan and bloodwork, and since, I've all but terrorized the Blue Ridge staff and her oncologist at this point in demanding the results back.

Especially after realizing how much weight she's lost in the last three weeks. Something she didn't mention, but I've been vigilant about monitoring since she got her first clear scan.

It's the fear of what the sudden shift might mean that's had me glued to her side day and night. The fact that there is a one- to two-week fucking wait for imaging results for someone who might be or has been ill is fucking bullshit to me. You would think that after billions of dollars have been raised, donated, and spent for both treatment and cure, someone would, at the very least, have found a quicker route to get results.

The fact that it takes so fucking long for anyone that could be terminally ill to gain that life-changing information feels unbelievably and unnecessarily cruel.

I've been keeping us as busy as I can with tasks at the orchard, filling every minute with new memories, but tonight, my anxiety refuses to abate. I'm even more on edge because we only have a week before Dom and Sean's homecoming. Until they discover what Delphine and I now know. That Tobias, too, has fallen for Cecelia Horner. And worse? She's fallen for him. Not only that, but they've set up house at Roman's.

It's too much of a mind fuck for me to decipher what feelings to have about it, so I blink it out, instead concentrating on my own love story.

"Soldier," Delphine draws out sleepily as I rock us with my foot, my leg hanging just out of the hammock to keep us going. The night noise starts to surround us as the sun vanishes. The fireflies already sparking up, looking like a blinking blanket hovering over the surrounding grass. The atmosphere peaceful in contrast to the riot in my head and chest with the verdict looming. I don't want her to fucking suffer anymore, in any fucking capacity, for any reason. She's been through enough.

"Yeah, baby?"

"Do you believe in God?"

When I instantly tighten my grip—giving myself away—she immediately speaks up. "No, Soldier, this isn't fear. This is a conversation we've never had because I do fear your answer."

"You think I don't?" I deduce.

"I think you are brilliant, but for you, science and reasoning overrules spirituality."

"I debate it often," I tell her honestly. "I guess you could say for now I'm agnostic."

"This makes me happy. I hope every day that God wins, that He convinces you He's real," she says.

"Why do you believe?" I ask, knowing whether or not she's admitting it, she's scared. Her thoughts on God are because of the fear she's not voicing because, for her and so many others, simply believing is comforting.

"I believe because I have felt God's presence with me many times in my life. Even after I numbed. It was not Matis's rules about cleanliness, or anything else to abide by that kept me faithful. It was feeling His presence with me during good days and bad. I feel it so much sometimes with you, and because of you, my miracle, that He is often with us. But sometimes my logic-necessary brain makes me doubt. It is ironic though, that even during those times, I believe."

"You can talk to me if you're scared," I whisper.

She piles her palms on my chest before resting her chin on them, staring at me for long seconds before speaking softly. "Soldier, we both *know*."

"For once, could you not be so intuitive?" I drawl around the instant burn searing my chest as I force the question out. "Do you feel sick?"

"No, not yet." She bites her lip before she speaks. "But, Soldier, I *know*."

The burning inside goes straight to inferno as she does her best to calm it. "I have won this battle before, and I have never been more ready to fight. For us, for our heaven on earth here. Soldier, I promise you. You said our thoughts are powerful, right?"

"Right," I manage around the scald—this particular mental fight fucking horrific.

"Then I will believe myself to win again."

Fear mutes me briefly as I nod until I can speak. "Then I will, too."

"If I am right, I promise you, Soldier. I will fight so very hard."

"Stop trying to console me. I believe *in you, in your words*, always have," I whisper low because if I don't, she'll hear the crack of fear winning. Instead, I grin back at her, palming her crown and running my thumb along her hairline and down her cheek.

"I love it when you do this," she whispers, nuzzling into my touch.

"I know," I tell her, "and I have faith in you. That *you are* going to beat it, and that's only *if* you're right, General," I state, managing to rein it in. "You've been wrong before and lost money during the Super Bowl." I quirk a brow.

"I made a bet," she grumbles, "*that* was the point. It was a therapy breakthrough," she justifies.

"Is my little tightwad still sore she lost a thousand bucks betting on the Broncos to my Uncle Gray?"

"Shut up, asshole."

"Oof," I chuckle. "But I told you to always bet on the *birds*." I wink.

"I love you so much," she blurts, seemingly out of nowhere, thankful that the arrival of her declaration works like a cool balm to my stinging soul.

"Well, I was hoping you did. Especially tonight," I tell her.

"Oh? Why?"

"Because I have something I want to give you." I adjust her so I can reach into my pocket and pull it out, keeping it clenched in my fist.

"What is it?"

"Someday, we're going to have to make you understand the *fun part* of gift-giving," I chuckle.

"You have given me too much already," she says, eyeing my fist.

"Don't want it?" I ask. "Because I'll give you a little background on when I got it. It was the same day you tried to kill me with the saltiest fucking enchiladas in world history," I quip before we both burst into laughter. My lips burn in remembrance of the night I ate two of them just to keep her laughing, as she refused more than our first mouthful before making a frozen pizza.

"What do you have for me, Soldier?"

"Again, this is to be revealed, that is, *if* you can get my fist *open*."

"Argh," she drawls, "impossible. I surrender already. You are a brute."

"And you are the most brilliant strategist on the planet," I tell her. "You'll think of *something*."

"This is true," she says confidently.

"Modest, too," I chuckle as she starts to try and pry my fist open. Within a minute, she's full-on straddling me in the swinging hammock, her temple covered in sweat as I egg her on.

"Guess you don't want it badly enough," I quip just before she shoves her tiny bare foot into my armpit while trying to rip my arm off.

"Ok-kay, ouch, shit." I jerk as she indirectly draws a tickled laugh from me. "I'm b-beginning to think you want it."

"Give it to me!" she orders in exasperation.

"Who's the brute now?" I muse as she wrestles me for another minute until she finally collapses on top of me, her aggravated muffle sounding in my chest. "You, Soldier, are an *asshole*."

"And you are the love of my life," I murmur before she lifts her head and stares for lingering seconds. The way she always does when I relay any sentiment of the like toward her. Taking my words to heart, her silver eyes shine with happiness as the dim light of the porch dances along her profile.

"You already know you are mine, too," she admits freely. "You bring me so much happiness, Soldier."

"Hey, this is *my speech*."

"You are giving a speech to me? Why?"

"Because I want you to have this," I whisper, lifting my closed fist and opening my fingers slowly, angling my wrist to capture the nearby porchlight as the ring comes into view. She gasps at the sight of it, darting her eyes from me to the ring and back.

"Soldier . . . what does this mean?" she asks, openly gaping at the solid band made up of diamonds.

"This is my forever," I whisper, emotion clear in my voice. "And there's only one woman on earth I will ever want to give it to. I just hope she really wants it."

"Oh! I want it so much!" she admonishes tearfully as she sinks back onto me, nestled in my arms before holding up her left hand, which sparks hope in my chest. Gripping the ring, I flirt the glittering circle onto the top of each of her fingers without sliding it onto any of them, repeating the motion until she sounds up.

"Which one, Soldier?"

"Which one do you want it to be?" I murmur to her temple.

"This one." She wiggles *the* ring finger as my heart thunders, and I slide it on. The fit is perfect as she keeps her hand up, the two of us admiring it for long seconds.

"What would you have done if I wanted it on my *middle* finger?" she laughs.

"I would have had it resized," I tell her honestly, elation covering me about the finger she chose. "But since I got the right finger, will you lift your beautiful eyes to mine so I can pose the question that goes with it?"

She rolls back over, tears slipping down her cheeks as she clears her eyes, adamant about not missing any part.

"Can I have your forever, too, baby?" I murmur. "Will you marry me?"

She nods and nods. "Yes, yes, yes. Soldier, you've always had my forever, my miracle, my love, you are why I have faith." She barely manages to get the words out before we're kissing to seal the deal. My elation easing some of the anxiety as we spend long minutes reveling in our decision, until I give her my delayed reply.

"Then maybe you'll be the reason I have faith too."

"When will we get married?" she asks.

"That's up to my forever," I tell her honestly. "But when you decide the where and when for me to show up in a penguin suit, I'll be there."

"No, I am not falling for *that*," she states, "that is not a metaphor for *anything*."

"Yes, it is," I chuckle, "I promise you it is. Look it up on Google."

"Non," she retorts instantly.

"What is your damn issue with the internet already?"

"It has no appeal for me," she states. "And stand by for that order, Soldier, penguin suit bullshit to me or not." She nestles back into my arms and lifts her newly donned finger for us both to admire. Even in the dim light, it sparkles incredibly, matching the emotion in my chest.

"Mon Dieu, I am so very lucky. I love you." She kisses my throat and my jaw before pulling me under her spell. And I dive into her kiss, filling up on it before she pulls away. "I've always wanted to marry a *real* soldier. Now, you've given me every single dream I've ever wanted. This is the best night of my life, Tyler," she declares, as she so often does, and I reply like I always do.

"No, it's not. I promise you, it's not."

Not long after, we both doze off, and my pocket vibrates as Delphine nestles against me, clearly irritated by the disturbance. I quickly retrieve my phone from my pocket, dread filtering in when I see who's calling. Hitting the button on the second ring, I put the phone on speaker, knowing Delphine will want to hear whatever he's calling for. "Dom?"

"Tyler." His voice is a mix of anguish and panic before he calls my name again. "Tyler, I fucked up. I instantly perk up at his admission, as does Delphine, who is already tense in my arms, as her head lifts, her fear-filled eyes drilling into mine. All the peace we had minutes ago feeling stripped as I prod him.

"What's going on?" I ask, as panic for my brother quickly filters in. The few words he's spoken already reeking of utter depletion as a short silence ensues. "Dom?"

"I need a favor," he expels, his tone just as tortured as Delphine quickly stirs fully awake. I get to my feet, helping her out of the hammock and keeping the phone lifted between us as she follows me inside the house and into the kitchen. She stands idly by, listening intently and watching me as I start to pace. Within a minute of our exchange, she retrieves my laptop from the living room as Dom begs me to bring him and Sean home. Within seconds, I'm searching for direct flights from Paris to Charlotte, even as I try to reason with him to wait, knowing whatever pain he's in will seem like nothing compared to what he's in for when he gets home.

It's during our exchange that Dom starts to talk to me in a way I've never heard him speak before. The changes in him becoming more evident as he speaks so adamantly, utterly solidified in his convictions. Completely unapologetic about loving Cecelia and determined to claim the love he deserves. The way he's conversing so openly about his feelings jarring us both as Delphine and I hold one another's stunned gazes.

"I fell in love, and it's not a fucking crime, and *you*, of all people, know it's nondiscriminatory about the fucking *who*," Dom states as Delphine's eyes widen. "How is she?"

Delphine's lips part as I remain mute.

"We're fucking grownups, Tyler. Let's stop with the bullshit. I don't fault you the same way you're not faulting me right now. How is Delphine?"

Making my question clear in my expression, Delphine nods in permission. "She just got her latest scan done, and we will get the results tomorrow or the day after, but she's gone almost eleven months without a sip."

"You're fucking kidding me," Dom rasps out as Delphine cups her mouth to hold her cries, her eyes spilling over. "I . . . I don't know what to say."

I stare over at her, pride filling me, never happier than to give her this moment, or rather that Dom's giving it to her, even unknowingly.

"*She* kicked it, Dom. *Not me,* and she's still fighting. She's fucking happy," I relay truthfully as Delphine continues to nod her head, the tears gliding down her cheeks so beautiful it steals my breath away. Pride for my brother's growth multiplies, even as my trepidation for him sets in.

"*Good.* You both deserve it. Especially her. We all fucking do. And my bill here is settled. I'm not paying for it another goddamned day for loving her, do you hear me?"

Delphine and I stare off as Dom's question rings out between us. "What? What aren't you telling me?"

I hold and keep silent. The secret I'm holding for Tobias now is just as fucking painful as when I withheld it from him. Back on my laptop, I start to type in their info into the flight I'm booking, deciding I'll never hold a secret that harbors this much fucking weight for any of them again. Not this way. It's the gnawing in my gut that tells me I likely won't have to because of the damage this one will cause. The truth of it being that our dynamic truly changed last year, the second Cecelia Horner drove into Triple Falls.

Briefly, I resent Cecelia for being the catalyst that very well might destroy us. Even if I do love her as a friend and would protect her at all costs. Dread settles in for the days ahead as I glance over to Delphine while addressing Dom. "There's a direct flight leaving in a few hours."

Silence lingers, and I can hear his stuttered breaths over the line, his emotion coming directly through. "Dom?"

"Book it," he finally says.

I let out a loaded exhale as he cuts the call before pulling Delphine into me as silent, conflicting emotions run between the two of us. Relief being one for her because she now knows Dom's feelings about her—of his genuine care for her. Her worry for her nephews and their future relationship undoubtedly another. Not long after, she pulls away, her expression having shifted, matching the one she wore the day she won her war. Grabbing her phone off the counter, she shoots me a look, and I dip my chin, knowing her reasoning before she speaks it. Dom had asked me to work my magic to get them out of Paris without flagging Tobias, but it's my general who's got this one.

"I will call Ormand."

Chapter Fifty-Five

Delphine

THE SCREEN DOOR creaks open behind me, the familiarity of the telling sound always drawing mixed emotions, especially in *this house*. A house that now contains so much history, its walls and doors laying witness to so much of my life and of those who once dwelled here. Used now only to store the boxed remnants of our pasts.

But despite the horrors it's witnessed and the extreme mixture of memories this house hosts and can evoke, as of tonight, unexpectedly, it has been declared a gathering point. Even more unbelievably, a temporary place of *refuge* for Dominic and Sean, whom Tyler gathered and brought here after their confrontation with Tobias at King's. Shortly after, Dom fled, and I arrived just after to witness Sean's devastation firsthand, which was telling enough of my nephew's state.

All has been quiet as the hours have passed as I wait in hope of his return. *Too quiet*, and because of it, it's the familiar snap of the door closing, one I've heard a thousand times or more, that manages to bring some comfort. As does the strong, warm hand that covers my shoulder as Tyler takes the step behind me, encasing me with his legs before pulling me back into his chest. Bending, he gently nuzzles my neck as he speaks.

"He might not come back tonight, baby. He's gutted."

When he hesitates briefly just after, I know he's holding more news, and I gently nudge him to continue. "I just got off the phone with Jimmy," he emits low, knowing I'm aware Jimmy is the one who tattoos all local Ravens. "He passed Dom as he was leaving Roman's house."

"Dom tried to stop it?" I ask.

"I'm thinking he wanted to. Dom is still parked at Roman's now."

"Mon Dieu," *My God*, "Tyler, this is too much," I croak, my eyes watering as the surrealness of the situation sets in. My fear increasing for all involved—especially my nephews. As of this morning, after Sean and Dom discovered Ezekiel and Cecelia's relationship, they are all at odds *indefinitely*. Ezekiel's latest claiming act of marking Cecelia only damning any near future chance of reconciliation.

"I feel this hurt for them both, for Jean Dominic especially. In his voice last night . . ." I utter, feeling the desperation of my nephews' words during their call while taking comfort in my love's arms as they circle my waist. "I feel *so much*, Soldier . . . it's worry and this *horrible ache* that won't subside as if it's happening to *me*."

"You know what that sounds like?" he asks before pressing a slow kiss to my temple.

"What?"

"Like the love of a *parent*." He turns my chin with his finger to face him. "You weren't nearly as bad as you've convinced yourself you were. As pointless as it might be to voice, Dom was more of an unbearable teenager than most. Hell, Tobias could barely stand him back then."

"He *was* such an *asshole*," I laugh lightly as I lean back into him. "I will admit that." I stare into my love's eyes. "Thank you for saying that."

"I'm not saying it to be kind," he assures, "it's just the truth."

I blow out a long breath. "I have this horrible feeling."

"It'll be okay," he assures, "it'll take time, but they'll get through it."

"Is Sean sleeping?" I ask, his heartbreak palpable, bleeding through the walls and doors from where we both sit.

"No, he's in T's room," he replies, "it's quiet, but I can smell a fresh cigarette burning every few minutes."

"I could use a cigarette myself," I sigh, "too bad I only smoked when I drank." His answering grin is filled with pride before he releases me.

"I'll go check on him . . . fuck, I hate this," he groans.

"Should we have spoken up, Soldier? Maybe tried to somehow stop this?"

"The results would have been the same. At least, that's what I tell myself. It's times like this that any justification we come up with won't make it any easier to deal with." He pinches my chin lightly, turning my face to his. "One more hour, General, then you come to bed, okay?"

He leaves me with a chaste kiss before making his way back into the house. Seconds after, I follow, quietly opening the storm door before pausing in wait. It's when I hear Tyler and Sean's muffled exchange drifting from Ezekiel's room that I pull both front doors firmly closed before resuming my place on the steps.

Staring out at the quiet street from the porch, only the crickets sing as I pray for the sound of his engine, willing Dominic to return and hating that I'm slightly winded from so little physical activity. The gnawing inside me is telling enough. Then again, I've slept so little since I heard Dom's pained voice last night. My youngest nephew's words replaying in my mind throughout the day.

The war I started with Jean Dominic started so long ago that all I want now is to put a permanent end to it. To try to be here for him as he suffers this heartache. When he took me to see that sunset last summer, it felt like a start, but it was my guilt-fueled confession about how I had wronged Cecelia that quickly ruined that progress. My darkest secret. One I have yet to fully forgive myself for. But it was the *man* who spoke to Tyler last night—a man who sounded very much like Dominic—

who voiced words I never imagined he'd ever say. Words that sparked my hope that our war could finally end.

As the minutes tick by, I replay dozens of clear memories of Jean Dominic. Vivid memories captured in my mind before the haze, before Celine's and Beau's deaths. In searching them, I manage to pinpoint the memory of the last time I saw my sister and her youngest son together.

Though almost too big for her frame, Dominic bounced on Celine's hip as they danced in her kitchen. Their foreheads and noses touching, dark hair tangling as Dominic widened his eyes at her in animation. His heart was wide open back then, and he didn't care who noticed how he loved and adored his mother. Neither did Ezekiel.

That recollection brings instant tears to my eyes as I track that memory to the next, up to the months after Celine and Beau died. Of the devastation on Jean Dominic's face and just how carefully he *watched me*—heartbreak and confusion in his expression as I lashed out. Even back then, he was my mirror. Through the reflection in his eyes, I *saw* the comparison of the Tatie he once knew to the unhinged mess I was quickly becoming, and in turn, I *hurt him* for it.

Guilty tears sting my eyes as I recall not long after, when his own expression started to harden, his heart's door starting to narrow further and further for me as he began to fight back. Painful realization sets in that though Cecelia might have broken his heart today, I had a hand in breaking it long ago.

That truth glides down my cheeks as I sort through the years of our ensuing war after, up to the last day we truly had ill words between us. Mere months before he left for college. Back to the morning where a marijuana cloud trailed him as he walked through the sliding glass door to find me standing at the foot of the kitchen table.

"What are you doing awake?"

"Waiting on you," *I answer instantly, taking the chair at the table as he opens the fridge.* "How did it go?"

"I'm not handcuffed," he spouts sarcastically as he bends to search the shelves, "so I would say well enough."

Keeping my eyes lowered, my heart pounds in remembrance of the hours before, experiencing the most intense lovemaking of my life—with Tyler. Shame threatens to take hold as my body continues to hum, my lips still tingling from his kiss as my heart begs me to believe his words, promises, and declarations. Never in my life have I felt so much with and for another. Yet, am I a fucking fool to believe, to put faith in, the declarations of someone so young?

Fueled by the war that instantly started my mind racing as my body continued to buzz when I woke alone, I left my mattress in search of Tyler. Heart alight and in a haze, I found myself in the kitchen staring blankly at the maps, utterly consumed by what just transpired and his constantly circulating words.

"... There will be no other women for me because there is no other woman meant for me ... I love you. I fucking love you."

It's when I glance over to see Dominic staring at me curiously at the open refrigerator that I jar myself out of my stupor. Cursing my stupidity for leaving my room while furiously trying to put my mask back in place.

"You seem rather"—he tilts his head—"chipper this morning."

My heart starts to pound, but I speak up instantly with false bravado.

"Because I want to show you something," I tell him, hoping my tone is convincing. "I am making maps of Triple Falls. Many have hidden spots for refuge. Tyler thought it would be a good idea and that it would benefit you all. What do you think?"

Slowly closing the fridge, he approaches the table to hover over me as I continue.

"Look, here." I point to the map before I brave a glance at him. "See? The location of a forgotten underground entrance on Main Street. Maybe it will be useful for the club at some point in the future?"

The weight of his stare has me rattling with anxiety while trying my best to push away all thoughts of what it felt like to be with Tyler so intimately. But it's Dominic's unforgiving scrutiny that forces me to finally acknowledge it. "What? Dominic, what?"

"Are you really going to ruin his fucking life because you're afraid to date a man your own age? I'm not a fucking idiot. Whatever is happening with Tyler, you need to end it. Now."

"Hmm, you are acting like one. I don't even know where Tyler is."

"He went for a run because he's fucked up and dealing with a lot right now. He doesn't need you fucking with his head. End it."

I still, keeping my eyes lowered. "We are friends, very good friends who care very much for each other—"

"Come on, Tatie, surely you can find someone your own age to play games with and deal with your bullshit." His adamance to confront me forces me to lift my face to him. Panic rips through me as he stares back at me, utterly determined.

"I care for Tyler so much"—I swallow—"I would never hurt—"

"He's not some lab rat for you to fucking experiment with." Dom relights his joint and opens the sliding glass door. Keeping his eyes on me, he exhales a cloud of smoke, his searing judgment strangling me as I search for and spot my bottle on the counter, craving the numbness it promises.

"I am trying to change, Dominic. I am changing. I do not drink as much. I am doing all I can to—"

"Jesus, you're so fucking selfish," he spits, "fucking disgusting." He flicks his joint before stalking past to slam himself into his room. Music blares from behind his door a second after I pass. My bottle is already at my lips before I close my bedroom door and drain every drop.

Dominic's Camaro sounds a few streets over, jarring me from the memory of that morning, before it appears and he pulls up to the curb. With the porch light off, I know he can't see me as he remains idle for several minutes before finally cutting his engine. When he exits, I stand to announce myself, hoping my white flag is evident in my expression as he begins to stalk toward the house, head cast down. Just as he approaches and lifts his head, he pauses when he sees me as I clear fresh tears from my eyes.

"I thought you didn't live here anymore, Tatie?" he utters softly, not a trace of animosity to be found in his question. Relief sets in at his gentle reception as I answer.

"I don't. I'm here to wait for you." My eyes start to sting again as he draws in, and just as I think he'll pass me, he takes a seat on the bottom porch step instead. I immediately join him, taking in the changes in his appearance with what little light filters on us from the lamppost across the street. His build is far more muscular, his hair shorter, and his jaw more defined. He smells of marijuana, but both his posture and expression reek of pain and defeat. Pain he's not making much effort to conceal, or worse, that he can't, which has my eyes welling again. "I'm so sorry, Dominic."

He gives me a slow nod before granting me an ironic half smile as he speaks. "Well . . . silver lining for you is that your prediction came true, and karma got me on your behalf pretty fucking good."

"No, Dom, shh." I lift my palms to him in surrender as tears glide down my cheeks. "Please don't speak of *that* out loud. This is not me gloating. That's *not* how I feel."

I lift a shaking hand to his shoulder, and he doesn't deny my gesture as I will myself to speak again. "Through much, *much* therapy, I can now say things I never thought I would, and what I want you to take to your heart is that I never wish for your pain."

He stares back at me as I release his shoulder to help

clear my eyes. "Well, I'll take your word for it because you're *leaking again*."

I can't help laughing. "I have been nothing but an *emotional woman* since I stopped drinking, and I hate it. But if you can believe it, no matter how much I leak now, I am so much happier."

"I see it in you. You look well . . . healthy," he rasps out, "I almost couldn't believe it when Tyler told me"—he tilts his head—"but then I remembered noticing a real difference in you when I took you to Pretty Place for that sunset. You were sober that day."

"Oui." I smile. "I had just gotten sober. I have worked very hard to stay sober. Very close to a year now."

"It shows," he whispers low before a rare apprehension fills his eyes. "You know, Ormand personally escorted me and Sean to the airport last night."

"Oh?" I say, dread settling low. "Good, he owes me many favors."

"Tatie," he drags out, his tone confirming that Ormand did much more than give him a ride. Fury instantly fills me as I gape over at him.

"What did Ormand tell you?"

"A lot that you omitted. You undersold the shit out of your past when Tobias forced the conversation between us before I left for MIT." He nudges me. "Jesus . . . fuck, Tatie, why didn't you tell us?"

"Because you were *children*, and it was my job to protect you from such vile truths. Of all my failures, it's the *one thing* I successfully managed to guard you from, even as I failed to shield you from myself. As you both grew older, I decided I never wanted you to know." I shake my head in fury. "Ezekiel still does not know, and it was not Ormand's place to tell you anything," I whisper shakily, "he had no fucking right, the fucking imbecile."

"Well, you might be pissed at him, but I got the impression you're his hero," he relays ironically. "I don't think he meant any harm because he got pretty choked up as he rambled on about how he had wronged you. He looked fucking terrified, too, like he had the fear of God put in him. He kissed mine and Sean's collective asses the whole ride. So, while you might hate it, I'm glad I know what little he did tell us, Tatie, and that you're here because I already decided *months ago* that I was coming to you after I got back."

My heart lights at his admission. "You did?"

"Through a coincidence—I'm now positive is named *Tyler*—I stumbled upon my grandfather," he confesses.

"You met *Francis*?" I gasp.

"And his son, Ranier, briefly, but yeah, and my conversation with him changed a lot of my perception of you." He shakes his head, his expression dimming. "After hearing Ormand last night . . . you're not the only one who has an overdue apology. I fucking"—he swallows—"I fucking made fun of you, antagonized you, and you . . ." His remorseful gaze prompts me to answer his unspoken question.

"No." I shake my head. "This is not the conversation I wanted to have. I have put that in the past behind me, and you are suffering enough."

"Tatie," he urges. "This is the conversation I need to have. I have bits and pieces, but I need to hear the truth from you." He watches me carefully as if through new eyes. "I remember you before, Delphine. The aunt you were to me before my parents died. You weren't a ball of sunshine, but you played with me and Tobias in the yard. You read to me a lot to practice your English. *'One Fish, Two Fish, Red Fish, Blue Fish,'*" he says as I mouth the last of the title with him. "It was our favorite book, even if you did have a love-hate relationship with Dr. Seuss."

I palm my mouth to hold in my emotion as he nudges me. "Tatie, tell me what happened."

"You were a child," I tell him. "Please let it be."

"I can't. Tell me what he did."

Closing my eyes briefly, I nod. "If I tell you this, Dominic, you must promise never to share it with Ezekiel."

He nods.

"I will not give you all the details, but to keep it short, Alain took a heavy ashtray from the kitchen table, a very heavy ashtray, and struck me here"—I point to my left temple—"causing permanent damage . . . he almost killed me, but it was Beau, your father, who saved me from that fate," I relay in hopes it brings him pride. "Beau terrorized Alain enough to scare him into hiding, and he never contacted me again."

"Jesus Christ," he utters. "All those times I fucked with you about it," he darts his eyes away, "and that morning . . . I was so fucking vicious with you about Tyler."

"Shh, Dom, no"—I glance back at the door in fear—"please don't speak of this. I don't want Tyler to hear or to know. *Not ever.*"

"Fuck that," he says, not lowering his tone by a fraction. "I know you broke it off with him after I went off on you that morning," he relays, guilt clear in his eyes, "because he enlisted just after and would never come near this house. That's . . . on me, and I'm fucking sorry for that, but I swear to God, Tatie, I thought I was protecting him." He palms the back of his neck. "Or maybe I was just too much of a fucking asshole to see it."

"You weren't wrong, Dom. You weren't right, either, but time told us differently. Tyler and I are very happy now. You just wanted your friend to have the best life. It's not so hard to understand why you had so many doubts . . . I shared them with you, but *please*, please let's not speak of this . . . you know he has the hearing of a bat."

He nudges me again. "He really doesn't suspect?"

"No, and he will *never know*," I vow.

"I don't know if I can live with it. He deserves to know, and I deserve his wrath for it."

"No," I say adamantly. "No. Self-punishment is the absolute *worst torture*. Let it be, Jean Dominic, and don't credit yourself so much. You may have had something to do with my decision that morning, but you did not make the decision. *I did*, and don't forget that. You did not drink all those bottles, self-sabotage, and hurt your nephews. I did. So, take the blame from yourself, make peace that you were young and acted like a natural asshole teenager, and let it be over. We have all suffered enough from our past mistakes and circumstances, so enough of this," I state again. "You thrive on your relationships with your brothers. I do not want this to be another divide between what you hold so dear. Hear me, Jean Dominic, let it be, let it go, and *never speak* of this again. Do you understand?"

He stares at me for a long minute before he finally nods.

"But I will ask you for *one thing*, nephew. Just one thing."

"I'm listening," he mutters, exhaustion and ache in his eyes.

"Do you remember what I told you about forgiveness when you took me to the sunset?

"Yeah," he says. "I do."

"My ask is that you don't let this go on so long that you and Ezekiel lose one another. Your heartbreak is one thing, but the loss of your relationship with your brother will be the true tragedy. I still, to this day, love your mother so much for loving me when I thought no one could. I'm sure now that is why she remains so deep in my heart, and you have her heart, Dominic."

"I'm feeling a lot right now, Tatie, but I heard you." He lets out a long breath. "You really don't hold it against me?"

"No. I'm okay with things as they happened because he's an incredible soldier, and I helped to rear the soldier inside of him to care for you both, which is my contribution and repentance. And look what you all have become! I have so much pride that you are all the soldiers I wanted so much to be . . . but please try to forgive as fast as you can so you don't lose the time I have because it is damning," I warn. "So damning."

He studies me for several heartbeats before he finally nods again.

"Okay, that's all I wanted to say." I stand. "Good night . . . je t'aime, Jean Dominic," I exhale shakily. "I am so glad you remember me . . . before."

Turning from him to relieve him of any response to my affection, he grips my forearm to stop me when I take the first step up. Looking down, I see his eyes filled with pain before he poses his question.

"Do you want to play a game?"

"Do you mean Battle?" I perk up.

"Yeah." He stands, "I don't see myself sleeping anytime soon."

"Okay." I smile. "Let me go find some soldiers."

***

The feel of little hands has me opening my eyes to follow their movements. They carefully strip away the plastic before the adhesive is pressed to my skin, covering the fingerprint-shaped bruises on my arm. The little fingers attached to little hands continually pluck from a box of Band-Aids that are propped against my drawn knee where I lay in bed. It's when he starts to hum "Alouette" that a sting I swore I was incapable of since I woke begins to burn my eyes, nose, throat, and chest. A sting that increases as I continue to rouse.

"Tobias . . . you can't go," Tyler calls from yards away, trailing Ezekiel as he stalks toward his Jag.

"Where is she?" Ezekiel snaps in response.

Jean Dominic remains diligent in his task to cover me in strips of plastic where I lay on my side, facing him. With every bandage he successfully secures, he darts his eyes up to mine, sensing he's being watched, and I close them just as quickly before he resumes his work.

As Jean Dominic attaches another bandage at the base of my neck, I ignore the tickle. Fighting hard not to release the burning tears desperately trying to escape my closed eyes. Slitting them open, I catch glimpses of the little boy at my bedside, who is doing his very best to cover every visible mark, every hurt on my body.

"You know you can't—" Tyler tries to reason with Ezekiel as he, in turn, demands his answer.

"Where is she?" Ezekiel orders a second time.

"Je te plumerai la tête... oh, oh, oh, oh," Jean Dominic squeaks as he carries on, as feelings I haven't once experienced—nor been able to draw out since I woke in that hospital—start to crash into me like a tidal wave. Emotion that I haven't yet been able to summon. Not once since Ormand looked over to me, sobbing with red-rimmed eyes. Not once since Celine began to spoon-feed me, her eyes haunted as she assured me Alain was long gone and would never be back. Feelings that did not arise the day I isolated myself in my bathroom, staring for long minutes at the damage my husband left in his wake.

Confusion has been present since I woke, as well as irritation with Beau, who did not heed my warning about Abel. Insisting he would deal with Ezekiel's grandfather if he did become a threat. That our Ravens would stand guard and that we had the upper hand here in the States.

More irritation as well for the haze that now surrounds my vision, my memory. For being so helpless and unable to care for myself. For being unable to speak. But as far as real, genuine emotion, especially anger—not a trace. However, it's the loss of something essential inside of me that plagues and puzzles me. The mystery of what was taken that sometimes outweighs the pain. Something I know now is not emotion.

But it's Jean Dominic's continued gentle touch and humming that has emotion threatening to overcome me now. Through slow cleansing breaths, as I gaze upon him,

I manage to stifle the threatening cries so as not to scare him, though I want so much to free them.

"You don't want to do this," Tyler warns, his voice more urgent. "It will only—"

"Where is she?!" Ezekiel shouts as a tense silence passes.

"At school," my love hesitantly replies, his curse floating up to me shortly after Ezekiel's car door slams, and my nephew turns his engine over before racing away.

Jean Dominic hums as I keep up my charade, stealing glimpses at my nephew, where he stands at my bedside, bandaging me in an effort to heal me. Inching my head back to gain more view, I glance down to see my pajama top is covered as well—but in only one place. I count six Band-Aids lined up in a neat row across my pajama top, above where my heart lies. The number is ironic to me because Jean Dominic could never possibly know that's the number of years I was trapped in hell. It's when he finally works his way up to my face that I allow him to see my open eyes as his own widen in surprise. "Tatie!" *he exclaims.* "You are awake!"

I nod as he scans the work he's done before he brings his gaze back to me. "Maman said you were so very sick and sad and that you can't talk!" *He shouts as if I'm deaf, too.* "Do you feel better?"

His innocent eyes search mine in hope as I will myself to answer.

"Oui!" *I manage, my voice unrecognizable with that one word.*

"Maman!" *Dominic calls loudly for her, and I know it's to boast that he got me talking. As he calls her a second time, I note the beauty of Celine's youngest son. Where Ezekiel is just as beautiful in his own right, Jean Dominic's is ethereal . . . almost otherworldly in a sense. I decide it has to be his youth and that all children are probably beautiful in the same way. I have not paid attention to many children, but I have noticed it in Celine's boys. In their translucent newborn skin, the tiny veins just beneath their perfect pinkness, and their silky hair. Which shines on its own without the added reflection of light.*

Their souls just as flawless. Perfect and pure, free of debris and the filth of life. Their tiny bodies and hearts utterly untarnished. As I stare at Jean Dominic as he waits for his mother's praise in those short few seconds, for the first time, I take a different meaning in the Word, which conveys God's love for all his children. Words which declare we are seen and loved by Him the very same way—new babes with translucent skin, tiny veins—and shine for Him without the reflection of light. That His love keeps us safely in that veil and viewed the way I view Jean Dominic right now.

The idea that this could be the truth has my chest roaring in pain and longing, in desperate want of that love. Where just days ago, I was made to believe that love is the greatest deceiver of all and could never exist in such a way for me. But in my nephew—during those short seconds—I see God's love. Just as I think it, a shudder runs the length of my body before it erupts in chills. A presence takes hold of every one of my senses, surreal warmth filtering throughout my heart as my mind goes utterly silent. And with my mind quieted, I feel a soothing balm surrounding the riot roaring within my rupturing soul, a half breath before it's snuffed out. Within the length of a few heartbeats, all pain leaves me, and I experience a peace I never thought myself capable of. Just after, I'm gently released back into reality. That utter state of peace coming and going so quickly that I instantly wonder if I experienced it at all. It's the relaxed state that remains in the aftermath that convinces me it did happen—that I didn't imagine it.

In that aftermath, the sight of Celine popping her head into my bedroom door, eyes comically widening a second before her jaw unhinges, has a smile threatening—a smile!

The mere notion of that expression seeming impossible

to me, a feat I never planned on taking on after I woke. Never to be fought for or mustered up, or a priority or remote possibility mere minutes ago that suddenly becomes knowledge. A knowledge that someday, maybe not soon, but someday, I will smile again.

Celine's eyes widen further as she draws near and lifts the box of empty Band-Aids, her voice light but scolding.

"My God, Dominic, did you have to use every single one?" Celine's mortified eyes dart to mine in apology as she kneels before him and grips his tiny, healing hands. "And what did I tell you?"

"To leave Tatie alone," Jean Dominic speaks, mimicking her voice. "But she said she feels better now, Maman!" he argues before he turns to me, his silver-gray eyes imploring mine. "She told me so. She talked to me, Maman! Didn't you?"

"Oui," I answer through the rusted blades in my throat as I manage my first words for him since I woke in that hospital. "Oui, m-m-much better."

My sister's eyes instantly fill with tears as we hold our stare for long seconds, both moved by the gesture of her beautiful little boy. Hope bouncing between us for the very same reason—that we will survive this dark time and escape the lingering fear and pain together as we have every other obstacle we've faced since we became sisters.

"Come on," Celine sighs, guiding Jean Dominic by the palm through my bedroom door as I call after him. They both stop at the threshold as I whisper the truth.

"You heal me."

"Oui, Tatie," he pronounces proudly. "Then I will bring more tomorrow!"

"No," Celine laughs, ushering him out. "You will not. Come on, little prince," she says, giving me a wink before they disappear from sight. Just after, I release the tears of hope I've been holding as I stare after the angel who just left my bedside.

Tyler surrounds me in his comfort as I stare down at

Dominic's solid white casket, pinpointing precisely what Alain took that night—the naïve sense of safety God gifted us. The blissful ignorance that veils and shields us from the evils of men. Of being naturally blind to such evil. Of believing in Band-Aids.

A veil that no one, once exposed to it, can ever get back. And in seeing that evil, feeling it, and becoming intimate with it, I can task myself to battle it like my nephew did before he lost that fight. As more cars begin to turn over, I allow myself to mourn the loss of that veil for the last time. To grieve the boy who stole my heart and brought me light and hope during one of my darkest times. It's then I collapse into my love's arms and allow that grief briefly to take hold . . . but only for a moment.

Years before that veil was taken, I charged myself to fight the evils of men. And as I will the last of that grief out of me, I decide to reforge the soldier within and charge her to rejoin the battle she left long ago.

Fury begins to take hold, taking ownership of my grief as the restlessness that's been prodding me since the day Jean Dominic died becomes recognizable. Inside that recognition, a mold starts to take shape. The inferno of anger blazing inside, pouring itself into it just after. The base of my designed wrath precise for wielding. The opposing edge sharpening to a point capable of penetrating any armor. The tip of it coated in a venom so toxic it will unapologetically take down any barrier that threatens to interfere with its purpose. As I gather my rage to poise it—to take aim—I feel the coil beginning within, growing tighter and tauter as I start to straighten my spine, denying another tear.

Tyler tenses briefly, sensing the change happening inside me before releasing me just as I lift my eyes to his.

In an instant, he recognizes what's in my expression. And though my days as this newly forged soldier are numbered, I lift my chin in defiance of that number, determined to take aim as long as I'm capable. Not an ounce of fear remaining as I stare at the man who not only recognizes the fire now burning inside me but stokes it with the return fire in his own. No words necessary as we solidify our new mission.

Our collective flames and darkness brushing before merging together as we mentally start to strategize. Though they declared it, they'll soon die painfully regretting it because, as of this moment, we're taking it back and declaring it *our own war*. As my soldier and I walk hand in hand from Dom's graveside, we blaze together down that hillside with a matching search for vengeance in our rippling souls and wrath beating between our synced hearts.

Chapter Fifty-Six

TYLER

BLINK.
Exhausted and reeling from these last relentless weeks, images of my latest mission threaten to shutter in as I lower my truck windows, allowing the breeze in. Fall announcing its imminent arrival as brisk air filters throughout the cabin. Restless and unable to sleep, I left Delphine in bed to take a drive, and since then, I have ended up aimlessly roaming the streets of Triple Falls as I did years ago. Only vaguely aware I've lost time due to the visions continually threatening to batter me.

Eyeing the clock on my dash, I see it's a little past 3 a.m. Since the day we buried Dom, Delphine and I have been vigilantly trying to stop the hemorrhaging that started with that gunfight—and after, an attack on every southeast chapter, resulting in the death of at least one bird in each.

So while Tobias spun out, figuratively and literally, leaving Dom's casket to race toward Cecelia, it was mine and Delphine's back-and-forth during the drive home that birthed my first mission. Our first step toward retribution. A minute into the drive, Delphine had deduced one of the reasons Miami had been so quiet. They were scoping us out to the point that they put a strategy together to start their attack and used the contract on Roman to kick it off.

Terrified that was the truth of it, both of us became hellbent on coming up with a plan.

"*There was someone in that car that escaped with too much intel,*" she expels confidently, as the truth of it guts me.

"Even with a practical cannon in my fucking hands, I didn't have a clear shot due to the glint of the sun, and I don't fucking miss, Delphine." I glance over at her, seeing the wrath in her posture in my passenger seat. "But I did miss that day, and it cost us dearly. I should have taken them out when I had the chance."

"*Try not to doubt Ezekiel's reasoning, Soldier. He's as trained as you are and spent just as many days at that kitchen table with me. His biggest hesitance in taking out Miami was their mafia connections. There is reason there, and we need to get to the bottom of it so we can move forward. But first, do you remember the make and model?*"

"Yeah, hard to miss. It was an obnoxiously painted street-illegal performance car—an orange and lime green Honda. One I didn't recognize from the meetups, which means fuck all. They were too far clear of the gate by the time I made it there, so I didn't get the license plate. I've put a call in with Phillip to track it, but chances are slim he'll find it."

"*We start there. Grab your Miami ledger and hunt down that fucking singing canary, if he exists, and I will help you,*" Delphine relays, her whisper lethal. "*If it's one source, you'll find he's one of the most established in the Miami chapter, probably closest to Matteo and Andre in ranks if he has so much knowledge of our club. Once you do, silence him and all his closest in a very messy way.*" She turns to me in the seat. "*It's time to send a message, Soldier—one they cannot ignore and will have them rethinking they have the position of high ground. Compile a list of possibles if you can't locate the car or the owner, and I will help you find a way to narrow it down.*"

As we pull up to the house, she immediately opens her door before rounding the truck to meet me at mine. "No, Soldier. Go, now. Find the source."

"Baby, but your treatment—"

"*Is the only reason you're going alone,*" *she states emphatically, forcing me to drop it.* "We've already lost too much time and need to find that canary. If you track him and decide to move in before getting back to me, make him sing his last song for you. For intel on Miami and the extent of their connections. Including what branch of mafia before he bellows his last note. If he refuses, find personal leverage against him." *Her comment hangs in the air between us.* "Which will be very messy," *she warns.*

"I excel at messy," *I assure her.*

"I know," *she whispers, her worry for me evident.* "I will work on a strategy while you're gone. One that will get our birds back home in their own beds, but . . ." *When she reaches for me, I bend, giving her access while pulling her to me.* "One last order."

"I'm listening," *I murmur against her lips.*

"Come home to me, Soldier. That is a priority order."

I didn't argue with her, selfishly in need of a way to purge my grief. Within hours of zeroing in, I found the bird, one that hypocritically wore our fucking ink, and a Miami veteran. For him, I had taken my most trusted of the Triple chapter and called in a few of our inked military before carrying her order out to the letter in Florida.

Though I was gone for too many days, we left a brutal blood trail in our wake while delivering our intended message. A trail I'm still processing now as I pull up to the darkened, abandoned garage. The second I've parked, a vivid flash of Dom behind the hood of his Camaro crashes into me before another surfaces, followed by another, until I'm flooded by them. Every day, I feel the added weight against my bulging levee, but so far, I've held it, keeping myself upright for my birds. Tonight, that task is especially taxing, and I fear that if I let so much as a drop through,

I won't be able to get upright again. Working through the burn, I stare at the dark, abandoned garage from where I sit, the need for release briefly paralyzing me.

We promptly shut down King's after the attacks started on our southeast chapters and have yet to get the garage back up and running.

Not that any of us are anxious or have the fucking time anymore to keep the ruse going as we fight to keep our birds safe and get our club back to functioning on some level. Right now, Tobias has been forced to play the role of politician in damage control and is, at present, a moving target. A target at his wit's end to try to restore peace in our club. We've been so busy scrambling on the offensive as Miami continues its assault that none of us have had time to grieve. But with my most recent mission, their advances have slowed slightly. To the point that several birds have migrated back to their houses from Denny's compound since I ordered us all there the morning of the gunfight.

As of now, we've taken every imaginable step to safeguard Triple Falls.

With eyes fucking everywhere, and thanks to the digitization and access by the club to Delphine's maps, we've got birds posted at every single vantage point to detect any possible threat or motorcade that looks even remotely suspect. Her strategy, combined with the police vigilantly monitoring every major road in and out of Triple Falls—thanks to Roman—has me feeling confident in some respects. While feeling utterly helpless in others, Delphine's sickness being the first.

But with the added help of Beekman and the rest of our rapidly increasing number of feathered Feds currently scouring the media and everything in circulation to keep our street war unlinked, if control wasn't an illusion, I might feel some sense of it this side of the half hour. Delphine's and my new reality so far from the hammock-swinging, snooze-inducing state of bliss we were in not so long ago. A place and state I would do anything to get back to for the moment, but this war is far too close to home.

At this point, I would do anything to erase the days between that night and this one for any other outcome than Dom's permanent absence. The echo of his death haunting my every waking hour. But it's the image of Dom's lifeless body in Tobias's arms as he brought him down Roman's staircase that morning that keeps the rage lacing the blood pumping through my heart. That keeps me in constant need of an outlet. It's that need that now fuels my strategies and upcoming plans for retaliation. For the purpose to purge on the motherfuckers who took him from us in an effort to shift this war in our favor and bring Tobias back. Though, day by day, Tobias becomes more and more lost to us.

As does Sean. That sting becoming harder to ignore.

Knowing I won't be able to sleep anytime soon—and in need of mindless work—I stalk into the garage. Letting Delphine witness my anxiety isn't something I want right now, but the idea that her treatment won't take—of losing her . . .

Tamping that fear down, I enter the side door of the garage and stop at the open hood of the closest car, needing the mind-numbing work to help me sort my shit. Fully aware that I, too, am a moving fucking target, I keep the main bay lights off and pop on the shop light already hanging over the engine. Shortly after, I flip open a toolbox, ready to assess what needs fixing. An instant later, my Glock is drawn and pointed at a . . . kid whose eyes bug out of his head as he gapes back at me just as a soft "Russell?" leaves his lips.

"The fuck?" I say, immediately tucking my Glock back into my jeans. "Who in the hell are you?" I ask, darting my eyes to the couch to see a blanket and pillow discarded there.

"I-I'm—I thought you w—" he says, backing slowly

away from me, his palms up. "I d-d . . . I'm sorry." He skitters toward the couch as I slowly trail him.

"You can't fucking be here, kid," I bark, confusion setting in.

When he glances back and sees me on his heels, he does a one-eighty before stumbling backward and falling on his ass, palms still up as he speaks rapidly.

"R-Russell was c-coming back to g-get me. He j-just, he couldn't get a-ahold of anyone to k-keep me while he ran an errand b-but he's coming right b-back." He lets this all out in a terrified but stuttered rush as I realize I'm towering over him, my posture threatening and tense.

"That explains shit," I expel, the tension in me due to his own safety as I offer my hand to help him up. Denying my outstretched hand, he palms the concrete before standing on shaking legs as I pull out my phone. "Who are you?"

"Zach," he expels, eyes darting to the side door.

"That still explains nothing. Why are you sleeping on our couch, Zach?"

He bites his lip, the fear in him palpable, terror in his eyes, which look slightly familiar. It's the rest of him that I can't place. I gauge him carefully, seeing signs of extreme fatigue. Even beneath the dim shop light, I can see his complexion is gaunt, and he's extremely malnourished by the looks of him. Pocketing my phone, I decide to act first and ask Russell questions later, knowing this situation could go further south if the garage is being watched—which is likely.

Adrenaline kicking in, I stalk over and kill the shop light and cock my head. Just after, I start to bark my orders rapidly while walking over to the door to ensure it is fully pulled to and locked. "You need to get your shoes on and your shit and come with me right now."

Even in the blacked-out bay, I manage to catch his nod and a telling sniff before letting out a heavy exhale.

"Hustle, please," I manage as gently as I can, knowing

I might have just put this kid in direct fire. Subconsciously, I came here to pick a fight with anyone who might have snuck past our borders, knowing damn well this garage is a hot spot and neon sign for Miami.

Zach promptly kicks into his shoes, grabbing a tattered backpack at the end of the couch before stopping a good five feet from me when I lift my hand to halt him. Easing open the side door, Glock drawn, I scour the corners of the building before turning to him. "Stay right here until I come back for you," I utter low. "Only open this fucking door if you hear four rapid knocks. If you don't hear those knocks when you count to a hundred and twenty, call Russell, got it?"

"Got it." His voice breaks on the words, confirming I've terrorized this kid within minutes of meeting him while racking my brain on who he could be and why he's here. After clearing the building, I quickly knock and retrieve him before rushing him to the cab of my truck.

A heartbeat later, we're shooting out of the parking lot and racing away from the garage as I continually dart my gaze between the road and my rearview. Rapidly becoming pissed at myself that I'd just so recklessly risked my well-being when I have a woman at home who needs me. Who is fighting to stay here, all the while growing more pissed at Russell, who put the kid shaking next to me in harm's way as my need increases for his explanation.

"Jesus . . . fuck," I grit out, relief filtering in when I catch no signs of life behind us. Glancing over, I see Zach plastered to his passenger door, a pang of guilt stinging me. Pulling out my cell, I dial Russell, who doesn't answer. Irritation growing, I manage to compose a menacing text, threat included. Russell's not a fucking fool by any means. His every step is just as calculated as mine. So why would he leave a fucking kid so vulnerable in the garage?

"Tell me why you're sleeping on a couch," I prompt, keeping eagle eyes on our rearview while I press a little harder on the gas.

"D-Dom was my friend," he utters. "You're Tyler, r-right?"

"Yeah, sorry, I'm a little on edge and don't normally go around pulling guns on kids. You just scared the shit out of me," I tell him as he stares at me, eyes bugged wide. "But I'm guessing I returned the favor. I'm really sorry if I scared you, but I wasn't expecting you . . . and am going to kill Russell," I grumble.

"Please don't," he says, eyeing me as if I may see it through.

"Not like that, man," I say through a chuckle I can't help as I glance between him and the road, my anxiety easing slightly with every mile I put between us and the garage. By his uneasy disposition—even after our introduction and the look of him as he continues to white-knuckle the passenger door handle—it's obvious he's experienced some heavy-handed trauma. It's everywhere on his person, which has my chest squeezing as I do my best to put us both more at ease. "So, Dom was your friend, how?"

He lowers his head as he settles slightly in my seat. "He . . . looked out for me a lot up until about a year ago. Then he just . . . disappeared. He d-didn't answer my calls. But for a long time, as I was growing up, he would check on me even after he left for college. He used to help me when my dad would—" He falters before he speaks again. "C-can you please call Russell? I accidentally left my phone at the garage."

Feeling his hesitance and urgent need to be in the company he trusts—which isn't mine—I do my best to shuffle myself into that fold. "Look, I'll admit that was a shit fucking introduction for the two of us, but I swear to God, I'm not going to hurt you, okay? Things are pretty tense right now."

"I know about Miami," Zach relays as my body draws tight.

"You *what*?" I utter in disbelief as my cell phone buzzes. "Hold up, okay?"

Zach nods as I answer Russell's call without speaking a word while sliding to a stop under the cover of some trees clustered on the roadside. Quickly circling the truck to the passenger door to stand guard, when I'm confident enough we're as safe as we can be for the moment, I finally lift the phone with a— "You want to explain to me why the fuck you left a ten-year-old kid in a hot spot for Miami?"

"I know I fucked up," Russell replies instantly, "but I've got your twenty, and I'm coming straight to you . . . and he's not ten. He just turned *thirteen*."

"What? Not this kid, he's . . ." I trail off, glancing toward the truck.

"Yeah, man," Russell sounds, "he's thirteen."

"Explain," I snap.

"Dom kind of took him in, took care of him since he was young. His dad is this piece of shit who used him as a punching bag. Dom would buy him clothes and shoes, you know how he is . . . *was*," Russell corrects, his verbiage stinging us both as a short silence ensues. "When Zach popped up at Dom's funeral after everyone left and told me that Dom said to come to him if things got bad, I made the judgment call and took him with me. I kept him at the compound at first. I finally took him home with me a few days ago, but Mom flipped shit tonight, had one of her moments. You know how she gets. Zach's been through enough, Tyler. I don't want him around her when she's like that. Just after we left my house to get a hotel for the night, I got pinged by Peter. I had to think on my toes and tucked him away at the garage because I had no choice."

"Why in the fuck didn't you fucking call me!"

"You know why," he counters defensively. "Everyone is dealing with so much, man, and I had a threat to take care of. I didn't have the luxury of time, and I couldn't fucking leave him streetside in the middle of the night. Nothing around me was open. I've only been gone twenty minutes," he says in exasperation.

"Everyone okay?"

"Yeah, false alarm. Peter thought Miami was at Eddie's."

"You sure it wasn't them?" I snap in question.

"Yeah, brother," he says, "positive, just some asshole causing shit, but Peter swore it was, so I raced to him."

"Fuck!" I kick the gravel with my boots and the fact that I can't be the eyes and ears I was months ago or stretch myself any further. I can't be there for all of Delphine's treatments and carry out her orders. I'm already breaking my promise to revolve the club around the two of us. A promise I made years ago that she and I would come first. Ironically, breaking that promise now at her insistence. Due to her unrelenting thirst for revenge, which conveniently matches my own, but has us losing precious time.

One thing at a time, Jennings.

But that's the problem—as it is now, my multitasking days are getting more limited and seem over until we can start to anticipate Miami's moves. As of now, we're stuck on the offensive—something Delphine is working diligently to rectify.

Shifting my gaze to the kid who's staring through the windshield in a daze, my chest tightens again at the sight of him. Brown hair and eyes, looking utterly lost, he briefly reminds me of a younger me.

"So . . . he's got no place to go?"

"All he had was his dad, and he's not going back to him, Tyler. I'll take him in. I'll do what has to be done. Dom wanted him with *us*, brother. I'll take responsibility. I'm not letting him—"

"This should have been brought to me. Period. What if his dad sets off an Amber Alert?"

"His dad hasn't called his phone *once* since he left. Hasn't bothered looking for him, man. I know I made the wrong call tonight, but Peter was bugging out."

"Son of a bitch," I grit out, feeling helpless to the fact we don't have enough birds to cover every business and guard our borders. Peter's state is indicative that we're already stretched thin.

Severed Heart

"Just sit tight, I'll be there in five." Russell misconstrues my frustration. "I've got him. I should have brought him to Denny's, but I had no fucking time," he rushes out. "Tyler . . . I'm telling you, that kid has been through enough." Russell continues to sputter out more explanations as my mind races with solutions until a few of his words cut into my thoughts.

". . . dad owns some gas station."

"What?" I stop pacing and turn to stare at the kid who's currently peering back at me through the passenger window of my truck. I now realize exactly why his eyes are familiar, even as I ask. "You say he's *thirteen*? Where is his mother?"

"Yeah, man, just turned last week. He's been through hell. Says his mother left him when he was like three or four, had some affair or something, and his dad's been fucking punishing *him* for it since."

All the blood drains from my face as I keep the kid's gaze while a fear-filled tear slowly trickles down his cheek. "Russell . . . this is important," I utter hoarsely, "was his mother's name Grace? His dad's name, Tim?"

"Yeah, I think so. You know them?"

"Yeah," I manage as the gravity of who I'm peering at through the passenger glass sinks into me. His eyes familiar because they belong to the toddler who squirmed in Grace's arms nine years ago, his arms reaching out to me. *For me.* An image forever burned into my memory. "I've got him," I hear myself speak, disbelieving of the words but feeling the decision in my gut. "I'll get him safe . . . I've got him."

"What . . . you sure? I'm good with him. We get along well. I—"

"Please trust me on this. I've got him. Just . . . we'll talk later but lock down that fucking garage. No one goes in or out until I say otherwise. And meet me at Denny's tomorrow at noon. It's time to get more aggressive."

"I'll be there," he says, "but . . . there's a few things you need to know." Russell's tone has dread seizing me before he speaks. "Zach... can't at all handle human touch, Tyler. At all, okay? Do not touch him."

"His dad abused him that badly?"

"He left home because his dad beat him with an extension cord before he made him wrap it around his own neck... Jesus, man, I—"

"Tell me," I order, chest seizing unbearably.

"Then he ordered Zach to sit tight while he went to scout the perfect spot for him to hang himself from."

I drop my phone instantly, turning my back to Zach as the grief I've been holding at bay spills over my levee. A breath later, I make a beeline for the cover of the trees, giving myself a few seconds of collection. Fisting my hands at my sides, I absorb the latest blow and addition to the list of collateral damage left in the wake of Carter Jennings's *mistakes*.

***

Half an hour later, I bend to press a kiss to Delphine's temple as I murmur in her ear. "Hey baby, can you wake up for me, please," I whisper hoarsely. Delphine slowly rouses from sleep before opening her gorgeous silver-gray eyes. I see the happiness in her expression just before it dims, and I know it has nothing to do with any loss of enthusiasm in seeing me—but that she's just realized within a blink that she's living in an altered world. One that Dom no longer exists in. My own grief is evident, along with the fear of the alteration I'm bringing to her as she gauges my expression. In an instant, she's lifting to sit, her eyes scouring me with concern.

"Soldier, what's wrong?" She begins frantically searching me for any wounds as I grip her frantic, explorative hands.

"I'm fine, baby," I assure her as her eyes dart to mine.

"Is Ezekiel—"

"He's fine, too. I'm sorry, I didn't mean to scare you,"

I whisper. "It's not that serious," I relay and then shake my head. "Actually, yeah, it is."

"I am here, Soldier. Please tell me," she utters.

Her expression remains guarded, and it's then I wonder if we'll ever experience real joy in full again without Dom. If either of us will be capable of forgetting, for just a few seconds, about the matching hole now and forever punched into our gaping hearts. Wanting more than anything to blink myself out, if only for a day, instead, I exhale a loaded breath.

"Please, Soldier, tell me what's wrong."

"I'm sad. I'm really sad right now, *gutted*," I admit honestly. "And I need my best friend. I need you, and I mean I *really need* you. I need both your permission and help. I-I, *fuck*."

"I'm here, I'm here, Soldier," she assures, covering me in her voice, her caress. I glance back toward the closed bedroom door, knowing Zach is probably feeling more ill at ease in his skin than he ever has as he sits in our living room—isolated. Probably wondering why the hell he's been passed off by Russell and thinking he did something wrong to end up here. Pushing all apprehension aside in my ask because of that fact alone. For the way he must be feeling, the words begin to pour from my lips. Ten minutes later, Delphine is fully dressed and pulling on her robe.

Clearing her eyes one last time, she glances back at me before opening our bedroom door and stalking down the hall toward the lost boy rattling with fear on our couch.

Chapter Fifty-Seven

Tyler

FALL 2015

BLINK. Zach laughs maniacally at Delphine's stunned expression where they sit at our small kitchenette as he animatedly takes a good portion of her flank down in an air raid. Shaking her head, she catches my gaze over his shoulder, eyes narrowing on me where I'm propped, arms crossed at the threshold. "You asshole, you warned him!"

"Knowledge is power, baby, and he's on my side," I quip around the boulder in my throat. Hearing me, Zach turns in his chair, his brown eyes shining with mischief, far more life in the smile he's flashing me than last week and the week before. His color and overall well-being have improved dramatically in the short time he's been with us due to our collective efforts to get him to a healthier mental space and weight.

Along with healthy sugars, we've been feeding him lots of proteins in combination with the vegetables Delphine grew and harvested this summer. Still about a month or so before the first real frost, Delphine took part in the Jenningses' annual canning day last weekend with Mom and Aunt Rhonda. Thanks to the hellfire-filled grenades we've been forced to take cover from, she hasn't moved forward in making wedding plans since I ringed her finger, but it's evident Delphine is already a Jennings through and through.

Since Zach's been here, he's been equally inducted into the family fold and regarded as one of our own. Even by Mom, who, despite knowing who he is, or maybe especially because of it, started working with Zach right away, as did Delphine—here in our place of healing. A safe haven we both decided we wanted and needed to share with him the night I brought him home.

Though Zach never really got an explanation for our invitation and ask to stay with us—if it becomes permanent, and it looks that way—I plan on coming clean at some point. For now, I take pride that we've started slow. Using our mutual love of baseball, I've eased into his company by way of playing catch with him in the orchard like I did with Dad when I was a kid. Recently, he's started participating in the Jenningses' Sunday baseball games at the orchard after church. Church that Zach and Delphine regularly attend now because she's crazy about Pastor Ron, who she claims is 'so very wise.' A Sunday ritual I miss consistently to run club errands while they're occupied to get shit done so I can get right back to them.

I've been on two more missions to retaliate on Miami, both ordered by my general, and I hated every single minute because home is where I want to be. But as I stare at the two of them, bantering and talking, the need to escape right now is threatening to take over. It's the ease and peace in which the two of them interact now—in contrast to the white-hot pain currently raging inside me—that has me making a quick excuse.

"I think I'll toss something on the grill," I manage in the perfect tone. "You guys want chicken or burgers?"

"Burgers," both demand in unison as I feign a smile I don't feel and don't know if I ever will again, having just ended a call with Delphine's oncologist. Despite targeted radiation and the most potent imaginable chemo, her cancer has leapt from her ureters and kidneys to her lymph nodes, putting her at stage IV-B.

Terminal.

Mere weeks into her fight and grueling treatment, her oncologist recommended we stop all efforts, as one would suggest I might need an umbrella today in case of rain. Knowing if he had been in front of me, I would have fucking killed him; instead, I told him I would be seeking a second opinion.

In turn, he relayed that he understood and was sorry to be the bearer of bad news. What he didn't realize is that he just passed out two death sentences. And by the look of growing adoration on Zach's rapidly plumping face as he engages her across the table, he might have added another.

As I soak her in myself, I realize her quality of life today, right now, might be the best it will ever get again. That she's dying, in real time, before my eyes.

Blink out, Jennings. Blink out. Right fucking now!

My chest seizes again when she stokes the emotion I'm desperately trying to camouflage with the silver love she's showering me with over Zach's shoulder. Utterly unaware of what that look is doing to me.

But as she continues to peer back at me with so much unguarded affection, a suspicion spikes that maybe the love she's fusing into me right now is for comfort she thinks I might need. Deep down, a large part of me believes she was certain she was leaving me when she accepted my marriage proposal and after, starting the unforgiving treatment for my sake alone.

That her intuition is just as fucking damning as her nephew's was, who knew too that his time on earth would be cut short. That she already knew that in a matter of months, this life we have, this heaven we made together, will be stolen—robbed from us. A priceless fortune gained by and meant for others.

Unbearable pain starts to unfurl through every one of

my veins as I cement my mask in place. Hellfire burning inside my skin as the woman I'd move heaven and earth for sits with a boy who looks a lot like me. Nurturing and bringing forth his inner soldier the same way she did mine. Saving him while becoming his refuge from his father's cruelty and mistakes—just like she did for me.

Which is what I asked her for the night that I brought him home and pled with her to save him the same way.

Though it took little to convince her after hearing why he'd fled his father, and even less once she laid eyes on him. Just after, we settled him into what we deemed his room as we lay in bed, hands clasped, a decision brewing between us as she echoed my own thoughts about him. *"He's a younger you, Tyler, just like you."*

With that decision now solidified, but with her God's decision to take her, He's threatening to relinquish the family we just became. Unable to handle another second of our new reality, I stalk over to the fridge to continue the charade as I plot my escape. Albeit temporary, I need a reprieve to gain my bearings and reinforce my levee, which feels obliterated in my mind as my body threatens to follow.

Grabbing some hamburger meat, I mentally summon a list of people I could call. He's just one oncologist. There are specialists all over the world I can contact for additional help. I have millions in the bank that mean fuck all to me, but that money will buy an audience and has the power to gain the attention of those people. People who can tell me different words. Miracles happen every day. She still calls me hers, and I want more than anything now to make that true.

"I can help you after this game," Zach offers.

"That'd be cool," I hear myself reply in the perfect tone. I've mastered this.

Blink out, Jennings. Blink the fuck out!

"I've always wanted to learn how to grill," Zach adds.

"Then I'm your man," my voice deceives in jest as I miraculously speak again, my delivery just as convincing.

"God knows that French menace in front of you can't cook for shit."

"Asshole," she spouts as I glance over at her and lie again with the wink she loves so much. How in the fuck did I fake *that*? More so, how did she accept it without knowing I'm dying too, right along with her?

Or is she actively deceiving me as well?

Though none of those answers matter because she's . . .

The burn wins as I take measured steps outside, the steps of a man in no hurry, gait typical. The easy strides of a man who's going to cook dinner for his fiancé, and . . . what Zach is or will become to me, not yet definable. Just as I step out of the front door, I think I might be made when she calls my name, until I turn back to see her smiling.

"*Imbecile*," she drawls lovingly, "I may burn and over-salt everything, but even I know you have to make the patties first!"

She bought it, she's buying it. I can fake my way through this, but for how long? That question is answered a second later as the sledgehammer swings again—the doctor's words slamming into me full force, damn near taking me to my knees, hastening my decision to temporarily retreat.

"I'm aware, General," I drawl dryly, the deceptive execution professional as my heart continually seizes, threatening to give out. "Shit, I forgot," I lie, stalking back to the fridge to ditch the meat, "I have an errand to run. I'll only be a few hours and will cook when I get back." I quirk a brow. "Unless you two want to brave it?"

Both grant me easy nods before dismissing me, the two of them already sparring in their shit talk by the time I'm taking more measured steps out the front door. The instant I'm clear of their line of sight, a slight relief sets in, which is promptly annihilated by the sight of the porch swing—a swing I installed to watch a lifetime of sunsets with my general. With that added fuel, I go up in a blaze and free myself with the sweep of my eyes.

BLINK. *BLACK.*

***

BLINK.

"'I'm your Huckleberry,'" Jeremy quips the *Tombstone* quote to Peter as the two clown around in the bay. Their banter reminding me of Cecelia and our game, the guilt-filled tug in my heart promptly following. Our last interaction was horrific. An interaction in which Cecelia stood covered in my brother's blood, destroyed by Dom's death, and consumed by fear while begging me not to turn my back on her.

That gnawing guilt increases as I pull my cell to check on her and see that she's parked at school. No doubt going through the motions while replaying the trauma and questioning if we truly are the cruel deceivers we led her to believe we were. Who left her flailing and utterly isolated in the dark, cast out and grief-stricken. Our current war only reinforcing Tobias's initial decision to keep her away from the club. A decision seemingly heartless, but in truth, fueled by his love and dire need to protect her to his own paralyzing detriment.

If Cecelia knew that Tobias fights himself every fucking day to keep from going to her, she'd put herself in harm's way to be here, and they'd both be moving targets. So, while I feel it's unusually cruel to have alienated her, *again*, even I agree it's for the best—for now.

Jeremy's hysterical laughter jars me out of thoughts of her, as does Sean's curse before he noisily tosses a tool on the concrete in response. His accusatory eyes cutting toward them both as they play oblivious—the tension growing thick. Even from where I stand at the counter in the lobby, I can feel the anger rattling off him. After sealing the last envelope as they continue to crack on one another, I walk into the bay to join them for a few. I need a little more time to level myself out, to keep capable of faking what remains of the day for Delphine, who will get the results tomorrow.

I blinked back when I pulled up to the garage, the roar returning with a vengeance, no breathing technique capable of taming it. But because the woman I love has to endure it—as does everyone else without access to my created loophole—I decided to man up and do the same.

As I continue watching Sean rattle in his skin, I realize that when you're experiencing the same discomfort and pain, it's easily identifiable in others. That truth ringing clearer as I observe him, knowing I'm not the only one in the garage currently raging against the hand life has recently dealt. Even from feet away, it's obvious Sean is seconds away from implosion. Then again, he has been in this state since the day Dom died.

Though we're somewhat functioning at this point—having managed to open the garage just yesterday—I'm still uneasy about trying to attempt club life as usual, or whatever the fuck that might have meant before I was wasted an hour ago by a doctor's words. It's when I see Sean glower at them both that I recognize he, too, has no idea what *as usual* is, either. Not anymore.

"The fuck is so fucking funny?" Sean demands a second before their laughter ceases, and they both turn to see him bristling feet away.

"Chill out, man," Jeremy says, "we were just cutting up, having a laugh."

"Yeah? Well, maybe *I want to laugh, too*," Sean prompts in a voice I don't recognize.

"Something tells me you're not in the mood," Jeremy says with a sigh, his delivery lacking sarcasm but baiting enough for Sean—who's begging for any reason to lash out, his thinning patience already threadbare.

"Sean," I bark in warning, with enough bite behind it that he immediately shifts his glare to me, "you're behaving badly."

In the next second, I'm dismissed as he cocks his head at them both, his tone condemning with audacity. "How can you fucking laugh? How can you two fucking idiots laugh at *anything*?"

"How can you not?" Jeremy counters lifelessly, eyes dimming, but Sean's already stalking across the bay, keeping his glare on them both as he pulls his smokes from his jeans before blasting through the side door.

"It's all right, man," I relay on Sean's heels. "I've got him," I offer as both sets of wary eyes trail me until I push through.

Just outside of it, I find Sean crouched against the building, his cigarette already burnt in half as I study the hard lines etched into his expression. Lines I'm certain didn't exist before France.

"Unless you're out here to bum a smoke," he delivers in that alien voice, "I have nothing for you."

"Pain seems to be the only vehicle you're operating right now, brother. But I can't say shit, I'm driving the same one."

"*Are* we still brothers?" he counters sarcastically, "because we've only spent, what, maybe a year together collectively since you left." He gives me a wary side-eye. "I knew you well *once* . . . but let's be honest, Dom was my brother."

"So, I guess that in death, Dom gets a pass for his own extended absence, huh? That's quite an unfair edge."

Silence.

"Well, I guess it's a good thing I'm not competing and wouldn't try to, but that fucking stung, so congratulations, Sean. Would you like another?"

I take a step forward. "Tell you what, you can escalate this and swing at me too if you think it'll make you feel better, but the alternative feeling you're looking for right now does not exist in you drawing upon or causing the pain of the people closest to you. And yeah, we might not know each other as well as we once did, but that's not you, no matter how things change or what you've been through." Remorse fills his gaze briefly before his expression morphs back to unapologetic. "And you've always made it obvious who your favorite is."

"He was," he clips.

"That's common knowledge to even a village idiot, but that stung, too. You want some more?"

"I don't know what I want. No." He exhales a cloud of smoke. "That's bullshit, I know I don't want to fucking be here right now, or tomorrow, or maybe ever." He takes another exaggerated drag. "I know I don't want to glimpse this fucking tattoo every day thinking only one thing—that I'm forever linked to that motherfucker. Or continue to work with him to see this war through, and I sure as fuck don't want your judgmental ass telling me how I need to act right now because I know you still pledge allegiance to him." He lifts his chin in dismissal. "So why don't you run along and go be *his brother.*"

"Before you fire another shot or go a step further with an agenda that won't work no matter what bullshit you hurl at me today, I'm going to tell you right now I just found out Delphine is terminally ill. If I'm *lucky*, she's got six months. So, you should know I'm standing here because I still consider you brother enough to give you a few of *her* precious remaining minutes."

"Jesus . . . *fuck.*" His eyes instantly water as regret pours from his lips. "Tyler, I'm so—"

"Why? You weren't sorry a second ago, so don't be sorry now. Dom's your favorite, and you're pissed at me for staying loyal to my ink and to T, and that's your prerogative. But know my stance on those things aren't changing no matter how big of a fit you pitch, so stay mad. But for the sake of today, let me have the win in the grievances department. Though, right now, we're talking about you."

"Fuck that man, you're right"—his eyes spill over as he runs a palm over his mouth and jaw—"I am so out of line . . . I'm so fucking sorry. I didn't mean any of that."

"You meant some of it, there's always a little truth mixed in with your lash outs, but rest assured, I don't give a shit what part you meant most because, again, I'm operating the same vehicle you are. But we need to be talking about *you* because, for one, selfishly, it's distracting me, and two, so you stop pointlessly attempting to alienate your brothers... because like it or not, Sean, if either of them goes down tomorrow, you're going to grieve them just as hard even if you do successfully manage to push them away."

"Jesus, is that what I'm doing?" He shakes his head. "That's... sadly predictable."

"It's *natural*." I shrug. "In thinking that if you distance yourself enough, you'll never feel like this again. But it's not going to work. Not for you. Your heart won't have it. You can't cut off your hand and think you'll still have the use of your fingers because *you're all heart*, Sean."

A tear slides down his jaw as he stares up at me, looking utterly lost before he inhales more of his cigarette. "I don't know how to manage this, Tyler. I don't know how people manage this... and go on living. I'm so fucked up," he croaks. "I can't sleep. I can't concentrate on shit. I got a new place, bought a house... thinking it would be a project to keep my mind occupied, but I haven't done anything to fix it up. I haven't unpacked a single box or suitcase. I just keep buying new shirts and underwear." He glances back at the garage. "I've got two jobs I don't want anymore. I don't know if I want this life without him."

"So, switch it up and see what sticks." I shrug.

"What does that look like?" he asks as his silent tears track his cheeks while he lights another cigarette.

"You want a plan?"

He nods. "I could use one, yeah."

"I'm thinking you switch vehicles, and the opposite of the vehicle you're in, of pain, would be *pleasure*. How about you start with food you love or hike a trail you never have. Not here in Triple, but miles away. Something new, uncharted. The point is to start small... and instead of looking for a way to escape the pain, start searching for pleasure while you feel that pain. Little by little. Day by day."

"Sounds like slogan advice," he harrumphs, "and I don't see that happening," he dismisses.

"Because the pain is taking up your headspace, and you're allowing it. So, try to edge it back just enough to seek its opposite. And while you're at it, add some structure for yourself. Force yourself to do one thing to fix that house every day without fail—to unpack *one* box and then leave that house and go seek out *one* thing that brings you some pleasure, no matter how small."

"And you think that'll work?"

"I think it's better than what you're doing. You wanted a solution, and that's the only one I can think of that might help." I palm the back of my neck. "And while you're at it, maybe you could help me. I could use a little extra time at home today, so I have an errand I want to opt out of, which may kill two birds for us both. It will get me back to Delphine, and in helping me, you might be able to draw upon other people's happiness."

"Name it," he says, standing, his posture perking slightly.

"There's an envelope on the checkout desk full of your blessings. I've got about fifteen business owners eagerly waiting for those checks. Why don't you deliver them today? And while you're at it, Layla has been telling me about this dress shop called Retro Stitch. You know the one on Main?"

"Yeah, I know where it is."

"Go there and ask for the shop owner, her name is Tessa. Layla said she's good people. Maybe you could feel her out and see if she's a good fit for future bird commerce."

"Done . . ." He scours me, and I can feel the shift in him the second his worry for me begins to override his selfish pain because I do know him that well, and I've already forgiven him. "What else can I do for you?"

"Cure cancer." I shake my head ironically. "Stop smoking."

"Anything but those?" he counters, the harder shell he's growing accustomed to temporarily discarded as his worry for me kicks in.

"Take care of, and do your best to get back to some semblance of your true self, Sean . . . That's the best thing you can do for us both because I might need to call in that favor soon." I scrape my lip as he nods in understanding before pulling me to him, his whisper hoarse.

"I'm so fucking sorry," he croaks before releasing me. "Please, brother, please take my apology."

"Accepted, and we both know it won't be the last time you lash out at me and vice versa. That's the way of things, but . . . Sean, I know some of the reasons it's hard for you to draw full breaths right now, and you do too." I hesitate briefly, knowing what reception it'll bring, but push it anyway. "You won't even try talking to him?"

"He can call every day for the ink, and I'll answer for that reason, but I'm done with him otherwise." He gives me a pointed stare.

"Don't say it," I warn, "Sean, don't—"

"I wish it was him," he spits. "I do. I wish it would have been him."

"And now you have to *live with that*," I sigh. "Go." I pull my truck keys from my pocket, feeling the weight of his stare. Keeping my eyes averted, I refuse to get drawn any further into his dark, bleak headspace while still battling my own. "Get that envelope and go," I repeat, my anger for his admission evident in my delivery. "I'm here for you no matter what," I add with the grudge I feel, "but do us all a favor and check your shit before approaching anyone for any more face-to-face today."

A few stunted heartbeats later, he mutes whatever words he was summoning and disappears into the garage as I make a beeline for my truck. Turning over the engine, I idle for a few seconds to warm it up and scan the garage, not wanting to be here, either. No matter how much pain it brings me to face my newly doled out future, I'd rather face it with her. So, when Sean fires up and pulls out, I file in behind him, eager to get back to the woman who owns the majority of my heart's real estate, along with the boy who's quickly stealing some of his own.

As I near the orchard, a trail of leaves spills across my

hood and windshield, bringing me back to the memory of a hilltop a year ago. To the day Delphine confessed her love for me—one of the best moments, days of my life. Pressing the gas to hasten my return, I decide to steal our heaven back from all threats. To take the power back from the war looming over us, continually dividing us, and from that doctor's condemning words. From anything threatening to steal any more of the peace we fought so fucking hard to find. It's then I realize that though our time is limited, what happiness we created and the memories we made can't be taken or stolen unless we allow it. As much of a mental fuck as it might be, it's not only possible to keep what we have but to make more peace, more of those memories in abundance, during what seasons remain.

As I eye the heavily veined, light-yellow leaf now plastered to my windshield, I task myself with a new mission to do just that for as long as I'm capable. Mission sorted, by the time my tires cut into the gravel to meet and return the collective smiles through my windshield, I'm no longer faking anything.

Chapter Fifty-Eight

TYLER

Blink. Pulling up the driveway, I revel in the sight of the calming view ahead of me. Of the soft porch light and the lights inside the house beyond the windows. Of the peak of the low-lit fire burning through the glass. Of the plaid blanket folded on the plush couch and the memories it now evokes. Of the trees encompassing the house framing this picture. Of the definition of this vision and place—heaven.

It's when I cut my engine and step outside, hearing a shatter, that my body tenses. Within seconds, I'm inside the door and at the threshold of the kitchen in time to see Delphine hurl another plate at the floor. The force of her anger has it shattering to nothing but splinters as she plucks another dish from the cabinet. It's not the mess around her or the glass piling up, but her expression that guts me as I counter my gun.

"Delphine," I call, but she doesn't hear me, fury and devastation shifting along her gorgeous features as she continues to destroy our dishes one by one before picking up a marble rolling pin and hoisting it up like a bat. I approach her slowly as she swings at the glass canisters, destroying them with one vicious blow, her outraged cry as she does echoing throughout the kitchen as well as my rapidly hemorrhaging heart.

Softly, I repeat her name again and again until she exhausts herself, chest heaving with silent sobs. It's been a month since she was sentenced by the *third* opinion we sought out, and I knew a reckoning was coming at some point. I've felt the restless struggle within her but decided to let it come naturally rather than force it. I've caught many of her lingering looks and returned them with an open-door expression, which she hasn't taken me up on. She's kicking that door wide open now, and while I'm ready, I can't handle the sight of her destroying the one room of the house she loves most. Knowing she'll regret it if she goes any further, I speak up to stop her.

"Please, baby. Please stop," I insert between the next shatter, loud enough for her to hear. This plea has her instantly ceasing before she scours the damage. Upon seeing it, she immediately crumbles before me. When I take a cautious step toward her around some of the debris, she holds up a hand to stop me.

"I hate her!"

"Who?"

Her chin wobbles as she shakes her head. "I hate her so much!"

"Who, Delphine? Who do you hate?"

"The woman . . . who gets to have you after me. The woman who"—her voice cracks—"the woman who deserved you all along. Who will give you children—I hate her!"

My heart splinters as she drops her weapon, which I consider useless compared to her words. "I told you long ago, there's no woman—"

"Oh, *there is*, Tyler, and for you, she'll be fucking exceptional because you are . . . everything any woman could ever want . . . and, and s-she'll be everything I wasn't. That I'm not, and I couldn't be for you. She'll love you better. She'll be far less selfish. Look how selfish I am! Look how selfish I'm being right now!" Her silver eyes pierce me as she palms her chest with both hands as if its beat is physically paining her. "I needed more time to prove myself to you. To deserve you. To convince you. So you will remember, will *know* just how much I . . . love you . . . I'm so in love with you. So in love with you."

My heart cracks at her confession. "Delphine—"

"I wanted to make you feel what you make me feel. I just needed time." She lowers her palms to her stomach as if she's been kicked. "Do you think I deserved you? Never. Never once have I deserved you, but I was going to try to. I was going to try so hard to make all you've sacrificed, all the pain, and your patience for me worth it. But *she* gets to have you. *She* gets to be worthy of you. I just wanted to *deserve* you before I die!"

"You do, Delphine, you do, and I don't want her," I whisper hoarsely.

"You won't be able to help yourself." She bursts into tears with that, and my own eyes sting. "You'll use me as an excuse at first, but you'll love her. You'll love her, and I hate her for that. Please just let me hate her. Just for a minute."

"Come here," I order.

"No, I can't." She palms her chest again as my own batters me. "I can't, this pain, this anger. I was okay with dying because I didn't have . . . you. Merde, damn it, Tyler, damn you, I was ready to die."

"No, you weren't," I state bluntly, "and you're not ready now."

"Why did you do this to me!? Give me the life I dreamed of?"

"Because *I'm selfish*," I admit.

"I'm going to die," she spits bluntly, her eyes not wavering. "You're a romantic fool. That's how this ends, you know, I *die*."

"I know."

"Oh, you know." She slaps at her cheeks, rebuking her tears. "Well, I'm glad you know."

"You're far from dead right now," I challenge. "So, instead of starting on the CorningWare, let's go to bed."

She gapes at me as though I've slapped her. "You care so little about this?"

"Not tonight and not right now."

"So easy for you to say," she counters, "you get to—"

"To what?" I snap back. "I get to live? You aren't that ignorant. I have to bury you while you'll be completely unaware of any of that pain. God or no God, you'll be in a perpetual state of bliss or ignorance while I reject any life without you, fucking forcing myself through every breath. So no, I don't feel sorry for you, Delphine, because you get to die, and you won't be the one left behind. I wish . . . fuck what I wish." I swallow. "I have to fucking survive losing you. I have to live through it, and if I ever do pray to the God you believe in, it'll be that it won't be long-term."

Tears stream down her cheeks at my admission and the fact that she knows I mean every word.

"So no, I have no intention of living the full life I have only imagined with you. That future you're dreaming up for me is fucking fictional and was created out of jealousy, the same jealousy I would have if I was the one dying and I imagined you moving on. But know this—*my future* is being *stolen* right along with yours the minute you leave me."

"That's not what I want for you," she croaks before quickly backpedaling. "You're right. I'm simply jealous. So jealous, but I don't want you to deny yourself. At all, because you're right, I'll be in bliss. I don't want this bleak existence you see for yourself at all, Soldier."

"And I don't want to bury you, but neither of us is getting our way, so instead of fighting with me about what we can't control, let me show you just how alive you still are."

Her expression collapses as she sobs in her hands. Unable to handle another minute of the space between us, I stalk toward her before lifting her from the remains of what was formerly our kitchen and hauling her back toward our bedroom. By the time we reach the door, our mouths are molded together. Blindly, I walk toward the bed as I thrust my tongue into her mouth, and she meets my kiss, just as frenzied.

The second we're undressed, and she's spread beneath me, I bury myself in her wet heat. Her moans fueling me as I fuck her aggressively, pinning her hands beside her head and grinding my length against her clit.

Within minutes, she's tightening around me and crying out through her release. Heart thundering, I fuck her at a frantic pace until she's completely wrung out, her body a trembling mess of aftermath, her skin soaked and covered in afterburn. It's when she whispers my name and palms my face that I slow, throat and nose burning from the fight roaring in my chest.

"Tyler," she whispers urgently, commanding my eyes as I waste myself inside her, fighting her, fighting fate, and fucking away the enemy neither of us can defeat. Her soldier I may be, but I'm useless in defending or protecting her from this. For the first time since we got the news, I allow her to glimpse my grief, coming apart at the seams as I milk every ounce of pleasure from her that I can. Fighting for our peace as I thrust in, again and again, groaning filthy words into her tear-streaked face before licking her salted lips.

Licking my own tears, I dig my fingernails into her while inhaling what I can of her scent, memorizing her, submerging myself fully into her until I'm drenched, drowning, and beyond as grief seizes me whole.

"Tyler," she demands, refusing to back down until I bring my gaze to hers. I slow and still when I see the expression on her face . . . a peaceful resolve and acceptance I've been dreading.

"Don't baby, don't. Please don't," I rasp out. "Keep fighting with me, please."

She digs her heels into my back, refusing me, stilling me while running her hands along my shoulders and down my arms in a soothing motion.

"You brought me back to life," she murmurs, her voice

full of awe as she gazes up at me like I'm the only thing that matters.

"Please don't stop fighting," I cry openly as she shakes her head and gives me a blinding smile.

"It's okay, it's okay now, Soldier, don't you see?"

I shake my head, hearing the agitation and anger in my voice. "See what?"

"We won. We've already won," she declares victoriously.

"No, I don't see," I bite out bitterly. "And I never will. This will never fucking be okay."

"Have faith, my soldier. You will." She lifts and places the gentlest of kisses on my lips. "One day, you will see."

After freeing me, I work us both until we're a heaving mess, our hearts pounding in unison with our cries until we're utterly taxed. After a shower of murmured words and tender kisses I order her to dress.

"For what?" she asks, her eyes half-closed from exhaustion.

"And meet me at the Ranger in ten minutes," I add without answering.

"Why?"

"Because."

"Fine, Soldier. Would you like fries with that order?" she mumbles sarcastically, and I gape at her.

"*Perfect execution*, baby, well done," I compliment with a grin.

"Tyler, I'm tired," she whines. "Do we have to leave?"

"Yes. Nine minutes left now, General Whiney," I chuckle. "Get moving."

Climbing into her Ranger *twenty minutes later*, she turns and glimpses the haul I loaded in the back seat. "We're camping tonight?"

"Possibly," I mutter, "and just so we're clear, you're a nightmare when it comes to presents and surprises." I turn the Ranger over to start it as her voice carries over it.

"I love you, best friend," she drawls out as I turn to see her gazing back at me, a peaceful twinkle in her eyes. "And if I have to kick buckets, then I'm so glad it's with you."

I bite my lip and shake my head just as she shouts, making us both jump. "Bucket, it's 'kick the bucket!'" she corrects herself.

"This is . . . a pretty morbid start," I sigh, "and not how I want this portion of our night to go."

"So what," she states. "Neither of us wants to talk about it, so let's get it all out now and be done with it. I never meant for you to find me like that. I sent Zach away for the night and didn't expect you home so early. But I wasn't expecting to redecorate the kitchen," she whispers mournfully. "Fuck it, I'm glad because it's out there now. I'm sad, you're sad, we're both mad, so let's just say what we feel and truly be done." Her eyes widen with an idea. "But we're going to say it really fast."

"Why fast?" I ask.

"So that we reveal our most brash, most honest thoughts."

"Fine," I concede, "but the minute this Ranger stops, so does the conversation, deal?"

"Deal," she says. I give the Ranger some gas as she speaks up first after a few seconds of the ride. "I'm scared it will hurt, and I don't want to be in pain the *whole time*."

"I'm scared you'll be in pain too, so I'm going to make sure that's not an issue," I counter just as quickly while steering us onto the path.

"I'm scared you won't find faith," she says.

"I'm scared I won't be strong for Zach," I admit.

"I'm not scared about that at all, Tyler. I know you'll be exactly what you're supposed to be for him."

"I'm glad you're so confident," I utter.

"I am." She nudges me as I slow us down, knowing we need to get this out and the trek to our destination is a short one. "This is good, see?"

"I don't share your enthusiasm, but go," I tell her.

"Bury me close to my sister and nephew . . . and don't pick an ugly casket. I'm scared you'll pick an ugly casket."

"Hey, I have good taste," I defend hoarsely, hating this exchange with every fiber of my being. "But I promise I'll buy the most expensive light blue Cadillac-quality casket available," I clip, my eyes stinging.

"Soldier," she whispers, sensing the pain this is causing me, and I shake my head.

"Keep going," I demand. "I'll deal."

"Get him in school," she orders as we roll over a divot in the trail. We decided right away to let Zach skip this semester because of the legalities we haven't gotten to yet and to acclimate him to us to see if it was where this was going. Also, to protect me for serving time, because if I meet Tim right now, I'll kill him. No question in my mind about that.

Along with therapy, and after the holidays, Mom is giving Zach an aptitude test she's securing from a school counselor friend so we can see what we're dealing with. But before we get him back into population, Delphine and I decided we want Zach back in good health, which will give him some needed confidence and some added tools in dealing with the company he's been forced to keep. From what he's told us, he loves school, but his classmates, not so much.

"What else?" I prompt, realizing we both went silent as the headlights beam ahead, lighting up our path, along with the added help of the three-quarter moon blazing above us. A moon I'm thankful for, which helped cement the decision to bring her here tonight—timing everything, especially with us as emotional as we are.

"No internet," she states firmly.

"That's just not possible, baby. It's consuming the world."

"That's a problem. Mark my words, Soldier, it is evil and will cause much destruction."

"Sean would agree with you, but tell me why you think so," I ask, taking a turn and slowing even further—our destination an easy four- to five-minute walk, at most, from the house.

"Because I finally got online when you gave me that stupid smartphone, putting my feelings aside to be objective."

"And?" I prompt.

"And within minutes, I had watched a cat video, a cute baby video, an inspirational video full of beautiful images, before I watched a train crash into a car with people inside it, which killed them. Then I was exposed to another video where a suicidal soldier begged a cop for a hug."

Her point strikes where intended, and I swallow as our eyes meet.

"All of that, that chaos, the beautiful mixed with the tragic, to the depraved, is a deity's view, Tyler. It's a god's view, not meant for us. We are not built for such exposure to things like this, capable of processing so many extremes in such a short time. It's already causing so much harm to young minds, who are now harming themselves. While it is disguised as a good tool, I *feel* it's evil and know it will do great harm."

"How about limited internet, monitored social media?" I barter.

"Limited internet, *no social media* until he's graduated."

"You just caused me hours of fighting with him," I relent.

"I know, but please for me, Soldier. Please. Don't expose him to that. Make him spend some time in the sun every day and form real relationships *in person*."

"You love him," I state as we take one last dip and round the bend of trees, and I stop just short of breaching them.

"You do, too," she says, scanning our path.

"I'm starting to," I admit before she takes a second look around.

"He's special, Tyler, like you. There is far more to him that he is revealing ... hey"—she frowns, realizing the path we're on—"this was blocked before, with many, many large tree limbs."

I flash her a grin. "I know."

"You blocked me?"

"Oui," I spout.

"So, we're camping here?"

"No, we're finishing this conversation here," I state and

turn to her. "I have something to say, but I'm not saying it fast."

"Oh, no"—she licks her lips—"okay. Tell me."

"The reason I'm not showing you my pain is because I decided the day I found out not to mourn you until you're gone. Not to let your illness steal our happiness and peace. I don't know how long I can make it last, but I want to try to hold onto it for as long as possible."

"I agree, Soldier. I agree."

"I was hoping you would, but it's not my decision. We can do this any way you want."

"I want it exactly the way you decided. It's perfect"—she nods for emphasis—"it's the perfect strategy."

"Okay, and one more thing." I swallow. "I know how much you love me, Delphine. I feel it and always have. Even when you fought so hard to conceal it, I felt it." She nods, eyes watering. "Believe me, I know, okay?"

I can see the relief in her eyes as she scours the grounds, and the night noise surrounds us.

"But if you want to suck my cock *exactly like* you did this morning every *day* to prove your love, I will not object to any effort—" She slaps at my chest cutting me short, and we both laugh before I shrug. "You wanted *brash*."

"Ha-ha." She rolls her eyes. "Now, take me to camp," she sighs, and I feel the weight of the conversation start to leave us, even as the ache lingers. When I hit the gas, she clamps my arm. "Last thing," she says, and I sigh and stomp the brakes, knowing I wasn't going to get away with ending the discussion so easily.

"Please don't mourn me. Please let me go when the time comes. I want you to live a full life. You are too young to limit yourself so much. Let me be and remain your first love, Tyler, not your only. Promise me."

"I can't promise that." I shake my head. "I'm sorry. I can't."

She stares at me for a long beat. "Fine, imbecile, but if you can't promise me, then you have to give me one last wish."

"Anything you want," I swear.

"Anything?" she prompts.

"Anything," I repeat with a nod.

"Hmm, then"—she sits back in her seat—"I'll let you know."

"I may have granted that too easily, and now I'm scared," I chuckle, "are we done?"

"Yes . . . no, Ezekiel," she whispers.

"I've got him," I assure, "well, as much as *anyone can* have him." I shake my head with a grin.

"I know." She nods. "I know, Soldier . . . and"—she glances down at her ring—"I want you to know I would have planned the most ridiculous wedding for a forty-one-year-old kissing tramp," she laughs. The vision of her blowing out her candles not even a week ago re-stoking the relentless ache. "I would have embarrassed you, Soldier."

"Do it," I dare. "Embarrass me."

"No, that's a gift I'm giving to your future wife."

"Stop," I grit out, "there is no after you."

"Oh, but there is," she assures with a smile, "have faith, my Soldier." She palms my jaw. "Have faith."

Deciding the conversation is pointless and futile, I pull her reassuring hand from my jaw, kissing it before tethering our fingers and holding them in my lap. Pressing the gas, I steer us around a winding corner of clustered evergreens before pulling to a stop at the foot of the field. Thankful when I see the moon doing my bidding as it casts a surreal glow over the endless acres of wildflowers.

She palms her mouth with both hands at the sight of them, and I gently lower them to take in her expression. Having decided to save the reveal for a night just like this one, where we needed our spirits lifted. A plan seemingly executed as her wide eyes glitter along the expanse of the valley, which is blanketed by every imaginable stem fit for the region. Many of the blooms are already reaching knee height, and the flowers dance and sway with the sweep of the cool breeze filtering through as if summoning us both that it's playtime. Proud of my handiwork, but even more so by the wonder and shock in Delphine's expression, she only furthers the zing in my chest when she turns to me, gasping out her familiar sentiment. "Okay, Soldier, *this is the best night of my life.*"

A deep ache surfaces when, for the first time, I allow her sentiment to pass without my typical rebuttal. "Then it'll be the best night of my life, too."

Briefly, I allow the burn of that defeat to do its thing while turning on the Ranger's radio before rounding it to stand at her door. Hand extended as the soft music croons through the crisp night air, I finally utter the question I've been anticipating asking since I plowed and planted the field last fall. "General, can I have this dance?"

Chapter Fifty-Nine

TYLER

WINTER 2015
Christmas Eve

BLINK.
Palming the tile, streaming hot water pelts my back where I stand beneath the shower head in an attempt to cleanse myself, *body and mind*, of the last few days due to my latest mission. Intent on calming or, at the very least, *muting* all lingering restlessness, even as a flurry of activity takes place down the hall.

Judy Garland croons throughout the house as my mom helps Delphine put up some last-minute decorations to add to the already festive, cozy décor while covertly helping me make sure Delphine doesn't burn the turkey. Not just for our selfish sakes but for her own due to the amount of time she's spent in preparation. Despite her rapidly deteriorating health since Thanksgiving, she's mustered an inhuman, determined amount of energy, transforming our house into a twinkling, glittering haven of comfort.

Her finishing touches include three old-school sock stockings, our names freshly embroidered on them where they're strung alongside our antique-stove fireplace. The stove currently houses a low-lit fire, completing her ideal picture while chasing out any winter chill.

Outside, I can faintly hear Zach enjoying the hell out of his early Christmas present from Delphine, who gifted him the keys and ownership of her Ranger. Though it stung to see her relinquish them and pass on the gift, it was a moment to witness as Zach's eyes lit up, but not on the Ranger, on Delphine. I could see it then—his need to embrace her in some way in gratitude, but even better, his desire to do it, though he's not quite there yet.

It's been a cumulative mix of peaceful and hellacious months, but with Delphine's latest brainchild hatched, as of this morning, we've maimed Miami in a way they aren't going to recover from anytime soon. In fact, I'm certain that any move Miami ponders on making now, they'll be second-guessing, rethinking, and most likely shitting their pants before carrying anything out. In addition, her latest scheme brought a much-needed break for our club and exhausted Ravens.

The brilliant strategy my general came up with derived from an interaction Tobias recounted, in painstaking detail, only once for Delphine and me about what transpired the night Dom died. The exchange between Matteo, Andre, Dom, Tobias, and Cecelia. An exchange in which Delphine had memorized and concocted a revenge plot consisting of the things typical in drawing out the evils of most men—money, greed, and power.

Our temporary solution laying within Andre's own spoken confession of 'things getting a little too light down south.'

In ruminating on that, Delphine decided we should finally share some of our hard-earned wealth in her devised game of tit for tat. To lure in and sprinkle some of our blessings to Miami's most desperate and bloodthirsty bottom feeders. To those who get crumbs of intake from the lion's share—and are treated with the least respect—to do *our bidding*.

And because Miami so effectively fucked with our club's morale in *tit*, she decided we should deliver just as effectively in *tat*. It took a little time, but together, Tobias and I lured in the lowest on Miami's totem pole and offered them a small fortune to flip on their own to deliver some epic payback.

I was wary of the plan at first. However, fifteen of Miami's runners and mistreated gophers flipped on them overnight. Not only giving us intel but taking a few of the raven-inked defective out with our offered added bonus. Ultimately, it turned out to be the best money our club has ever spent. The best part? Tobias and I made calls after boarding our plane home to the personal, private cell phone numbers of those now highest in their ranks while they were in the midst of actively plotting against us.

Once they answered, we were both able to wish them a heartfelt Merry Christmas, our calls ending as Ravens blew holes through their front doors before spreading the rest of our Christmas cheer.

Not only was her tactical plan fucking brilliant, but it ended up in a lot less bloodshed for our Ravens as Miami practically slew themselves. The downside is that when they finally do sum up the nerve and come back for us, we know they'll make it hurt. But this is war, and with blinks of Dom still heavily flashing through my mind and his words in my psyche, regret and remorse will never factor in.

Rinsing off, I step out and grab a towel as my phone rumbles with a message. Checking it for the first time in months without apprehension, I make quick work of dressing before setting off to join the festivities. Pausing my footing at the end of the hall, just a step outside the living room, I spot Mom opening a familiar box and retrieving my cotton ball ornament before presenting it to Delphine.

"I was always going to gift this to him when Tyler made his own family," Mom relays, emotion clear in her voice. "These are yours now."

Delphine bites her lip at the sight of it before she speaks. "Oh, Regina, I appreciate this. But it's clear you have so much pride and mother's love for him, and why you want to rid yourself of it because this is *ugly*." She tosses her head back at Mom's answering frown and laughs, and I join in. Delphine's eyes widen as she turns and sees me, her expression dimming with a little guilt. "I was joking, Sold—"

"Oh, no," I quip, loving that she'll forever remain her brash self in any situation. "You can't take it back now that you're busted"—I stalk toward her—"and I was five when I made that, you *asshole*."

"Five or not, you're going to ruin our beautiful tree when you hang that monstrosity." She extends it toward me, covering her eyes with her free palm. "But I love you enough to suffer if you hang your ugly ornament." Mom laughs at this, staring between me and Delphine, eyes softening at our back and forth as I give as good as I'm getting.

"I never claimed to be Picasso, just like you can't claim to be an Iron Chef." Delphine lowers her palm to glower at me as I wink at Mom. "But if *my mommy* says I'm talented, I believe her."

"You better take that false confidence because I won't be encouraging you to paint or participate in any other artistic endeavor," she jokes before taking more decorations out of Mom's offered box and unwrapping one surrounded by tissue.

"Oops, that's baby's first ornament," Mom says, snatching that one back. "It's a mother's right to keep this one," Mom joins the razzing, darting her eyes between us. "So, let's not make this fight physical because I will," she warns playfully as a knock sounds on the door.

"Uh, oh, we locked Zach out," Delphine says as she walks over with a wince. Opening it, she stiffens in surprise when she sees a Marine dressed to the nines in his blues on the other side.

"You're not Zach," she chuckles as he grins down at her. "Soldier," she calls, glancing back at me. "I think it's for you."

"Actually, Delphine," he replies, "I'm here to see you."

"Me?" she says, glancing back at me in confusion before addressing him again. "Here for me, why? Who are you?"

I can't help but chuckle at her frank candor and reception. He grins down at her before spotting me over her shoulder. I grin back, giving him a shrug and *'good luck, pal'* eyes.

"Well," he chuckles in amusement, and I can tell she's intimidated him a little, which is comical because he's a good foot and half taller and is currently towering over her. "I'm First Sergeant Eric Shultz, and this," he says, extending a neatly pressed jacket to her, "is for you."

"Shultz," she mimics, very familiar with the name. "You are here for me?" she repeats, darting her eyes over her shoulder to me before turning back to him. "I know who you are."

"Likewise, I've been anxious to meet you for some time now, and it's the reason I'm here. Today, I came from Albany, New York, to thank you for saving my life."

The air tenses briefly as he stares down at her, his expression sincere as shock registers in her posture.

"You came from New York? . . . But I-I did no such thing," she argues, though I can hear the effect of his words in her voice. Already armed and ready for her objection, Shultz pulls up his cell phone.

"This is my daughter, Amy, and I almost didn't get to be her father." Delphine takes the phone, stares down at the picture, and studies it for long seconds, which I know she's using to gain her composure.

"She's beautiful," Delphine says.

"She is, and thanks to you, I'm going to help her blow out her fourth birthday candle next week."

"I appreciate you . . . the jacket, really, but—"

"Delphine," Shultz delivers in his no-bullshit tone, "I would have missed her birth, her life, being her father if you wouldn't have trained the man behind you. If you hadn't taken the time to teach him exactly how the hell to get us out of a situation we *should not* have survived. So—"

He takes the jacket and opens it, and Delphine turns, pushing her arms through as he covers her with it. "This is yours because it's what I was wearing when you saved me."

"I—oh, Merci, thank you"—I can see the mist in her eyes as she glances back at me again—"but truly, I did nothing—"

"Well, I'm afraid we don't share your opinion, ma'am," he says, grabbing her hand and squeezing it before releasing it. "So, thank you, Delphine. Truly, thank you."

"Okay, I don't know . . . what," she chuckles nervously, "you are welcome, I guess," she whispers, the rattle in her voice thinly concealed as she pauses. "Wait, *we*?"

"Yes, ma'am," he says, stepping back and opening the door wide just as Mom takes her cue and clicks on the porch light. Delphine gasps as she scans the row of uniformed soldiers in varying branches of the military lined in our front yard.

"Mon Dieu," *My God*, she croaks before turning back to me, instant tears shimmering in her eyes. "Soldier, what is this?"

"This is a long overdue and much deserved thank you," Shultz replies for me. "Merry Christmas, Delphine," he says before turning and stalking off the porch, passing Ramirez as he steps up, lifting his chin toward me in greeting before his eyes glitter down on her.

"Hi Delphine, I'm—"

"Ramirez," she whispers, her voice full of incredulity just as Zach enters the back door.

"Hey, what's going on out—oh," he says, as I hold up a hand and usher him toward me with the wave of my fingers. A second later, Zach joins me at my side as Ramirez voices his own gratitude while Delphine rattles in shock at the front door.

"Watch this, buddy," I say, careful not to nudge Zach the way I'm naturally inclined to.

"They're all here for her?" he whispers.

"I think the better way to put it would be—they're *still here because* of her."

"She saved them all?" He gawks, and I nod before nodding toward the exchange at the front door.

". . . ten-year veteran, husband of fifteen, and father of

Severed Heart

five who also thanks you for bringing their father home—but my wife especially because, well—" Ramirez bulges his eyes—"*five children.*"

We all laugh as, one by one, my buddies begin to pay homage to the soldier whose endless efforts to educate and mentor me played a major role in getting us all home.

"Merry Christmas, General," he tells her, and I can see her physically start to shake as they continue to come, one by one, showering her with tokens of thanks and praise.

McCormick delivers his thanks next, his words visibly affecting her before he nods to me just after in greeting. "Merry Christmas, brother."

"Merry Christmas, man," I call back before he turns and heads off the porch.

When Delphine palms her face, overwhelmed, a "Mon Dieu" leaving her in a rush in McCormick's wake, I join her. Cradling her in my arms, pride fills me as she finally gets the well-deserved props.

"What have you done, Soldier?" she whispers, utterly shaken, as I hold her steady while they continue to address her one by one, as the others patiently wait for their turn. Fully shaken when one of them gifts her his Purple Heart, which she tried to refuse. Battle lost, the ribbon now hangs from one of the lapels of the jacket, swallowing her. Each takes their time, giving her detailed testaments of how they escaped with their lives by carrying out my orders. Her orders.

"Tyler," Delphine croaks, becoming increasingly overwhelmed as they continue to approach her, all of them in their best dress to honor the woman who saved them. Pride thrums through me that not one of them made an excuse and showed up for her. Mom beams equally with pride, her eyes continually watering as Zach inches closer, just as affected, hanging onto their every word. The last to step up is a mid-forties man with a ruddy complexion and a shitty disposition, who manages a smile for Delphine as she greets him by name.

"You are Phillip," she declares, and he nods and extends his hand, and she takes it.

"It's nice to finally meet you, General." He gives her a wink after using her pet name. "I came to personally thank you for building the soldier capable of saving my sister's son. My nephew is the closest to a son I'll ever have, and if it weren't for you, for Tyler, he wouldn't be home tonight spending Christmas with his fiancée. So, thank you sincerely, Delphine. And . . . if you ever find yourself bored and need a way to pass the time, get my number from him," he says, only half joking. "I'd love to pick your brain and—"

"Don't push it," I mutter before we share a smile. "Thanks for coming."

Phillip steps off the porch just as Shultz rings out a "Company, attennn-*tion*!"

In an instant, a collective snap of boots sounds. Releasing Delphine, I round her before walking down the step, doing an about-face and snapping my own boots as Ramirez cracks a joke. "Where are your blues, asshole?"

My grin wiped clean as Shultz sounds out a second later.

"Company, join me in wishing the general a very Merry Christmas!"

"We wish you a very Merry Christmas, General!" we shout in unison as Mom snaps a dozen photos and Zach stands back in shock.

"Company, salute!" Shultz shouts as we all snap our hands to our brows, and tears flow over Delphine's cheeks as she soaks us all in, one by one, before Shultz breaks us up with a final order. "Company . . . dismissed! . . . And *Merry Christmas, fuckers!*"

Delphine crashes into my mom's waiting arms as I razz her from where I stand at the foot of the porch. "You're embarrassing me," I taunt as she buries her head in Mom's chest while flipping me the bird.

A second later, my view of her is blocked before I'm surrounded by some of my old company and GRS team. We spend a few minutes greeting one another, as I thank every one of them individually. Not long after, they all start to pile into vans and trucks they used to carpool here in an attempt to keep their cover and approach the house undetected.

Exhaling a contented sigh of relief as the last car speeds off, happy with how it went down, I turn back toward the house to see Mom and Zach have made themselves scarce while my newly and highly decorated general waits for me on the porch. Tears continue spilling down her cheeks as I walk up the step, and she stalks toward me, gripping me to her before burying her head in my chest. "You . . ." Her voice is hoarse as she speaks. ". . . just . . . can this be the second-best night of my life, Soldier?" she whispers.

"It can be whatever you want it to be. Merry Christmas, General."

"I can't believe this. I have no words . . . no words. Tyler, how did you do this?"

She stares up at me with splotched cheeks, wearing a priceless smile, and I could tell her that her expression alone is why I did it. Instead, I give her the second reason. "Because no matter how many times I tried to tell you that you saved us, you refused to believe me. I had an argument to win, so I guess the question is . . . do you believe me *now*?"

***

Locking up the house later that night, I look out the front door to see Zach standing in the middle of the yard and frown. He'd wished us both a good night an hour ago and disappeared into his room. Delphine and I have been wrapping presents for him in our bedroom since. Stepping out, Zach tenses when he hears the creak of the door. It's then I see his chest bouncing involuntarily as his hand flies to his face. Heart aching at the knowledge he's crying, I give him his personal space as I speak at his back. "We can talk about it, about anything, and I'll be straight with you, I promise."

Silence ensues, and I know it's because he's gathering

himself. I scan the orchard, the night moonless but star-littered, the porch light illuminating the frost on the ground. Thankful it's been a mild winter, I remain patiently in wait until he finally speaks.

"She's really going to die," he croaks. "She looks okay... I mean, she's getting weak and is starting to look... but she seems okay."

"She is okay tonight. She is, Zach. She's not in any pain right now."

"She's hiding it so well," he whispers.

"So are you," I tell him. "And I wish you wouldn't, if I'm honest."

"You don't think you're dealing with enough?" He looks back to me then, and I hold his eyes, studying what I can of him under the dim porch light.

"I'm dealing with what I chose to, and that includes whatever you want to give me." I take a step toward him. "You know, she never wanted to be a mother, ever. But if she could, she would take on that role for you, Zach. Since minute one, she's wanted to. And she loves you"—his back bounces as I admit that—"and I know because she's preparing you the exact same way she prepared me when I was a few years older than you. That's how she loves."

"I got her a stupid present," he croaks. "It's so stupid. I wish I had gotten her a better present. And I won't ever get to give her a better one."

"She'll love whatever it is. I promise you she will. She gets so damned excited about the littlest things."

He turns back to me, a laugh on his lips. "She does, doesn't she?" He chuckles. "I said 'mater sandwiches' the other day, and I think she peed her pants laughing. She ran out of the room."

I wince as urinary incontinence is a sign that her body is starting to fail her, but if she had to have that embarrassing moment, I'm glad it was laughter that caused it. This I keep to myself. "It's getting pretty cold out here, buddy. Do you want to go inside and talk for a little while?"

"I don't want her to know I'm upset," he sniffs. "She worked so hard to make this Christmas perfect for us. I don't want to ruin it."

"It is perfect. You're not ruining anything. Nothing will or could ruin it, mark my words." The instant I release that declaration, a French shrill sounds from the house and fills the yard.

"MERDE! PUTAIN! MY FUCKING YAMS ARE BURNT! DAMN IT, TYLER! I TOLD YOU TO TELL ME WHEN IT WAS FORTY-FIVE MINUTES!"

Zach and I hit the ground, laughter erupting from both of us as more shrieks ring out.

"ALL FUCKING DAY I WAIT TO COOK THESE LAST SO NOTHING GETS BURNED... THEY ARE POTATOES... HOW DO THEY BURN?... I HEAR YOU LAUGHING AT ME, ASSHOLES!"

Chapter Sixty

Tyler

SPRING 2016

BLINK. Zach tightens the bolt as I watch on, pride filling me for his progress, even as the gnaw that's been tugging at me since we left for King's this morning threatens to again set in. The two of us ordered to march by our general, thrust away from her bedside after pancakes, and her insistence we get 'sun on our faces.' A sun which remains concealed under the blanket of clouds hovering over the garage outside of the bay.

Batting down the unease that's been threatening since we left her, my solace is found in Zach's answering grin when I commend him, knowing he finds the same satisfaction in fixing things the way I do. Another commonality we've been bonding over recently while doing maintenance on the equipment at the farm. This spring fighting for every bloom as winter temperatures continue to linger. Over the long, cold season, and as Delphine started to take more frequent, lengthy naps, I taught him the ins and outs of hunting, which also had us gravitating more toward each other.

Though his grins have become scarcer in recent months. Fewer and far between, as have mine *because of* said nap frequency while Delphine began to dissolve before our collective eyes. Every smile between us now hard-won while rewarding in its own right. The kid I collided with months ago in this garage vastly different now in demeanor and appearance than the one I'm stealing glances of this morning. A kid who speaks so little, yet knows so much, as I marvel at the changes in him, and the knowledge Delphine was right.

Zach is a genius.

According to his first staggering aptitude test results, as well as his fifth—which annoyed him—he's got the potential of becoming a Rhodes Scholar and beyond. Not that we ever doubted his intelligence, it was just the opposite, and it's now confirmed.

Delphine had known he was special, that he had potential we probably hadn't realized, but he'd tested off the charts. For weeks now, I've been pondering big decisions when it comes to him. Along with having lengthy conversations with Delphine about how to move forward in raising him. Daily, I'm becoming more impatient to start the conversation I've been mulling over, while growing more eager to pose the question.

"Are you happy living at the orchard, Zach?" I blurt outright, while marveling over the truth that some things work out for the better—no matter where they stemmed from. Or how they *might* work out if Zach agrees to claim the place Delphine and I have made in our home and our hearts. Now unable to imagine what these past months would have been like without him. The idea of finally having *the* talk staving off the gnaw that's trying to sneak its way back in.

Pausing the tool, he looks over to me for motive to see my inquiry is genuine before releasing an easy reply. "Yeah, I am. Your family is awesome. I love Barrett and Charlie, but Jasper and Jessie are a trip," he laughs.

It's your family too, if you'll have us.

But instead of voicing my thought, I keep it light. "I'm

ashamed to admit I don't know my younger cousins very well," I tell him honestly.

"Because you never come to the Sunday baseball games," he reminds me.

I nod. "I'll make it a point to come to the next one."

"They would love it. They ask about you all the time."

"It's crazy that you know my family better than I do." I grin. "But I'm glad you know that—" The premonition takes over mid-sentence, the gnawing crashing over me in a tidal wave a nanosecond before my cell phone buzzes in my pocket. Or maybe it's simultaneous. Either way and without looking to see who's calling, I identify the gnawing. Knowing it to be a certainty because I feel it in every fiber of my being now—*she's leaving me.*

She's leaving me.

"Tyler, what's up man? Tyler," Russell sounds, jarring me from the darkness shrouding my vision as Zach's eyes dart to mine.

"Fuck." I lower my eyes to my watch to buy time, summoning the expertise of the liar within for my biggest trial yet. "I just forgot I had to pick up that part from Spellman's by ten this morning. Shit. Russell, can you take me? I'm going to let Zach stay back and work on my truck."

Reading into my lie instantly, Russell pulls out his keys, an easy "sure" leaving him as Jeremy, standing a bay over, speaks up, following as well. "I've got him, bro," he assures, giving nothing away as I glance back at Zach.

"You good for twenty?"

Zach nods, his eyes lingering too fucking long as I will myself the strength to pull this off, keeping my steps measured as Russell and I stalk toward the parking lot. It's when the reality of what's happening registers a mere step outside of the garage—the truth of it far too debilitating—that I trip up, stumbling between strides.

She's leaving me.

Russell catches my slip instantly, hoisting me against him. A heartbeat later, Zach speaks up with a "Can I come?"

"Next time," I call out from Russell's passenger door before I snap it closed, managing to clip out my order. "Get me home."

Within a blink, Russell is whipping us out of the parking lot and has us idling roadside. As a car passes, blocking our quick exit, my eyes dart to Russell's rearview—to the kid now running towards us before Russell stomps on the gas, turning in the direction of the orchard. As we take off, Zach's shouts and pleas seep through the passenger glass, and straight into my seizing heart.

"I'm sorry," I whisper to his reflection, "I'm so sorry," I choke out as Zach piles his hands on his head, face twisted in anguish. Knowing he feels betrayed, I try to make peace with our future fallout, to protect him from one of life's biggest cruelties. To keep his last memory of her as one of us departing her room, smiling as she shooed us away, her own attempt to protect us both. That truth setting in as Russell races me toward the orchard. Toward home. A home that's disappearing as the seconds tick by and a mental image of our front door shutters in, as do dozens of images of her on either side of it. Of the first time she raced to it with the key in hand. As she grinned over at me while lining the kitchen shelves with paper. Of her meeting me at the tractor with tea. Of the two of us bundled on the porch swing to watch the sunset last night, squeezing one another's hands tightly—knowing. Knowing today was coming. All those memories reflecting in eyes of silver, in the call of my name. The call of home. One I can hear so clearly now.

"*Soldier,*" she summons, finding me as she always does in the dark.

"I'm on my way," I whisper back. "Please don't go."

"*Soldiers don't stay,*" I hear eighteen-year-old me echo back through to the first time I asked her to wait—just as she asked me to stay.

"Tyler," Russell says in a steady voice, "talk to me."

"Delphine's about to die," I deliver point-blank to both of us.

"How do you know?"

"I just do, please," I croak, "get me home."

"Jesus, man, I'm so—"

Shaking my head adamantly to cut off any condolences, I issue my first order. "Call Tobias and Dom—" I cut my words as he stares over at me, realizing just how far I've already slipped as agony lances through me. I'm already traveling to the place the sensible me can't reach. Dom's not here to call. He's not here. Dom's gone too. Everything feels gone . . . feels wrong. She's dying. She's leaving me.

Go.

GO.

GO!

Russell's words filter in from somewhere in a faraway place. In response, I grip the handle of his door and clip out my order. "Repeat that."

"I'll call Tobias . . ."

"*Soldier,*" Delphine summons.

". . . hold everything down. Don't give it a second thought," Russell assures. "Don't lose a second worrying about us, brother."

I nod as a tidal wave of awareness crashes into me. The next time I see Russell, she'll be gone. The next time I drive my truck, she'll be gone. Everything will change. Everything has already changed.

Darkness threatens to engulf me, but I order its release just as quickly, refuting its ability to claim me. It's Russell's curse before he barks my name that brings me somewhat back to. His words becoming more muffled as my ears thunder, filling with my pulsing heartbeat. Spinning, I'm fucking spinning out, and she needs me. As I fight to keep myself upright in my seat, Russell presses his palm into my chest. "Tyler, you good? You just blacked out, man."

"Get me to her," I beg, "please," I add, knowing I need

to gather myself to be there for her, for Zach, but I can feel my ability to balance has already left me.

"Tyler!" Russell shouts as I blank out again, feeling myself sink in the seat. In the next second I'm focused on the asphalt we're consuming as Russell races us toward the orchard, somehow already engaged in a phone call. I pull my own cell out of my pocket, unsure if I want to know if she's already gone. Utterly helpless, darkness again threatens to cloud my vision as my psyche begs me to allow it in. To blink myself out of the state I'm in. I kissed her before I left. Told her I loved her. Palmed her head and whispered my fingers over her crown. Did she feel it? Did she feel my love? Would what I left her with be enough? My chest rages with the answer as I speak to her God.

Please, please don't take her yet. Let me say goodbye. It's my one ask. One. If you're there, this is all I'll ever ask of you.

"Peter, listen to me," Russell rattles off as my own cell rings in my hand. *Sheila*, her hospice nurse's name appearing on screen. Whatever words she has for me having the power to dismantle me within the length they're spoken. I can still feel her. She can't be gone. She can't be.

"*Soldier,*" I hear her call as if she's right next to me.

"I'm coming," I whisper back.

I stare at the phone as it rings in my hand and swipe as the seconds start to tick by, reminding God of my one request.

Please, God, just this one thing.

"Sheila," I whisper.

"Tyler, she's fading—"

Thank you.

"How long?" I ask.

"Within the hour, maybe less," she replies.

Fighting the urge to yell at her for not alerting me sooner, I knew the risk in leaving this morning. Of complications that can arise in the final days. The touch and go.

I was always going to lose her. I haven't slept in days because of that knowledge. The idea of sleep beckons me, and selfishly I allow that fatigue in. Maybe if I let it take me under, this pain will subside, and my heart will give out. Or maybe life will be merciful enough to complicate that sleep so I can go with her. Knowing that mercy isn't an option, I lift my phone and manage to catch some of Sheila's words.

"... Tobias just arrived."

He must have been close or going to see her. He's been haunting our house for months. Haunting because he drifts in, stays mere minutes, and drifts right back out. As if he can't handle anything more. As much as I know it hurts Delphine to see him in that state, it would have hurt her more without his ghost visits.

I stare out the window as the trees blur, and flinch when I see snow flurries start to drift toward me as my one ask backfires.

"Don't you fucking dare," I snap at the clouds, at her God, "don't you dare do this to her," I say as Russell jerks his head in my direction.

"What? What is it, brother?"

"Pardon?" Sheila asks.

I shake my head, the story too long to tell. Her life story. She's lived so much life, a lot of it I've been witness to, but not enough.

"She's only forty-one," I whisper, lowering the phone. "She's only forty-one," I release in exhale, disbelieving that's the truth of it. That I came into her life when she'd already lived half of it.

"I'm so fucking sorry," Russell emits low, and I know it's my state that's making him emotional. None of the birds really know her. They don't know how incredible she is, or of her true nature. Most of them only glimpsing the formidable alcoholic she was. Which was only a mask and shield she held in place—that she fought to hold. But my life with her, my whole relationship with her took place behind both. It's as I reflect on that truth that Tobias's words from our conversation drift back to me.

"Do we ever really know people?"

We do, the people we truly love and memorize, and God, how I memorized her.

"Russell," I prompt, my unspoken request immediately answered as he floors the gas, using every bit of horsepower beneath his hood to get me to her. It's then I realize I'm still on the phone, the seconds ticking by as Sheila patiently waits. Inside these seconds, I find life irrevocably cruel to take her this way, on this day. A day without the sun she so loves while hoping she hasn't seen the snow. She'll think of Matis. I don't want her mind there when she takes her last breath. Her final thoughts to be on the man who started the slow break of her heart, only for me to do everything to try and seal it, to mend it, to soothe it.

She's finally whole, she's finally . . .

"Sheila, close her drapes right now, do you hear me? Close them. Don't let her see it's snowing." This year, winter was charitable, only granting us a few inches that didn't stick. While it snowed, I kept her in our bedroom to watch a Star Wars marathon.

"She's not very cognizant—"

"Close them," I snap, more determined than ever to protect her from it. "Sheila, it's important," I beg. "Please."

"Already done," she assures.

A weak French curse sounds, and I'm slapped back into reality by her voice, remembering my promise not to mourn her until she's gone and she's still here. She's still here. "Please put the phone to her ear."

"Doing it now."

"Soldier," Delphine utters weakly. "I am okay."

"Hey baby," I croak, hearing the gutting taking place inside of me. "Can you try," I utter, "t-to wait for me?" My eyes burn as I try to hold in the ache that wants to leave me. While also silencing any condemnation for her order to take Zach out of the house this morning. An order to leave her side. Because she knew, of course she knew. But I don't dare condemn her for it. If I could protect her from this, I would. And I've just done it to Zach, who will probably never forgive me. Staving that down to concentrate on the precious seconds remaining, I speak what I can manage. "If you can't wait," I release in a pained exhale, "it's okay, baby. It's okay."

An empathy-fueled grunt sounds from next to me as Russell torpedoes us through the backroads. His effort feeling futile because we're too far out. We're still too fucking far out.

"You did so good, General," I relay as my heart starts to hemorrhage, "do you hear me? You fought so well. You made us safe again. We're all home now because of you, and sleeping more soundly. You're the reason we're okay. All your strategies paid off."

Russell's head snaps toward me because, to this day, my birds, her birds, and army know very little of her involvement. Of who their true leader was and is. Because she's always been an unsung hero in her story and never wanted the credit, only the journey of a soldier.

"Through you, I fulfilled my dreams," she proclaims, "and I will wait, Soldier, as long as you promise me something in return."

"*Anything*," I manage through the burn in my throat.

"Ne me pleure pas. Promis moi. Do not mourn me so long it hurts you, Tyler. Steal your life back the first chance you get. Win again. And when you find her, or when she finds you, let yourself love her as you loved me. Live as both *man and my soldier*. Win again."

"Are you in pain?"

"Promise me you'll try," she insists.

"I can't," I counter brokenly, as my heart starts to muddle its beat, utterly confused in rhythm.

"Please try," she urges softly. "You are so young."

"You are my forever," I declare, knowing this is our last fight and one I can't let her win, and I fucking hate myself for it. But I feel its truth to my core. No woman will ever be able to match her. It's pointless to conceive of it.

"You haven't seen it yet. But you will. That is why I'm okay to go."

"Are you... in pain?" I rasp out, unable to mask my own.

"Not bad, Soldier," she assures. "I promise."

"Okay. Give the phone to Sheila."

When Sheila comes on the line, I don't bother with anything other than my order as precious seconds tick by. "Give her as much as she can handle while keeping her as cognizant as possible."

"I'll administer now."

"Thank you. Please put her back on the phone."

A few seconds pass as I try to find worthy words for the woman on the other end of the line, and miraculously, they begin pouring out of me.

"I first took notice of you at fourteen. I'd be lying if I said I didn't recognize how beautiful you were. But in my eyes, you were just another parent. Someone's mom—" I crack briefly but muster the strength, refusing the hurt to deny me any confession.

"The way you spoke. Jesus, you did not mince words. At times, it was ruthless, but it was addictive hearing the truth from someone who voiced it so often—in every conversation. I respected you so much for it. Because it's so fucking brave. You were no saint, but I could tell you were trying with Dom. After so many failed attempts, I couldn't figure out why you kept trying so hard—until one day, it dawned on me. I realized that *your normal* wasn't your normal at all. I don't know when I finally grasped it, but I understood that you hadn't been yourself *in years*." I grip the passenger handle as Russell takes a dicey turn before rocketing us forward.

"Somehow I *knew* the woman I originally met wasn't exactly you. It wasn't your beauty that day, but a shift. It was like seeing the sun for the first time. It was too bright to get a clear view of. That was what my first look at you was, getting a glimpse of the sun. I know now that I met the true you the day I wandered into your house, and you taught me how to breathe through my anger and pain . . . but fuck, baby." I swallow. "When I finally did get my first real look at you, God, did I fucking ever lose myself in those seconds. And that's what it was like staring at you *after*, what if *felt* like. Looking at something you're not supposed to gaze upon for too long, something you're not allowed to have. And fuck, how it hurt, but I just kept looking, kept falling. Your beauty overwhelmed me, though you tried so fucking hard to conceal it, so hard. But it was the day you wore that sundress and brought home those plants that you stole my forever."

"I remember that day," she rasps. "You were walking up the driveway. Tyler, I *felt it*."

"When you looked up and smiled at me, I lost all the fight I had left. We'd been spending so much time together, but *that day*, in that moment, I knew I was just fucking done. Done searching the faces of any girl for what I had already found with you. Done searching for someone to share my thoughts with, my pain with. My heart had already decided, and though my mind fought me, that war was long over. You'd already captured me utterly because of who you were. With the playful glint in your eyes. I hung on every word you spoke. And when Dom dismissed your efforts that day without a thought, and didn't spare you, I watched as your expression went bleak. *Felt* your defeat before you drank right from the bottle. As you did, I *saw* you miss *her*. The girl you were, the girl you were trying so hard to get back to. The girl who smiled at me in the driveway. It broke something in me that no one noticed your struggle, but baby, I did. Though I was enchanted, I respected you so much for fighting so hard to get back to her."

Silence.

"Baby, you there?"

"I'm here," she exhales in a shaky rush.

"From then on, you fascinated me. I couldn't take my

eyes off you. I couldn't understand how a creature so beautiful was so angry and defeated, but I never really pitied you. I rooted for you. I can honestly claim that because I fucking *knew* you were fighting to get back to *yourself*, even then. To become the woman you revealed to me, the woman I fell for, the woman you are now. It's been a long, long battle for you, baby. Such a long road." I crack a little as a sob bursts from her mouth. "But you have existed as that woman since the day I walked back into your house." I swallow. "You need to know, Delphine, that building a true home with you, being with you as that woman, has given me the happiest months of my life. We've had years together combined, and I'm going to spend the rest of my days thankful for every sunset we had. You were worth waiting for. You were so worth waiting for. So fucking worth it" — my voice cracks — "so worth it."

"I never thought I would know happiness, but I'm taking so many good days with me. Thank you for seeing me, Tyler."

"Don't thank me, baby, just wait for me *there*," I croak. "I'll meet you. We'll be together in your place. I'll try so hard to have faith . . . I'll try so hard, I promise."

"How . . . far are you?" she whispers.

Fuck. Fuck. Fuck.

She's fading and fighting her hardest. "I'm with you. Do you feel me? I'm already with you."

"I feel you," she murmurs.

"Are you scared?" I choke out.

"Non. Nothing to be afraid of," she utters instantly.

"Because you're a true soldier. Always have been. Fearless," I murmur. "I'm sorry—" My voice cracks on every word, and I hate the fact that Russell can hear every one of them as I turn away from him. "I'm so sorry I'm not there. I shouldn't have left."

"Hang in," Russell utters in assurance as he guns us down a straightaway before Delphine sounds over the line.

"I watched you leave, Soldier," she relays, as if each word is hard-won, "the day you left for Paris Island."

"What?" Shock filters in, and my heart stutters in response.

"I followed Dom that morning . . . because I knew you were leaving. I watched you toss your pack over your shoulder. You paused, but you didn't look back." Her voice is barely audible now, and I can feel her fighting for every word. "I came to tell you . . . I don't know what I would have said. Maybe 'I'm sorry,' maybe that I would wait, but I was there."

"You were," I rasp out. "You were there?"

"Oui. Because I believed you. I saw you, too. As the man you are now. The man I love. Maybe that is what I would have told you . . . I saw you too, Tyler, and always have."

Implosion.

It's the only way to describe it, and it happens so suddenly I can't catch myself. I feel the weight of Russell's stare as I grunt through the pain.

"Tyler?"

"I'm here, baby. Please try to hold on. I want to look into your eyes."

"I will wait."

Six of the most excruciating minutes of my life later, I fling myself out of Russell's Mustang before it comes to a stop. Passing Tobias on the porch, I fly straight through the front door. A heartbeat later, I'm standing at the threshold of our bedroom, white-knuckling the phone still at my ear.

Terrified because she stopped speaking in the last few minutes, I take a step in as Sheila eyes me with trepidation. She's seen this time and time again, the loss. Grieving families pouring out their goodbyes. To her, I'm just another widower. Probably no more memorable than the last.

Walking over to where Delphine lies, I lift her into my arms along with the patched quilt covering her and cradle her to me as Sheila hands me the IV bag attached to her arm. Too terrified to look down, Delphine remains utterly limp in my arms as I walk her out of the door, past Russell and Tobias who give me a wide berth, both their heads cast down. Stalking past a blur of approaching people—one I make out as Barrett—I head straight to the pasture filled with our wildflowers, which, to my surprise, have already bloomed. The colorful flowers vivid in contrast to the gray sky as snow begins to pour out of it.

Once on the ground, the flurries start to coat us both as I glimpse the surrounding hillsides. Oddly, the land has never been more beautiful to me. Surrounded by a strange sense of peace, I brave whatever fate awaits as I finally look down to gaze upon her face.

"You waited," I gasp out in relief at seeing her silver eyes open. The look inside them taking my breath away.

Love, so much fucking love.

Knowing she no longer has the strength to speak, I lock our gazes, willing my own devotion through. Hoping she can see it even as my vision blurs, and I blink to clear it, not wanting to miss a second as I explain myself.

"It's snowing, and I didn't want you to miss it. I didn't want you to miss it because I wanted the last thing you see to be the man who loves you more than any selfish need, more than himself, more than life, and take that with you as the absolute truth," I say in hopes to finally mend the start of the slow break Matis started all those years ago. In hope of replacing all other visions she's had of the pain-filled precipitation with one of the man who loves her with everything he has. Who never broke a single promise to her, abused her love, or took it for granted. To replace the images that have haunted her for so much of her life with the man who loved her as she hoped. To mend that hurt once and for all.

Despite my fear of not making it in time, she doesn't fade away quickly or peacefully. She struggles for breath several times as I grip her tightly to me, talking her through it the best I can, doing my best to maintain and be the strength she needs during her very last fight. She keeps my eyes the whole time, every second, trusting me wholly to help her through it as I try to soothe any discomfort. Each unmerciful bout breaking me a little more until she stops struggling altogether.

Agonizing minutes later, as the snow-coated wildflowers whisper on the breeze around us, unexplainably, I *feel* her start to slip away. Grunting through the most painful moment of my life, I summon the last of my strength to say the words she deserves.

"I loved you through space and time before, and I'll do it again. I'll do it again. I'm with you, I'm with you, always," I croak in promise. As her last breath leaves her, I bend to whisper in her ear. "Forever," I murmur, her weight sinking further into me as she departs.

Agony rips through me when I pull back to see the telling, faraway look in her glazed eyes, my apology coming out in a rush for the one thing I couldn't protect her from. "I'm sorry," I cry as our war ends, and the illness that consumed her claims its victory. "I'm so sorry."

Years of images start to cloud my vision as I clutch her to me. Images of her, of us, and of our short time in heaven. Reliving every blink as they come, I take precious inventory because I'll never be granted another to add to them. It's in living that knowledge that I break.

A roar of outrage erupts from me, echoing along the hillsides as my heart cracks clear in half without an ounce of fight. No slow shatter, or slow splintering, nor resistance. As my heart starts to clang with its new beat, my front door closes and begins to dissolve before it disappears entirely, once again leaving me a homeless soldier.

Chapter Sixty-One

Tyler

Funeral-appropriate, morbid, and bitter thoughts circulate through my mind as I stare at the light blue casket surrounded by hallowed ground. Knowing there's only darkness beneath the box, I resist the urge to collect her body from within it, even if it's no longer hosting her. Despite that, I fucking loathe the thought of leaving her in a hole. Of some stranger that doesn't know her worth tossing dirt on a body that, just weeks ago, I worshipped. A body which contained the spirit, heart, and brilliant mind of a woman I'll go to my own death loving.

I don't want her here. I don't want her last home to be a dark place without a trace of light. I don't want any of this.

But life has a sick fucking way of ignoring those wants. I decide then that when I separate from my own body, and if my soul resides elsewhere, I want no trace of my remains anywhere for anyone to visit.

Though it may be a selfish decision, when I perish from this earth, I want *memories* to be where I reside in the minds and hearts of those who knew me, without a trace of the host to be found. I follow that line of thinking into a darker place as the crowd begins to disperse.

It's then I also understand that funerals really and truly are for the living, and am only aggravated as I'm approached with apology after apology. Condolences by people who are probably thinking to themselves that one day, I'll heal. That one day, I'll live again. But how can I? She's not here.

"I'm so sorry for your loss."

The ricocheting condolence doled out by so many has me screaming inside. Screaming with my unvoiced reply. *It's not my loss. It's everyone's fucking loss!*

The saying grates on me like no other because it's a bullshit acknowledgment. A polite pass-off. The person still breathing, saying those words, is forgetting about the person they're giving condolences to in the next breath, their next blink, while your entire life stutters in their wake. Forever altered by all the collective breaths in their life path. The in-passing, parting remark more demeaning than any other I can think of when half your fucking soul is torn from you. Spit out in routine by those who just want to say the right thing, to seem sincere, but they don't fucking know it's not just my loss, it's theirs too. Even if corrected, they will never truly know the gravity and weight of that person's life and what they sacrificed for them.

Just like my fallen military brothers who get a day or two of recognition per calendar year but lived every day of their fucking lives for others who are *"sorry for your loss."*

The woman I loved shaped soldiers of her own, soldiers who will save countless lives for generations to come.

Her loss is not just my loss. She's everyone's loss. The world's loss. Just like Dom's is, and I won't let the world forget them. I won't let the world be sorry for *my loss*. I'll make sure they're *sorry for theirs*.

One day, I'll find a way to make it known exactly what two souls helped shape the fate of our country.

Someday, somehow, I'll find a fucking way.

Faintly acknowledging the long hug and damp tears my mother stains my jaw with and the prolonged palm of my father's hand on my shoulder, one by one, they file up to me. All ready with an offered hug, or a handshake. All of my birds there in support, their own words muted by the clanging in my chest. Their muddled condolences and lingering stares following my every move, save one... Not long after the cars turn over, I finally sense his presence behind me.

He doesn't say a word but just stands a few feet to my side, a silent support despite his own extended absence. Truthfully, it feels like his soul departed the day we laid his brother to rest a few feet over. Maybe he's wordless because he already resides in the same wasteland I've just gained entrance to. The land of broken heartbeats and lost dreams. The land of unconscionable pain.

Resigned to the fate and path of a loveless man, I tear my gaze away from the place I know my beloved isn't. She's more present in that field of wildflowers than she'll ever be here. She'll never be here, and therefore, I have no reason to be.

"I don't know which of us has it worse," I finally say to Tobias, my fury quickly rising to the surface. "You because Cecelia still breathes, or me because Delphine wasn't granted that privilege." I toss the handful of wildflowers I picked from our field onto her casket and, with one last lingering look, begin to walk toward my truck.

She's not here, she's not in that hallowed ground, keep walking, Soldier.

Her host betrayed her, and I have no use for a place she doesn't exist.

She's not here. I could search the entirety of this earth, and I won't find her. That's death.

"Tyler," Tobias barks on my heels, a one-eighty from the last funeral we attended where I was on his heels to keep him from fleeing to Cecelia. When I buried another of the closest people to me. Not even a year. I couldn't even get a fucking year between them thanks to this unmerciful fucking life.

The life of a soldier, Jennings, keep walking.

"You won't be alone tonight," he says in more order than request, which only pisses me off more.

"That's not your decision, but no, I won't."

"I don't want to fight," he rasps from beside me, "please brother, let's not fight."

"Yeah, well, *I'm sorry for your loss*, but I don't give a fuck about what you want," I snap.

"Tyler, stop," T utters in a pathetic order. One I don't follow.

"I've got somewhere to be," I lie as Zach meets my eyes from where he waits for me at the hood of my truck. He stayed at the back of the crowd purposefully because he didn't want condolences. He's too raw for that right now. I didn't want so much distance between us during the funeral, but I respected it. This loss will no doubt change his makeup if it hasn't started already, and I have to keep that in mind, *him* in mind.

Keep marching, Soldier.

"You have nowhere to be," Tobias says, calling my bluff.

I scoff. "I have a thousand places to be, and I don't need you to return the favor." It's a low blow, but I was the only one who was able to reason with him once he imploded after Dom's funeral.

Dom.

Delphine.

Tobias is the last living member of his whole goddamned family. In a sick way, I envy him. He has nothing holding him back from being the emotionless monster he's trying his best to become. Getting closer by the day in succeeding, his concern for me is surprising, considering he's a living ghost at this point. But my whole being has an aversion to him right now, and I say as much.

"I'm going home with Zach. If you really want to be there for me, then stop walking," I snap. He stops his footing instantly. The pain in his exhale is evident, but I ignore it, focusing on my own for once. Unsure of how I'll ever resemble a fraction of the man I was.

I'm a soldier now. Nothing more. But it's then I look back into the eyes of the boy I've come to love in mere months and know that I'll have to be more than that.

Left. Right. Keep marching.

Thankful. I'm supposed to be thankful for the time I had and for the memories we made, but I hate each second as it passes because of the distance it puts between the time she was breathing and the reality now in which she isn't.

That's fucking death. Each breath I take becomes agonizing as I will myself to stay in the moment, not to blink out for the kid standing curbside at my truck, looking as broken and lost as I feel. Will this be his life if he stays with me? Who will fucking protect him if I don't? I can't fail him.

"Tyler—" Tobias calls after me.

"Hey, get in the truck, okay?" I tell Zach, who doesn't move, sensing something's afoot.

"Please, Zach. Please don't make today harder," I ask him, knowing our day of reckoning is coming. The grudge in his eyes in the days after her death still there even as he does my bidding and climbs into the cab.

"Brother," Tobias clips behind me, "let me—"

"I'm all soldier right now, T," I snap back at him, rounding my truck and opening my door. "Don't expect anything else anytime soon."

On my heels, he palms my open door shut, crowding me against the truck. "Don't do this," I grit out. "Don't fucking do this, T."

"You aren't alone tonight. I'll be a shadow, I won't say a fucking word, but you aren't alone tonight."

"I know your place, but so do you," I grit out. "This is personal, and I'm not asking permission."

Both our cell phones rattle as we're summoned for another battle, and I find relief in a new mission, a distraction to keep me from coming apart. "I've got it," I say.

He pins me with his stare. "You're sitting this one out, Tyler."

"I don't sit shit *out*. In case you've conveniently forgotten *again*, we're in the middle of a fucking war."

"You are sitting this one out today. You just buried the love of your life, and I just buried my last relative."

"You hated her," I spit at him, slapping his chest with my palms. He doesn't so much as flinch, his lifeless eyes peering back at me even as he speaks words of contradiction.

"I loved her, and she knew that, and so do you," he admits without pause.

"Tyler," Zach calls through the partially lowered window of the truck, his eyes watering as I realize he's watching me lose my shit. In seeing his state, all the past months I've spent trying to give him a stable home, stable footing start to feel tarnished.

"It's all good," I grit out, my plea clear as I lift a palm in temporary truce while eyeing Tobias, who nods and steps away to disengage. It's the fear in Zach's eyes as I enter the truck that damn near levels me. Because it's not fear of me, it's fear *for* me. Of what I might do. I'm becoming unhinged, and it's apparent. He's a reason. He's a reason to endure another second.

A reason to keep my now misshapen heart beating.

A reason Delphine and I shared during our precious seconds together.

Something worth fighting for.

And so for her, for him, I'll force myself to soldier on.

***

"Tyler." My name is called as I try to register the familiarity of the man kneeling in front of me. His face coming into focus as he calls my name a second time. Or a third. "Please, Tyler, look at me," Sean pleads. "Please, brother, you're scaring the fuck out of me," he croaks as I fully focus on him.

"What?"

"You've been sitting here for a solid twenty-four hours." He darts his eyes over my shoulder. "Zach is terrified. He called me and told me you haven't gone into the house."

I glance back at the brick and mortar before peering through the glass door at the boy with fear-filled eyes, who's staring right back at me. When we pulled up from the funeral, I told Zach to go inside. That I'd be right in, but I never made it past the front porch step.

"Fuck," I rasp out.

"I've got everything handled," Sean assures, "but you have got to get ahold of yourself, for him. Okay?"

I nod.

"Russell is delegating, but I came to ask what you need. Tell me."

Checking myself, terrified of what I've already done to Zach, I go through a mental list of shit I know has to be done. "You need to pass out blessings."

"No, *you*, brother. What do *you* need?"

A *silver return stare*. "Nothing," I utter.

"We can argue that lie later, but for now, for Zach, can you try to get to your feet?" he asks, as I glance over to his idling Nova to see Tessa sitting in the passenger seat, her anxious eyes glued to us both.

"Not yet," I tell him. "Just give me a minute."

"I'll be back in a few hours," Sean releases, not bothering to conceal the concern in his tone, "but if you're not in that house by the time I get back, we're going to have to figure something out. You're scaring him."

"Fuck, I didn't realize." I palm my neck and nod. "All right."

"He'll be fine, okay? Just try to make it into the house. I'll be back. I love you, brother."

The second Sean pulls out I hear the noise of another vehicle passing and glance up to see my dad's F-150 pulling to a stop. Dread settles into me as I look back to see the fear in Zach's eyes before he pushes through the storm door.

Of all the people to call, kid. Seriously?

My dad exits his truck and stalks over to me as I finally stand, my legs tight from being idle for so long as I step toward him.

"I don't know what he told you, but we're fine here. You can go."

"Son, I held back at the funeral, but I'm begging you to let me stay today."

Zach chooses that moment to walk out as I attempt to get to some sort of healthier headspace while running interference on Carter.

"What are you doing?" I prompt Zach as he stalks down the porch to stand next to my dad.

"You need him," Zach declares.

"You have no idea what you're talking about. You don't know him," I counter. "Look, bud," I relay on exhale, "now isn't the time—"

"Yes, I do know him," he interjects. "We spend every Sunday together," he proclaims. "Who do you think taught me that mean curveball?"

"What?" I ask, gaping at him before glaring at my father. "You've been sneaking behind my fucking back?"

"No," Zach defends. "He's just been coming to his family gatherings, and we got close. And I like him . . . no, I love him, and he told me he wants so bad to be your dad again."

I keep my hardening stare on my father. "Really smooth, Carter, using a kid to try and get to me?"

"That's not what this is," Dad clips, but without offense.

"Zach, get in the house," I say. "We'll talk about this later."

"You've been out h-here for a whole d-day," Zach relays shakily. "I don't think you're okay. You need somebody—" his voice cracks as his face contorts. But it's when he starts to cry that my heart sinks.

"Fuck . . ." I run my hands through my hair. "I'm sorry I scared you, buddy, I am, but I'm just sad, okay? It's you. You're all I need, I promise. I just want to hang with you."

Zach sniffs, staring back at me, his eyes filled with a mix of concern and affection.

"I promise I'm coming," I assure as best I can. "Please just get in the house. I'll be right behind you. Are you hungry?"

Zach nods, looking between Dad and me, and anger builds that my father's opinion matters. That adding to the sting of Zach openly admitting he loves him.

"There's a bunch of casseroles in the fridge. Will you heat one up for us?"

He nods and turns to my father, who palms his shoulder briefly in encouragement. "Go on, I'll see you Sunday," Dad says, and Zach dips his chin. Not long after, shoulders slumped, Zach disappears into the house as Dad approaches me.

"Seriously?" I shake my head. "You know that Mom knows who he is, right? Don't you have any fucking shame?"

"Grace left him, Tyler, not me. That's something I would never do. Of course I didn't know the situation. If I did, I would have done what I could. I've paid for my past mistakes dearly, so you don't get to turn this around on me today. I'm very aware of what a bastard I am, but that's not why I'm here," he relays evenly. "I'm here because that boy fucking worships you, and I love him back, but I love the man in front of me more so."

"Well, your loyalty is a bit unwarranted considering I've barely minced words with you in—"

"Ten years," he finishes, the words biting, "sound familiar? I thought you weren't going to repeat my mistakes."

"Fuck you," I spit venomously, and he flinches. "How about that? Will that do it?"

Cringing inside, I lower my eyes and turn my back, thankful for the anger over the pain as I manage to put one foot in front of the other.

"No," he finally speaks. "It won't do it. It's unforgivable, but I guess I'm owed one or two of those from you. Please, don't turn me away. Please, Tyler. I love you."

"You don't fucking know me."

"Yes, I do," he calls after me. "You think I didn't reach out to everyone I fucking knew to see where you were at all times while you were in the service? Do you think I wasn't sitting beside your mother during every call? Hoping that just once you'd ask to speak to me? I've been looking after you every fucking day since you walked out of that house and biting my tongue for close to a decade as you treated me as an acquaintance, but I can't do it anymore."

"Then stop," I utter, willing my feet forward, over the porch and toward the door.

"I need to be your father again, more than the air I breathe because I do know you, Tyler. And I'm so proud of you. You've become my hero, Son."

I snort derisively as I stalk toward the door, using my anger as fuel to override everything else. "Look, Dad, I'm sorry about the disrespect, and *I am* sorry—" I glance back to see his eyes red-rimmed—"and I appreciate the sentiment and all, but I've got a scared kid inside—"

"My kid is scared!" he shouts. "My kid is hurting, and just suffered the worst blow of his life!" His voice cracks. "Goddamnit, Tyler, stop running from me and fucking face me, please," he utters, the break in his voice pausing my steps.

"I appreciate that you're here and showed up for me, but now isn't the time," I utter, palming the front door.

"Yes, it is," he counters, "and I'm not the only one who thinks so, Son. I have a message from your *wife*."

I pause the turn of the knob and glance back at him. A few tense heartbeats pass before I manage my reply. "What did you just say?"

He doesn't hesitate, taking a step toward the porch as he speaks. "I said I have a message from your wife, Tyler. I have a message from Delphine."

He maintains his stance as I stalk toward him. His expression remaining adamant, even as his eyes water when I come to a stop a foot away. "I'm Delphine's last wish, Son."

I go utterly still while soaking him in thoroughly for the first time in a decade. "What do you mean y—"

"I mean I both knew and loved Delphine, and I was her last recruit."

I shake my head in denial as he elevates his voice.

"Her purpose in doing so is that you would need a new best friend."

"Stop—"

"No," he claps back, digging his heels in. "We've spent a lot of time together in the last six months. It started with the few chemo appointments you couldn't be there for before she stopped treatment. I've been with her every second you weren't or couldn't be. While you worked or were on missions in Miami. I got to know her very well. She taught me how to play Battle. And it was because she purposely took the time to get to know me. She told me everything, Son, and my job is to be here for you because she can't anymore." He keeps his gaze zeroed on me as his eyes spill over. "I *loved* Delphine, and while you're devastated and grieving your wife, I'm grieving my friend, and honestly, I'm miserable she's gone."

I shake my head, disbelieving she would relay so much and spill so many secrets. A woman with an iron jaw who never slips. Even if it's to her own detriment. "What do you mean she told you everything?"

"She told me the most incredible story I've ever heard. Of her past, of Matis and Alain. Of how the two of you started working together and bonded after I broke your trust, your heart. Of how you fought some dark places and the way you relentlessly trained. She told me about how close the two of you got and became fishin' buddies while you fell in love here on our land."

I stand reeling, disbelieving of his words as each one pummels me, re-stoking my hurts.

"She told me you went into the service to investigate it,

mostly because of me and for *me*," he croaks, "she told me all about your missions while you were in and about your time in the GRS. About Phillip. About losing Armstrong. She explained the history behind your tattoos, Son, *both* of them."

I gape back at him, utterly stupefied that the woman whose trust is unbreakable, whose secrecy is unsurmountable, broke mine to the one man I've been purposely mute to for a decade. She wouldn't. But it's the look in my father's eyes and his admissions that have me believing otherwise as he stares at me with pride I'd long forgotten. Pride I forgot I so desperately wanted and worked for half my life. A pride and respect I lived for.

"She told me she wanted me to be the only one to know all of your secrets because she knows I'm the only other person on earth you would have once trusted with them."

My vision blurs as he steps closer. His unease and hope palpable and rolling from him as I start to break further apart. Piece by piece.

"She wanted me to remind you that the true brilliance of any strategist lies within the *surprise* . . . and I am her last wish, Tyler."

Tears roll down my cheeks as I hit my knees, and he instantly crouches down next to me, palming my shoulder as I grip both of his.

"Because she wanted you to know me again, because she knows I'm the wound she could never heal. She asked me to come here long before today, before Zach called, and relay this to you because she trusted me to be able to do this, to be here for you. Which is why I'm the only other person on this earth aside from Pastor Ron that knows the two of you God married in the wildflowers last fall, but filed no paperwork because it was your promise to her to have—"

"Faith," we both say simultaneously.

Fingers tightening on his jacket, I shake my head at his

admissions, too stunned, too filled with emotion to utter any other word, but one.

"Dad," I croak before he crushes me to him, going blind with pain as it unleashes inside me. Agony lights my veins as I lose myself in my grief, shattering in his arms, coming apart as he keeps me firmly in his grip, keeps me upright, whispering assurances over and over again as I break against him.

"You're an incredible man, Tyler. I'm so fucking proud of you. So proud. I'm so in awe of you. Of what you've done . . . I want so badly to fill the role she gave me. I want so much to be your friend again, your best friend and father . . . I'm begging you, Son," he whispers, "please, please, let me stay. Please let me stay."

Crushed in my father's hold, all I can do is nod.

Epilogue

Tyler

BLINK. Russell pulls up in the King's tow truck as my mangled hood comes into view. I clamp my hand over my mouth to conceal my lady-like gasp as fury lights in my veins. Zach eyes me from behind the windshield, where he sits in the passenger seat of the tow truck as Russell hops out and stalks toward me.

"Shit, brother," Russell utters, reading my expression. "You might want to take a breath before you . . . do the daddy thing."

"I'm good," I lie, both shaken and furious. "He's okay?"

"Yeah, he's fine," Russell assures, "he's scared shitless but hiding it well."

The passenger door closes and Zach comes into view behind Russell's shoulder before he attempts to speed past the two of us to get to the house.

"Stop your feet, *now*," I snap. Zach barely acknowledges my order but obeys, stopping feet ahead of us.

"Annnnd, that's my cue to leave," Russell chuckles.

"Thanks for the heads-up, and for bringing him home," I say.

"No problem, but damn does he have a set of balls on him," Russell muses.

"Which haven't yet fucking dropped," I counter, knowing Zach can hear us.

"I'll drop it off in the barn. Text you later, man," Russell says before getting back into the tow truck. The sight of my mangled hood as he drives away brings actual stinging fucking tears to my eyes before I shift my gaze to scan Zach.

"Okay. You meant to hurt me, and I'm hurt, so mission accomplished, but you could have fucking killed yourself, kid. You can barely reach the fucking pedals, which is no doubt why you wrecked. What in the hell were you thinking?"

He stands mute, which is infuriating. The only thing I'm thankful for is that there's no real fear in him. Maybe not enough.

"What is going on with you?" I ask. "I thought we were good."

"I'll pay for it," he offers dryly.

"That's a given. You'll be working it off with double your chores and no Ranger for six months."

His mouth pops open. "You can't do that."

"Want to make it a year? You're delusional. You're thirteen years old and drove my fucking classic forty minutes across town."

"I was just riding," he says in shit excuse. I cross my arms as he shakes his head. "Whatever."

"Tell me what's going on," I say. Tell me why you're so pissed at me."

"I'm not."

"And I'm a ballet dancer," I utter dryly. "You can go all night bullshitting me, and I can play along, or you can simplify this for us both."

"You didn't let me say goodbye," he snaps. "You didn't let me say shit!"

I manage to stave off my flinch. "I apologized for that."

"Fuck your apology," he snaps. "You don't get to apologize for things like that."

"Watch your mouth," I warn, palming my neck. "You need to back it up and speak to me with respect, right now."

"Fine, sorry."

"Sorry what?"

"Oh, fuck this, *sorry, sir*." He stalks off. I'm instantly on his heels as he continually spouts off, "You're not my dad . . . I don't know why in the hell I'm here."

"I told you why," I counter, undeterred, "because I want you here, and I asked you to stay."

"Because your girlfriend died," he tosses over his shoulder, the blow landing as intended.

"Please don't go there, not that low," I utter hoarsely. At my tone, he stops and turns to me, his eyes watering as mine threaten to follow. "I did what I thought was best, and I'm sorry."

"You could have let me talk to her on the phone," he condemns, tears falling. The pain still fresh for us both. Her funeral barely a month ago.

"I'm sorry. I am," I offer hoarsely, my eyes filling at the utter devastation in his face. "I could have, should have put you on with her, but I was running out of time. I was so fucking sad, Zach, and maybe it was selfish, but she didn't want you there. She didn't want you to see her go. But she loved you. I miss her too. Every fucking day. So much."

"It isn't your job to protect me. You're not my father," he repeats.

"Yeah, you keep saying that." I swallow.

"Because it's true." He kicks at the dirt between us. "You're not. I'm not your son, Tyler."

"Do you want to be?" His eyes widen slightly as a pained gasp leaves him. "Because in my heart, that's who you are to me now. What you've become. And what I want you to be."

His face twists again as he releases a suppressed grunt. Tears shimmer in his eyes as I find the strength to fight for the first time since she passed. For us. For him.

"I love you, and I want you in my life. I want you here. With me."

He openly cries now as I fist my hands at my sides. It's then the clear image of the toddler wiggling in his mother's arms comes to mind. As does the sound of the demand which accompanied the engrained image from a decade ago.

"Hole me."

The burn in my throat mutes me briefly until the fight for him wins out.

"Zach, I'm losing my shit right now because I really want to pull you to me, to hug you. Just tell me if you—" He launches himself at me, cutting me off, and I capture him in my arms, holding him for long seconds as his body shakes, his grief palpable. I keep him tightly gripped, my whispers fueled by my heart. By the truth.

"You're saving me," I tell him honestly. "You may think I did you a favor, but you're saving me, Zach. And all I want to do now is spend my life being your father. I can't promise to save you back because that's a promise no one can make to another, but I promise you everything else a father can offer. I'll be there for you as long as I have breath in me. You're golden. You're everything that's good about my life now, and you were for her too. And God, how she loved you."

He buckles as I keep him upright. "I'm right here. I'm not going anywhere. You have to grow up and let go of my hand first, but I'm not letting go. That's the promise I made her, and it belongs *to you now.*"

He sobs uncontrollably as I shield him from it all. From the eyes that have shamed him. Playing barrier to the pain that has plagued him, never lessening my grip. "I'm yours if you'll have me. I'll show up for you. I promise. I swear it, I swear it. I love you, Zach, and I need you. I want you here. With me."

His sobs come harder, and he clutches me tighter and breaks against me, with me, my own face soaked when he finally releases me.

"D-do you believe in G-God like she does?"

"I will never lie to you. Not ever, so I can't bullshit you on something I've struggled with for years because of the things I've seen. But when I looked at her, at you, I want to believe. I want to because you both deserve a place like that. I want to believe so badly she's there. So for you, and for her, I'll try."

He nods, his chest pumping with his cries. Once he's spent, I wordlessly follow him to his room and remain at his door until he falls into a fitful sleep. I wake in the morning to see him sleeping on the floor next to me, his hand gripping my sheet at the side of my bed. Bending, I lift him onto the mattress to lay next to me and stare at him until I'm lights out. When we both wake, he turns to me and gives me my answer. And within a blink, I'm a father.

BLINK.

Glaring down at my brother where he lays in the hospital bed, I fight the anger and resentment threatening to destroy what's left of us. "You take for granted the breath in your body while I watched her struggle for every single one. She wanted those breaths because it meant having another day—with me. You want to line up with the rest of your family, go right on ahead, but I will not fucking be there to witness it if you don't fight for your own breaths anymore. They deserve better . . . I deserve better. So, if you give a fuck about me at all," I plead with him for the last fucking time, "wake the fuck up! Wake the fuck up, T."

BLINK.

Standing in my penguin suit, I wink at Zach, who tugs at the collar of his shirt where he sits in the first row, loosening his tie. Catching his eyes, I jerk my chin as we start our mental conversation exchange.

Not yet, kid.

It's uncomfortable.

Deal with it.
Shit.
Manners.
Fine!
Love you.
You too.

I can even hear him grumbling it, and can't help but smile with how far we've come. Shifting my focus on my brother, and the love shining in his eyes, I take in the moment, being there with him, for him, as my own ache surfaces in remembrance of the time I took similar vows.

"I, Sean, take you, Tessa, to be my lawfully wedded wife."

BLINK.

Zach winds up on the mound as I palm Dad's shoulder, my heart in my throat as we hold our collective breath. A heartbeat later, the ump calls it as we explode out of our seats.

BLINK.

Dad and I stare, standing side by side, dressed in our blues, as the shots are fired. Granddad's picture standing nearby as the flag is folded.

BLINK.

My phone rings as I stand idly by the gas pump when my name is called. Turning, I see Layla holding her daughter, Lily, prompting her to wave to me just outside the station door. Grinning, I wave back as I answer.

"Hey man, long time."

"I've got it on good authority that you're being called up, buddy," Beekman imparts, and I can hear the smile in his voice.

"No shit? Now?"

"Affirmative. I hope you have a realtor in DC."

"I'm hoping you have one," I retort absently, as it starts to sink in.

"Matter of fact, I do," he boasts.
"I prefer to have one you haven't jilted," I quip.
"Oh, then you're on your own."
"Figures," I jibe.
"Pack your bags, brother, and your kid, and let him know Uncle Beekman is picking you both up soon, secret agent man."

BLINK.

Zach tosses his duffle into his truck, his gaze lingering on our DC house for long seconds as I rattle feet away. Glancing over to me, he easily reads my expression before pulling me to him. "Don't worry, Dad," his whisper reaches me. "I swear I've got this. You made sure of it. Love you."

Just after he pulls away, I place the knife in his palm speaking around the lump in my throat. "She would have wanted you to have it." His eyes fix on the knife as he swallows, the sting evident before he nods.

"Thank you."

"Call me as soon as you can."

"I'll call you in ten minutes," he says before he pulls away.

My phone rings in five.

BLINK.

"Zuzu's petals, there they are!" Jimmy Stewart rings out on screen as Zach feasts on Mom's Christmas tree-shaped Rice Krispie treats, his size twelve boots hanging over her ottoman. Scouring the living room, I chuckle as Dad catches flies, mouth gaping in his second nap today. In the corner, I watch as Mom pulls out a familiar box from a large plastic bin. Inside is an ornament that gives me both a nostalgia kick and stokes my constant heartache. At the sight of it, I'm transported back into our little house as silver eyes stare back at me, her lips twisted in a grin.

"It's my ugly ornament," I utter to Mom who looks

back over to me, concern in her eyes. "I'm okay," I assure in a rough whisper. "Let me hang it?"

She gives me an easy nod, her eyes misting before she turns to stare at her glittering tree. "I miss her all the time, Son."

BLINK.

Standing in the doorway of Tobias's office, he looks over to me, utter devastation on his face. Reason being, Cecelia accepted another man's ring. "Talk to me," I prompt, the sweat from hauling ass here cooling on my back.

"No need," he states.

"You can continue to lie," I counter, remaining idle, "and maybe I'll pretend to believe it, or we can talk, really talk this out. Choice is yours."

We stare off for a few silent seconds before he speaks.

"Tell me why she accepted." He pours a finger full of gin in his tumbler.

"He wasn't sure she would say yes, so he did it in a room full of people who knew them both as a couple and as successful business partners. To remind her of what they've built together—also what she stands to lose if she didn't take the ring. It's a little manipulative, but he worships her."

"That's not what I asked," Tobias snaps.

I sigh, knowing he doesn't want the truth even as he demands it with the lift of his chin. "Because he's both good to and for her."

He rakes his lip, but it doesn't lessen any of the blow in his expression. Pressing in, for him, for her, I give him more of the brutal truth.

"This is what you decided for her when you sent her back to Georgia. A normal life, non-club related."

He nods, even as sweat breaks out on his brow.

"You know your choices," I remind him. "You either go get her and risk losing her to our life, or you let her go"—I cut my hand through the air to stop his bullshit objection—"I mean, *really* let her go."

"I have . . ." He spares me a glance as I flat out call bullshit with my eyes alone. ". . . Enough to make her believe I have," he grits out.

"You still love her, Tobias," I deliver point-blank.

"I'm with Alicia."

"No," I scoff, "you fucking aren't. Alicia knows that, too. And like Alicia with you, Collin knows Cecelia's not *all in* with him. That there's something or someone from her past holding her back. I'm willing to bet my life that Collin has absolutely no knowledge of you. Even without mention of the club, and that's because she's holding out hope just like you are. If you truly are her past, she would have told him about you, and she hasn't, which makes her all the more alluring to him."

"You seem certain of all of this," he says, tossing more gin back.

"I am." I shrug.

"Simply because of the way he proposed?" he asks.

"There's a lot to be said about approach, but there's more, there's always more, and you know damn well I watch out for her, so don't play fucking ignorant," I warn, done with his excuses.

"Subtlety is no longer a trait you possess," he says, swallowing another healthy sip of gin. A numbing I'm all too familiar with. "She doesn't love him," he insists.

"Maybe not in the same way she did you," I agree. "A way she no doubt now identifies as unhealthy thanks to you, but she does love him."

I hold his stare, intent on seeing this through. "She loves him enough to marry him, and if you don't stop it, *she will* marry him, T."

"She's too smart to trap herself in the lie she's living, and make no mistake, she's living a lie," he argues.

"Which makes you birds of a feather," I drop, a second

before he shatters his keyboard with his fist. Blood drips from his hand as all pretense of calm flies out the window.

"The risk is still too great," he argues weakly.

"Tessa can endure it," I counter, "and you've seen that for yourself. There are marriages that last in this fucking club . . . but I'm not here to talk you into going to her."

"Then why are you?" he snaps.

"I'm here to tell you *she will marry* him if you don't stop it."

Tobias's eyes flare as I become the enemy, his temporary scapegoat for the pain lancing through him.

"Since we're being honest, why don't you come clean about being happy to deliver this news to me."

"Fuck you," I bite out. "Despite your current skewed perception, not everyone is your enemy."

"No, but you're no friend of mine since I've disappointed you so greatly. Your grudge is still there. Tell me it doesn't please you to tell me this," he hisses as I turn to take my leave. "That it doesn't please you that I live as you do, as a fucking dead man."

Turning on a dime, I stalk toward him, done with the hand-holding. "You want to go blow for blow? Think it will make you feel better?" I stop short of his desk. "We both know it won't, but today, I'm fucking up for it, you fucking prick. So, say the word."

He tilts his head, eyes filling with concern as I jerk my chin.

"Save it. Don't play big brother right now. You're not the one who just fucking flew across Charlotte to watch you implode."

"I'm not," he denies.

"You are, and every single bit of what you're feeling right now is on you, and you know it."

"She'll die," he whispers fearfully.

"She might," I agree, "and that's the chance we all take when we get inked. You *inked her*, you dumb bastard.

But while we've been mopping up our mess, she's been embracing that ink—earning it. You know as well as I do that we can talk club safety all night, but we both know there's no fucking guarantee and never will be. We learned that the hard way. But that was years ago, and now you're standing behind excuses that are becoming less and less relevant while still playing the fucking martyr with your broken heart." Annoyed, I stare him down as the last of my patience starts to thin. "Look, sulk, cry, whine, and continue to remain in denial, but your lack of future with her is completely your fucking decision and less about her safety at this point."

"She won't forgive me."

"She's not a young tender anymore, Tobias. She's a goddamn force to be reckoned with, and my money is that she'll give you the hell you deserve before you get to glimpse the peace you found with her again. You were willing to risk losing your brothers over her, so what is the risk now?"

"Her fucking life!"

"That's your PTSD talking," I counter.

"Fuck you."

"You were hurt, bad, and almost died, and it scared you and only reinforced your decision to keep her away, but you're still breathing, and so is she. The coast is as clear as it's going to get, and you know all too fucking well she's starting to stack enemies of her own. Now more than ever, she needs your protection."

"She has it."

"No, she has *mine*," I draw out, "which is better than yours, but it's not mine she wants." Done with the conversation, I glance back at the door. "Look, go to her, or don't, but this is it. I've watched you get up from concrete you shouldn't have been able to grow roots from, but you did."

"I can't watch her die," he finally admits.

"You're dying watching her fucking live without you,

brother. The thing is . . . I know you'll eventually go to her, whether it's today or a dozen years from now. But what my gut tells me now is that there's a chance she'll still be there for you, though I have and have had a feeling that the clock is ticking out. This engagement only proves as much. A woman like Cecelia—with a heart like hers—you and I both know she won't let it wither. One day, she will succeed in finding someone to help her put it to use, even if it isn't Collin. She's not going to waste much more of it on you. Do what you will, but you know I'm right."

Stalking over to the door, knowing I've done and said all I can for my brother, I slam the door behind me.

**

US PRESIDENT: PRESTON J MONROE | 2021 -2029
FALL 2021

BLINK.

Chest heaving due to exertion, I toss away the last of the brush before getting into the cab of the backhoe. With no choice but to look at the house standing twenty feet in front of me, I finally face it head-on. An immediate vision of Delphine on the porch, watering can in hand, flits to mind. The hem of her sundress catching on the breeze, blowing around her, along with wisps of her long, black hair as she glances my way, her lips curving up due to my arrival. Just after, the feel of our connection when our eyes met and held through my windshield.

The late summer sun beams down, and I clear the sweat from my brow with the exposed part of my wrist beneath my work gloves as I swallow down that vision. In vain, because a second later, it's promptly replaced by another. Zach manning the grill as Delphine chatted to him from where she sat at the porch swing while I chopped wood. I can still see them so clearly—comfortable, smiling, content. That image brings the ache back tenfold, the loss of it crippling.

The facts are, once upon a short time ago, and only briefly, I had a family. A family I didn't try or petition for but came together naturally—a gift. A gift that was promptly snatched right back like a favorite toy in cruel taunt.

"Christ," I rasp out as I put the backhoe into gear and lower the bucket, fury driving me on as I head in the direction of the small house she made a home, intent on erasing it.

It's the speeding car on the road next to me blurring into my periphery that has me halting the demolition and kicking back in the bucket seat to weigh going through with it.

Seconds later, Tobias pulls up right next to me, our eyes meeting from where I sit a few feet above in the tractor to his driver's seat. I know the second he glances toward the house and back at me that he's reading my intent, and I mutter a curse before exiting.

Sighing as he exits his newest Jag, I lean against the tractor as he approaches, noticing that the usual confidence in his gait is completely absent, and I know why. Right now, we're in the same type of hell.

Two months after Tobias summoned Cecelia with an email to buy Horner Tech, Cecelia came, fought the good fight, and went. To her utter detriment, Tobias did everything he could to see her out the door. Despite my warnings and her attempts to salvage them, his fear won out. It's apparent it's winning now as he approaches me, eyeing me intently.

"Don't judge my actions," I snap.

"Like I have any right," he scoffs, relenting easily—too easily, and I hate it, missing my brother as I have since the night he was forever altered. I want this fight. I've wanted it for years, but as it stands now, we both look and feel defeated. "But know you'll only destroy an empty home, not the memories."

I abandoned any life in Triple Falls years ago, including this place, but it's always nagged at me that this house remains here, unoccupied.

"If it's a mistake, I'll learn from it after. Not in the mood to be preached to," I relay. "Not today."

"Understood," he answers, his accent a little thicker due to the emotion emanating from him, which he's doing nothing to hide. It dawns on me then.

"You're finally going to her," I state with an ironic shake of my head. It's then I notice his dress, nothing but jeans and a T-shirt.

"I'm terrified she'll take me back, but more terrified she won't."

"I hope she gives you hell," I relay.

His eyes narrow on me. "You want me to suffer."

"Some, but don't forget that I washed my hands of this months ago."

He scans the expansive farm, the hills and valleys for long seconds before he looks back to me, eyes misting. "Have you washed your hands of me, Tyler? Do you find me redeemable?"

"That's up to you," I dismiss.

"I miss the beginning," he whispers, gaze and voice distant. "I would have done so many things differently."

"I think we all would," I relay truthfully.

"If I could go back, I would, Tyler, I would." He looks over to me. "And not just for myself," he relays hoarsely, with no sort of manipulative preempt in the delivery. He's living in his mistakes, in his personal prison, and this is his first step in trying to break free. He's finally fucking ready. That truth angers me more than it relieves me. Sensing my burgeoning disposition, he studies me carefully.

Stepping up to me, he lets me see his pain, his regret. "Answer me, brother, please. Are we salvageable? But before you do, I came to tell you that I understand you more than I ever have. I understand"—he nods toward the house—"this. The why of it all in a way I never have before. That's not a reason for you to forgive me, but I want you to know that much."

"So, what you're really asking is that because I needed you, and you weren't there, can I be the same prick to you?"

"I guess so," he says, a tear shaking free and gliding down his cheek. "And if you can be, I would deserve it." He shakes his head. "You know I love Cecelia, but you don't know why. We never shared those details, and I never asked what you had with Delphine, nor do I know of any memories you harbor. I never let you share your happiness with me or fucking asked. I never knew what this"—he gestures toward the house—"was like for you."

"Heaven," I manage around the burn in my throat. "Only miles away, it was, felt, seemed untouchable by the club, by everyone. Even by our war. During my time with her, I knew real peace." I lick my lips and glance away. "I knew what it was to have a family . . . until it was ripped away."

Tobias stares at the front porch for long seconds. "You gave her that same happiness, family. Something she lacked in her own life, but you know that."

I palm my neck and nod.

"Thank you for that, Tyler. Thank you for caring for her, for loving her. For not giving up on her, for being more her family than we were."

"Well," I say, tightening my gloves on my hands, "thanks for stopping by on the apology tour, but—"

"Goddamnit," he steps up to me, and I react, landing a solid blow on his chin, with nothing behind it. His head snaps right, but it doesn't stop him as he crowds me, palming my shoulder, his eyes pleading. "I'm sorry! I'm sorry! Hear me, see me, and know I'm sincere. I haven't acted like a brother to you in so long, and I'm sorry. I'm so fucking sorry." He pulls me to him and keeps me there, his words coming out rapid but unrehearsed. "As selfish as I've been, I need you just as much. Have needed you, and now I need the one I trust the most on this earth to tell me that a life other than what we're living is possible because I can't take this reality any longer."

"For you," I choke out, palming his back, "for you, you stupid son of a bitch, but not for me, and it's all up to you."

We break apart, and I run my glove along my jaw to wipe at the weakness lining it. I swallow again, the heaviness in the air between us lifting substantially as my anger takes a back seat. Glancing up and over, I gaze at my brother, who's looking back at me with fresh eyes—new perspective. Who sees the man and not the boy.

"The life you get to live from here on out is entirely what you make of it once you reach her, T. There's no quick fix. You decide. She decides, and then you decide the rest together. That's all there is."

He nods. "And for you?"

"I'm all booked up," I sniff, unable to stand the sight of the house any longer. "But when it's over, this is my future." I gesture. "You have St. Jean de Luz, and I have this little piece of heaven to make whatever life I want after. Until then, I'm letting the earth swallow it up."

He searches me for long minutes and sees my resolve. "When do you return to DC?"

"Tomorrow," I answer.

He fingers the back pockets of his jeans. "Can I catch a ride with you?"

I draw my brows.

"I want to go to her with nothing but the clothes on my back. She deserves that."

It's admirable, considering the man's fetishes for the finer things and the knowledge that he's going to have to go without his little indulgences.

"Sure you can do without your morning espresso?" I tease.

"Fuck no, but for her," he says, no humor in his voice, "I'll do anything."

"Know that I'll so be the fly on the wall for this shit show, and I'll be close if you need me," I assure him. "Either of you."

"I know that. I just don't want you to resent me for it any longer," he says.

"Something tells me I won't," I admit. "That's if you do the work and finally get to the place of deserving her again."

"I can't live without her," he whispers, his voice distant but filled with surety, "and I won't."

"That's apparent."

"No, Tyler." His eyes lock with mine, and I take a step back at what I see. I'd read it all wrong. "I *won't* live without her. If my decisions or this club cost her life . . ." He trails off, but his implication is clear, and he's completely of sound mind.

"You're serious?" I ask, though I know better.

"Before I take a step near her, I need your word that will remain the case."

"Jesus Christ, T—"

"I don't breathe a day without her, Tyler, fucking promise me. Promise me. I don't last a minute past her last breath if it's possible."

Swallowing, I see his ask and his resolution. It's one thing about Tobias that can't ever be bent or swayed or bartered. Well, unless your name is Cecelia Horner. She's his only weakness, but his weakness is both damning and caustic, hence this request. But this is the nature of Tobias and his absolutes—of how his heart works, of his devotion.

I know this because I'm very much the same man in that respect.

I don't bother to try and talk him out of it, and he's all too aware of my capabilities.

"Can you live with it?" he asks.

The question is also pointless. He knows I can. That I've got capabilities others don't. That compartmentalization is my biggest strength. That I grieve Delphine *by choice*. He's well aware I can turn my emotions on and off like a switch under any circumstance and reads that truth in my return gaze.

"Promise me, Tyler. Promise me," he prods, unrelenting in his quest. Knowing he won't survive her loss, I bat away all emotion and flip that switch before reasoning through my decision for long minutes before answering.

"You have my word, brother."

He nods, perfectly content with his decision, and adds another life-altering secret to my bill before turning back to me. "So, do you have another set of gloves?"

"I'm good, just let me . . ." I trail off as Tobias nods and steps back.

Turning back to the house, I stare at the brick and mortar ahead of me that at one time was more than a house, but a home. Engine idling, bucket lowered, I allow myself a few more seconds to back out of the emotional decision to destroy the only true home I've ever known.

I'm already years into the road ahead of me, the road that begins after her. Reliving the memories and peace of the time we spent here, I allow the bittersweet emotions to swarm me.

This part of my life is over, and for the next seven years, I have no room for emotional attachment. The inkling to erase what could have been fills me with surety as I aim the bucket at the front door.

It's over. Death took away all illusions of moving forward in the life we made.

Now, I'm an image of who others expect me to be, a falsity, an illusion, a liar, manipulator, and the keeper of all secrets. A protector and her soldier, nothing more.

The reason I breathe now is to make sure those I'm loyal to don't have to desperately search for the rise and fall of the chest of those they love. From that, I can and will protect them the way I wasn't.

Because it was heaven to love her, too, though I was in a sacrificial type of state. In order to have it, I had to give my heart permission to love her, though her loss altered my soul.

So I'll protect them, so these questions don't fucking haunt them. I'll keep their secrets and watch them fuck up and lose their chances to stupidity. I'll watch them hurt each other and take each other for granted. Knowing the cost, I won't say a fucking word, but fight for their individual breaths in between so they don't ever fucking realize that their naïveté could cost them their sanity.

For a time, I swore she was my one weakness, but the truth is, now I draw breath for them. They are my weakness and reason. For them, I'll breathe and will my heart to keep beating.

Only for them.

Because if I fail them, I'll cease to have a reason to anymore.

Bucket lowered, I'm feet from the house when my son steps out of the front door, challenge in his eyes. Panic and shock seizing me, I all but stand on the brakes and kill the engine, jumping out as Zach squares off with me.

"What the fuck are you doing, Dad?"

Guilt washes over me as he steps forward demanding an answer.

"Did you maybe think for *one fucking second* that by totaling this place, you'd be wiping the memories of the only mother I've ever had away from me!"

Zach's fury radiates from him as I stand in shock at his reaction. "You're selfish in your pain with her. You've tried, but you're still fucking selfish!"

"I'm sorry," I offer pathetically as guilt and shame wash over me. "I thought you'd build a new—"

"I don't want to erase my past. I'm embracing it. Even the parts I don't want to remember. It's part of being a well-rounded human. You taught me that, and what are you doing? . . . She's gone, and yeah, we need to move on with living, but what is this? You want to forget her now, too?"

I shake my head. "I can't."

"Dad," he sighs, "I've sat back and watched you suffer year after year, but enough is enough. You know good and fucking well she didn't want this! She told you specifically not to take mourning her this far, and here you are well over half a decade later, and you're not even trying!"

"I can't!" I admit, the pain lancing through me at that truth. "I can't."

"That's the first time I've ever heard those words come out of your mouth," he says. "Words you *refused* to let me use."

Zach steps up to me, and even as he scorns me, I can't help the pride I feel, even as he hands my ass to me. Which inside, I know, is deserved. She didn't want this—me to mourn her this far—but my heart still isn't beating the same. My breaths are still shallow, and I miss her with every single one.

"Dad, I want to make this *my home* one day. When I find the girl for me, I want to bring her here, to the place where I witnessed firsthand what kind of love I wanted. It's one of my dreams. So please, don't tear it down."

I nod, utterly speechless at his display. He rarely gets so emotional anymore, and I know it's not because he doesn't have a heart. It's because he takes good care of it. In doing so, he's now taking care of mine.

"Promise me," he prompts, his eyes drilling mine.

"I promise, Son. Fuck, I'm sorry. It's just—" I crack a little as I admit the truth. "I can't reason my way out of this fucking grief. I can't. I just need—"

"Faith, Dad. That's all she asked of you. You need faith. Real faith. She asked you to believe her and you need to start. I heard her give you that order more than once before she died. I heard it. An order you're not following.

So you need to know you're not going to find the peace you want until you do."

"I'll try, Son. I'll try."

"Okay," he releases on a long exhale before glancing back at the house. "Let's—" He nods toward the door. "Let's spend the night with her, here, before you go back?"

I give him a slow nod. "Yeah, she would love that."

Eyes still full of concern, his expression relaxes slightly as he glances over a Tobias. "Hey Uncle T, you staying?"

T nods. "Hey, and yes, if it's okay with you."

"Of course . . . no, Uncle T, put your fucking wallet away." Zach rolls his eyes before turning to me. "I'll go grab something to grill." He eyes the newly vacant porch. "And I guess get a new fucking grill," he utters dryly, shaking his head before stalking to my truck. Easily finding the keys where I pinned them above the tire, he turns it over before driving away. Tobias and I stand mute for a few minutes as Zach speeds down the gravel drive. I remain zeroed on the truck until it's out of sight, utterly in awe of the son I raised when Tobias speaks up behind me.

"It's so wild watching you be a father, but I always saw it in you. Since the day we met and you mowed my lawn."

"Yeah." I grin and turn to him. "You ever think about it?"

"I was blessed to be brother and father."

"You aren't going to try with Cecelia?"

He gives me an imperceptible expression. "That's a complicated question considering she wrote me off. One step at a time, brother."

"This is going to be epic," I muse. "Just know Russell and I will be popping popcorn every night to tune in for this shit show."

"Fuck you," he utters, even as a grin plays on his lips.

***

Later that night we honor Delphine in a way that would actually please her. Laughing hysterically about her antics and salty cooking. Pausing heavily when it starts to sting. After sipping my beers a little longer and when the pain becomes too much, I cut myself off before any buzz can set in. Determined to stay sharp when I start on Preston's security detail tomorrow. As I remind them of that, we all part ways for lights-out. But when the two of them head for the bedrooms, I decide to take a walk, which turns into a moonlit trek toward the pasture of wildflowers.

"*Breathe, Soldier,*" her whisper reaches me as the trees sway with the crisp arrival of fall. Visions of her swarm me just after, leaving me aching as her whispers continually reach me.

"*Je t'aime, my miracle, soldier of my heart,*" she whispers.

Turning the corner, I'm stopped by the sight that greets me. The wildflowers I planted so long ago eat up the entire hillside having grown wildly in the years since our departure. Nature doing its thing, the overabundance renders me speechless.

In a blink I'm surrounded by them, by her, as faint music fills my senses, carrying over the breeze. Getting lost in time, I become absorbed in the night I married the love of my life. In remembrance of the feel of her. Of her silken hair and skin against my palms as we danced on our wedding night. Her lilted whispers engulfing me as I turn slowly to inhale the sight before me. Raw and aching, the pain remains unrelenting, as the dark beckons me, forever promising a way out. But this pain, this pain could never be fully blinked away. Just as I think it, the breeze flutters over the tips of the wildflowers as her whisper reaches me.

"*Close your eyes, Tyler.*"

"They're closed," I whisper back.

"*See your way out, Soldier, do you see it?*"

"I see it, baby," I croak, cracking wide as the blades of the Blackhawk sound in the distance, the *thwomp thwomp thwomp* announcing its rapid approach.

"Have faith, Soldier. Have faith."

"I'll have faith, baby . . . I love you."

"My one true love," she whispers.

"I miss you so much." I slap my fingers against my salted cheeks.

The helicopter touches down yards away as Tobias approaches the field, and I hold the moment for as long as I can, feeling her everywhere for those brief seconds.

"Open your eyes, Soldier of my heart. Go."

A peace washes over me as I inhale her one last time and exhale her slowly. Not completely, but enough to take another full breath since the last time she took one of her own.

"Go, Soldier," she orders through time and space as I approach the bird and Zach appears, waving us off from the side of the house. Her voice echoes back to me one last time as my severed heart beats soundly for the first time in years. Even if it remains in pieces.

"Win again, Soldier. Win again."

THE END . . . but truthfully, it's just the beginning.

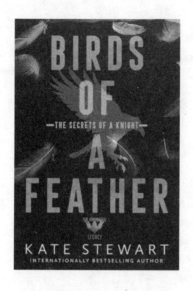

Read the rest of Tyler and more
of our Ravens' story in
Birds of Feather: The Secrets of a Knight.